George Sand

Two Biographies and Three Novels

By

George Sand
Bertha Thomas
Justin M'Carthy

Cover Artwork: Portrait de George Sand en 1838, by: Auguste Charpentier

ISBN: 978-1-78139-422-9

Contents

GEORGE SAND.

GEORGE SAND.

THE DEVIL'S POOL

APPENDIX

MAUPRAT

INDIANA

PART FIRST

PART SECOND

PART THIRD

PART FOURTH

CONCLUSION

GEORGE SAND.

BY BERTHA THOMAS.

PREFATORY NOTE.

THE authentic materials available for an account of the life of George Sand, although lately increased by the publication of a large part of her correspondence, are still incomplete. Her memoirs by her own hand, dealing fully with her early life alone, remain unsupplemented by any entire and detailed biography, for which, indeed, the time seems hardly yet come. Hence one among many obvious difficulties in the way of this attempt to prepare for English readers a brief sketch that shall at least indicate all the more salient features of a life of singularly varied aspect.

Much, though of interest in itself, must here be omitted, as beyond the scope of the present study. There are points again into which, as touching persons still living or quite recently deceased, it would be premature to enter. But none seem of such importance as to forbid the endeavor, by a careful review of those facts in the life of George Sand which most justly represent her character as a whole, and were the determining influences on her career and on her work, to arrive at truth and completeness of general outline, the utmost it is possible to hope to accomplish in this little volume.

Bertha Thomas.

CHAPTER I. - EARLY YEARS.

IN naming George Sand we name something more exceptional than even a great genius. Her rise to eminence in the literature of her century, is, if not without a parallel, yet absolutely without a precedent, in the annals of women of modern times.

The origin of much that is distinctive in the story of her life may be traced in the curious story of her lineage.

George Sand was of mixed national descent, and in her veins ran the blood of heroes and of kings. The noble and the artist, the *bourgeoisie* and the people, all had their representatives among their immediate ancestors. Her grandmother, the guardian of her girlhood, was the child of Maurice, Marshal Saxe, that favorite figure in history and romance, himself son of the famous Augustus II., Elector of Saxony, and King of Poland, and the Swedish Countess Aurora von Königsmark. The Marshal's daughter Aurore, though like her father of illegitimate birth—her mother, who was connected with the stage, passed by her professional name of Mlle. Verrieres—obtained after the Marshal's death the acknowledgment and protection of his relatives in high places, notably of his niece, the Dauphin of France, grand-daughter of Augustus of Poland, and mother of the three kings—Louis XVI., Louis XVIII., and Charles X.

Carefully educated at St. Cyr, Mlle. de Saxe was married, when little more than a child, to the Count de Horn, who was also of partly royal but irregular origin. He very shortly afterward fell in a duel. His widow, at thirty, became the wife of M. Dupin de Franceuil, an old gentleman of good provincial family and some fortune. Maurice, their only child, was the father of George Sand.

Madame Dupin (the suffix de Franceuil was afterwards dropped by her husband) appears to have inherited none of the adventurous and erratic tendencies of her progenitors. Aristocratic in her sympathies, philosophic in her intellect, and strictly decorous in her conduct, throughout the whole of her long and checkered life she was regarded with respect. Left a widow again, ten years after her second marriage, she concentrated her hopes and affections on her handsome and amiable son Maurice. Though fondly attached to her, he was yet to be the cause of her heaviest sorrows, by his more than hazardous marriage, and by his premature and tragical fate.

His strongest natural leanings seem to have been towards art in general, music and the drama in particular, and of his facile, buoyant, artist temperament there is ample evidence; but the political conditions of France under the Directory in 1798 left him no choice but to enter the army, where he served under Dupont, winning his commission on the field of Marengo in 1800. It was during this Italian campaign that the young officer met with the woman who, four years later, became his wife, and the mother of his illustrious child.

Mademoiselle Sophie Victorie Delaborde, was, emphatically speaking, a daughter of the people. Her father had been a poor bird-seller at Paris, where she herself had worked as a milliner. Left unprotected at a very early age, thoroughly uneducated and undisciplined, gifted with considerable beauty, and thrown on the world at a time when the very foundations of society seemed to be collapsing, she had been exposed to extreme dangers, and without any of the ordinary safeguards against them. That she proved herself not undeserving of the serious attachment with which she inspired Maurice Dupin, her least favorable judges were afterwards forced to admit; though, at the time this infatuation of the lieutenant of six-and-twenty for one four years his senior, and of the humblest extraction, and whose life hitherto had not been blameless, was naturally regarded as utterly disastrous by his elders.

The devoted pair were married secretly at Paris in 1804; and on the 5th of July in the same year—the last of the French Republic and the first of the Empire—their daughter entered the world, receiving the name of Amantine-Lucile-Aurore.

The discovery of the *mésalliance* she had been dreading for some time, and which her son had not dared to confess to her, was a heavy blow to old Madame Dupin. However, she schooled herself to forgive what was irrevocable, and to acknowledge this most unwelcome daughter-in-law, the infant Aurore helping unconsciously to effect the reconciliation. But for more than three years M. Dupin's mother and his wife scarcely ever met. Madame Dupin *mère* was living in a retired part of the country, in the very centre of France, on the little property of Nohant, which she had bought with what the Revolution had left her out of her late husband's fortune. Maurice, now Captain Dupin and *aide-de-camp* to Murat, resided, when not on service, in Paris, where he had settled with his wife and child. The union, strange though it may seem, continued to be a happy one. Besides a strong attachment there existed a real conformity of disposition between the two. The mother of George Sand was also, in her way, a remarkable woman. She has been described by her daughter as "a great artist lost for want of development"; showing a wonderful dexterity in whatever she put her hand to, no matter if practiced in it or not. "She tried everything, and always succeeded"—sewing, drawing, tuning the piano—"she would have made shoes, locks, furniture, had it been necessary." But her tastes were simple and domestic. Though married out of her rank, she was entirely without any vain ambition to push herself into fashionable society, the constraint of which, moreover, she could not bear. "She was a woman for the fire-side, or for quick, merry walks and drives. But in the house or out of doors, what she wanted was intimacy and confidence, complete sincerity in her relations with those around her, absolute liberty in her habits and the disposal of her time. She always led a retired life, more anxious to keep aloof from tiresome acquaintance than to seek such as might be advantageous. That was just the foundation of my father's character; and in this respect never was there a better-assorted couple. They could never be happy except in their own little *ménage*. Everywhere out of it they had to stifle their melancholy yawns, and they have transmitted to me that secret shyness which has always made the gay world intolerable, and home a necessity to me."

In a modest *bourgeois* habitation in the Rue Meslay, afterwards transferred to the Rue Grange-Batelière, Aurore Dupin's infancy passed tranquilly away, under the wing of her warmly affectionate mother who, though utterly illiterate, showed intuitive tact and skill in fostering the child's intelligence. "Mine," says her daughter, "made no resistance; but was never beforehand with anything, and might have been very much behindhand if left to itself."

Aurore was not four years old when adventures began for her in earnest. In the spring of 1808, her father was at Madrid, in attendance upon Murat; and Madame Maurice Dupin, becoming impatient of prolonged separation from her husband, started off with her little girl to join him. The hazards and hardships of the expedition, long mountain drives and wild scenery, strange fare and strange sights, could not fail vividly to impress the child, whose imagination from her cradle was extraordinarily active. Her mother ere this had discovered that Aurore, then little more than a baby, and pent up within four chairs to keep her out of harm's way, would make herself perfectly happy, plucking at the basket-work and babbling endless fairy tales to herself, confused and diluted versions of the first fictions narrated to her. A picturesque line in a nursery song was enough to bring before her a world of charming wonders; the figures, birds, and flowers on a Sèvres china candelabrum would call up enchanting landscapes; and the sound of a flageolet played from some distant attic start a train of melodious fancies and throw her into musical raptures. Her daily experiences, after reaching Madrid with her mother, continued to be novel and exciting in the extreme. The palace of the Prince de la Paix, where Murat and his suite had their quarters, was to her the realization of the wonder-land of Perrault and d'Aulnoy; Murat, the veritable Prince Fanfarinet. She was presented to him in a fancy court-dress, devised for the occasion by her mother, an exact imitation of her father's uniform in miniature, with spurs, sword, and boots, all complete. The Prince was amused by the jest, and took a fancy to the child, calling her his little *aide-de-camp*. After a residence of several weeks in this abode, whose splendor was alloyed by not a little discomfort and squalor, the return-journey had to be accomplished in the height of summer, amid every sort of risk; past reeking battle-fields, camps, sacked and half-burnt villages and beleaguered cities. Captain Dupin succeeded, however, in escorting his family safely back into France again, the party halting to recruit awhile under his mother's roof.

Nohant, a spot that has become as famous through its associations as Abbotsford, lies about three miles from the little town of La Châtre, in the department of the Indre, part of the old province of Berry. The manor is a plain gray house with steep mansard roofs, of the time of Louis XVI. It stands just apart from the road, shaded by trees, beside a pleasure ground of no vast extent, but with its large flower-garden and little wood allowed to spread at nature's bidding, quite in the English style. Behind the house cluster a score of cottages of the scattered hamlet of Nohant; in the centre rises the smallest of churches, with a tiny cemetery hedged around and adjoining the wall of the manor garden.

At this country home the tired travellers gladly alighted; but they had barely a few weeks in which to recover from the fatigues of their Spanish campaign, when a terrible calamity overwhelmed the household. Maurice Dupin, riding home one night from La Châtre, was thrown from his horse and killed on the spot.

The story of Aurore Dupin's individual life opens at once with the death of her father—a loss she was still too young to comprehend, but for which she was soon to suffer through the strange, the anomalous position, in which it was to place her. Maurice Dupin's patrician mother and her plebeian daughter-in-law, bereft thus violently of him who had been the only possible link between them, found themselves hopelessly, actively, and increasingly at variance. Their tempers clashed, their natures were antipathetic, their views contradictory, their positions irreconcilable. Aurore was not only thrust into an atmosphere of strife, but condemned to the apple of discord. She was to grow up between two hostile camps, each claiming her obedience and affection.

The beginning was smooth, and the sadness which alone kept the peace was not allowed to weigh on the child. She ran wild in the garden, the country air and country life strengthening a naturally strong constitution; and her intelligence, though also allowed much freedom in its development, was not neglected. A preceptor was on the spot in the person of the fourth inmate of Nohant, an old pedagogue, Deschartres by name, formerly her father's tutor, who had remained in Madame Dupin's service as "intendant." The serio-comic figure of this personage, so graphically drawn by George Sand herself in the memoirs of her early life, will never be forgotten by any reader of those reminiscences. Pedant, she says, was written in every line of his countenance and every movement that he made. He was possessed of some varied learning, much narrow prejudice, and a violent, crotchety temper, but had proved during the troubles of the Revolution his sincere and disinterested devotion to the family he served, and Aurore and "the great man," as she afterwards nicknamed her old tutor, were always good friends.

Before she was four years old she could read quite well; but she remarks that it was only after learning to write that what she read began to take a definite meaning for her. The fairy-tales perused but half intelligently before were re-read with a new delight. She learnt grammar with Deschartres, and from her grandmother took her first lessons in music, an art of which she became passionately fond; and it always remained for her a favourite source of enjoyment, though she never acquired much proficiency as a musical performer. The educational doctrines of Rousseau had then brought into fashion a *régime* of open-air exercise and freedom for the young, such as we commonly associate with English, rather than French, child-life; and Aurore's early years—when domestic hostilities and nursery tyrannies, from which, like most sensitive children, she suffered inordinately, were suspended—were passed in the careless, healthy fashion approved in this country. A girl of her own age, but of lower degree, was taken into the house to share her studies and pastimes. Little Ursule was to become, in later years, the faithful servant of her present companion, who had then become lady of the manor, and who never lost sight of this humble friend. Aurore had also a boy playmate in a *protégé* of her grandmother's, five years her senior, who patronised and persecuted her by turns, in his true fraternal fashion. This boy, Hippolyte, the son of a woman of low station, was in fact Aurore's half-brother, adopted from his birth and brought up by Madame Dupin the elder, whose indulgence, where her son was concerned, was infinite. With these, and the children of the farm-tenants and rural proprietors around, Aurore did not want for companions. But the moment soon arrived when the painful family dispute of which she was the object, was to become the cause of more distress to the child than to her elders. There were reasons which stood in the way of Madame Maurice Dupin's fixing her residence permanently under her mother-in-law's roof. But the mind of the latter was set on obtaining the guardianship of her grand-daughter, the natural heir to her property, and on thus assuring to her social and educational privileges of a superior order. The child's heart declared unreservedly for her mother, whose passionate fondness she returned with the added tenderness of a deeper nature, and all attempts to estrange the two had only drawn them closer together. But the pecuniary resources of Maurice Dupin's widow were of the smallest, and the advantages offered to her little girl by the proposed arrangement so material, that the older lady gained her point in the end. Madame Maurice settled in Paris. Aurore grew up her grandmother's ward, with Nohant for her home; a home she was to keep, knowing no other, till the end of her life.

The separation was brought about very gradually to the child. The first few winters were spent in Paris, where her grandmother had an establishment. Then she could pass whole days with her mother, who, in turn, spent summers at Nohant, and Aurore for years was buoyed up by the hope that a permanent reunion would still be brought about. But meantime domestic jealousy and strife, inflamed by the unprincipled meddling of servants, raged more fiercely than ever, and could not but be a source of more than ordinary childish misery to their innocent object. It was but slowly that she became attached to her grandmother, whose undemonstrative temper, formal habits and condescending airs were little calculated to win over her young affections, or fire her with gratitude for the anxiety displayed by this guardian to form her manners and cultivate her intellect. Nay, the result was rather to implant in her a premature dislike and distrust for conventional ideals. From the standard of culture and propriety, from the temptations of social rank and wealth held up for her preference, she instinctively turned to the simple, unrestrained affection of the despised mother, and the greater freedom and expansion enjoyed in such company. In vain did disdainful lady's-maids try to taunt her into precocious worldly wisdom, asking if she could really want to go and eat beans in a little garret. Such a condition, naturally, she began to regard as the equivalent of a noble and glorious existence!

Meantime, throughout all these alternations of content and distress, Nohant and its surroundings were perforce becoming dear to her, as only the home of our childhood can ever become. The scenery and characteristics of that region are familiar to all readers of the works of George Sand; a quiet region of narrow, winding, shady lanes, where you may wander long between the tall hedges without meeting a living creature but the wild birds that start from the honey-suckle and hawthorn, and the frogs croaking among the sedges; a region of soft-flowing rivers with curlew-haunted reed beds, and fields where quails cluck in the furrows; the fertile plain studded with clumps of ash and alder, and a rare farm-habitation standing amid orchards and hemp-fields, or a rarer hamlet of a dozen cottages grouped together. The country is flat, and, viewed from the rail or high road, uŋimpressive. But those fruitful fields have a placid beauty, and it needs but to penetrate the sequestered lanes and explore the thicket-bound courses of the streams, to meet with plenty of those pleasant solitudes after a poet's own heart, whose gift is to seize and perpetuate transient effects, and to open the eyes of duller minds to charms that might pass unnoticed. In this sense only can George Sand be said to have idealized for us the landscapes she loved.

The thoughtful, poetic side of her temperament showed itself early, leading her to seek long intervals of solitude, when she would bury herself in books or dreams, to satisfy the cravings of her intellect and imagination. On the other hand, her vigorous physical organization kept alive her taste for active amusements and merry companionship. So the child-squire romped on equal terms with the little rustics of Nohant, sharing their village sports and the occupations of the seasons as they came round: hay-making and gleaning in summer; in winter weaving bird-nets to spread in the snowy fields for the wholesale capture of larks; anon listening with mixed terror and delight to the picturesque legends told by the hemp-beaters, as they sat at their work out of doors on September moonlight evenings—to all the traditional ghost-stories of the "Black Valley," as she fancifully christened the country round about. Tales were these of fantastic animals and goblins, the *grand'-bête* and the *levrette blanche*, Georgeon, that imp of mischief, night apparitions of witches and charmers of wolves, singing Druidical stones and mysterious portents—a whole fairy mythology, then firmly believed in by the superstitious peasantry.

As a signal contrast to this way of life came for a time the annual visits to Paris—suspended after she was ten years old. There liberty ended, and the girl was transported into a novel and most uncongenial sphere. Her grandmother's friends and relatives were mostly old people, who clung to antiquated modes and customs; and distinguished though such circles might be, the youngest member only found out that they were intolerably dull. The wrinkled countesses with their elaborate toilettes and ceremonious manners, the *abbés* with their fashionable tittle-tattle and their innumerable snuff-boxes, the long dinners, the accomplishment-lessons, notably those in dancing and deportment, were repugnant to the soul of the little hoyden. She made amends to herself by observing these new scenes and characters narrowly, with the acute natural perception that was one of her leading gifts. From this artificial atmosphere of constraint, it was inevitable that she should welcome hours of escape into her mother's unpretending domestic circle; and already at ten years old she had pronounced the lot of a scullery-maid enviable, compared to that of an old *marquise*.

Nevertheless the fact of her having, at an age when impressions are strongest, and most lasting, mixed freely and on equal terms with the upper classes of society, was a point in her education not without its favorable action on her afterwards as a novelist. Despite her firm republican sympathies, emphatic disdain for mere rank and wealth, and her small mercy for the foibles of the fashionable world, she can enter into its spirit, paint its allurements without exaggeration, and indicate its shortcomings with none of that asperity of the outsider which always suggests some unconscious envy lurking behind the scorn.

The despised accomplishment-lessons, in themselves tending only to so much agreeable dabbling, proved useful to her indirectly by creating new interests, and as an intellectual stimulus. There seems to have been little or no method about her early education. The study of her own language was neglected, and the time spent less profitably, she considered in acquiring a smattering of Latin with Deschartres. She took to some studies with avidity, while others remained wholly distasteful to her. For mere head-work she cared little. Arithmetic she detested; versification, no less. Her imagination rebelled against the restrictions of form. Nowhere, perhaps, except in the free-fantasia style of the novel, could this great prose-poet have found the right field in which to do justice to her powers. The dry *technique* in music was a stumbling-block of which she was impatient. History and literature she enjoyed in whatever they offered that was romantic, heroic, or poetically suggestive. In her Nohant surroundings there was nothing to check, and much to stimulate, this dominant, imaginative faculty. Her youthful attempts at original composition she quickly discarded in disgust; but it seemed almost a law of her mind that whatever was possessing it she must instinctively weave into a romance. Thus in writing her history-epitome she must improve on the original, when too dry, by exercising her fancy in the description of places and personages. The actual political events of that period were of the most exciting character; Napoleon's Russian campaign, abdication, retreat to Elba, the Hundred Days, Waterloo, the Restoration, following each other in swift succession. Old Madame Dupin was an anti-Bonapartist, but Aurore had caught from her mother something of the popular infatuation for the emperor, and her fancy would create him over again, as he might have been had his energies been properly directed. Her day-dreams were often so vivid as to effect her senses with all the force of realities.

Such a visionary life might have been most dangerous and mentally enervating had her organization been less robust, and the tendency to reverie not been matched by lively external perception and plentiful physical activity. As it was, if at one moment she was in a cloud-land of her own, or poring over the stories of the Iliad, the classic mythologies, or Tasso's *Gerusalemme*, the next would see her scouring the fields with Ursule and Hippolyte, playing practical jokes on the tutor, and extemporizing wild out-of-door games and dances with her village companions.

Of serious religious education she received none at all. Here, again, the authorities were divided. Her mother was pious in a primitive way, though holding aloof from priestly influences. The grandmother, a disciple of Jean-Jacques Rousseau and of Voltaire, had renounced the Catholic creed, and was what was then called a Deist. But beyond discouraging a belief in miraculous agencies she preserved a neutrality with her ward on the subject, and Aurore was left free to drift as her nature should decide. Instinctively she felt more drawn toward her mother's unreasoning, emotional faith than toward a system of philosophic, critical inquiry. But on both sides what was offered her to worship was too indefinite to satisfy her strong religious instincts. Once more she filled in the blank with her imagination, which was forthwith called upon to picture a being who should represent all perfections, human and divine; something that her heart could love, as well as her intelligence approve.

This ideal figure, for whom she devised the name *Corambé*, was to combine all the spiritual qualities of the Christian ideal with the earthly grace and beauty of the mythological deities of Greece. For very many years she cherished this fantasy, finding there the scope she sought for her aspirations after superhuman excellence. It is hardly too much to say that the Christianity which had been expressly left out in her teaching she invented for herself. She erected a woodland altar in the recesses of a thicket to this imaginary object of her adoration, and it is a characteristic trait that the sacrifices she chose to offer there were the release of birds and butterflies that had been taken prisoners—as a symbolical oblation most welcome to a divinity whose essential attributes were infinite mercy and love. It will be remembered that a somewhat similar anecdote is related of the youthful Goethe.

Aurore, as the years went on, had grown sincerely fond of Madame Dupin; but her mother still held the foremost place in her heart, and she had never ceased to cherish the belief that if they two could live together she would be perfectly happy. The discovery of this deeply irritated her grandmother, who at length was provoked to intimate to the girl something of the real motive for insisting on this separation—namely, that her mother's antecedents were such as, in the eyes of Aurore's well-wishers, rendered it desirable to establish the daughter's existence apart from that of her parent. Sooner or later such a revelation must have been made; but made as it was, thus precipitately, in a moment of jealous anger, the chief result was of necessity to cause a painful and dangerous shock to the sensitive young mind. It brought about an unnatural discord in her moral nature, forbidden all at once to respect what she had loved most, and must continue to love, in spite of all. On the injurious effects of the over-agitation to which she was subjected in her childhood she has laid much stress in her remarkable work, "The Story of My Life." Much of this book, written when she was between forty and fifty, reads like a romance; and had a certain amount of retrospective imagination entered into the treatment of these reminiscences it would not be surprising. The tendency to impart poetical color and significance to whatever was capable of taking it was her mastering impulse, and may sometimes have led her to lose the distinction between fancy and reality, especially as by her own confession her memory was never her strong point. But she had an excellent memory for impressions, and no reader whose own recollections of childhood have not grown faint, but will feel the profound truth of the spirit of the narrative, which is of a kind that occasional exaggerations in the letter cannot depreciate in value as a psychological history. For an account of her early life it must always remain the most important source.

Aurore was now thirteen, and though she had read a good deal of miscellaneous literature her instruction had been mostly of a desultory sort; she was behindhand in the accomplishments deemed desirable for young ladies; and her country manners, on the score of etiquette, left something to be desired. To school, therefore, it was decided that she must go; and her grandmother selected that held by the nuns of the "English convent" at Paris, as the most fashionable institution of the kind.

This *Convent des Anglaises* was a British community, first established in the French capital in Cromwell's time. It has now been removed, and its site, the Rue St. Victor, has undergone complete transformation. In 1817, however, it was in high repute among conventual educational establishments. To this retreat Aurore was consigned and there spent more than two years, an untroubled time she has spoken of as in many respects the happiest of her life. There is certainly nothing more delightful in her memoirs than the vivid picture there drawn of the convent-school interior, drawn without flattery or malice, and with sympathy and animation.

The nunnery was an extensive building of rambling construction—with parts disused and dilapidated—quite a little settlement, counting some 150 inmates, nuns, pupils and teachers; with cells and dormitories, long corridors, chapels, kitchens, distillery, spiral staircases and mysterious nooks and corners; a large garden planted with chestnut trees, a kitchen garden, and a little cemetery without gravestones, over-grown with evergreens and flowers. The sisters were all English, Irish, or Scotch, but the majority of the pupils and the secular mistresses were French. Of the nuns the ex-scholar speaks with respect and affection, but their religious exercises left them but the smaller share of their time and attention to devote to the pupils. The girls almost without exception were of high social rank, the *bourgeois* element as yet having scarcely penetrated this exclusive seminary. Aurore formed warm friendships with many of her school-fellows, and seems to have been decidedly popular with the authorities as well, in spite of the high spirits which amid congenial company found vent in harmless mischief and a sort of organized playful insubordination. The school had two parties: the *sages* or good girls, and the *diables*, their opposites. Among the latter Aurore conscientiously enrolled herself and became a leader in their escapades, acquiring the sobriquet of "Madcap." These outbreaks led to nothing more heinous than playing off tricks on a tyrannical mistress, or making raids on the forbidden ground of the kitchen garden. But the charm that held together the confraternity of *diables* was a grand, long-cherished design, to which their best energy and ingenuity were devoted—a secret, heroic-sounding enterprise, set forth as "the deliverance of the victim." A tradition existed among them that a captive was kept languishing miserably in some remote cell, and they had set themselves the task of discovering and liberating this hapless wretch.

It is needless to say that prisoner and dungeon existed in their girlishly romantic brains alone, but easy to see how such a legend might possess itself of their imaginations, and to what bewitching exploits it might invite firm believers. The supervision was not so very strict but that a *diable* of spirit might sometimes play truant from the class-room unnoticed. The truants would then start on an exciting journey of discovery through the tortuous passages, exploring the darkest recesses of the more deserted portions of the convent; now penetrating into the vaults, now adventuring on the roofs, regardless of peril to life or limb. This sublimely ridiculous undertaking, half-sport, half-earnest, so fascinated Aurore as to become the most important occupation of her mind!

The teaching provided for the young ladies appears to have been of the customary superficial order—of everything a little; a little music, a little drawing, a little Italian. With English she had the opportunity of becoming really conversant, as it was the language commonly spoken in the convent, where also she could not fail to acquire some insight into the English character. This she has treated more fairly than England for long was to treat her. Few of her gifted literary countrymen have done such justice to the sterling good qualities of our nation. Even when, in delineating the Briton, she caricatures those peculiarities with which he is accredited abroad, her blunders seem due to incomplete knowledge rather than to any inability to comprehend the spirit of a people with whom, indeed, she had many points of sympathy. She could penetrate that coldness and constraint of manner so repelling to French natures, and has said of us, with unconventional truth, that our character is in reality more vehement than theirs; but with less mastery over our emotions themselves, we have more mastery over the expression of our emotions. Among her chosen school-comrades were several English girls, but on leaving the convent their paths separated, and in her after life she had but rare opportunities for renewing these early friendships.

Some eighteen months had elapsed in this fashion when Aurore began to tire of *diablerie*. The victim remained undiscoverable. The store of practical jokes was exhausted. Her restless spirit, pent up within those convent walls, was thirsting for a new experience,—something to fill her heart and life.

It came in the dawn of a religious enthusiasm—different from her mystical dream of *Corambé*, which however poetical was out of harmony with the spirit and ritual of a Catholic convent. But monastic life had its poetical aspects also; and through these it was that its significance first successfully appealed to her. An evening in the chapel, a Titian picture representing Christ on the Mount of Olives, a passage chanced upon in the "Lives of the Saints," brought impressions that awoke in her a new fervor, and inaugurated a period of ardent Catholicism. All vagueness was gone from her devotional aspirations, which now acquired a direct personal import. The change brought a revolution in her general behavior. She was understood to have been "converted." "Madcap" was now nicknamed "Sainte Aurore" by her profane school-fellows, and she formed the serious desire and intention of becoming a nun.

The sisters, a practical-minded community, behaved with great good sense and discretion. Without distressing the youthful proselyte by casting doubts on her "vocation," they reminded her that the consideration was a distant one, as for years to come her first duty would be to her relatives, who would never sanction her present determination. Her confessor, the Abbé Prémord, a Jesuit and man of the world, was likewise kindly discouraging; and perceiving that her zeal was leading her to morbid self-accusation and asceticism of mood, he shrewdly enjoined upon her as a penance to take part in the sports and pastimes with the rest as heretofore, much to her dismay. But she soon found her liking for these return, and with it her health of mind. Unshaken still in her private belief that she would take the veil in due time, she was content to wait, and in the interval to be a useful and agreeable member of society. No more insubordination, no more mischievous freaks, yet "Sainte Aurore" remained the life and soul of all recreations recognized by authority, which even included little theatrical performances now and then.

She had become more regular in her studies since her mind had taken a serious turn, but her heart was less in them than ever. Considering this, and the deficiencies in the system of instruction itself, it is hardly surprising that when, in the spring of 1820, her grandmother fearing that the monastic idea was taking hold of Aurore in good earnest decided to remove her from the *Couvent des Anglaises*, she knew little more than when first she had entered it.

CHAPTER II. - GIRLHOOD AND MARRIED LIFE.

AURORE DUPIN was now fifteen, and so far, though somewhat peculiarly situated, she and her life had presented no very extraordinary features, nor promise of the same. Her energies had flowed into a variety of channels, and manifestly clever and accustomed to take the lead though she might be, no one, least of all herself, seems to have thought of regarding her as a wonder. The Lady Superior of the *Couvent des Anglaises*, who called her "Still Waters," had perhaps an inkling of something more than met the eye, existent in this pupil. But a dozen years were yet to elapse before the moment came when she was to start life afresh for herself, on a footing of independence and literary enterprise, and by her first published attempts raise her name at once above the names of the mass of her fellow-creatures.

Old Madame Dupin, warned by failing health that her end was not far off, would gladly have first assured a husband's protection for her ward, whom she had now succeeded in really dissociating from her natural guardian. The girl's bringing-up, and an almost complete separation for the last five years, had made a gap—in habits of mind and feeling—such as could hardly be quite bridged over, between her mother and herself. But though beginning to be sadly aware of this and of the increasing violence and asperities of poor Madame Maurice Dupin's temper, which made peace under one roof with her a matter of difficulty, Aurore hung back from the notion of marriage, and clearly was much too young to be urged into taking so serious a step. So to Nohant she returned from the convent in the spring of 1820. There she continued to strike that judicious compromise between temporal and spiritual duties and pleasures enjoined on her by her clerical adviser. Still bent on choosing a monastic life, when free to choose for herself, she was reconciled in the meantime to take things as they came, and to make herself happy and add to the happiness of her grandmother in the ordinary way. So we find her enjoying the visit of one of her school friends, getting up little plays to amuse the elders, practicing the harp, receiving from her brother Hippolyte—now a noisy hussar—during his brief visit home, her first initiation into the arts of riding—for the future her favorite exercise—and of pistol-shooting; and last, but not least, beginning to suspect that she had learned nothing whatever while at school, and setting to work to educate herself, as best she could, by miscellaneous reading.

In the spring of the following year Madame Dupin's health and mental faculties utterly broke down. But she lived on for another ten months. Aurore for the time was placed in a most exceptional position for a French girl of sixteen. She was thrown absolutely on herself and her own resources, uncontrolled and unprotected, between a helpless, half imbecile invalid, and the eccentric, dogmatic pedagogue, Deschartres. Highly susceptible to influences from without, her mind, during their sudden and complete suspension, seemed as it were invited to discover and take its own bent.

Piqued by the charge of dense ignorance flung at her by her ex-tutor, and aware that there was truth in it, she would now sit up all night reading, finding her appetite for the secular knowledge she used to despise grow by what it fed upon. The phase of religious exaltation she had recently passed through still gave the tone to her mind, and it was with the works of famous philosophers, metaphysicians, and Christian mystics that she began her studies. Comparing the "Imitation of Christ" with Châteaubriand's "Spirit of Christianity," and struck here and elsewhere with the wide discrepancies and contradictions of opinion manifest between great minds ranging themselves under one theological banner, she was led on to speculations that alarmed her conscience, and she appealed to her spiritual director, the Abbé Prémord, for advice, fearing lest her faith might be endangered if she read more. He encouraged her to persevere, telling her in no wise to deny herself these intellectual enjoyments. But her rigid Catholicism was doomed from that hour. Hers was that order of mind which can never give ostensible adhesion to a creed whilst morally unconvinced; never accept that refuge of the weak from the torment of doubt, in abdicating the functions of reason and conscience, shifting the onus of responsibility on to others, and agreeing to believe, as it were, by proxy. She had plunged fearlessly and headlong into Aristotle, Bacon, Locke, Condillac, Mably, Leibnitz, Bossuet, Pascal, Montaigne, Montesquieu; beginning to call many things in question, and, through the darkness and confusion into which she was sometimes thrown, trying honestly and sincerely to feel her way to some more glorious faith and light.

In the convent she had been familiarized with Romanism under its most attractive aspects. The moral refinement, the mystery, the seclusion, and picturesque beauties of that abode had a poetic charm that had carried her irresistibly away. But, confronted with the system in its practical working, she was staggered by many of its features. In the country churches around her she saw the peasantry encouraged in their grossest superstitions, and the ritual, carelessly hurried through, degenerate often into mere mockery. The practice of confession, moreover—her ultimate condemnation of which, as an institution whose results for good are scanty, its dangers excessive, will be endorsed by most persons in this country—and the Church's denial of the right of salvation to all outside its pale, revolted her; and she caught at the teaching of those who claimed liberty of conscience. "Reading Leibnitz," she observes, "I became a Protestant without knowing it." That purer and more liberal Christianity she dreamed of had, she discovered, been the ideal of many great men. The step brought her face to face with fresh and grave problems of which, she truly observes, the solutions were beyond her years, and beyond that era. There came to her rare moments of celestial calm and concord, but she owed them to other and indirect sources of inspiration. The study of philosophy, indeed, was not much more congenial to her at sixteen than arithmetic had been at six. In what merely exercised memory and attention she took comparatively but languid interest. Instruction, to bring her its full profit, must be conveyed through the medium of moral emotion, but the mysterious power of feeling to stimulate intellect was with her immense. She turned now to the poets—Shakespeare, Byron, Dante, Milton, Virgil, Pope. A poet herself, she discovered that these had more power than controversialists to strengthen her religious convictions, as well as to enlarge her mind. Above all, the writings of the poet-moralist, Jean-Jacques Rousseau, helped her towards resolving the question that occupied her, of her true vocation in life, now that her determination to take the veil was not a little shaken.

The midnight student was by turns Amazon and sick-nurse as well. From the fatigue of long watches over her books or by the invalid's bedside, she found a better and more invigorating refreshment than sleep in solitary morning rides across country. Her fearlessness on horseback was madness in the eyes of the neighbors. Riding, then and there, was almost unheard of for ladies, a girl in a riding-habit regarded as simply a Cossack in petticoats, and Mademoiselle Dupin's delight in horse-exercise sufficed to stamp her as eccentric and strong-minded in the opinion of the country gentry and the towns-folk of La Châtre. They had heard of her studies, too, and disapproved of them as unlady-like in character. Philosophy was bad enough, but anatomy, which she had been encouraged to take up by Deschartres, himself a proficient in medical science, was worse—sacrilegious, for a person understood to be professedly of a devotional turn of mind. She went game-shooting with the old tutor; he had a mania for the sport, which she humored though she did not share. But when quails were the object, she owns to have enjoyed her part in the chase, which was to crouch in the furrows among the green corn, imitating the cry of the birds to entice them within gunshot of the sportsman. Lastly, finding in the feminine costume-fashions of that period a dire impediment to out-door enterprise of the sort, in a region of no roads, or bad roads, of rivers perpetually in flood, turning the lanes into water-courses for three-fourths of the year, of miry fields and marshy heaths, she procured for herself a suit of boy's clothes, donning blouse and gaiters now and then without compunction for these rough country walks and rambles.

Here, indeed, was more than enough to raise a hue-and-cry at La Châtre, a small provincial town, probably neither better nor worse than the rest of its class, a class never yet noted for charity or liberality of judgment. The strangest stories began to be circulated concerning her, stories for the most part so false and absurd as to inspire her with a sweeping contempt for public opinion. By a very common phenomenon, she was to incur throughout her life far more censure through freaks, audacious as breaches of custom, but intrinsically harmless, nor likely to set the fashion to others, than is often reserved for errors of a graver nature. The conditions of ordinary middle-class society are designed, like ready-made clothes, to fit the vast majority of human beings, who live under them without serious inconvenience. For the future George Sand to confine her activities within the very narrow restrictions laid down by the social code of La Châtre was, it must be owned, hardly to be expected. It was perhaps premature to throw down the gauntlet at sixteen, but her inexperience and isolation were complete. The grandmother in her dotage was no counsellor at all. Deschartres, an oddity himself, cared for none of these things. Those best acquainted with her at La Châtre, families the heads of which had known her father well and whose younger members had fraternized with her from childhood upwards, liked her none the less for her unusual proceedings, and defended her stoutly against her detractors.

"You are losing your best friend," said her dying grandmother to her when the end came, in December, 1821. Aurore was, indeed, placed in a difficult and painful situation. She had inherited all the property of the deceased, who, in her will, expressed her desire that her own nearest relations by her marriage with M. Dupin, a family of the name of de Villeneuve, well-off and highly connected, should succeed her as guardians to her ward. But it was impossible to dispute the claims of Madame Maurice Dupin to the care of her own daughter if she chose to assert them, which she quickly did, bearing off the girl with her to Paris—Nohant being left under the stewardship of Deschartres—and by her unconciliatory behavior further alienating the other side of the family from whom Aurore, through no fault of her own, was virtually estranged at the moment when she stood most in need of a friend. Twenty years later they came forward to claim kinship and friendship again: it was then with George Sand, the illustrious writer, become one of the immortals.

Thus her lot was cast for her in her mother's home and plebeian circle of acquaintance. So much the worse, it was supposed, for her prospects, social and matrimonial. This did not distress her, but none the less was the time that followed an unhappy one. The mother whom she had idolized, and of whom she always remained excessively fond, appears to have been something of a termagant in her later years. The heavy troubles of her life had aggravated one of those irascible and uncontrollable tempers that can only be soothed by superior violence. Aurore, saddened, gentle, and submissive, only exasperated her. Her fitful affection and fitful rages combined to make her daughter's life miserable, and to incline the girl unconsciously to look over-favorably on any recognized mode of escape that should present itself.

A long visit to the country-house of some friends near Melun, was hailed as a real relief by both. Here there were young people, and plenty of cheerful society. Aurore became like one of the family, and her mother was persuaded to allow her to prolong her stay indefinitely. Among the new acquaintance she formed whilst on this visit was one that decided her future.

M. Casimir Dudevant was a young man on terms of intimacy with her hosts, the Duplessis family. From the first he was struck by Mlle. Dupin, who on his further acquaintance was not otherwise than pleased with him. The sequel, before long, came in an offer of marriage on his part, which she accepted with the approval of her friends.

He was seven-and-twenty, had served in the army, and studied for the law; but had expectations which promised an independence. His father, Colonel Dudevant, a landed proprietor in Gascony, whose marriage had proved childless, had acknowledged Casimir, though illegitimate, and made him his heir. It was reckoned not a brilliant *parti* for the *châtelaine* of Nohant, but a perfectly eligible one. It was not a *mariage de convenance*; the young people had chosen freely. Still less was it a love match. Romantic sentiment—counted out of place in such arrangements by the society they belonged to—seems not to have been dreamed of on either side. But they had arranged it for themselves, which to Aurore would naturally seem, as indeed it was, an improvement on the usual mode of procedure, according to which the burden of choice would have rested with her guardians. It was a *mariage de raison* founded, as she and he believed, on mutual friendliness; in reality on a total and fatal ignorance of each other's characters, and probably, on Aurore's side, of her own as well. She was only just eighteen, and had a wretched home.

The match was sanctioned by their parents, respectively. In September, 1822, Aurore Dupin became Madame Dudevant, and shortly afterwards she and her husband established themselves at Nohant, there to settle down to quiet country life.

If tranquillity did not bring all the happiness that was expected, it was at least unbroken by such positive trials as those to come, and whatever was lacking to Madame Dudevant's felicity she forgot for a while in her joy over the birth of her son Maurice, in the summer of 1823—a son for whom more than ordinary treasures of maternal affection were in store, and who, when his childhood was past, was to become and remain until the time of her death a sure consolation and compensation to her for the troubles of her life.

The first two years after her marriage were spent almost without interruption in the still monotony of Nohant. "We live here as quietly as possible," she writes to her mother in June, 1825, "seeing very few people, and occupying ourselves with rural cares." That absolute dependence on each other's society that might have had its charm for a really well-assorted couple was, however, not calculated to prolong any illusions that might exist as to the perfect harmony of their dispositions. Already in the summer of 1824 the Dudevants had sought a change from seclusion in a long visit to their friends the Duplessis, after which they rented a villa in the environs of Paris for a short while. The spring found them back at Nohant, and the summer of 1825 was marked by a tour to the Pyrenees, undertaken in concert with some old school-fellows of Aurore's, two sisters, who with their father were starting for Cauterets. The pleasure of girlish friendships renewed gave double charm to the trip, and her delight in the mountain scenery knew no bounds.

"I am in such a state of enthusiasm about the Pyrenees," she writes to her mother, "that I shall dream and talk of nothing but mountains and torrents, caves and precipices, all the rest of my life." She joined eagerly in every excursion on foot and horseback, but even moderate feats of mountaineering, such as are now expected of the quietest English lady-tourists by their husbands and brothers, were then deemed startlingly eccentric, and got her into fresh trouble on this head.

Her letters and the fragments of her journal kept during this time, and in which she tried to commit to paper her impressions, whilst fresh and vivid, of the Pyrenees, show the same peculiar descriptive power that distinguished her novels—that art of seizing grand general effects together with picturesque detail, and depicting them in a simple and straightforward manner, in which she was an adept. It must be added that the diffuseness which characterizes her fiction, also pervades her correspondence. Neither can be adequately represented by extracts. Her composition is like a gossamer web, that must be shown in its entirety, as to split it up is to destroy it.

The ensuing winter and spring were passed agreeably in visits with her husband to his family at Nérac, Gascony, and to friends in the neighborhood. In the summer of 1826 their wanderings ended. Once more they settled down at Nohant, where Madame Dudevant, except for a few brief absences on visits to friends, or to health resorts in the vicinity, remained stationary for the next four years, during which her after-destiny was unalterably shaping itself.

It is perfectly idle to speculate on what might have happened had her lot in marriage turned out a fortunate one, or had she married for love, or had the moral character of the partner of her life preserved any solid claim on her respect, since the contrary was unhappily the case. Their situation, no doubt, was anomalous. In the young girl of barely eighteen, country-bred and intellectually immature, whom M. Dudevant had chosen to marry, who could have discerned one of the greatest poetical geniuses and most powerful minds of the century? Some commiseration might *à priori* be felt for the petty squire's son who had taken the hand of the pretty country-heiress, promising himself, no doubt, a comfortable jog-trot existence in the ordinary groove, to discover in after years that he was mated with the most remarkable woman that had made herself heard of in the literary world since Sappho! But he remained fatally blind to the nature of the development that was taking place under his eyes, preserving to the last the serenest contempt for his wife's intelligence. Her large mind and enthusiastic temperament sought in vain for moral sympathy from a narrow common spirit, and in proportion as her faculties unfolded, increasing disparity between them brought increasing estrangement. Such a strong artist-nature may require for its expansion an amount of freedom not easily compatible with domestic happiness. But of real domestic happiness she never had a fair chance, and for a time the will to make the best of her lot as it was cast appears not to have been wanting.

The Dudevants, after their return home in 1826, began to mix more freely in such society as La Châtre and the environs afforded, and at certain seasons there was no lack of provincial gayeties. Aurore Dudevant all her life long was quite indifferent to what she has summarily dismissed as "the silly vanities of finery"—"*Souffrir pour être belle*" was what from her girlhood she declined to do. Regard for the brightness of her eyes, her complexion, the whiteness of her hands, the shape of her foot, never made her sacrifice her midnight study, her walks in the sunshine, or her good country sabots for the rough lanes of Berry. "To live under glass, in order not to get tanned, or chapped, or faded before the time, is what I have always found impossible," she for her part has acknowledged. And she cared very moderately for general society. She writes to her mother in spring, 1826: "It is not the thing of all others that reposes, or even that amuses me best; still there are obligations in this life, which one must take as they come." She was not yet two-and-twenty, and carnival-tide with its social "obligations" in the form of balls and receptions was not unwelcome. They snatched her away from her increasing depression. She writes of these diversions to her mother in a lively strain, describing how one ball was kept up till nine o'clock the next day, how every Sunday morning the *curé* preaches against dancing, but in the evening the dance goes on in despite of him—how this cross *curé* is not their own parish *curé* of St. Chartier,—a very old friend and a "character" who, when Madame Dudevant was five-and-thirty, used to say of her, "Aurore is a child I have always been fond of." "As for him, if only he were sixty years younger," she adds, "I would undertake to make him dance himself if I set about it." Then follows an amusing sketch of a rustic bridal, the double marriage of two members of the Nohant establishment:

> The wedding-feast came off in our coach-houses—there was dinner in one, dancing in the other. The splendor was such as you may imagine; three tallow candle-ends by way of illumination, lots of home-made wine for refreshment; the orchestra consisting of a bagpipe and a hurdy-gurdy, the noisiest and, therefore, the best appreciated in the country side. We invited some friends over from La Châtre, and made fools of ourselves in a hundred thousand ways; as, for instance, dressing up as peasants in the evening and disguising ourselves so well as not to recognize each other. Madame Duplessis was charming in a red petticoat; Ursule, in a blue blouse and a big hat was a most comical fellow; Casimir, got up as a beggar, had some halfpence given him in all good faith; Stephane, whom I think you know, as a spruce peasant, made believe to have been drinking, stumbled against our *sous-prèfet* and accosted him—he is a nice fellow, and was just going to depart when all of a sudden he recognized us. Well, it was a most farcical evening, and would have amused you I will engage. Perhaps you, too, would have been tempted to put on the country-cap, and I will answer for it that there would not have been a pair of black eyes to compete with yours.

In other letters written in a vein of charming good humor, her facility and spirit are shown in her treatment of trivial incidents, or sketches of local characters, as this, for example, of an ancient female servant in her employ:

> The strangest old woman in the world—active, industrious, clean and faithful, but an unimaginable grumbler. She grumbles by day, and I think by night, when asleep. She grumbles whilst making the butter, she grumbles when feeding the poultry, she grumbles even at

> her meals. She grumbles at other people, and when she is alone she grumbles at herself. I never meet her without asking her how her grumbling is getting on, and she grumbles away more than ever.

And elsewhere she has her fling at the little squabbles and absurdities of provincial society, the "sets" and petty distinctions, giving a humorous relation of the collapse of her well-meaning efforts, in conjunction with friends at the *sous-prèfecture*, to do away with some of these caste prejudices, of the horror and indignation created in the oligarchy of La Châtre by the apparition of an inoffensive music-master and his wife at the *sous-prèfet's* reception, horror so great that on the next occasion, the *salon* of the official was unfurnished with guests, except for the said music-master and the Dudevants themselves. She wrote a poetical skit to commemorate the incident, which created great amusement among her friends.

In the autumn, 1828, her daughter Solange was born. The care of her two children, to whom she was devoted, occupied her seriously. Maurice's education was beginning, a fresh inducement to her to study that she might be better able to superintend his instruction. His least indisposition put her into a fever of anxiety. Her own health during all these years had repeatedly given cause for alarm. Symptoms of chest-disease showed themselves, but afterwards disappeared, her constitutional vigor triumphing in the end over complaints which seem to a great extent to have been of a nervous order. Meantime her domestic horizon was becoming overcast at many points.

Her brother, Hippolyte Chatiron, now married, came with his family to settle in the neighborhood, and spent some time at Nohant. He had fallen into the fatal habit of drinking, in which he was joined by M. Dudevant to the degradation of his habits and, it would be charitable to suppose, to the confusion of his intelligence. This grave ill came to make an open break in the household calm, hitherto undisturbed on the surface. Low company and its brutalizing influences were tending to bring about a state of things to which the most patient of wives might find it hard to submit. A rôle of complete self-effacement was not one it was in her power long to sustain, and the utter moral solitude into which she was thrown consolidated those forces inclining her to the extreme of self-assertion. For together with trials without came the growing sense of superiority, the *ennui* and unrest springing from mental faculties with insufficient outlet, and moreover, denied the very shadow of appreciation at home, where she saw the claim to her deference and allegiance co-exist with a repudiation she resented of all idea of the reciprocity of such engagements.

She had voluntarily handed over the management of her property—the revenue of which was hardly proportionate to the necessary expenses and required careful economy—to her husband, an arrangement which left her, even for pocket money, dependent on him. She now set herself to devise some means of adding to her resources by private industry. The more ambitious project of securing by her own exertions a separate maintenance for herself and her children would at this time have seemed chimerical, but it haunted her as a dream long before it took definite shape.

It was not in literature that she first fancied she saw her way to earning an independent income. She had begun to make amateur essays in novel-writing, but was as dissatisfied with them as with the compositions of her childhood, and with a religious novelette she had produced whilst in the convent, and speedily committed to the flames. Again, alluding to her attempts, in 1825, at descriptions of the Pyrenees, she says: "I was not capable then of satisfying myself by what I wrote, for I finished nothing, and did not even acquire a taste for writing."

But she had dabbled in painting, and remained fond of it. "The finest of the arts," she calls it, writing to her mother in 1830, "and the most pleasant, as a life-occupation, whether taken up for a profession, or for amusement merely. If I had real talent, I should consider such a lot the finest in the world." But neither did the decoration of fans and snuff-boxes nor the production of little water-color likenesses of her children and friends, beyond which her art did not go, promise anything brilliant in the way of remuneration.

In her circle of friends at La Châtre—old family friends who had known her all her life—were those who had recognized and admired her superior ability. Here, too, she met more than one young spirit with literary aspirations, and one, at least, M. Jules Sandeau, who was afterwards to achieve distinguished literary success. The desire to go and do likewise came and took hold of her, together with the conviction of her capability to make her mark. However discontented with her essays in novel-writing hitherto, she began to be conscious she was on the right track. The Revolution of July, 1830, had just been successfully accomplished, and new hopes and ambitions for the world in general, and their own country in particular, lent a stimulus to the intellectual activity of the youth of France—a movement too strong not to make itself felt, even in Berry.

The state of things at Nohant for the last two years had, as we have seen, been tending rather to stifle than to keep alive any hesitation or compunction Madame Dudevant might have felt at breaking openly from her present condition. In a letter, dated October, 1830, to her son's private tutor, M. Boucoiran, who had then been a year under their roof in that capacity, she remarks, significantly:

> You often wonder at my mobility of temper, my flexible character. What would become of me without this power of self-distraction? You know all in my life, and you ought to understand that but for that happy turn of mind which makes me quickly forget a sorrow, I should be disagreeable and perpetually withdrawn into myself, useless to others, insensible to their affection.

The distance between herself and her husband had, indeed, been widening until now the sole real link between them was their joint love for the children. No pretence of mutual affection existed any longer. Madame Dudevant's feeling seems to have been of indifference merely; M. Dudevant's of dislike, mingled, probably, with a little fear. It appears that he committed to paper his sentiments on the subject, and that this document, ostensibly intended by him not to be opened till after his death, was found and perused by his wife. It was the provocation thus occasioned her, and the certainty thus acquired of her husband's aversion to her society, that brought matters to a climax; so, at least, she asserted in the heat of the moment. But nothing, we imagine, could long have deferred her next step, strange and venturesome though it was. Violent in acting on a determination when taken, after the manner, as she observes, of those whose determinations are slow in forming, she declared her intentions to her husband, and obtained his consent to her plan.

According to this singular arrangement she was to be permitted to spend every alternate three months in Paris, where she proposed to try her fortune with her pen. She looked forward to having her little girl to be there with her as soon as she was comfortably settled, supposing the experiment to succeed. For half the year she would continue to reside, as hitherto, at Nohant, so as not to be long separated from her son, who was old enough to miss her, and to part from whom, on any terms, cost her dear. But he was to be sent to school in two years, and for the meantime she had secured for him the care and services of M. Boucoiran, whom she thoroughly trusted.

Her husband was to allow her £120 a year out of her fortune, and on condition that the allowance should not be exceeded, he left her at liberty to get on as she chose, abstaining from further interference.

It seems obvious that this compromise, whilst postponing, could only render more inevitable a future separation on less amicable terms, though neither appear to have realized it at the time. Madame Dudevant can have had no motive to blind her in the matter beyond her desire, in detaching herself from her present position, not to disconnect her life from that of her children. The freedom she demanded it was probably too late to deny. Those about her, her husband and M. Chatiron, who, with his family, was temporarily domesticated at Nohant, and who so far supported her as to offer her the loan of rooms held by him in Paris, for the first part of her stay, thought her resolution but a caprice. And viewed by the light of her subsequent success it is hard now to realize the boldness of an undertaking whose consequences, had it failed, must have been humiliating and disastrous. She had no practical knowledge of the world, had received no artistic training, and enjoyed none of the advantages of intellectual society. But she had extraordinary courage, spirit, and energy, springing no doubt from a latent sense of extraordinary powers, almost matured, though as yet but half-manifest. So much she knew of herself, and states modestly: "I had discovered that I could write quickly, easily, and for long at a time without fatigue; that my ideas, torpid in my brain, woke up and linked themselves together deductively in the flow of the pen; that in my life of seclusion, I had observed a good deal, and understood pretty well the characters I had chanced to come across, and that, consequently, I knew human nature well enough to describe it." A most moderate estimate, in which, however, she had yet to convince people that she was not self-deceived.

CHAPTER III. - DÉBUT IN LITERATURE.

IN the first days of January 1831, the Rubicon was passed. The step, though momentous in any case to Madame Dudevant, was one whose ultimate consequences were by none less anticipated than by herself, when to town she came, still undecided whether her future destiny were to decorate screens and tea-caddies, or to write books, but resolved to give the literary career a trial.

For actual subsistence she had her small fixed allowance from home; for credentials she was furnished with an introduction or two to literary men from her friends in the country who had some appreciation, more or less vague, of her intellectual powers. Though courageous and determined, she was far from self-confident; she asked herself if she might not be mistaking a mere fancy for a faculty, and her first step was to seek the opinion of some experienced authority as to her talent and chances.

M. de Kératry, a popular novelist, to whom she was recommended, spoke his mind to her without restraint. It was to the crushing effect that a woman ought not to write at all. Her sex, Madame Dudevant was informed, can have no proper place in literature whatsoever. M. Delatouche, proprietor of the *Figaro*, poet and novelist besides, and cousin of her old and intimate friends the Duvernets, of La Châtre, was a shade more encouraging, even so far committing himself as to own that, if she would not let herself be disgusted by the struggles of a beginner, there might be a distant possibility for her of making some sixty pounds a year by her pen. Such specimens of her fiction as she submitted to him he condemned without appeal, but he encouraged her to persevere in trying to improve upon them, and advised her well in advising her to avoid imitation of any school or master, and fearlessly to follow her own bent.

Meantime he took her on to the staff of his paper, then in its infancy and comparative obscurity. Journalism however was the department of literature least suited to her capabilities, and her fellow-contributors, though so much less highly gifted than Madame Dudevant, excelled her easily in the manufacture of leaders and paragraphs to order. To produce an article of a given length, on a given subject, within a given time, was for her the severest of ordeals; here her exuberant facility itself was against her. She would exhaust the space allotted to her, and find herself obliged to break off just at the point when she felt herself "beginning to begin." But she justly valued this apprenticeship as a professional experience, bringing her into direct relations with the literary world she was entering as a perfect stranger. Once able to devote herself entirely to composition and to live for her work, she found her calling begin to assert itself despotically. In a letter to a friend, M. Duteil, at La Châtre, dated about six weeks after her arrival in Paris, she writes:—

> If I had foreseen half the difficulties that I find, I should not have undertaken this enterprise. Well, the more I encounter the more I am resolved to proceed. Still, I shall soon be returning home again, perhaps without having succeeded in launching my boat, but with hopes of doing better another time, and with plans of working harder than ever.

Three weeks later we find her writing to her son's tutor, M. Boucoiran, in the same strain:—

> I am more than ever determined to follow the literary career. In spite of the disagreeables I often meet with, in spite of days of sloth and fatigue that come and interrupt my work, in spite of the more than humble life I lead here, I feel that henceforth my existence is filled. I have an object, a task, better say it at once, a passion. The profession of a writer is a violent one, and so to speak, indestructible. Once let it take possession of your wretched head, you cannot stop. I have not been successful; my work was thought too unreal by those whom I asked for advice.

But still she persisted, providing, as best she could, "copy" for the *Figaro*, at seven francs a column, and trying the experiment of literary collaboration, working at fictions and magazine articles, the joint productions of herself and her friend and fellow-student, Jules Sandeau, who wrote for the *Revue de Paris*. It was under his name that these compositions appeared, Madam Dudevant, in these first trial-attempts, being undesirous to bring hers before the public.

"I have no time to write home," she pleads, petitioning M. Boucoiran for news from the country, "but I like getting letters from Nohant, it rests my heart and my head."

And alluding to her approaching temporary return thither, in accordance with the terms of her agreement with M. Dudevant, she writes to M. Charles Duvernet:—

> I long to get back to Berry, for I love my children more than all besides, and, but for the hopes of becoming one day more useful to them with the scribe's pen than with the housekeeper's needle, I should not leave them for so long. But in spite of innumerable obstacles I mean to take the first steps in this thorny career.

In her case it was really the first step only that cost dear; whilst against the annoyances with which, as a new comer, she had to contend, there was ample compensation to set in the novel interests of the intellectual, political, and artistic world stirring around her. Country life and peasant life she had had the opportunity of studying from her youth up; of middle-class society she had sufficient experience; she counted relatives and friends among the *noblesse*, and had moved in those charmed circles; but the republic of art and letters, to which by nature and inclination she emphatically belonged, was a land of promise first opened up to her now. She was eager and impatient to deprovincialize herself.

In the art galleries of the Louvre, at the theatre and the opera, in the daily interchange of ideas on all kinds of topics with her little circle of intelligent acquaintance, her mind grew richer by a thousand new impressions and enjoyments, and rapidly took fresh strength together with fresh knowledge. The heavy practical obstacles that interfere with such self-education on the part of one of her sex were seriously aggravated in her case by her narrow income. How she surmounted them is well known; assuming on occasion a disguise which, imposing on all but the initiated, enabled her everywhere to pass for a collegian of sixteen, and thus to go out on foot in all weathers, at all hours, alone if necessary, unmolested and unobserved, in theatre or restaurant, boulevard or reading-room. In defense of her adoption of this strange measure, she pleads energetically the perishable nature of feminine attire in her day,—a day before double-soles or ulsters formed part of a lady's wardrobe,—its incompatibility with the incessant going to and fro which her busy life required, the exclusion of her sex from the best part of a Paris theatre, and so forth; the ineffable superiority of a costume which, economy and comfort apart, secured her equal independence with her men competitors in the race, and identical advantages as to the rapid extension of her field of observation. The practice, though never carried on by her to such an extent as very commonly asserted, was one to which she did not hesitate to resort now and then in later years, as a mere measure of convenience—a measure the world will only tolerate in the Rosalinds and Violas of the stage. The career of George Sand was, like her nature, entirely exceptional, and any attempt to judge it in any other light lands us in hopeless moral contradictions. She had extraordinary incentives to prompt her to extraordinary actions, which may be condemned or excused, but which there could be no greater mistake than to impute to ordinary vulgar motives. It must also be remembered that fifty years ago, the female art student had no recognized existence. She was shut out from that modicum of freedom and of practical advantages it were arbitrary to deny, and which may now be enjoyed by any earnest art aspirant in almost any great city. However unjustifiable the proceeding resorted to for a time by George Sand and Rosa Bonheur may be held to be, it cannot possibly be said they had no motive for it but a fantastic one.

Writing to her mother from Nohant, whither she had returned in April for a length of time as agreed, Madam Dudevant speaks out characteristically in defense of her love of independence:—

> I am far from having that love of pleasure, that need of amusement with which you credit me. Society, sights, finery, are not what I want,—you only are under this mistake about me,—it is liberty. To be all alone in the street and able to say to myself, I shall dine at four or at seven, according to my good pleasure; I shall go to the Tuileries by way of the Luxembourg instead of going by the Champs Elysées;

this is what amuses me far more than silly compliments and stiff drawing-room assemblies.

Such audacious self-emancipation, she was well aware, must estrange her from her friends of her own sex in the upper circles of Parisian society, and she anticipated this by making no attempt to renew such connections. For the moment she thought only of taking the shortest, and, as she judged, the only way for a "torpid country wife," like herself, to acquire the freedom of action and the enlightenment she needed. Those most nearly related to her offered no opposition. It was otherwise with her mother-in-law, the *baronne* Dudevant, with whom she had a passage-of-arms at the outset on the subject of her literary campaign, here disapproved *in toto*.

"Is it true," enquired this lady, "that it is your intention to *print books*?"

"Yes, madame."

"Well, I call that an odd notion!"

"Yes, madame."

"That is all very good and very fine, but I hope you are not going to put the name that I bear on the *covers of printed books*?"

"Oh, certaintly not, madame, there is no danger."

The liberty to which other considerations were required to give way was certainly complete enough. The beginning of July found her back at work in the capital. On the Quai St. Michel—a portion of the Seine embankment facing the towers of Notre Dame, the Sainte Chapelle, and other picturesque monuments of ancient Paris—she had now definitely installed herself in modest lodgings on the fifth story. Accepted and treated as a comrade by a little knot of fellow *literati* and colleagues on the *Figaro*, two of whom—Jules Sandeau and Félix Pyat—were from Berry, like herself; and with Delatouche, also a Berrichon, for their head-master, she served thus singularly her brief apprenticeship to literature and experience;—sharing with the rest both their studies and their relaxations, dining with them at cheap restaurants, frequenting clubs, studios, and theatres of every degree; the youthful effervescence of her student-friends venting itself in such collegians' pranks as parading deserted quarters of the town by moonlight, in the small hours, chanting lugubrious strains to astonish the shopkeepers. The only great celebrity whose acquaintance she had made was Balzac, himself the prince of eccentrics. Although he did not encourage Madame Dudevant's literary ambition, he showed himself kindly disposed towards her and her young friends, and she gives some amusing instances that came under her notice of his oddities. Thus, once after a little Bohemian dinner at his lodgings in the Rue Cassini, he insisted on putting on a new and magnificent dressing-gown, of which he was exceedingly vain, to display to his guests, of whom Madame Dudevant was one; and not satisfied therewith, must needs go forth, thus accoutred, to light them on their walk home. All the way he continued to hold forth to them about four Arab horses, which he had not got yet, but meant to get soon, and of which, though he never got them at all, he firmly believed himself to have been possessed for some time. "He would have escorted us thus," says Madame Dudevant, "from one extremity of Paris to another, if we had let him."

Twice again before the end of the year, faithful to her original intentions, we find her returning to her place as mistress of the house at Nohant, occupying herself with her children, and working at the novel *Indiana*, which was to create her reputation the following year.

Meanwhile, a novelette, *La Prima Donna*, the outcome of the literary collaboration with Jules Sandeau, had found its way into a magazine, the *Revue de Paris*; and was followed by a longer work of fiction, of the same double authorship, entitled *Rose et Blanche*, published under Sandeau's *nom de plume* of Jules Sand.

This literary partnership was not to last long, and to-day the novel will be found omitted in the list of the respective works of its authors. Its perusal will hardly repay the curious. The powerful genius of Madame Dudevant, the elegant talent of the author of *Mlle. de la Seiglière*, are mostly conspicuous by their absence in *Rose et Blanche*, or *La Comédienne et la Réligieuse*, an imitative attempt, and not a happy one, in the style of fiction then in vogue.

Madame Dudevant had stepped into the literary world at the moment of the most ardent activity of the Romantic movement. The new school was on the point of achieving its earliest signal triumphs. Victor Hugo's first poems had just been followed by the dramas *Hernani* and *Marion Delorme*. Dumas' *Antony* was drawing crowded and enthusiastic houses. A few months before the publication of *Rose et Blanche* appeared *Notre Dame de Paris*. The passion for innovation which had seized on all the younger school of writers was leading many astray. The strange freaks of Hugo's genius had, to quote Madame Dudevant's own expression, excited a "ferocious appetite" for whatever was most outrageous, and set taste, precedent, and probability most flatly at defiance. From those aberrations into which the great master's imitators had been betrayed Madame Dudevant's fine art-instincts were calculated to preserve her; but she had not yet learned to trust to them implicitly.

Rose et Blanche, though containing many clever passages—waifs and strays of shrewd observation, description and character analysis,—is in the main ill-conceived, ill-constructed, and unreal. The two authors have sacrificed their individualities in a mistaken effort to follow the fashion's lead, resulting in a most ineffective compound of tameness and sensationalism. Amazing adventures are undergone by each heroine before she is one-and-twenty. Angels of innocence, they are doomed to have their existences crushed out by the heartless conduct of man, Blanche expiring of dismay almost as soon as she is led from the altar, Rose burying herself and her despair in a convent. The then favorite heroes of romance were of the French Byronic type—young men of fortune who have exhausted life before they are five-and-twenty, whose minds are darkened by haunting memories of some terrific crime, but who are none the less capable of all the virtues and great elevation of sentiment on occasion. None of these requisitions are left unfulfilled by the unamiable hero of *Rose et Blanche*, a work which did little to advance the fortunes of its authors, and whose intrinsic merits offer little warrant for dragging it out of the oblivion into which it has been suffered to drop.

To escape the influences of the literary revolution everywhere then triumphant was of course impossible. To make them serve her individual genius instead of enslaving her individuality was all Madame Dudevant needed to learn. Her friend Balzac had done this for himself, suiting his genius to the period without any sacrifice of originality. Although not yet at the height of his fame he had produced many most successful works, and Madame Dudevant, according to her own account, derived great profit from the study of his method, although with no inclination to follow in his direction. Yet he afterwards observed to her, "Our two roads lead to the same goal."

Rose et Blanche, though little noticed by the public, brought a publisher to the door, one Ernest Dupuy, with an order for another novel by the same authors. *Indiana* was ready-written, and came in response to the demand. But as Sandeau had had no hand whatever in this composition, the signature had of course to be varied. The publisher wishing to connect the new novel with its predecessor it was decided to alter the prefix only. She fixed on George, as representative of Berry, the land of husbandmen; and George Sand thus became pseudonym of the author of *Indiana*, a pseudonym whose origin imaginative critics have sought far afield and some have discovered in her alleged sympathy with Kotzebue's murderer, Karl Sand, and political assassination in general! Its assumption was to inaugurate a new era in her life.

In the last days of April, 1832, appeared *Indiana*, by George Sand. "I took," says Madame Dudevant, in her account of the transaction, "the 1,200 francs paid me by the publisher, which to me were a little fortune, hoping he would see his money back again." She had recently returned from one of her periodical visits to Nohant, accompanied this time by her little girl, whom the progress already achieved enabled her now to take into her charge, and was living very quietly and studiously in her humble establishment on the Quai St. Michel, when she awoke to find herself famous.

Her success, for which indeed there had been nothing to prepare her—neither flattery of friends, nor vain-glorious ambition within herself—was immediate and conclusive. Whatever differences of opinion might exist about the book, critics agreed in recognizing there the revelation of a new writer of extraordinary power. "One of those masters who have been gifted with the enchanter's wand and mirror," wrote Sainte-Beuve, a few months later, when he did not hesitate to compare the young author to Madame de Staël. The novel of sentimental analysis, a style in which George Sand is unsurpassed, was then a fresh and promising field. *Indiana*, without the aid of marvellous incidents, startling crimes, or iniquitous mysteries, riveted the attention of its readers as firmly as the most thrilling tales of adventure and horror. It is a "soul's tragedy," and that is all—the love-tragedy vulgarized since by repeated treatment by inferior novelists, of a romantic, sensitive, passionate, high-natured girl, hopelessly ill-mated with a somewhat tyrannical and stupid, yet not entirely ill-disposed old colonel, and exposed to the seductions of a Lovelace—the truth about whose unloveable character, in its profound and heartless egoism, first bursts upon her at the moment when, maddened by brutal insult, she is driven to claim the generous devotion he has proffered a thousand times. Side by side with the ideal of selfishness, Raymon stands in contrast with the ideally chivalrous Ralph, Indiana's despised cousin, who, loving her disinterestedly and in silence, has watched over her as a guardian-friend to the last, and does save her ultimately. The florid descriptions, the high-flown strains of emotion, which now strike as blemishes in the book, were counted beauties fifty years since; and even to-day, when reaction has brought about an extreme distaste for emotional writing, they cannot conceal the superior ability of the novelist. The sentiment, however extravagantly worded, is genuine and spontaneous, and has the true ring of passionate conviction. The characters are vividly, if somewhat closely drawn and contrasted, the scenes graphic; every page is colored by fervid imagination, and despite some violations of probability in the latter portion, out of keeping artistically with the natural character of the rest of the book, the whole has the strength of that unity and completeness of conception which is the distinguishing stamp of a genius of the first order. The *entrain* of the style is irresistible. It was written, she tells us, *tout d'un jet*, under the force of a stimulus from within. Ceasing to counterfeit the manner of anyone, or to consult the exigencies of the book-market, she for the first time ventures to be herself responsible for the inspiration and the mode of expression adopted.

The papers spoke of the new novel in high tones of praise, the public read it with avidity. The authorship, for a time, continued to perplex people. In spite of the masculine pseudonym, certain feminine qualities, niceties of perception and tenderness, were plainly recognized in the work, but the possibility that so vigorous and well-executed a composition could come from a feminine hand was one then reckoned scarcely admissible. Even among those already in the secret were sceptics who questioned the author's power to sustain her success, since nearly everybody, it is said, can produce one good novel.

"The success of *Indiana* has thrown me into dismay," writes Madame Dudevant, in July, 1832, to M. Charles Duvernet, at La Châtre. "Till now, I thought my writing was without consequence, and would not merit the slightest attention. Fate has decreed otherwise. The unmerited admiration of which I have become the object must be justified." And *Valentine* was already in progress; and its publication, not many months after *Indiana*, to be a conclusive answer to the challenge.

The season of 1832, in which George Sand made her *début* in literature, was marked, in Paris, by public events of the most tragic character. In the spring, the cholera made its appearance, and struck panic into the city. Six people died in the house where Madame Dudevant resided, but neither she nor any of her friends were attacked. She was next to be a witness of political disturbances equally terrible. The disappointment felt by the Liberals at the results of the Revolution of 1830, and of the establishment of Louis Philippe's Government, upon which such high hopes had been founded, was already beginning to assert itself in secret agitation, and in the sanguinary street insurrections, such as that of June, 1832, sanguinarily repressed. Madame Dudevant at this time had no formulated political creed, and political subjects were those least attractive to her. But though born in the opposite camp she felt all her natural sympathies incline to the Republican side. They were further intensified by the scenes of which she was an eye-witness, and which roused a similar feeling even among anti-revolutionists. Thus Heine, in giving an account of the struggle mentioned above, and speaking of the enthusiasts who sacrificed their lives in this desperate demonstration, exclaims: "I am, by God! no Republican. I know that if the Republicans conquer they will cut my throat, and all because I don't admire all they admire; but yet the tears came into my eyes as I trod those places still stained with their blood. I had rather I, and all my fellow-moderates, had died than those Republicans."

Amid such disturbing influences it is not surprising that we find her complaining in the letter last quoted that her work makes no progress; but the lost time was made up for by redoubled industry during her summer visit to Nohant.

In the autumn appeared *Valentine*. This second novel not only confirmed the triumph won by the first, but was a surer proof of the writer's calibre, as showing what she could do with simpler materials. Here, encouraged by success, she had ventured to take her stand entirely on her own ground—dispensing even with an incidental trip to the tropics, which, in *Indiana*, strikes as a misplaced concession to the prevalent craze for Oriental coloring—and to lay the scene in her own obscure province of Berry, her first descriptions of which show her rare comprehension of the poetry of landscape. Like *Indiana*, *Valentine* is a story of the affections; like *Indiana*, it is a domestic tragedy, of which the girl-heroine is the victim of a pernicious system that makes of marriage, in the first instance, a mere commercial speculation. Indeed, the extreme painfulness of the story would render the whole too repulsive but for the charm of the setting, which relieves it not a little, and a good deal of humor in the treatment of the minor characters, notably the eighteenth century *marquise*, and the Lhéry family of peasant-*parvenus*. The personages are drawn with more finish than those in *Indiana*; the tone is more natural in its pitch. It is the work of one who finds in every-day observation, as well as in such personal emotions as come but once in a lifetime, the inspiration that smaller talents can derive from the latter alone.

In both her consummate art, or rather natural gift of the art of narrative, is the mainstay of the fabric her imagination has reared. That incomparable style of hers is like some magic fairy-ring, that bears the wearer, safe and victorious, through manifold perils—perils these of prolixity, exaggeration, and disdain of careful construction. Both *Indiana* and *Valentine*, moreover, contain scenes and passages offensive to English taste, but it is impossible fairly to criticise the fiction of a land where freer expression in speech and in print than with us is habitually recognized and practiced, from our own standpoint of literary decorum. It was not for this feature that French criticism had already begun to charge her books with dangerous tendencies (thus contributing largely to noise her fame abroad), as breathing rebellion against the laws of present society; charges which, so far as *Indiana* and *Valentine* are concerned, had, as is now generally admitted, but little foundation. Each is the story of an unhappy marriage, but there is no attempt whatever to throw contempt on existing institutions, or to propound any theory, unless it be the idea—no heresy or novelty in England at least—that marriage, concluded without love on either side, is fraught with special dangers to the wife, whose happiness is bound up with her affections. It was the bold and uncompromising manner in which this plain fact was brought forward, the energy of the protest against a real social abuse, which moved some critics to sound a war-cry for which, as yet, no just warrant had been given.

Besides these two novels, containing full proof of her genius, if not of its highest employment, there appeared, late in 1832, that remarkable novelette, *La Marquise*, revealing fresh qualities of subtle penetration and clear analysis. The flexibility of her imagination, the variety in her modes of its application, form an essential characteristic of her work. Not by any single novel, nor, indeed by half-a-dozen taken at random, can she be adequately represented.

When in the winter of 1832 Madame Sand returned with her little girl to Paris after spending the autumn, as usual, at Nohant, it was to rather more comfortable quarters, on the Quai Malplaquet. The rapid sale of her books was placing her in comparatively easy circumstances, and giving fresh spur to her activity. But her situation was transforming itself fast; the freedom of obscurity was lost to her for ever from the day when the unknown personage, George Sand, became the object of general curiosity—of curiosity redoubled in Paris by the rumors current there of her exceptional position, eccentric habits, and interesting personality.

The celebrated portrait of her by Eugène Delacroix was painted in the year 1833. It is a three-quarter view, and represents her wearing her *quasi* masculine *redingote*, with broad *revers* and loosely knotted silk neck-tie. Of somewhat later date is a highly interesting drawing by Calamatta, well-known by engravings; but of George Sand in her first youth no likeness unfortunately has been left to the world. She has been most diversely described by her different contemporaries. But that at this time she possessed real beauty is perfectly evident; for all that she denies it herself, and that, unlike most women, and nearly all French women, she scorned to enhance it by an elaborated toilette. Heine, though he never professed himself one of her personal adorers, compares the beauty of her head to that of the Venus of Milo, saying, "It bears the stamp of ideality, and recalls the noblest remaining examples of Greek art." Her figure was somewhat too short, but her hands and feet were very small and beautifully shaped. His acquaintance with her dates from the early years of her literary triumphs, and his description is in harmony with Calamatta's presentation. She had dark curling hair, a beauty in itself, falling in profusion to her shoulders, well-formed features, pale olive-tinted complexion, the countenance expressive, the eyes dark and very fine, not sparkling, but mild and full of feeling. The face reminds us of the character of "Still Waters," attributed to the Aurore Dupin of fifteen by the Lady Superior of the English convent. Her voice was soft and muffled, and the simplicity of her manner has been remarked on by those who sought her acquaintance, as a particular charm. Yet, like all reserved natures, she often failed to attract strangers at a first meeting. In general conversation she disappointed people, by not shining. Men and women, immeasurably her inferiors, surpassed her in ready wit and brilliant repartee. Her taciturnity in society has been somewhat ungenerously laid to a *parti pris*. She was one, it is said, who took all and gave nothing. That she was intentionally chary of her passing thoughts and impressions to those around her, is, however, sufficiently disproved by her letters. Here she shows herself lavish of her mind to her correspondents. Conversation and composition necessitate a very different brain action, and her marvellous facility in writing seems really to have been accompanied with no corresponding readiness of speech and reply. Probably it was only, as she herself states, when she had a pen in her hand that her lethargic ideas would arise and flow in order as they should. And the need of self-expression felt by all those who have not the gift of communicating themselves fully and easily in speech or manner, a strong need in her case, from her having so much to express, was the spur that drove her to seek and find the mode of so doing in art.

Her silence in company certainly did not detract from her fascination upon a closer acquaintance. Of those who fell under the spell, the more fortunate came at once to terms of friendship with her, which remained undisturbed through life. Thus, of one among this numerous brotherhood, François Rollinat, with whom she would congratulate herself on having realized the perfection of such an alliance of minds, she could write when recording their friendship, then already a quarter of a century old, that it was still young as compared with some that she counted, and that dated from her childhood.

Others fell in love with her, and found her unresponsive. With some of these, jealousies and misunderstandings arose, and led to estrangements, for the most part but temporary. Yet the winner of her heart was scarcely to be envied. She was apt—she has herself thus expressed it—to see people through a prism of enthusiasm, and afterwards to recover her lucidity of judgment. Great, no doubt, was her power of self-illusion; it betrayed her into errors that have been unsparingly judged. For her power of calm and complete disillusion she was perhaps unique among women, and it is no wonder if mankind have found it hard to forgive.

CHAPTER IV. - LÉLIA.—ITALIAN JOURNEY.

IT was less than two years since she had come up to the capital, to seek her fortunes there in literature. Aurore Dudevant, hereafter to be spoken of as George Sand (for she made her adopted name more her own than that she had borne hitherto, and became George Sand for her private friends as well as for the public,) found herself raised to eminence among the eminent. And it was at an exceptionally brilliant epoch in French imaginative literature that the distinction had been won. Such a burst of talent as that which signalized the opening years of Louis Philippe's reign is unexampled in French literary history. With Hugo, Dumas, De Musset, Balzac, not to mention lesser stars, the author of *Indiana* and *Valentine*, although a woman, was acknowledged as worthy to rank. The artist in her, a disturbing element in her inner life which had driven her out of the spiritual bondage and destitution of a petty provincial environment to secure for herself freedom and expansion, had justified the audacity of the move by a triumphant artistic success. From this time onward her artistic faculty dominated her life, often, probably, unknown to herself an invincible force of instinct she obeyed, whilst assigning, in all good faith, other motives for her course of action, and for real or apparent inconsequences, that have been constantly misrepresented and misunderstood.

So sudden and abrupt a change would have turned all heads but the strongest. Publishers competed with one another to secure her next work. Buloz, proprietor of the *Revue des Deux Mondes*, engaged her to write regularly for his periodical, to which, for the next ten years, she never ceased to be a regular and extensive contributor. Although the scale of remuneration was not then very high she was clearly secure, so long as she allowed nothing to interfere with her literary work, of earning a sufficient income for her own needs. She had learnt the importance of pecuniary independence, and never pretended to despise the reward of her industry. To luxury she was indifferent, but the necessity of strict economy was a burden she was impatient of; she liked to have plenty to give away, and was always excessively liberal to the poor. Her little dwelling on the Quai Malplaquet was no longer the hermitage of an anonymous writer of no account. The great in art and letters, leading critics, such as Sainte-Beuve and Gustave Planche, came eager to seek her acquaintance, and delighting to honor the obscure student of a year ago.

Writing to M. Boucoiran after her return to Paris in December, 1832, she describes her altered position:—

> All day long I am beset with visitors, who are not all entertaining. It is a calamity of my profession, which I am partly obliged to bear. But in the evening I shut myself up with my pens and ink, Solange, my piano, and a fire. With all these I pass some right pleasant hours. No noise but the sounds of a harp, coming I know not whence, and of the playing of a fountain under my window. This is highly poetical—pray don't make game of me!

There was another side to her success. Fame brought trials and annoyances that fell with double severity on her as a woman. Her door was besieged by a troop of professional beggars, impostors, impertinent idlers, and inquisitive newsmongers. Jealousy and ill-will, inevitably attendant on sudden good fortune such as hers, busied themselves with direct calumny and insidious misrepresentation. No statement so unfounded, so wildly improbable about her, but it obtained circulation and credit. Till the end of her life she remained the centre of a cloud of myths, many, to the present day, accepted as gospel. People insisted on identifying her with the heroines of her novels. Incidents, personal descriptions, nay, whole letters extracted from these novels will be found literally transcribed into alleged biographies of herself and her friends, as her own statement of matters of fact. Now, though the spirit of her life is strongly and faithfully represented by her fiction taken as a whole, those who would read in any special novel the literal record of any of the special events of her existence cannot be too much on their guard. Whatever the material under treatment, George Sand must retouch, embellish, transform, artist-fashion, as her genius shall dictate, till often little resemblance is left between the original and the production it has done no more than suggest. Romance and reality are so fused together in these apparent outpourings of spirit that her nearest friends were at a loss how to separate them. As an actress into many a favorite part, so could she throw herself into her favorite characters; but seldom if ever will much warrant be found in actual fact for identifying these creations with their creatress.

How, indeed, could so many-sided a nature as hers be truly represented in a single novel? Her rare physical and mental energies enabled her to combine a life of masculine intellectual activity with the more highly emotional life of a woman, and with vigilance in her maternal cares. Maurice was placed in the spring of 1833 at the College Henri IV., at Paris; thus she had now both son and daughter near her, and watched indefatigably over them, their childish illnesses and childish amusements, their moral and intellectual training absorbing a large share of her time and attention. Heine, a friendly visitor at her house, says:—

> I have often been present for hours whilst she gave her children a lesson in French, and it is a pity that the whole of the French Academy could not have been present too, as it is quite certain that they might have derived great profit from it.

Not all the distractions of fame and work, of passionate pleasure or passionate sorrow, ever relaxed her active solicitude for the present and future welfare of her two young children. "They give me the only real joys of my life," she repeats again and again.

Lélia, begun immediately after *Valentine* was published in the spring of 1833, and created an immense sensation. Hailed by her admirers as a sign of an accession of power, of power exerted in quite a new direction, it brought down on the writer's head a storm of hostile criticism, as a declared enemy of religion and domestic morality—enhancing her celebrity not a little.

Lélia, a lyrical novel—an outburst of poetical philosophy in prose, stands alone among the numerous productions of George Sand. Here she takes every sort of poetical license, in a work without the restrictions of poetic form, which are the true conditions of so much latitude. "Manfred" and "Alastor" are fables not further removed from real life than is *Lélia*. The personages are like allegorical figures, emblematic of spiritual qualities on a grand scale, the scenes like the paradisiacal gardens that visited the fancy of Aurore Dupin when a child. There is no action. The interest is not in the characters and what they do, but in what they say. The declamatory style, then so popular, is one the taste for which has so completely waned that *Lélia* will find comparatively few readers in the present day, fewer who will not find its perusal wearisome, none perhaps whose morality, however weak, will be seriously shaken by utterances ever and anon hovering on the perilous confines of the sublime and the ludicrous.

Lélia, a female Faust or Manfred, a mysterious muse-like heroine, who one night sleeps on the heathery mountain-side, the next displays the splendor of a queen in palaces and fairy-like villas; her sorely tried and hapless lover, Sténio, the poet, who pours forth odes to his own accompaniment on the harp, and lingers the night long among Alpine precipices brooding over the abyss; Trenmor, the returned gentleman convict and Apostle of the Carbonari, whose soul has been refreshed, made young and regenerated at the galleys; and the mad Irish priest, Magnus, are impossible personages, inviting to easy ridicule, and neither wisdom nor folly from their lips is likely to beguile the ears of the present generation.

It is no novel, but a poetical essay, fantastically conceived and executed with the *sans gêne* of an improvisatore. For those who admire the genius of George Sand its interest as a psychological revelation remains unabated. Into *Lélia*, she owns, she put more of her real self than into any other of her books—of herself, that is, and her state of mind at the dawn of a period of moral disturbance and revolt. All must continue to recognize there an extraordinary exhibition of poetical power and musical style. As a work of art George Sand has herself pronounced it absurd, yet she always cherished for it a special predilection, and, as will be seen, took the trouble to rewrite it some years later, when in a happier and healthier frame of mind than that which inspired this unique and most characteristic composition.

The note of despair struck in *Lélia*, the depth of bitter feeling, the capacity for mental and moral speculation and suffering it seemed to disclose, astounded many of her familiar acquaintance. "*Lélia* is a fancy-type," so writes to the author her friend and neighbor in Berry, Jules Néraud, an ardent naturalist, whose botanical and entomological pursuits she had often shared: "it is not like you—you who are merry, dance the *bourrée*, appreciate lepidoptera, do not despise puns, who are not a bad needlewoman, and make very good preserves. Is it possible you should have thought so much, felt so much, without anyone having any idea of it?"

Lélia was certainly the expression of a new phase in her mind's history, a moral crisis she could not escape, which was all the more severe for her having, as she remarks, reached her thirtieth year without having opened her eyes to the realities of life. Till the time of her coming to Paris, for very dearth of outward impressions, she had lived chiefly in dreams, the life of all others most favorable to the prolongation of ignorance and credulity. The liberty and activity she had enjoyed for the last two years were fatal to Utopian theories.

It was not only the bitterness that springs from disenchantment in individuals, the sense of the miserable insufficiency of human love to satisfy her spiritual aspirations producing "that widely concluding unbelief which," as her sister in greatness has said, "we call knowledge of the world, but which is really disappointment in you and in me." George Sand was one to whom scepticism was intolerable. Pessimistic doctrines were fatal to her mind's equilibrium, and private experience and outward intellectual influences were driving her to distrust all objects of her previous worship, human and divine. The moment was one when the most fundamental social and religious principles were being called in question.

"Nothing in my old beliefs," she writes, "was sufficiently formulated in me, from a social point of view, to help me to struggle against this cataclysm; and in the religious and socialistic theories of the moment I did not find light enough to contend with the darkness." The poet's creed, with which her mind had hitherto rested satisfied, was shaken, and appeared to prove a false one. She was staggered by the infinity of evil, misery, and injustice, which dwellers in great cities are not allowed to forget, the problem of humanity, the eternal mystery of suffering and wrong predominant in a world on the beneficence of whose Supreme Power all her faiths were founded.

Her mental revolt and suffering found vent in *Lélia*, which it was an immense relief to her to write. Characteristic as an exhibition of feeling and of mastery of language, it is not in the least typical of her fiction. Yet, but for *Lélia*, and its successor *Jacques*, it is impossible to point to a work of hers that would ever have lastingly stamped her, in the public mind, as an expounder of dangerous theories. In *Lélia*, however, which is strongly imbued with Byronic coloring, she had chosen to pose somewhat as the proud angel in rebellion; and the immediate effect of hostile criticism was to confirm her in the position taken up. Neither *Lélia* nor *Jacques* combined the elements of lasting popularity with those of instant success; but they roused a stir and strife which created an impression of her as a writer systematically inimical to religion and marriage—an impression almost ludicrously at variance with facts, taking her fiction as a whole, but which has only recently begun to give way, in this country, to a juster estimate of its tendencies.

The morality of *Lélia*, which it is rather difficult to discuss seriously in the present day, both the personages and their environment being too preternatural for any direct application to be drawn from them, as reflecting modern society, found indiscreet champions as determined as its aggressors. Violently denounced by M. Capo de Feuillide, of the *Europe littéraire*, it was warmly defended by M. Gustave Planche, in the *Revue des Deux Mondes*. The war of words grew so hot between them that a challenge and encounter were the result—surely unique in the annals of duelling. The swords of the critics fortunately proved more harmless than their words.

From the morbid depression that had tormented her mind and imagination, and has its literary memorial in *Lélia*, she was to find a timely, though but a temporary rescue, in the charm of a new acquaintance—the delighting society of a poetic mind of an order not inferior to her own.

It was in August, 1833, at a dinner given by Buloz to the staff of the *Revue des Deux Mondes*, that George Sand first made the personal acquaintance of Alfred de Musset, then in his twenty-third year, and already famous through his just published poem, *Rolla*, and his earlier dramas, *Andrea del Sarto* and *Les Caprices de Marianne*. He rapidly became enamored of the author of *Lélia*, who for her part felt powerfully the attraction of his many admirable qualities, mutual enchantment leading them so far as to believe they could be the hero and heroine of a happy love tale. In a letter of September 21, addressed to her friend and correspondent Sainte-Beuve, whom she had made the confidant of her previous depression and strange moods of gloom, she writes of herself as lifted out of such dangers by a happiness beyond any she had imagined, restoring youth to her heart—the happiness accorded her by the poet's society and his preference for her own. De Musset, at this time, would have given the world to have been able to make her his wife.

The story of their short-lived infatuation and of the swift-following mutual disenchantment,—a story which, says Sainte-Beuve, has become part of the romance of the nineteenth century,—is perhaps of less consequence here than in the life of De Musset,[1] in whom the over-sensitiveness of genius was not allied with the extraordinary healthy vitality which enabled George Sand to come out of the most terrible mental experiences unembittered, with the balance of her mind unshaken, and her powers unimpaired. Yet that he acquired an empire over her no other ever acquired there is much to indicate. It took her from France for a while, from her children, her friends—and the breaking of the spell set her at war, not only with him, but for a while with herself, with life, and her fellow creatures.

In the last days of 1833, she and the author of *Rolla* started on a journey to Italy, where George Sand spent six months, and where she has laid the scene of a number of her novels: the first and best part of *Consuelo*, *La Dernière Aldini*, *Leone*, *Leoni*, *La Daniella*, and others. The spirit of that land she has caught and reproduced perhaps more successfully than any other of the many novelists who have chosen it for a frame—of Italy as the artist's native country, that is—not the

---

[1] The biography of Alfred De Musset, by Paul De Musset, translated from the French by Harriet W. Preston. Boston, Roberts Brothers.

Italy of political history, nor of the Medici, but the Italy that is the second home of painters, poets, and musicians. Can anything be more enjoyable, and at the same time more vividly true, than George Sand's delineations of Venice; and, in the first of the *Lettres d'un Voyageur*, the pictures given of her wanderings on the shores of the Brenta, of Bassano, the Brenta valley, Oliero, Possagno, Asolo, a delicious land, till quite recently as little tourist-trodden as in 1834? What a contrast to the purely imaginary descriptions in *Lélia*, written before those beauties had appeared to her except in dreams!

From Genoa the travellers journeyed to Pisa, Florence, and thence to Venice, where first George Sand felt herself really at home in Italy. The architecture, the simplicity of Venetian life and manners, the theatres—from the opera-houses, where Pasta and Donzelli were singing, down to the national drama of Pulchinello—the pictures, the sea, the climate, combined to make of it a place of residence so perfectly to her mind, that again and again in her letters she expresses her wish that she could bring over her children and there fix her abode.

"It is the only town I can love for its own sake," she says of it. "Other cities are like prisons, which you put up with for the sake of your fellow-prisoners." This Italian journey marks a fresh stage in her artistic development, quite apart from the attendant romantic circumstances, the alleged disastrous consequences to a child of genius less wise and fortunate than herself, which has given an otherwise disproportionate notoriety to this brief episode.

George Sand was no doubt fatally in error when she persuaded herself, and even succeeded in persuading the poet's anxious mother, that she had it in her to be his guardian angel, and reform him miraculously in a short space of time; and that because he had fallen in love with her she would know how to make him alter a way of life he had no abiding desire to abandon. Such a task demands a readiness not merely for self-sacrifice, but for self-suppression; and her individuality was far too pronounced to merge itself for long in ministering to another's. She never seems to have possessed the slightest moral ascendancy over him, beyond the power of wounding him very deeply by the change in her sentiments, however much he might feel himself to blame for it.

The history of the separation of the lovers—of De Musset's illness, jealousy, and departure from Venice alone—is a thrice-told tale. Like the subject of "The Ring and the Book," it has been set forth, by various persons, variously interested, with correspondingly various coloring. The story, as told by George Sand in her later novel, *Elle et Lui*, is substantially the same as one related by De Musset in his *Confession d'un Enfant du Siècle*, published two years after these events, and in which, if it is to be regarded as reflecting personal idiosyncrasies in the slightest degree, the poet certainly makes himself out as the most insupportable of human companions. None the less did the publication of *Elle et Lui*, a quarter of a century later, provoke a savage retort from the deceased poet's brother, in *Lui et Elle*. Finally, in *Lui*, a third novelist, Madame Colet, presented the world with a separate version of the affair from one who imagined she could have made up to the poet for what he had lost.

But it needs no deep study of human nature, or yet of these novels, to understand the impracticability of two such minds long remaining together in unity. Genius, in private life, is apt to be a torment—its foibles demanding infinite patience, forbearance, nay, affectionate blindness, in those who would minister to its happiness, and mitigate the worst results of those foibles themselves. Certainly George Sand, for a genius, was a wonderfully equable character; her "satanic" moods showed themselves chiefly in pen and ink; her nerves were very strong, the balance of her physical and mental organization was splendidly even, as one imagines Shakespeare's to have been. But the very vigor of her character, its force of self-assertion, unfitted her to be the complement to any but a very yielding nature. The direct influence a passive, merely receptive spirit would have accepted, and gratefully, was soon felt as an intolerable burden by a mind in many ways different from her own, but with the same imperious instinct of freedom, and as little capable of playing anvil to another mind for long. He rebelled against her ascendancy, but suffered from the spell. She was no Countess Guiccioli, content to adore and be adored, and exercise an indirect power for good on a capricious lover. Her logical mind, energetic and independent, grew impatient of the seeming inconsistencies of her gifted companion; and when at last she began to perceive in them the fatal conditions of those gifts themselves, only compassion survived in her, as she thought, and compassion was cold.

How could De Musset, with such an excellent example of prudence, regular hours, good sense, calm self-possession, and ceaseless literary industry as hers before his eyes, not be stirred up to emulate such admirable qualities? But her reason made him unreasonable; the indefatigability of her pen irritated his nerves, and made him idle out of contradiction; her homilies provoked only fresh imprudences—as though he wanted to make proof of his independence whilst secretly feeling her dominion—a phenomenon with which highly nervous people will sympathize not a little, but which was perfectly inexplicable to George Sand.

His genius was of a more delicate essence than hers; he has struck, at times, a deeper note. But his nature was frailer, his muse not so easily within call, his character as intolerant of restraint as her own, but less self-sufficing; and the morbid taint of thought then prevalent, and which her natural optimism and better balanced faculties enabled her to throw off very shortly, had entered into him ineffaceably. Whether or not she brought a fresh blight on his mind, she certaintly failed to cure it.

The spring had hardly begun when De Musset was struck down by fever. George Sand, who had previously been very ill herself, nursed him through his attack with great devotion; and in six weeks' time he was restored to health, if not to happiness. Theirs was at an end, as they recognized, and agreed to part—"for a time, perhaps, or perhaps for ever," she wrote,—with their attachment broken but not destroyed.

It was early in April that De Musset started on his homeward journey. George Sand saw him on his way as far as Vicenza, and ere returning to Venice, made a little excursion in the Alps, along the course of the Brenta. "I have walked as much as four-and-twenty miles a day," she writes to M. Boucoiran, "and found out that this sort of exercise is very good for me, both morally and physically. Tell Buloz I will write some letters for the *Revue*, upon my pedestrian tours. I came back into Venice with only seven centimes in my pocket, otherwise I should have gone as far as the Tyrol; but the want of baggage and money obliged me to return. In a few days I shall start again, and cross over the Alps by the gorges of the Piave."

And the spring's delights on the Alpine borders of Lombardy are described by her *con amore*, in the promised letters:—

> The country was not yet in its full splendor; the fields were of a faint green, verging on yellow, and the leaves only coming into bud on the trees. But here and there the almonds and peaches in flower mixed their garlands of pink and white with the dark clumps of cypress. Through the midst of this far-spreading garden the Brenta flowed swiftly and silently over her sandy bed, between two large banks of pebbles, and the rocky *débris* which she tears out of the heart of the Alps, and with which she furrows the plains in her days of anger. A semi-circle of fertile hills, overspread with those long festoons of twisting vine that suspend themselves from all the trees in Venetia, made a near frame to the picture; and the snowy mountain-heights, sparkling in the first rays of sunshine, formed an immense second border, standing, as if cut out in silver, against the solid blue of the sky.

None of these excursions, however, were ever carried very far. For the next three months she remained almost entirely stationary at Venice, her head-quarters. She had taken apartments for herself in the interior of the city, in a little low-built house, along the narrow, green, and yet limpid canal, close to the Ponte dei Barcaroli. "There," she tells us, "alone all the afternoon, never going out except in the evening for a breath of air, working at night as well, to the song of the tame nightingales that people all Venetian balconies, I wrote *André*, *Jacques*, *Mattea*, and the first *Lettres d'un Voyageur*."

None can read the latter and suppose that the suffering of the recent parting was all on one side. The poet continued to correspond with her, and the consciousness of the pain she had inflicted she was clearly not sufficiently indifferent herself to support. But neither De Musset nor any other in whom, through the "prism of enthusiasm," she may have seen awhile a hero of romance, was ever a primary influence on her life. These were two. Firstly, her children, who although at a distance were seldom absent from her thoughts. Of their well-being at school and at home respectively, she was careful to keep herself informed, down to the minutest particulars, by correspondents in Paris and at Nohant, whence no opposition whatever was raised by its occupier to her prolonged absence abroad. Secondly, her art-vocation. She wrote incessantly; and independently of the pecuniary obligations to do so which she put forward, it is obvious that she had become wedded to this habit of work. "The habit has become a faculty—the faculty a need. I have thus come to working for thirteen hours at a time without making myself ill; seven or eight a day on an average, be the task done better or worse," she writes to M. Chatiron, from Venice, in March. Sometimes, as with *Leone Leoni*, she would complete a novel in a week; a few weeks later it was in the *Revue des Deux Mondes*. Such haste she afterward deprecated, and, like all other workers, she aspired to a year's holiday in which to devote herself to the study of the masterpieces of modern literature; but the convenient season for such suspension of her own productive activity never came. And whilst at Venice she found herself literally in want of money to leave it. Buloz had arranged with her that she should contribute thirty-two pages every six weeks to his periodical for a yearly stipend of £160. She had anticipated her salary for the expenses of her Italian journey, and must acquit herself of the arrears due before she could take wing.

Jacques, the longest of the novels written at Venice, afforded fresh grounds to those who taxed her works with hostility to social institutions. Without entering into the vexed question of the right of the artist in search of variety to exercise his power on any theme that may invite to its display, and of the precise bearing of ethical rules on works of imagination, it is permissible to doubt that *Jacques*, however bitter the sentiments of the author at that time regarding the marriage tie, ever seriously disturbed the felicity of any domestic household in the past or present day. It is too lengthy and too melancholy to attract modern readers, who care little to revel in the luxuries of woe, so relished by those of a former age. We cannot do better than quote the judgment pronounced by Madame Sand herself, thirty years later, on this work of pure sentimentalism—generated by an epoch thrown into commotion by the passionate views of romanticism—the epoch of René, Lara, Childe Harold, Werther, types of desperate men; life weary, but by no means weary of talking. "*Jacques*," she observes, "belonged to this large family of disillusioned thinkers; they had their *raison d'être*, historical and social. He comes on the scene in the novel, already worn by deceptions; he thought to revive through his love, and he does not revive. Marriage was for him only the drop of bitterness that made the cup overflow. He killed himself to bequeath to others the happiness for which he cared not, and in which he believed not."

Jacques, taken as a *plaidoyer* against domestic institutions, singularly misses its aim. As critics have remarked, some of the most eloquent pages are those that treat of married bliss. Our sympathies are entirely with the wronged husband against his silly little wife. It is a kindred work to *Lélia*, and its faults are the same; but whilst dealing ostensibly with real life and possible human beings it cannot, like *Lélia*, be placed apart, and retain interest as a literary curiosity.

André is a very different piece of work and a little masterpiece of its kind. The author, in her preface, tells us how, whilst mechanically listening to the incessant chatter of the Venetian sempstresses in the next room to her own, she was struck by the resemblance between the mode of life and thought their talk betrayed, and that of the same class of girls at La Châtre; and how in the midst of Venice, to the sound of the rippling waters stirred by the gondolier's oar, of guitar and serenade, and within sight of the marble palaces, her thoughts flew back to the dark and dirty streets, the dilapidated houses, the wretched moss-grown roofs, the shrill concerts of the cocks, cats, and children of the little French provincial town. She dreamt also of the lovely meadows, the scented hay, the little running streams, and the floral researches she had been fond of. This tenacity of her instincts was a safeguard she may have sometimes rebelled against as a chain; it was with her an essential feature, and, despite all vagaries, gave a great unity to her life.

"Venice," she writes to M. Chatiron in June, "with her marble staircases and her wonderful climate, does not make me forget anything that has been dear to me. Be sure that nothing in me dies. My life has its agitations; destiny pushes me different ways, but my heart does not repudiate the past. Old memories have a power none can ignore, and myself less than another. I love on the contrary to recall them, and we shall soon find ourselves together again in the old nest at Nohant." *André* she considered the outcome of this feeling of nostalgia. In it she has put together the vulgar elements of inferior society in a common-place country town, and produced a poem, though one of the saddest. If the florist heroine, Genevieve, is a slightly idealized figure, the story and general character-treatment are realistic to a painful degree. There is more power of simple pathos shown here than is common in the works of George Sand. *André* is a refreshing contrast, in its simplicity and brevity, to the inflation of *Lélia* and *Jacques*. It was an initial essay, and a model one, in a style with better claims to enduring popularity.

As the summer advanced, George Sand found herself free to depart, and started on her way back to France, famishing, as she tells us, for the sight of her children. Her grand anxiety was to reach her destination in time for the breaking-up day and distribution of prizes at the College Henri IV. "I shall be at Paris before then," she writes from Milan, to her son, "if I die on the way, and really the heat is such that one might die of it." From Milan she journeyed over the Simplon to the Rhone valley, Martigny, Chamounix, and Geneva, performing great part of the way on foot. She reached Paris in the middle of August, and a few days later started with her boy for Nohant, where Solange had spent the time during her mother's absence, and where they remained together for the holidays. Here too she was in the midst of a numerous circle of friends of both sexes, in whose staunch friendliness she found a solace of which she stood in real need.

CHAPTER V. - MENTAL DEVELOPMENT.

THE period immediately following George Sand's return from Italy in August 1834, was a time of transition, both in her outer and inner life. If undistinguished by the production of any novel calculated to create a fresh sensation, it shows no abatement of literary activity. This, as we have seen, had become to her a necessity of nature. Neither vicissitudes without nor commotions within, though they might direct or stimulate, seem to have acted as a check on the flow of her pen.

During the first twelvemonth she continued to reside alternately at Nohant, whither she came with her son and daughter for their holidays—Solange being now placed in a children's school kept by some English ladies at Paris,—and her "poet's garret," as she styled her third floor *appartement* on the Quai Malplaquet.

This winter saw the ending for herself and De Musset of their hapless romance. An approach to complete reconciliation—for the existing partial estrangement had been discovered to be more unbearable than all besides—led to stormy scenes and violent discord, and resulted before very long in mutual avoidance, which was to be final. It is said that forgiveness is the property of the injured, and it should be remembered that whenever De Musset's name is mentioned by George Sand it is with the admiring respect of one to whom his genius made that name sacred, and who refused to the end of his life to use the easy weapon offered her by his notorious frailties for vindicating herself at his expense. And, however pernicious the much talked of effect on De Musset's mind, it is but fair to the poet to recollect that it is no less true of him than of George Sand that his best work, that with which his fame has come chiefly to associate itself, was accomplished after this painful experience.

Into her own mental state—possibly at this time the least enviable of the two—we get some glimpses in the *Lettres d'un Voyageur* of the autumn 1834, and winter 1834-35. Here, again, we should be content with gathering a general impression, and not ingenuously read literal facts in all the self-accusations and recorded experiences of the "*voyageur*"—a semi-fictitious personage whose improvisations were, after all, only a fresh exercise which George Sand had invented for her imagination taking herself and reality for a starting-point merely, a suggestive theme.

But the despair and disgust of life, to which both these and her private letters give such uncompromising and eloquent expression, indubitably reflect her feelings at this moral crisis—the feelings of one who having openly braved the laws of society, to become henceforward a law unto herself, recognizes that she has only found her way to fresh sources of misery. Never yet had she had such grave and deep causes of individual mental torment to blacken her views of existence, and incline her to abhor it as a curse. "Your instinct will save you, bring you back to your children," wrote a friend who knew her well. But her maternal love and solicitude themselves were becoming a source of added distress and apprehension.

The extraordinary arrangement she and M. Dudevant had entered into four years before with regard to each other, was clearly one impossible to last. It will be recollected that she at that time had relinquished her patrimony to those who had thought it no dishonor to continue to enjoy it; and the terms of that agreement had since been nominally undisturbed. But besides that, the control of the children remained a constant subject of dissension. M. Dudevant was beginning to get into pecuniary difficulties in the management of his wife's estate. Sometimes he contemplated resigning it to her, and retiring to Gascony, to live with his widowed stepmother on the property which at her death would revert to him. But unfortunately he could not make up his mind to this course. No sooner had he drawn up an agreement consenting to a division of property, than he seemed to regret the sacrifice; upon which she ceased to press it.

Meantime Madame Dudevant, whose position at Nohant was that of a visitor merely, and becoming untenable, felt her hold on her cherished home and her children becoming more precarious day by day.

Some of her friends had strongly advised her to travel for a length of time, both as offering a mortal remedy, and as a temporary escape from the practical perplexities of the moment. Her rescue, however, was to be otherwise effected, and a number of new intellectual interests that sprang up for her at this time all tended to retain her in her own country.

It was in the course of this spring that she made the acquaintance of M. de Lamennais, introduced to her by their common friend, the composer, Franz Liszt. The famous author of the *Paroles d'un Croyant* had virtually severed himself from the Church of Rome by his recent publication of this little volume, pronounced by the Pope, "small in size, immense in perversity!" The eloquence of the poet-priest, and the doctrines of the anti-Catholic and humanitarian Christianity of which he came forward as the expounder, could not fail powerfully to impress her intelligence. Here seemed the harbor of refuge her half-wrecked faiths were seeking, and what the abbé's antagonists denounced as the "diabolical gospel of social science," came to her as the teachings of an angel of light. Christianity as preached by him was a sort of realization of the ideal religion of Aurore Dupin—faith divorced from superstition and the doctrine of Romish infallibility. Complete identity of sentiments between herself and the abbé was out of the question. But his was the right mind coming to her mind at the right moment, and exercised a healing influence over her troubled spirits. For *Le Monde*, a journal founded by him shortly after this time, she wrote the *Lettres à Marcie*, an unfinished series, treating of moral and spiritual problems and trials. Finally, the position M. de Lamennais had taken up as the apostle of the people further enlisted her sympathies in his cause, which made religious one with social reform, and amalgamated the protest against moral enslavement with the liberation-schemes then fermenting in young and generous minds all over Europe.

The belief in the possibility of their speedy realization was then wide-spread—a conviction that, as Heine puts it, some grand recipe for freedom and equality, invented, well drawn up, and inserted in the *Moniteur*, was all that was needed to secure those benefits for the world at large. If George Sand, led afterwards into searching for this empirical remedy for the wrongs and sufferings of the masses, believed the elixir to have been found in the establishment of popular sovereignty by universal suffrage, it was through the persuasive arguments of the leaders of the movement, with whom at this period she was first brought into personal relations. Her own unbiassed judgment, to which she reverted long years after, when she had seen these illusions perish sadly, was less sanguine in its prognostications for the immediate future, as appears in her own reflections in a letter of this time:—

> What I see in the midst of the divergencies of all these reforming sects is a waste of generous sentiments and of noble thoughts, a tendency towards social amelioration, but an impossibility for the time to bring forth through the want of a head to that great body with a hundred hands, that tears itself to pieces, for not knowing what to attack. So far the struggles make only dust and noise. We have not yet come to the era that will construct new societies, and people them with perfected men.

She had recently been introduced to a political and legal celebrity of his day, the famous advocate Michel, of Bourges. He was then at the height of his reputation, which, won by his eloquent and successful defense of political prisoners on various occasions, was considerable. Madame Sand had been advised to consult him professionally about her business affairs, and for this purpose went over one day with some of her Berrichon friends to see him at Bourges. But the man of law had, it appears, been reading *Lélia*, and instead of talking of business with his distinguished client, dashed at once into politics, philosophy, and social science, overpowering his listeners with the strength of his oratory. His sentiments were those of extreme radicalism, and he carried on a little private propaganda in the country around. The force of his character seems to have spent itself in oratorical effort. He could preach revolution, but not suggest reform; denounce existing abuses, but do nothing towards the remodelling of social institutions; and in after years he failed, as so many leading men in his profession have failed, to make any impression as a speaker in Parliament. The author of *Lélia* was overwhelmed, if not all at once converted, by the tremendous rhetorical power of this singular man. She was a proselyte worth the trouble of making, and Michel was bent on drawing her more closely into active politics, with which hitherto she had occupied herself very little. He began a correspondence, writing her long epistles, the sum of which, she says, may thus be resumed:—"Your scepticism springs from personal unhappiness. Love is selfish. Extend this solicitude for a single individual to the whole human race." He certainly succeeded in inspiring her with a strong desire to share his passion for politics, his faith, his revivifying hopes of a speedy social renovation, his ambition to be one of its apostles. To Michel, under the sobriquet of "Everard," are addressed several of the *Lettres d'un Voyageur* of the spring and summer of 1835, letters which she defines as "a rapid analysis of a rapid conversion."

But Michel's work was a work of demolition only; and when his earnest disciple wanted new theories in place of the old forms so ruthlessly destroyed, he had none to offer. There were others, however, who could. She was soon to be put into communication with a number of the active workers for the republican cause throughout the country. They counted many of the best hearts and not the worst heads in France, and were naturally eager to enlist her energies on their side.

Foremost, by right of the influence exercised over her awhile by his writings, was the philosopher Pierre Leroux, with whom her acquaintance dates from this same year. In spite of the wide divergence between her pre-eminently artistic spirit and a mind of the rougher stamp of this born iconoclast, he was to indoctrinate her with many new opinions. His disinterested character won her admiration; he was a practical philanthropist as well as a critical thinker, one whose life and fighting power were devoted to promoting the good of the working classes to whom he belonged, having been brought up as a printer. He was regarded as the apostle of communism, as then understood, or rather not understood—for the form under which it suggested itself to the social reformers of the period in question was entirely indefinite.

Meantime the novelist's pen was far from idle. One or two pleasant glimpses she has given us into her manner of working belong to this year. In the summer the heat in her "poet's garret" becoming intolerable, she took refuge in a congenial solitude offered by the ground-floor apartments of the house, then in course of reconstruction, dismantled and untenanted. The works had been temporarily suspended, and Madame Sand took possession of the field abandoned by the builders and carpenters. The windows and doors opening into the garden had been taken away, and the place thus turned into an airy, cool retreat. Out of the apparatus of the workmen, left behind, she constructed her writing-establishment, and here, secure from interruption, denying herself to all visitors, never going out except to visit her children at their respective schools, she completed her novel with no companions but the spiders crawling over the planks, the mice running in and out of the corners, and the blackbirds hopping in from the garden; the deep sense of solitude enhanced by the roar of the city in the very heart of which she had thus voluntarily isolated herself.

As an artistic experience she found it refreshing, and repeated it more than once. Soon after, a friend offered her the loan of an empty house at Bourges, a town that had been suggested to her as a desirable place of residence, should the circumstances at Nohant ever force her to abandon it entirely. As a home she saw and disapproved of Bourges, but she thoroughly enjoyed a brief retreat spent there in an absolutely deserted, vine-covered dwelling, standing in a garden enclosed by stone walls. Her meals were handed in through a wicket. A few friends came to see her in the evenings. The days, and often the nights, she passed in study and meditation, shut up in the library reading Lavater, expatiating on her impressions of his theories in a letter addressed to Franz Liszt (inserted among the *Lettres d'un Voyageur*), or strolling in the flower garden—"forgotten," she tells us, "by the whole world, and plunged into oblivion of the actualities of my own existence."

Of her numerous letters of advice to her boy at school, we quote one written during this summer of 1835, when their future relations to each other were in painful uncertainty:—

> Work, be strong and proud; despise the little troubles supposed to belong to your age. Reserve your strength of resistance for deeds and facts that are worth the effort. If I am here no longer, think of me who worked and suffered cheerfully. We are like each other in mind and in countenance. I know already from this day what your intellectual life will be. I fear for you many and deep sorrows. I hope for you the purest of joys. Guard within yourself that treasure, kindness. Know how to give without hesitation, how to lose without regret, how to acquire without meanness. Know how to replace in your heart, by the happiness of those you love, the happiness that may be wanting to yourself. Keep the hope of another life. It is there that mothers meet their sons again. Love all God's creatures. Forgive those who are ill-conditioned, resist those who are unjust, and devote yourself to those who are great through their virtue. Love me. I will teach you many, many things if we live together. If that blessing (the greatest that can befall me, the only one that makes me wish for a long life) is not to be, you must pray for me, and from the grave itself, if anything remains of me in the universe, the spirit of your mother will watch over you.

In the autumn, 1835, Madame Dudevant, under legal advice, and supported by the approval of friends of both parties, determined to apply to the courts for a judicial separation from her husband, on the plea of ill-treatment. She had sufficient grounds to allege for her claim, and had then every reason to hope that her demand would not even be contested by M. Dudevant, who, on former occasions, had voluntarily signed but afterwards revoked the agreement she hereby only desired to make valid and permanent, and which, ensuring to him a certain proportion of her income, gave her Nohant for a place of habitation, and established the children under her care.

Pending the issue of this suit, which, unexpectedly protracted, dragged on until the summer of the next year, she availed herself of the hospitality of a family at La Châtre, friends of old standing, and from under whose roof she awaited, as from a neutral ground, the decision of her judges. During this year she saw little of Paris, and less of Nohant, except for a brief visit which, profiting by a moment when its walls were absolutely deserted by every other human being, she paid to her house—not knowing then whether she would ever, so to speak, inhabit it again in her own right.

On the result of the legal proceedings depended her future home and the best part of her happiness. Sooner than be parted from her children, she contemplated the idea, in case of the decision going against her, of escaping with them to America! Yet, in the midst of all this suspense, we find her industrious as ever, joining in the daytime in the family life of the household with which she was domesticated, helping to amuse the children among them, retiring to her room at ten at night, to work on at her desk till seven in the morning, according to her wont. A more cheerful tone begins to pervade her effusions. The clouds were slowly breaking on all sides at once, and a variety of circumstances combining to restore to her mind its natural tone—faith, hope, and charity to her heart, and harmony to her existence. She began to perceive what she was enabled afterwards more fully to acknowledge as follows:—

> As to my religion, the ground of it has never varied. The forms of the past have vanished, for me as for my century, before the light of study and reflection. But the eternal doctrine of believers, of God and His goodness, the immortal soul and the hopes of another life, this is what, in myself, has been proof against all examination, all discussion, and even intervals of despairing doubt.

It is significant that during these months, spent for the most part at La Châtre, we find her rewriting *Lélia*, trying, as she expressed her intention, "to transform this work of anger into a work of gentleness." *Engelwald*, a novel of some length on which she was engaged, was destined never to see the light.

To the Comtesse d'Agoult, better known by her *nom de plume* of Daniel Stern, whose acquaintance she had recently made in Paris, she writes in May, 1836:—

> I am still at La Châtre, staying with my friends, who spoil me like a child of five years old. I inhabit a suburb, built in terraces against the rock. At my feet lies a wonderfully pretty valley. A garden thirty feet square and full of roses, and a terrace extensive enough for you to walk along it in ten steps, are my drawing-room, my study, and gallery. My bed-room is rather large—it is decorated with a red cotton curtained bed—a real peasant's bed, hard and flat, two straw chairs, and a white wooden table. My window is situated six feet above the terrace. By the trellised trees on the wall I can get out and in, and stroll at night among my thirty feet of flowers without having to open a door or wake anyone.
>
> Sometimes I go out riding alone, at dusk. I come in towards midnight. My cloak, my rough hat, and the melancholy trot of my nag, make me pass in the darkness for a commercial traveller, or a farm-boy.
>
> One of my grand amusements is to watch the transition from night to day; it effects itself in a thousand different manners. This

revolution, apparently so uniform, has every day a character of its own.

The summer that had set in was unusually hot and sultry. Writing to Madame d'Agoult, July 10, 1836, she thus describes her enjoyment of a season that allowed of some of the pleasures of primitive existence:—

> I start on foot at three in the morning, fully intending to be back by eight o'clock; but I lose myself in the lanes; I forget myself on the banks of the river; I run after butterflies; and I get home at midday in a state of torrefaction impossible to describe.

Another time the sight of the cooling stream is more than she can resist, and she walks into the Indre fully dressed; but a few minutes more and the sun has dried her garments, and she proceeds on her walk of ten or twelve miles—"Never a cockchafer passes but I run after it."

> You have no idea of all the dreams I dream during my walks in the sun. I fancy myself in the golden days of Greece. In this happy country where I live you may often go for six miles without meeting a human creature. The flocks are left by themselves in pastures well enclosed by fine hedges; so the illusion can last for some time. One of my chief amusements when I have got out to some distance, where I don't know the paths, is to fancy I am wandering over some other country with which I discover some resemblance. I recollect having strolled in the Alps, and fancied myself for hours in America. Now I picture to myself an Arcadia in Berry. Not a meadow, not a cluster of trees which, under so fine a sun, does not appear to me quite Arcadian.

We give these passages because they seem to us very forcibly to portray one side, and that the strongest and most permanent, of the character of George Sand: the admixture of a child's simplicity of tastes, a poet's fondness for reverie, and that instinctive independence of habits—an instinct stronger than the restraints of custom—which her individuality seemed to demand.

In the letter last quoted to Madame d'Agoult, the new ideal which was arising out of these contemplations is thus resumed:—

> To throw yourself into the lap of mother nature: to take her really for mother and sister; stoically and religiously to cut off from your life what is mere gratified vanity; obstinately to resist the proud and the wicked; to make yourself humble with the unfortunate, to weep with the misery of the poor; nor desire another consolation than the putting down of the rich; to acknowledge no other God than Him who ordains justice and equality upon men; to venerate what is good, to judge severely what is only strong, to live on very little, to give away nearly all, in order to re-establish primitive equality and bring back to life again the Divine institution: that is the religion I shall

> proclaim in a little corner of my own, and that I aspire to preach to my twelve apostles under the lime-trees in my garden.

The judgment of the court, first pronounced in February, 1836, and given in her favor by default, no opposition having been raised to her claims to the proposed partition of property by the defendant, placed her in legal possession of her house and her children. Appeal was made, however, prolonging and complicating the case, but without affecting its termination. In the war of mutual accusations thus stirred up, M. Dudevant's *rôle* as accuser, yet objecting in the same breath to the separation, had an appearance of insincerity that could not fail to withdraw sympathy from his side, irrespective of any judgment that might be held on the conduct of the wife, whose absence and complete independence he had authorized or acquiesced in. Before the actual conclusion of the law-suit his appeal was withdrawn. As a result, the previous judgment in favor of Madame Dudevant was virtually confirmed, and the details were settled by private agreement.

It is almost impossible to overrate the importance to George Sand of a conclusion that gave her back her old home of Nohant, and secured to her the permanent companionship of her children. The present pecuniary arrangement left M. Dudevant some hold over Maurice and his education, concerning which his parents had long disagreed, and which for another year remained a source of contention.

The affair thus concluded, Madame Sand entered formally into possession of Nohant; and early in September she started with her two children for Switzerland, where they spent the autumn holidays in a long-contemplated visit to her friend the Comtesse d'Agoult, then at Geneva. This tour is fancifully sketched in a closing number of the *Lettres d'un Voyageur*, a volume which stands as a sort of literary memorial of two years of unsettled, precarious existence, material and spiritual—a time of trial now happily at an end.

Simon, a tale dedicated to Madame d'Agoult, and published in the *Revue des Deux Mondes*, 1836—a graceful story, of no high pretentions—is noticeable as marking the commencement of a decided and agreeable change in the tone of George Sand's fiction. Hitherto the predominant note struck had been most often one of melancholy, if not despair—the more hopelessly painful the subject, the more fervent, apparently, the inspiration to the writer. In *Indiana* she had portrayed the double victim of tyranny and treachery; in *Valentine*, a helpless girl sacrificed to family ambition and social prejudice; in *Lélia* and *Jacques*, the incurable *Weltschmerz*, heroism unvalued and wasted; in *Leone Leoni*, the infatuation of a weak-minded woman for a phenomenal scoundrel; in *André*, the wretchedness which a timid, selfish character, however amiable, may bring down on itself and on all connected with it. Henceforward she prefers themes of a pleasanter nature. In *Simon* she paints the triumph of true and patient love over social prejudice and strong opposition. In *Mauprat*,[1] written in 1837, at Nohant, she exerts all the force of her imagination and language to bring before us vividly

[1] Mauprat, translated by Miss Vaughan. Boston, Roberts Brothers.

the gradual redemption of a noble but degraded nature, through the influence of an exclusive, passionate and indestructible affection. The natural optimism of her temperament, not her incidental misfortunes, began and continued to color her compositions.

From Switzerland she returned for part of the winter to Paris. She had given up her "poet's garret," and occupied for a while a suite of rooms in the Hôtel de France, where resided also Madame d'Agoult. The *salon* of the latter was a favorite *rendezvous* of cosmopolitan artistic celebrities, whose general *rendezvous* just then was Paris. A very Pantheon must have been an intimate circle that included, among others, George Sand, Daniel Stern, Heine, the Polish poet Mickiewicz, Eugène Delacroix, Meyerbeer, Liszt, Hiller, and Frédéric Chopin.

The delicate health of her son forced Madame Sand to leave with him shortly for Berry, where he soon became convalescent. Later in the season, some of the same party of friends that had met in Paris met again at Nohant. It was during this summer that George Sand wrote for her child the well-known little tale, *Les Maîtres Mosaïstes*, in which the adventures of the Venetian mosaic-workers are woven into so charming a picture. "I do not know why, but it is seldom that I have written anything with so much pleasure," she tells us. "It was in the country, in summer weather, as hot as the Italian climate I had lately left. I have never seen so many birds and flowers in my garden. Liszt was playing the piano on the ground floor, and the nightingales, intoxicated with music and sunshine, were singing madly in the lilac-trees around."

The party was abruptly dispersed upon the intelligence that reached Madame Sand of her mother's sudden, and, as it proved, fatal illness. She hurried to Paris, and remained with Madame Maurice Dupin during her last days. The old fond affection between them, though fitful in its manifestations on the part of the mother, had never been impaired, and the breaking of this old link with the past was very deeply felt by Madame Sand.

Before returning to Nohant, she spent a few weeks at Fontainebleau with her son, from whom she never liked to separate. They passed their days in exploring the forest, then larger and wilder than now, botanizing and butterfly-hunting. At night she sat up writing, when all was quiet in the inn. Just as, whilst at Venice, her fancy flew back to the scenes and characters of French provincial life, and *André* was the result, so here, amid the forest landscapes of her own land, her imagination rushed off to Venice and the shores of the Brenta, and produced *La Dernière Aldini.*

This constant industry, which had now become her habit of life, was more of a practical necessity than ever. Nohant, as already mentioned, barely repaid the owner the expenses of keeping it up. Madame Sand, who desired to be liberal besides, to travel occasionally, to gratify little artistic fancies as they arose, must look to her literary work to furnish the means.

"Sometimes," she writes from Nohant, in October, 1837, to Madame d'Agoult, then in Italy, "I am tempted to realize my capital, and come and join you; but out there I should do no work, and the galley-slave is chained up. If Buloz lets him go for a walk it is on *parole*, and *parole* is the cannon-ball the convict drags on his foot."

Nor was it for herself only that she worked in future, but for her children, the whole responsibility of providing for both of whose education she was now about definitely to take on her own shoulders. The power of interference left to M. Dudevant by the recent legal decision had been exercised in a manner leading to fresh vexatious contention, and continual alarm on Madame Sand's part lest the boy should be taken by force from her side. These skirmishes included the actual abduction of Solange from Nohant by M. Dudevant during her mother's absence at Fontainebleau; a foolish and purposeless trick, by which nothing was to be gained, except annoyance and trouble to Madame Sand, whose right to the control of her daughter had never been contested. A final settlement entered into between the parties, in 1838, placed these matters henceforward on a footing of peace, fortunately permanent. By this agreement Madame Sand received back from M. Dudevant—who had lately succeeded to his father's estate—some house property that formed part of her patrimony, and paid down to him the sum of £2,000; he ceding to her the remnant of his paternal rights; she freeing him from all charges for Maurice's education, her authority over which, in future, was recognized as complete.

CHAPTER VI. - SOLITUDE, SOCIETY AND SOCIALISM.

THE charge of both children now resting entirely in her hands, Madame Sand was enabled to fulfill her desire of permanently removing her boy, now fourteen years of age, from the college Henri IV. Not only was she opposed to the general *régime* and educational system pursued in French public schools of this type, she felt persuaded of its special unsuitability to her son, whose tastes and temperament were artistic, like her own, and whose classical studies had been repeatedly interrupted by illness. His delicate health determined her to spend the winter of 1838-9 abroad with her family. Having heard the climate and scenery of Majorca highly praised, she selected the island for their resort; tempted herself by the prospect of a few months absolute quiet, where, with neither letters to answer, nor newspapers to read, she would enjoy some rare leisure, which she proposed to spend in studying history and teaching French to her children.

Just at this time her friend and ardent admirer, Frédéric Chopin, was recovering from a chest attack, the first presage of the illness that caused his early death. The eminent pianist and composer had also been recommended to winter in the South, and greatly needed repose and change of air to recruit him from the fatigues of the Parisian season. It was arranged that the convalescent should make one of the expedition to Majorca. He joined Madame Sand and her children at Perpignan, and they embarked for Barcelona, whence the sea-voyage to the island was safely accomplished, the party reaching Palma, the capital, in magnificent November weather, and never suspecting how soon they would have cause to repent their choice of a retreat.

But their practical information about the island proved lamentably insufficient. With the scenery, indeed, they were enraptured. "We found," says Madame Sand in her little volume, *Un Hiver à Majorque*, published the following year, "a green Switzerland under a Calabrian sky, with all the solemnity and stillness of the East." But though a painter's Elysium, Majorca was wanting in the commonest comforts of civilized life. Inns were non-existent, foreigners viewed and treated with suspicion. The party thought themselves fortunate in securing a villa some miles from Palma, furnished, though scantily. "The country, nature, trees, sky, sea, and mountains surpass all my dreams," she writes in the first days, "it is the promised land; and as we have succeeded in housing ourselves pretty well, we are delighted."

CHAPTER VI. - SOLITUDE, SOCIETY AND SOCIALISM.

The delight was of brief duration. That Madame Sand's manuscripts took a month to reach the editor of the *Revue des Deux Mondes*; that the piano ordered from Paris for Chopin took two months to get to Majorca, were the least among their troubles. A rainy season of exceptional severity set in, and the villa quickly became uninhabitable. It was not weatherproof. Chopin fell alarmingly ill. Good food and medical attendance were hardly to be procured for him; and finally, the villa proprietor, having heard that his tenant was suffering from consumption—an illness believed to be infectious by the Majorcans—gave the whole party notice to quit. The invalid improving somewhat, though still too weak to attempt the return journey to France, Madame Sand transported her ambulance, as she styled it, to some tolerable quarters she had already discovered in the deserted Carthusian monastery of Valdemosa—"a poetical name and a poetical abode," she writes; "an admirable landscape, grand and wild, with the sea at both ends of the horizon, formidable peaks around us, eagles pursuing their prey even down to the orange-trees in our garden, a cypress walk winding from the top of our mountain to the bottom of the gorge, torrents over-grown with myrtles, palm-trees below our feet, nothing could be more magnificent than this spot."

Parts of the old monastic buildings were dilapidated; the rest were in good order, being frequented as a summer retreat by the inhabitants of Palma. Now, in December, the Chartreuse was entirely abandoned, except by a housekeeper, a sacristan and a lone monk, the last offshoot of the community—a kind of apothecary, whose stock-in-trade was limited to guimauve and dog-grass.

The rooms into which the travellers moved had just been vacated by a Spanish family of political refugees departing for France. These lodgings were at least provided with doors, window-panes, and decent furniture; but the luxury of chimneys was unknown, and a stove, which had to be manufactured at an enormous price on purpose for the party, is described as "a sort of iron cauldron, that made our heads ache and dried up our throats." Continuous stormy weather having suspended steam traffic with the mainland, the visitors had no choice but to remain prisoners some two months more, during which the deluge went on with little intermission.

Still, to young and romantic imaginations the island and life in the ex-monastery offered considerable charm. Madame Sand and her children were delighted with the unfamiliar vegetation, the palms, aloes, olives, almond and orange trees, the Arab architecture, and picturesque costumes. Valdemosa itself was splendidly situated among the mountains, in a stone-walled garden surrounded with cypress trees and planted with palms and olives. In the morning, Madame Sand gave lessons to the children; in the afternoon, they ran wild out of doors whilst she wrote—when the invalid musician was well enough to be left. In the evenings she and the young people went wandering by moonlight through the cloisters, exploring the monkish cells and chapels. Maurice had fortunately recovered his health completely, but poor Chopin's state, aggravated by the damp weather and privations—for the difficulties in obtaining a regular supply of provisions were immense—remained throughout their stay a constant and terrible cause of anxiety and responsibility to Madame Sand. From the islanders no sort of help or even sympathy was forthcoming, and thievish servants and extortionate traders were not the least of the annoyances with which the strangers had to contend. In a letter to François Rollinat she gives a graphic account of their misfortunes:—

> It has rightly been laid down as a principle that where nature is beautiful and generous, men are bad and avaricious. We had all the trouble in the world to procure the commonest articles of food, such as the island produces in abundance; thanks to the signal dishonesty, the plundering spirit of the peasants, who made us pay for everything three times what it was worth, so that we were at their mercy under the penalty of dying of hunger. We could get no one to serve us, because we were not *Christians* [the travellers passed for being "sold to the Devil" because they did not go to Mass], and, besides, nobody would attend on a consumptive invalid. However, for better for worse, we were established.... The place was incomparably poetical; we did not see a living soul, nothing disturbed our work; after waiting two months, and paying three hundred francs extra, Chopin had at last received his piano, and delighted the vaults of his cell with his melodies. Health and strength were visibly returning to Maurice; as for me, I worked as tutor seven hours a day: I sat up working on my own account half the night; Chopin composed masterpieces, and we hoped to put up with the remainder of our discomforts by the aid of these compensations.

It was in the cells of Valdemosa that Madame Sand completed her novel of Monastic life, *Spiridion*, then publishing in the *Revue des Deux Mondes*. "For heaven's sake not so much mysticism!" prayed the editor of her, now and then; and assuredly those readers for whom George Sand was simply a purveyor of passionate romances, those critics who set her down in their minds as exclusively a glorifier of mutinous emotion and the apologist of lawless love, must have been taken aback by these pages, in which she had devoted her most fervent energies to tracing the spiritual history, *peu récréatif*, as she dryly observes, of a monk who, in the days of the decadence of the monastic orders, retained earnestness and sincerity; whose mind, revolted by the hypocrisy and worldliness around him, passes through the successive stages of heresy and philosophic doubt, and to whom is finally revealed an eternal gospel, which lies at the core of his old religion, but which later growths have stifled, and which outlasts all shocks and changes, and is to generate the religion of the future.

The compositions of Chopin above alluded to, include the finest of his well-known Preludes, which may easily be conceived of as suggested by the strange mingling of contrasting impressions in the Chartreuse. "Several of these Preludes," writes Madame Sand, "represent the visions that haunted him of deceased monks, the sounds of funeral chants; others are soft and melancholy; these came to him in his hours of sunshine and health, at the sound of the children's laughter beneath the window, the distant thrum of guitars and the songs of the birds under the damp foliage; at the sight of the pale little roses in bloom among the snow."

The loneliness and melancholy beauty of the spot, however congenial to the romance writer or inspiring to the composer, were not the right tonics for the nerves of the over-sensitive, imaginative invalid. The care and nursing of Madame Sand made amends for much, and by her good sense she saved him from being doctored to death by local practitioners. But his fortitude, which bore up heroically against his personal danger, was not proof against the dreary influences of Valdemosa in bad weather, the fogs, the sound of the hurricane sweeping through the valley, and bringing down portions of the dilapidated building, the noise of the torrents, the cries of the scared sea-birds and the roar of the sea.

The elevation of the Chartreuse made the climate peculiarly disagreeable at this season. She writes on:—

> We lived in the midst of clouds, and for fifty days were unable to get down into the plains; the roads were changed to torrents, and we saw nothing more of the sun. I should have thought it all beautiful if poor Chopin could only have got on. Maurice was none the worse. The wind and the sea sung sublimely as they beat against the rocks. The vast and empty cloisters cracked over our heads. If I had been there when I wrote the portion of *Lélia* that takes place in the convent, I should have made it finer and truer. But my poor friend's chest got worse and worse. The fine weather did not return.... A maid I had brought over from France, and who so far had resigned herself, on condition of enormous wages, to cook and do the housework, began to refuse attendance, as too hard. The moment was coming when after having wielded the broom and managed the *pot au feu*, I was ready to drop with fatigue—for besides my work as tutor, besides my literary labor, besides the continual attention necessitated by the condition of my invalid, I had rheumatism in every limb.

The return of spring was hailed as offering a tardy release from their island. The steamers were running again, and the party determined to leave at all risks; for though Chopin's state was more precarious than ever, nothing could be worse for him than to remain. They departed, feeling, she admits, as though they were escaping from the tender mercies of Polynesian savages, and once safely on board a French vessel at Barcelona, they thankfully welcomed the day that restored them to comfort and civilization, and saw the end of an expedition that had turned out in most respects so disastrous a *fiasco*.

They remained throughout April at Marseilles, where Chopin, in the hands of a good doctor, became convalescent. From Marseilles they made a short tour in Italy, visiting Genoa and the neighborhood, and returning to France in May, Chopin apparently on the high road to complete recovery. It was in the following year that his illness returned in a graver form, and unmistakable symptoms of consumption showed themselves. The life of a fashionable pianist in Paris, the constant excitement, late hours, and heavy strain of nervous exertion, were fatal to his future chances of preserving his health; but it was a life to which he had now become wedded, and which he never willingly left, except for his long annual visits to Nohant.

Madame Sand repeatedly contemplated settling herself entirely in the country. She had no love for Paris. "Parisian life strains our nerves and kills us in the long run," she writes from Nohant to one of her correspondents. "Ah, how I hate it, that centre of light! I would never set foot in it again, if the people I like would make the same resolution." And again, speaking of her "Black Valley, so good and so stupid," she adds, "Here I am always more myself than at Paris, where I am always ill, in body and in spirit."

Paris, however, afforded greater facilities for her children's education. She had a strong desire to see her son an artist, and he was already studying painting in Delacroix's studio. Also her income at this moment did not suffice to enable her to live continuously at Nohant where, she frankly confessed, she had not yet found out how to live economically, expected as she was to keep open house, regarded as grudging and unneighborly if she did not maintain her establishment on a scale to which her resources as yet were unequal. Her expenses in the country she calculated as double those in Paris, where, as she writes to M. Chatiron,—

> Everyone's independence is admirable. You invite whom you like, and when you don't wish to receive anyone you let the porter know you are not at home. Yet I hate Paris in all other respects. There I grow stout, and my mind grows thin. You know how quiet and retired my life there is, and I do not understand why you tell me, as they say in the provinces, that glory keeps me there. I have no glory, I have never sought for it, and I don't care a cigarette for it. I want to breath fresh air and live in peace. I am succeeding, but you see and you know on what conditions.

Her Paris residence, a few seasons later, she fixed in the Cour d'Orléans Rue St. Lazare, in a block of buildings one-third of which was occupied by herself and her family; another belonged to her friend, Madame Marliani, wife of the Spanish Consul, the third to Frédéric Chopin.

With respect to Chopin's long and deep attachment to Madame Sand, and its requital, concerning which so much has been written, there can surely be no greater misstatement than to speak of her as having blighted his life. This last part of his life was indeed blighted, but by ill-health and consequent nervous irritability and suffering; but such mitigation as was possible he found for eight years in the womanly devotion and genial society of Madame Sand—real benefits to one whose strange and delicate individuality it was not easy to befriend—and which the breach that took place between them shortly before his death should not allow us to forget.

"Chopin," observes Eugène Delacroix, "belongs to the small number of those whom one can both esteem and love." Madame Sand joined a sympathetic appreciation of the refinement of his nature, and an enthusiastic admiration of his genius—feelings she shared with his numberless female worshippers—to a strength of character that lent the support no other could perhaps so fully have given, or that he would accept from no other, to the fragile, nervous, suffering tone-poet. Her sentiments towards him seem to resolve themselves into a great tenderness rather than a passionate fervor—a placid affection for himself, and an adoration for his music.

All the time their existences, so far from having been united, flowed in different, nay divergent channels. Chopin, the idol of Paris society, moved constantly in the aristocratic and fashionable world, from which Madame Sand lived aloof. She for her part had heavy domestic cares and anxieties that did not touch him, and with the political party which was absorbing more and more of her energies he had no sympathy whatever. Whether the cause were the false start she had made at the outset by her marriage, forbidding her the realization of a woman's ideal, the non-separation of the gift of her heart from that of her whole life, or whether that her masculine strength of intellect created for her serious public interests and occupations, beside which personal pleasures and pains are apt to become of secondary moment, certain it appears that with George Sand, as with many an eminent artist of the opposite sex, such *affaires de cœur* were but ripples on the sea of a large and active existence.

The year after her return from Majorca was marked by her first appearance before the public as a dramatic author. Although it was a line in which she afterwards obtained successes, as will be seen in a future chapter, the result of this initial effort, *Cosima*, a five-act drama, was not encouraging. It was acted at the Théâtre Français in the spring of 1840, and proved a failure. It betrays no insufficient sense of dramatic effect, nor lack of the means for producing it, but decided clumsiness in the adaptation of these means to that end. The plot and personages recall those of *Indiana*, with the important differences that the *beau rôle* of the piece falls to the husband, and that the scene is transported back to Florence in the Middle Ages—an undoubted error, as giving to a play essentially modern and French in its complexities of sentiment and motive a strong local coloring of a past time and another people, making the whole seem unreal. It has a psychological subject which Emile Augier or Dumas *fils* would know how to handle dramatically; but as treated by George Sand, we are perpetually being led to anticipate too much in the way of action, to have our expectations dissipated the next moment. A wet blanket of disappointment on this head dampens any other satisfaction that the merits of the play might otherwise afford.

Hitherto she had continued to write regularly for the *Revue des Deux Mondes*. As her revolutionary opinions became more pronounced, they began to find utterance in her romances. Her conversion by Michel had not only been complete, but the disciple had outstripped the master. The study of the communistic theories of Pierre Leroux had familiarized her with the speculations in social science of those who at this time were devoting their attention to criticising the existing social organization, and seeking, and sometimes imagining they had found, the secret of creating a better. George Sand's strong admiration for the writings of Leroux, always praised by her in the highest terms, strikes us now as extravagant, but was shared to some extent by not a few leading men of the time, such as Sainte-Beuve and Lamartine. Her intellect had eagerly followed this bold and earnest pioneer in new-discovered worlds of thought; "I do not say it is the last word of humanity, but, so far, it is its most advanced expression," she states of his philosophy. The study of it had brought a clearness into her own views, due, probably, much more to the action of her own mind upon the novel ideas suggested than to the lucidity of a system of social science as yet undetermined in some of its main points.

She writes, when looking back on this period from a long distance of time,—

> After the despairs of my youth, I was governed by too many illusions. Morbid scepticism was succeeded in me by too much kindliness and ingenuousness. A thousand times over I was duped by dreams of an archangelic fusion of the opposing forces in the great strife of ideas.

Her novel *Horace*, written for the *Revue des Deux Mondes*, was rejected—as subversive of law and order—by the editor, except on condition of alterations which she declined to make.

After this temporary rupture with Buloz, Madame Sand's services were largely appropriated by the *Revue Indépendante*, a new journal founded in 1840 by her friends Pierre Leroux and Louis Viardot, in conjunction with whose names hers appears on the title page as leading contributor. For this periodical no theories could be too advanced, no fictitious illustrations too audacious, and to its pages accordingly was *Horace* transferred. Among the secondary characters in this novel figure a young couple, immaculate otherwise in principle and in conduct, but who as converts to St. Simonism have dispensed with the ordinary legal sanction to their union. Perhaps a more solid objection to its insertion in the *Revue des Deux Mondes* was the picture introduced of the *émcute* of June 1832, painted in heroic colors. Both these features, however, are purely incidental. The main interest and the real strength of the book lie in a remarkable study of character-development—that of the chief personage, Horace. It is a cleverly painted portrait of a type that reappears, with slight modifications, in all ages; a moral charlatan, who half imposes on himself, and entirely for a while on other people. A would-be hero, genius, and chivalrous lover, he has none of the genuine qualities needed for sustaining the parts. Nonchalant and inert of temperament, he is capable of nothing beyond a short course of successful affectation. The imposition breaking down at last, he sinks helplessly into the unheroic mediocrity of position and pretension for which alone he is fit.

A veritable attempt at a Socialist novel is the *Compagnon du Tour de France* written in the course of 1840, which must surely be ranked as one of the weakest of George Sand's productions. Exactly the converse of *Horace* may be said of this book. In the former, those most repelled by the revolutionary doctrines flashing out here and there, will yet be struck and interested by the masterly piece of character-painting that makes of the novel a success. The utmost fanaticism for the ideas ventilated in the *Compagnon du Tour de France* can reconcile no reader to the dullness and unreality of the story which make of it a failure. For her socialism itself, as set forth in her writings, dispassionate examination of what she actually inculcated, leaves but little warrant, in the state of progress now reached, for echoing the mighty outcry raised against it at the time. No doubt she thought that a complete reorganization of society on a new basis was eminently to be desired. But what she definitely advocated was, first, free education for the poor, and secondly, some fairer adjustment of the relations to each other of capital and labor. As to the first, authority has already sanctioned her opinion; the second question, if unsettled, has become a first preoccupation with statesmen and philosophers of all denominations in the present day.

With regard to the complete solution of the problem, she leaves her socialist heroes, as she herself felt, in doubt and perplexity. There was something in the schemes and doctrines she conscientiously approved, irreconcilable with her artist-nature—a materialistic tendency which clashed with her poetical instincts. When the stern demagogue Michel denounced the whole tribe of artists as a corrupting influence, enervating to the courage and will of a nation, she rose up energetically in defense of the confraternity to which she was born:—

> Will you tell me, pray, what you mean, with your declamations against artists? Cry out against them as much as you please, but respect art. Oh, you Vandal! I like that stern sectarian who wants to dress Taglioni in a stuff-gown and *sabots*, and set Liszt's hands to turn the machinery of a wine-press, and who yet, as he lies on the grass, finds the tears come into his eyes at the least linnet's song, and who makes a disturbance in the theatre to stop Othello from murdering Malibran! The austere citizen would suppress artists as social excrescences that absorb too much of the sap; but this gentleman is fond of vocal music, and so will spare the singers. Let us hope that painters will find one among your strong heads who appreciates painting, and won't wall up all studio windows. And as for the poets, they are your cousins; and you don't despise their forms of language and their rhythmical mechanism when you want to make an impression on the idle crowd. You will go to them to take lessons in metaphor, and how to make use of it.
>
> Unfortunately for the cause of the superiority of antiquity, whenever you go to hear Berlioz's *Funeral March*, the least that can happen to you will be to confess that this music is rather better than what they used to give us in Sparta, when we served under Lycurgus; you will think that Apollo, displeased to see us sacrificing to Pallas exclusively, has played us a trick in giving lessons to that *Babylonian*, so that by the exercise of a magnetic and disastrous power over us, he may lead our spirits astray.

And she would prove to the demagogue, out of his own mouth, that everything cannot be reduced to "bread and shoes all round," as the grand desideratum. Give these to men, it will not suffice. The eloquent orator instinctively seeks besides to impart "hallowed emotions and mystic enthusiasm to those who toil and sweat—

he teaches them to hope, to dream of God, to take courage and lift themselves above the sickening miseries of human conditions by the thought of a future, chimerical it may be, but strengthening and sublime."

For a period, however, she was too fascinated by the new ideas to judge them, and she straightway sought in her art a means of popularizing them. "These ideas," she writes in a later preface to her socialist novel, *Le Péché de M. Antoine*, "at which, as yet but a small number of conservative spirits had taken alarm, had, as yet, only really begun to sprout in a small number of attentive, laborious minds. The government, so long as no actual form of political application was assumed, was not to be disquieted by theories, and let every man make his own, put forth his dream, and innocently construct his city of the future, by his own fire-side, in the garden of his imagination."

She was aware that her readers thought her novels getting more and more tedious, in proportion as she communicated to her fictitious heroes and heroines the pre-occupations of her brain, and that she was thus stepping out of the domain of art. But she affirmed she could never help writing of whatever was absorbing her thoughts and feelings at the moment, and must take her chance of boring the public. Fortunately for *Le Péché de M. Antoine*, nature and human nature are here allowed to claim the larger share of our attention, and philosophy is a secondary feature. The scene is laid in the picturesque Marche country on the confines of Berry, a day's journey from Nohant, and we are glad to linger with her along the rocky banks of the Creuse, or among the ruined castles of Crozant and Châteaubrun. The novel contains much that is original and admirable in the drawing of characters of the most opposite classes.

Finally, in *Le Meunier d'Angibault*,[1] written as was the last-mentioned work some four or five years later (1844-45), but which may be named here, as making up with *Le Compagnon du Tour de France* the trio of "socialist" novels, the *Tendenz* does not interfere to the detriment of the artistic plan of the book. In it the romantic elements of the remote country nook she inhabited are cleverly brought together, without departing too widely from probability. The dilapidated castle, the picturesque mill, the traditions of brigandage two generations ago, all these were realities familiar to her notice. The painting of the country and country people is masterly; and there is not a passage in the book to offend the taste of the most scrupulous reader. Nor can it be justly impugned on the ground of inculcating disturbing political principles. The personages, in their preference of poverty and obscurity to rank and wealth, may, in the judgment of some, think and conduct themselves like chimerical dreamers, but their actions, however quixotic, concern themselves alone.

But, previous to either of the two novels last named, she had presented the world with a more ambitious work, whose merit was to compel universal acknowledgment—the most important, in fact, she had produced for eight years.

[1] The Miller of Angibault. Translated by M. E. Dewey. Boston, Roberts Brothers.

CHAPTER VII. - CONSUELO—HOME LIFE AT NOHANT.

CONSUELO first appeared in the *Revue Indépendante*, 1842-43. This noble book might not be inaptly described as,

> —a whole which, irregular in parts,
> Yet left a grand impression on the mind.

Its reckless proportions naturally "shocked the connoisseurs" among literary critics, especially in her own land; but nevertheless it became, and deservedly, one of her most popular productions, and did more than any other single novel she ever wrote to spread her popularity abroad. If *Indiana*, *Valentine*, and *Lélia* had never been written to create the fame of George Sand, *Consuelo* would have done so, and may be said to have established it over again, on a better and more lasting basis. Upon so well-known a work lengthened comment here would be superfluous. Originally intended for a novelette,—the opening chapters appear in the *Revue* under the modest heading, *Consuelo, conte*,—the beginning was so successful that the author was urged to extend her plan beyond its first proposed limits. The novel is an ephemeral form of art, no doubt, but it is difficult to conceive of a stage of social and intellectual progress when the first part of *Consuelo* will cease to be read with interest and delight.

The heroine once transported from the lagunes of Venice to the frontier of Bohemia and the castle of Rudolstadt, the character of the story becomes less naturalistic; the storyteller loses herself somewhat in subterranean passages and the mazes of adventure generally. She wrote on, she acknowledges, at hap-hazard, tempted and led away by the new horizons which the artistic and historical researches her work required kept opening to her view. But the powerful contrast between the two pictures,—of bright, sunshiny, free, sensuous, careless Venetian folk-life, and of the stern gloom of the mediæval castle, where the more spiritual consolations of existence come into prominence—is singularly effective and original. So also is the charming way in which an incident in the boyhood of young Joseph Haydn is treated by her fancy, in the episode of Consuelo's flight from the castle, when he becomes her fellow-traveller, and their adventures across country are told with such zest and *entrain*, in pages where life-sketches of character, such as the good-natured, self-indulgent canon, the violent, abandoned Corilla, make us forget the wildest improbabilities of the fiction itself. The concluding portion of the book, again entirely different in frame, with its delineation of art-life in a fashionable capital, Vienna, is as true as it is brilliant. It teems with suggestive ideas on the subject of musical and dramatic art, and with excellently drawn types. The relations of professional and amateur, the contradictions and contentions to which, in a woman's nature, the rival forces of love and of an artistic vocation may give rise, have never been better portrayed in any novel. The heroine, Consuelo, is of course an ideal character: her achievements partake of the marvellous; and there are digressions in the book which are diffuse in the extreme; but nowhere is the author's imagination more attractively displayed and her style more engaging. The tone throughout is noble and pure. To look on *Consuelo* as an agreeable story merely is to overlook the elevation of the moral standard of the book, in which much of its power resides. It marks more strongly than *Mauprat* the change that had come over the spirit of George Sand's compositions.

In the continuation, *La Comtesse de Rodolstadt*, which followed immediately in the *Revue Indépendante*, 1843, the novelist strays further and further from reality—the *terra firma* on which her fancy improvises such charming dances. Here she only touches the ground now and then, and between whiles her imagination asks ours to accompany it on the most extraordinary flights. As a novel of adventure, it is written with unflagging spirit; and in the rites and doctrines of the *Illuminati*, an idealization of the feature of the secret sects of the last century, she found a new medium of expression for her sentiments regarding the present abuses of society and the need of thorough renovation. Secret societies, at that time, were extremely numerous and active among the Republican workers in France. Madame Sand seems thoroughly to have appreciated their dangers, and has expressly stated that she was no advocate of such sects; that though under a tyranny, such as that which oppressed Germany in the times of which she wrote, they may be a necessity, elsewhere they are an abuse if not a crime. "The custom indeed I have never regarded as applicable for good in our time and our country; I have never believed that it can bring forth anything in future but a dictatorship, and the dictatorial principle is one I have never accepted." (*Histoire de ma Vie.*)

But the romance of the subject was irresistibly tempting to her inventive faculty. "Tell Leroux to send me some more books on freemasonry, if he can find any," she writes to a correspondent at Paris whilst working at the *Comtesse de Rudolstadt* at Nohant; "I am plunged into it over head and ears. Tell him also that he has there thrown me into an abyss of follies and absurdities, but that I am dabbling about courageously though prepared to extract nothing but nonsense."

For the musical miracles which it is given to Madame Sand's heroes and heroines to perform at a trifling cost, she may well at this time have come to regard them as almost in the natural order. She had received her second, and her best musical education through the contemplation of original musical genius, of the rarest quality, among her most intimate friends, her constant guests at Paris and Nohant. The vocal and instrumental feats of Consuelo and Count Albert themselves are not more astonishing than the actual recorded achievements of Liszt, pronounced a perfect *virtuoso* at twelve years old—and no wonder! The boy had so carried away his accompanyists, the band of the Italian opera at Paris, by his performance of the solo in an orchestral piece, that when the moment came for them to strike in, one and all forgot to do so, but remained silent, petrified with amazement. And Liszt when in the full development of his genius, had, as we have seen, been the art-comrade of George Sand; he had spent the whole of the summer season of 1837 at Nohant, transcribing Beethoven's symphonies for the piano-forte whilst she wrote her romances; she was familiar with his marvellous improvisations. In her "Trip to Chamounix" (*Lettres d'un Voyageur*, No. VI.) she has drawn a vivid picture of their extraordinary effect, describing his unrehearsed organ recital in the Cathedral of Freibourg to his little party of travelling companions. Nor was the charm of Chopin's gift less magical. The well-known anecdotes related on this subject are like so many glimpses into a musical paradise. Madame Sand has given us an amusing one herself. It is evening in her *salon* at Paris. At the piano is Chopin; and she, her son, Eugène Delacroix, and the Polish poet Mickiewicz sit listening whilst the composer, in an inspired mood, is extemporizing in the sublimest manner to the little circle. All are in silent raptures; when the servant breaks in with the alarm—the house is on fire. They rush to the room where the flames are, and succeed after a time in extinguishing them. Then they perceive that the poet Mickiewicz is missing. On returning to the *salon* they find him as they left him, rapt, entranced, unconscious of the stir around him, of the scare that had driven all the rest from the room. "He did not even know we had gone and left him alone. He was listening to Chopin, he had continued to hear him." Nor could the bewitched poet be brought down from the clouds that evening. He remained deaf to their banter, to Madame Sand's laughing admonition, "Next time I am with you when the house takes fire, I must begin by putting you into a safe place, for I see you would get burnt like a mere faggot, before you knew what was going on."

Eugène Delacroix, one of Madame Sand's earliest and most valued friends in the artist-world, and one of the many with whom she enjoyed along and unclouded friendship, gives in his letters some agreeable pictures of life at Nohant, during his visits there in the successive summers of 1845 and 1846:—

> When not assembled together with the rest for dinner, breakfast, a game of billiards, or a walk, you are in your room reading, or lounging on your sofa. Every moment there come in through the window open on the garden, "puffs of music" from Chopin, working away on one side, which mingle with the song of nightingales and the scent of the roses.

He describes a quiet, monastic-like existence, simple and studious: "We have not even the distraction of neighbors and friends around. In this country everybody stays at home, to look after his oxen and his land. One would become a fossil in a very short time."

The greatest event for the visitor was a village-festival—a wedding or a Saint's day—when the rustic dances went on under the tall elms to the roaring of the bagpipes. Peasant youths and peasant maids joined hands in the *bourrée*, the characteristic dance of the country; now, we fear, surviving in tradition only, but then still popular. The great artist was fired to paint a "Ste. Anne," patron-saint of Nohant, in honor of the place, but his work progressed but slowly. He writes in August, 1846:—"I am frightfully lazy, I can do nothing, I hardly read; and yet the days pass too quickly, for I must soon renounce this *vie de chanoine*, and return into the furnace of stirring ideas, good and bad. In Berry they have very few ideas, but they do just as well without." Then he adds, "Chopin has been playing Beethoven to me divinely well. That is worth all æstheticism."

Little theatrical entertainments of an original kind, presided over by Madame Sand, and carried out by herself, her children, and their young friends, became in time a prominent feature of life at Nohant. She thus describes their nature and commencements:—

> During the long evenings I took it into my head to devise for my family theatricals on the old Italian pattern—*commedia dell'arte*—plays in which the dialogue, itself extemporized, yet follows the outlines of a written plan, placarded behind the scenes. It is something like the charades acted in society, the development of which depends on the talent contributed by the actors. It was with these that we began, but little by little the word of the charade disappeared. We acted wild *saynètes*, afterwards comedies of plot and intrigue, finally dramas of event and emotion.
>
> All began with pantomime; and this was Chopin's invention. He sat at the piano and extemporized, whilst the young people acted scenes in dumb show and danced comic ballets. These charming improvisations turned the children's heads and made their legs nimble. He led them just as he chose, making them pass, according to his fancy, from the amusing to the severe, from burlesque to solemnity—now graceful, now impassioned. We invented all kinds of costumes, so as to play different characters in succession. No sooner did the artist see them appear than he adapted his theme and rhythm to the parts wonderfully. This would be repeated for two or three evenings; after which the *maestro*, departing for Paris, would leave us quite excited, exalted, determined not to let the spark be lost with which he had electrified us.

Chopin was possessed of much dramatic talent himself, and was an admirable mimic. When a boy it had been said of him that he was born to be a great actor. His capacity for facial expressions was something extraordinary; he often amused his friends by imitations of fellow-musicians, reproducing their manner and gestures to the life; so well as actually on more than one occasion to take in the spectator.

Madame Sand thus gives account of the even tenor of her way, in a letter of September, 1845:—

> I have been in Paris till June, and since then am at Nohant until the winter, as usual; for henceforward my life is ruled as regularly as

> music paper. I have written two or three novels, one of which is just going to appear.
>
> My son is still thin and delicate, but otherwise well. He is the best being, the gentlest, most equable, industrious, simple-minded, and straightforward ever seen. Our characters, like our hearts, agree so well that we can hardly live a day apart. He is entering his twenty-third year, Solange her eighteenth. We have our ways of merriment, not noisy, but sustained, which bring our ages nearer together, and when we have been working hard all the week we allow ourselves, by way of a grand holiday, to go and eat our cake out of doors some way off, in a wood or an old ruin, with my brother, who is like a sturdy peasant, full of fun and good nature, and who dines with us every day, seeing that he lives not two miles off. Such are our grand pranks.

Sometimes these little outings would originate a novel, as with the *Meunier d'Angibault*, which she ascribes to "a walk, a discovery, a day of leisure, an hour of idleness." On a ramble with her children she came upon what she calls "a nook in a wild paradise;" a mill, whose owner had allowed everything to grow around the sluices that chose to spring up, briar and alder, oaks and rushes. The stream, left to follow its devices, had forced its way through the sand and the grass in a network of little waterfalls, covered below in the summer time with thick tufts of aquatic plants.

It was enough; the seed was sown and the fruit resulted. "The apple falling from the tree led Newton to the discovery of one of the grand laws of the universe.... In scientific works of genius, reflection derives the causes of things from a single fact. In art's humbler fancies, that isolated fact is dressed and completed in a dream."

The picture given by Madame Sand and her guests of these years of her life is charming enough, and in certain ways seems an ideal kind of existence, amid beloved children, friends, pleasant and calm surroundings, and the sweets of successful literary activity. But if it had its bright lights, it had also its deep shadows. For every fresh pleasure and interest crowded into her existence, there entered a fresh source of anxiety and trouble. Age, in bringing her more power of endurance, had not blunted her sensibilities. As usual with the strongest natures in their hours of depression—and none so strong as to escape these—she could then look for no help except from herself. Those accustomed, like her, to shirk no responsibility, no burden, to invite others to lean on them, and to ask no support, if their fortitude gives way find the allowance, help and sympathy so easily accorded to their weaker fellow-creatures nowhere ready for them. The exclamation wrung from one of the characters in a later work of Madame Sand's, may be but a faithful echo of the cry of her own nature in some moment of mental torment. "Let me be weak; I have been seeming to be strong for so long a time!"

Chopin, though the study of his genius had freshly inspired her own, and greatly extended her comprehension of musical art, was a being to whom the burden of his own life was too painful to allow him to lighten the troubles of another; a partial invalid, a prey to nervous irritation, he was dependent on her to soothe and cheer him at the best of times, and to be nurse and secretary besides when he was prostrated by illness or despondency. One is loth to call selfish a nature so attractive in its refinement, so unhappy in its over-susceptibility. But it is obvious that such a one might easily become a trial to those he loved. With all its vigor her nervous system could not escape the exhaustion and disturbance that attend on incessant brain-work. "Those who have nothing to do," she remarks, "when they see artists produce with facility, are ready to wonder at how few hours, how few instants, these can reserve for themselves. For such do not know how these gymnastics of the imagination, if they do not affect your health, yet leave an excitation of your nerves, an obsession of mental pictures, a languor of spirit, that forbid you to carry on any other kind of work."

Although her constitution was even stronger than in her youth, she had for some years been subject to severe attacks of neuralgia. "Madame Sand suffers terribly from violent headaches and pain in her eyes," remarks Delacroix, in one of the letters above quoted, "which she takes upon herself to surmount as far as possible, with a great effort, so as not to distress us by what she goes through." Her habit of writing principally at night and contenting herself with the least possible allowance of repose, few could have persisted in for so long without breaking down. For many years she never took more than four hours sleep. The strain began to tell on her eye-sight at last, and already in a letter of 1842 she speaks of being temporarily compelled to suspend this practice of night-work, to her great regret, as in the daylight hours she was never secure from interruption. Only her abnormal power of activity and of bearing fatigue could have enabled her to fulfill so strenuously the responsibilities she had undertaken to her children, her private friends, and the public. The pressure of literary work was incessant, and whatever her dislike to accounts and arithmetic she is said to have fulfilled her engagements to editors and publishers with the regularity and punctuality of a notary. Her large acquaintance, relations with various classes, various projects, literary, political, and philanthropical, involved an immense amount of serious correspondence in addition to that arising from the postal persecution from which no celebrity escapes. Ladies wrote to consult her on sentimental subjects—to inquire of her, as of an oracle, whether they should bestow their heart, their hand, or both, upon their suitors; poets, to solicit her patronage and criticism. In the course of a single half-year, 153 manuscripts were sent her for perusal! She replied when it seemed fit, conscientiously and ungrudgingly; but experience had made her less expansive than formerly to those whose overtures she felt to be prompted by curiosity or some such idle motive, in the absence of any sympathy for her ways of thinking. "I am not to be caught in my words with indifferent persons," she writes to M. Charles Duvernet, describing how, when in her friend Madame Marliani's *salon* in Paris she heard herself and her political allies or their opinions attacked, she was not to be provoked into argument or indignant denial, but went on quietly with her work of hemming pocket-handkerchiefs. "To such people one speaks through the medium of the Press. If they will not attend, no matter."

Her sex, her anomalous position, her freedom of expression and action, exposed her to an extent quite exceptional, even for a public character, to the shafts of malice and slander. Accustomed to have to brave the worst from such attacks, she might and did arrive at treating them with an indifference that was not, however, in her nature, which shrank from the observation and personal criticism of the vulgar.

To a young poet of promise in whose welfare she took interest, she writes, August, 1842:—

> Never show my letters except to your mother, your wife, or your greatest friend. It is a shy habit, a mania I have to the last degree. The idea that I am not writing for those alone to whom I write, or for those who love them thoroughly, would freeze my heart and my hand directly. Everyone has a fault. Mine is a misanthropy in my outward habits—for all that I have no passion left in me but the love of my fellow-creatures; but with the small services that my heart and my faith can render in this world, my personality has nothing to do. Some people have grieved me very much, unconsciously, by talking and writing about me personally and my doings, even though favorably, and meaning well. Respect this malady of spirit.

Madame Sand, being naturally undemonstrative, was commonly more or less tongue-tied and chilled in the presence of a stranger, and she had a frank dread of introductions and first interviews, even when the acquaintance was one she desired to make. Sometimes she asks her friends to prepare such new comers for receiving an unfavorable first impression, and to beg them not to be unduly prejudiced thereby. Such a one would find the persecution of lion-hunters intolerable, and now and then this drove her to extremities. Great must, indeed, have been the wrath of one of these irrepressibles, who, more obstinate than the rest, failing by fair means to get an introduction to George Sand, calmly pushed his way into Nohant unauthorized by anyone, whereupon her friends conspired to serve him the trick it must be owned he deserved; and which we give in the words of Madame Sand, writing to the Comtesse d'Agoult. The story is told also by Liszt in his letters:—

> M. X. is ushered into my room. A respectable-looking person there receives him. She was about forty years of age, but you might give her sixty at a pinch. She had had beautiful teeth, but had got none left. All passes away! She had been rather good-looking, but was so no longer. All changes! Her figure was corpulent, and her hands were soiled. Nothing is perfect!
>
> She was clad in a gray woolen gown spotted with black, and lined with scarlet. A silk handkerchief was negligently twisted round her black hair. Her shoes were faulty, but she was thoroughly dignified.

> Now and then she seemed on the point of putting an *s* or a *t* in the wrong place, but she corrected herself gracefully, talked of her literary works, of her excellent friend M. Rollinat, of the talents of her visitor which had not failed to reach her ears, though she lived in complete retirement, overwhelmed with work. M. G. brought her a foot-stool, the children called her mamma, the servants Madame.
>
> She had a gracious smile, and much more distinguished manners than that fellow George Sand. In a word X. was happy and proud of his visit. Perched in a big chair, with beaming aspect, arm extended, speech abundant, there he stayed for a full quarter of an hour in ecstasies, and then took leave, bowing down to the ground to—Sophie!

It was the maid that had thus been successfully passed off as the mistress, who with her whole household enjoyed a long and hearty laugh at the expense of the departed unbidden guest. "M. X. has gone off to Châteauroux," she concludes, "on purpose to give an account of his interview with me, and to describe me personally in all the *cafés*."

This anecdote however belongs to a much earlier period of her life, the year 1837. Of her cordiality and kindliness to those who approached her in a right spirit of sincerity and simplicity, many have spoken. For English readers we cannot do better than quote Mr. Matthew Arnold's interesting account, given in the *Fortnightly*, 1877, of his visit to her in August, 1846. Desirous of seeing the green lanes of Berry, the rocky heaths of Bourbonnais, the descriptions of which in *Valentine* and *Jeanne* had charmed him so strongly, the traveller chose a route that brought him to within a few miles of her home:—"I addressed to Madame Sand," he tells us, "the sort of letter of which she must in her lifetime have had scores—a letter conveying to her, in bad French, the youthful and enthusiastic homage of a foreigner who had read her works with delight." She responded by inviting him to call at Nohant. He came and joined a breakfast-party that included Madame Sand and her son and daughter, Chopin, and other friends—Mr. Arnold being placed next to the hostess. He says of her:—

> As she spoke, her eyes, head, bearing were all of them striking, but the main impression she made was one of simplicity, frank, cordial simplicity. After breakfast she led the way into the garden, asked me a few kind questions about myself and my plans, gathered a flower or two and gave them to me, shook hands heartily at the gate, and I saw her no more.

During the eight years of successful literary activity, lying between Madame Sand's return from Majorca and the Revolution of February, 1848, the profits of her work had, after the first, enabled her freely to spend the greater part of the year at Nohant, and to provide a substantial dowry for her daughter. But the amassing of wealth suited neither her taste nor her principles. She writes to her poet-protégé M. Poncy, in September, 1845:—

> We are in easy circumstances, which enables us to do away with poverty in our own neighborhood, and if we feel the sorrow of being unable to do away with that which desolates the world—a deep sorrow, especially at my age, when life has no intoxicating personality left, and one sees plainly the spectacle of society in its injustices and frightful disorder—at least we know nothing of *ennui*, of restless ambition and selfish passions. We have a sort of relative happiness, and my children enjoy it with the simplicity of their age.
>
> As for me, I only accept it in trembling, for all happiness is like a theft in this ill-regulated world of men, where you cannot enjoy your ease or your liberty, except to the detriment of your fellow-creatures—by the force of things, the law of inequality, that odious law, those odious combinations, the thought of which poisons my sweetest domestic joys and revolts me against myself at every moment. I can only find consolation in vowing to go on writing as long as I have a breath of life left in me, against the infamous maxim, "*Chacun chez soi, chacun pour soi.*" Since all I can do is to make this protest, make it I shall, in every key.

Her republican friends in Berry had founded in 1844 a local journal for the spread of liberal ideas—such as Lamartine at the time was supporting at Macon. Madame Sand readily contributed her services to a cause where she labored for the enlightenment of the masses on all subjects—truth, justice, religion, liberty, fraternity, duties, and rights. The government of Louis Philippe, so long as such utterances attacked no definite institution, allowed an almost illimitable freedom in expression of opinion. The result was that thought had advanced so far ahead of action that social philosophers had grown to argue as though practical obstacles had no existence—to be rudely reminded of their consequence, when brought to the front in 1848, and acting somewhat too much as if on that supposition.

It is impossible not to make concerning Madame Sand, the reflection made on other foremost workers in the same cause of organic social reform—namely, that her character and her instincts were in curious opposition to her ideas. What was said by Madame d'Agoult of Louis Blanc applies with even greater force to George Sand: "The sentiment of personality was never stronger than in this opposer of individualism, communist theories had for their champion one most unfit to be absorbed into the community." For no length of time was the idea of "communism" accepted, and never was it advocated by her except in the most restricted sense. The land-hunger, or rather land-greed, of the small proprietors in her neighborhood had, it is true, given her a certain disgust for these contested possessions. But from the preference of a small child for a garden of its own however small, to another's however large, she characteristically infers the instinct of property as a law of nature it were preposterous to disallow, and furthermore she lays down as an axiom that, "in treating the communistic idea it is necessary first to distinguish what is essential in liberty and work to the complete existence of the individual, from what is collective." When forced by actual experience to point out what she holds to be the rightful application of the idea, she limits it to voluntary association; and she hoped great things from the co-operative principle, as tending to eliminate the ills of extreme inequalities in the social structure, and to preserve everything in it that is worth preserving.

CHAPTER VIII. - NOVELIST AND POLITICIAN.

BY her novels classed as "socialistic," Madame Sand had, as we have seen, incurred the public hostility of those whom her doctrines alarmed. And yet her "communist" heroes and heroines are the most pacific and inoffensive of social influences. They merely aspire to isolate themselves, and personally to practice principles and virtues of the highest order; unworldliness such as, if general, might indeed turn the earth into the desired Utopia. Nothing can be said against their example, unless that it is too good, and that there is little hope of its being widely followed.

Charges of another sort, no less bitter, and though exaggerated, somewhat better founded, assailed her after the appearance in 1847 of *Lucrezia Floriani*, a novel of character-analysis entirely, but into which she was accused of having introduced an unflattering portrait of Frédéric Chopin, whose long and long-requited attachment to her entitled him to better treatment at her hands.

With respect to the general question of such alleged fictitious reproductions, few novelists escape getting into trouble on this head. It has been aptly observed by Mr. Hamerton that the usual procedure of the reading public in such cases is to fix on some real personage as distinctly unlike the character in the book as possible, for the original, and then to complain of the unfaithfulness of the resemblance. Madame Sand's taste and higher art-instincts would have revolted against the practice—now unfortunately no longer confined to inferior writers—of forcing attention to a novel by making it the gibbet of well-known personalities, with little or no disguise; and Chopin himself, morbidly sensitive and fanciful though he was, read her work without perceiving in it any intention there to portray their relations to each other, which, indeed, had differed essentially from those of the personages in the romance.

Lucrezia Floriani is a *cantatrice* of genius, who, whilst still young, has retired from the world, indifferent to fame, and effectually disenchanted—so she believes—with passion. Despite an experience strange and stormy, even for a member of her Bohemian profession, Lucrezia has miraculously preserved intact her native nobility of soul, and appears as a meet object of worship to a fastidious young prince on his travels, who becomes passionately enamored of her. He over-persuades Lucrezia into trusting that they will find their felicity in each other. Their happiness is of the briefest duration, owing to the unreasonable character of the prince, who leads the actress a miserable life; his love taking the form of petty tyranny and retrospective jealousy. After long years of this material and moral captivity, the heroic Lucrezia fades and dies.

Not content with identifying the intolerable, though it must be owned severely-tested, Prince Karol with Chopin, imaginative writers have gone so far as to assert that the book was conceived and written from an express design on the novelist's part to bring about the breach of a link she was beginning to find irksome!

Madame Sand has described how it was written—as are all such works of imagination—in response to a sort of "call"—some striking yet indefinable quality in one idea among the host always floating through the brain of the artist, that makes him instantly seize it and single it out as inviting to art-treatment. It would be preposterous to doubt her statement. But whether the inspiration ought not to have been sacrificed is another question. Her gift was her good angel and her evil angel as well, but in any case something of her despot. Here, assuredly, it ruled her ill. It is indisputable that, as she had pointed out, the sad history of the attachment of Lucrezia the actress and Karol the prince deviates too widely from that which was supposed to have originated it for just comparisons to be drawn between the two, that Karol is not a genius, and therefore has none of the rights of genius—including, we presume, the right to be a torment to those around him—that to talk of a portrait of Chopin without his genius is a contradiction in terms, that he never suspected the likeness assumed until it was insinuated to him, and so forth. But there remains this, that in the work of imagination she here presented to the public there was enough of reality interwoven to make the world hasten to identify or confound Prince Karol with Chopin. This might have been a foregone conclusion, as also that Chopin, the most sensitive of mortals, would be infinitely pained by the inferences that would be drawn. Perhaps if only as a genius, he had the right to be spared such an infliction; and one must wish it could have appeared in this light to Madame Sand. It seems as though it were impossible for the author to put himself at the point of view of the reader in such matters. The divine spark itself, that quickens certain faculties, deadens others. When Goethe, in *Werther*, dragged the private life of his intimate friends, the Kestners, into publicity, and by falsifying the character of the one and misrepresenting the conduct of the other, in obedience to the requisitions of art, exposed his beloved Charlotte and her husband to all manner of annoyances, it never seems to have entered into his head beforehand but that they would be delighted by what he had done. Nor could he get over his surprise that such petty vexations on their part should not be merged in a proud satisfaction at the literary memorial thus raised by him to their friendly intercourse! This seems incredible, and yet his sincerity leaves no room for doubt.

Madame Sand's transgressions on this head, though few, have obtained great notoriety, on account of the extraordinary celebrity of two of the personages that suggested characters she has drawn. To the supposed originals, however obscure, the mortification is the same. But what often passes uncommented on when the individuals said to be traduced are unknown to fame, sets the whole world talking when one of the first musicians or poets of the century is involved; so that Madame Sand has incurred more censure than other novelists, though she has deserved it more rarely. But regret remains that for the sake of *Lucrezia Floriani*, one of the least pleasant though by no means the least powerful of her novels, she should have exposed herself to the charge of unkindness to one who had but a short while to live.

Other causes had latterly been combining to lead to differences of which it would certainly be unfair to lay the whole blame on Madame Sand. The tie of personal attachment between Chopin and herself was not associated by identity of outward interests or even of cares and family affections, such as, in the case of husband and wife, make self-sacrifice possible under conditions which might otherwise be felt unbearable, and help to tide over crises of impatience or wrong. Madame Sand's children were now grown up; cross-influences could not but arise, hard to conciliate. Without accrediting Chopin with the self-absorption of Prince Karol, it is easy to see here, in a situation somewhat anomalous, elements of probable discord. It was impossible that he should any longer be a first consideration; impossible that he should not resent it.

For some years his state of health had been getting worse and worse, and his nervous susceptibilities correspondingly intensified. Madame Sand betrayed some impatience at last of what she had long borne uncomplainingly, and their good understanding was broken. As was natural, the breach was the more severely felt by Chopin, but that it was of an irreparable nature, one is at liberty to doubt. He bitterly regretted what he had lost, for which not all the attentions showered on him by his well-wishers could afford compensation, as his letters attest.

But outward circumstances prolonged the estrangement till it was too late. They met but once after the quarrel, and that was in company in March, 1848. Madame Sand would at once have made some approach, but Chopin did not then respond to the appeal; and the reconciliation both perhaps desired was never to take place. Political events had intervened to widen the gap between their paths. Chopin had neither part nor lot in the revolutionary movement that just then was throwing all minds and lives into a ferment, and which was completely to engross Madame Sand's energies for many months to come. It drove him away to England, and he only returned to Paris, in 1849, to die.

In May, 1847, the tranquility of life at Nohant had been varied by a family event, the marriage of Madame Sand's daughter Solange with the sculptor Clésinger. The remainder of the twelvemonth was spent in the country, apparently with very little anticipation on Madame Sand's part that the breaking of the political storm, that was to draw her into its midst, was so near.

The new year was to be one of serious agitations, different to any that had yet entered into her experience. Political enterprise for the time cast all purely personal interests and emotions into the background. "I have never known how to do anything by halves," she says of herself very truly; and whatever may be thought of the tendency of her political influence and the manner of its exertion, no one can tax her with sparing herself in a contest to which, moreover, she came disinterested; vanity and ambition having, in one of her sex, nothing to gain by it. But in political matters it seems hard for a poet to do right. If, like Goethe, he holds aloof in great crises, he is branded for it as a traitor and a bad patriot. The battle of Leipzig is being fought, and he sits tranquilly writing the epilogue for a play. If, like George Sand, he throws the whole weight of his enthusiastic eloquence into what he believes to be the right scale, it is ten to one that his power, which knows nothing of caution and patience, may do harm to the cause he has at heart.

Madame Sand rested her hopes for a better state of things, for the redemption of France from political corruption, for the amelioration of the condition of the working classes, and reform of social institutions in general, on the advent to power of those placed at the head of affairs by the collapse of the government of Louis Philippe, a crisis long threatened, long prepared, and become inevitable.

"The whole system," wrote Heine prophetically of the existing monarchy, five years before its fall, "is not worth a charge of powder, if indeed some day a charge of powder does not blow it up." February, 1848, saw the explosion, the flight of the Royal Family, and the formation of a Provisional Government, with Lamartine at its head.

It is hard to realize in the present day, when we contemplate these events through the sobering light of the deplorable sequel, how immense and wide-spreading was the enthusiasm that at this particular juncture seemed to put the fervent soul of a George Sand or an Armand Barbès into the most lukewarm and timid. "More than one," writes Madame d'Agoult, "who for the last twenty years had been scoffing at every grand thought, let himself be won by the general emotion." The prevailing impression can have fallen little short of the conviction that a sort of millennium was at hand for mankind in general and the French in particular, and that all human ills would disappear because a bad government had been got rid of, and that without such scenes of blood and strife as had disfigured previous revolutions.

The first task was firmly to establish a better one in its place. Madame Sand, though with a strong perception of the terrible difficulties besetting a ministry which, to quote her own words, would need, in order to acquit itself successfully, "the genius of a Napoleon and the heart of Christ," never relaxed an instant in the enforcement, both by example and exhortation, of her conviction that it was the duty of all true patriots and philanthropists to consecrate their energies to the cause of the new republic.

"My heart is full and my head on fire," she writes to a fellow-worker in the same cause. "All my physical ailments, all my personal sorrows are forgotten. I live, I am strong, active, I am not more than twenty years old." The exceptional situation of the country was one in which, according to her opinion, it behooved men to be ready not only with loyalty and devotion, but with fanaticism if needed. She worked hard with her son and her local allies at the ungrateful task of revolutionizing Le Berry, which, she sighs, "is very drowsy." In March she came up to Paris and placed her services as journalist and partizan generally at the disposal of Ledru-Rollin, Minister of the Interior under the new Government. "Here am I already doing the work of a statesman," she writes from Paris to her son at Nohant, March 24. Her indefatigable energy, enabling her as it did to disdain repose, was perhaps the object of envy to the statesmen themselves. At their disgust when kept up all night by the official duties of their posts, she laughs without mercy. Night and day her pen was occupied, now drawing up circulars for the administration, now lecturing the people in political pamphlets addressed to them. To the *Bulletin de la République*, a government journal started with the laudable purpose of preserving a clear understanding between the mass of the people in the provinces and the central government, she became a leading contributor. For the festal invitation performances given to the people at the "Théâtre de la République," where Rachel sang the Marseillaise and acted in *Les Horaces*, Madame Sand wrote a little "occasional" prologue, *Le Roi Attend*, a new and democratic version of Molière's *Impromptu de Versailles*. The outline is as follows:—Molière is discovered impatient and uneasy; the King waits, and the comedians are not ready. He sinks asleep, and has a vision, in which the muse emerges out of a cloud, escorted by Æschylus, Sophocles, Euripides, Shakespeare, and Beaumarchais, to each of whom are assigned a few lines—where possible, lines of their own—in praise of equality and fraternity. They vanish, and Molière awakes; his servant announces to him that the King waits—but the King this time is, of course, the people, to whom Molière now addresses his flattering speech in turn.

But the fervor of heroism that fired everybody in the first days of successful revolution, that made the leaders disinterested, the masses well-behaved, reasonable, and manageable, was for the majority a flash only; and the dreamed-of social ideal, touched for a moment was to recede again into the far distance. It was Madame Sand's error, and no ignoble one, to entertain the belief that a nation could safely be trusted to the guidance of a force so variable and uncontrollable as enthusiasm, and that the principle of self-devotion could be relied upon as a motive power. The divisions, intrigues, and fatal complications that quickly arose at head-quarters confirmed her first estimation of the practical dangers ahead. She clung to her belief in the sublime virtues of the masses, and that they would prove themselves grander, finer, more generous than all the mighty and the learned ones upon earth. But each of the popular leaders in turn was pronounced by her tried and found wanting. None of the party chiefs presented the desirable combination of perfect heroism and political genius. Michel, the apostle who of old had converted her to the cause, she had long scorned as a deserter. Leroux, in the moment of action, was a nonentity. Barbès "reasons like a saint," she observes, "that is to say, very ill as regards the things of this world." Lamartine was a vain trimmer; Louis Blanc, a sectarian; Ledru-Rollin, a weathercock. "It is the characters that transgress," she complains naïvely as one after the other disappointed her. Her own shortcomings on the score of patience and prudence were, it must be owned, no less grave. Her clear-sightedness was unaccompanied by the slightest dexterity of action. Years before, in one of the *Lettres d'un Voyageur*, she had passed a criticism on herself as a political worker, the accuracy of which she made proof of when carried into the vortex. "I am by nature poetical, but not legislative, warlike, if required, but never parliamentary. By first persuading me and then giving me my orders some use may be made of me, but I am not fit for discovering or deciding anything."

Such an influence, important for raising an agitation, was null for controlling and directing the forces thus set in motion. In the application of the theories she had accepted she was as weak and obscure as she was emphatic and eloquent in the preaching of them. Little help could she afford the republican leaders in dealing with the momentous question how to fulfill the immense but confused aspirations they had raised, how to show that their principles could answer the necessities of the moment.

The worst, perhaps, that can be said of Madame Sand's political utterances is that they encouraged the people in their false belief—which belief she shared—that the social reforms so urgently needed could be worked rapidly by the Government, providing only it were willing. Over-boldness of expression on the part of advanced sections only increased the timidity and irresolution of action complained of in the administration. As the ranks of the Ministry split up into factions, Madame Sand attached herself to the party of Ledru-Rollin—in whom at that time she had confidence,—a party that desired to see him at the head of affairs, and that included Jules Favre, Étienne Arago, and Armand Barbès. No more zealous political partizan and agent than Madame Sand. The purpose in view was to preserve a cordial *entente* between these trusted chiefs and the masses whose interests they represented and on whose support they relied. To this end she got together meetings of working-men at her temporary Parisian abode, addressing them in speech and in print, and seemingly blind in the heat of the struggle to the enormous danger of playing with the unmanageable, unreasoning instincts of the crowd. She still cherished the chimera dear to her imagination—the prospective vision of the French people assembling itself in large masses, and deliberately and pacifically giving expression to its wishes.

Into the *Bulletin de la République* there crept soon a tone of impatience and provocation, improper and dangerous in an official organ. The 16th number, which appeared on April 16, at a moment when the pending general elections seemed likely to be overruled by reactionaries, contained the startling declaration that if the result should thus dissatisfy the Paris people, these would manifest their will once more, by adjourning the decision of a false national representation.

This sentence, which came from the pen of Madame Sand, was interpreted into a threat of intimidation from the party that would make Ledru-Rollin dictator, and created a considerable stir. There was, indeed, no call for a fresh brand of discord in the republican ranks. Almost simultaneously came popular demonstrations of a menacing character. Ledru-Rollin disavowed the offending *Bulletin*; but the growing uneasiness of the *bourgeoisie*, the unruly discontent among the workmen, the Government, embarrassed and utterly disorganized, was powerless to allay. Madame Sand began to perceive that the republic of her dreams, the "republican republic," was a forlorn hope, though still unconscious that even heavier obstacles to progress existed in the governed many than in the incapacity or personal ambition of the governing few. She writes to her son from Paris, April 17:—

> I am sad, my boy. If this goes on, and in some sense there should be no more to be done, I shall return to Nohant to console myself by being with you. I shall stay and see the National Assembly, after which I think I shall find nothing more here that I can do.

At the *Fête de la Fraternité*, April 20th, the spectacle of a million of souls putting aside and agreeing to forget all dissensions, all wrongs in the past and fears for the future, and uniting in a burst of joyous exultation, filled her with enthusiasm and renewed hope. But the demonstration of the 15th of May, of which she was next a spectator, besides its mischievous effect in alarming the quiet classes and exciting the agitators afresh, gave fatal evidence of the national disorganization and uncontrollable confusion everywhere prevailing, that had doomed the republic from the hour of its birth.

Madame Sand, though she strenuously denied any participation or sympathy with this particular manifestation, was closely associated in the public mind with those who had aided and abetted the uprising. During the gathering of the populace, which she had witnessed, mingling unrecognized among the crowd, a female orator haranguing the mob from the lower windows of a *café* was pointed out to her, and she was assured that it was George Sand. During the repressive measures the administration was led to take she felt uncertain whether the arrest of Barbès might not be followed by her own. Some of her friends advised her to seek safety in Italy, where at that time the partisans of liberty were more united and sanguine. She turned a deaf ear. But she was severed now from all influential connection with those in authority. Before the end of May she left for Nohant, with her hopes for the rapid regeneration of her country on the wane. "I am afraid for the future," she writes to the imprisoned Barbès, shortly after these events. "I suffer for those who do harm and allow harm to be done without understanding it.... I see nothing but ignorance and moral weakness preponderating on the face of the globe."

Through the medium of the press, notably of the journal *La Vraie République*, she continued to give plain expression to her sentiments, regardless of the political enmities she might excite, and of the personal mortification to which she was exposed, even at Nohant, which with its inmates had recently become the mark for petty hostile "demonstrations." Alluding to these, she writes:—

> Here in this Berry, so romantic, so gentle, so calm and good, in this land I love so tenderly, and where I have given sufficient proof to the poor and uneducated that I know my duties towards them, I myself in particular am looked upon as the enemy of the human race; and if the Republic has not kept its promises, it is I, clearly, who am the cause.

The term "communist," caught up and passed from mouth to mouth, was flung at Madame Sand and her son by the peasants, whose ideas as to its significance were not a little wild. "A pack of idiots," she writes to Madame Marliani, "who threaten to come and set fire to Nohant. Brave they are not, neither morally nor physically; and when they come this way and I walk through the midst of them they take off their hats; but when they have gone by they summon courage to shout, 'Down with the communists.'"

The ingratitude of many who again and again had received succor from her and hers, she might excuse on account of their ignorance, but the extent of their ignorance was an obstacle to immediate progress whose weight she had miscalculated.

"I shall keep my faith," she writes to Joseph Mazzini at this crisis—"the idea, pure and bright, the eternal truth will ever remain for me in my heaven, unless I go blind. But hope is a belief in the near triumph of one's faith. I should not be sincere if I said that this state of mind had not been modified in me during these last months."

The terrible insurrection of June followed, and overwhelmed her for the time. It was not only that her nature, womanly and poetical, had the greatest horror of bloodshed. The spectacle of the republicans slaughtering each other, of the evil passions stirred, the frightful anarchy, ended but at a frightful cost, the complete extinction of all hopes,—nothing left rampant but fear, rancor and distrust,—was heart-rendering to her whose heart had been thrown into the national troubles. Great was the panic in Berry, an after-clap of the disturbances in the capital. Madame Sand's position became more unpleasant than ever. She describes herself as "*blasée d outrages*—threatened perpetually by the coward hatreds and imbecile terrors of country places." But to all this she was well-nigh insensible in her despair over the public calamities oppressing her nation—the end of all long-struggling aspirations in "frightful confusion, complete moral anarchy, a morbid condition, in most which the courageous of us lost heart and wished for death.

"You say that the *bourgeoisie* prevails," she writes to Mazzini, in September, 1848, "and that thus it is quite natural that selfishness should be the order of the day. But why does the *bourgeoisie* prevail, whilst the people is sovereign, and the principle of its sovereignty, universal suffrage, is still standing? We must open our eyes at last, and the vision of reality is horrible. The majority of the French people is blind, credulous, ignorant, ungrateful, wicked, and stupid; it is *bourgeoisie* itself!"

Under no conceivable circumstances is it likely that Madame Sand would not very soon have become disgusted with active politics, for which her temperament unfitted her in every respect. Impetuous and uncompromisingly sincere, she was predestined to burn her fingers; proud and independent, to become something of a scape-goat, charged with all the follies and errors which she repudiated, as well as with those for which she was more or less directly responsible.

For some time to come she remained in comparative seclusion at Nohant. She had not ceased her propaganda, though obliged to conduct it with greater circumspection. After the horrors of civil warfare, had come the cry for order at any price, and France had declared for the rule of Louis Bonaparte. During the course of events that consolidated his power, Madame Sand withdrew more and more from the strife of political parties. She had been, and we shall find her again, inclined to hope for better things for France from its new master than time showed to be in store. Other republicans besides herself had been disposed to build high their hopes of this future "saviour of society" in his youthful days of adversity and mysterious obscurity. When in confinement at the fortress of Ham, in 1844, Louis Napoleon sent to George Sand his work on the Extinction of Pauperism. She wrote back a flattering letter in which, however, with characteristic sincerity, she is careful to remind him that the party to which she belonged could never acknowledge any sovereign but the people; that this they considered to be incompatible with the sovereignty of one man; that no miracle, no personification of popular genius in a single individual, could prove to them the right of that individual to sovereign power.

Since then she had seen the people supreme, and been forced to own that they knew not what they wanted, nor whither they were going, divided in mind, ferocious in action. Among the leaders, she had seen some infatuated by the allurements of personal popularity, and the rest showing, by their inability to cope with the perplexities of administrative government, that so far philosophical speculations were of no avail in the actual solution of social problems.

The result of her disenchantment was in no degree the overthrow of her political faith. A conviction was dawning on her that her social ideal was absolutely impracticable in any future that she and her friends could hope to live to see. But the belief on which she founded her social religion was one in which she never wavered; a certainty that a progress, the very idea of which now seemed chimerical, would some day appear to all as a natural thing; nay, that the stream of tendency would carry men towards this goal in spite of themselves.

CHAPTER IX. - PASTORAL TALES.

"So you thought," wrote Madame Sand to a political friend, in 1849, "that I was drinking blood out of the skulls of aristocrats. Not I! I am reading Virgil and learning Latin." And her best propaganda, as by and by she came to own, was not that carried on in journals such as *La Vraie République* and *La Cause du Peuple*. Through her works of imagination she has exercised an influence more powerful and universal, if indirect.

Among the more than half a hundred romances of George Sand, there stands out a little group of three, belonging to the period we have now reached—the *mezzo cammin* of her life—creations in a special style, and over which the public voice, whether of fastidious critics or general readers, in France or abroad, has been and remains unanimous in praise.

In these, her pastoral tales, she hit on a new and happy vein which she was peculiarly qualified to work, combining as she did, intimate knowledge of French peasant life with sympathetic interest in her subject and lively poetic fancy. Here she affronts no prejudices, advances no startling theories, handles no subtle, treacherous social questions, and to these compositions in a perfectly original *genre* she brought the freshness of genius which "age cannot wither," together with the strength and finish of a practiced hand.

Peasants had figured as accessories in her earlier works. The rustic hermit and philosopher, Patience, and Marcasse the rat-catcher, in *Mauprat*, are note-worthy examples. In 1844 had appeared *Jeanne*, with its graceful dedication to Françoise Meillant, the unlettered peasant-girl who may have suggested the work she could not read—one of a family of rural proprietors, spoken of by Madame Sand in a letter of 1843 as a fine survival of a type already then fast vanishing—of patriarchally constituted family-life, embodying all that was grand and simple in the forms of the olden time.

In *Jeanne*, Madame Sand had first ventured to make a peasant-girl the central figure of her novel, though still so far deferring to the received notions of what was essential in order to interest the "gentle" reader as to surround her simple heroine with personages of rank and education. Jeanne herself, moreover, is an exceptional and a highly idealized type—as it were a sister to Joan of Arc, not the inspired warrior-maid, but the visionary shepherdess of the Vosges. Yet the creation is sufficiently real. The author had observed how favorable was the life of solitude and constant communion with nature led by many of these country children in their scattered homesteads, to the development of remarkable and tenacious individuality. So with the strange and poetical Jeanne, too innately refined to prosper in her rough human environment, yet too fixedly simple to fare much better in more cultivated circles. She is the victim of a sort of celestial stupidity we admire and pity at once. In this study of a peasant heroine resides such charm as the book possesses, and the attempt was to lead on the author to the productions above alluded to, *La Mareau Diable*, *François le Champi*, and *La Petite Fadette*. Of this popular trio the first had been published already two years before the Revolution, in 1846; the second was appearing in the Feuilleton of the *Journal des Débats* at the very moment of the breaking of the storm, which interrupted its publication awhile. When those tumultuous months were over, and Madame Sand, thrown out of the hurly-burly of active politics, was brought back by the course of events to Nohant, she seems to have taken up her pen very much where she had laid it down. The break in her ordinary round of work made by the excitements of active statesmanship was hardly perceptible, and in 1849 *Le Champi* was followed by *La Petite Fadette*.

La Mare au Diable, George Sand's first tale of exclusively peasant-life, is usually considered her masterpiece in this *genre*. It was suggested to her, she tells us, by Holbein's dismal engraving of death coming to the husbandman, an old, gaunt, ragged, over-worked representative of his tribe—grim ending to a life of cheerless poverty and toil!

Here was the dark and painful side of the laborer's existence—a true picture, but not the whole truth. There was another and a bright side, which might just as allowably be represented in art as the dreary one, and which she had seen and studied. In Berry extreme poverty was the exception, and the agriculturist's life appeared as it ought to be, healthy, calm, and simple, its laboriousness compensated by the soothing influences of nature, and of strong home affections.

This little gem of a work is thoroughly well-known. The ploughing-scene in the opening—ploughing as she had witnessed it sometimes in her own neighborhood, fresh, rough ground broken up for tillage, the plough drawn by four yoke of young white oxen new to their work and but half-tamed, has a simplicity and grandeur of effect not easy to parallel in modern art. The *motif* of the tale is that you often go far to search for the good fortune that lies close to your door. Never was so homely an adage more freshly and prettily illustrated; yet how slight are the materials, how plain is the outline! Germain, the well-to-do, widowed laborer, in the course of a few miles' ride, a journey undertaken in order to present himself and his addresses to the rich widow his father desires him to woo, discovers the real life-companion he wants in the poor girl-neighbor, whom he patronizingly escorts on her way to the farm where she is hired for service. It all slowly dawns upon him, in the most natural manner, as the least incidents of the journey call out her good qualities of head and heart—her helpfulness in misadventure, forgetfulness of self, unaffected fondness for children, instinctively recognized by Germain's little boy, who, with his unconscious childish influence, is one of the prettiest features in the book. Germain, by his journey's end, has his heart so well engaged in the right quarter that he is proof against the dangerous fascinations of the coquettish widow.

There is a breath of poetry over the picture, but no denaturalization of the uncultured types. Germain is honest and warm-hearted, but not bright of understanding; little Marie is wise and affectionate, but as unsentimentally-minded as the veriest realist could desire. The native caution and mercenary habit of thought of the French agricultural class are indicated by many a humorous touch in the pastorals of George Sand.

Equally pleasing, though not aiming at the almost antique simplicity of the *Mare au Diable*, is the story of *François le Champi*, the foundling, saved from the demoralization to which lack of the softening influences of home and parental affection predestine such unhappy children, through the tenderness his forlorn condition inspires in a single heart—that of Madeline Blanchet, the childless wife, whose own wrongs, patiently borne, have quickened her commiseration for the wrongs of others. Her sympathy, little though it lies in her power to manifest it, he feels, and its incalculable worth to him, which is such that the gratitude of a whole life cannot do more than repay it.

Part of the narrative is here put into the mouth of a peasant, and told in peasant language, or something approaching to it. Over the propriety of this proceeding, adopted also in *Les Maîtres Sonneurs*, French critics are disagreed, though for the most part they regret it. It is not for a foreigner to decide between them. One would certainly regret the absence of some of the extremely original and expressive words and turns of speech current among the rural population, forms which such a method enabled her to introduce into the narrative as well as into the dialogue.

La Petite Fadette is not only worthy of its predecessors but by many will be preferred to either. There is something particularly attractive in the portraits of the twin brothers—partly estranged by character, wholly united by affection,—and in the figure of Fanchon Fadet, an original in humble life, which has made this little work a general favorite wherever it is known.

These prose-idylls have been called "The Georgics of France." It is curious that in a country so largely agricultural, and where nature presents more variety of picturesque aspect than perhaps in any other in Europe, the poetic side of rural life should have been so sparingly represented in her imaginative literature. French poets of nature have mostly sought their inspiration out of their own land, "In France, especially," observes Théophile Gautier, "all literary people live in town, that is in Paris the centre, know little of what is unconnected with it, and most of them cannot tell wheat from barley, potatoes from beetroot." It was a happy inspiration that prompted Madame Sand to fill in the blank, in a way all her own, and her task as we have seen was completed, revolutions notwithstanding. She owns to having then felt the attraction experienced in all time by those hard hit by public calamities, "to throw themselves back on pastoral dreams, all the more naïve and childlike for the brutality and darkness triumphant in the world of activity." Tired of "turning round and round in a false circle of argument, of accusing the governing minority, but only to be forced to acknowledge after all that they were put there by the choice of the majority," she wished to forget it all: and her poetic temperament which unfitted her for success in politics assisted her in finding consolation in nature.

Moreover a district like Le Berry, singularly untouched by corruptions of the civilization, and preserving intact many old and interesting characteristics, was a field in which she might draw from reality many an attractive picture. She was as much rallied by town critics about her shepherdesses as though she had invented them. And yet she saw them every day, and they may be seen still by any wanderer in those lanes, and at every turn, Fanchons, Maries, Nanons, as she described them, tending their flock of from five to a dozen sheep, or a few geese, a goat and a donkey, all day long between the tall hedgerows, or on the common, spinning the while, or possibly dreaming. A certain refinement of cast distinguishes the type. Eugène Delacroix, in a letter describing a village festival at Nohant, remarks that if positive beauty is rare among the natives, ugliness is a thing unknown. A gentle, passive cast of countenance prevails among the women: "They are all St. Annes," as the artist expresses it. The inevitable changes brought about by steam-communication, which have as yet only begun to efface the local habits and peculiarities, must shortly complete their work. George Sand's pastoral novels will then have additional value, as graphic studies of a state of things that has passed away.

It does not appear that the merit of these stories was so quickly recognized as that of *Indiana* and *Valentine*. The author might abstract herself awhile from passing events and write idylls, but the public had probably not yet settled down into the proper state of mind for fully enjoying them. Moreover Madame Sand's antagonists in politics and social science, as though under the impression that she could not write except to advance some theory of which they disapproved, presupposed in these stories a set purpose of exalting the excellence of rustic as compared with polite life—of exaggerating the virtues of the poor, to throw into relief the vices of the rich. The romances themselves do not bear out such a supposition. In them the author chooses exactly the same virtues to exalt, the same vices to condemn, as in her novels of refined society. She shows us intolerance, selfishness, and tyranny of custom marring or endangering individual happiness among the working-classes, as with their superiors. There are Philistines in her thatched cottages, as well as in her marble halls. Germain, in *La Mare au Diable*, has some difficulty to discover for himself, as well as to convince his family and neighbors, that in espousing the penniless Marie he is not marrying beneath him in every sense. François le Champi is a pariah, an outcast in the estimation of the rustic world. Fanchon Fadet, by her disregard of appearances and village etiquette, scandalizes the conservative minds of farmers and millers very much as Aurore Dupin scandalized the leaders of society at La Châtre. Most prominence is given to the more pleasing characters, but the existence of brutality and cupidity among the peasant classes is nowhere kept out of sight. Her long practical acquaintance with these classes indeed was fatal to illusions on the subject. The average son of the soil was as far removed as any other living creature from her ideal of humanity, and at the very time when she penned *La Petite Fadette* she was experiencing how far the ignorance, ill-will, and stupidity of her poorer neighbors could go.

Thus she writes from Nohant to Barbès at Vincennes, November 1848: "Since May, I have shut myself up in prison in my retreat, where, though without the hardships of yours, I have more to suffer than you from sadness and dejection, ... and am less in safety." Threatened by the violence and hatred of the people, she had painfully realized that she and her party had their most obstinate enemies among those whom they wished and worked to save and defend.

Her profound discouragement finds expression in many of her letters from 1849 to 1852. The more sanguine hopes of Mazzini and other of her correspondents she desires, but no longer expects, to see fulfilled. She compares the moral state of France to the Russian retreat; the soldiers in the great army of progress seized with vertigo, and seeking death in fighting with each other.

To her son, who was in Paris at the time of the disturbances in May, 1849, she writes:—

> Come back, I implore you. I have only you in the world, and your death would be mine. I can still be of some small use to the cause of truth, but if I were to lose you it would be all over with me. I have not got the stoicism of Barbès and Mazzini. It is true they are men, and they have no children. Besides, in my opinion it is not in fight, not by civil war, that we shall win the cause of humanity in France. We have got universal suffrage. The worse for us if we do not know how to avail ourselves of it, for that alone can lastingly emancipate us, and the only thing that would give us the right to take up arms would be an attempt on their part to take away our right to vote.

During the two years preceding the *coup d'état* of December, 1851, life at Nohant had resumed its wonted cheerfulness of aspect. Madame Sand was used to surround herself with young people and artistic people; but now, amid their lightheartedness, she had for a period to battle with an extreme inward sadness, confirmed by the fresh evidence brought by these years of the demoralization in all ranks of opinion. "Your head is not very lucid when your heart is so deeply wounded," she had remarked already, after the disasters of 1848, "and how can one help suffering mortally from the spectacle of civil war and the slaughter among the people?"

To that was now added a loss of faith in the virtues of her own party, as well as of the masses. It is no wonder if she fell out of love for awhile with the ideals of romance, with her own art of fiction, and the types of heroism that were her favorite creations. But if the shadow of a morbid pessimism crept over her mind, she could view it now as a spiritual malady which she had yet the will and the strength to live down; as years before she had surmounted a similar phase of feeling induced by personal sorrow.

Already, in 1847, she had begun to write her *Memoirs*, and reverting to them now, she found there work that suited her mood, as dealing with the past, more agreeable to contemplate just then than the present or the future.

However, in September, 1850, we find her writing to Mazzini,—after dwelling on the present shortcomings of the people, and the mixture of pity and indignation with which they inspired her: "I turn back to fiction and produce, in art, popular types such as I see no longer; but as they ought to be and might be." She alludes to a play on which she was engaged, and continues: "The dramatic form, being new to me, has revived me a little of late; it is the only kind of work into which I have been able to throw myself for a year."

The events of December, 1851, surprised her during a brief visit to Paris. Her hopes for her country had sunk so low, that she owns herself at the moment not to have regarded the *coup d'état* as likely to prove more disastrous to the cause of progress than any other of the violent ends which threatened the existing political situation. She left the capital in the midst of the cannonade, and with her family around her at Nohant awaited the issue of the new dictatorship.

The wholesale arrests that followed immediately, and filled the country with stupefaction, made havoc on all sides of her. Among the victims were comrades of her childhood, numbers of her friends and acquaintance and their relatives—as well in Berry as in the capital—many arrested solely on suspicion of hostility to the President's views, yet none the less exposed to chances of death, or captivity, or exile.

The crisis drove Madame Sand once more to quit the privacy of her country life, but this time in the capacity of intercessor with the conqueror for his victims. She came up to Paris, and on January 20, 1852, addressed a letter to the President, imploring his clemency for the accused generally in an admirably eloquent appeal to his sentiments as well of justice as of generosity. The plea she so forcibly urged, that according to his own professions mere opinion was not to be prosecuted as a crime, whereas the so-called "preventive measures" had involved in one common ruin with his active opponents those who had been mere passive spectators of late events, was, of course, unanswerable. The future Emperor granted her two audiences within a week at the Elysée, in answer to her request, and he succeeded on the first occasion in convincing her that the acts of iniquity and intimidation perpetrated as by his authority were as completely in defiance of his public intentions as of his private principles. As a personal favor to herself, he readily offered her the release of any of the political prisoners that she choose to name, and promised that a general amnesty should speedily follow. She left him, reassured to some extent as to the fate in store for her country. The second interview she had solicited in order to plead the cause of one of her personal friends, condemned to transportation. The mission was a delicate one, for her client would engage himself to nothing for the future, and Madame Sand, in petitioning for his release, saw no better course open to her than as expressed by herself, frankly to denounce him to the President as his "incorrigible personal enemy." Upon this the President granted her the prisoner's full pardon at once. Madame Sand was naturally touched by this ready response of the generous impulse to which she had trusted. To those who cast doubts on the sincerity of any good sentiment in such a quarter, she very properly replied that it was not for her to be the first to discredit the generosity she had so successfully appealed to.

But between her republican friends, loth to owe their deliverance to the tender mercies of Louis Napoleon, and her own desire to save their lives and liberties, and themselves and their families from ruin and despair, she found her office of mediator a most unthankful one. She persisted however in unwearying applications for justice and mercy, addressed both to the dictator directly, and through his cousin, Prince Napoleon (Jerome), between whom and herself there existed a cordial esteem. She clung as long as she could to her belief in the public virtue of the President, or Emperor as he already began to be called here and there. But the promised clemency limited itself to a number of particular cases for whom she had specially interceded.

The subsequent conditions of France precluded all free emission of socialist or republican opinions, but Madame Sand desired nothing better than to send in her political resignation; and it is impossible to share the regret of some of her fellow-republicans at finding her again devoting her best energies to her art of fiction, and in November, 1853, writing to Mazzini such words of wisdom as these:—

> You are surprised that I can work at literature. For my part, I thank God that he has let me preserve this faculty; for an honest and clear conscience like mine still finds, apart from all debate, a work of moralization to pursue. What should I do if I relinquish my task, humble though it be? Conspire? It is not my vocation; I should make nothing of it. Pamphlets? I have neither the wit nor the wormwood required for that. Theories? We have made too many, and have fallen to disputing, which is the grave of all truth and all strength. I am, and always have been, artist before everything else. I know that mere politicians look on artists, with great contempt, judging them by some of those mountebank-types which are a disgrace to art. But you, my friend, you well know that a real artist is as useful as the *priest* and the *warrior*, and that when he respects what is true and what is good, he is in the right path where the divine blessing will attend him. Art belongs to all countries and to all time, and its special good is to live on when all else seems to be dying. That is why Providence delivers it from passions too personal or too general, and has given to its organization patience and persistence, an enduring sensibility, and that contemplative sense upon which rests invincible faith.

Her novel, *Les Maîtres Sonneurs*, the first-fruits of the year 1853, is what most will consider a very good equivalent for party pamphlets and political diatribes.

When composing *La Mare au Diable*, in 1846, Madame Sand looked forward to writing a series of such peasant tales, to be collectively entitled *Les Veillées du Chanvreur*, the hemp-beaters being, as will be recollected, the Scheherazades of each village. Their number was never to be thus augmented, but the idea is recalled by the chapter-headings of *Les Maîtres Sonneurs*, in which Étienne Despardieu, or Tiennet, the rustic narrator, tells, in the successive *veillées* of a month, the romance of his youth. It is a work of a very different type to the rural tales that had preceded it, and should be regarded apart from them. It is longer, more complex in form and sentiment, more of an ideal composition. *Les Maîtres Sonneurs*, is a delightful pastoral, woodland fantasy, standing by itself among romances much as stands a kindred work of imagination, "As You Like It," among plays, yet thoroughly characteristic of George Sand, the nature-lover, the seer into the mysteries of human character, and the imaginative artist. The agreeable preponderates in the story, but it has its tragic features and its serious import. A picturesque and uncommon setting adds materially to its charm. Every thread tells in this delicate piece of fancy-work, and the weaver's art is indescribable. But one may note the ingenuity with which four or five interesting yet perfectly natural types are brought into a group and contrasted; improbable incidents so handled as not to strike a discordant note, the characteristics of the past introduced without ever losing hold of the links, the points of identity between past and present. The scene is the hamlet of Nohant itself; the time is a century ago, when the country, half covered with forest, was wilder, the customs rougher, the local coloring stronger than even Madame Sand in her childhood had known them. The personages belong to the rural proprietor class. The leading characters are all somewhat out of the common, but such exist in equal proportions in all classes of society, and there is ample evidence besides George Sand's of notable examples among the French peasantry. The plot and its interest lie in the development of character and the fine tracing of the manner in which the different characters are influenced by circumstances and by each other. If the beauty of rustic maidens, and of rustic songs and dance-music, as here described, seem to transcend probability, it must be remembered it is a peasant who speaks of these wonders, and as wonders they might appear to his limited experience. As a musical novel, it has the ingenious distinction of being told from the point of view of the sturdy and honest, but unartistic and non-musical Tiennet; a typical Berrichon. Madame Sand was of opinion that during the long occupation of Berry by the English the two races had blended extensively, and she would thus account for some of the heavier, more inexpansive qualities of our nation having become characteristic of this French province.

More than one English reader of *Les Maîtres Sonneurs* may have been struck by the picture there presented of peasant-folk in a state of peace and comfort, such as we do not suppose to have been common in France before the Revolution. Madame Sand has elsewhere explained how, as a fact, Nohant, and other estates in the region round about, had enjoyed some immunity from the worst abuses of the *ancien régime*. Several of these properties, as it happened, had fallen to women or minors—widows, elderly maiden ladies, who, and their agents, spared the holders and cultivators of the soil the exactions which, by right or by might, its lords were used to levy. "So the peasants," she writes, "were accustomed not to put themselves to any inconvenience; and when came the Revolution they were already so well relieved virtually from feudal bonds that they took revenge on nobody." A new *seigneur* of Nohant, coming to take possession, and thinking to levy his utmost dues, in cash and in kind, found his rustic tenants turn a deaf ear to his summons. Ere he could insist the storm burst, but it brought no convulsion, and merely confirmed an independence already existing.

Les Maîtres Sonneurs, whilst illustrating some of the most striking merits of George Sand, is free from the defects often laid to her charge; and although of all her pastorals it must suffer the most when rendered in any language but the original, it is much to be regretted that some good translation of this work should not put it within the reach of all English readers.

CHAPTER X. - PLAYS AND LATER NOVELS.

THERE are few eminent novelists that have not tried their hands at writing for the stage; and Madame Sand had additional inducements to do so, beyond those of ambition satiated with literary success, and tempted by the charm of making fresh conquest of the public in a more direct and personal fashion.

From early childhood she had shown a strong liking for the theatre. The rare performances given by travelling acting-companies at La Châtre had been her greatest delight when a girl. At the convent-school she had arranged Molière from memory for representation by herself and her school-fellows, careful so to modify the piece as to avoid all possibility of shocking the nuns. Thus the Sisters applauded *Le Malade Imaginaire* without any suspicion that the author was one whose works, for them, were placed under a ban, and whose very name they held in devout abhorrence. She inherited from her father a taste for acting, which she transmitted to her children. We have seen her during her literary novitiate in Paris, a studious observer at all theatres, from the classic boards of the Français down to the lowest of popular stages, the Funambules, where reigned at that time a real artist in pantomime, Débureau. His Pierrot, a sort of modified Pulchinello, was renowned; and attracted more fastidious critics to his audience than the Paris artisans whose idol he was. Since then Madame Sand had numbered among her personal friends such leading dramatic celebrities as Madame Dorval, Bocage, and Pauline Garcia. "I like actors," she says playfully, "which has scandalized some austere people. I have also been found fault with for liking the peasantry. Among these I have passed my life, and as I found them, so have I described them. As these, in the light of the sun, give us our daily bread for our bodies, so those by gaslight give us our daily bread of fiction, so needful to the wearied spirit, troubled by realities." Peasants and players seem to be the types of humanity farthest removed from each other, and it is worthy of remark that George Sand was equally successful in her presentation of both.

Her preference for originality and spontaneity before all other qualities in a dramatic artist was characteristic of herself, though not of her nation. Thus it was that Madame Dorval, the heroine of *Antony* and *Marion Delorme*, won her unbounded admiration. Even in Racine she clearly preferred her to Mlle. Mars, as being a less studied actress, and one who abandoned herself more to the inspiration of the moment. The effect produced, as described by Madame Sand, will be understood by all keenly alive, like herself, to the enjoyment of dramatic art. "She" (Madame Dorval) "seemed to me to be myself, more expansive, and to express in action and emotion all that I seek to express in writing." And compared with such an art, in which conception and expression are simultaneous, her own art of words and phrases would at such moments appear to her as but a pale reflection.

Bocage, the great character actor of his time, was another who likewise appealed particularly to her sympathies, as the personation, on the boards, of the protest of the romantic school against the slavery of convention and tradition. Her acquaintance with him dated from the first representation of Hugo's *Lucrèce Borgia*, February, 1833, when Bocage and the author of *Indiana*, then strangers to each other, chanced to sit side by side. In their joint enthusiasm over the play they made the beginning of a thirty years' friendship, terminated only by Bocage's death in 1862. "It was difficult not to quarrel with him," she says of this popular favorite; "he was susceptible and violent; it was impossible not to be reconciled with him quickly. He was faithful and magnanimous. He forgave you admirably for wrongs you had never done him, and it was as good and real as though the pardon had been actual and well-founded, so strong was his imagination, so complete his good faith."

The assistance of Madame Dorval, added to the strength of the Comédie Française company, did not, however, save from failure Madame Sand's first drama, *Cosima*, produced, as will be remembered, in 1840. She allowed nearly a decade to elapse before again seriously competing for theatrical honors, by a second effort in a different style, and more satisfactory in its results.

This, a dramatic adaptation by herself of her novel, *François le Champi*, was produced at the Odéon in the winter of 1849. Generally speaking, to make a good play out of a good novel, the playwright must begin by murdering the novel; and here, as in all George Sand's dramatic versions of her romances, we seem to miss the best part of the original. However, the curious simplicity of the piece, the rustic scenes and personages, here faithfully copied from reality, unlike the conventional village and villager of opera comique, and the pleasing sentiment that runs through the tale, were found refreshing by audiences upon whom the sensational incidents and harrowing emotions of their modern drama were already beginning to pall. The result was a little stage triumph for Madame Sand. It helped to draw to her pastoral tales the attention they deserved, but had not instantly won in all quarters. Théophile Gautier writes playfully of this piece: "The success of *François le Champi* has given all our vaudeville writers an appetite for rusticity. Only let this go on a little, and we shall be inundated by what has humorously been called the 'ruro-drama.' Morvan hats and Berrichon head-dresses will invade the scenes, and no language be spoken but in dialect."

Madame Sand was naturally encouraged to repeat the experiment. This was done in *Claudie* (1851) and *Le Pressoir* (1853), ruro-dramas both, and most favorably received. The first-named has a simple and pathetic story, and, as usual with Madame Sand's plays, it was strengthened at its first production by the support of some of the best acting talent in Paris—Fechter, then a rising *jeune premier*, and the veteran Bocage ably representing, respectively, youth and age.

Old Berrichon airs were introduced with effect, as also such picturesque rustic festival customs as the ancient harvest-home ceremony, in which the last sheaf is brought on a wagon, gaily decked out with poppies, cornflowers and ribbons, and receives a libation of wine poured by the hand of the oldest or youngest person present.

"But what the theatre can never reproduce," laments Madame Sand, "is the majesty of the frame—the mountain of sheaves solemnly approaching, drawn by three pairs of enormous oxen, the whole adorned with flowers, with fruit, and with fine little children perched upon the top of the last sheaves."

Henceforward a good deal of her time and interest continued to be absorbed by these dramatic compositions. But though mostly eliciting during her lifetime a gratifying amount of public favor and applause, the best of them cannot for an instant be placed in the same high rank as her novels. For with all her wide grasp of the value of dramatic art and her exact appreciation of the strength and weakness of the acting world, her plays remain, to great expectations, uniformly disappointing. Her specialty in fiction lies in her favorite art of analyzing and putting before us, with extreme clearness, the subtlest ramifications, the most delicate intricacies of feeling and thought. A stage audience has its eyes and ears too busy to give its full attention to the finer complications of sentiment and motive; or, at least, in order to keep its interest alive and its understanding clear, an accentuation of outline is needed, which she neglects even to seek.

Her assertion, that the niceties of emotion are sufficient to found a good play upon, no one now will dream of disputing. But for this an art of execution is needed of which she had not the instinct. The action is insufficient, or rather, the sense of action is not conveyed. The slightness of plot—a mere thread in most instances—requires that the thread shall at least be never allowed to drop. But she cuts or slackens it perpetually, long arguments and digressions intervening, and the dialogue, whose monotony is unrelieved by wit, nowhere compensates for the limited interest of the action. Awkward treatment is but half felt when subject and situations are dramatically strong; but plays with so airy and impalpable a basis as these need to be sustained by the utmost perfection of construction, concision and polish of dialogue.

Her novel *Mauprat* has many dramatic points, and she received a score of applications for leave to adapt it to the stage. She preferred to prepare the version herself, and it was played in the winter of 1853-4, with moderate success. But it suffers fatally from comparison with its original. An extreme instance is *Flaminio* (1854), a protracted drama, drawn by Madame Sand from her novelette *Teverino*. This is a fantasy-piece whose audacity is redeemed, as are certain other blemishes, by the poetic suggestiveness of the figure of Madeline, the bird-charmer; whilst the picturesque sketch of Teverino, the idealized Italian bohemian, too indolent to turn his high natural gifts to any account, has proved invaluable to the race of novelists, who are not yet tired of reproducing it in large. The work is one addressed mainly to the imagination.

In the play we come down from the clouds; the poetry is gone, taste is shocked, fancy uncharmed, the improbabilities become grotesque, and the whole is distorted and tedious. Madame Sand's personages are never weary of analyzing their sentiments. Her flowing style, so pleasant to read, carries us swiftly and easily through her dissertations in print, before we have time to tire of them. On the stage such colloquies soon appear lengthy and unnatural. The climax of absurdity is reached in *Flaminio*, where we find the adventurer expatiating to the man of the world on "the divinity of his essence."

There is scarcely a department of theatrical literature in which Madame Sand does not appear as an aspirant. She was a worshipper of Shakespeare, acknowledging him as the king of dramatic writers. For her attempt to adapt "As You Like It" to suit the tastes of a Parisian audience, she disarms criticism by a preface in the form of a letter to M. Régnier, of the Comédie Française, prefixed to the printed play. Here she says plainly that to resolve to alter Shakespeare is to resolve to murder, and that she aims at nothing more than at giving the French public some idea of the original. In "As You Like It" the license of fancy taken is too wide for the piece to be safely represented to her countrymen, since it must jar terribly on "that French reason which," remarks Madame Sand, "we are so vain of, and which deprives us of so many originalities quite as precious as itself." The fantastic, which had so much attraction for her (possibly a result of her part German origin), is a growth that has hard work to flourish on French soil. The reader will remember the fate of Weber's *Freischütz*, outrageously hissed when first produced at Paris in its original form. Nine days later it was reproduced, having been taken to pieces and put together again by M. Castil-Blaze, and thus as *Robin des Bois* it ran for 357 nights. The reckless imagination that distinguishes the Shakespearian comedy and does not shrink before the introduction of a lion and a serpent into the forest of Arden, and the miraculous and instantaneous conversion of the wretch Oliver into a worthy suitor for Celia, needed to be toned down for acceptance by the Parisians. But Madame Sand was less fortunate than M. Castil-Blaze. Her version, produced at the Théâtre Français, in 1856, failed to please, although supported by such actors as Delaunay, Arnold-Plessy, and Favart. Macready, who had made Madame Sand's acquaintance in 1845, when he was giving Shakespearian performances in Paris, and whom she greatly admired, dedicating to him her little theatrical romance *Le Château des Désertes*, was present at this representation and records it as a failure. But of her works for the stage, which number over a score, few like her *Comme il vous plaira* missed making some mark at the time, the prestige of her name and the exceptionally favorable circumstances under which they were produced securing more than justice for their intrinsic merit. It was natural that she should over-estimate their value and continue to add to their number. These pieces would be carefully rehearsed on the little stage in the house at Nohant, often with the aid of leading professional actors; and there, at least, the success was unqualified.

Her ingenious novel *Les Beaux Messieurs Bois Doré*, dramatized with the aid of Paul Meurice and acted in 1862, was a triumph for Madame Sand and her friend Bocage. The form and spirit of this novel seem inspired by Sir Walter Scott, and though far from perfect, it is a striking instance of the versatility of her imaginative powers. The leading character of the septuagenarian Marquis, with his many amiable virtues, and his one amiable weakness, a longing to preserve intact his youthfulness of appearance as he has really preserved his youthfulness of heart, is both natural and original, comic and half pathetic withal. The part in the play seemed made for Bocage, and his heart was set upon undertaking it. But his health was failing at the time, and the manager hesitated about giving him the rôle. "Take care, my friend," wrote Bocage to Madame Sand; "perhaps I shall die if I play the part; but if I play it not, I shall die of that, to a certainty." She insisted, and play it he did, to perfection, she tells us. "He did not act the Marquis de Bois Doré; he was the personage himself, as the author had dreamt him." It was to be his last achievement, and he knew it. "It is my end," he said one night, "but I shall die like a soldier on the field of honor." And so he did, continuing to play the rôle up till a few days before his death.

More lasting success has attended Madame Sand in two of the lightest of society comedies, *Le Mariage de Victorine* and *Le Marquis de Villemer*, which seem likely to take a permanent place in the *répertoire* of the French stage. The first, a continuation that had suggested itself to her of Sedaine's century-old comedy, *Le Philosophe sans le savoir*, escapes the ill fate that seems to attend sequels in general. It is of the slightest materials, but holds together, and is gracefully conceived and executed. First produced at the Gymnase in 1851, it was revived during the last year of Madame Sand's life in a manner very gratifying to her, being brought out with great applause at the Comédie Française, preceded on each occasion by Sedaine's play, and the same artists appearing in both.

The excellent dramatic version of her popular novel *Le Marquis de Villemer*, first acted in 1864, is free from the defects that weaken most of her stage compositions. It is said that in preparing it she accepted some hints from Alexander Dumas the younger. Whatever the cause, the result is a play where characters, composition and dialogue leave little to be desired.

L'autre, her latest notable stage success, brings us down to 1870, when it was acted at the Gymnase, Madame Sarah Bernhardt impersonating the heroine. This not very agreeable play is derived, with material alterations, from Madame Sand's agreeable novel *La Confession d'une jeune Fille*, published in 1864.

If, however, her works for the stage, which fill four volumes, added but little, in proportion to their quantity, to her permanent fame, her dramatic studies added fresh interest and variety to her experience, which brought forth excellent fruit in her novels. Actors, their art and way of life have fared notoriously badly in fiction. Such pictures have almost invariably fallen into the extreme of unreality or that of caricature, whether for want of information or want of sympathy in those who have drawn them.

The subject, always attractive for Madame Sand, is one in which she is always happy. Already in the first year of her literary career her keen appreciation of the art and its higher influences had prompted her clever novelette *La Marquise*. Here she illustrates the power of the stage as a means of expression—of the truly inspired actor, though his greatness be but momentary, and his heroism a semblance, to strike a like chord in the heart of the spectator—and, in a corrupt and artificial age, to keep alive some latent faith in the ideal. Since then the stage and players had figured repeatedly in her works. Sometimes she portrays a perfected type, such as Consuelo, or Impéria in *Pierre qui roule*, but always side by side with more earthly and faulty representatives such as Corilla and Anzoleto, or Julia and Albany, in Narcisse, incarnations of the vanity and instability that are the chief dangers of the profession, drawn with unsparing realism. In *Le Château des Désertes* we find further many admirable theories and suggestive ideas on the subject of the regeneration of the theatre. But it fared with her theatrical as with her political philosophy: she failed in its application, not because her theories were false, but for want of practical aptitude for the craft whose principles she understood so well.

It is impossible here to do more than cast a rapid glance over the literary work accomplished by George Sand during the first decade of the empire. It includes more than a dozen novels, of unequal merit, but of merit for the most part very high. The *Histoire de ma Vie* was published in 1855. It is a study of chosen passages out of her life, rather than a connected autobiography. One out of the four volumes is devoted to the story of her father's life before her birth; two more to the story of her childhood and girlhood. The fourth rather indicates than fully narrates the facts of her existence from the time of her marriage till the Revolution of 1848. It offers to her admirers invaluable glimpses into her life and mind, and is a highly interesting and characteristic composition, if a most irregular chronicle. It has given rise to two most incompatible-sounding criticisms. Some have been chiefly struck by its amazing unreserve, and denounced the over-frankness of the author in revealing herself to the public. Others complain that she keeps on a mask throughout, and never allows us to see into the recesses of her mind. Her passion for the analysis of sentiment has doubtless led her here, as in her romances, to give very free expression to truths usually better left unspoken. But her silence on many points about which her readers, whether from mere curiosity or some more honorable motive, would gladly have been informed, was then inevitable. It could not have been broken without wounding the susceptibilities of living persons, which she did right in respecting, at the cost of disappointment to an inquisitive public.

In January, 1855, a terrible domestic sorrow befell her in the loss of her six-years-old grandchild, Jeanne Clésinger, to whom she was devoted. It affected her profoundly. "Is there a more mortal grief," she exclaims, "than to outlive, yourself, those who should have bloomed upon your grave?" The blow told upon her mentally and physically; she could not rally from its effects, till persuaded to seek a restorative in change of air and scene, which happily did their work.

"I was ill," she says, when writing of these events to a lady correspondent, later in the same year; "my son took me away to Italy.... I have seen Rome, revisited Florence, Genoa, Frascati, Spezia, Marseilles. I have walked a great deal, been out in the sun, the rain, the wind, for whole days out of doors. This, for me, is a certain remedy, and I have come back cured."

Those who care to follow the mind of George Sand on this Italian journey may safely infer from *La Daniella,* a novel written after this tour, and the scene of which is laid in Rome and the Campagna, that the author's strongest impression of the Eternal City was one of disillusion. Her hero, a Berrichon artist on his travels, confesses to a feeling of uneasiness and regret rather than of surprise and admiration. The ancient ruins, stupendous in themselves, seemed to her spoilt for effect by their situation in the center of a modern town. "Of the Rome of the past not enough exists to overwhelm me with its majesty; of the Rome of the present not enough to make me forget the first, and much too much to allow me to see her."

But the Baths of Caracalla, where the picture is not set in a frame of hideous houses, awakened her native enthusiasm. "A grandiose ruin," she exclaims, "of colossal proportions; it is shut away, isolated, silent and respected. There you feel the terrific power of the Cæsars, and the opulence of a nation intoxicated with its royalty over the world."

So in the Appian Way, the road of tombs, the fascination of desolation—a desolation there unbroken and undisfigured by modern buildings or otherwise—she felt to the full. But whatever came under her notice she looked on with the eye of the poet and artist, not of the archæologist, and approved or disapproved or passed over it accordingly.

The beauties of nature, at Tivoli and Frascati, appealed much more surely to her sympathies. But of certain sites in the Campagna much vaunted by tourists and hand-books she remarks pertinently: "If you were to pass this village" (Marino) "on the railway within a hundred miles of Paris, you would not pay it the slightest attention." Such places had their individuality, but she upheld that there is not a corner in the universe, "however common-place it may appear, but has a character of its own, unique in this world, for any one who is disposed to feel or comprehend it." In one of her village tales a sagacious peasant professes his profound contempt for the man who cannot like the place he belongs to.

Neither the grottoes and cascades of Tivoli, the cypress and ilex gardens of Frascati and Albano, nor the ruins of Tusculum, were ever so pleasant to her eyes as the poplar-fringed banks of the Indre, the corn-land sand hedgerows of Berry, and the rocky borders of the Creuse at Crozant and Argenton. She had not ceased making fresh picturesque discoveries in her own neighborhood. Of these she records an instance in her pleasant *Promenades autour d'un village*, a lively sketch of a few days' walking-tour on the banks of the Creuse, undertaken by herself and some naturalist friends in June, 1857. In studying the interesting and secluded village of Gargilesse, with its tenth-century church and crypt with ancient frescoes, its simple and independent-minded population, in following the course of a river whose natural wild beauties, equal to those of the Wye, are as yet undisfigured here by railroad or the hand of man, lingering on its banks full of summer flowers and butterflies, exploring the castles of Châteaubrun and La Prugne au

Pot, George Sand is happier, more herself, more communicative than in Rome, "the museum of the universe."

The years 1858 to 1861 show her to us in the fullest conservation of her powers and in the heyday of activity. The group of novels belonging to this period, the climax of what may be called her second career, is sufficiently remarkable for a novelist who was almost a sexagenarian, including *Elle et Lui, L'Homme de Neige, La Ville Noire, Constance Verrier, Le Marquis de Villemer* and *Valvèdre. Elle et Lui*, in which George Sand at last broke silence in her own defense on the subject of her rupture with Alfred de Musset, first appeared in the *Revue des Deux Mondes*, 1859. Though many of the details are fictitious, the author here told the history of her relations with the deceased poet much too powerfully for her intention to be mistaken or to escape severe blame. That a magnanimous silence would have been the nobler course on her part towards the child of genius whose good genius she had so signally failed to be, need not be disputed. It must be remembered, however, that De Musset on his side had not refrained during his lifetime from denouncing in eloquent verse the friend he had quarreled with, and satirizing her in pungent prose. Making every possible allowance for poetical figures of speech, he had said enough to provoke her to retaliate. It is impossible to suppose that there was not another side to such a question. But Madame Sand could not defend herself without accusing her lost lover. She often proved herself a generous adversary—too generous, indeed, for her own advantage—and in this instance it was clearly not for her own sake that she deferred her apology.

It is even conceivable that the poet, when in a just frame of mind, and not seeking inspiration for his *Nuit de Mai* or *Histoire d'un Merle blanc*, would not have seen in *Elle et Lui* a falsification of the spirit of their history. The theorizing of the outside world in such matters is of little worth; but the novel bears, conspicuously among Madame Sand's productions, the stamp of a study from real life, true in its leading features. And the conduct of the heroine, Therèse, though accounted for and eloquently defended, is by no means, as related, ideally blameless. After an attachment so strong as to induce a seriously-minded person, such as she is represented, to throw aside for it all other considerations, the hastiness with which, on discovering her mistake, she entertains the idea of bestowing her hand, if not her heart, on another, is an exhibition of feminine inconsequence which no amount of previous misconduct on the part of her lover, Laurent, can justify. Further, Therèse is self-deceived in supposing her passion to have died out with her esteem. She breaks with the culprit and engages her word to a worthier man. But enough remains over of the past to prevent her from keeping the promise she ought never to have made. When she sacrifices her unselfish friend to return to the lover who has made her miserable, she is sincere, but not heroic. She is too weak to shake off the influence of the fatal infatuation and shut out Laurent from her life, nor yet can she accept her heart's choice for better or worse, even when experience has left her little to learn with regard to Laurent. Clearly both friend and lover, out of a novel, would feel wronged. Therèse's excuse lies in the extremely trying character of her companion, whose vagaries may be supposed to have driven her beside herself at times, just as her airs of superiority and mute reproach may have driven him not a little mad. Those who wish to know in what spirit Madame Sand met the attacks upon her provoked by this book, will find her reply in a very few words at the conclusion of her preface to *Jean de la Roche*, published the same year.

Most readers of *Elle et Lui* have been so preoccupied with the question of the rights and wrongs of the originals in their behavior to each other, so inclined to judge of the book according to its supposed accuracy or inaccuracy as a matter of history, that its force, as a study of the attraction that so often leads two exceptional but hopeless, irreconcilable spirits to seek in each other a refuge from the isolation in which their superiority places them, has been somewhat overlooked. Laurent, whether a true portrait or not, is only too true to nature; excessive in his admirable powers and in his despicable weakness. Therèse is an equally faithful picture of a woman not quite up to the level of her own principles, which are so high that any lapse from them on her part brings down more disasters on herself and on others than the misdemeanors of avowedly unscrupulous persons.

Within a few months of *Elle et Lui* had appeared *L'Homme de Neige*,[1] a work of totally different but equally characteristic cast. The author's imagination had still all its old zest and activity, and readers for whom fancy has any charm will find this Scandinavian romance thoroughly enjoyable. The subject of the marionette theater, here introduced with such brilliant and ingenious effect, she had studied both historically and practically. She and her son found it so fascinating that, years before this time, a miniature stage had been constructed by the latter at Nohant, over which he presided, and which they and their friends found an endless source of amusement. Madame Sand wrote little dramas expressly for such representations, and would sit up all night, making dresses for the puppets. In an agreeable little article she has devoted to the subject, she describes how from the crudest beginnings they succeeded in elaborating their art to a high pitch; the *répertoire* of their lilliputian theater including more than twenty plays, their "company" over a hundred marionettes.

To the next year, 1860, belong the pleasant tale of artisan life, *La Ville Noire*, and the well-known and popular *Marquis de Villemer*, notable as a decided success in a *genre* seldom adopted by her, that of the purely society novel.

Already Madame Sand had outlived the period of which she was so brilliant a representative. After the Romantic movement had spent its force, a reaction had set in that was influencing the younger school of writers, and that has continued to give the direction to successful talent until the present day. Of the so-called "realism," Madame Sand said that it was nothing new. She saw there merely another form of the same revolt of nature against affectation and convention which had prompted the Romantic movement, whose disciples had now become guilty of affectation in their turn. *Madame Bovary* she pronounced with truth to be but concentrated Balzac. She was ready to perceive and do justice to the great ability

---

[1] The "Snow Man," translated by Virginia Vaughan. Boston: Roberts Brothers.

of the author, as to original genius in any school; thus of Tourguénief she speaks with enthusiasm: "Realist to see all, poet to beautify all, great heart to pity and understand all." But she deplored the increasing tendency among artists to give the preference among realities to the ugliest and the most painful. Her personal leanings avowedly were towards the other extreme; but she was too large-minded not to recognize that truth in one form or another must always be the prime object of the artist's search. The manner of its presentation will vary with the age.

> Let the realists, if they like, go on proclaiming that all is prose, and the idealists that all is poesy. The last will have their rainy days, the first their days of sunshine. In all arts the victory remains with a privileged few, who go their own ways; and the discussions of the "schools" will pass away like old fashions.

On the generation of writers that George Sand saw growing up, any opinion pronounced must be premature. But with regard to herself, it should now be possible to regard her work in a true perspective. As with Byron, Dickens, and other popular celebrities, a phase of infinite enthusiasm for her writings was duly succeeded by a phase of determined depreciation. The public opinion that survives when blind friendship and blind enmity have done their worst is likely to be the judgment of posterity.

CHAPTER XI. - ARTIST AND MORALIST.

ON what, in the future, will the fame of George Sand mainly rest? According to some critics, on her gifts of fertile invention and fluent narration alone, which make her novels attractive in spite of the chimerical theories, social, political and religious, everywhere interwoven. According to other judges again, her fictions transcend and are likely to outlive other fictions by virtue of certain eternal philosophic verities which they persistently set forth, and which give them a serious interest the changes in novel-fashions cannot effect.

The conclusion seems inevitable that whilst the artistic strength of George Sand's writings is sufficient to command readers among those most out of harmony with her views, to minds in sympathy with her own these romances, because they express and enforce with earnestness, sincerity and fire, the sentiments of a poetic soul, a generous heart, and an immense intelligence, on subjects of consequence to humanity, have a higher value than can attach to skillful development of plot and intrigue, mere display of literary cleverness, or of the storings of minute observation.

Her opinions themselves have been widely misapprehended, perhaps because her personality—or rather that imaginary personage, the George Sand of the myths—has caused a confusion in people's minds between her ideal standard and her individual success in keeping up to it. We would not ignore the importance of personal example in one so famous as herself. We may pass by eccentricities not inviting to imitation; for if any of her sex ever thought to raise themselves any nearer to the level of George Sand by smoking or wearing men's clothes, such puerility does not call for notice. Still, the influence she strenuously exerted for good as a writer for the public would have worked more clearly had she never seemed to swerve from the high principles she expressed, or been led away by the disturbing forces of a nature calm only on the surface. Nothing is more baffling than the incomplete revelations of a very complex order of mind, with its many-sided sympathies and its apparent contradictions. The self-justification she puts forward for her errors is sometimes sophistical, but not for that insincere. She is not trying to make us her dupes; she is the dupe herself of her dangerous eloquence. But her moral worth so infinitely outweighed the alloy as to leave but little call, or even warrant, for dwelling on the latter. "If I come back to you," said her old literary patron Delatouche, into whose disfavor she had fallen awhile, when he came years after to ask for the restitution of the friendship he had slighted, "it is that I cannot help myself, and your qualities surpass your defects."

To pass from herself to her books, no one has made more frank, clear and unchanging confession of their heart's faith or their head's principles. Her creed was that which has been, and ever will be in some guise, the creed of minds of a certain order. She did not invent it. Poets, moralists, theologians, have proclaimed it before her and after her. She found for it a fresh mode of expression, one answering to the needs of the age to which she belonged.

It is in the union of rare artistic genius with an almost as rare and remarkable power of enthusiasm for moral and spiritual truth that lies her distinguishing strength. Most of her novels—all her best novels—share this characteristic of seeming to be prompted by the double and equal inspiration of an artistic and a moral purpose. Wherever one of these preponderates greatly, or is wanting altogether, the novel falls below her usual standard.

For in several qualities reckoned important her work is open to criticism. "Plan, or the want of it," she acknowledges, with a sort of complacency, "has always been my weak point." Thus whilst in many of her compositions, especially the shorter novels, the construction leaves little to be desired, *Consuelo* is only one among many instances in which all ordinary rules of symmetry and proportion are set at naught. Sometimes the leading idea assumed naturally and easily a perfect form; if simple, as in *André* and her pastorals, it usually did so; but if complex, she troubled herself little over the task of symmetrical arrangement. M. Maxime Du Camp reports that she said to him: "When I begin a novel I have no plan; it arranges itself whilst I write, and becomes what it may." This fault shocks less in England, where genius is apt to rebel against the restrictions of form, and such irregularity has been consecrated, so to speak, by the masterpieces of the greatest among our imaginative writers. And even the more precise criticism of her countrymen has owned that this carelessness works by no means entirely to her disadvantage. In fictions more faultless as literary compositions the reader, whilst struck with admiration for the art with which the whole is put together, is apt to lose something of the illusion—the impression of nature and conviction. The faults of no writer can be more truly defined as the *défauts de ses qualités* than those of George Sand. Shorn of her spontaneity, she would indeed be shorn of her strength. We are carried along by the pleasant, easy stream of her musical eloquence, as by an orator who knows so well how to draw our attention that we forget to find him too long. Her stories may be read rapidly, but to be enjoyed should be read through. Dipped into and their parts taken without reference to the whole, they can afford comparatively but little pleasure.

In translation no novelist loses more than George Sand,—who has so much to lose! The qualities sacrificed, though almost intangible, are essential to the force of her charm. The cement is taken away and the fabric coheres imperfectly; and whilst the beauties of her manner are blurred, its blemishes appear increased; the lengthiness, over-emphasis of expression, questionable taste of certain passages, become more marked. Although nevertheless many of her tales remain pleasant reading, they suffer as much as translated poetry, and only a very inadequate impression of her art as a novelist can be arrived at from any rendering of it in a foreign tongue.

Her dialogue has neither brilliancy nor variety. Her characters characterize themselves by the sentiments they express; their manner of expression is somewhat uniform—it is the manner of George Sand; and although pleasant humor and good-natured fun abound in her pages, these owe none of their attractions to witty sayings, being curiously bare of a *bon mot* or an epigram.

But we find there the rarer merits of a poetic imagination, a vast comprehension of nature, admirable insight into human character and power of clear analysis; a whole science of sentiment and art of narrative, and a charm of narrative style that soothes the nerves like music.

She has given us a long gallery of portraits of extraordinary variety. It is true that her creations for the most part affect us rather as masterly portraits than as living, walking men and women. This is probably owing to the above-noted sameness of style of dialogue, and the absence generally of the dramatic quality in her novels. On the other hand they are extremely picturesque, in the highest sense, abounding in scenes and figures which, without inviting to the direct illustration they are too vivid to need, are full of suggestions to the artist. The description in *Teverino* of Madeleine, the bird-charmer, kneeling at prayer in the rude mountain chapel, or outside on the rocks, exercising her natural magic over her feathered friends; in *Jeanne*, of the shepherd-girl discovered asleep on the Druidical stones; the noon-day rest of the rustic fishing-party in *Valentine*—Benedict seated on the felled ash-tree that bridges the stream, Athenaïs gathering field-flowers on the banks, Louise flinging leaves into the current, Valentine reclining dreamily among the tall river-reeds,—are a few examples taken at random, which it would be easy to multiply *ad infinitum*.

Any classification of her works in order of time that professes to show a progressive change of style, a period of super-excellence or of distinct decadence, seems to us somewhat fanciful. From *Indiana* and its immediate successors, denounced by so many as fraught with peril to the morals of her nation, down to *Nanon* (1872), which might certainly carry off the prize of virtue in a competition in any country, George Sand can never be said to have entirely abandoned one "manner" for another, or for any length of time to have risen above or sunk below a certain level of excellence. *André*, extolled by her latest critics as "a delicious eclogue of the fields," was contemporary with the bombastic, false Byronism of *Jacques*; the feeble narrative of *La Mare au Diable* with the passion-introspection of *Lucrezia Floriani*. The ever-popular *Consuelo* immediately succeeded the feeble *Compagnon du Tour de France*. *La Marquise*, written in the first year of her literary life, shows a power of projection out of herself, and of delicate analysis, hardly to be surpassed; but *Francia*, of forty years' later date, is an equally perfect study. From the time of *Indiana* onwards she continued to produce at the rate of about two novels a year; and at intervals, rare intervals, the product was a failure. But we shall find her when approaching seventy still writing on, without a trace of the weakness of old age.

The charge of "unreality" so commonly brought against her novels it may be well briefly to examine. Such little fantasy-pieces in Hoffmann's manner as *Le Château des Désertes*, *Teverino*, and others, making no pretense to be exact studies of nature, cannot fairly be censured on this head. Like fairy tales they have a place of their own in art. One of the prettiest of these is *Les Dames Vertes*, in which the fable seems to lead us over the borders of the supernatural; but the secret of the mystification, well kept till the last, is itself so pleasing and original that the reader has no disappointing sense as of having had a hoax played upon his imagination.

In character drawing no one can, on occasion, be a more uncompromising realist than George Sand. André, Horace, Laurent in *Elle et Lui*, Pauline, Corilla, Alida in *Valvèdre*, might be cited as examples. But her theory was unquestionably not the theory which guides the modern school of novel writers. She wrote, she states explicitly, for those "who desire to find in a novel a sort of ideal life." She made this her aim, but without depreciation of the widely different aims of other authors. "You paint mankind as they are," she said to Balzac; "I, as they ought to be, or might become. You write the comedy of humanity. I should like to write the eclogue, the poem, the romance of humanity." She has been taxed with flattering nature and human nature because her love of beauty—defined by her as the highest expression of truth—dictated her choice of subjects. An artist who paints roses paints from reality as entirely as he who paints mud. Her principle was to choose among realities those which seemed best worth painting.

The amount of idealization in her peasant sketches was naturally overestimated by those who, never having studied the class, could not conceive of a peasant except conventionally, as a drunken boor. The very just portrait of Cecilia Boccaferri, the conscientious but obscure artist in *Le Château des Désertes*, might seem over-flattered to such as imagine that all opera-singers must be persons of riotous living. The types she prefers to present, if exceptional, are not impossible or non-existent. An absolutely faultless heroine, such as Consuelo, she seldom attempts to bring before us; an ideal hero; never.

Further, even when the idealism is greatest the essence is true. Her most fanciful conceptions, most improbable combinations, seem more natural than do everyday scenes and characters treated by inferior artists. This is only partly due to the inimitable little touches of nature that renew the impression of reality at every page. Her imagination modified her material, but only in order the more vividly to illustrate truths positive and everlasting. So did Shakespeare when he drew Prospero and Miranda, Caliban and Ariel. Art, as regarded by George Sand, is a search for ideal truth rather than a study of positive reality. This principle determined the spirit of her romances. She was the highest in her *genre*; let the world decide which *genre* is the highest.

When, after the publication of *Indiana*, *Valentine*, *Lélia* and *Jacques*, the moral tendency of her works was so sharply attacked, it was contended on her behalf by some friendly critics that art and social morality have no necessary connection—a line of defense she would have been the last to take up for herself. In the present day her judges complain rather of her incessant moralizing, and on the whole with more reason. She indignantly denied that her novels had the evil tendencies imputed to them. Certainly the supposition of the antagonistic spirit of her writings to Christianity and marriage vanishes in proportion to the reader's acquaintance with her works. But against certain doctrines and practices of the Roman Catholic Church which she believed to be pernicious in their influence, she from the first declared war, and by her frank audacity made bitter enemies. M. Renan relates that when he was a boy of fifteen his ecclesiastical superiors showed him George Sand, emblematically portrayed for the admonition of the youth under their care, as a woman in black trampling on a cross! Now, it is not merely that her own faith was eminently Christian in character, and that the Christian ideal seemed to her the most perfect that has yet presented itself to the mind of man; but if unable to accept for herself the doctrine of revelation as commonly interpreted, she is utterly without the aggressiveness of spirit, the petty flippancy, that often betray the intellectual bigot under the banner of free thought. She was too large-minded to incline to ridicule the serious convictions of earnest seekers for truth, and she respected all sincerity of belief—all faith that produced beneficence in action.

The alleged hostility of her romances to marriage resumes itself into a declared hostility to the conventional French system of match-making. Much that she was condemned for venturing to put forward we should simply take for granted in England, where—whichever system work the best in practice—to the strictest Philistine's ideas of propriety there is nothing unbecoming in a love-match. The aim and end of true love in her stories is always marriage, whether it be the simple attachment of Germain, the field-laborer, for the rustic maiden of his choice, the romantic predilection of the rich young widow in *Pierre qui roule* for the handsome actor Laurence, or the worship of Count Albert for the *cantatrice* Consuelo. Her ideal of marriage was, no doubt, a high one, "the indissoluble attachment of two hearts fired with a like love;" a love "great, noble, beautiful, voluntary, eternal." Among French novelists she should rather be noted for the extremely small proportion of her numerous romances that have domestic infelicity for a theme.

Her remark that their real offense was that they were a great deal too moral for some of their critics, hit home, inasmuch as in her attack on the ordinary marriage system of France she struck directly at the fashionable immorality which is its direct result, and which she saw, both in life and in literature, pass free of censure. It is the selfish intriguer who meets with least mercy in her pages, and who is there held up, not only to dislike, but to ridicule.

Persons perplexed by the fact that particular novels of hers which, judged by certain theories, ought to be morally hurtful, do yet produce a very different effect, have accounted for it in different ways. One explains it by saying that if there is poison on one page there is always the antidote on the next. Another observes that a certain morality of misfortune is never absent from her fictions. In other words, she nowhere presents us with the spectacle of real happiness reaped at the expense of a violation of conscience. And in the rare cases where the purpose of the novel seems questionable, she defeats her own end. For truth always preponderates over error in her conceptions, and the result is a moral effect.

The want of delicacy that not unfrequently disfigures her pages and offends us, offends also as an artistic fault. As a fact it is taste rather than conscience that she is thus apt to shock. For the almost passing coarseness of expression or thought is nothing more than the overflow, the negligent frankness of a rich and active but healthy nature, not the deliberate obliquity of a corrupt fancy or perverted mind. Such unreserve, unfortunately, has too commonly been the transgression of writers of superabundant energy. But her sins are against outward decorum rather than against the principles upon which the rules of decorum are based. No one was better capable of appreciating and indicating with fine touches, delicacy and niceties of taste and feeling in others. Her sympathy with such sensitiveness is a corrective that should render harmless what might vitiate taste if that qualification were absent. And her stories, though including a very few instances where the subject chosen seems to most English minds too repulsive to admit of possible redemption, and the frequent incidental introduction of situations and frank discussion of topics inadmissible in English fiction of that period—an honorable distinction it seems in some danger of losing in the present—can hardly be censured from the French standpoint, as fair critics now admit. It is inconceivable that a public could be demoralized by *Indiana* and *Valentine*, at a time when no subject seemed wicked and morbid enough to satisfy popular taste. The art of George Sand in the main was sound and healthy, and in flat opposition to the excesses both of the ultra-romantic and ultra-realist schools.

Clear-sighted critics, perceiving that the impression produced by her works is not one to induce men and women to defy the laws of their country, nor likely to undermine their religious faith, have gone more to the heart of the matter. The dangerous tendency is more insidious, they say, and more general. Virtue, and not vice, is made attractive in her books; but it is an easy virtue, attained without self-conquest. All her characters, good and bad, act alike from impulse. Those who seek virtue seek pleasure in so doing, and her philosophy of life seems to be that people should do as they like. The morality she commends to our sympathy and admiration is a morality of instinct and emotion, not of reason and principle. Self-renunciation, immolation of desire in obedience to accepted precept, is ignored. Sentiment is supreme. Duty, as a motive power, is set aside.

George Sand, who as a writer from first to last appeared as a crusader against the evil, injustice and vice that darken the world, did undoubtedly choose rather to speak out of her heart to our hearts, than out of her head to our heads, and considered moreover that such was the more effectual way. Her idea of virtue lay not in the curbing of evil instincts, but in their conversion or modification by the evoking of good impulses, that "guiding and intensifying of our emotions by a new ideal" which has been called the great work of Christianity.

It is not—or not in the first place—that people should do as they like, but that they should like to do right; and further, that human nature in that ideal life the sentiment of which pervades her works, and in which she saw "no other than the normal life as we are called to know it," does not desire what is hurtful to it.

The goodness that consists in doing right or refraining from doing wrong reluctantly, or in obedience to prescribed rules, or from mechanical habit, had for her no life or charm. The object to be striven for should be nothing less than the "perfect harmony of inward desire and outward obligation."

Virtue should be chosen, though we seem to sacrifice happiness; but that the two are in the beginning identical, that, as expressed by Mr. Herbert Spencer, "whether perfection of nature, virtuousness of action, or rectitude of motive, be assigned as the proper aim, the definition of perfection, virtue, rectitude, brings us down to happiness experienced in some form, at some time, by some person as the fundamental idea," is a philosophic truth of which a large *aperçu* is observable in the works of George Sand. Self-sacrifice should spring from direct desire, altruism be spontaneous—a need—becoming a second and better nature; not won by painful effort, but through the larger development of the principle of sympathy. Strong in her own immense power of sympathy, she applied herself to the task of awakening and extending such sympathies in others. This she does by the creation of agreeable, interesting and noble types, such as may put us out of conceit with what is mean and base. Goodness, as understood and portrayed by her, must recommend itself not only to the judgment but to the heart. She worked to popularize high sentiments, and to give shape and reality to vague ideas of human excellence. Her idea of virtue as a motive, not a restraint, not the controlling of low and evil desires, but the precluding of all temptations to yield to these, by the calling out of stronger, higher desires, so far from being a low one, is indeed the very noblest; yet not on that account a chimera to those who hold, like her, to the conviction that "what now characterizes the exceptionally high may be expected eventually to characterize all. For that which the highest human nature is capable of is within the reach of human nature at large." "We gravitate towards the ideal," she writes, "and this gravitation is infinite, as is the ideal itself." And her place remains among those few great intelligences who can be said to have given humanity an appreciable impulse in the direction of progress.

CHAPTER XII. - LATER YEARS.

WHEN, in 1869, Madame Sand was applied to by M. Louis Ulbach—a literary friend who proposed to write her biography—for some account of her life from that time onwards where her memoirs break off, she replied, in a letter now appended to those memoirs, as follows:—

> For the last five-and-twenty years there is nothing more that is of interest. It is old age, very quiet and very happy, *en famille*, crossed by sorrows entirely personal in their nature—deaths, defections, and then the general state of affairs in which we have suffered, you and I, from the same causes. My time is spent in amusing the children, doing a little botany, long walks in summer—I am still a first-rate pedestrian—and writing novels, when I can secure two hours in the daytime and two in the evening. I write easily and with pleasure. This is my recreation, for my correspondence is numerous, and there lies work indeed! If one had none but one's friends to write to! But how many requests, some touching, some impertinent! Whenever there is anything I can do, I reply. Those for whom I can do nothing I do not answer. Some deserve that one should try, even with small hope of succeeding. Then one must answer that one will try. All this, with private affairs to which one must really give attention now and then, makes some ten letters a day.

The old age of George Sand, brighter, fuller and more active than the youth of most men and women, was in itself a most signal proof of the stability and worth of her mental organization. Life, which deteriorates a frail character, told with a perfecting and elevating power upon hers.

Of her earlier personal beauty few traces remained after middle age except a depth of expression in her eyes, the features having become thickened by age. Some among those who, like Dickens, first saw her in her later years and still looked for the semblance of a heroine of romance, failed to find the muse Lélia of their imaginations under the guise of a middle-aged *bourgeoise*. But such impressions were superficial. Her portrait in black and white by Couture, engraved by Manceau, seems to reconcile these apparent discrepancies. Beauty is not here, but the face is so powerful and comprehensive that we perceive there at once the mirror of a mind capable of embracing both the prose and the poetry of life; and by many this portrait is preferred to the earlier likenesses.

Nor is there anything more remarkable in her correspondence than the extremely interesting series of letters, extending from February, 1863, to within three months of her death in 1876, and addressed to Gustave Flaubert, at this period her familiar friend. The intercourse of two minds of so different an intellectual and moral order as those of the authors of *Consuelo* and of *Madame Bovary* offers to all a curious study. To the admirers of George Sand these letters are invaluable, both from a literary point of view and as a record of her inner life from that time onwards, when, as expressed by herself, she resolutely buried youth, and owned herself the gainer by an increasing calm within. The secret of her future happiness she found in living for her children and her friends. That she retained her zest for intellectual pleasures she ascribed to the very fact that she never allowed herself to be absorbed for long in these and in herself.

"Artists are spoilt children," she writes to Flaubert, "and the best of them are great egoists. You tell me I love them too well; I love them as I love woods and fields, all things, all beings that I know a little and make my constant study. In the midst of it all I pursue my calling; and how I love that calling of mine, and all that nourishes and renovates it!"

We must now take up the thread of outward events again, which we have slightly anticipated.

In the autumn of 1860 Madame Sand had a severe attack of typhoid fever. She was then on the point of beginning her little tale, *La Famille de Germandre*; "*le roman de ma fièvre*," she playfully terms it afterwards, when retracing the circumstances in a letter to her old friend François Rollinat:—

> The day before that upon which I was suddenly taken very seriously ill, I had felt quite well. I had scribbled the beginning of a novel; I had placed all my personages; I knew them thoroughly; I knew their situations in the world, their characters, tendencies, ideas, relations to each other. I saw their faces. All that remained to be known was what they were going to do, and I did not trouble my head about that, having time to think it over to-morrow.

Struck down on the morrow, she was for many days in a precarious condition; and in the confused fancies of fever found herself wandering with *La Famille de Germandre* about the country, alighting in ruined castles, and encountering the most whimsical adventures in flood and field.

It would have been an easy death, she remarked afterwards, had she died then, as she might, in her dream; but she came to herself to find her son and friends in such anxiety on her account, so overjoyed at her convalescence, that she could not but be glad of the life that was given back to her. Early in 1861 we find her recruiting her forces by a stay at Tamaris, near Toulon, completing the novel interrupted by illness; resuming her long walks and botanic studies, and thoroughly enjoying the sense of returning vital powers.

She stood always in great dread of the idea of possibly losing her activity as she advanced in years. The infirmities of old age, however, she was happily to be spared, preserving her energy and mental faculties, as will be seen, till just before her death. But though she was restored to health and strength, this illness seems to have left its traces on her constitution.

Her son's marriage to Mdlle. Calamatta, spoken of by Madame Sand as a heart's desire of hers at length fulfilled, took place in 1862, not many months after his return from half a year of travel in Africa and America, in the company of Prince Napoleon. The event proved a fresh source of the purest happiness to her, and was not to separate her from her son. The young people settled at Nohant, which remained her head-quarters. There a few years later we find her residing almost exclusively, except when called by matters of business to her *pied-à-terre* in Paris, where she never lingered long. To the two little grand-daughters, Aurore and Gabrielle, whom she saw spring up in her home, she became passionately devoted. Most of her compositions henceforward are dated from Nohant, where, indeed, more than fifty years of her life were spent.

As regards decorum of expression and temperance of sentiments, the later novels of George Sand have earned more praise than censure; but some readers may feel that in fundamental questions of taste the comparison between them and their forerunners is not always entirely to their advantage. The fervor of youth has a certain purifying power to redeem from offense matter, even though over-frankly treated, which becomes disagreeable in cold analysis, however sober the wording, and clear and admirable the moral pointed.

Mademoiselle La Quintinie, which appeared in 1863, was suggested by M. Octave Feuillet's *Sibille*. The point of M. Feuillet's novel is, that Sibille, an ardent Catholic, stifles her love, and renounces her lover on account of his heterodox opinions. Madame Sand gives us the reverse—a heroine who is reflectively rather than mystically inclined, and whose lover by degrees succeeds in effecting her conversion to his more liberal views. Here, as elsewhere, the author's mind shows a sympathetic comprehension of the standpoint of enlightened Protestantism curiously rare among those who, like herself, have renounced Romanism for the pursuit of free thought and speculation. But even those who prefer the *dénoûment* of George Sand's novel to that of M. Feuillet's will not rank *Mademoiselle La Quintinie* very high among the author's productions. It is colorless, and artistically weak, however controversially strong.

Madame Sand, according to her own reckoning in 1869, had made at least £40,000 by her writings. Out of this she had saved no fortune. She had always preferred to live from day to day on the proceeds of her work, regulating her expenses accordingly, trusting her brain to answer to any emergency and bring her out of the periodical financial crises in which the uncertainty of literary gains and the liberality of her expenditure involved her. She continued fond of travelling, especially of exploring the nooks and corners of France, felt by her to be less well known than they deserve, and fully as picturesque as the spots tourists go far to visit. Here she sought fresh frames for her novels. "If I have only three words to say about a place," she tells us, "I like to be able to refer to it in my memory so as to make as few mistakes as possible."

CHAPTER XII. - LATER YEARS.

In January, 1869, we find her writing of herself in a playful strain to her friend Flaubert:—

> The individual called George Sand is quite well, enjoying the marvelous winter now reigning in Berry, gathering flowers, taking note of interesting botanic anomalies, stitching at dresses and mantles for her daughter-in-law, costumes for the marionettes, dressing dolls, reading music, but, above all, spending hours with little Aurore, who is a wonderful child. There is not a being on earth more tranquil and happier in his home than this old troubadour retired from business, now and then singing his little song to the moon, singing well or ill he does not particularly care, so long as he gives the *motif* that is running in his head.... He is happy, for he is at peace, and can find amusement in everything.

M. Plauchut, another literary friend and a visitor at Nohant during this last decade of her lifetime, gives a picture of the order of her day; it is simplicity itself.

Nine o'clock, in summer and in winter alike, was her hour of waking. Letters and newspapers would then occupy her until noon, when she came down to join the family *déjeûner*. Afterwards she would stroll for an hour in the garden and the wood, visiting and tending her favorite plants and flowers. At two o'clock she would come indoors to give a lesson to her grandchildren in the library, or work there on her own account, undistracted by the romps around her. Dinner at six was followed by a short evening walk, after which she played with the children, or set them dancing indoors. She liked to sit at the piano, playing over to herself bits of music by her favorite Mozart, or old Spanish and Berrichon airs. After a game of dominoes or cards she would still sit up so late, occupying herself with water-color painting or otherwise, that sometimes her son was obliged to take away the lights. These long evenings, the same writer bears witness, sometimes afforded rare opportunities of hearing Madam Sand talk of the events and the men of her time. In the absolute quiet of the country, among a small circle of responsive minds, she, so silent otherwise, became expansive. "Those who have never heard George Sand at such hours," he concludes, "have never known her. She spoke well, with great elevation of ideas, charming eloquence, and a spirit of infinite indulgence." When at length she retired, it was to write on until the morning hours according to her old habit, only relinquished when her health made this imperative.

She had allowed her son and her daughter-in-law to take the cares of household management off her hands. This left her free, as she expressed it, to be a child again, to hold aloof from things immediate and transitory, reserving her thoughts and contemplations for what is general and eternal. She found a poet's pleasure in abstracting herself from human life, saying: "There are hours when I escape from myself, when I live in a plant, when I feel myself grass, a bird, a tree-top, a cloud, a running stream." Shaking off, as it were, the sense of personality, she felt more freely and fully the sense of kinship with the life and soul of the universe.

It was her habit every evening to sum up in a few lines the impressions of the day, and this journal, for the conspicuous absence of incident in its pages, she compares to the log-book of a ship lying at anchor. But one terrible and little anticipated break in its tranquil monotony was yet to come.

George Sand lived to see her country pass through every imaginable political experience. Born before the First Republic had expired, she had witnessed the First Empire, the restored Monarchy, the Revolution of 1830, the reign of Louis Philippe, the convulsions of 1848, the presidency of Louis Bonaparte, and the Second Empire. She was still to see and outlive its fall, the Franco-German War, the Commune, and to die, as she was born, under a republic.

To some of her friends who had reproached her with showing too much indulgence for the state of things under Imperial rule, she replied that the only change in her was that she had acquired more patience in proportion as more was required. The *régime* she condemned—and amid apparent prosperity had foretold the corrupting influence on the nation of the established ideal of frivolity, and that a crash of some kind must ensue. Her judgment on the Emperor, after his fall, is worth noting, if only because it is dispassionate. Since his elevation to the Imperial dignity she had lost all old illusions as to his public intentions. With regard to these, on the occasion of her interviews with him at the Elysée, he had completely deceived her, and designedly, she had at first thought. Nor had she concealed her disgust.

> I left Paris, and did not come to an appointment he had offered me. They did not tell me "The King might have had to wait!" but they wrote "The Emperor waited." However, I continued to write to him, whenever I saw hopes of saving some victim, to ponder his answers and watch his actions; and I became convinced that he did not intentionally impose upon any one. He imposed on himself and on everybody else.... In private life he had genuine qualities. I happened to see in him a side that was really generous and sincere. His dream of grandeur for France was not that of a sound mind, but neither of an ordinary mind. Really France would have sunk too low if she had submitted for twenty years to the supremacy of a *crétin*, working only for himself. One would then have to give her up in despair for ever and ever. The truth is that she mistook a meteor for a star, a silent dreamer for a man of depth. Then seeing him sink under disasters he ought to have foreseen, she took him for a coward.

George Sand's *Journal d'un Voyageur pendant la guerre* has a peculiar and painful interest. It is merely a note-book of passing impressions from September, 1870, to January, 1871; but its pages give a most striking picture of those effects of war which have no place in military annals.

The army disasters of the autumn were preceded by natural calamities of great severity. The heat of the summer in Berry had been tremendous, and Madame

Sand describes the havoc as unprecedented in her experience—the flowers and grass killed, the leaves scorched and yellowed, the baked earth under foot literally cracking in many places; no water, no hay, no harvest, but destructive cattle-plague, forest-fires driving scared wolves to seek refuge in the courtyard of Nohant itself—the remnant of corn spared by the sun, ruined by hail-storms. She and all her family had suffered from the unhealthiness of the season. Thus the political catastrophe found her already weakened by anxiety and fatigue, and feeling greatly the effort to set to work again. Finally, an outbreak of malignant small-pox in the village forced her to take her little grandchildren and their mother from Nohant out of reach of the infection. September and October were passed at or in the neighborhood of Boussac, a small town some thirty miles off. Sedan was over, and the worst had begun; the protracted suspense, the long agony of hope.

Those suffered most perhaps who, like herself, had to wait in enforced inaction, amid the awful dead calm that reigned in the provinces, yet forbidden to forget their affliction for a moment. The peasant was gone from the land—only the old and infirm were left to look after the flocks, to till and sow the field. Madame Sand notes, and with a kind of envy, the stolid patience and industry, the inextinguishable confidence, of poor old Jacques Bonhomme when things are at the worst. "He knows that in one way or another it is he who will have to pay the expenses of the war; he knows next winter will be a season of misery and want, but he believes in the spring"—in the bounty of nature to repair war's ravages.

During this time of unimaginable trouble some of the strongest minds were unhinged. It is no small honor to George Sand that hers should have preserved its balance. The pages of this journal are distinguished throughout by a wonderful calm of judgment and an equitable tone—not the calm of indifference, but of a broad and penetrating intelligence, no longer to be blinded by the wild excitement and passions of the moment, or exalted by childish hopes one hour to be thrust into the madness of despair the next.

Although tempted now and then to regret that she had recovered from her illness ten years ago, surviving but to witness the abasement of France, she was not, like others, panic-struck at the prospect of invasion, as though this meant the end of their country. "It will pass like a squall over a lake," she said.

But it was a time when they could be sure of nothing except of their distress. The telegraph wires were cut; rumors of good news they feared to believe would be succeeded by tales of horror they feared to discredit. Tidings would come that three hundred thousand of the enemy had been disposed of in a single engagement and King William taken prisoner; then of fatal catastrophes befallen to private friends—stories which often proved equally unfounded.

She had friends shut up in Paris of whom she knew not whether they were alive or dead. The strain of anxiety and painful excitement made sleep impossible to her except in the last extremity of fatigue. Yet she had her little grandchildren to care for; and when they came around her, clamoring for the fairy tales she was used to supply, she contented them as well as she could and gave them their lessons as usual, anxious to keep them from realizing the sadness the causes of which they were too young to understand.

It was the first time that she had known a distress that forbade her to find a solace in nature. She describes how one day, walking out with some friends and following the course of the river Tarde, she had half abandoned herself to the enjoyment of the scene—the cascade, the dragon-flies skimming the surface, the purple scabious flowers, the goats clambering on the boulders of rock that strewed the borders and bed of the stream—when one of the party remarks: "Here's a retreat pretty well fortified against the Prussians."

And the present, forgotten for an instant in reverie, came back upon her with a shock.

Letters in that district took three or four days to travel thirty miles. Newspapers were rarely to be procured; and when procured, made up of contradictions, wild suggestions, and the pretentious speeches of national leaders, meant to be reassuring, but marked by a vagueness and violence from which Madame Sand rightly augured ill.

The red-letter days were those that brought communications from their friends in Paris by the aerial post. On October 11, two balloons, respectively called "George Sand" and the "Armand Barbès," left the capital. "My name," she remarks, "did not bring good luck to the first—which suffered injuries and descended with difficulty, yet rescued the Americans who had gone up in it." The "Barbès" had a smoother but a more famous flight; alighting and depositing M. Gambetta safely at Tours.

As the autumn advanced Madame Sand and her family were enabled to return to Nohant. But what a return was that! The enemy were quartered within forty miles, at Issoudun; the fugitives thence were continually seen passing, carrying off their children, their furniture and their merchandise to places of security. Already the enemy's guns were said to have been heard at La Châtre. Madame Sand walked in her garden daily among her marigolds, snapdragon and ranunculus, making curious speculations as to what might be in store for herself and her possessions. She remarks:—

> You get accustomed to it, even though you have not the consolation of being able to offer the slightest resistance.... I look at my garden, I dine, I play with the children, whilst waiting in expectation of seeing the trees felled roots upwards; of getting no more bread to eat, and of having to carry my grandchildren off on my shoulders; for the horses have all been requisitioned. I work, expecting my scrawls to light the pipes of the Prussians.

But the enemy, though so near, never passed the boundaries of the "Black Valley." The department of the Indre remained uninvaded, though compassed on all sides by the foreign army; and George Sand was able to say afterwards that she at least had never seen a Prussian soldier.

A sad Christmas was passed. On the last night of 1870 a meeting of friends at Nohant broke up with the parting words, "All is lost!"

CHAPTER XII. - LATER YEARS.

"The execrable year is out," writes Madame Sand, "but to all appearances we are entering upon a worse."

On the 15th of January, 1871, her little drama *François le Champi*, first represented in the troublous months of 1849, was acted in Paris for the benefit of an ambulance. She notes the singular fate of this piece to be reproduced in time of bombardment. A pastoral!

The worst strain of suspense ended January 29, with the capitulation of Paris. Here the *Journal d'un Voyageur* breaks off. It would be sad indeed had her life, like that of more than one of her compeers, closed then over France in mourning. Although it was impossible but that such an ordeal must have impaired her strength, she outlived the war's ending, and the horrible social crisis which she had foreseen must succeed the political one. Happier than Prosper Mérimée, than Alexandre Dumas, and others, she saw the dawn of a new era of prosperity for her country, whose vital forces, as she had also foretold, were to prevail in the end over successive ills—the enervation of corruption, of military disaster, and the "orgie of pretended renovators" at home, that signalized the first months of peace abroad.

In January, 1872, we again find her writing cheerily to Flaubert:—

> Mustn't be ill, mustn't be cross, my old troubadour. Say that France is mad, humanity stupid, and that we are unfinished animals every one of us, you must love on all the same, yourself, your race, above all, your friends. I have my sad hours. I look at my blossoms, those two little girls smiling as ever, their charming mother, and my good, hard-working son, whom the end of the world will find hunting, cataloguing, doing his daily task, and yet as merry as Punch in his rare leisure moments.

In a later letter she writes in a more serious strain:—

> I do not say that humanity is on the road to the heights; I believe it in spite of all, but I do not argue about it, which is useless, for every one judges according to his own eyesight, and the general outlook at the present moment is ugly and poor. Besides, I do not need to be assured of the salvation of our planet and its inhabitants in order to believe in the necessity of the good and the beautiful; if our planet departs from this law it will perish; if its inhabitants discard it they will be destroyed. As for me, I wish to hold firm till my last breath, not with the certainty or the demand to find a "good place" elsewhere, but because my sole pleasure is to maintain myself and mine in the upward way.

The last five years of her life saw her pen in full activity. In the *Revue des Deux Mondes*, *Malgrétout*, the novel of 1870, was succeeded by *Flamarande* and *Les Deux Frères*—compositions executed with unflagging energy and animation of style; *La Tour de Percemont*, and a series of graceful fairy-stories entitled *Contes d'une grand'mère*. *Nanon* (1872), a rustic romance of the First Revolution, is a highly remarkable little work, possibly suggested by her recent experiences of the effect of public disturbances on remote country places.

She was also a constant contributor to the newspaper *Le Temps*. A critical notice by her hand of M. Renan's *Dialogues et Fragments Philosophiques*, reprinted from those columns, bears date May, 1876, immediately before she succumbed to the illness which in a few days was to cut short her life.

At the beginning of this year she had written on this subject to Flaubert, in the brave spirit she would fain impart to her weaker brethren:—

> Life is perhaps eternal, and work in consequence eternal. If so, let us finish our march bravely. If otherwise, if the individual perish utterly, let us have the honor of having done our task. That is duty, for our only obvious duties are to ourselves and our fellow-creatures. What we destroy in ourselves we destroy in them. Our abasement abases them; our falls drag them down; we owe to them to stand fast, to save them from falling. The desire to die early is a weakness, as is the desire to live long.

George Sand, like most persons of an exceptional constitution, had little faith in the efficacy for herself of medical science. She was persuaded that the prescribed remedies did her more harm than good, and on more than one occasion, when her health had caused her children uneasiness, they had had to resort to an affectionate *ruse* to induce her to take advice. Her habit of disregarding physical ailments, fighting against them as a weakness, and working on in their despite, led her to neglect for too long failing health that should have been attended to. During the whole of May, 1876, Madame Sand, though suffering from real illness, continued to join in the household routine and to proceed with her literary work as usual. Not till the last days of the month did she, unable any longer to make light of her danger, at length consent to send for professional advice. It was then too late. She was suffering from internal paralysis. The medical attention which, sought earlier, might, in the opinion of the doctors, have prolonged her life for years, could now do nothing to avert the imminent fatal consequences of her illness. "It is death," she said; "I did not ask for it, but neither do I regret it." For beyond the sorrow of parting it had no particular terrors for her; she had viewed and could meet it in another spirit. "Death is no more," she had written; "it is life renewed and purified."

She lingered for a week, in great suffering, but bearing all with fortitude and an unflinching determination not to distress those around her by painful complaining. Up to her last hour she preserved consciousness and lucidity. The words, "*Ne touchez pas à la verdure*," among the last that fell from her lips, were understood by her children, who knew her wish that the trees should be undisturbed under which, in the village cemetery, she was soon to find a resting-place—a wish that had been sacredly respected.

Her suffering ceased a short while before death, which came to her so quietly that the transition was almost imperceptible to the watchers by her side. It was on the morning of the 8th of June. She was within a month of completing her seventy-second year. Although her life's work had long since been mainly accomplished, yet the extinction of that great intelligence was felt by many—as fitly expressed by M. Renan—"like a diminution of humanity."

Two days later she was buried in the little cemetery of Nohant, that adjoins her own garden wall. The funeral was conducted with extreme simplicity, in accordance with her taste and spirit. The scene was none the less a memorable one. The rain fell in torrents, but no one seemed to regard it; the country-people flocking in from miles around, old men standing bare-headed for hours, heedless of the deluge. The peasant and the prince, Parisian leaders of the world of thought and letters, and the humblest and most unlearned of her poorer neighbors, stood together over her grave.

Six peasants carried the bier from the house to the church, a few paces distant. The village priest came, preceded by three chorister-boys and the venerable singing-clerk of the parish, to perform the ceremony. A portion of the little churchyard, railed off from the rest and planted with evergreen-trees, contains the graves of her grandmother, her father, and the two little grandchildren she had lost. A plain granite tomb in their midst now marks the spot where George Sand was laid, literally buried in flowers.

A great spirit was gone from the world; and a good spirit, it will be generally acknowledged: an artist in whose work the genuine desire to leave those she worked for better than she found them, is one inspiring motive. Such endeavor may seem to fail, and she affirmed: "A hundred times it does fail in its immediate results. But it helps, notwithstanding, to preserve that tradition of good desires and of good deeds, without which all would perish."

GEORGE SAND.

By

JUSTIN M'CARTHY.

GEORGE SAND.

We are all of us probably inclined, now and then, to waste a little time in vaguely speculating on what might have happened if this or that particular event had not given a special direction to the career of some great man or woman. If there had been an inch of difference in the size of Cleopatra's nose; if Hannibal had not lingered at Capua; if Cromwell had carried out his idea of emigration; if Napoleon Bonaparte had taken service under the Turk,—and so on through all the old familiar illustrations dear to the minor essayist and the debating society. I have sometimes felt tempted thus to lose myself in speculating on what might have happened if the woman whom all the world knows as George Sand had been happily married in her youth to the husband of her choice. Would she ever have taken to literature at all? Would she, loving as she does, and as Frenchwomen so rarely do, the changing face of inanimate nature,—the fields, the flowers and the brooks,—have lived a peaceful and obscure life in some happy country place, and been content with home, and family, and love, and never thought of fame? Or if, thus happily married, she still had allowed her genius to find an expression in literature, would she have written books with no passionate purpose in them,—books which might have seemed like those of a good Miss Mulock made perfect,—books which Podsnap might have read with approval, and put without a scruple into the hands of that modest young person, his daughter? Certainly one cannot but think that a different kind of early life would have given a quite different complexion to the literary individuality of George Sand.

Bulwer Lytton, in one of his novels, insists that true genius is always quite independent of the individual sufferings or joys of its possessor, and describes some inspired youth in the novel as sitting down, while sorrow is in his heart, and hunger gnawing at his vitals, to throw off a sparkling and gladsome little fairy tale. Now this is undoubtedly true, in general, of any high order of genius; but there are at least some great and striking exceptions. Rousseau and Byron are, in modern days, remarkable illustrations of genius, admittedly of a very high rank, governed and guided almost wholly by the individual fortunes of the men themselves. So, too, must we speak of the genius of George Sand. Not Rousseau, not even Byron, was in this sense more egotistic than the woman who broke the chains of her ill-assorted marriage with a crash that made its echoes heard at last in every civilized country in the world. Just as people are constantly quoting *nous avons changé tout cela* who never read a page of Molière, or *pour encourager les autres* without even being aware that there is a story of Voltaire's called "Candide," so there have been thousands of passionate protests uttered in America and Europe, for the last twenty years, by people who never saw a volume of George Sand, and yet are only echoing her sentiments and even repeating her words.

In a former number of *The Galaxy*, I expressed casually the opinion that George Sand is probably the most influential writer of our day. I am still, and deliberately, of the same opinion. It must be remembered that very few English or American authors have any wide or deep influence over peoples who do not speak English. Even of the very greatest authors this is true. Compare, for example, the literary dominion of Shakespeare with that of Cervantes. All nations who read Shakespeare read Cervantes: in Stratford-upon-Avon itself Don Quixote is probably as familiar a figure in people's minds as Falstaff; but Shakespeare is little known indeed to the vast majority of readers in the country of Cervantes, in the land of Dante, or in that of Racine and Victor Hugo. In something of the same way we may compare the influence of George Sand with that of even the greatest living authors of England and America. What influence has Charles Dickens or George Eliot outside the range of the English tongue? But George Sand's genius has been felt as a power in every country of the world where people read any manner of books. It has been felt almost as Rousseau's once was felt; it has aroused anger, terror, pity, or wild and rapturous excitement and admiration; it has rallied around it every instinct in man or woman which is revolutionary; it has ranged against it all that is conservative. It is not so much a literary influence as a great disorganizing force, riving the rocks of custom, resolving into their original elements the social combination which tradition and convention would declare to be indissoluble. I am not now speaking merely of the sentiments which George Sand does or did entertain on the subject of marriage. Divested of all startling effects and thrilling dramatic illustrations, these sentiments probably amounted to nothing more dreadful than the belief that an unwedded union between two people who love and are true to each other is less immoral than the legal marriage of two uncongenial creatures who do not love and probably are not true to each other. But the grand, revolutionary idea which George Sand announced was that of the social independence and equality of woman,—the principle that woman is not made for man in any other sense than as man is made for woman. For the first time in the history of the world woman spoke out for herself with a voice as powerful as that of man. For the first time in the history of the world woman spoke out as woman, not as the servant, the satellite, the pupil, the plaything, or the goddess of man.

Now, I intend at present to write of George Sand rather as an individual, or an influence, than as the author of certain works of fiction. Criticism would now be superfluously bestowed on the literary merits and peculiarities of the great woman whose astonishing intellectual activity has never ceased to produce, during the last thirty years, works which take already a classical place in French literature. If any reputation of our day may be looked upon as established, we may thus regard the reputation of George Sand. She is, beyond comparison, the greatest living novelist of France. She has won this position by the most legitimate application of the gifts of an artist. With all her marvellous fecundity, she has hardly ever given to the world any work which does not seem, at least, to have been the subject of the most elaborate and patient care. The greatest temptation which tries a story-teller is perhaps the temptation to rely on the attractiveness of story-telling, and to pay little or no attention to style. Walter Scott's prose, for example, if regarded as mere prose, is rambling, irregular, and almost worthless. Dickens's prose is as bad a model for imitation as a musical performance which is out of tune. Of course, I need hardly say that attention to style is almost as characteristic of French authors in general, as the lack of it is characteristic of English authors; but, even in France, the prose of George Sand stands out conspicuous for its wonderful expressiveness and force, its almost perfect beauty. Then, of all modern French authors,—I might, perhaps, say of all modern novelists of any country,—George Sand has added to fiction, has annexed from the worlds of reality and of imagination the greatest number of original characters,—of what Emerson calls new organic creations. Moreover, George Sand is, after Rousseau, the one only great French author who has looked directly and lovingly into the face of Nature, and learned the secrets which skies and waters, fields and lanes, can teach to the heart that loves them. Gifts such as these have won her the almost unrivalled place which she holds in living literature; and she has conquered at last even the public opinion which once detested and proscribed her. I could therefore hope to add nothing to what has been already said by criticism in regard to her merits as a novelist. Indeed, I think it probable that the majority of readers in this country know more of George Sand through the interpretation of the critics than through the pages of her books. And in her case criticism is so nearly unanimous as to her literary merits, that I may safely assume the public in general to have in their minds a just recognition of her position as a novelist. My object is rather to say something about the place which George Sand has taken as a social revolutionist, about the influence she has so long exercised over the world, and about the woman herself. For she is assuredly the greatest champion of woman's rights, in one sense, that the world has ever seen; and she is, on the other hand, the one woman out of all the world who has been most commonly pointed to as the appalling example to scare doubtful and fluttering womanhood back into its sheepfold of submissiveness and conventionality. There is hardly a woman's heart anywhere in the civilized world which has not felt the vibration of George Sand's thrilling voice. Women who never saw one of her books,—nay, who never heard even her *nom de plume*, have been stirred by emotions of doubt or fear, or repining or ambition, which they never would have known but for George Sand, and perhaps but for George Sand's uncongenial marriage. For, indeed, there is not now, and has not been for twenty years, I venture to think, a single "revolutionary" idea, as slow and steady-going people would call it, afloat anywhere in Europe or America, on the subject of woman's relations to man, society, and destiny, which is not due immediately to the influence of George Sand, and to the influence of George Sand's unhappy marriage upon George Sand herself.

GEORGE SAND.

The world has of late years grown used to this extraordinary woman, and has lost much of the wonder and terror with which it once regarded her. I can quite remember,—younger people than I can remember,—the time when all good and proper personages in England regarded the authoress of "Indiana" as a sort of feminine fiend, endowed with a hideous power for the destruction of souls, and an inextinguishable thirst for the slaughter of virtuous beliefs. I fancy a good deal of this sentiment was due to the fearful reports wafted across the seas, that this terrible woman had not merely repudiated the marriage bond, but had actually put off the garments sacred to womanhood. That George Sand appeared in men's clothes was an outrage upon consecrated proprieties far more astonishing than any theoretical onslaught upon old opinions could be. Reformers, indeed, should always, if they are wise in their generation, have a care of the proprieties. Many worthy people can listen with comparative fortitude when sacred and eternal truths are assailed, who are stricken with horror when the ark of propriety is never so lightly touched. George Sand's pantaloons were, therefore, regarded as the most appalling illustration of George Sand's wickedness. I well remember what excitement, scandal, and horror were created in the provincial town where I lived, some twenty years ago, when the editor of a local Panjandrum (to borrow Mr. Trollope's word) insulted the feelings and the morals of his constituents and subscribers by polluting his pages with a translation from one of George Sand's shorter novels. Ah me! the little novel might, so far as morality was concerned, have been written every word by Miss Phelps, or the authoress of the "Heir of Redcliff"; it had not a word, from beginning to end, which might not have been read out to a Sunday-school of girls; the translation was made by a woman of the purest soul, and, in her own locality, of the highest name; and yet how virtue did shriek out against the publication! The editor persevered in the publishing of the novel, spurred on to boldness by some of his very young and therefore fearless coadjutors, who thought it delightful to confront public opinion, and liked the notion of the stars in their courses fighting against Sisera, and Sisera not being dismayed. That charming, tender, touching little story! I would submit it to-day cheerfully to the verdict of a jury of matrons, confident that it would be declared a fit and proper publication. But at that time it was enough that the story bore the odious name of George Sand; public opinion condemned it, and sent the magazine which ventured to translate it to an early and dishonored grave. I remember reading, about that time, a short notice of George Sand by an English authoress of some talent and culture, in which the Frenchwoman's novels were described as so abominably filthy that even the denizens of the Paris brothels were ashamed to be caught reading them. Now, this declaration was made all in good faith, in the simple good faith of that class of persons who will pass wholesale and emphatic judgment upon works of which they have never read a single page. For I need hardly tell any intelligent person of to-day that, whatever may be said of George Sand's doctrines, she is no more open to the charge of indelicacy than the authoress of "Romola." I cannot, myself, remember any passage in George Sand's novels which can be called indelicate; and, indeed, her severest and most hostile critics are fond of saying, not without a certain justice, that one of the worst characteristics of her works is the delicacy and beauty of her style, which thus commends to pure and innocent minds certain doctrines that, broadly stated, would repel and shock them. Were I one of George Sand's inveterate opponents, this, or something like it, is the ground I would take up. I would say: "The welfare of the human family demands that a marriage, legally made, shall never be questioned or undone. Marriage is not a union depending on love or congeniality, or any such condition. It is just as sacred when made for money, or for ambition, or for lust of the flesh, or for any other purpose, however ignoble and base, as when contracted in the spirit of the purest mutual love. Here is a woman of great power and daring genius, who says that the essential condition of marriage is love and natural fitness; that a legal union of man and woman without this is no marriage at all, but a detestable and disgusting sin. Now, the more delicately, modestly, plausibly she can put this revolutionary and pernicious doctrine, the more dangerous she becomes, and the more earnestly we ought to denounce her." This was, in fact, what a great many persons did say; and the protest was at least consistent and logical.

But horror is an emotion which cannot long live on the old fuel, and even the world of English Philistinism soon ceased to regard George Sand as a mere monster. Any one now taking up "Indiana," for example, would perhaps find it not quite easy to understand how the book produced such an effect. Our novel-writing women of to-day commonly feed us on more fiery stuff than this. Not to speak of such accomplished artists in impurity as the lady who calls herself Ouida, and one or two others of the same school, we have young women, only just promoted from pantalettes, who can throw you off such glowing chapters of passion and young desire as would make the rhapsodies of "Indiana" seem very feeble milk-and-water brewage by comparison. Indeed, except for some of the descriptions in the opening chapters, I fail to see any extraordinary merit in "Indiana"; and toward the end it seems to me to grow verbose, weak, and tiresome. "Leone Leoni" opens with one of the finest dramatic outbursts of emotion known to the literature of modern fiction; but it soon wanders away into discursive weakness, and only just toward the close brightens up into a burst of lurid splendor. It is not those which I may call the questionable novels of George Sand,—the novels which were believed to illustrate in naked and appalling simplicity her doctrines and her life,—that will bear up her fame through succeeding generations. If every one of the novels which thus in their time drew down the thunders of Society's denunciation were to be swept into the wallet wherein Time, according to Shakespeare, carries scraps for oblivion, George Sand would still remain where she now is,—at the head of the French fiction of her day. It is true, as Goethe says, that "miracle-working pictures are rarely works of art." The books which make the hair of the respectable public stand on end are not often the works by which the fame of the author is preserved for posterity.

It is a curious fact that, at the early time to which I have been alluding, little or nothing was known in England (or, I presume, in America) of the real life of Aurora Amandine Dupin, who had been pleased to call herself George Sand. People knew, or had heard, that she had separated from her husband, that she had written novels which depreciated the sanctity of legal marriage, and that she sometimes wore male costume in the streets. This was enough. In England, at least, we were ready to infer any enormity regarding a woman who was unsound on the legal marriage question, and who did not wear petticoats. What would have been said had people then commonly known half the stories which were circulated in Paris,—half the extravagances into which a passionate soul, and the stimulus of sudden emancipation from restraint, had hurried the authoress of "Indiana" and "Lucrezia Floriani"? For it must be owned that the life of that woman was, in its earlier years, a strange and wild phenomenon, hardly to be comprehended, perhaps, by American or English natures. I have heard George Sand bitterly arraigned even by persons who protested that they were at one with her as regards the early sentiments which used to excite such odium. I have heard her described by such as a sort of Lamia of literature and passion,—a creature who could seize some noble, generous, youthful heart, drain it of its love, its aspirations, its profoundest emotions, and then fling it, squeezed and lifeless, away. I have heard it declared that George Sand made "copy" of the fierce and passionate loves which she knew so well how to awaken and to foster; that she distilled the life-blood of youth to obtain the mixture out of which she derived her inspiration. The charge so commonly (I think unjustly) made against Goethe, that he played with the girlish love of Bettina and of others in order to obtain a subject for literary dissection, is vehemently and deliberately urged in an aggravated form,—in many aggravated forms,—against George Sand. Where, such accusers ask, is that young poet, endowed with a lyrical genius rare indeed in the France of later days,—that young poet whose imagination was at once so daring and so subtle,—who might have been Béranger and Heine in one, and have risen to an atmosphere in which neither Béranger nor Heine ever floated? Where is he, and what evil influence was it which sapped the strength of his nature, corrupted his genius, and prepared for him a premature and shameful grave? Where is that young musician, whose pure, tender, and lofty strains sound sweetly and sadly in the ears, as the very hymn and music of the Might-Have-Been,—where is he now, and what was the seductive power which made a plaything of him and then flung him away? Here and there some man of stronger mould is pointed out as one who was at the first conquered, and then deceived and trifled with, but who ordered his stout heart to bear, and rose superior to the hour, and lived to retrieve his nature and make himself a name of respect; but the others, of more sensitive and perhaps finer organizations, are only the more to be pitied because they were so terribly in earnest. Seldom, even in the literary history of modern France, has there been a more strange and shocking episode than the publication by George Sand of the little book called "Elle et Lui," and the rejoinder to it by Paul de Musset, called "Lui et Elle." I can hardly be accused of straying into the regions of private scandal when I speak of two books which had a wide circulation, are still being read, and may be had, I presume, in any New York book-store where French literature is sold. The former of the two books, "She and He," was a story, or something which purported to be a story, by George Sand, telling of two ill-assorted beings whom fate had thrown together for awhile, and of whom the woman was all tenderness, love, patience, the man all egotism, selfishness, sensuousness, and eccentricity. The point of the whole business was to show how sublimely the woman suffered, and how wantonly the man flung happiness away. Had it been merely a piece of fiction, it must have been regarded by any healthy mind as a morbid, unwholesome, disagreeable production,—a sin of the highest æsthetic kind against true art, which must always, even in its pathos and its tragedy, leave on the mind exalted and delightful impressions. But every one in Paris at once hailed the story as a chapter of autobiography, as the author's vindication of one episode in her own career,—a vindication at the expense of a man who had gone down, ruined and lost, to an early grave. Therefore the brother of the dead man flung into literature a little book called "He and She," in which a story, substantially the same in its outlines, is so told as exactly to reverse the conditions under which the verdict of public opinion was sought. Very curious indeed was the manner in which the same substance of facts was made to present the two principal figures with complexions and characters so strangely altered. In the woman's book the woman was made the patient, loving, suffering victim; in the man's reply this same woman was depicted as the most utterly selfish and depraved creature the human imagination could conceive. Even if one had no other means whatever of forming an estimate of the character of George Sand, it would be hardly possible to accept as her likeness the hideous picture sketched by Paul de Musset. No woman, I am glad to believe, ever existed in real life so utterly selfish, base, and wicked as his bitter pen has drawn. I must say that the thing is very cleverly done. The picture is at least consistent with itself. As a character in romance it might be pronounced original, bold, brilliant, and, in an artistic sense, quite natural. There is something thoroughly French in the easy and delicate force of the final touch with which de Musset dismisses his hideous subject. Having sketched this woman in tints that seem to flame across the eyes of the reader,—having described with wonderful realism and power her affectation, her deceit, her reckless caprices, her base and cruel coquetries, her devouring wantonness, her soul-destroying arts, her unutterable selfishness and egotism,—having, to use a vulgar phrase, "turned her inside out," and told her story backwards,—the author calmly explains that the hero of the narrative in his dying hour called his brother to his bedside, and enjoined him, if occasion should ever arise, if the partner of his sin should ever calumniate him in his grave, to vindicate his memory, and avenge the treason practised upon him. "Of course," adds the narrator, "the brother made the promise,—and I have since heard that he has kept his word." I can hardly hope to convey to the reader any adequate idea of the effect produced on the mind by these few simple words of compressed, whispered hatred and triumph, closing a philippic, or a revelation, or a libel of such extraordinary bitterness and ferocity. The whole episode is, I believe and earnestly hope, without precedent or imitation in literary controversy. Never, that I know of, has a living woman been publicly exhibited to the world in a portraiture so hideous as that which Paul de Musset drew of George Sand. Never, that I know of, has any woman gone so near to deserving and justifying such a measure of retaliation.

For if it be assumed,—and I suppose it never has been disputed,—that in writing "Elle et Lui" George Sand meant to describe herself and Alfred de Musset, it is hard to conceive of any sin against taste and feeling,—against art and morals,—more flagrant than such a publication. The practice, to which French writers are so much addicted, of making "copy" of the private lives, characters, and relationships of themselves and their friends, seems to me in all cases utterly detestable. Lamartine's sins of this kind were grievous and glaring; but were they red as scarlet, they would seem whiter than snow when compared with the lurid monstrosity of George Sand's assault on the memory of the dead poet who was once her favorite. The whole affair, indeed, is so unlike anything which could occur in America or in England, that we can hardly find any canons by which to try it, or any standard of punishment by which to regulate its censure. I allude to it now because it is the only substantial evidence I know of which does fairly seem to justify the worst of the accusations brought against George Sand; and I do not think it right, when writing for grown men and women, who are supposed to have sense and judgment, to affect not to know that such accusations are made, or to pretend to think that it would be proper not to allude to them. They have been put forward, replied to, urged again, made the theme of all manner of controversy in scores of French and in some English publications. Pray let it be distinctly understood that I am not entering into any criticism of the morality of any part of George Sand's private life. With that we have nothing here to do. I am now dealing with the question, fairly belonging to public controversy, whether the great artist did not deliberately deal with human hearts as the painter of old is said to have done with a purchased slave,—inflicting torture in order the better to learn how to depict the struggles and contortions of mortal agony. In answer to such a question I can only point to "Lucrezia Floriani" and to "Elle et Lui," and say that unless the universal opinion of qualified critics be wrong, these books, and others too, owe their piquancy and their dramatic force to the anatomization of dead passions and discarded lovers. We have all laughed over the pedantic surgeon in Molière's "Malade Imaginaire", who invites his *fiancée*, as a delightful treat, to see him dissect the body of a woman. I am afraid that George Sand did sometimes invite an admiring public to an exhibition yet more ghastly and revolting,—the dissection of the heart of a dead lover.

But, in truth, we shall never judge George Sand and her writings at all, if we insist on criticising them from any point of view set up by the proprieties or even the moralities of Old England or New England. When the passionate young woman,—in whose veins ran the wild blood of Marshal Saxe,—found herself surrendered by legality and prescription to a marriage bond against which her soul revolted, society seemed for her to have resolved itself into its original elements. Its conventionalities and traditions contained nothing which she held herself bound to respect. The world was not her friend, nor the world's law. By one great decisive step she sundered herself forever from the bonds of what we call "society". She had shaken the dust of convention from her feet; the world was all before her where to choose. No creature on earth is so absolutely free as the Frenchwoman who has broken with society: There, then, stood this daring young woman, on the threshold of a new, fresh, and illimitable world; a young woman gifted with genius such as our later years have rarely seen, and blessed or cursed with a nature so strangely uniting the most characteristic qualities of man and woman, as to be in itself quite unparalleled and unique. Just think of it,—try to think of it! Society and the world had no longer any laws which she recognized. Nothing was sacred; nothing was settled. She had to evolve from her own heart and brain her own law of life. What wonder if she made some sad mistakes? Nay, is it not rather a theme for wonder and admiration that she did somehow come right at last? I know of no one who seems to me to have been open at once to the temptations of woman's nature and man's nature, except this George Sand. Her soul,—her brain,—her style may be described, from one point of view, as exuberantly and splendidly feminine; yet no other woman has ever shown the same power of understanding, and entering into the nature of a man. If Balzac is the only man who has ever thoroughly mastered the mysteries of a woman's heart, George Sand is the only woman, so far as I know, who has ever shown that she could feel as a man can feel. I have read stray passages in her novels which I would confidently submit to the criticism of any intelligent men unacquainted with the text, convinced that they would declare that only a man could have thus analyzed the emotions of manhood. I have in my mind, just now especially, a passage in the novel "Piccinino" which, were the authorship unknown, would, I am satisfied, secúre the decision of a jury of literary experts that the author must be a man. Now this gift of entire appreciation of the feelings of a different sex or race is, I take it, one of the rarest and highest dramatic qualities. Especially is it difficult for a woman, as our social life goes, to enter into the feelings of a man. While men and women alike admit the accuracy of certain pictures of women drawn by such artists as Cervantes, Molière, Balzac, and Thackeray, there are few women,—indeed, perhaps there are no women but one,—by whom a man has been so painted as to challenge and compel the recognition and acknowledgment of men. In "The Galaxy", some months ago, I wrote of a great Englishwoman, the authoress of "Romola", and I expressed my conviction that on the whole she is entitled to higher rank, as a novelist, than even the authoress of "Consuelo". Many, very many men and women, for whose judgment I have the highest respect, differed from me in this opinion. I still hold it, nevertheless; but I freely admit that George Eliot has nothing like the dramatic insight which enables George Sand to enter into the feelings and experiences of a man. I go so far as to say that, having some knowledge of the literature of fiction in most countries, I am not aware of the existence of any woman but this one, who could draw a real, living, straggling, passion-tortured man. All other novelists of George Sand's sex,—even including Charlotte Brontë,—draw only what I may call "women's men". If ever the two natures could be united in one form,—if ever a single human being could have the soul of man and the soul of woman at once,—George Sand might be described as that physical and psychological phenomenon. Now the point to which I wish to direct attention, is the peculiarity of the temptation to which a nature such as this was necessarily exposed at every turn when, free of all restraint and a rebel against all conventionality, it confronted the world and the world's law, and stood up, itself alone, against the domination of custom and the majesty of tradition. I claim, then, that when we have taken all these considerations into account, we are bound to admit that Aurora Dudevant deserves the generous recognition of the world for the use which she made of her splendid gifts. Her influence on French literature has been, on the whole, a purifying and strengthening power. The cynicism, the recklessness, the wanton, licentious disregard of any manner of principle, the debasing parade of disbelief in any higher purpose or nobler restraint, which are the shame and curse of modern French fiction, find no sanction in the pages of George Sand. I remember no passage in her works which gives the slightest encouragement to the "nothing new, and nothing true, and it don't signify" code of ethics which has been so much in fashion of late years. I find nothing in George Sand which does not do homage to the existence of a principle and a law in everything. This daring woman, who broke with society so early and so conspicuously, has always insisted, through every illustration, character, and catastrophe in her books, that the one only reality, the one only thing that can endure, is the rule of right and of virtue. Nor has she ever, that I can recollect, fallen into the enfeebling and sentimental theory so commonly expressed in the works of Victor Hugo, that the vague abstraction society is always to bear the blame of the faults committed by the individual man or woman. Of all persons in the world, Aurora Dudevant might be supposed most likely to adopt this easy and complacent theory as her guiding principle. She had every excuse, every reason for endeavoring to preach up the doctrine that our errors are society's and our virtues our own. But I am not aware that she ever taught any lesson save the lesson that men and women must endeavor to be heroes and heroines for themselves, heroes and heroines though all the world else were craven, and weak, and selfish, and unprincipled. Even that wretched and lamentable "Elle et Lui" affair, utterly inexcusable as it is when we read between the lines its secret history, has, at least, the merit of being an earnest and powerful protest against the egotistical and debasing indulgence of moral weaknesses and eccentricities which mean and vulgar minds are apt to regard as the privilege of genius. "Stand upon your own ground; be your own ruler; look to yourself, not to your stars, for your failure or success; always make your standard a lofty ideal, and try persistently to reach it, though all the temptations of earth, and all the power of darkness strive against you"—this, and nothing else, if I have read her books rightly, is the moral taught by George Sand. She may be wrong in her principle sometimes, but, at least, she always has a principle. She has a profound and generous faith in the possibilities of human nature; in the capacity of man's heart for purity, self-sacrifice, and self-redemption. Indeed, so far is she from holding counsel with wilful weakness or sin, that I think she sometimes falls into the noble error of painting her heroes as too glorious in their triumph over temptation, in their subjugation of every passion and interest to the dictates of duty and of honor. Take, for instance, that extraordinary book which has just been given to the American public in Miss Virginia Vaughan's excellent translation, "Mauprat". If I understand that magnificent romance at all, its purport is to prove that no human nature is ever plunged into temptation beyond its own strength to resist, provided that it really wills resistance; that no character is irretrievable, no error inexpiable, where there is sincere resolve to expiate, and longing desire to retrieve. Take, again, that exquisite little story, "La Dernière Aldini"; I do not know where one could find a finer illustration of the entire sacrifice of man's natural impulse, passion, interest, to what might almost be called an abstract idea of honor and principle. I have never read this little story without wondering how many men one ever has known who, placed in the same situation as that of Nello, the hero, would have done the same thing; and yet so simply and naturally are the characters wrought out, and the incidents described, that the idea of pompous, dramatic self-sacrifice never enters the mind of the reader, and it seems to him that Nello could not do otherwise than as he is doing. I speak of these two stories particularly, because in both of them there is a good deal of the world and the flesh; that is, both are stories of strong human passion and temptation. Many of George Sand's novels, the shorter ones especially, are as absolutely pure in moral tone, as entirely free from even a taint or suggestion of impurity, as they are perfect in style. Now, if we cannot help knowing that much of this great woman's life was far from being irreproachable, are we not bound to give her all the fuller credit, because her genius, at least, kept so far the whiteness of its soul? Revolutions are not to be made with rose-water; you cannot have omelettes without breaking of eggs. I am afraid that great social revolutionists are not often creatures of the most pure and perfect nature. It is not to patient Griselda you must look for any protest against even the uttermost tyranny of social conventions. One thing I think may, at least, be admitted as part of George Sand's vindication,—that the marriage system in France is the most debased and debasing institution existing in civilized society, now that the buying and selling of slaves has ceased to be a tolerated system. I hold that the most ardent advocates of the irrevocable endurance of the marriage bond are bound, by their very principles, to admit that, in protesting against the so-called marriage system of France, George Sand stood on the side of purity and right. Assuredly, she often went into extravagances in the other direction. It seems to be the fate of all French reformers to rush suddenly to extremes; and we must remember that George Sand was not a Bristol Quakeress, or a Boston transcendentalist, but a passionate Frenchwoman, the descendant of one of the maddest votaries of love and war who ever stormed across the stage of European history.

Regarding George Sand, then, as an influence in literature, and on society, I claim for her at least four great and special merits: First, she insisted on calling public attention to the true principle of marriage; that is to say, she put the question as it had not been put before. Of course, the fundamental principle she would have enforced is always being urged more or less feebly, more or less sincerely; but she made it her own question, and illuminated it by the fervid, fierce rays of her genius and her passion. Secondly, her works are an exposition of the tremendous reality of the feelings which people who call themselves practical are apt to regard with indifference or contempt as mere sentiments. In the long run, the passions decide the life-question one way or the other. They are the tide which, as you know or do not know how to use it, will either turn your mill and float your boat, or drown your fields and sweep away your dwellings. Life and society receive no impulse and no direction from the influences out of which the novels of Dickens, or even of Thackeray, are made up. These are but pleasant or tender toying with the playthings and puppets of existence. George Sand constrains us to look at the realities through the medium of her fiction. Thirdly, she insists that man can and shall make his own career; not whine to the stars, and rail out against the powers above, when he has weakly or wantonly marred his own destiny. Fourthly,—and this ought not to be considered her least service to the literature of her country,—she has tried to teach people to look at Nature with their own eyes, and to invite the true love of her to flow into their hearts. The great service which Ruskin, with all his eccentricities and extravagances, has rendered to English-speaking peoples by teaching them to use their own eyes when they look at clouds, and waters, and grasses, and hills, George Sand has rendered to France.

I hold that these are virtues and services which ought to outweigh even very grave personal and artistic errors. We often hear that this or that great poet or romancist has painted men as they are; this other as they ought to be. I think George Sand paints men as they are, and also not merely as they ought to be, but as they can be. The sum of the lesson taught by her books is one of confidence in man's possibilities, and hope in his steady progress. At the same time she is entirely practical in her faith and her aspirations. She never expects that the trees are to grow up into the heavens, that men and women are to be other than men and women. She does not want them to be other; she finds the springs and sources of their social regeneration in the fact that they are just what they are, to begin with. I am afraid some of the ladies who seem to base their scheme of woman's emancipation and equality on the assumption that, by some development of time or process of schooling, a condition of things is to be brought about where difference of sex is no longer to be a disturbing power, will find small comfort or encouragement in the writings of George Sand. She deals in realities altogether; the realities of life, even when they are such as to shallow minds may seem mere sentiments and ecstacies; the realities of society, of suffering, of passion, of inanimate nature. There is in her nothing unmeaning, nothing untrue; there is in her much error, doubtless, but no sham.

I believe George Sand is growing into a quiet and beautiful old age. After a life of storm and stress, a life which, metaphorically at least, was "worn by war and passion", her closing years seem likely to be gilded with the calm glory of an autumnal sunset. One is glad to think of her thus happy and peaceful, accepting so tranquilly the reality of old age, still laboring with her unwearied pen, still delighting in books, and landscapes, and friends, and work. The world can well afford to forget as soon as possible her literary and other errors. Of the vast mass of romances, stories, plays, sketches, criticisms, pamphlets, political articles, even, it is said, ministerial manifestoes of republican days, which she poured out, only a few comparatively will perhaps be always treasured by posterity; but these will be enough to secure her a classic place. And she will not be remembered by her writings alone. Hers is probably the most powerful individuality displayed by any modern Frenchwoman. The influence of Madame Roland was but a glittering unreality, that of Madame de Staël only a boudoir and coterie success, when compared with the power exercised over literature, human feeling, and social law, by the energy, the courage, the genius, even the very errors and extravagances of George Sand.

THE DEVIL'S POOL

By George Sand

Translated From The French By Jane Minot Sedgwick And Ellery Sedgwick

With An Etching By E. Abot

THE AUTHOR TO THE READER

A la sueur de ton visaige,
Tu gagnerais ta pauvre vie.
Après long travail et usaige,
Voicy la mort qui te convie[1].

---

[1] In toil and sorrow thou shalt eat
The bitter bread of poverty.
After the burden and the heat,
Lo! it is Death who calls for thee.

THIS quaint old French verse, written under one of Holbein's pictures, is profoundly melancholy. The engraving represents a laborer driving his plow through the middle of a field. Beyond him stretches a vast horizon, dotted with wretched huts; the sun is sinking behind the hill. It is the end of a hard day's work. The peasant is old, bent, and clothed in rags. He is urging onward a team of four thin and exhausted horses; the plowshare sinks into a stony and ungrateful soil. One being only is active and alert in this scene of toil and sorrow. It is a fantastic creature. A skeleton armed with a whip, who acts as plowboy to the old laborer, and running along through the furrow beside the terrified horses, goads them on. This is the specter Death, whom Holbein has introduced allegorically into that series of religious and philosophic subjects, at once melancholy and grotesque, entitled "The Dance of Death."

In this collection, or rather this mighty composition, where Death, who plays his part on every page, is the connecting link and predominating thought, Holbein has called up kings, popes, lovers, gamesters, drunkards, nuns, courtesans, thieves, warriors, monks, Jews, and travelers,—all the people of his time and our own; and everywhere the specter Death is among them, taunting, threatening, and triumphing. He is absent from one picture only, where Lazarus, lying on a dunghill at the rich man's door, declares that the specter has no terrors for him; probably because he has nothing to lose, and his existence is already a life in death.

Is there comfort in this stoical thought of the half-pagan Christianity of the Renaissance, and does it satisfy religious souls? The upstart, the rogue, the tyrant, the rake, and all those haughty sinners who make an ill use of life, and whose steps are dogged by Death, will be surely punished; but can the reflection that death is no evil make amends for the long hardships of the blind man, the beggar, the madman, and the poor peasant? No! An inexorable sadness, an appalling fatality brood over the artist's work. It is like a bitter curse, hurled against the fate of humanity.

Holbein's faithful delineation of the society in which he lived is, indeed, painful satire. His attention was engrossed by crime and calamity; but what shall we, who are artists of a later date, portray? Shall we look to find the reward of the human beings of to-day in the contemplation of death, and shall we invoke it as the penalty of unrighteousness and the compensation of suffering?

No, henceforth, our business is not with death, but with life. We believe no longer in the nothingness of the grave, nor in safety bought with the price of a forced renunciation; life must be enjoyed in order to be fruitful. Lazarus must leave his dunghill, so that the poor need no longer exult in the death of the rich. All must be made happy, that the good fortune of a few may not be a crime and a curse. As the laborer sows his wheat, he must know that he is helping forward the work of life, instead of rejoicing that Death walks at his side. We may no longer consider death as the chastisement of prosperity or the consolation of distress, for God has decreed it neither as the punishment nor the compensation of life. Life has been blessed by Him, and it is no longer permissible for us to leave the grave as the only refuge for those whom we are unwilling to make happy.

There are some artists of our own day, who, after a serious survey of their surroundings, take pleasure in painting misery, the sordidness of poverty, and the dunghill of Lazarus. This may belong to the domain of art and philosophy; but by depicting poverty as so hideous, so degraded, and sometimes so vicious and criminal, do they gain their end, and is that end as salutary as they would wish? We dare not pronounce judgment. They may answer that they terrify the unjust rich man by pointing out to him the yawning pit that lies beneath the frail covering of wealth; just as in the time of the Dance of Death, they showed him his gaping grave, and Death standing ready to fold him in an impure embrace. Now, they show him the thief breaking open his doors, and the murderer stealthily watching his sleep. We confess we cannot understand how we can reconcile him to the human nature he despises, or make him sensible of the sufferings of the poor wretch whom he dreads, by showing him this wretch in the guise of the escaped convict or the nocturnal burglar. The hideous phantom Death, under the repulsive aspect in which he has been represented by Holbein and his predecessors, gnashing his teeth and playing the fiddle, has been powerless to convert the wicked and console their victims. And does not our literature employ the same means as the artists of the Middle Ages and the Renaissance?

The revelers of Holbein fill their glasses in a frenzy to dispel the idea of Death, who is their cup-bearer, though they do not see him. The unjust rich of our own day demand cannon and barricades to drive out the idea of an insurrection of the people which Art shows them as slowly working in the dark, getting ready to burst upon the State. The Church of the Middle Ages met the terrors of the great of the earth with the sale of indulgences. The government of to-day soothes the uneasiness of the rich by exacting from them large sums for the support of policemen, jailors, bayonets, and prisons.

Albert Durer, Michael Angelo, Holbein, Callot, and Goya have made powerful satires on the evils of their times and countries, and their immortal works are historical documents of unquestionable value. We shall not refuse to artists the right to probe the wounds of society and lay them bare to our eyes; but is the only function of art still to threaten and appall? In the literature of the mysteries of iniquity, which talent and imagination have brought into fashion, we prefer the sweet and gentle characters, which can attempt and effect conversions, to the melodramatic villains, who inspire terror; for terror never cures selfishness, but increases it.

We believe that the mission of art is a mission of sentiment and love, that the novel of to-day should take the place of the parable and the fable of early times, and that the artist has a larger and more poetic task than that of suggesting certain prudential and conciliatory measures for the purpose of diminishing the fright caused by his pictures. His aim should be to render attractive the objects he has at heart, and, if necessary, I have no objection to his embellishing them a little. Art is not the study of positive reality, but the search for ideal truth, and the "Vicar of Wakefield" was a more useful and healthy book than the "Paysan Perverti," or the "Liaisons Dangereuses."

Forgive these reflections of mine, kind reader, and let them stand as a preface, for there will be no other to the little story I am going to relate to you. My tale is to be so short and so simple, that I felt obliged to make you my apologies for it beforehand, by telling you what I think of the literature of terror.

I have allowed myself to be drawn into this digression for the sake of a laborer; and it is the story of a laborer which I have been meaning to tell you, and which I shall now tell you at once.

I — The Tillage of the Soil

I HAD just been looking long and sadly at Holbein's plowman, and was walking through the fields, musing on rustic life and the destiny of the husbandman. It is certainly tragic for him to spend his days and his strength delving in the jealous earth, that so reluctantly yields up her rich treasures when a morsel of coarse black bread, at the end of the day's work, is the sole reward and profit to be reaped from such arduous toil. The wealth of the soil, the harvests, the fruits, the splendid cattle that grow sleek and fat in the luxuriant grass, are the property of the few, and but instruments of the drudgery and slavery of the many. The man of leisure seldom loves, for their own sake, the fields and meadows, the landscape, or the noble animals which are to be converted into gold for his use. He comes to the country for his health or for change of air, but goes back to town to spend the fruit of his vassal's labor.

On the other hand, the peasant is too abject, too wretched, and too fearful of the future to enjoy the beauty of the country and the charms of pastoral life. To him, also, the yellow harvest-fields, the rich meadows, the fine cattle represent bags of gold; but he knows that only an infinitesimal part of their contents, insufficient for his daily needs, will ever fall to his share. Yet year by year he must fill those accursed bags, to please his master and buy the right of living on his land in sordid wretchedness. Yet nature is eternally young, beautiful, and generous. She pours forth poetry and beauty on all creatures and all plants that are allowed free development.

She owns the secret of happiness, of which no one has ever robbed her. The happiest of men would be he who, knowing the full meaning of his labor, should, while working with his hands, find his happiness and his freedom in the exercise of his intelligence, and, having his heart in unison with his brain, should at once understand his own work and love that of God, The artist has such delights as these in contemplating and reproducing the beauties of nature; but if his heart be true and tender, his pleasure is disturbed when he sees the miseries of the men who people this paradise of earth. True happiness will be theirs when mind, heart, and hand shall work in concert in the sight of Heaven, and there shall be a sacred harmony between God's goodness and the joys of his creatures. Then, instead of the pitiable and frightful figure of Death stalking, whip in hand, across the fields, the painter of allegories may place beside the peasant a radiant angel, sowing the blessed grain broadcast in the smoking furrow. The dream of a serene, free, poetic, laborious, and simple life for the tiller of the soil is not so impossible that we should banish it as a chimera. The sweet, sad words of Virgil: "Oh, happy the peasants of the field, if they knew their own blessings!" is a regret, but, like all regrets, it is also a prophecy. The day will come when the laborer too may be an artist, and may at least feel what is beautiful, if he cannot express it,—a matter of far less importance. Do not we know that this mysterious poetic intuition is already his, in the form of instinct and vague reverie? Among those peasants who possess some of the comforts of life, and whose moral and intellectual development is not entirely stifled by extreme wretchedness, pure happiness that can be felt and appreciated exists in the elementary stage; and, moreover, since poets have already raised their voices out of the lap of pain and of weariness, why should we say that the labor of the hands excludes the working of the soul? Without doubt this exclusion is the common result of excessive toil and of deep misery; but let it not be said that when men shall work moderately and usefully there will be nothing but bad workers and bad poets. The man who draws in noble joy from the poetic feeling is a true poet, though he has never written a verse all his life.

My thoughts had flown in this direction, without my perceiving that my confidence in the capacity of man for education was strengthened by external influences. I was walking along the edge of a field, which some peasants were preparing to sow. The space was vast as that in Holbein's picture; the landscape, too, was vast and framed in a great sweep of green, slightly reddened by the approach of autumn. Here and there in the great russet field, slender rivulets of water left in the furrows by the late rains sparkled in the sunlight like silver threads. The day was clear and mild, and the soil, freshly cleft by the plowshare, sent up a light steam. At the other extremity of the field, an old man, whose broad shoulders and stern face recalled Holbein's plowman, but whose clothes carried no suggestion of poverty, was gravely driving his plow of antique shape, drawn by two placid oxen, true patriarchs of the meadow, tall and rather thin, with pale yellow coats and long, drooping horns. They were those old workers who, through long habit, have grown to be *brothers*, as they are called in our country, and who, when one loses the other, refuse to work with a new comrade, and pine away with grief. People who are unfamiliar with the country call the love of the ox for his yoke-fellow a fable. Let them come and see in the corner of the stable one of these poor beasts, thin and wasted, restlessly lashing his lean flanks with his tail, violently breathing with mingled terror and disdain on the food offered him, his eyes always turned toward the door, scratching with his hoof the empty place at his side, sniffing the yokes and chains which his fellow used to wear, and incessantly calling him with melancholy lowings. The ox-herd will say: "There is a pair of oxen gone;' this one will work no more, for his brother is dead. We ought to fatten him for the market, but he will not eat, and will soon starve himself to death." The old laborer worked slowly, silently, and without waste of effort His docile team were in no greater haste than he; but, thanks to the undistracted steadiness of his toil and the judicious expenditure of his strength, his furrow was as soon plowed as that of his son, who was driving, at some distance from him, four less vigorous oxen through a more stubborn and stony piece of ground.

My attention was next caught by a fine spectacle, a truly noble subject for a painter. At the other end of the field a fine-looking youth was driving a magnificent team of four pairs of young oxen, through whose somber coats glanced a ruddy, glow-like name. They had the short, curry heads that belong to the wild bull, the same large, fierce eyes and jerky movements; they worked in an abrupt, nervous way that showed how they still rebelled against the yoke and goad, and trembled with anger as they obeyed the authority so recently imposed. They were what is called "newly yoked" oxen. The man who drove them had to clear a corner of the field that had formerly been given up to pasture, and was filled with old tree-stumps; and his youth and energy, and his eight half-broken animals, hardly sufficed for the Herculean task.

A child of six or seven years old, lovely as an angel, wearing round his shoulders, over his blouse, a sheepskin that made him look like a little Saint John the Baptist out of a Renaissance picture, was running along in the furrow beside the plow, pricking the flanks of the oxen with a long, light goad but slightly sharpened. The spirited animals quivered under the child's light touch, making their yokes and head-bands creak, and shaking the pole violently. Whenever a root stopped the advance of the plowshare, the laborer would call every animal by name in his powerful voice, trying to calm rather than to excite them; for the oxen, irritated by the sudden resistance, bounded, pawed the ground with their great cloven hoofs, and would have jumped aside and dragged the plow across the fields, if the young man had not kept the first four in order with his voice and goad, while the child controlled the four others. The little fellow shouted too, but the voice which he tried to make of terrible effect, was as sweet as his angelic face. The whole scene was beautiful in its grace and strength; the landscape, the man, the child, the oxen under the yoke; and in spite of the mighty struggle by which the earth was subdued, a deep feeling of peace and sweetness reigned over all. Each time that an obstacle was surmounted and the plow resumed its even, solemn progress, the laborer, whose pretended violence was but a trial of his strength, and an outlet for his energy, instantly regained that serenity which is the right of simple souls, and looked with fatherly pleasure toward his child, who turned to smile back at him. Then the young father would raise his manly voice in the solemn and melancholy chant that ancient tradition transmits, not indeed to all plowmen indiscriminately, but to those who are most perfect in the art of exciting and sustaining the spirit of cattle while at work. This song, which was probably sacred in its origin, and to which mysterious influences must once have been attributed, is still thought to possess the virtue of putting animals on their mettle, allaying their irritation, and of beguiling the weariness of their long, hard toil. It is not enough to guide them skilfully, to trace a perfectly straight furrow, and to lighten their labor by raising the plowshare or driving it into the earth; no man can be a consummate husbandman who does not know how to sing to his oxen, and that is an art that requires taste and especial gifts. To tell the truth, this chant is only a recitative, broken off and taken up at pleasure. Its irregular form and its intonations that violate all the rules of musical art make it impossible to describe.

But it is none the less a noble song, and so appropriate is it to the nature of the work it accompanies, to the gait of the oxen, to the peace of the fields, and to the simplicity of the men who sing it, that no genius unfamiliar with the tillage of the earth, and no man except an accomplished laborer of our part of the country, could repeat it. At the season of the year when there is no work or stir afoot except that of the plowman, this strong, sweet refrain rises like the voice of the breeze, to which the key it is sung in gives it some resemblance. Each phrase ends with a long trill, the final note of which is held with incredible strength of breath, and rises a quarter of a tone, sharping systematically. It is barbaric, but possesses an unspeakable charm, and anybody, once accustomed to hear it, cannot conceive of another song taking its place at the same hour and in the same place, without striking a discord.

So it was that I had before my eyes a picture the reverse of that of Holbein, although the scene was similar. Instead of a wretched old man, a young and active one; instead of a team of weary and emaciated horses, four yoke of robust and fiery oxen; instead of death, a beautiful child; instead of despair and destruction, energy and the possibility of happiness.

Then the old French verse, "À la sueur de ton vis-aige," etc., and Virgil's "O fortunatos... agricolas," returned to my mind, and seeing this lovely child and his father, under such poetic conditions, and with so much grace and strength, accomplish a task full of such grand and solemn suggestions, I was conscious of deep pity and involuntary respect. Happy the peasant of the fields! Yes, and so too should I be in his place, if my arm and voice could be endowed with sudden strength, and I could help to make Nature fruitful, and sing of her gifts, without ceasing to see with my eyes or understand with my brain harmonious colors and sounds, delicate shades and graceful outlines; in short, the mysterious beauty of all things. And above all, if my heart continued to beat in concert with the divine sentiment that presided over the immortal sublimity of creation.

But, alas! this man has never understood the mystery of beauty; this child will never understand it. God forbid that I should not think them superior to the animals which are subject to them, or that they have not moments of rapturous insight that soothe their toil and lull their cares to sleep. I see the seal of the Lord upon their noble brows, for they were born to inherit the earth far more truly than those who have bought and paid for it. The proof that they feel this is that they cannot be exiled with impunity, that they love the soil they have watered with their tears, and that the true peasant dies of homesickness under the arms of a soldier far from his native field. But he lacks some of my enjoyments, those pure delights which should be his by right, as a workman in that immense temple which the sky only is vast enough to embrace. He lacks the consciousness of his sentiment. Those who condemned him to slavery from his mother's womb, being unable to rob him of his vague dreams, took away from him the power of reflection.

Yet, imperfect being that he is, sentenced to eternal childhood, he is nobler than the man in whom knowledge has stifled feeling. Do not set yourselves above him, you who believe yourselves invested with a lawful and inalienable right to rule over him, for your terrible mistake shows that your brain has destroyed your heart, and that you are the blindest and most incomplete of men! I love the simplicity of his soul more than the false lights of yours; and if I had to narrate the story of his life, the pleasure I should take in bringing out the tender and touching side of it would be greater than your merit in painting the degradation and contempt into which he is cast by your social code.

I knew the young man and the beautiful child; I knew their history, for they had a history. Everybody has his own, and could make the romance of his life interesting, if he could but understand it. Although but a peasant and a laborer, Germain had always been aware of his duties and affections. He had related them to me clearly and ingenuously, and I had listened with interest. After some time spent in watching him plow, it occurred to me that I might write his story, though that story were as simple, as straightforward, and unadorned as the furrow he was tracing.

Next year that furrow will be filled and covered by a fresh one. Thus disappear most of the footprints made by man in the field of human life. A little earth obliterates them, and the furrows we have dug succeed one another like graves in a cemetery. Is not the furrow of the laborer of as much value as that of the idler, even if that idler, by some absurd chance, have made a little noise in the world, and left behind him an abiding name?

I mean, if possible, to save from oblivion the furrow of Germain, the skilled husbandman. He will never know nor care, but I shall take pleasure in my talk.

II — Father Maurice

"GERMAIN," said his father-in-law one day, "you must decide about marrying again. It is almost two years now since you lost my daughter, and your eldest boy is seven years old! You are almost thirty, my boy, and you know that in our country a man is considered too old to go to housekeeping again after that age; you have three nice children, and thus far they have not proved a burden to us at all. My wife and my daughter-in-law have looked after them as well as they could, and loved them as they ought. Here is Petit-Pierre almost grown up. He goads the oxen very well; he knows how to look after the cattle; and he is strong enough to drive the horses to the trough. So it is not he that worries us. But the other two, love them though we do, God knows the poor little innocents give us trouble enough this year; my daughter-in-law is about to lie in, and she has yet another baby to attend to. When the child we are expecting comes, she will not be able to look after your little Solange, and above all your Sylvain, who is not four years old, and who is never quiet day or night. He has a restless disposition like yours; that will make a good workman of him, but it makes a dreadful child, and my old wife cannot run fast enough to save him when he almost tumbles into the ditch, or when he throws himself in front of the tramping cattle. And then with this other that my daughter-in-law is going to bring into the world, for a month at least her next older child will fall on my wife's hands. Besides, your children worry us, and give us too much to do; we hate to see children badly looked after, and when we think of the accidents that may befall them, for want of care, we cannot rest. So you need another wife, and I another daughter-in-law. Think this over, my son. I have called it to your mind before. Time flies, and the years will not wait a moment for you. It is your duty to your children and to the rest of us, who wish all well at home, to marry as soon as you can." "Very well, father," answered the son-in-law, "if you really wish it, I must do as you say. But I do not wish to hide it from you that it will make me very sad, and that I hardly wish for anything but to drown myself. We know who it is we lose, we never know whom we find. I had a good wife, a pretty wife, sweet, brave, good to her father and mother, good to her husband, good to her children, good to toil in the fields and in the house, well fitted to work,—in short, good for everything; and when you had given her to me, and I took her, we did not place it among our promises that I should go and forget about her if I had the misfortune to lose her."

"What you say shows your good heart, Germain," answered Father Maurice. "I know that you loved my daughter and that you made her happy, and that had you been able to satisfy Death by going in her place, Catherine would be alive today, and you would be in the graveyard. She deserved all your love, and if you are not consoled, neither are we. But I do not speak to you of forgetting her: God wished her to leave us, and we do not let a day go by without telling him in our prayers and thoughts, and words and actions, that we keep her memory and still sorrow for her loss. But if she could speak to you from the other world, and let you know what she wishes, she would tell you to find a mother for her little orphans. So the question is to find a woman who will be worthy to take her place. It will not be easy, but it is not impossible. And when we shall find her for you, you will love her as you used to love my daughter, because you are a good man, and because you will be thankful to her for helping us and for loving your children."

"Very well, Father Maurice, I shall do as you wish, as I have always done."

"It is only justice, my son, to say that you have always listened to the friendly advice and good judgment of the head of the house. So let us consult about your choice of a new wife. First, I don't advise you to take a young girl. That is not what you need. Youth is careless, and, as it is hard work to bring up three children, especially when they are of another bed, you must have a good soul, wise and gentle, and well used to work. If your wife is not about the same age as you, she will have no reason to accept such a duty. She will find you too old and your children too young. She will be complaining, and your children will suffer."

"This is just what makes me uneasy. Suppose the poor little things should be badly treated, hated, beaten?"

"God grant not," answered the old man. "But bad women are more rare with us than good, and we shall be stupid if we cannot pick out somebody who will suit us."

"That is true, father. There are good girls in our village. There is Louise, Sylvaine, Claudie, Marguerite—yes, anybody you want."

"Gently, gently, my boy. All these girls are too young, or too poof, or too pretty; for surely we must think of that top, my son. A pretty woman is not always as well behaved as another!"

"Then you wish me to take an ugly wife?" said Germain, a little uneasy.

"No, not ugly at all, for this woman will bear you other children, and there is nothing more miserable than to have children who are ugly and weak and sickly. But a woman still fresh and in good health, who is neither pretty nor ugly, would suit you exactly."

"I am quite sure," said Germain, smiling rather sadly, "that to get such a woman as you wish, you must have her made to order. All the more because you don't wish her to be poor, and the rich are not easy to get, particularly for a widower."

"And suppose she were a widow herself, Germain? A widow without children and with a good portion?"

"For the moment, I cannot think of anybody like this in our parish."

"Nor I either. But there are others elsewhere."

"You have somebody in mind, father. Then tell me, at once, who it is."

III — Germain, the Skilled Husbandman

"YES, I have somebody in mind," replied Father Maurice. "It is a Leonard, the widow of a Guérin. She lives at Fourche."

"I know neither the woman nor the place," answered Germain, resigned, but growing more and more melancholy.

"Her name is Catherine, like your dead wife's."

"Catherine? Yes, I shall be glad to have to pronounce that name, Catherine; and yet if I cannot love one as much as the other, it will pain me all the more. It will bring her to my mind more often."

"I tell you, you will love her. She is a good soul, a woman with a warm heart. I have not seen her for a long time. She was not an ugly girl then. But she is no longer young. She is thirty-two. She comes of a good family, honest people all of them, and for property she has eight or ten thousand francs in land which she would sell gladly in order to invest in the place where she settles. For she, too, is thinking of marrying again, and I know that if your character pleases her, she will not be dissatisfied with your situation."

"So you have made all the arrangements?"

"Yes, except that I have not had an opinion from either of you, and that is what you must ask each other when you meet. The woman's father is a distant connection of mine, and he has been a good friend to me. You know Father Leonard well?"

"Yes, I have seen you two talking at the market, and at the last you lunched together. Then it was about her that he spoke to you so long?"

"Certainly. He watched you selling your cattle and saw that you drove a shrewd bargain, and that you were a good-looking fellow and appeared active and intelligent; and when I told him what a good fellow you were and how well you have behaved toward us, without one word of vexation or anger during the eight years we have been living and working together, he took it into his head to marry you to his daughter. This suits me, too, I admit, when I think of her good reputation and the honesty of her family and the prosperous condition I know her affairs are in."

"I see, Father Maurice, that you have an eye to money."

"Of course I do; you have, too, have you not?"

"I do look toward it, if you wish, for your sake; but you know that, for my own part, I don't worry whether I gain or not in what we make. I don't understand about profit-sharing; I have no head for that sort of thing. I understand the ground;

I understand cattle, horses, carts, sowing, threshing, and provender. As for sheep, and vineyards, and vegetables, petty profits, and fine gardening, you know that is your son's business. I don't have much to do with it. As to money, my memory is short, and I should rather give up everything than fight about what is yours and what is mine. I should be afraid of making some mistake and claiming what does not belong to me, and if business were not so clear and simple I should never find my way in it."

"So much the worse, my son; and this is the reason I wish you to have a wife with a clear head to fill my place when I am gone. You never wished to understand our accounts, and this might lead you into a quarrel with my son, when you don't have me any longer to keep you in harmony and decide what is each one's share."

"May you live long, Father Maurice. But do not worry about what will happen when you die. I shall never quarrel with your son. I trust Jacques as I do you; and as I have no property of my own, and all that might accrue to me comes from your daughter and belongs to our children, I can rest easy, and you, too. Jacques would never rob his sister's children for the sake of his own, for he loves them all equally."

"You are right, Germain. Jacques is a good son, a good brother, and a man who loves the truth. But Jacques may die before you, before your children grow up; and in a family we must always remember never to leave children without a head to look after them and govern their disagreements; otherwise, the lawyer-people mix themselves up in it, stir them up to fight, and make them eat up everything in law-suits. So we ought not to think of bringing home another person, man or woman, without remembering that some day or other that person may have to control the behavior and business of twenty or thirty children and grandchildren, sons-in-law and daughters-in-law. We never know how big a family can grow, and when a hive is so full that the bees must form new swarms, each one wishes to carry off her share of the honey. When I took you for my son, although my daughter was rich and you were poor, I never reproached her for choosing you. I saw that you were a hard worker, and I knew very well that the best fortune for people in such a country as ours is a pair of arms and a heart like yours. When a man brings these into a family, he brings enough. But with a woman it is different. Her work indoors saves, but it does not gain. Besides, now that you are a father, looking for a second wife, you must remember that your new children will have no claim on the property of your children by another wife; and if you should happen to die they might suffer very much—at least, if your wife had no money in her own right. And then the children which you will add to our colony will cost something to bring up. If that fell on us alone, we should surely take care of them without a word of complaint; but the comfort of everybody would suffer, and your eldest children would bear their share of hardship. When families grow too large, if money does not keep pace, misery comes, no matter how bravely you bear up. This is what I wished to say, Germain; think it over, and try to make the widow Guérin like you; for her discretion and her dollars will help us now and make us feel easy about the future."

"That is true, Father. I shall try to please her and to like her."

"To do that you must go to find her, and see her."

"At her own place? At Fourche? That is a great way from here, is it not? And we scarcely have time to run off at this season of the year."

"When it is a question of a love-match you must make up your mind to lose time, but when it is a sensible marriage of two people, who take no sudden fancies and know what they want, it is very soon decided. To-morrow is Saturday; you will make your day's work a little shorter than usual. You must start after dinner about two o'clock. You will be at Fourche by nightfall. The moon rises early. The roads are good, and it is not more than three leagues distant. It is near Magnier. Besides, you will take the mare."

"I had just as lief go afoot in this cool weather."

"Yes, but the mare is pretty, and a suitor looks better when he comes well mounted. You must put on your new clothes and carry a nice present of game to Father Leonard. You will come from me and talk with him, pass all of Sunday with his daughter, and come back Monday morning with a yes or no."

"Very well," answered Germain calmly, and yet he did not feel very calm.

Germain had always lived soberly, as industrious peasants do. Married at twenty, he had loved but one woman in his life, and after her death, impulsive and gay as his nature was, he had never played nor trifled with another. He had borne a real sorrow faithfully in his heart, and it was not without misgiving nor without sadness that he yielded to his father-in-law; but that father had always governed the family wisely, and Germain, entirely devoted as he was to the common welfare and so, by consequence, to the head of the house, who represented it, could not understand that he might have wronged his own good sense and hurt the interests of all. Nevertheless, he was sad. Few days went by when he did not cry in secret, for his wife, and although loneliness began to weigh on him, he was more afraid of entering into a new marriage than desirous of finding a support in his sorrow. He had a vague idea that love might have consoled him by coming to him of a sudden, for this is the only way love can console. We never find it when we seek it; it comes over us unawares.

This cold-blooded scheme of marriage that Father Maurice had opened to him, this unknown woman he was to take for his bride, perhaps even all that had been said to him of her virtue and good sense, made him pause to think. And he went away musing as men do whose thoughts are too few to divide into hostile factions, not scraping up fine arguments for rebellion and selfishness but suffering from a dull grief, submissive to ills from which there is no escape.

Meanwhile, Father Maurice had returned to the farm, while Germain, between sunset and dark, spent the closing hour of the day in repairing gaps the sheep had made in the hedge of a yard near the farm-buildings. He lifted up the branches of the thorn-bushes and held them in place with clods of earth, whilst the thrushes chattered in the neighboring thicket and seemed to call to him to hurry, for they were eager to come and see his work as soon as he had gone.

IV — Mother Guillette

FATHER MAURICE found at his house an old neighbor who had come to talk with his wife, seeking at the same time to secure a few embers to light her fire. Mother Guillette lived in a wretched hut two gunshots away from the farm. Still she was a willing and an orderly woman. Her poor dwelling was clean and neat, and the care with which her clothes were mended showed that she respected herself in the midst of her penury.

"You have come to fetch your evening fire, Mother Guillette," said the old man to her. "Is there anything else you want?"

"No, Father Maurice," answered she; "nothing for the present. I am no beggar, as you know, and I take care not to abuse the kindness of my friends."

"That is very true. Besides, your friends are always ready to do you a service."

"I was just talking to your wife, and I was asking her if Germain had finally decided to marry again."

"You are no gossip," replied Father Maurice; "we can talk in your presence without having any foolish tale-bearing to fear. So I will tell my wife and you that Germain has made up his mind absolutely. To-morrow morning he starts for the farm at Fourche."

"Good enough!" cried Mother Maurice; "poor child! God grant he may find a woman as good and true as he."

"So he is going to Fourche?" remarked Mother Guillette; "how lucky that is! It is exactly what I want. And since you were just asking me if there were anything I wished for, I am going to tell you, Father Maurice, how you can do me a service."

"Tell me what it is; we like to help you."

"I wish Germain would be so kind as to take my daughter along with him."

"Where? To Fourche?"

"No, not to Fourche, but to Ormeaux. She is to stay there the rest of the year."

"What!" exclaimed Mother Maurice, "are you going to separate from your daughter?"

"She must go out to work and earn her living. I am sorry enough, and she is too, poor soul. We could not make up our minds to part Saint John's Day, but now that Saint Martin's is upon us, she finds a good place as shepherdess at the farms at Ormeaux. On his way home from the fair the other day, the farmer passed by here. He caught sight of my little Marie tending her three sheep on the common.

"'You have hardly enough to do, my little girl,' said he; 'three sheep are not enough for a shepherdess: would you like to take care of a hundred? I will take you along. Our shepherdess has fallen sick. She is going back to her family, and if you will be at our farm before a week is over, you shall have fifty francs for the rest of the year up to Saint John's Day.'

"The child refused, but she could not help thinking it over and telling me about it, when she came home in the evening, and found me downhearted and worried about the winter, which was sure to be hard and long; for this year the cranes and wild ducks were seen crossing the sky a whole month before they generally do. We both of us cried, but after a time we took heart. We knew that we could not stay together, since it is hard enough for one person to get a living from our little patch of ground. Then since Marie is old enough,—for she is going on to sixteen,—she must do like the rest, earn her own living and help her poor mother."

"Mother Guillette," said the old laborer, "if it were only fifty francs you needed to help you out of your trouble, and save you from sending away your daughter, I should certainly find them for you, although fifty francs is no trifle for people like us. But in everything we must consult common sense as well as friendship. To be saved from want this year will not keep you from want in the future, and the longer your daughter takes to make up her mind, the harder you both will find it to part. Little Marie is growing tall and strong. She has not enough at home to keep her busy. She might get into lazy habits..."

"Oh, I am not afraid of that!" exclaimed Mother Guillette. "Marie is as active as a rich girl at the head of a large family can be. She never sits still with her arms folded for an instant, and when we have no work to do, she keeps dusting and polishing our old furniture until it shines like a mirror. The child is worth her weight in gold, and I should much rather have her enter your service as a shepherdess than go so far away to people I don't know. You would have taken her at Saint John's Day; but now you have hired all your hands, and we cannot think of that till Saint John's Day next year."

"Yes, I consent with all my heart, Guillette. I shall be very glad to take her. But in the mean time she will do well to learn her work, and accustom herself to obey others."

"Yes, that is true, no doubt. The die is cast. The farmer at Ormeaux sent to ask about her this morning; we consented, and she must go. But the poor child does not know the way, and I should not like to send her so far alone. Since your son-in-law goes to Fourche to-morrow, perhaps he can take her. It seems that Fourche is close to her journey's end. At least, so they tell me, for I have never made the trip myself."

"It is very near indeed, and my son will show her the way. Naturally, he might even take her up behind him on the mare. That will save her shoes. Here he comes for supper. Tell me, Germain, Mother Guillette's little Marie is going to become a shepherdess at Ormeaux. Will you take her there on your horse?"

"Certainly," answered Germain, who, troubled as he was, never felt indisposed to do a kindness to his neighbor.

In our community a mother would not think of such a thing as to trust a girl of sixteen to a man of twenty-eight. For Germain was really but twenty-eight, and although according to the notions of the country people he was considered rather old to marry, he was still the best-looking man in the neighborhood. Toil had not wrinkled and worn him as it does most peasants who have passed ten years in tilling the soil. He was strong enough to labor for ten more years without showing signs of age, and the prejudices of her time must have weighed heavily on the mind of a young girl to prevent her from seeing that Germain had a fresh complexion, eyes sparkling and blue as skies in May, ruddy lips, fine teeth, and a body well shaped and lithe as a young horse that has never yet left his pasture.

But purity of manners is a sacred custom in some districts far distant from the corrupted life of great cities, and amongst all the households of Belair, the family of Maurice was known to be honest and truth-loving. Germain was on his way to find a wife. Marie was a child, too young and too poor to be thought of in this light, and unless he were a heartless and a bad man he could not entertain one evil thought concerning her. Father Maurice felt no uneasiness at seeing him take the pretty girl on the crupper. Mother Guillette would have thought herself doing him a wrong had she asked him to respect her daughter as his sister. Marie embraced her mother and her young friends twenty times, and then mounted the mare in tears. Germain, sad on his own account, felt all the more sympathy for her sorrow, and rode away with a melancholy air, while all the people of the neighborhood waved good-by to Marie without a thought of harm.

V — Petit-Pierre

THE gray was young, good-looking, and strong. She carried her double burden with ease, laying back her ears and champing her bit like the high-spirited mare she was. Passing in front of the pasture, she caught sight of her mother, whose name was the Old Gray as hers was the Young Gray, and she whinnied in token of good-by. The Old Gray came nearer the hedge, and striking her shoes together she tried to gallop along the edge of the field in order to follow her daughter; then seeing her fall into a sharp trot, the mare whinnied in her turn and stood in an uneasy attitude, her nose in the air and her mouth filled with grass that she had no thought of eating.

"That poor beast always knows her offspring," said Germain, trying to keep Marie's thoughts from her troubles. "That reminds me, I never kissed Petit-Pierre before I started. The naughty boy was not there. Last night he wished to make me promise to take him along, and he wept for an hour in bed. This morning again, he tried everything to persuade me. Oh, how sly and coaxing he is! But when he saw that he could not gain his point, the young gentleman got into a temper. He went off to the fields, and I have not seen him all day."

"I have seen him," said little Marie, striving to keep back her tears; "he was running toward the clearing with Soulas' children, and I felt sure that he had been away from home a long time, for he was hungry and was eating wild plums and blackberries. I gave him the bread I had for lunch, and he said, 'Thank you, dear Marie; when you come to our house, I will give you some cake.' He is a dear little child, Germain."

"Yes, he is," answered the laborer; "and there is nothing I would not do for him. If his grandmother had not more sense than I, I could not have helped taking him with me, when I saw him crying as though his poor little heart would burst."

"Then why did you not take him, Germain? He, would have been very little trouble. He is so good when you please him."

"He would probably have been in the way in the place where I am going. At least Father Maurice thought so. On the other hand, I should have thought it well to see how they received him. For no one could help being kind to such a nice child. But at home they said that I must not begin by showing off all the cares of the household. I don't know why I speak of this to you, little Marie; you can't understand."

"Oh, yes, I do; I know that you are going away to marry; my mother spoke to me about it, and told me not to mention it to a soul, either at home or at my destination, and you need not be afraid; I shall not breathe a word about it."

"You are very right. For the deed isn't done yet. Perhaps I shall not suit this woman."

"I hope you will, Germain; why should you not suit her?"

"Who knows? I have three children, and that is a heavy burden for a woman who is not their mother."

"Very true. But are not your children like other children?"

"Do you think so?"

"They are lovely as little angels, and so well brought up that you can't find better children."

"There 's Sylvain. He is none too obedient."

"He is so very little. He can't help being naughty. But he is very bright."

"He is bright it is true, and very brave. He is not afraid of cows nor bulls, and if he were given his own way, he would be climbing on horseback already with his elder brother."

"Had I been in your place, I would have taken the eldest boy along. Surely people would have liked you at once for having such a pretty child."

"Yes, if a woman is fond of children. But if she is not."

"Are there women who don't love children?"

"Not many, I think, but still there are some, and that is what troubles me."

"You don't know this woman at all, then?"

"No more than you, and I fear that I shall not know her better after I have seen her. I am not suspicious. When people say nice things to me, I believe them, but more than once I have had good reason to repent, for words are not deeds."

"They say that she is a very good woman."

"Who says so? Father Maurice?"

"Yes, your father-in-law."

"That is all very well. But he knows her no more than I."

"Well, you will soon see. Pay close attention, and let us hope that you will not be deceived."

"I have it. Little Marie, I should be very much obliged if you would come into the house for a minute before you go straight on to Ormeaux. You are quick-witted; you have always shown that you are not stupid, and nothing escapes your notice. Should you see anything to rouse your suspicions, you must warn me of it very quietly."

"Oh! no, Germain, I will not do that; I should be too much afraid of making a mistake; and, besides, if a word lightly spoken were to turn you against this marriage, your family would bear me a grudge, and I have plenty of troubles now without bringing any more on my poor dear mother."

As they were talking thus, the gray pricked up her ears and shied; then returning on her steps, she approached the bushes, where she began to recognize something which had frightened her at first. Germain cast his eye over the thicket, and in a ditch, beneath the branches of a scrub-oak, still thick and green, he saw something which he took for a lamb.

"The little creature is strayed or dead, for it does not move. Perhaps some one is looking for it; we must see."

"It is not an animal," cried little Marie; "it is a sleeping child. It is your Petit-Pierre."

"Heavens!" exclaimed Germain; "see the little scamp asleep so far away from home, and in a ditch where a snake might bite him!"

He lifted up the child, who smiled as he opened his eyes and threw his arms about his father's neck, saying: "Dear little father, you are going to take me with you."

"Oh, yes; always the same tune. What were you doing there, you naughty Pierre?"

"I was waiting for my little father to go by. I was watching the road, and I watched so hard that I fell asleep."

"And if I had passed by without seeing you, you would have been out of doors all night, and a wolf would have eaten you up."

"Oh, I knew very well that you would see me," answered Petit-Pierre, confidently.

"Well, kiss me now, bid me good-by, and run back quickly to the house, unless you wish them to have supper without you."

"Are you not going to take me, then?" cried the little boy, beginning to rub his eyes to show that he was thinking of tears.

"You know very well that grandpapa and grand-mama do not wish it," said Germain, fortifying himself behind the authority of his elders, like a man who distrusts his own.

The child would not listen. He began to cry with all his might, saying that as long as his father was taking little Marie, he might just as well take him too. They replied that they must pass through great woods filled with wicked beasts who eat up little children. The gray would not carry three people; she had said so when they were starting, and in the country where they were going there was no bed and no supper for little boys. All these good reasons could not persuade Petit-Pierre; he threw himself on the ground, and rolled about, shrieking that his little father did not love him any more, and that if he did not take him he would never go back to the house at all, day or night.

Germain had a father's heart, as soft and weak as a woman's. His-wife's death, and the care which he had been obliged to bestow all alone on his little ones, as well as the thought that these poor motherless children needed a great deal of love, combined to make him thus. So such a sharp struggle went on within him, all the more because he was ashamed of his weakness and tried to hide his confusion from little Marie, that the sweat started out on his forehead, and his eyes grew red and almost ready to weep. At last he tried to get angry, but as he turned toward little Marie in order to let her witness his strength of mind, he saw that the good girls face was wet with tears; all his courage forsook him and he could not keep back his own, scold and threaten as he would.

"Truly your heart is too hard," said little Marie at last, "and for myself I know that I never could refuse a child who felt so badly. Come, Germain, let 's take him. Your mare is well used to carrying two people and a child, for you know that your brother-in-law and his wife, who is much heavier than I, go to market every Saturday with their boy on this good beast's back. Take him on the horse in front of you. Besides, I should rather walk on foot all alone than give this little boy so much pain."

"Never mind," answered Germain, who was dying to allow himself to give way. "The gray is strong, and could carry two more if there were room on her back. But what can we do with this child on the way? He will be cold and hungry, and who will take care of him to-night and tomorrow, put him to bed, wash him, and dress him? I don't dare give this trouble to a woman I don't know, who will think, doubtless, that I am exceedingly free and easy with her to begin with."

"Trust me, Germain, you will know her at once by the kindness or the impatience that she shows. If she does not care to receive your Pierre, I will take charge of him myself. I will go to her house and dress him, and I will take him to the fields with me to-morrow. I will amuse him all day long, and take good care that he does not want for anything."

"He will tire you, my poor girl, and give you trouble. A whole day is a long time."

"Not at all; it will give me pleasure; he will keep me company, and that will make me less sad the first day that I must pass in a new place. I shall fancy that I am still at home."

Seeing that little Marie was pleading for her, the child seized upon her skirt and held it so tight that they must have hurt him in order to tear it away. When he perceived that his father was weakening, he took Marie's hand in both his tiny sunburned fists and kissed her, leaping for joy, and pulling her toward the mare with the burning impatience children feel in their desires.

"Come along," said the young girl, lifting him in her arms; "let us try to quiet his poor little heart. It is fluttering like a little bird; and if you feel the cold when night comes on, tell me, my Pierre, and I will wrap you in my cape. Kiss your little father, and beg his pardon for being naughty. Tell him that you will never, never be so again. Do you hear?"

"Yes, yes, provided that I always do just as he wishes. Isn't it so?" said Germain, drying the little boy's eyes with his handkerchief. "Marie, you are spoiling the little rascal. But really and truly, you are too good, little Marie. I don't know why you did not come to us as shepherdess last Saint John's Day. You would have taken care of my children, and I should much rather pay a good price for their sake than try to find a woman who will think, perhaps, she is doing me a great kindness if she does not detest them."

"You must not look on the dark side of things," answered little Marie, holding the horse's bridle while Germain placed his son in front of the big pack-saddle covered with goatskin. "If your wife does not care for children, take me into your service next year, and you may be sure I shall amuse them so well that they will not notice anything."

VI — On the Heath

"DEAR ME," said Germain, after they had gone a few steps farther, "what will they think at home when they miss the little man? The family will be worried, and will be looking everywhere for him."

"You can tell the man who is mending the road up there that you are taking him along, and ask him to speak to your people."

"That is very true, Marie; you don't forget anything. It never occurred to me that Jeannie must be there."

"He lives close to the farm, and he will not fail to do your errand."

When they had taken this precaution, Germain put the mare to a trot, and Petit-Pierre was so overjoyed that for a time he forgot that he had gone without his dinner; but the motion of the horse gave him a hollow feeling in his stomach, and at the end of a league, he began to gape and grow pale, and confessed that he was dying of hunger.

"This is the way it begins," exclaimed Germain. "I was quite sure that we should not go far without this young gentleman crying with hunger or thirst."

"I am thirsty, too!" said Petit-Pierre.

"Very well, then, let 's go to Mother Rebec's tavern at Corlay, the sign of 'The Dawn'—a pretty sign, but a poor lodging. You will take something to drink, too, will you not, Marie?"

"No, no; I don't want anything. I will hold the mare while you go in with the child."

"But I remember, my good girl, that this morning you gave the bread from your own breakfast to my Pierre. You have had nothing to eat. You would not take dinner with us at home; you would do nothing but cry."

"Oh, I was not hungry; I felt too sad, and I give you my word that even now I have no desire to eat."

"You must oblige yourself to eat, little girl, else you will fall sick. We have a long way to go, and it will not do to arrive half-starved and beg for bread before we say how d' ye do. I shall set you a good example myself, although I am not very hungry: and I am sure that I can, for, after all, I did not eat any dinner. I saw you crying, you and your mother, and it made me feel sad. Come along. I am going to tie the gray at the door. Get down; I wish you to."

All three entered the inn, and in less than fifteen minutes the fat, lame hostess was able to place before them a nice-looking omelette, some brown bread, and a bottle of light wine.

VI — On the Heath

Peasants do not eat quickly, and little Pierre had such a good appetite that a whole hour passed before Germain could think of starting out again. At first little Marie ate in order to be obliging; then little by little she grew hungry. For, at sixteen, a girl cannot fast for long, and country air is dictatorial.

The kind words with which Germain knew how to comfort her and strengthen her courage, produced their effect. She tried hard to persuade herself that seven months would soon be over, and to think of the pleasure in store for her when she saw once more her family and her hamlet; for Father Maurice and Germain had both promised to take her into their service. But just as she began to cheer up and play with little Pierre, Germain was so unfortunate as to point out to her from the inn window the lovely view of the valley which can all be seen from this height, and which looks so happy and green and fertile.

Marie looked and asked if the houses of Belair were in sight.

"No doubt," said Germain, "and the farm, too, and even your house—see! that tiny gray spot not far from Godard's big poplar, below the belfry."

"Ah, I see it," said the little girl; and then she began to cry.

"I ought not to have made you think of it," said Germain. "I can do nothing but stupid things today. Come along, Marie; let 's start, and in an hour, when the moon rises, it will not be hot."

They resumed their journey across the great heath, and for fear of tiring the young girl and the child by too rapid a trot, Germain did not make the gray go very fast. The sun had set when they left the road to enter the wood.

Germain knew the way as far as Magnier, but he thought it would be shorter to avoid the Chantaloube road and descend by Presles and La Sépulture, a route he was not in the habit of taking on his way to the fair. He lost his way, and wasted more time before he reached the wood. Even then he did not enter it on the right side, although he did not perceive his mistake, so that he turned his back on Fourche, and took a direction higher up on the way to Ardente.

He was prevented still further from finding his way by a thick mist which rose as the night fell; one of those mists which come on autumn evenings when the whiteness of the moonlight renders them more undefined and more treacherous. The great pools of water scattered through the glades gave forth a vapor so dense that when the gray crossed them, their presence was known only by a splashing noise, and the difficulty with which she drew her feet from the mud.

At last they found a good straight road, and when they came to the end of it, and Germain tried to discover where he was, he saw that he was lost. For Father Maurice had told him, when he explained the way, that on leaving the wood he must descend a very steep hillside, cross a wide meadow, and ford the river twice. He had even warned him to cross this river carefully; for, early in the season, there had been great rains, and the water might still be higher than usual. Seeing neither hillside nor meadows, nor river, but a heath, level and white as a mantle of snow, Germain stopped, looked about for a house, and waited for a passer-by, but could find nothing to set him right. Then he retraced his steps and reentered the wood. But the mist thickened yet more, the moon was completely hidden, the roads were execrable, and the quagmires deep. Twice the gray almost fell. Her heavy load made her lose courage, and although she kept enough sagacity to avoid the tree-trunks, she could not prevent her riders from striking the great branches which overhung the road at the height of their heads and caused them great danger. In one of these collisions Germain lost his hat, and only recovered it after much difficulty. Petit-Pierre had fallen asleep, and, lying like a log in his father's arms, hampered him so that he could no longer hold up nor direct the horse.

"I believe we are bewitched," exclaimed Germain, stopping; "for the wood is not large enough to get lost in, if a man is not drunk, and here we have been turning round and round for two hours at least, without finding a way out. The gray has but one idea in her head, and that is to get home. It is she who is deceiving me. If we wish to go home, we have only to give her the bit. But when we are perhaps but two steps from our journey's end, it would be foolish to give up and return such a long road; and yet I am at a loss what to do. I can't see sky or earth, and I am afraid that the child will catch the fever if we remain in this cursed fog, or that he will be crushed beneath our weight if the horse falls forward."

"We must not persist longer," said little Marie. "Let 's dismount, Germain. Give me the child; I can carry him perfectly well, and I know better than you how to keep the cloak from falling open and leaving him exposed. You lead the mare by her bridle. Perhaps we shall see more clearly when we are nearer the ground."

This precaution was of service only in saving them from a fall, for the fog hung low and seemed to stick to the damp earth.

Their advance was painfully slow, and they were soon so weary that they halted when they reached a dry spot beneath the great oaks.

Little Marie was in a violent sweat, but she uttered not a word of complaint, nor did she worry about anything. Thinking only of the child, she sat down on the sand and laid it upon her knees, while Germain explored the neighborhood, after having fastened the gray's reins to the branch of a tree.

But the gray was very dissatisfied with the journey. She reared suddenly, broke the reins loose, burst her girths, and giving, by way of receipt, half a dozen kicks higher than her head, she started across the clearing, showing very plainly that she needed no one to show her the way home.

"Well, here we are afoot," said Germain, after a vain attempt to catch the horse, "and it would do us no good now if we were on the good road, for we should have to ford the river on foot, and since these paths are filled with water, we may be sure that the meadow is wholly submerged. We don't know the other routes. We must wait until this fog clears. It can't last more than an hour or two; as soon as we can see clearly, we shall look about for a house, the first we come to near the edge of the wood. But for the present we can't stir from here. There is a ditch and a pond over there. Heaven knows what is in front of us, and what is behind us is more than I can say now, for I have forgotten which way we came."

VII — Underneath the Big Oaks

"WELL, we must be patient, Germain," said little Marie. "We are not badly off on this little hillock. The rain does not pierce the leaves of these big oaks, and we can light a fire, for I can feel old stumps which stir readily and are dry enough to burn. You have a light, Germain, have you not? You were smoking your pipe a few minutes ago."

"I did have; my tinderbox was in my bag on the saddle with the game that I was bringing to my bride that is to be, but that devilish mare has run away with everything, even with my cloak, which she will lose and tear to bits on every branch she comes to." "No, no, Germain; saddle and cloak and bag are all there on the ground at your feet. The gray burst her girths, and threw off everything as she ran away."

"That's true, thank God," exclaimed the laborer; "if we can grope about and find a little dead wood, we shall be able to dry ourselves and get warm."

"That's not difficult," said little Marie; "dead wood always cracks when you step on it. But will you give me the saddle?"

"What do you want of it?"

"To make a bed for the child. No, not that way. Upside down. He will not roll off into the hollow, and it is still very warm from the horse's back. Prop it up all around with the stones that you see there."

"I can't see a stone; you must have cat's eyes."

"There, it is all done, Germain. Hand me your cloak so that you can wrap up his little feet, and throw my cape over his body. Just see if he is not as comfortable as though he were in his own bed, and feel how warm he is."

"You certainly know how to take care of children, Marie."

"I need not be a witch to do that; now get your tinderbox from your bag, and I will arrange the wood."

"This wood will never catch fire; it is too damp."

"You are always doubting, Germain. Don't you remember when you were a shepherd, and made big fires in the fields right in the midst of the rain?"

"Yes, that is a knack that belongs to children who take care of sheep; but I was made to drive the oxen as soon as I could walk."

"That is what has made your arms strong and your hands quick! Here, the fire is built; you shall see whether it does not burn. Give me the light and a handful of dry ferns. That is all right Now blow; you are not consumptive, are you?"

"Not that I know of," said Germain, blowing like a smith's bellows. In an instant the flame leaped up, and throwing out a red glare, it rose finally in pale blue jets under the oak branches, battling with the fog, and gradually drying the atmosphere for ten feet around.

"Now I am going to sit by the child, so that the sparks may not fall on him," said the young girl. "Pile on the wood and stir up the fire, Germain; we shall not catch cold nor fever here, I will answer for it."

"Upon my word, you are a clever girl," said Germain; "and you know how to make a fire like a little fairy of the night. I feel quite revived, and my courage has come back again; for with my legs drenched up to the knees, and with the thought of staying this way till daylight, I was in a very bad temper just now."

"And when people are in a bad temper they don't think of anything," answered little Marie.

"And are you never bad-tempered?"

"No, never; what is the good of it?"

"Oh, of course, there is no good; but how can you help it when you have troubles? Yet Heaven knows that you have not lacked them, my little girl; for you have not always been happy."

"It is true that my mother and I have suffered. We have had sorrows, but we have never lost heart."

"I should never lose heart, no matter how hard my work was," said Germain, "but poverty would make me very sad; for I have never wanted for anything. My wife made me rich, and I am rich still; I shall be so as long as I work on the farm; and that will be always, I hope. But everybody must suffer his share! I have suffered in another way."

"Yes; you have lost your wife. That is very sad."

"Isn't it?"

"Oh! Germain, I have wept for her many a time. She was so very kind! But don't let us talk about her longer, for I shall burst out crying. All my troubles are ready to come back to me to-day."

"It is true, she loved you dearly, little Marie. She used to make a great deal of you and your mother. Are you crying? Come, my girl, I don't want to cry...."

"But you are crying, Germain! You are crying as hard as I. Why should a man be ashamed to weep for his wife? Don't let me trouble you. That sorrow is mine as well as yours."

"You have a kind heart, Marie, and it does me good to weep with you. Put your feet nearer the fire; your skirts are all soaked, too, poor little girl. I am going to take your place by the boy. You move nearer the fire."

"I am hot enough," said Marie; "and if you wish to sit down, take a corner of the cloak. I am perfectly comfortable."

"The truth is that it is not so bad here," said Germain, as he sat down beside her. "Only I feel very hungry again. It is almost nine o'clock, and I have had such hard work in walking over these vile roads that I feel quite tired out. Are you not hungry, too, little Marie?"

"I?—not at all. I am not accustomed like you to four meals a day, and I have been to bed so often without my supper that once more does not trouble me."

"A woman like you is very convenient; she costs nothing," said Germain, smiling.

"I am not a woman," exclaimed Marie, naïvely, without perceiving the direction the husbandman's ideas had taken. "Are you dreaming?"

"Yes, I believe I must be dreaming," answered Germain. "Perhaps hunger is making my mind wander."

"How greedy you are," answered she, brightening in her turn. "Well, if you can't live five or six hours without eating, have you not game in your bag and fire to cook it?"

"By Jove, that's a good idea! But how about the present to my future father-in-law?"

"You have six partridges and a hare! I suppose you do not need all of them to satisfy your appetite."

"But how can we cook them without a spit or andirons. They will be burned to a cinder!"

"Not at all," said little Marie; "I warrant that I can cook them for you under the cinders without a taste of smoke. Have you never caught larks in the fields, and cooked them between two stones? Oh! that is true—I keep forgetting that you have never been a shepherd. Come, pluck the partridge. Not so hard! You will tear the skin."

"You might be plucking the other to show me how!"

"Then you wish to eat two? What an ogre you are! They are all plucked. I am going to cook them."

"You would make a perfect little sutler's girl, Marie, but unhappily you have no canteen, and I shall have to drink water from this pool!"

"You would like some wine, would you not? Possibly you might prefer coffee. You imagine yourself under the trees at the fair. Call out the host. Some wine for the good husbandman of Belair!"

"You little witch, you are making fun of me! Would not you drink some wine if you had it?"

"I? At Mother Rebec's, with you to-night, I drank some for the second time in my life. But if you are very good, I shall give you a bottle almost full, and excellent too."

"What? Marie, I verily believe you are a witch!"

"Were you not foolish enough to ask for two bottles of wine at the inn? You and your boy drank one, and the other you set before me. I hardly drank three drops, yet you paid for both without looking."

"What then?"

"Why, I put the full one in my basket, because I thought that you or your child would be thirsty on the journey. And here it is."

"You are the most thoughtful girl I have ever met. Although the poor child was crying when we left the inn, that did not prevent her from thinking of others more than of herself. Little Marie, the man who marries you will be no fool."

"I hope not, for I am not fond of fools. Come, eat up your partridges; they are done to a turn; and for want of bread, you must be satisfied with chestnuts."

"Where the deuce did you find chestnuts, too?"

"It is extraordinary! All along the road I picked them off the branches as we went along, and filled my pockets."

"And are they cooked, too?"

"Where would my wits have been had I not had sense enough to put the chestnuts in the fire as soon as it was lighted? That is the way we always do in the fields."

"So we are going to take supper together, little Marie. I want to drink your health and wish you a good husband, just the sort of a man that will suit you. Tell me what kind you want."

"I should find that very difficult, Germain, for I have not thought about it yet."

"What, not at all? Never?" said Germain, as he began to eat with a laborer's appetite, yet stopping to cut off the more tender morsels for his companion, who persisted in refusing them and contented herself with a few chestnuts.

"Tell me, little Marie," he went on, seeing that she had no intention of answering him, "have you never thought of marrying? Yet you are old enough?"

"Perhaps," she said, "but I am too poor. I need at least a hundred crowns to marry, and I must work five or six years to scrape them together."

"Poor girl, I wish Father Maurice were willing to give me a hundred crowns to make you a present of."

"Thank you kindly, Germain. What do you suppose people would say of me?"

"What do you wish them to say of you? They know very well that I am too old to marry you. They would never believe that I—that you—"

"Look, Germain, your child is waking up," said little Marie.

VIII — The Evening Prayer

PETIT-PIERRE had raised his head and was looking about him with a thoughtful air.

"Oh, that is the way he always does, whenever he hears the sound of eating," said Germain. "The explosion of a cannon would not rouse him, but if you work your jaws near him, he opens his eyes at once."

"You must have been just like him at his age," said little Marie, with a sly smile. "See! my Petit-Pierre, you are looking for your canopy. To-night it is made all of green, my child; but your father eats his supper none the less. Do you wish to sup with him? I have not eaten your share; I thought that you might claim it."

"Marie, I wish you to eat," cried the husbandman; "I shall not touch another morsel. I am a greedy glutton. You are depriving yourself for our sake. It is not fair. I am ashamed. It takes away all my appetite. I will not have my son eat his supper unless you take some too."

"Leave us alone," said little Marie; "you have not the key to our appetites. Mine is tight shut to-day, but your Pierre's is as wide open as a little wolfs. Just see how he seizes his food. He will be a strong workman too, some day!"

In truth, Petit-Pierre showed very soon whose son he was, and though scarcely awake and wholly at a loss to know where he was and how he had come there, he began to eat ravenously. As soon as his hunger was appeased, feeling excited as children do who break loose from their wonted habits, he had more wit, more curiosity, and more good sense than usual. He made them explain to him where he was, and when he found that he was in the midst of a forest, he grew a little frightened.

"Are there wicked beasts in this forest?" he demanded of his father.

"No, none at all. Don't be afraid."

"Then you told a story when you said that if I went with you into the great forest, the wolves would carry me off."

"Just see this logician," said Germain, embarrassed.

"He is right," replied little Marie. "That is what you told him. He has a good memory, and has not forgotten. But, little Pierre, you must learn that your father never tells a story. We passed through the big forest whilst you were sleeping, and now we are in the small forest where there are no wicked beasts."

"Is the little forest very far away from the big one?"

"Far enough; besides, the wolves never go out of the big forest. And then, if some of them should come here, your father would kill them."

"And you too, little Marie?"

"Yes, we, too, for you would help also, my Pierre. You are not frightened, are you? You would beat them soundly?"

"Yes, indeed, I would," said the child, proudly, as he struck a heroic attitude; "we would kill them."

"There is nobody like you for talking to children and for making them listen to reason," said Germain to little Marie. "To be sure, it is not long ago since you were a small child yourself, and you have not forgotten what your mother used to say to you. I believe that the younger one is, the better one gets on with children. I am very much afraid that a woman of thirty who does not yet know what it is to be a mother, would find it hard to prattle to children and reason with them."

"Why, Germain? I don't know why you have such a bad idea of this woman; you will change your mind."

"The devil take the woman!" exclaimed Germain. "I wish I were going away from her forever. What do I want of a wife whom I don't know?"

"Little father," said the child, "why is it that you speak so much of your wife to-day, since she is dead?"

"Then you have not forgotten your poor, dear mother?"

"No; for I saw her placed in a beautiful box of white wood, and my grandmother led me up to her to kiss her and say good-by. She was very white and very stiff, and every evening my aunt made me pray God that she might go to him in Heaven and be warm. Do you think that she is there now?"

"I hope so, my child; but you must always pray. It shows your mother that you love her."

"I am going to say my prayers," answered the boy. "I forgot them to-night. But I can't say them all alone, for I always forget something. Little Marie must help me."

"Yes, my Pierre, I will help you," said the young girl. "Come and kneel down in my lap."

The child knelt down on the girl's skirt. He clasped his little hands and began to say his prayers, at first with great care and earnestness, for he knew the beginning very well, then slowly and with more hesitation, and finally repeating word by word after Marie, when he came to that place in his prayer where sleep overtook him so invariably that he had never been able to learn the end. This time again the effort of close attention and the monotony of his own accent produced their wonted effect. He pronounced the last syllables with great difficulty, and only after they were thrice repeated.

His head grew heavy and fell on Marie's breast; his hands unclasped, divided, and fell open on his knees. By the light of the camp-fire, Germain watched his little darling hushed at the heart of the young girl, who, as she held him in her arms and warmed his fair hair with her sweet breath, had herself fallen into a holy reverie, and prayed in quiet for the soul of Catherine.

Germain was touched. He tried to express to little Marie the grateful esteem which he felt for her, but he could find no fitting words.

He approached her to kiss his son, whom she held close to her breast, and he could scarcely raise his lips from little Pierre's brow.

"You kiss too hard," said Marie, gently pushing away the husbandman's head. "You will wake him. Let me put him back to bed, for the boy has left us already for dreams of paradise."

The child allowed Marie to lay him down, but feeling the goatskin on the saddle, he asked if he were on the gray. Then opening his big blue eyes, and keeping them fixed on the branches for a minute, he seemed to be dreaming, wide-awake as he was, or to be struck with an idea which had slipped his mind during the daytime, and only assumed a distinct form at the approach of sleep.

"Little father," said he, "if you wish to give me a new mother, I hope it will be little Marie."

And without waiting for an answer, he closed his eyes and slept.

IX — Despite the Cold

LITTLE MARIE seemed to give no more heed to the child's odd words than to regard them as a proof of friendship. She wrapped him up with care, stirred the fire, and as the fog resting on the neighboring pool gave no sign of lifting, she advised Germain to lie near the fire and take a nap.

"I see that you are sleepy already," said she, "for you don't say a word and you gaze into the fire, just as your little boy was doing."

"It is you who must sleep," answered the husbandman, "and I will take care of both of you, for I have never felt less sleepy than I do now. I have fifty things to think of."

"Fifty is a great many," said the little girl, with a mocking accent. "There are lots of people who would be delighted to have one."

"Well, if I am too stupid to have fifty, I have one, at least, which has not left me for the past hour."

"And I shall tell it to you as well as I told you those you thought of before."

"Yes, do tell me if you know, Marie. Tell me yourself. I shall be glad to hear."

"An hour ago," she answered, "your idea was to eat—and now it is to sleep."

"Marie, I am only an ox-driver, but, upon my word, you take me for an ox. You are very perverse, and it is easy to see that you do not care to talk to me, so go to sleep. That will be better than to pick flaws in a man who is out of sorts."

"If you wish to talk, let 's talk," said the girl, half reclining near the child and resting her head against the saddle. "You torment yourself, Germain, and you do not show much courage for a man. What would n't I say if I did n't do my best to fight my own troubles?"

"Yes, that's very true, and that's just what I am thinking of, my poor child. You are going to live, away from your friends, in a horrid country full of moors and fens, where you will catch the autumn fevers. Sheep do not pay well there, and this is always discouraging for a shepherdess if she means well. Then you will be surrounded by strangers who may not be kind to you and will not know how much you are worth. It makes me more sorry than I can tell you, and I have a great desire to take you home to your mother instead of going on to Fourche."

"You talk very kindly, but there is no reason for your misgivings, my poor Germain. You ought not to lose heart on your friend's account, and instead of showing me the dark side of my lot, you should show me the bright side, as you did after lunch at Rebec's."

"What can I do? That's the way it appeared to me then, and now my ideas are changed. It is best for you to take a husband."

"That cannot be, Germain, and as it is out of the question, I think no more about it."

"Yet such a thing might happen. Perhaps if you told me what kind of a man you want, I might imagine somebody."

"Imagining is not finding. For myself, I never imagine, for it does no good."

"You are not looking for a rich man?"

"Certainly not, for I am as poor as Job."

"But if he were comfortably off, you would n't be sorry to have a good house, and good food, and good clothes, and to live with an honest family who would allow you to help your mother."

"Oh, yes indeed! It is my own wish to help my mother."

"And if this man were to turn up, you would not be too hard to please, even if he were not so very young."

"Ah! There you must excuse me, Germain. That is just the point I insist on. I could never love an old man."

"An old man, of course not; but a man of my age, for example!"

"Your age is too old for me, Germain. I should like Bastien's age, though Bastien is not so good-looking as you."

"Should you rather have Bastien, the swineherd?" said Germain, indignantly. "A fellow with eyes shaped like those of the pigs he drives!"

"I could excuse his eyes, because he is eighteen."

Germain felt terribly jealous.

"Well," said he, "it's clear that you want Bastien, but, none the less, it's a queer idea."

"Yes, that would be a queer idea," answered little Marie, bursting into shouts of laughter, "and he would make a queer husband. You could gull him to your heart's content. For instance, the other day, I had picked up a tomato in the curate's garden. I told him that it was a fine, red apple, and he bit into it like a glutton. If you had only seen what a face he made. Heavens! how ugly he was!"

"Then you don't love him, since you are making fun of him."

"That would n't be a reason. But I don't like him. He is unkind to his little sister, and he is dirty." "Don't you care for anybody else?" "How does that concern you, Germain?" "Not at all, except that it gives me something to talk about. I see very well, little girl, that you have a sweetheart in your mind already."

"No, Germain, you 're wrong. I have no sweetheart yet. Perhaps one may come later, but since I cannot marry until I have something laid by, I am destined to marry late in life and with an old man." "Then take an old man without delay." "No. When I am no longer young, I shall not care; for the present, it is different." "I see that I displease you, Marie; that's clear enough," said Germain, impatiently, and without stopping to weigh his words.

Little Marie did not answer. Germain bent over her. She was sleeping. She had fallen back, overcome, stricken down, as it were, by slumber, as children are who sleep before they cease to babble.

Germain was glad that she had not caught his last words. He felt that they were unwise, and he turned his back to distract his attention and change his thoughts.

It was all in vain. He could neither sleep nor think of anything except the words he had just spoken. He walked about the fire twenty times; he moved away; he came back. At last, feeling himself tremble as though he had swallowed gunpowder, he leaned against the tree which sheltered the two children, and watched them as they slept.

"I know not how it is," thought he; "I have never noticed that little Marie is the prettiest girl in the countryside. She has not much color, but her little face is fresh as a wild rose. What a charming mouth she has, and how pretty her little nose is! She is not large for her age, but she is formed like a little quail and is as light as a bird. I cannot understand why they made so much fuss at home over a big, fat woman with a bright red face. My wife was rather slender and pale, and she pleased me more than any one else. This girl is very frail, but she is healthy, and she is pretty to watch as a white kid. And then she has such a gentle, frank expression. You can read her good heart in her eyes even though they are closed in sleep. As to wit, I must confess she has more than ever my dear Catherine had, and she would never become wearisome. She is gay, wise, industrious, loving, and she is amusing. I don't know what more I could wish for....

"But what is the use of thinking of all this?" Germain went on, trying to look in another direction. "My father-in-law would not hear of it, and all the family would think me mad! Besides, she would not have me herself, poor child! She thinks me too old; she told me so. She is unselfish, and does not mind poverty and worry, wearing old clothes, and suffering from hunger for two or three months every year, so long as she can satisfy her heart some day and give herself to the man she loves. She is right. I should do the same in her place, and even now, if I had my own way, instead of marrying a wife whom I don't care for, I would choose a girl after my own heart."

The more Germain tried to compose himself by reasoning, the further he was from succeeding. He walked away a dozen steps, to lose himself in the fog; then, all of a sudden, he found himself on his knees beside the two sleeping children. Once he wished to kiss Petit-Pierre, who had one arm about Marie's neck, and made such a mistake that Marie felt a breath, hot as fire, cross her lips, and awaking, looked about her with a bewildered expression, totally ignorant of all that was passing within his mind.

"I did n't see you, my poor children," said Germain, retreating rapidly. "I almost stumbled over you and hurt you."

Little Marie was so innocent that she believed him, and fell asleep again. Germain walked to the opposite side of the fire, and swore to God that he would not stir until she had waked. He kept his word, but not without a struggle. He thought that he would go mad.

At length, toward midnight, the fog lifted, and Germain could see the stars shining through the trees. The moon freed herself from the mist which had hidden her, and began to sow her diamonds over the damp moss. The trunks of the oak-trees remained in impressive darkness, but beyond, the white branches of the birch-trees seemed a long line of phantoms in their shrouds. The fire cast its reflection in the pool; and the frogs, growing accustomed to the light, hazarded a few shrill and uneasy notes; the rugged branches of the old trees, bristling with dim-colored lichens, crossed and intertwined themselves, like great gaunt arms, above the travelers' heads. It was a lovely spot, but so lonely and so sad that Germain, unable to endure it more, began to sing and throw stones into the water to forget the dread weariness of solitude. He was anxious also to wake little Marie, and when he saw her rise and look about at the weather, he proposed that they start on their journey.

"In two hours," said he, "the approach of morning will chill the air so that we can't stay here in spite of our fire. Now we can see our way, and we shall soon find a house which will open its doors to us, or at least a barn where we can pass the rest of the night under shelter."

Marie had no will of her own, and although she was longing to sleep, she made ready to follow Germain. The husbandman took his boy in his arms without awaking him, and beckoned Marie to come nearer, in order to cover her with his cloak. For she would not take her own mantle, which was wrapped about the child.

When he felt the young girl so close to him, Germain, who for a time had succeeded in distracting his mind and raising his spirits, began to lose his head once more. Two or three times he strode ahead abruptly, leaving her to walk alone. Then seeing how hard it was for her to follow, he waited, drew her quickly to his side, and pressed her so tight that she was surprised, and even angry, though she dared not say so.

As they knew not the direction whence they had come, they had no idea of that in which they were going. So they crossed the wood once more, and found themselves afresh before the lonely moor. Then they retraced their steps, and after much turning and twisting they spied a light across the branches.

"Good enough! Here 's a house," exclaimed Germain. "And the people are already astir, for the fire is lighted. It must be very late."

It was no house, but the camp-fire, which they had covered before they left, and which had sprung up in the breeze.

They had tramped for two hours, only to find themselves at the very place from which they had started.

X — Beneath the Stars

"THIS time I give up," said Germain, stamping I his foot. "We are bewitched, that is certain, and we shall not get away from here before broad day. The devil is in this place!"

"Well, it's of no use to get angry," said Marie. "We must take what is given us. Let us make a big fire. The child is so well wrapped up that he is in no danger, and we shall not die from a single night out of doors. Where have you hidden the saddle, Germain? Right in the midst of the holly-bushes,—what a goose you are! It's very convenient to get it from there!"

"Stop, child; hold the boy while I pull his bed from the thorns. I did n't want you to scratch your hands."

"It's all done. Here 's the bed, and a few scratches are not saber-cuts," replied the brave girl.

She proceeded to put the child to bed again, and Petit-Pierre was so sound asleep this time that he knew nothing of his last journey. Germain piled so much wood on the fire that the forest all about glowed with the light.

Little Marie had come to the end of her powers, and although she did not complain, her legs would support her no longer. She was white, and her teeth chattered with cold and weakness. Germain took her in his arms to warm her. The uneasiness, the compassion, the tenderness of movement he could not repress, took possession of his heart and stilled his senses. As by a miracle his tongue was loosened, and every feeling of shame vanished.

"Marie," said he, "I like you, and I am very sorry that you don't like me. If you would take me for your husband, there are no fathers, nor family, nor neighbors, nor arguments which could prevent me from giving myself to you. I know how happy you would make my children, and that you would teach them to love the memory of their mother, and with a quiet conscience I could satisfy the wishes of my heart. I have always been fond of you, and now I love you so well that were you to ask me to spend all my life in doing your pleasure, I would swear to do it on the instant. Please think how much I love you, and try to forget my age. Think that it is a wrong notion to believe that a man of thirty is old. Besides, I am but twenty-eight. A young girl is afraid that people will talk about her if she takes a man ten or twelve years older than she, simply because that is not the custom in our country, but I have heard say that in other countries people don't look at it in this light, and that they had rather allow a sensible man of approved courage to support a young girl, than trust her to a mere boy, who may go astray, and, from the honest fellow they thought him, turn into a good-for-nothing. And then years don't always make age. That depends on the health and strength a person has. When a man is used up by overwork and poverty, or by a bad life, he is old before twenty-five. While I—but Marie, you are not listening...." "Yes I am, Germain; I hear you perfectly," answered little Marie, "but I am thinking over what my mother used to tell me so often: that a woman of sixty is to be pitied greatly when her husband is seventy or seventy-five and can no longer work to support her. He grows feeble, and it becomes her duty to nurse him at the very age when she begins to feel great need of care and rest herself, and so it is that the end comes in a garret."

"Parents do well to say so, I admit," answered Germain, "but then they would sacrifice all their youth, the best years of their life, to calculating what will become of them at the age when a person is no longer good for anything, and when it is a matter of indifference which way death comes. But I am in no danger of starving in my old age. I am even going to lay by something, since I live with my wife's parents and spend nothing. And then, you see, I shall love you so well that I can never grow old. They say that when a man is happy he keeps sound, and I know well that in love for you, I am younger than Bastien; for he does not love you; he is too stupid, too much of a child to understand how pretty and how good you are, and how you were made for people to court. Do not hate me, Marie. I am not a bad man. I made my Catherine happy, and on her death-bed she swore before God that she had had only happiness of me, and she asked me to marry again. Her spirit must have spoken to her child to-night. Did you not hear the words he said? How his little lips quivered as his eyes stared upward, watching something that we could not see! He was surely looking at his mother, and it was she who made him say that he wished you to take her place."

"Germain," answered Marie, amazed and yet thoughtful, "you speak frankly, and everything that you say is true. I am sure that I should do well to love you if it did not displease your parents too much. But what can I do? My heart does not speak for you. I am very fond of you, but though your age does not make you ugly, it makes me afraid. It seems as if you were some such relation to me, as an uncle or a godfather, that I must be respectful toward you, and that there might be moments when you would treat me like a little girl rather than like your wife and your equal. And perhaps my friends would make fun of me, and although it would be silly to give heed to that, I think that I should be a little sad on my wedding-day."

"Those are but childish reasons, Marie; you speak like a child."

"Yes, that is true; I am a child," said she, "and it is on that account I am afraid of too sensible a man. You must see that I am too young for you, since you just found fault with me for speaking foolishly. I can't have more sense than my age allows."

"O Heavens! How unlucky I am to be so clumsy and to express so ill what I think!" cried Germain. "Marie, you don't love me. That is the long and short of it.

You find me too simple and too dull. If you loved me at all, you would not see my faults so clearly. But you do not love me. That is the whole story."

"That is not my fault," answered she, a little hurt that he was speaking with less tenderness. "I am doing my best to hear you, but the more I try the less I can get it into my head that we ought to be husband and wife."

Germain did not answer. His head dropped into his hands, and little Marie could not tell whether he wept or sulked or was fast asleep. She felt uneasy when she saw him so cast down, and could not guess what was passing in his mind. But she dared not speak to him more, and as she was too astonished at what had passed to have any desire to sleep, she waited impatiently for dawn, tending the fire with care and watching over the child, whose existence Germain appeared to forget. Yet Germain was not asleep. He did not mope over his lot. He made no plans to encourage himself, nor schemes to entrap the girl. He suffered; he felt a great weight of grief at his heart. He wished that he were dead. The world seemed to turn against him, and if he could have wept at all, his tears would have come in floods. But mingled with his sorrow there was a feeling of anger against himself, and he felt choked, without the power or the wish to complain.

When morning came, and the sounds of the country brought it to Germain's senses, he lifted his head from his hands and rose. He saw that little Marie had slept no more than he, but he knew no words in which to tell her of his anxiety. He was very discouraged. Hiding the gray's saddle once more in the thicket, he slung his sack over his shoulder and took his son by the hand.

"Now, Marie," said he, "we are going to try to end our journey. Do you wish me to take you to Ormeaux?"

"Let us leave the woods together," answered she, "and when we know where we are, we shall separate, and go our different ways."

Germain did not answer. He felt hurt that the girl did not ask him to take her as far as Ormeaux, and he did not notice that he had asked her in a tone well fitted to provoke a refusal.

After a few hundred steps, they met a wood-cutter, who pointed out the high-road, and told them that when they had crossed the plain, one must turn to the right, the other to the left, to gain their different destinations, which were so near together that the houses of Fourche were in plain sight from the farm of Ormeaux, and *vice versa.*

When they had thanked him and passed on, the wood-cutter called them back to ask whether they had not lost a horse.

"Yes," he said, "I found a pretty gray mare in my yard, where perhaps a wolf had driven her to seek refuge; my dogs barked the whole night long, and at day-break I saw the mare under my shed. She is there now. Come along with me, and if you recognize her, you may take her."

When Germain had given a description of the gray, and felt convinced that it was really she, he started back to find his saddle. Little Marie offered to take his child to Ormeaux, whither he might go to get him after he had introduced himself at Fourche.

"He is rather dirty after the night that we have passed," said she. "I will brush his clothes, wash his pretty face, and comb his hair, and when he looks neat and clean, you can present him to your new family."

"Who told you that I wish to go to Fourche?" answered Germain, petulantly. "Perhaps I shall not go."

"But truly, Germain, it is your duty to go there. You will go there," replied the girl.

"You seem very anxious to have me married off, so that you may be quite sure that I shall not trouble you again?"

"Germain, you must not think of that any more. It is an idea which came to you in the night, because this unfortunate mishap took away your spirits. But now you must come to your senses. I promise you to forget everything that you said to me, and not to breathe it to a soul."

"Oh, say what you wish. It is not my custom to deny what I have spoken. What I told you was true and honest, and I shall not blush for it before anybody."

"Yes, but if your wife were to know that just before you came you were thinking of another woman, it would prejudice her against you. So take care how you speak now. Don't look at me before everybody with such a rapt expression. Think of Father Maurice, who relies on your obedience, and who would be enraged at me if I were to turn you from his will. Good-by, Germain. I take Petit-Pierre in order to force you to go to Fourche. He is a pledge which I keep on your behalf."

"So you want to go with her?" said the husbandman to his son, seeing that the boy had clasped Marie's hands and was following her resolutely.

"Yes, father," answered the child, who had heard the conversation and understood after his own fashion the words spoken so unguardedly before him. "I am going away with my dearest little Marie. You shall come to find me when you have done marrying, but I wish Marie to be my little mother."

"You see how much he wishes it," said Germain to the girl. "Listen to me, Petit-Pierre," he added. "I wish her to be your mother and to stay with you always. It is she who does not wish to. Try to make her grant you what she has denied me."

"Don't be afraid, father, I shall make her say yes. Little Marie does everything that I wish."

He walked away with the young girl. Germain stood alone, sadder and more irresolute than ever.

XI — The Belle of the Village

AND after all, when he had brushed the dust of travel from his clothes and from his horse's harness, when he had mounted the gray, and when he had learned the road, he felt that there was no retreat and that he must forget that anxious night as though it had been a dangerous dream.

He found Father Leonard seated on a trim bench of spinach-green. The six stone steps leading up to the door showed that the house had a cellar. The walls of the garden and of the hemp-field were plastered with lime and sand. It was a handsome house, and might almost have been mistaken for the dwelling of a bourgeois.

Germain's future father-in-law came forward to meet him, and having plied him, for five minutes, with questions concerning his entire family, he added that conventional phrase with which one passer-by addresses another concerning the object of his journey: "So you are taking a little trip in this part of the country?"

"I have come to see you," replied the husbandman, "to give you this little present of game with my father's compliments, and to tell you from him that you ought to know with what intentions I come to your house."

"Oh, ho!" said Father Leonard, laughing and tapping his capacious stomach, "I see, I understand, I am with you, and," he added with a wink, "you will not be the only one to pay your court, young man. There are three already in the house dancing attendance like you. I never turn anybody away, and I should find it hard to say yes or no to any of them, for they are all good matches. Yet, on account of Father Maurice and for the sake of the rich fields you till, I hope that it may be you. But my daughter is of age and mistress of her own affairs. She will do as she likes. Go in and introduce yourself. I hope that you will draw the prize."

"I beg your pardon," answered Germain, amazed to find himself an extra when he had counted on being alone in the field. "I was not aware that your daughter was supplied already with suitors, and I did not come to quarrel over her."

"If you supposed that because you were slow in coming, my daughter would be left unprovided for, you were greatly mistaken, my son," replied Father Leonard with unshaken good humor. "Catherine has the wherewithal to attract suitors, and her only difficulty lies in choosing. But come in; don't lose heart. The woman is worth, a struggle."

And pushing in Germain by the shoulders with boisterous gaiety, he called to his daughter as they entered the house:

"So, Catherine, here is another!"

This cordial but unmannerly method of introduction to the widow, in the presence of her other devotees, completed Germain's distress and embarrassment. He felt the awkwardness of his position, and stood for a few moments without daring to look upon the beauty and her court.

The Widow Guérin had a good figure and did not lack freshness, but her expression and her dress displeased Germain the instant he saw her. She had a bold, self-satisfied look, and her cap, edged with three lace flounces, her silk apron, and her fichu of fine black lace were little in accord with the staid and sober widow he had pictured to himself.

Her elaborate dress and forward manners inclined Germain to judge the widow old and ugly, although she was certainly not either. He thought that such finery and playful manners might well suit little Marie's years and wit, but that the widow's fun was labored and over bold, and that she wore her fine clothes in bad taste.

The three suitors were seated at a table loaded with wines and meats which were spread out for their use throughout the Sunday morning; for Father Leonard liked to show off his wealth, and the widow was not sorry to display her pretty china and keep a table like a rich lady. Germain, simple and unsuspecting as he was, watched everything with a penetrating glance, and for the first time in his life he kept on the defensive when he drank. Father Leonard obliged him to sit down with his rivals, and taking a chair opposite he treated him with great politeness, and talked to him rather than to the others.

The present of game, despite the breach Germain had made on his own account, was still plenteous enough to produce its effect. The widow did not look unaware of its presence, and the suitors cast disdainful glances in its direction.

Germain felt ill at ease in this company, and did not eat heartily. Father Leonard poked fun at him.

"You look very melancholy," said he, "and you are ill-using your glass. You must not allow love to spoil your appetite, for a fasting lover can make no such pretty speeches as he whose ideas are brightened with a drop of wine."

Germain was mortified at being thought already in love, and the artificial manner of the widow, who kept lowering her eyes with a smile as a woman does who is sure of her calculations, made him long to protest against his pretended surrender; but fearing to appear uncivil, he smiled and held his peace.

He thought the widow's beaus, three bumpkins. They must have been rich for her to admit of their pretensions. One was over forty, and fat as Father Leonard; another had lost an eye, and drank like a sot. The third was a young fellow, and nice-looking too; but he kept insisting on displaying his wit, and would say things so silly that they were painful to hear. Yet the widow laughed as though she admired all his foolishness, and made small proof of her good taste thereby. At first Germain thought her infatuated with him, but soon he perceived that he himself was especially encouraged, and that they wished him to make fresh advances. For this reason he felt an increasing stiffness and severity which he took no pains to conceal.

The time came for mass, and they rose from table to go thither in company. It was necessary to walk as far as Mers, a good half-league away, and Germain was so tired that he longed to take a nap before they went; but he was not in the habit of missing mass, and he started with the others.

The roads were filled with people, and the widow marched proudly along, escorted by her three suitors, taking an arm, first of one and then of another, and carrying her head high with an air of importance. She was eager to display the fourth to the eyes of the passers-by; but Germain felt so ridiculous to be dragged along in the train of a petticoat where all the world might see, that he kept at a respectable distance, chatting with Father Leonard, and succeeded in occupying his attention so well that they did not look at all as if they belonged to the party.

XII — The Master

WHEN they reached the village, the widow halted to allow them to catch up. She was bent upon making her entry with all her train; but Germain, denying her this pleasure, deserted Father Leonard, and after conversing with several acquaintances, he entered the church by another door. The widow was vexed.

When mass was over, she made her appearance in triumph on the lawn, where dancing was going on, and she began her dance with her three lovers in turn. Germain watched her and saw that she danced well, but with affectation.

"So, you don't ask my daughter?" said Leonard, tapping him on the shoulder. "You are too easily frightened."

"I have not danced since I lost my wife," answered the husbandman.

"But now that you are looking for another, mourning 's over in heart as well as in clothes."

"That's no reason, Father Leonard. Besides, I am too old and I don't care for dancing."

"Listen," said Father Leonard, drawing him toward a retired corner, "when you entered my house you were vexed to see the place already besieged, and I see that you are very proud. But that is not reasonable, my boy. My daughter is used to a great deal of attention, particularly since she left off her mourning two years ago, and it is not her place to lead you on."

"Has your daughter been thinking of marrying for two years already without making her choice?" asked Germain.

"She does n't wish to hurry, and she is right. Although she has lively manners, and although you may not think that she reflects a great deal, she is a woman of excellent common sense, and knows very well what she is about."

"It does not appear to me so," said Germain ingenuously, "for she has three suitors in her train, and if she knew her own mind, there are two of them, at least, whom she would find superfluous and request to stay at home."

"Why, Germain, you don't understand at all. She does n't wish the old man, nor the blind man, nor the young man, I am quite certain; yet if she were to turn them off, people would think that she wished to remain a widow, and nobody else would come."

"Oh, I see. These three are used for a guide-post."

"As you like. What is the harm if they are satisfied?"

"Every man to his taste," said Germain.

"I see that yours is different. Now supposing that you are chosen, then they would leave the coast clear."

"Yes, supposing! and meanwhile how much time should I have to whistle?"

"That depends on your persuasive tongue, I suppose. Until now, my daughter has always thought that she would pass the best part of her life while she was being courted, and she is in no hurry to become the servant of one man when she can order so many others about. So she will please herself as long as the game amuses her; but if you please her more than the game, the game will cease. Only you must not lose courage. Come back every Sunday, dance with her, let her know that you are amongst her followers, and if she finds you more agreeable and better bred than the others, some fine day she will tell you so, no doubt."

"Excuse me, Father Leonard. Your daughter has the right to do as she pleases, and it is not my business to blame her. If I were in her place, I should do differently. I should be more frank, and should not waste the time of men who have, doubtless, something better to do than dancing attendance on a woman who makes fun of them. Still, if that is what amuses her and makes her happy, it is no affair of mine. Only there is one thing I must tell you which is a little embarrassing, since you have mistaken my intentions from the start, for you are so sure of what is not so, that you have given me no chance to explain. You must know, then, that I did not come here to ask for your daughter in marriage, but merely to buy a pair of oxen which you are going to take to market next week, and which my father-in-law thinks will suit him."

"I understand, Germain," answered Leonard very calmly; "you changed your plans when you saw my daughter with her admirers. It is as you please. It seems that what attracts some people repels others, and you are perfectly welcome to withdraw, for you have not declared your intentions. If you wish seriously to buy my cattle, come and see them in the pasture, and whether we make a bargain or not, you will come back to dinner with us before you return."

"I don't wish to trouble you," answered Germain. "Perhaps you have something to do here. I myself am tired of watching the dancing and standing idle. I will go to see your cattle, and I will soon join you at your house."

Then Germain made his escape, and walked away toward the meadows where Leonard had pointed out to him some of his cattle. It was true that Father Maurice intended to buy, and Germain thought that if he were to bring home a fine pair of oxen at a reasonable price, he might more easily receive a pardon for wilfully relinquishing the purpose of his journey. He walked rapidly, and soon found himself at some distance from Ormeaux. Then of a sudden, he felt a desire to kiss his son and to see little Marie once again, although he had lost all hope and even had chased away the thought that he might some day owe his happiness to her. Everything that he had heard and seen: this woman, flirtatious and vain; this father, at once shrewd and short-sighted, encouraging his daughter in habits of pride and untruth; this city luxury, which seemed to him a transgression against the dignity of country manners; this time wasted in foolish, empty words; this home so different from his own; and above all, that deep uneasiness which comes to a laborer of the fields when he leaves his accustomed toil: all the trouble and annoyance of the past few hours made Germain long to be with his child and with his little neighbor. Even had he not been in love, he would have sought her to divert his mind and raise his spirits to their wonted level.

But he looked in vain over the neighboring meadows. He saw neither little Marie nor little Pierre, and yet it was the hour when shepherds are in the fields. There was a large flock in a pasture. He asked of a young boy who tended them whether the sheep belonged to the farm of Ormeaux.

"Yes," said the child.

"Are you the shepherd? Do boys tend the flocks of the farm, amongst you?"

"No, I am taking care of them to-day, because the shepherdess went away. She was ill."

"But have you not a new shepherdess, who came this morning?"

"Yes, surely; but she, too, has gone already."

"What! gone? Did she not have a child with her?"

"Yes, a little boy who cried. They both went away after they had been here two hours."

"Went away! Where?"

"Where they came from, I suppose. I did n't ask them."

"But why did they go away?" asked Germain, growing more and more uneasy.

"How the deuce do I know?"

"Did they not agree about wages? Yet that must have been settled before."

"I can tell you nothing about it I saw them come and go, nothing more."

Germain walked toward the farm and questioned the farmer. Nobody could give him an explanation; but after speaking with the farmer, he felt sure that the girl had gone without saying a word, and had taken the weeping child with her.

"Can they have been ill-treating my son?" cried Germain.

"It was your son, then? How did he happen to be with the little girl? Where do you come from, and what is your name?"

Germain, seeing that after the fashion of the country they were answering him with questions, stamped his foot impatiently, and asked to speak with the master.

The master was away. Usually, he did not spend the whole day when he came to the farm. He was on horseback, and he had ridden off to one of his other farms.

"But, honestly," said Germain, growing very anxious, "can't you tell me why this girl left?"

The farmer and his wife exchanged an odd smile. Then the former answered that he knew nothing, and that it was no business of his. All that Germain could learn was that both girl and child had started off toward Fourche. He rushed back to Fourche. The widow and her lovers were still away; so was Father Leonard. The maid told him that a girl and a child had come to ask for him, but that as she did not know them, she did not wish to let them in, and had advised them to go to Mers.

"And why did you refuse to let them in?" said Germain, angrily. "People are very suspicious in this country, where nobody opens the door to a neighbor."

"But you see," answered the maid, "in a house as rich as this, I must keep my eyes open. When the master is away, I am responsible for everything, and I cannot open the door to the first person that comes along."

"It is a bad custom," said Germain, "and I had rather be poor than to live in constant fear like that. Good-by to you, young woman, and good-by to your vile country."

He made inquiries at the neighboring house. The shepherdess and child had been seen. As the boy had left Belair suddenly, carelessly dressed, with his blouse torn, and his little lambskin over his shoulders, and as little Marie was necessarily poorly clad at all times, they had been taken for beggars. People had offered them bread. The girl had accepted a crust for the child, who was hungry, then she had walked away with him very quickly, and had entered the forest.

Germain thought a minute, then he asked whether the farmer of Ormeaux had not been at Fourche.

"Yes," they answered, "he passed on horseback a few seconds after the girl."

"Was he chasing her?"

"Oh, so you understand?" answered the village publican, with a laugh. "Certain it is that he is the devil of a fellow for running after girls. But I don't believe that he caught her; though, after all, if he had seen her—"

"That is enough, thank you!" And he flew rather than ran to Leonard's stable. Throwing the saddle on the gray's back, he leaped upon it, and set off at full gallop toward the wood of Chanteloube.

His heart beat hard with fear and anger; the sweat poured down his forehead; he spurred the mare till the blood came, though the gray needed no pressing when she felt herself on the road to her stable.

XIII — The Old Woman

GERMAIN came soon to the spot where he had passed the night on the border of the pool. The fire was smoking still. An old woman was gathering the remnants of the wood little Marie had piled there. Germain stopped to question her. She was deaf and mistook his inquiries.

"Yes, my son," said she, "this is the Devil's Pool. It is an evil spot, and you must not approach it without throwing in three stones with your left hand, while you cross yourself with the right. That drives away the spirits. Otherwise trouble comes to those who go around it."

"I am not asking about that," said Germain, moving nearer her, and screaming at the top of his lungs. "Have you seen a girl and a child walking through the wood?"

"Yes," said the old woman, "a little child was drowned there."

Germain shook from head to foot; but happily the hag added:

"That happened a long time ago. In memory of the accident they raised a handsome cross there. But one stormy night, the bad spirits threw it into the water. You can still see one end of it. If anybody were unlucky enough to pass the night here, he could never find his way out before daylight. He must walk and walk, and though he went two hundred leagues into the forest, he must always return to the same place."

The peasant's imagination was aroused in spite of himself, and the thought of the evils that must come in order that the old woman's assertions might be vindicated, took so firm a hold of his mind that he felt chilled through and through. Hopeless of obtaining more news, he remounted, and traversed the woods afresh, calling Pierre with all his might, whistling, cracking his whip, and snapping the branches that the whole forest might reëcho with the noise of his coming; then he listened for an answering voice, but he heard no sound save the cowbells scattered through the glades, and the wild cries of the swine as they fought over the acorns.

At length Germain heard behind him the noise of a horse following in his traces, and a man of middle age, dark, sturdy, and dressed after the city fashion, called to him to stop. Germain had never seen the farmer of Ormeaux, but his instinctive rage told him at once that this was the man. He turned, and eyeing him from head to foot, waited for him to speak.

"Have not you seen a young girl of fifteen or sixteen go by with a small boy?" asked the farmer, with an assumed air of indifference, although he was evidently ill at ease.

"What do you want of her?" answered Germain, taking no pains to conceal his anger.

"I might tell you that that is none of your business, my friend. But as I have no reasons for secrecy, I shall tell you that she is a shepherdess whom I engaged for a year, before I knew her. When I saw her, she looked too young and frail to work on the farm. I thanked her, but I wished to pay the expenses of her short journey, and while my back was turned, she went off in a huff. She was in such a hurry that she forgot even some of her belongings and her purse, which has certainly not much in it, probably but a few pennies; but since I was going in this direction, I hoped to meet her, and give her back the things which she left behind, as well as what I owe her."

Germain had too honest a heart not to pause at hearing a story which, however unlikely, was not impossible. He fastened his penetrating gaze on the farmer, who submitted to the examination with a plentiful supply of impudence or of good faith.

"I wish to get at the bottom of this matter," said Germain; "and," continued he, suppressing his indignation, "the girl lives in my village. I know her. She can't be far away. Let 's ride on together; we shall find her, no doubt."

"You are right," said the farmer; "let's move on; but if we do not find her before we reach the end of this road, I shall give up, for I must turn off toward Ardentes."

"Oh, oh!" thought the peasant, "I shall not part with you, even if I have to follow you around the 'Devil's Pool for twenty-four hours."

"Stop," said Germain suddenly, fixing his eyes on a clump of broom which waved in a peculiar manner. "Halloa! halloa! Petit Pierre, is that you, my child?"

The boy recognized his father's voice, and came out from the broom leaping like a young deer; but when he saw Germain in company with the farmer, he stopped dismayed, and stood irresolute. "Come, my Pierre, come. It is I," cried the husbandman, as he leaped from his horse and ran toward his boy to take him in his arms; "and where is little Marie?"

"She is hiding there, because she is afraid of that dreadful black man, and so am I."

"You need n't be afraid. I am here. Marie, Marie. It is I."

Marie crept toward them, but the moment she saw Germain with the farmer close behind, she sprang forward, and throwing herself into his arms, clung to him as a daughter to her father.

"Oh, my brave Germain!" she cried, "you will defend me. I am not afraid when you are near."

Germain shuddered. He looked at Marie. She was pale; her clothes were torn by the thorns which had scratched her as she passed, rushing toward the brake like a stag chased by the hunters. But neither shame nor despair were in her face.

"Your master wishes to speak to you," said he, his eyes fixed on her features.

"My master!" she exclaimed fiercely; "that man is no master of mine, and he never shall be. You, Germain, you are my master. I want you to take me home with you. I will be your servant for nothing."

The farmer advanced, feigning impatience. "Little girl," said he, "you left something behind at the farm, which I am bringing back to you."

"No, you are not, sir," answered little Marie. "I did n't forget anything, and I have nothing to ask of you."

"Listen a moment," returned the farmer. "It's I who have something to tell you. Come with me. Don't be afraid. It's only a word or two."

"You may say them aloud. I have no secrets with you."

"At any rate, do take your money."

"My money? You owe me nothing, thank God!"

"I suspected as much," said Germain under his breath, "but I don't care, Marie. Listen to what he has to say to you, for—I am curious to know. You can tell me afterward. Go up to his horse. I shall not lose sight of you."

Marie took three steps toward the farmer. He bent over the pommel of his saddle, and lowering his voice he said:

"Little girl, here is a bright golden louis for you. Don't say anything about it; do you hear? I shall say that I found you too frail to work on my farm. There will be no more talk about that. I shall be passing by your house one of these days; and if you have not said anything, I will give you something more; and then if you are more sensible, you have only to speak. I will take you home with me, or I will come at dusk and talk with you in the meadows. What present would you like me to bring you?"

"Here, sir, is the present I have for you," answered little Marie, aloud, as she threw the golden louis in his face with all her might. "I thank you heartily, and I beg that if you come anywhere near our house, you will be good enough to let me know. All the boys in the neighborhood will go out to welcome you, because, where I live, we are very fond of gentlemen who try to make love to poor girls. You shall see. They will be on the lookout for you."

"You lie with your dirty tongue," cried the farmer, raising his stick with a dangerous air. "You wish to make people believe what is not so, but you shall never get a penny out of me. We know what kind of a girl you are."

Marie drew back, frightened, and Germain sprang to the bridle of the farmer's horse and shook it violently.

"I understand now," said he; "it is easy to see what is going on. Get down, my man, get down; I want to talk to you."

The farmer was not eager to take up the quarrel. Anxious to escape, he set spurs to his horse and tried to loosen the peasant's grasp by striking down his hands with a cane; but Germain dodged the blow, and seizing hold of his antagonist's leg, he unseated him and flung him to the earth. The farmer regained his feet, but although he defended himself vigorously, he was knocked down once more. Germain held him to the ground. Then he said:

"Poor coward, I could thrash you if I wished. But I don't want to do you an injury, and, besides, no amount of punishment would help your conscience—but you shall not stir from this spot until you beg the girl's pardon, on your knees."

The farmer understood this sort of thing, and wished to take it all as a joke. He made believe that his offense was not serious, since it lay in words alone, and protested that he was perfectly willing to ask her pardon, provided he might kiss the girl afterward. Finally, he proposed that they go and drink a pint of wine at the nearest tavern, and so part good friends.

"You are disgusting!" answered Germain, rubbing his victim's head in the dirt, "and I never wish to see your nasty face again. So blush, if you are able, and when you come to our village, you had better slink along Sneak's Alley[1]."

He picked up the farmer's holly-stick, broke it over his knee to show the strength of his wrists, and threw away the pieces with disgust Then giving one hand to his son and the other to little Marie, he walked away, still trembling with anger.

---

[1] This is the road, which, diverging from the principal street at the entrance of villages, makes a circuit about them.. Persons who are in dread off receiving some well deserved insult, are supposed to take this route to escape attention.

XIV — The Return to the Farm

AT the end of fifteen minutes they had left the heath behind them. They trotted along the highroad, and the gray whinnied at each familiar object. Petit-Pierre told his father as much as he could understand of what had passed.

"When we reached the farm," said he, "that man came to speak to my Marie in the fold where we had gone to see the pretty sheep. I had climbed into the manger to play, and that man did not see me. Then he said good morning to Marie, and he kissed her."

"You allowed him to kiss you, Marie?" said Germain, trembling with anger.

"I thought it was a civility, a custom of the place to new-comers, just as at your farm the grandmother kisses the young girls who enter her service to show that she adopts them and will be a mother to them."

"And next," went on little Pierre, who was proud to have an adventure to tell of, "*that man* told you something wicked, which you have told me never to repeat and not even remember; so I forgot it right away. Still, if father wishes, I will tell him what it was—"

"No, Pierre, I don't wish to hear, and I don't wish you ever to think of it again."

"Then I will forget it all over again," replied the child. "Next, *that man* seemed to be growing angry because Marie told him that she was going away. He told her he would give her whatever she wanted,—a hundred francs! And my Marie grew angry too. Then he came toward her as if he wished to hurt her. I was afraid, and I ran to Marie and cried. Then *that man* said: 'What 's that? Where did that child come from? Put it out,' and he raised his cane to beat me. But my Marie prevented him, and she spoke to him this way: 'We will talk later, sir; now I must take this child back to Fourche, and then I shall return.' And as soon as he had left the fold, my Marie spoke to me this way: 'We must run, my Pierre; we must get away as quickly as we can, for this is a wicked man and he is trying to do us harm.' Then when we had gone back of the farm-houses, we crossed a little meadow, and we went to Fourche to find you. But you were not there, and they would n't let us wait. And then *that man*, riding his black horse, came behind us, and we ran on as fast as we could and hid in the woods. And then he followed us, and when we heard him coming, we hid again. And then, when he had passed, we began to run toward home, and then you came and found us, and that is how it all happened. I have n't forgotten anything, have I, my Marie?"

"No, my Pierre, that is the whole truth. Now, Germain, you must be my witness, and tell everybody in the village that if I did not stay there it was not from want of courage and industry."

"And, Marie, I want to ask of you whether a man of twenty-eight is too old when there is a woman to be defended and an insult to be revenged. I should like to know whether Bastien or any other pretty boy, ten years better off than I, would not have been knocked to pieces by *that man*, as Petit-Pierre says. What do you think?"

"I think, Germain, that you have done me a great service, and that I shall be grateful all my life."

"Is that all?"

"Little father," said the child, "I forgot to ask little Marie what I promised. I have not had time yet, but I will speak to her at home, and I will speak to my grandmother too."

The child's promise set Germain to thinking He must explain his conduct to his family and give his objections to the widow Guam, and all the while conceal the true reasons which had made him so judicious and so decided. When a man is proud and happy, it seems an easy task to thrust his happiness upon others, but to be repulsed on one side and blamed on the other is not a very pleasant position.

Fortunately, Petit-Pierre was fast asleep when they reached the farm, and Germain put him to bed undisturbed. Then he began upon all sorts of explanations, Father Maurice, seated on a three-legged stool before the door, listened with gravity; and, although he was ill-content with the result of the journey, when Germain told him about the widow's systematic coquetry, and demanded of his father-in-law whether he had the time to go and pay his court fifty-two Sundays in the year at the risk of being dismissed in the end, the old man nodded his head in assent and answered: "You were not wrong, Germain; that could never be." And then, when Germain described how he had been obliged to bring back little Marie, with the utmost haste, in order to protect her from the insults or perhaps from the violence of a wicked master, Father Maurice nodded approvingly again and said: "You were not wrong, Germain; that was right."

When Germain had told his story, and had set forth all his reasons, the old farmer and his wife heaved deep, simultaneous sighs of resignation, and looked at each other. Then the head of the house rose and said: "God's will be done. Love can't be made to order."

"Come to supper, Germain," said his mother-in-law. "It is unfortunate that this did not come to a better end, but, after all, it seems that God did not wish it. We must loök elsewhere."

"Yes," added the old man, "as my wife says, we must look elsewhere."

There was no more noise at the house, and on the morrow, when Petit-Pierre rose with the larks at dawn, he was no longer excited by the extraordinary events of the preceding days. Like other little peasants of his age, he became indifferent, forgot everything that had been running in his head, and thought only of playing with his brothers, and of pretending to drive the horses and oxen like a man. Germain plunged into his work, and tried to forget, too; but he became so absent-minded and so sad that everybody noticed it. He never spoke to little Marie, he never even looked at her, and yet had anybody asked him in what meadow she was, or by what road she had passed, there was not a moment in the day when he could not have answered if he would. He dared not ask his family to take her in at the farm during the winter, and yet he knew well how she must suffer from want. But she did not suffer; and Mother Guillette could not understand how her little store of wood never grew less, and how her shed was full in the morning, although she had left it almost empty at night It was the same with the wheat and potatoes. Somebody entered by the garret window, and emptied a sack on the floor without awaking a soul or leaving a trace of his coming. The widow was at once uneasy and delighted. She made her daughter promise to tell nobody, and said that were people to know of the miracle performed at her house they would take her for a witch. She felt confident that the devil had a share in it, but she was in no hurry to pick a quarrel with him by calling down the priest's exorcisms on the house. It would be time enough, she said, when Satan should come to demand her soul in return for his gifts.

Little Marie understood the truth better, but she dared not speak to Germain, for fear of seeing him return to his dreams of marriage, and, before him, she pretended to perceive nothing.

XV — Mother Maurice

ONE day, Mother Maurice was alone in the orchard with Germain, and spoke to him kindly:

"My poor son, I believe you are not well. You don't eat as well as usual; you never laugh; you talk less and less. Perhaps one of us, or all of us, have hurt your feelings, without knowing and without wishing it."

"No, my mother," answered Germain, "you have always been as kind to me as the mother who brought me into the world, and I should be very ungrateful if I were to complain of you or your husband, or of anybody in the household."

"Then, my child, it is the sorrow for your wife's death which comes back to you. Instead of growing lighter with time, your grief becomes worse, and as your father has said very wisely, it is absolutely necessary for you to marry again."

"Yes, my mother, that is my opinion, but the women whom you advised me to ask don't suit me. Whenever I see them, instead of forgetting my Catherine, I think of her all the more."

"Apparently that's because we have n't been able to understand your taste. You must help us by telling us the truth. There must be a woman somewhere who is made for you, for God does n't make anybody without placing his happiness in somebody else. So if you know where to find this woman whom you need, take her, and be she pretty or ugly, young or old, rich or poor, we have made up our minds, my husband and I, to give our consent, for we are tired of seeing you so sad, and we can never be happy while you are sorrowful."

"My mother, you are as kind as the kind Lord, and so is my father," answered Germain; "but your compassion brings small help to my troubles, for the girl I love does n't care for me."

"She is too young, then? It's foolish for you to love a young girl."

"Yes, mother dear, I have been foolish enough to love a young girl, and it's my fault. I do my best to stop thinking of it, but, working or sleeping, at mass or in bed, with my children or with you, I can think of nothing else."

"Then it's like a fate cast over you, Germain. There's but one remedy, and it is that this girl must change her mind and listen to you. It's my duty to look into this, and see whether it's practicable. Tell me where she lives, and what 's her name."

"Oh, my dear mother, I dare not," said Germain, "because you will make fun of me."

"I shall not make fun of you, Germain, because you are in trouble, and I don't wish to make it harder for you. Is it Fanchette?"

"No, mother, of course not."

"Or Rosette?"

"No."

"Tell me, then, for I shall never finish if I must name every girl in the country-side."

Germain bowed his head, and could not bring himself to answer.

"Very good," said Mother Maurice, "I shall let you alone for to-day; to-morrow, perhaps, you will be more confidential with me, or possibly your sister-in-law will question you more cleverly." And she picked up her basket to go and spread her linen on the bushes.

Germain acted like children who make up their minds when they see that they are no longer attracting attention. He followed his mother, and at length, trembling, he named Marie of Guillette.

Great was the surprise of Mother Maurice. Marie was the last person she would have dreamed of. But she had the delicacy not to cry out, and made her comments to herself. Then seeing that her silence hurt Germain, she stretched out her basket toward him and said:

"Is there any reason for not helping me at my work. Carry this load, and come and talk with me. Have you reflected well, Germain? Are you fully decided?"

"Alas, dear mother, you must n't speak in that way. I should be decided if I had a chance of success, but as I could never be heard, I have only made up my mind to cure myself, if I can."

"And if you can't."

"There is an end to everything, Mother Maurice: when the horse is laden too heavily, he falls, and when the cow has nothing to eat, she dies."

"Do you mean to say that you will die, if you do not succeed. God grant not, Germain. I don't like to hear a man like you talk of those things; for what he says, he thinks. You are very brave, and weakness is dangerous for strong men. Take heart; I can't conceive that a poverty-stricken girl, whom you have honored so much as to ask her to marry you, will refuse you."

"Yet it's the truth: she does refuse me."

"And what reasons does she give you?"

"That you have always been kind to her, and that her family owes a great deal to yours, and that she does n't wish to displease you by turning me away from a rich marriage."

"If she says that, she proves her good sense, and shows what an honest girl she is. But, Germain, she does n't cure you; for of course she tells you that she loves you and would marry you if we were willing?"

"That's the worst part of all. She says that her heart can never be mine."

"If she says what she does n't think in order to keep you at a safer distance, the child deserves our love, and we should pass over her youth on account of her great good sense."

"Yes," said Germain, struck by a hope he had never held before; "that would be very wise and right of her! But if she is so sensible, I am sure it is because I displease her."

"Germain," said Mother Maurice, "you must promise me not to worry for a whole week. Keep from tormenting yourself, eat, sleep, and be as gay as you used to be. For my part, I 'll speak to my husband, and if I gain his consent, you shall know the girl's real feelings toward you."

Germain promised, and the week passed without a single word in private from Father Maurice, who seemed to suspect nothing. The husbandman did his best to look calm, but he grew ever paler and more troubled.

XVI — Little Marie

AT length, on Sunday morning, when mass was over, his mother-in-law asked Germain what encouragement he had had from his sweetheart since the conversation in the orchard.

"Why, none at all," answered he; "I have n't spoken to her."

"How can you expect to win her if you don't speak to her?"

"I have spoken to her but once," replied Germain. "That was when we were together at Fourche, and since then I have n't said a single word. Her refusal gave me so much pain that I had rather not hear her begin again to tell me that she does n't love me."

"But, my son, you must speak to her now; your father gives his approval. So make up your mind. I tell you to do it, and, if need be, I shall order you to do it, for you can't rest in this uncertainty."

Germain obeyed. He reached Mother Guillette's house, hanging his head with a hopeless air. Little Marie sat alone before the hearth so thoughtful that she did not hear Germain's step. When she saw him before her, she started from her chair in surprise and grew very red.

"Little Marie," said he, sitting down near her, "I come to trouble you and to give you pain. I know it very well, but the man and his wife at home [it was thus after the peasant fashion that he designated the heads of the house] wish me to speak to you, and beg you to marry me. You don't care for me. I am prepared for it."

"Germain," answered little Marie, "are you sure that you love me?"

"It pains you, I know, but it isn't my fault. If you could change your mind, I should be so very happy, and certain it is that I don't deserve it. Look at me, Marie; am I very terrible?"

"No, Germain," she answered, with a smile, "you are better looking than I."

"Don't make fun of me; look at me charitably; as yet, I have never lost a single hair nor a single tooth. My eyes tell you plainly how much I love you. Look straight into my eyes. It is written there, and every girl knows how to read that writing."

Marie looked into Germain's eyes with playful boldness; then of a sudden she turned away her head and trembled.

"Good God," exclaimed Germain, "I make you afraid; you look at me as though I were the farmer of Ormeaux. Don't be afraid of me, please don't; that hurts me too much. I shall not say any bad words to you, I shall not kiss you if you will not have me, and when you wish me to go away, you have only to show me the door. Must I go in order to stop your trembling?"

Marie held out her hand toward the husbandman, but without turning her head, which was bent on the fireplace, and without saying a word.

"I understand," said Germain. "You pity me, for you are kind; you are sorry to make me unhappy; but you can't love me."

"Why do you say these things to me, Germain?" answered little Marie, after a pause. "Do you wish to make me cry?"

"Poor little girl, you have a kind heart, I know; but you don't love me, and you are hiding your face for fear of letting me see your dislike and your repugnance. And I? I dare not even clasp your hand! In the forest, when my boy was asleep and you were sleeping too, I almost kissed you very gently. But I would have died of shame rather than ask it of you, and that night I suffered as a man burning over a slow fire. Since that time I have dreamed of you every night. Ah! how I have kissed you, Marie! Yet during all that time you have slept without a dream. And now, do you know what I think? I think that were you to turn and look at me with the eyes I have for you, and were you to move your face close to mine, I believe I should fall dead for joy. And you, you think that if such a thing were to happen, you would die of anger and shame!"

Germain spoke as in a dream, not hearing the words he said. Little Marie was trembling all the time, but he was shaking yet more and did not notice it. Of a sudden, she turned. Her eyes were filled with tears, and she looked at him reproachfully. The poor husbandman thought that this was the last blow, and without waiting for his sentence, he rose to go, but the girl stopped him, and throwing both her arms about him, she hid her face in his breast.

"Oh, Germain," she sobbed, "did n't you feel that I loved you?"

Then Germain had gone mad, if his son, who came galloping into the cottage on a stick, with his little sister on the crupper, scourging the imaginary steed with a willow branch, had not brought him to his senses. He lifted the boy and placed him in the girl's arms.

"See," said he, "by loving me, you have made more than one person happy."

APPENDIX

I — A Country Wedding

HERE ends the history of Germain's marriage as he told it to me himself, good husbandman that he is. I ask your forgiveness, kind reader, that I know not how to translate it better; for it is a real translation that is needed by this old-fashioned and artless language of the peasants of the country "that I sing," as they used to say. These people speak French that is too true for us, and since Rabelais and Montaigne, the advance of the language has lost for us many of its old riches. Thus it is with every advance, and we must make the best of it. Yet it is a pleasure still to hear those picturesque idioms used in the old districts in the center of France; all the more because it is the genuine expression of the laughing, quiet, and delightfully talkative character of the people who make use of it. Touraine has preserved a certain precious number of patriarchal phrases. But Touraine was civilized greatly during the Renaissance, and since its decline she is filled with fine houses and highroads, with foreigners and traffic. Berry remained as she was, and I think that after Brittany and a few provinces in the far south of France, it is the best preserved district to be found at the present day. Some of the costumes are so strange and so curious that I hope to amuse you a few minutes more, kind reader, if you will allow me to describe to you in detail a country wedding—Germain's, for example—at which I had the pleasure of assisting several years ago.

For, alas! everything passes. During my life alone, more change has taken place in the ideas and in the customs of my village than had been seen in the centuries before the Revolution. Already half the ceremonies, Celtic, Pagan, or of the Middle Ages, that in my childhood I have seen in their full vigor, have disappeared. In a year or two more, perhaps, the railroads will lay their level tracks across our deep valleys, and will carry away, with the swiftness of lightning, all our old traditions and our wonderful legends.

It was in winter about the carnival season, the time of year when, in our country, it is fitting and proper to have weddings. In summer the time can hardly be spared, and the work of the farm cannot suffer three days' delay, not to speak of the additional days impaired to a greater or to a less degree by the moral and physical drunkenness which follows a gala-day. I was seated beneath the great mantelpiece of the old-fashioned kitchen fireplace when shots of pistols, barking of dogs, and the piercing notes of the bagpipe told me that the bridal pair were approaching. Very soon Father and Mother Maurice, Germain, and little Marie, followed by Jacques and his wife, the closer relatives, and the godfathers and godmothers of the bride and groom, all made their entry into the yard.

Little Marie had not yet received her wedding-gifts,—favors, as they call them,—and was dressed in the best of her simple clothes, a dress of dark, heavy cloth, a white fichu with great spots of brilliant color, an apron of carnation,—an Indian red much in vogue at the time, but despised nowadays,—a cap of very white muslin after that pattern, happily still preserved, which calls to mind the head-dress of Anne Boleyn and of Agnes Sorrel. She was fresh and laughing, but not at all vain, though she had good reason to be so. Beside her was Germain, serious and tender, like young Jacob greeting Rebecca at the wells of Laban. Another girl would have assumed an important air and struck an attitude of triumph, for in every rank it is something to be married for a fair face alone. Yet the girl's eyes were moist and shone with tenderness. It was plain that she was deep in love and had no time to think of the opinions of others. Her little air of determination was not absent, but everything about her denoted frankness and good-will. There was nothing impertinent in her success, nothing selfish in her sense of power. Never have I seen so lovely a bride, when she answered with frankness her young friends who asked if she were happy:

"Surely I have nothing to complain of the good Lord."

Father Maurice was spokesman. He came forward to pay his compliments, and give the customary invitations. First he fastened to the mantelpiece a branch of laurel decked out with ribbons; this is known as the *writ*—that is to say, the letter of announcement. Next he gave to every guest a tiny cross made of a bit of blue ribbon sewn to a transverse bit of pink ribbon—pink for the bride, blue for the groom. The guests of both sexes were expected to keep this badge to adorn their caps or their button-holes on the wedding-day. This is the letter of invitation, the admission ticket.

Then Father Maurice paid his congratulations. He invited the head of the house and all his *company*,—that is to say, all his children, all his friends, and all his servants,—to the benediction, *to the feast, to the sports, to the dance, and to everything that follows*. He did not fail to say, "I have come *to do you the honor of inviting you*"; a very right manner of speech, even though it appears to us to convey the wrong meaning, for it expresses the idea of doing honor to those who seem worthy of it.

Despite the generosity of the invitation carried from house to house throughout the parish, politeness, which is very cautious amongst peasants, demands that only two persons from each family take advantage of it—one of the heads of the house, and one from the number of their children.

After the invitations were made, the betrothed couple and their families took dinner together at the farm.

Little Marie kept her three sheep on the common, and Germain tilled the soil as though nothing had happened.

About two in the afternoon before the day set for the wedding, the music came. The music means the players of the bagpipe and hurdy-gurdy, their instruments decorated with long streaming ribbons, playing an appropriate march to a measure which would have been rather slow for feet foreign to the soil, but admirably adapted to the heavy ground and hilly roads of the country.

Pistol-shots, fired by the young people and the children, announced the beginning of the wedding ceremonies. Little by little the guests assembled, and danced on the grass-plot before the house in order to enter into the spirit of the occasion. When evening was come they began strange preparations; they divided into two bands, and when night had settled down they proceeded to the ceremony of the *favors*.

All this passed at the dwelling of the bride, Mother Guillette's cottage. Mother Guillette took with her her daughter, a dozen pretty shepherdesses, friends and relatives of her daughter, two or three respectable housewives, talkative neighbors, quick of wit and strict guardians of ancient customs. Next she chose a dozen stout fellows, her relatives and friends; and last of all the parish hemp-dresser, a garrulous old man, and as good a talker as ever there was.

The part which, in Brittany, is played by the bazvalon, the village tailor, is taken in our part of the country by the hemp-dresser and the wool-carder, two professions which are unusually combined in one. He is present at all ceremonies, sad or gay, for he is very learned and a fluent talker, and on these occasions he must always figure as spokesman, in order to fulfil with exactitude certain formalities used from time immemorial. Traveling occupations, which bring a man into the midst of other families, without allowing him to shut himself up within his own, are well fitted to make him talker, wit, storyteller, and singer.

The hemp-dresser is peculiarly skeptical. He and another village functionary, of whom we have spoken before, the grave-digger, are always the daring spirits of the neighborhood. They have talked so much about ghosts, and they know so well all the tricks of which these malicious spirits are capable, that they fear them scarcely at all. It is especially at night that all of them—grave-diggers, hemp-dressers, and ghosts—do their work. It is also at night when the hemp-dresser tells his melancholy stories. Permit me to make a digression.

When the hemp has reached the right stage, that is to say, when it has been steeped sufficiently in running water, and half dried on the bank, it is brought into the yard and arranged in little upright sheaves, which, with their stalks divided at the base, and their heads bound in balls, bear in the dusk some small resemblance to a long procession of little white phantoms, standing on their slender legs, and moving noiselessly along the wall.

It is at the end of September, when the nights are still warm, that they begin to beat it by the pale light of the moon. By day the hemp has been heated in the oven; at night they take it out to beat it while it is still hot. For this they use a kind of horse surmounted by a wooden lever which falls into grooves and breaks the plant without cutting it. It is then that you hear in the night that sudden, sharp noise of three blows in quick succession. Then there is silence; it is the movement of the arm drawing out the handful of hemp to break it in a fresh spot. The three blows begin again; the other arm works the lever, and thus it goes on until the moon is hidden by the early streaks of dawn. As the work continues but a few days in the year, the dogs are not accustomed to it, and yelp their plaintive howls toward every point of the horizon.

It is the time of unwonted and mysterious sounds in the country. The migrating cranes fly so high that by day they are scarcely visible. By night they are only heard, and their hoarse wailing voices, lost in the clouds, sound like the parting cry of souls in torment, striving to find the road to heaven, yet forced by an unconquerable fate to wander near the earth about the haunts of men; for these errant birds have strange uncertainties, and many a mysterious anxiety in the course of their airy flight. Sometimes they lose the wind when the capricious gusts battle, or come and go in the upper regions. When this confusion comes by day, you can see the leader of the file fluttering aimlessly in the air, then turn about and take his place at the tail of the triangular phalanx, while a skilful manoeuver of his companions forms them soon in good order behind him. Often, after vain efforts, the exhausted leader relinquishes the guidance of the caravan; another comes forward, tries in his turn, and yields his place to a third, who finds the breeze, and continues the march in triumph. But what cries, what reproaches, what protests, what wild curses or anxious questionings are exchanged in an unknown tongue amongst these winged pilgrims!

Sometimes, in the resonant night, you can hear these sinister noises whirling for a long time above the housetops, and as you can see nothing, you feel, despite your efforts, a kind of dread and kindred discomfort, until the sobbing multitude is lost in boundless space.

There are other noises too which belong to this time of year, and which sound usually in the orchards. Gathering the fruit is not yet over, and the thousand unaccustomed cracklings make the tree seem alive. A branch groans as it bends beneath a burden which has reached, of a sudden, the last stage of growth; or perhaps an apple breaks from the twig, and falls on the damp earth at your feet with a dull sound. Then you hear rush by, brushing the branches and the grass, a creature you cannot see; it is the peasant's dog, that prowling and uneasy rover, at once impudent and cowardly, always wandering, never sleeping, ever seeking you know not what, spying upon you, hiding in the brush, and taking flight at the sound of a falling apple, which he thinks a stone that you are throwing at him.

It is during those nights, nights misty and gray, that the hemp-dresser tells his weird stories of will-o'-the-wisps and milk-white hares, of souls in torment and wizards changed to wolves, of witches' vigils at the cross-roads, and screech-owls, prophetesses of the graveyard. I remember passing the early hours of such a night while the hemp-dressing was going on, and the pitiless strokes, interrupting the dresser's story at its most awful place, sent icy shivers through our veins. And often too the good man continued his story as he worked, and four or five words were lost, terrible words, no doubt, which we dared not make him repeat, and whose omission added a mystery yet more fearful to the dark mysteries of the story which had gone before. It was in vain the servants warned us that it was too late to stay without doors, and that bedtime had sounded for us long since; they too were dying to hear more; and then with what terror we crossed the hamlet on our way home! How deep did the church porch appear to us, and how thick and black the shadows of the old trees! The graveyard we dared not see; we shut our eyes tight as we passed it.

But no more than the sacristan is the hemp-dresser gifted solely with the desire of frightening; he loves to make people laugh; he is sarcastic and sentimental at need, when love and marriage are to be sung. It is he who collects and keeps stored in his memory the oldest songs, and who transmits them to posterity. And so it is he who acts at weddings the part we shall see him play at the presentation of little Marie's favors.

II — The Wedding Favors

WHEN all the guests were met together in the house, the doors and windows were closed with the utmost care; even the garret window was barricaded; boards and benches, logs and tables were placed behind every entrance, just as if the inhabitants were making ready to sustain a siege; and within these fortifications solemn stillness prevailed until at a distance were heard songs and laughter and the sounds of rustic music. It was the band of the bridegroom, Germain at the head, followed by his most trusty companions and by the grave-digger, relatives, friends, and servants, who formed a compact and merry train. Meanwhile, as they came nearer the house they slackened their pace, held a council of war, and became silent. The girls, shut up in the house, had arranged little loop-holes at the windows by which they could see the enemy approach and deploy in battle array. A fine, cold rain was falling, which added zest to the situation, while a great tire blazed on the hearth within. Marie wished to cut short the inevitable slowness of this well-ordered siege; she had no desire to see her lover catch cold, but not being in authority she had to take an ostensible share in the mischievous cruelty of her companions.

When the two armies met, a discharge of firearms on the part of the besiegers set all the dogs in the neighborhood to barking. Those within the house dashed at the door with loud yelps, thinking that the attack was in earnest, and the children, little reassured by the efforts of their mothers, began to weep and to tremble. The whole scene was played so well that a stranger would have been deceived, and would have made his preparations to tight a band of brigands. Then the grave-digger, bard and orator of the groom, took his stand before the door, and with a rueful voice, exchanged the following dialogue with the hemp-dresser, who was stationed above the same door:

The Grave-digger: "Ah, my good people, my fellow-townsmen, for the love of Heaven, open the door."

The Hemp-dresser: "Who are you, and what right have you to call us your dear fellow-townsmen? We don't know you."

The Grave-digger: "We are worthy folk in great distress. Don't be afraid of us, my friends. Extend us your hospitality. Sleet is falling; our poor feet are frozen, and our journey home has been so long that our sabots are split."

The Hemp-dresser: "If your sabots are split, you can look on the ground; you will find very soon a sprig of willow to make some *arcelets* [small curved blades of iron which are fastened on split sabots to hold them together]."

The Grave-digger: "Willow *arcelets* are scarcely strong enough. You are making fun of us, good people, and you would do better to open your doors. We can see a splendid fire blazing in your dwelling. The spit must be turning, and we can make merry with you, heart and belly. So open your doors to poor pilgrims who will die on the threshold if you are not merciful."

The Hemp-dresser: "Ah ha! so you are pilgrims? You never told us that. And what pilgrimage do you come from, may I ask?"

The Grave-digger: "We shall tell you that when you open the door, for we come from so far that you would never believe it."

The Hemp-dresser: "Open the door to you? I rather think not. We can't trust you. Tell us, is it from Saint Sylvain of Pouligny that you come?"

The Grave-digger: "We have been at Saint Sylvain of Pouligny, but we have been farther still."

The Hemp-dresser: "Then you have been as far as Saint Solange?"

The Grave-digger: "At Saint Solange we have been, sure enough, but we have been farther yet."

The Hemp-dresser: "You are lying. You have never been as far as Saint Solange."

The Grave-digger: "We have been farther, for now we are come from Saint Jacques of Compostelle."

The Hemp-dresser: "What absurdity are you telling us? We don't know that parish. We can easily see that you are bad people, brigands, nobodies, and liars. Go away with your nonsense. We are on our guard. You can't come in."

The Grave-digger: "Ah, my poor fellow, take pity on us. We are not pilgrims, as you have guessed, but we are unlucky poachers pursued by the keepers. Even the police are after us, and if you don't hide us in your hay-loft, we shall be taken and led off to prison."

The Hemp-dresser: "And who will prove you are what you say you are, this time? For you have told us one lie already that you can't maintain."

The Grave-digger: "If you will let us in, we shall show you a pretty piece of game we have killed."

The Hemp-dresser: "Show it right away, for we have our suspicions."

The Grave-digger: "All right, open the door or a window to let us pass the creature in."

The Hemp-dresser: "Oh, no, not quite so foolish. I am looking at you through a little chink, and I can see neither hunters nor game amongst you."

Here an ox-driver, a thick-set fellow of herculean strength, detached himself from a group where he had stood unperceived, and raised toward the window a plucked goose, spitted on a strong iron bar decorated with tufts of straw and ribbons.

"Ho, ho!" cried the hemp-dresser, after cautiously extending an arm to feel the roast. "That isn't a quail nor a partridge; it isn't a hare nor a rabbit; it's something like a goose or a turkey. Upon my word, you 're clever hunters, and that game did n't make you run very far. Move on, you rogues; we know all your lies, and you had best go home and cook your supper. You are not going to eat ours."

The Grave-digger: "O Heavens, where can we go to cook our game? It is very little for so many as we, and, besides, we have neither place nor fire. At this time every door is closed, and every soul asleep. You are the only people who are celebrating a wedding at home, and you must he hardhearted indeed to let us freeze outside. Once again, good people, open the door; we shall not cost you anything. You can see that we bring our own meat; only a little room at your hearth, a little blaze to cook with, and we shall go on our way rejoicing."

The Hemp-dresser: "Do you suppose that we have too much room here, and that wood is bought tor nothing?"

The Grave-digger: "We have here a small bundle of hay to make the fire. We shall be satisfied with that; only grant us leave to place the spit across your fireplace."

The Hemp-dresser: "That will never do. We are disgusted, and don't pity you at all. It is my opinion that you are drunk, that you need nothing, and that you only wish to come in and steal away our fire and our daughters."

The Grave-digger: "Since you won't listen to reason, we shall make our way in by force."

The Hemp-dresser: "Try, if you want; we are shut in well enough to have no fear of you, and since you are impudent fellows, we shall not answer you again."

Thereupon the hemp-dresser shut the garret window with a bang, and came down into the room below by a step-ladder. Then he took the bride by the hand, the young people of both sexes followed, and they all began to sing and chatter merrily, while the matrons sang in piercing voices, and shrieked with laughter in derision and bravado at those without who were attempting an attack.

The besiegers, on their side, made a great hubbub. They discharged their pistols at the doors, made the dogs growl, whacked the walls, shook the blinds, and uttered frightful shrieks. In short, there was such a pandemonium that nobody could hear, and such a cloud of dust that nobody could see.

And yet this attack was all a sham. The time had not come for breaking through the etiquette. If, in prowling about, anybody were to find an unguarded aperture, or any opening whatsoever, he might try to slip in unobserved, and then, if the carrier of the spit succeeded in placing his roast before the fire, and thus prove the capture of the hearth, the comedy was over and the bridegroom had conquered.

The entrances of the house, however, were not numerous enough for any to be neglected in the customary precautions, and nobody might use violence before the moment fixed for the struggle.

When they were weary of dancing and screams, the hemp-dresser began to think of capitulation. He went up to his window, opened it with precaution, and greeted the baffled assailants with a burst of laughter.

"Well, my boys," said he, "you look very sheep-faced. You thought there was nothing easier than to come in, and you see that our defense is good. But we are beginning to have pity on you, if you will submit and accept our conditions."

The Grave-digger: "Speak, good people. Tell us what we must do to approach your hearth."

The Hemp-dresser: "You must sing, my friends; but sing a song we don't know,—one that we can't answer by a better."

"That's not hard to do," answered the grave-digger, and he thundered in a powerful voice: "'Six months ago, 'twas in the spring...'"

"'I wandered through the sprouting grass,'" answered the hemp-dresser in a slightly hoarse but terrible voice. "You must be jesting, my poor friends, singing us such time-worn songs. You see very well that we can stop you at the first word."

"'She was a prince's daughter...'"

"'Right gladly would she wed,'" answered the hemp-dresser. "Come, move on to the next; we know that a little too well."

The Grave-digger: "How do you like this one?—

"'As I was journeying home from Nantes.'"

The Hemp-dresser:

"'Weary, oh, weary, was I, was I.'"

"That dates from my grandmother's time. Let's have another."

The Grave-digger:

"'One day I went a-walking...'"

The Hemp-dresser:

"'Along a lovely wood!'"

"That one is too stupid! Our little children would n't take the trouble to answer you. What! Are these all you know?"

The Grave-digger: "Oh, we shall sing you so many that you will never be able to hear them all."

In this way a full hour passed. As the two antagonists were champions of the country round in the matter of songs, and as their store seemed inexhaustible, the contest might last all night with ease, all the more because the hemp-dresser, with a touch of malice, allowed several ballads of ten, twenty, or thirty couplets to be sung through, feigning by his silence to admit his defeat. Then the bridegroom's camp rejoiced and sang aloud in chorus, and thought that this time the foe was worsted; but at the first line of the last couplet, they heard the hoarse croaking of the old hemp-dresser bellow forth the second rhyme. Then he cried:

"You need not tire yourselves by singing such a long one, my children—we know that one to our finger-tips."

Once or twice, however, the hemp-dresser made a wry face, contracted his brow, and turned toward the expectant housewives with a baffled air. The grave-digger was singing something so old that his adversary had forgotten it, or perhaps had never even heard it; but instantly the good gossips chanted the victorious refrain through their noses with voices shrill as a sea-mew's, and the grave-digger, forced to surrender, went on to fresh attempts.

It would have taken too long to wait for a decision of the victory. The bride's party declared itself disposed to be merciful, provided that the bride were given a present worthy of her.

Then began the song of the favors to a tune solemn as a church chant.

The men without sang together in bass voices:

"'Open the door, true love,
Open the door; I have presents for you, love,
Oh, say not adieu, love.'"

To this the women answered from within in falsetto, with mournful voices:

"'My father is sorry, my mother is sad,
And I am a maiden too kind by far
At such an hour my gate to unbar.'"

The men took up the first verse as far as the fourth line and modified it thus:

"'And a handkerchief new, love.'"

But, on behalf of the bride, the women answered in the same way as at first.

For twenty couplets, at least, the men enumerated all the wedding-presents, always mentioning something new in the last line: a handsome apron, pretty ribbons, a cloth dress, laces, a golden cross, and even a hundred pins to complete the modest list of wedding-presents. The refusal of the women could not be shaken, but at length the men decided to speak of

"A good husband, too, love."

And the women answered, turning toward the bride and singing in unison with the men:

"'Open the door, true love,
Open the door;
Here's a sweetheart for you, love,
Pray let us enter, too, love.'"

III — The Wedding

IMMEDIATELY the hemp-dresser drew back the wooden bolt which barred the door within. At this time it was still the only fastening known in most of the dwellings of our hamlet. The groom's band burst into the bride's house, but not without a struggle; for the young men quartered within, and even the old hemp-dresser and the gossips, made it their duty to defend the hearth. The spit-bearer, upheld by his supporters, had to plant the roast before the fireplace. It was a regular battle, although people abstained from striking, and there was no anger shown in this struggle. But everybody was pushing and shoving so hard, and there was so much playful pride in this display of muscular strength, that the results might well have been serious, although they did not appear so across the laughs and songs. The poor old hemp-dresser, fighting like a lion, was pinned to the wall and squeezed by the crowd until his breath almost left him. More than one champion was upset and trodden under foot involuntarily; more than one hand, jammed against the spit, was covered with blood. These games are dangerous, and latterly the accidents have been so severe that our peasants have determined to allow the ceremony of the favors to fall into disuse; I believe we saw the last at the marriage of François Meillant, although there was no real struggle on that occasion.

The battle was earnest enough, however, at Germain's wedding. It was a point of honor on one side to invade, on the other to defend, Mother Guillette's hearth. The great spit was twisted like a screw beneath the strong fists which fought for it A pistol-shot set fire to a small quantity of hemp arranged in sheaves and laid on a wicker shelf near the ceiling. This incident created a diversion, and while some of the company crowded about to extinguish the sparks, the grave-digger, who had climbed unbeknown into the garret, came down the chimney and seized the spit, at the very moment when the ox-driver, who was defending it near the hearth, raised it above his head to prevent it from being torn away. Some time before the attack, the women had taken the precaution to put out the fire lest in the struggle somebody should fall in and get burned. The jocular grave-digger, in league with the ox-driver, grasped the trophy and tossed it easily across the andirons. It was done! Nobody might interfere. The grave-digger sprang to the middle of the room and lighted a few wisps of straw, which he placed about the spit under pretense of cooking the roast, for the goose was in pieces and the floor was strewn with its scattered fragments.

Then there was a great deal of laughter and much boastful dispute. Everybody showed the marks of the blows he had received, and as it was often a friend's hand that had struck them, there was no word of complaint nor of quarreling. The hemp-dresser, half flattened out, kept rubbing the small of his back and saying that, although it made small difference to him, he protested against the ruse of his friend, the grave-digger, and that if he had not been half dead, the hearth had never been captured so easily. The women swept the floor and order was restored. The table was covered with jugs of new wine. When the contestants had drunk together and taken breath, the bridegroom was led to the middle of the chamber, and, armed with a wand, he was obliged to submit to a fresh trial.

During the struggle, the bride and three of her companions had been hidden by her mother, godmother, and aunts, who had made the four girls sit down in a remote corner of the room while they covered them with a large white cloth. Three friends of Marie's height, with caps of a uniform size, were chosen, so that when they were enveloped from head to toe by the cloth it was impossible to tell them apart.

The bridegroom might not touch them, except with the tip of his staff, and then merely to designate which he thought to be his wife. They allowed him time enough to make an examination with no other help than his eyes afforded, and the women, placed on either side, kept zealous watch lest cheating should occur. Should he guess wrong, he might not dance, with his bride, but only with her he had chosen by mistake.

When Germain stood in front of these ghosts wrapped in the same shroud, he feared he should make a wrong choice; and, in truth, that had happened to many another, so carefully and conscientiously were the precautions made. His heart beat loud. Little Marie did her best to breathe hard and shake the cloth a little, but her malicious companions followed her example, and kept poking the cloth with their fingers, so that there were as many mysterious signals as there were girls beneath the canopy. The square head-dresses upheld the cloth so evenly that it was impossible to discern the contour of a brow outlined by its folds.

After ten minutes' hesitation, Germain shut his eyes, commended his soul to God, and stretched out the wand at random. It touched the forehead of little Marie, who cast the cloth from her, and shouted with triumph. Then it was his right to kiss her, and lifting her in his strong arms, he bore her to the middle of the room, where together they opened the dance, which lasted until two in the morning. The company separated to meet again at eight. As many people had come from the country round, and as there were not beds enough for everybody, each of the village maidens took to her bed two or three other girls, while the men spread themselves pell-mell on the hay in the barn-loft. You can imagine well that they had little sleep, for they did nothing but wrestle and joke, and tell foolish stories. Properly, there were three sleepless nights at weddings, and these we cannot regret.

At the time appointed for departure, when they had partaken of milk-soup, seasoned with a strong dose of pepper to stimulate the appetite,—for the wedding-feast gave promise of great bounty,—the guests assembled in the farm-yard. Since our parish had been abolished, we had to go half a league from home to receive the marriage blessing. It was cool and pleasant weather, but the roads were in such wretched condition that everybody was on horseback, and each man took a companion on his crupper, whether she were young or old. Germain started on the gray, and the mare, well-groomed, freshly shod, and decked out with ribbons, pranced about and snorted fire from her nostrils. The husbandman went to the cottage for his bride in company with his brother-in-law, Jacques, who rode the old gray, and carried Mother Guillette on the crupper, while Germain returned to the farm-yard in triumph, holding his dear little wife before him.

Then the merry cavalcade set out, escorted by the children, who ran ahead and fired off their pistols to make the horses jump. Mother Maurice was seated in a small cart, with Germain's three children and the fiddlers. They led the march to the sound of their instruments. Petit-Pierre was so handsome that his old grandmother was pride itself. But the eager child did not stay long at her side. During a moment's halt made on the journey, before passing through a difficult piece of road, he slipped away and ran to beg his father to carry him in front on the gray.

"No, no," replied Germain, "that will call forth some disagreeable joke; we must n't do it."

"It's little that I care what the people of Saint Chartier say," said little Marie. "Take him up, Germain, please do; I shall be prouder of him than I am of my wedding-gown."

Germain yielded, and the pretty trio darted into the crowd borne by the triumphant gallop of the gray.

And so it was; the people of Saint Chartier, although they were very sarcastic, and somewhat disdainful of the neighboring parishes which had been annexed to theirs, never thought of laughing when they saw such a handsome husband, such a lovely wife, and a child that a king's wife might court. Petit-Pierre was all dressed in light blue cloth, with a smart red waistcoat so short that it descended scarcely below his chin. The village tailor had fitted his armholes so tight that he could not bring his two little hands together. But, oh, how proud he was! He wore a round hat, with a black-and-gold cord, and a peacock's plume which stuck out proudly from a tuft of guinea feathers. A bunch of flowers, bigger than his head, covered his shoulder, and ribbons fluttered to his feet The hemp-dresser, who was also the barber and hair-dresser of the district, had cut his hair evenly, by covering his head with a bowl, and clipping off the protruding locks, an infallible method for guiding the shears. Thus arrayed, the poor child was less poetic, certainly, than with his curls streaming in the wind, and his Saint John Baptist's sheepskin about him; but he knew nothing of this, and everybody admired him and said that he had quite the air of a little man. His beauty triumphed over everything, for what is there over which the exceeding beauty of childhood could not triumph?

His little sister, Solange, had, for the first time in her life, a peasant's cap in place of the calico hood which little girls wear until they are two or three years old. And what a cap it was! Longer and larger than the poor little thing's whole body. How beautiful she thought it! She dared not even turn her head; so she kept quite still and thought the people would take her for the bride.

As for little Sylvain, he was still in long clothes, and, fast asleep on his grandmother's knees, he did not even know what a wedding was.

Germain looked at his children tenderly, and when they reached the town hall, he said to his bride:

"Marie, I have come here with a happier heart than I had the day when I brought you home from the forest of Chanteloube, thinking that you could never love me. I took you in my arms to put you on the ground as I do here; but I thought that never again should we be mounted on the good gray with the child on our knees. I love you so dearly, I love these little creatures so dearly, I am so happy that you love me and that you love them, and that my family love you, and I love your mother so well and all my friends so well, and everybody else so well today, that I wish I had three or four hearts to fill all of them; for surely one is too small to hold so much love and so much happiness. It almost makes my stomach ache."

There was a crowd at the door of the town hall and another at the church to see the pretty bride. Why should we not tell about her dress? it became her so well. Her muslin cap, without spot and covered with embroidery, had lappets trimmed with lace. At that time peasant women never allowed a single lock to be seen, and, although they conceal beneath their caps splendid coils of hair tied up with tape to hold the coif in place, even to-day it would be thought a scandal and a shame for them to show themselves bareheaded to men. Nowadays, however, they allow a slender braid to appear over their foreheads, and this improves their appearance very much. Yet I regret the classic head-dress of my time; its spotless laces next the bare skin gave an effect of pristine purity which seemed to me very solemn; and when a face looked beautiful thus it was with a beauty of which nothing can express the charm and unaffected majesty.

Little Marie wore her cap thus, and her forehead was so white and so pure that it defied the whiteness of linen to cast it in the shade. Although she had not closed an eye the night before, the morning air and, yet more, the joy within of a soul pure as the heaven, and, more than all, a small secret flame guarded with the modesty of girlhood, caused a bloom to mount to her cheeks delicate as the peach-blossom in the first beams of an April sun.

Her white scarf, modestly crossed over her breast, left visible only the soft curves of a neck rounded like a turtle-dove's; her home-made cloth gown of myrtle-green outlined her pretty figure, which looked already perfect, yet which must still grow and develop, for she was but seventeen. She wore an apron of violet silk with the bib our peasant women were so foolish as to suppress, which added so much elegance and decency to the breast. Nowadays they display their scarfs more proudly, but there is no longer in their dress that delicate flower of the purity of long ago, which made them look like Holbein's virgins. They are more forward and more profuse in their courtesies. The good old custom used to be a kind of staid reserve which made their rare smile deeper and more ideal.

During the offertory, after the fashion of the day, Germain placed the "thirteen"—that is to say, thirteen pieces of silver—in his bride's hand. He slipped over her finger a silver ring of a form unchanged for centuries, but which is replaced for henceforth by the golden wedding-ring. As they walked out of church, Marie said in a low voice:

"Is this really the ring I wanted? Is it the one I asked you for, Germain?"

"Yes," answered he, "my Catherine wore it on her finger when she died. There is but one ring for both my weddings."

"Thank you, Germain," said the young woman, in a serious and impressive tone. "I shall die with it on, and if I go before you, you must keep it for the marriage of your little Solange."

IV — The Cabbage

THEY mounted and returned very quickly to Belair. The feast was bountiful, and, mingled with songs and dances, it lasted until midnight. For fourteen hours the old people did not leave the table. The grave-digger did the cooking, and did it very well. He was celebrated for this, and he would leave his fire to come in and dance and sing before and after every course. And yet this poor Father Bontemps was epileptic. Who would have thought it? He was fresh and strong, and merry as a young man. One day we found him in a ditch, struck down by his malady at nightfall. We carried him home with us, in a wheelbarrow, and we spent all night in caring for him. Three days afterward, he was at a wedding, singing like a thrush, jumping like a kid, and bustling about after his old fashion. When he left a marriage, he would go to dig a grave, and nail up a coffin. Then he would become very grave, and though nothing of this appeared in his gay humor, it left a melancholy impression which hastened the return of his attacks. His wife was paralyzed, and had not stirred from her chair for twenty years. His mother is living yet, at a hundred and forty, but he, poor man, so happy and good and amusing, was killed last year by falling from his loft to the sidewalk. Doubtless he died a victim to a fatal attack of his disease, and, as was his habit, had hidden in the hay, so as not to frighten and distress his family. In this tragic manner he ended a life strange as his disposition—a medley of things sad and mad, awful and gay; and, in the midst of all, his heart was ever good and his nature kind.

Now we come to the third day of the wedding, the most curious of all, which is kept to-day in all its vigor. We shall not speak of the roast which they carry to the bridal bed; it is a very silly custom, and hurts the self-respect of the bride, while it tends to ruin the modesty of the attendant girls. Besides, I believe that it is practised in all the provinces, and does not belong peculiarly to our own.

Just as the ceremony of the wedding favors is a symbol that the heart and home of the bride are won, that of the cabbage is a symbol of the fruit-fulness of marriage. When breakfast is over on the day after the wedding, this fantastic representation begins. Originally of Gallic derivation, it has passed through primitive Christianity, and little by little it has become a kind of mystery, or droll morality-play of the Middle Ages.

Two boys, the merriest and most intelligent of the company, disappear from breakfast, and after costuming themselves, return escorted by dogs, children, and pistol-shots. They represent a pair of beggars—husband and wife—dressed in rags. The husband is the filthier of the two; it is vice which has brought him so low; the wife is unhappy and degraded only through the misdeeds of her husband.

They are called the gardener and the gardener's wife, and they pretend it is their duty to guard and care for the sacred cabbage. The husband has several names, each with a meaning. Sometimes they call him the "scarecrow," because his head is covered with straw or hemp, and because his legs and a portion of his body are surrounded with straw to hide his nakedness, ill concealed by his rags. He has also a great belly, or hump, constructed of straw or hay underneath his blouse. Then he is known as the "ragamuffin," on account of his covering of rags. Lastly he is termed the "infidel," and this is most significant of all, because by his cynicism and his debauchery he is supposed to typify the opposite of every Christian virtue.

He comes with his face all smeared with soot and the lees of wine, and sometimes made yet more hideous by a grotesque mask. An earthenware cup, notched and broken, or an old sabot attached to his girdle by a cord, shows that he has come to beg for alms of wine. Nobody refuses him, and he pretends to drink; then he pours the wine on the ground by way of libation. At every step he falls, rolls in the mud, and feigns to be a prey to the most shameful drunkenness. His poor wife runs after him, picks him up, calls for help, arranges his hempen locks, which straggle forth in unkempt wisps from beneath his filthy hat, sheds tears over her husband's degradation, and pours forth pathetic reproaches.

"Wretched man," she cries, "see the misery to which your wickedness has brought us. I have to spend all my time sewing and working for you, mending your clothes. You tear and bedraggle yourself incessantly. You have eaten up all my little property; our six children lie on straw, and we are living in a stable with the beasts. Here we are forced to beg for alms, and, besides, you are so ugly and vile and despicable that very soon they will be tossing us bread as if we were dogs. Ah, my poor people, take pity on us! Take pity on me! I have n't deserved my lot, and never had woman a more dirty and detestable husband. Help me to pick him up, else the wagons will run over him as they run over broken bottles, and I shall be a widow, and that will end by killing me with grief, though all the world says it would be an excellent riddance for me." Such is the part of the gardener's wife, and her continued lamentations last during the entire play. For it is a genuine spontaneous comedy acted on the spur of the moment in the open air, along the roads and across the fields, aided by every chance occurrence that presents itself. Everybody shares in the acting, people within the wedding-party and people without, wayfarers and dwellers in houses, for three or four hours of the day, as we shall see. The theme is always the same, but the variations are infinite; and it is here that we can see the instinct of mimicry, the abundance of droll ideas, the fluency, the wit at repartee, and even the natural eloquence of our peasants.

The rôle of gardener's wife is intrusted commonly to a slender man, beardless and fresh of face, who can give a great appearance of truth to his personification and plays the burlesque despair naturally enough to make people sad and glad at once, as they are in real life. These thin, beardless men are not rare among us, and, strangely enough, they are sometimes most remarkable for their muscular strength.

When the wife's misfortunes have been explained, the young men of the company try to persuade her to leave her drunken husband and to amuse herself with them. They offer her their arms and drag her away. Little by little she gives way; her spirits rise, and she begins to run about, first with one and then with another, and grows more scandalous in her behavior: a fresh "morality"; the ill-conduct of the husband excites and aggravates the evil in the wife.

Then the "infidel" wakes from his drunkenness. He looks about for his companion, arms himself with a rope and a stick and rushes after her. They make him run, they hide, they pass the wife from one to another, they try to divert her attention and to deceive her jealous spouse. His friends try to get him drunk. At length he catches his unfaithful wife, and wishes to beat her. What is truest and most carefully portrayed in this play is that the jealous husband never attacks the men who carry off his wife. He is very polite and prudent with them, and wishes only to take vengeance on the sinning woman, because she is supposed to be too feeble to offer resistance.

At the moment, however, when he raises his stick and prepares his cord to strike the delinquent, all the men in the party interpose and throw themselves between husband and wife.

"Don't strike her! Never strike your wife," is the formula repeated to satiety during these scenes. They disarm the husband, and force him to pardon and to kiss his wife, and soon he pretends to love her better than ever. He walks along, his arm linked in hers, singing and dancing until, in a new access of drunkenness, he rolls upon the ground, and then begin all over again the lamentations of the wife, her discouragements, her pretended unfaithfulness, her husband's jealousy, the interference of the neighbors, and the reconciliation. In all this there is a simple and even coarse lesson, which, though it savors strongly of its Middle-Age origin, does not fail to fix its impression if not on the married folk, who are too loving or too sensible to have need of it, at least upon the children and the young people. The "infidel," racing after young girls and pretending to wish to kiss them, frightens and disgusts them to such a degree that they fly in unaffected terror. His dirty face and his great stick, harmless as it is, make the children shriek aloud. It is the comedy of customs in their most elementary but their most striking state.

When this farce is well under way, people make ready to hunt for the cabbage. They bring a stretcher and place upon it the "infidel," armed with a spade, a cord, and a large basket. Four powerful men raise him on their shoulders. His wife follows on foot, and after her come the "elders" in a body with serious and thoughtful looks; then the wedding-march begins by couples to a step tuned to music. Pistol-shots begin anew, and dogs bark louder than ever at the sight of the filthy "infidel" borne aloft in triumph. The children swing incense in derision with sabots fastened at the end of a cord.

But why this ovation to an object so repulsive? They are marching to the capture of the sacred cabbage, emblem of the fruitfulness of marriage, and it is this drunkard alone who can bear the symbolic plant in his hand. Doubtless, there is in it a pre-Christian mystery which recalls the Saturnalian feasts or some rout of the Bacchanals. Perhaps this "infidel," who is, at the same time, preeminently a gardener, is none other than Priapus himself, god of gardens and of drunkenness, a divinity who must have been pure and serious in his origin as is the mystery of birth, but who has been degraded bit by bit through license of manners and distraction of thought.

However this may be, the triumphal procession arrives at the bride's house, and enters the garden. Then they select the choicest cabbage, and this is not done very quickly, for the old people keep consulting and disputing interminably, each one pleading for the cabbage he thinks most suitable. They put it to vote, and when the choice is made the gardener fastens his cord to the stalk, and moves away as far as the size of the garden permits. The gardener's wife takes care that the sacred vegetable shall not be hurt in its fall. The wits of the wedding, the hemp-dresser, the grave-digger, the carpenter, and the sabot-maker, form a ring about the cabbage, for men who do not till the soil, but pass their lives in other people's houses, are thought to be, and are really, wittier and more talkative than simple farmhands. One digs, with a spade, a ditch deep enough to uproot an oak. Another places on his nose a pair of wooden or cardboard spectacles. He fulfils the duties of "engineer," walks up and down, constructs a plan, stares at the workmen through his glasses, plays the pedant, cries out that everything will be spoiled, has the work stopped and begun afresh as his fancy directs, and makes the whole performance as long and ridiculous as he can. This is an addition to the formula of an ancient ceremony held in mockery of theorists in general, for peasants despise them royally, or from hatred of the surveyors who decide boundaries and regulate taxes, or of the workmen employed on bridges and causeways, who transform commons into highways, and suppress old abuses which the peasants love. Be this as it may, this character in the comedy is called the "geometrician," and does his best to make himself unbearable to those who are toiling with pickaxe and shovel.

After a quarter of an hour spent in mummery, and difficulties raised in order to avoid cutting the roots, and to transplant the cabbage without injury, while shovelfuls of dirt are tossed into the faces of the onlookers,—so much the worse for him who does not retreat in time, for were he bishop or prince he must receive the baptism of earth,—the "infidel" pulls the rope, the "infidel's wife" holds her apron, and the cabbage falls majestically amidst the applause of the spectators. Then a basket is brought, and the "infidel" pair plant the cabbage therein with every care and precaution. They surround it with fresh earth, and support it with sticks and strings, such as city florists use for their splendid potted camellias; they fix red apples to the points of the sticks, and twist sprigs of thyme, sage, and laurel all about them; they bedeck the whole with ribbons and streamers; they place the trophy upon the stretcher with the "infidel," whose duty it is to maintain its equilibrium and preserve it from harm; and, at length, they move away from the garden in good order and in marching step.

But when they are about to pass the gate, and again when they enter the yard of the bridegroom's house, an imaginary obstacle blocks the way. The bearers of the burden stagger, utter loud cries, retreat, advance once more, and, as though crushed by a resistless force, they pretend to sink beneath its weight. While this is going on, the bystanders shout loudly, exciting and steadying this human team.

"Slowly, slowly, my child. There, there, courage! Look out! Be patient! Lower your head; the door is too low! Close up; it's too narrow! A little more to the left; now to the right; on with you; don't be afraid; you 're almost there."

Thus it is that in years of plentiful harvest, the ox-cart, loaded to overflowing with hay or corn, is too broad or too high to enter the barn door. Thus it is that the driver shouts at the strong beasts, to restrain them or to urge them on; thus it is that with skill and mighty efforts they force this mountain of riches beneath the rustic arch of triumph. It is, above all, the last load, called "the cart of sheaves," which requires these precautions, for this is a rural festival, and the last sheaf lifted from the last furrow is placed on the top of the cart-load ornamented with ribbons and flowers, while the foreheads of the oxen and the whip of the driver are decorated also. The triumphant and toilsome entry of the cabbage into the house is a symbol of the prosperity and fruitfulness it represents.

Safe within the bridegroom's yard, the cabbage is taken from its stretcher and borne to the topmost peak of the house or barn. Whether it be a chimney, a gable, or a dove-cote that crowns the roof, the burden must, at any risk, be carried to the very highest point of the building. The "infidel" accompanies it as far as this, sets it down securely, and waters it with a great pitcher of wine, while a salvo of pistol-shots and demonstrations of joy from the "infidel's wife" proclaim its inauguration.

Without delay, the same ceremony is repeated all over again. Another cabbage is dug from the garden of the husband and is carried with the same formalities and laid upon the roof which his wife has deserted to follow him. These trophies remain in their places until the wind and the rain destroy the baskets and carry away the cabbage. Yet their lives are long enough to give some chance of fulfilment to the prophecies which the old men and women make with bows and courtesies.

"Beautiful cabbage," they say, "live and flourish that our young bride may have a fine baby before a year is over; for if you die too quickly it is a sign of barrenness, and you will stick up there like an ill omen."

The day is already far gone when all these things are accomplished. All that remains undone is to take home the godfathers and godmothers of the newly married couple. When the so-called parents dwell at a distance, they are accompanied by the music and the whole wedding procession as far as the limits of the parish; there they dance anew on the highroad, and everybody kisses them good-by. The "infidel" and his wife are then washed and dressed decently, if the fatigue of their parts has not already driven them away to take a nap.

Everybody was still dancing and singing and eating in the Town Hall of Belair at midnight on this third day of the wedding when Germain was married. The old men at table could not stir, and for good reason. They recovered neither their legs nor their wits until dawn on the morrow. While they were regaining their dwellings, silently and with uncertain steps, Germain, proud and active, went out to hitch his oxen, leaving his young wife to slumber until daylight. The lark, caroling as it mounted to the skies, seemed to him the voice of his heart returning thanks to Providence. The hoar-frost, sparkling on the leafless bushes, seemed to him the whiteness of April flowers that comes before the budding leaves. Everything in nature was laughing and happy for him. Little Pierre had laughed and jumped so much the evening before that he did not come to help lead his oxen; but Germain was glad to be alone. He fell on his knees in the furrow he was about to plow afresh, and said his morning prayer with such a burst of feeling that two tears rolled down his cheeks, still moist with sweat.

Afar off he heard the songs of the boys from neighboring villages, who were starting on their return home, singing again in their hoarse voices the happy tunes of the night before.

THE END.

MAUPRAT

by George Sand

Translated by Stanley Young

GEORGE SAND

Napoleon in exile declared that were he again on the throne he should make a point of spending two hours a day in conversation with women, from whom there was much to be learnt. He had, no doubt, several types of women in mind, but it is more than probable that the banishment of Madame de Stael rose before him as one of the mistakes in his career. It was not that he showed lack of judgment merely by the persecution of a rare talent, but by failing to see that the rare talent was pointing out truths very valuable to his own safety. This is what happened in France when George Sand—the greatest woman writer the world has known, or is ever likely to know—was attacked by the orthodox critics of her time. They feared her warnings; they detested her sincerity—a sincerity displayed as much in her life as in her works (the hypocrite's Paradise was precisely her idea of Hell); they resented bitterly an independence of spirit which in a man would have been in the highest degree distinguished, which remained, under every test, untamable. With a kind of *bonhomie* which one can only compare with Fielding's, with a passion as great as Montaigne's for acknowledging the truths of experience, with an absence of self-consciousness truly amazing in the artistic temperament of either sex, she wrote exactly as she thought, saw and felt. Humour was not her strong point. She had an exultant joy in living, but laughter, whether genial or sardonic, is not in her work. Irony she seldom, if ever, employed; satire she never attempted. It was on the maternal, the sympathetic side that her femininity, and therefore her creative genius, was most strongly developed. She was masculine only in the deliberate libertinism of certain episodes in her own life. This was a characteristic—one on no account to be overlooked or denied or disguised, but it was not her character. The character was womanly, tender, exquisitely patient and good-natured. She would take cross humanity in her arms, and carry it out into the sunshine of the fields; she would show it flowers and birds, sing songs to it, tell it stories, recall its original beauty. Even in her moods of depression and revolt, one recognises the fatigue of the strong. It is never for a moment the lassitude of the feeble, the weary spite of a sick and ill-used soul. As she was free from personal vanity, she was also free from hysteria. On marriage—the one subject which drove her to a certain though always disciplined violence—she clearly felt more for others than they felt for themselves; and in observing certain households and life partnerships, she may have been afflicted with a dismay which the unreflecting sufferers did not share. No writer who was carried away by egoistic anger or disappointment could have told these stories of unhappiness, infidelity, and luckless love with such dispassionate lucidity.

With the artist's dislike of all that is positive and arbitrary, she was, nevertheless, subject rather to her intellect than her emotions. An insult to her intelligence was the one thing she found it hard to pardon, and she allowed no external interference to disturb her relations with her own reasoning faculty. She followed caprices, no doubt, but she was never under any apprehension with regard to their true nature, displaying in this respect a detachment which is usually considered exclusively virile. *Elle et Lui*, which, perhaps because it is short and associated with actual facts, is the most frequently discussed in general conversation on her work, remains probably the sanest account of a sentimental experiment which was ever written. How far it may have seemed accurate to De Musset is not to the point. Her version of her grievance is at least convincing. Without fear and without hope, she makes her statement, and it stands, therefore, unique of its kind among indictments. It has been said that her fault was an excess of emotionalism; that is to say, she attached too much importance to mere feeling and described it, in French of marvellous ease and beauty, with a good deal of something else which one can almost condemn as the high-flown. Not that the high-flown is of necessity unnatural, but it is misleading; it places the passing mood, the lyrical note, dependent on so many accidents, above the essential temperament and the dominant chord which depend on life only. Where she falls short of the very greatest masters is in this all but deliberate confusion of things which must change or can be changed with things which are unchangeable, incurable, and permanent. Shakespeare, it is true, makes all his villains talk poetry, but it is the poetry which a villain, were he a poet, would inevitably write. George Sand glorifies every mind with her own peculiar fire and tears. The fire is, fortunately, so much stronger than the tears that her passion never degenerates into the maudlin. All the same, she makes too universal a use of her own strongest gifts, and this is why she cannot be said to excel as a portrait painter. One merit, however, is certain: if her earliest writings were dangerous, it was because of her wonderful power of idealization, not because she filled her pages with the revolting and epicene sensuality of the new Italian, French, and English schools. Intellectual viciousness was not her failing, and she never made the modern mistake of confusing indecency with vigour. She loved nature, air, and light too well and too truly to go very far wrong in her imaginations. It may indeed be impossible for many of us to accept all her social and political views; they have no bearing, fortunately, on the quality of her literary art; they have to be considered under a different aspect. In politics, her judgment, as displayed in the letters to Mazzini, was profound. Her correspondence with Flaubert shows us a capacity for stanch, unblemished friendship unequalled, probably, in the biographies, whether published or unpublished, of the remarkable.

With regard to her impiety—for such it should be called—it did not arise from arrogance, nor was it based in any way upon the higher learning of her period. Simply she did not possess the religious instinct. She understood it sympathetically—in *Spiridion*, for instance, she describes an ascetic nature as it has never been done in any other work of fiction. Newman himself has not written passages of deeper or purer mysticism, of more sincere spirituality. Balzac, in *Seraphita*, attempted something of the kind, but the result was never more than a *tour de force*. He could invent, he could describe, but George Sand felt; and as she felt, she composed, living with and loving with an understanding love all her creations. But it has to be remembered always that she repudiated all religious restraint, that she believed in the human heart, that she acknowledged no higher law than its own impulses, that she saw love where others see only a cruel struggle for existence, that she found beauty where ordinary visions can detect little besides a selfishness worse than brutal and a squalor more pitiful than death. Everywhere she insists upon the purifying influence of affection, no matter how degraded in its circumstances or how illegal in its manifestation. No writer—not excepting the Brontes—has shown a deeper sympathy with uncommon temperaments, misunderstood aims, consciences with flickering lights, the discontented, the abnormal, or the unhappy. The great modern specialist for nervous diseases has not improved on her analysis of the neuropathic and hysterical. There is scarcely a novel of hers in which some character does not appear who is, in the usual phrase, out of the common run. Yet, with this perfect understanding of the exceptional case, she never permits any science of cause and effect to obscure the rules and principles which in the main control life for the majority. It was, no doubt, this balance which made her a popular writer, even while she never ceased to keep in touch with the most acute minds of France.

She possessed, in addition to creative genius of an order especially individual and charming, a capacity for the invention of ideas. There are in many of her chapters more ideas, more suggestions than one would find in a whole volume of Flaubert. It is not possible that these surprising, admirable, and usually sound thoughts were the result of long hours of reflection. They belonged to her nature and a quality of judgment which, even in her most extravagant romances, is never for a moment swayed from that sane impartiality described by the unobservant as common sense.

Her fairness to women was not the least astounding of her gifts. She is kind to the beautiful, the yielding, above all to the very young, and in none of her stories has she introduced any violently disagreeable female characters. Her villains are mostly men, and even these she invests with a picturesque fatality which drives them to errors, crimes, and scoundrelism with a certain plaintive, if relentless, grace. The inconstant lover is invariably pursued by the furies of remorse; the brutal has always some mitigating influence in his career; the libertine retains through many vicissitudes a seraphic love for some faithful Solveig.

Humanity meant far more to her than art: she began her literary career by describing facts as she knew them: critics drove her to examine their causes, and so she gradually changed from the chronicler with strong sympathies to the interpreter with a reasoned philosophy. She discovered that a great deal of the suffering in this world is due not so much to original sin, but to a kind of original stupidity, an unimaginative, stubborn stupidity. People were dishonest because they believed, wrongly, that dishonesty was somehow successful. They were cruel because they supposed that repulsive exhibitions of power inspired a prolonged fear. They were treacherous because they had never been taught the greater strength of candour. George Sand tried to point out the advantage of plain dealing, and the natural goodness of mankind when uncorrupted by a false education. She loved the wayward and the desolate: pretentiousness in any disguise was the one thing she suspected and could not tolerate. It may be questioned whether she ever deceived herself; but it must be said, that on the whole she flattered weakness—and excused, by enchanting eloquence, much which cannot always be justified merely on the ground that it is explicable. But to explain was something—all but everything at the time of her appearance in literature. Every novel she wrote made for charity—for a better acquaintance with our neighbour's woes and our own egoism. Such an attitude of mind is only possible to an absolutely frank, even Arcadian, nature. She did what she wished to do: she said what she had to say, not because she wanted to provoke excitement or astonish the multitude, but because she had succeeded eminently in leading her own life according to her own lights. The terror of appearing inconsistent excited her scorn. Appearances never troubled that unashamed soul. This is the magic, the peculiar fascination of her books. We find ourselves in the presence of a freshness, a primeval vigour which produces actually the effect of seeing new scenes, of facing a fresh climate. Her love of the soil, of flowers, and the sky, for whatever was young and unspoilt, seems to animate every page—even in her passages of rhetorical sentiment we never suspect the burning pastille, the gauze tea-gown, or the depressed pink light. Rhetoric it may be, but it is the rhetoric of the sea and the wheat field. It can be spoken in the open air and read by the light of day.

George Sand never confined herself to any especial manner in her literary work. Her spontaneity of feeling and the actual fecundity, as it were, of her imaginative gift, could not be restrained, concentrated, and formally arranged as it was in the case of the two first masters of modern French novel-writing. Her work in this respect may be compared to a gold mine, while theirs is rather the goldsmith's craft. It must not be supposed, however, that she was a writer without very strong views with regard to the construction of a plot and the development of character. Her literary essays and reviews show a knowledge of technique which could be accepted at any time as a text-book for the critics and the criticised. She knew exactly how artistic effects were obtained, how and why certain things were done, why realism, so-called, could never be anything but caricature, and why over-elaboration of small matters can never be otherwise than disproportionate. Nothing could be more just than her saying about Balzac that he was such a logician that he invented things more truthful than the truth itself. No one knew better than she that the truth, as it is commonly understood, does not exist; that it cannot be logical because of its mystery; and that it is the knowledge of its contradictions which shows the real expert in psychology.

Three of her stories—*La Petite Fadette*, *La Mare au Diable*, and *Les Maitres Mosaistes*—are as neat in their workmanship as a Dutch painting. Her brilliant powers of analysis, the intellectual atmosphere with which she surrounds the more complex characters in her longer romances, are entirely put aside, and we are given instead a series of pictures and dialogues in what has been called the purely objective style; so pure in its objectivity and detachment that it would be hard for any one to decide from internal evidence that they were in reality her own composition.

To those who seek for proportion and form there is, without doubt, much that is unsymmetrical in her designs. Interesting she always is, but to the trained eye scenes of minor importance are, strictly speaking, too long: descriptions in musical language sometimes distract the reader from the progress of the story. But this arose from her own joy in writing: much as she valued proportion, she liked expressing her mind better, not out of conceit or self-importance, but as the birds, whom she loved so well, sing.

Good nature is what we need above all in reading George Sand. It is there—infectious enough in her own pages, and with it the courage which can come only from a heart at peace with itself. This is why neither fashion nor new nor old criticism can affect the title of George Sand among the greatest influences of the last century and the present one. Much that she has said still seems untried and unexpected. Writers so opposite as Ibsen and Anatole France have expanded her themes. She is quoted unconsciously to-day by hundreds who are ignorant of their real source of inspiration. No woman ever wrote with such force before, and no woman since has even approached her supreme accomplishments.

PEARL MARY-TERESA CRAIGIE.

LIFE OF GEORGE SAND

George Sand, in whose life nothing was commonplace, was born in Paris, "in the midst of roses, to the sound of music," at a dance which her mother had somewhat rashly attended, on the 5th of July, 1804. Her maiden name was Armentine Lucile Aurore Dupin, and her ancestry was of a romantic character. She was, in fact, of royal blood, being the great-grand-daughter of the Marshal Maurice du Saxe and a Mlle. Verriere; her grandfather was M. Dupin de Francueil, the charming friend of Rousseau and Mme. d'Epinay; her father, Maurice Dupin, was a gay and brilliant soldier, who married the pretty daughter of a bird-fancier, and died early. She was a child of the people on her mother's side, an aristocrat on her father's. In 1807 she was taken by her father, who was on Murat's staff, into Spain, from which she returned to the house of her grandmother, at Nohant in Berry. This old lady adopted Aurore at the death of her father, in 1808. Of her childhood George Sand has given a most picturesque account in her "Histoire de ma Vie." In 1817 the girl was sent to the Convent of the English Augustinians in Paris, where she passed through a state of religious mysticism. She returned to Nohant in 1820, and soon threw off her pietism in the outdoor exercises of a wholesome country life. Within a few months, Mme. Dupin de Francueil died at a great age, and Aurore was tempted to return to Paris. Her relatives, however, were anxious that she should not do this, and they introduced to her the natural son of a retired colonel, the Baron Dudevant, whom, in September, 1822, she married. She brought him to live with her at Nohant, and she bore him two sons, Maurice and Solange, and a daughter. She quickly perceived, as her own intellectual nature developed, that her boorish husband was unsuited to her, but their early years of married life were not absolutely intolerable. In 1831, however, she could endure him no longer, and an amicable separation was agreed upon. She left M. Dudevant at Nohant, resigning her fortune, and proceeded to Paris, where she was hard pressed to find a living. She endeavoured, without success, to paint the lids of cigar-boxes, and in final desperation, under the influence of Jules Sandeau—who became her lover, and who invented the pseudonym of George Sand for her—she turned her attention to literature. Her earliest work was to help Sandeau in the composition of his novel, "Rose et Blanche" Her first independent novel, "Indiana," appeared at the close of 1831, and her second, "Valentine," two months later. These books produced a great and immediate sensation, and she felt that she had found her vocation. In 1833 she produced "Lebia"; in 1834 the "Lettres d'un Voyageur" and "Jacques"; in 1835 "Andre" and "Leone Leoni." After this her works become too numerous and were produced with too monotonous a regularity to be chronicled here. But it should be said that "Mauprat" was written in 1836 at Nohant, while she was pleading for a legal separation from her husband, which was given her by the tribunal of Bourges, with full authority over the education of her children. These early novels all reflect in measure the personal sorrows of the author, although George Sand never ceased to protest against too strict a biographical interpretation of their incidents. "Spiridion" (1839), composed under the influence of Lamennais, deals with questions of free thought in religion. But the novels of the first period of her literary activity, which came to a close in 1840, are mainly occupied with a lyrical individualism, and are inspired by the wrongs and disillusions of the author's personal adventures.

The years 1833 and 1834 were marked by her too-celebrated relations with Alfred de Musset, with whom she lived in Paris and at Venice, and with whom she quarrelled at last in circumstances deplorably infelicitous. Neither of these great creatures had the reticence to exclude the world from a narrative of their misfortunes and adventures; of the two it was fairly certainly the woman who came the less injured out of the furnace. In "Elle et Lui" (1859) she gave long afterward her version of the unhappy and undignified story. Her stay in Venice appears to have impressed her genius more deeply than any other section of her numerous foreign sojournings.

The writings of George Sand's second period, which extended from 1840 to 1848, are of a more general character, and are tinged with a generous but not very enlightened ardour for social emancipation. Of these novels, the earliest is "Le Compagnon du Tour de France" (1840), which is scarcely a masterpiece. In the pursuit of foreign modes of thought, and impelled by experiences of travel, George Sand rose to far greater heights in "Jeanne" (1842), in "Consuelo" (1842-'43), and in "La Comtesse de Rudolstade" (1844). All these books were composed in her retirement at Nohant, where she definitely settled in 1839, after having travelled for several months in Switzerland with Liszt and Mme. d'Agoult, and having lived in the island of Majorca for some time with the dying Chopin, an episode which is enshrined in her "Lucrezia Floriani" (1847).

The Revolution of 1848 appeared to George Sand a realization of her Utopian dreams, and plunged her thoughts into a painful disorder. She soon, however, became dissatisfied with the result of her republican theories, and she turned to two new sources of success, the country story and the stage. Her delicious romance of "Francois le Champi" (1850) attracted a new and enthusiastic audience to her, and her entire emancipation from "problems" was marked in the pages of "La Petite Fadette" and of "La Mare au Diable." To the same period belong "Les Visions de la Nuit des les Campagnes," "Les Maitres Sonneurs," and "Cosina." From 1850 to 1864 she gave a great deal of attention to the theatre, and of her numerous pieces several enjoyed a wide and considerable success, although it cannot be said that any of her plays have possessed the vitality of her best novels. The most solid of the former was her dramatization of her story, "Le Marquis de Villemer" (1864), which was one of the latest, and next to it "Le Mariage de Victorine" (1851), which was one of the earliest. Her successes on the stage, such as they are, appear mainly due to collaboration with others.

In her latest period, from 1860 to 1876, George Sand returned to her first lyrical manner, although with more reticence and a wider experience of life. Of the very abundant fruitage of these last years, not many rank with the masterpieces of her earlier periods, although such novels as "Tamaris" (1862), "La Confession d'une Jeune Fille" (1865), and "Cadio," seemed to her admirers to show no decline of force or fire. Still finer, perhaps, were "Le Marquis de Villemer" (1861) and "Jean de la Roche" (1860). Her latest production, which appeared after her death, was the "Contes d'une Grand'mere," a collection full of humanity and beauty. George Sand died at Nohant on the 8th of June, 1876. She had great qualities of soul, and in spite of the naive irregularities of her conduct in early middle life, she cannot be regarded otherwise than as an excellent woman. She was brave, courageous, heroically industrious, a loyal friend, a tender and wise mother. Her principle fault has been wittily defined by Mr. Henry James, who has remarked that in affairs of the heart George Sand never "behaved like a gentleman."

E. G.

PREFACE

When I wrote my novel *Mauprat* at Nohant—in 1846, if I remember rightly—I had just been suing for a separation. Hitherto I had written much against the abuses of marriage, and perhaps, though insufficiently explaining my views, had induced a belief that I failed to appreciate its essence; but it was at this time that marriage itself stood before me in all the moral beauty of its principle.

Misfortune is not without its uses to the thoughtful mind. The more clearly I had realized the pain and pity of having to break a sacred bond, the more profoundly I felt that where marriage is wanting, is in certain elements of happiness and justice of too lofty a nature to appeal to our actual society. Nay, more; society strives to take from the sanctity of the institution by treating it as a contract of material interests, attacking it on all sides at once, by the spirit of its manners, by its prejudices, by its hypocritical incredulity.

While writing a novel as an occupation and distraction for my mind, I conceived the idea of portraying an exclusive and undying love, before, during, and after marriage. Thus I drew the hero of my book proclaiming, at the age of eighty, his fidelity to the one woman he had ever loved.

The ideal of love is assuredly eternal fidelity. Moral and religious laws have aimed at consecrating this ideal. Material facts obscure it. Civil laws are so framed as to make it impossible or illusory. Here, however, is not the place to prove this. Nor has *Mauprat* been burdened with a proof of the theory; only, the sentiment by which I was specially penetrated at the time of writing it is embodied in the words of *Mauprat* towards the end of the book: "She was the only woman I loved in all my life; none other ever won a glance from me, or knew the pressure of my hand."

GEORGE SAND.

June 5, 1857.

TO GUSTAVE PAPET

Though fashion may proscribe the patriarchal fashion of dedications, I would ask you, brother and friend, to accept this of a tale which is not new to you. I have drawn my materials in part from the cottages of our Noire valley. May we live and die there, repeating every evening our beloved invocation:

SANCTA SIMPLICITAS! GEORGE SAND.

MAUPRAT

On the borders of La Marche and Berry, in the district known as Varenne, which is naught but a vast moor studded with forests of oak and chestnut, and in the most thickly wooded and wildest part of the country, may be found, crouching within a ravine, a little ruined chateau. The dilapidated turrets would not catch your eye until you were about a hundred yards from the principal portcullis. The venerable trees around and the scattered rocks above, bury it in everlasting obscurity; and you would experience the greatest difficulty, even in broad daylight, in crossing the deserted path leading to it, without stumbling against the gnarled trunks and rubbish that bar every step. The name given to this dark ravine and gloomy castle is Roche-Mauprat.

It was not so long ago that the last of the Mauprats, the heir to this property, had the roofing taken away and all the woodwork sold. Then, as if to give a kick to the memory of his ancestors, he ordered the entrance gate to be thrown down, the north tower to be gutted, and a breach to be made in the surrounding wall. This done, he departed with his workmen, shaking the dust from off his feet, and abandoning his domain to foxes, and cormorants, and vipers. Since then, whenever the wood-cutters and charcoal-burners from the huts in the neighbourhood pass along the top of the Roche-Mauprat ravine, if it is in daytime they whistle with a defiant air or hurl a hearty curse at the ruins; but when day falls and the goat-sucker begins to screech from the top of the loopholes, wood-cutter and charcoal-burner pass by silently, with quickened step, and cross themselves from time to time to ward off the evil spirits that hold sway among the ruins.

For myself, I own that I have never skirted the ravine at night without feeling a certain uneasiness; and I would not like to swear that on some stormy nights I have not given my horse a touch of the spur, in order to escape the more quickly from the disagreeable impression this neighbourhood made on me.

The reason is that in childhood I classed the name of Mauprat with those of Cartouche and Bluebeard; and in the course of horrible dreams I often used to mix up the ancient legends of the Ogre and the Bogey with the quite recent events which in our province had given such a sinister lustre to this Mauprat family.

Frequently, out shooting, when my companions and I have left our posts to go and warm ourselves at the charcoal fires which the workmen keep up all night, I have heard this name dying away on their lips at our approach. But when they had recognised us and thoroughly satisfied themselves that the ghosts of none of these robbers were hiding in our midst, they would tell us in a whisper such stories as might make one's hair stand on end, stories which I shall take good care not to pass on to you, grieved as I am that they should ever have darkened and pained my own memory.

Not that the story I am about to tell is altogether pleasant and cheerful. On the contrary, I must ask your pardon for unfolding so sombre a tale. Yet, in the impression which it has made on myself there is something so consoling and, if I may venture the phrase, so healthful to the soul, that you will excuse me, I hope, for the sake of the result. Besides this is a story which has just been told to me. And now you ask me for one. The opportunity is too good to be missed for one of my laziness or lack of invention.

It was only last week that I met Bernard Mauprat, the last of the line, the man who, having long before severed himself from his infamous connections, determined to demolish his manor as a sign of the horror aroused in him by the recollections of childhood. This Bernard is one of the most respected men in the province. He lives in a pretty house near Chateauroux, in a flat country. Finding myself in the neighbourhood, with a friend of mine who knows him, I expressed a wish to be introduced; and my friend, promising me a hearty welcome, took me to his house then and there.

I already knew in outline the remarkable history of this old man; but I had always felt a keen desire to fill in the details, and above all to receive them from himself. For me, the strange destiny of the man was a philosophical problem to be solved. I therefore noticed his features, his manners, and his home with peculiar interest.

Bernard Mauprat must be fully eighty-four, though his robust health, his upright figure, his firm step, and the absence of any infirmity might indicate some fifteen or twenty years less. His face would have appeared to me extremely handsome, had not a certain harshness of expression brought before my eyes, in spite of myself, the shades of his fathers. I very much fear that, externally at all events, he must resemble them. This he alone could have told us; for neither my friend nor myself had known any other Mauprat. Naturally, however, we were very careful not to inquire.

It struck us that his servants waited on him with a promptitude and punctuality quite marvellous in Berrichon domestics. Nevertheless, at the least semblance of delay he raised his voice, knitted his eyebrows (which still showed very black under his white hair), and muttered a few expressions of impatience which lent wings even to the slowest. At first I was somewhat shocked at this habit; it appeared to savour rather too strongly of the Mauprats. But the kindly and almost paternal manner in which he spoke to them a moment later, and their zeal, which seemed so distinct from fear, soon reconciled me to him. Towards us, moreover, he showed an exquisite politeness, and expressed himself in the choicest terms. Unfortunately, at the end of dinner, a door which had been left open and through which a cold air found its way to his venerable skull, drew from him such a frightful oath that my friend and I exchanged a look of surprise. He noticed it.

"I beg your pardon, gentlemen," he said. "I am afraid you find me an odd mixture. Ah, you see but a short distance. I am an old branch, happily torn from a vile trunk and transplanted into good soil, but still knotted and rough like the wild holly of the original stock. I have, believe me, had no little trouble in reaching the state of comparative gentleness and calm in which you behold me. Alas! if I dared, I should reproach Providence with a great injustice—that of having allotted me a life as short as other men's. When one has to struggle for forty or fifty years to transform one's self from a wolf into a man, one ought to live a hundred years longer to enjoy one's victory. Yet what good would that do me?" he added in a tone of sadness. "The kind fairy who transformed me is here no more to take pleasure in her work. Bah! it is quite time to have done with it all."

Then he turned towards me, and, looking at me with big dark eyes, still strangely animated, said:

"Come, my dear young man; I know what brings you to see me; you are curious to hear my history. Draw nearer the fire, then. Mauprat though I am, I will not make you do duty for a log. In listening you are giving me the greatest pleasure you could give. Your friend will tell you, however, that I do not willingly talk of myself. I am generally afraid of having to deal with blockheads, but you I have already heard of; I know your character and your profession; you are an observer and narrator—in other words, pardon me, inquisitive and a chatterbox."

He began to laugh, and I made an effort to laugh too, though with a rising suspicion that he was making game of us. Nor could I help thinking of the nasty tricks that his grandfather took a delight in playing on the imprudent busybodies who called upon him. But he put his arm through mine in a friendly way, and making me sit down in front of a good fire, near a table covered with cups—

"Don't be annoyed," he said. "At my age I cannot get rid of hereditary sarcasm; but there is nothing spiteful in mine. To speak seriously, I am delighted to see you and to confide in you the story of my life. A man as unfortunate as I have been deserves to find a faithful biographer to clear his memory from all stain. Listen, then, and take some coffee."

I offered him a cup in silence. He refused it with a wave of the arm and a smile which seemed to say, "That is rather for your effeminate generation."

Then he began his narrative in these words:

I

You live not very far from Roche-Mauprat, and must have often passed by the ruins. Thus there is no need for me to describe them. All I can tell you is that the place has never been so attractive as it is now. On the day that I had the roof taken off, the sun for the first time brightened the damp walls within which my childhood was passed; and the lizards to which I have left them are much better housed there than I once was. They can at least behold the light of day and warm their cold limbs in the rays of the sun at noon.

There used to be an elder and a younger branch of the Mauprats. I belong to the elder. My grandfather was that old Tristan de Mauprat who ran through his fortune, dishonoured his name, and was such a blackguard that his memory is already surrounded by a halo of the marvelous. The peasants still believe that his ghost appears, either in the body of a wizard who shows malefactors the way to the dwellings of Varenne, or in that of an old white hare which reveals itself to people meditating some evil deed. When I came into the world the only living member of the younger branch was Monsieur Hubert de Mauprat, known as the chevalier, because he belonged to the Order of the Knights of Malta; a man just as good as his cousin was bad. Being the youngest son of his family, he had taken the vow of celibacy; but, when he found himself the sole survivor of several brothers and sisters, he obtained release from his vow, and took a wife the year before I was born. Rumour says that before changing his existence in this way he made strenuous efforts to find some descendant of the elder branch worthy to restore the tarnished family name, and preserve the fortune which had accumulated in the hands of the younger branch. He had endeavoured to put his cousin Tristan's affairs in order, and had frequently paid off the latter's creditors. Seeing, however, that the only effect of his kindness was to encourage the vices of the family, and that, instead of respect and gratitude, he received nothing but secret hatred and churlish jealousy, he abandoned all attempts at friendship, broke with his cousins, and in spite of his advanced age (he was over sixty), took a wife in order to have heirs of his own. He had one daughter, and there his hopes of posterity ended; for soon afterward his wife died of a violent illness which the doctors called iliac passion. He then left that part of the country and returned but rarely to his estates. These were situated about six leagues from Roche-Mauprat, on the borders of the Varenne du Fromental. He was a prudent man and a just, because he was cultured, because his father had moved with the spirit of his century, and had had him educated. None the less he had preserved a firm character and an enterprising mind, and, like his ancestors, he was proud of hearing as a sort of surname the knightly title of Headbreaker, hereditary in the original Mauprat stock. As for the elder branch, it had turned out so badly, or rather had preserved from the old feudal days such terrible habits of brigandage, that it had won for itself the distinctive title of Hamstringer. [I hazard "Headbreaker" and "Hamstringer" as poor equivalents for the "Casse-Tete" and "Coupe-Jarret" of the French.—TR.] Of the sons of Tristan, my father, the eldest, was the only one who married. I was his only child. Here it is necessary to mention a fact of which I was long ignorant. Hubert de Mauprat, on hearing of my birth, begged me of my parents, undertaking to make me his heir if he were allowed absolute control over my education. At a shooting-party about this time my father was killed by an accidental shot, and my grandfather refused the chevalier's offer, declaring that his children were the sole legitimate heirs of the younger branch, and that consequently he would resist with all his might any substitution in my favour. It was then that Hubert's daughter was born. But when, seven years later, his wife died leaving him this one child, the desire, so strong in the nobles of that time, to perpetuate their name, urged him to renew his request to my mother. What her answer was I do not know; she fell ill and died. The country doctors again brought in a verdict of iliac passion. My grandfather had spent the last two days she passed in this world with her.

Pour me out a glass of Spanish wine; for I feel a cold shiver running through my body. It is nothing serious—merely the effect that these early recollections have on me when I begin to narrate them. It will soon pass off.

He swallowed a large glass of wine, and we did the same; for a sensation of cold came upon us too as we gazed at his stern face and listened to his brief, abrupt sentences. He continued:

Thus at the age of seven I found myself an orphan. My grandfather searched my mother's house and seized all the money and valuables he could carry away. Then, leaving the rest, and declaring he would have nothing to do with lawyers, he did not even wait for the funeral, but took me by the collar and flung me on to the crupper of his horse, saying: "Now, my young ward, come home with me; and try to stop that crying soon, for I haven't much patience with brats." In fact, after a few seconds he gave me such hard cuts with his whip that I stopped crying, and, withdrawing myself like a tortoise into my shell, completed the journey without daring to breathe.

He was a tall old man, bony and cross-eyed. I fancy I see him now as he was then. The impression that evening made on me can never be effaced. It was a sudden realization of all the horrors which my mother had foreshadowed when speaking of her execrable father-in-law and his brigands of sons. The moon, I remember, was shining here and there through the dense foliage of the forest. My grandfather's horse was lean, hardy, and bad-tempered like himself. It kicked at every cut of the whip, and its master gave it plenty. Swift as an arrow it jumped the ravines and little torrents which everywhere intersect Varenne in all directions. At each jump I lost my balance, and clung in terror to the saddle or my grandfather's coat. As for him, he was so little concerned about me that, had I fallen, I doubt whether he would have taken the trouble to pick me up. Sometimes, noticing my terror, he would jeer at me, and, to make me still more afraid, set his horse plunging again. Twenty times, in a frenzy of despair, I was on the point of throwing myself off; but the instinctive love of life prevented me from giving way to the impulse. At last, about midnight, we suddenly stopped before a small pointed gate, and the drawbridge was soon lifted behind us. My grandfather took me, bathed in a cold sweat as I was, and threw me over to a great fellow, lame and horribly ugly, who carried me into the house. This was my Uncle John, and I was at Roche-Mauprat.

At that time my grandfather, along with his eight sons, formed the last relic in our province of that race of petty feudal tyrants by which France had been overrun and harassed for so many centuries. Civilization, already advancing rapidly towards the great convulsion of the Revolution, was gradually stamping out the systematic extortions of these robbers. The light of education, a species of good taste reflected, however dimly, from a polished court, and perhaps a presentiment of the impending terrible awakening of the people, were spreading through the castles and even through the half-rustic manors of the lordlings. Ever in our midland provinces, the most backward by reason of their situation, the sentiment of social equality was already driving out the customs of a barbarous age. More than one vile scapegrace had been forced to reform, in spite of his privileges; and in certain places where the peasants, driven to desperation, had rid themselves of their overlord, the law had not dreamt of interfering, nor had the relatives dared to demand redress.

In spite of the prevailing tone of mind, my grandfather had long maintained his position in the country without experiencing any opposition. But, having had a large family, endowed like himself with a goodly number of vices, he finally found himself pestered and besieged by creditors who, instead of being frightened by his threats, as of old, were themselves threatening to make him suffer. He was obliged to devise some means of avoiding the bailiffs on the one hand, and, on the other, the fights which were continually taking place. In these fights the Mauprats no longer shone, despite their numbers, their complete union, and their herculean strength; since the whole population of the district sided with their opponents and took upon itself the duty of stoning them. So, rallying his progeny around him, as the wild boar gathers together its young after a hunt, Tristan withdrew into his castle and ordered the drawbridge to be raised. Shut up with him were ten or twelve peasants, his servants, all of them poachers or refugees, who like himself had some interest in "retiring from the world" (his own expression), and in finding a place of safety behind good stout walls. An enormous pile of hunting weapons, duck-guns, carbines, blunderbusses, spears, and cutlasses, were raised on the platform, and the porter received orders never to let more than two persons at a time approach within range of his gun.

From that day Mauprat and his sons broke with all civil laws as they had already broken with all moral laws. They formed themselves into a band of adventurers. While their well-beloved and trusty poachers supplied the house with game, they levied illegal taxes on the small farms in the neighbourhood. Now, without being cowards (and they are far from that), the peasants of our province, as you know, are meek and timid, partly from listlessness, partly from distrust of the law, which they have never understood, and of which even to this day they have but a scanty knowledge. No province of France has preserved more old traditions or longer endured the abuses of feudalism. Nowhere else, perhaps, has the title of the lord of the manor been handed down, as hitherto with us, to the owners of certain estates; and nowhere is it so easy to frighten the people with reports of some absurd and impossible political event. At the time of which I speak the Mauprats, being the only powerful family in a district remote from towns and cut off from communication with the outside world, had little difficulty in persuading their vassals that serfdom was about to be re-established, and that it would go hard with all who resisted. The peasants hesitated, listened timorously to the few among themselves who preached independence, then thought the matter over and decided to submit. The Mauprats were clever enough not to demand money of them, for money is what the peasant in such a district obtains with the greatest difficulty, and parts from with the greatest reluctance. "Money is dear," is one of his proverbs, because in his eyes money stands for something different from manual labour. It means traffic with men and things outside his world, an effort of foresight or circumspection, a bargain, a sort of intellectual struggle, which lifts him out of his ordinary heedless habits; it means, in a word, mental labour, and this for him is the most painful and the most wearing.

The Mauprats, knowing how the ground lay, and having no particular need of money any longer, since they had repudiated their debts, demanded payments in kind only. They ruled that one man should contribute capons, another calves, a third corn, a fourth fodder, and so on. They were careful, too, to tax judiciously, to demand from each the commodity he could provide with least inconvenience to himself. In return they promised help and protection to all; and up to a certain point they kept their word. They cleared the land of wolves and foxes, gave a welcome and a hiding-place to all deserters, and helped to defraud the state by intimidating the excise officers and tax-collectors.

They took advantage of their power to give the poor man a false notion of his real interests, and to corrupt the simple folk by undermining all sense of their dignity and natural liberty. They made the whole district combine in a sort of secession from the law, and they so frightened the functionaries appointed to enforce respect for it, that after a few years it fell into a veritable desuetude. Thus it happened that, while France at a short distance from this region was advancing with rapid strides towards the enfranchisement of the poorer classes, Varenne was executing a retrograde march and returning at full speed to the ancient tyranny of the country squires. It was easy enough for the Mauprats to pervert these poor folk; they feigned a friendly interest in them to mark their difference from the other nobles in the province whose manners still retained some of the haughtiness of their ancient power. Above all, my grandfather lost no opportunity of making the peasants share his own hatred of his own cousin, Hubert de Mauprat. The latter, whenever he interviewed his vassals, would remain seated in his arm-chair, while they stood before him bareheaded; whereas Tristan de Mauprat would make them sit down at his table, and drink some of the wine they had brought him as a sign of voluntary homage. He would then have them led home by his men in the middle of the night, all dead drunk, torches in hand, and making the forest resound with ribald songs. Libertinism completed the demoralization of the peasantry. In every family the Mauprats soon had their mistresses. This was tolerated, partly because it was profitable, and partly (alas! that it should have to be said) because it gratified vanity. The very isolation of the houses was favourable to the evil. No scandal, no denunciation were to be feared. The tiniest village would have been sufficient for the creation and maintenance of a public opinion. There, however, there were only scattered cottages and isolated farms; wastes and woods so separated the families from one another that the exercise of any mutual control was impossible. Shame is stronger than conscience. I need not tell you of all the bonds of infamy that united masters and slaves. Debauchery, extortion, and fraud were both precept and example for my youth, and life went on merrily. All notions of justice were scoffed at; creditors were defrauded of both interest and capital; any law officer who ventured to serve a summons received a sound thrashing, and the mounted police were fired on if they approached too near the turrets. A plague on parliament; starvation to all imbued with the new philosophy; and death to the younger branch of the Mauprats—such were the watchwords of these men who, to crown all, gave themselves the airs of knights-errant of the twelfth century. My grandfather talked of nothing but his pedigree and the prowess of his ancestors. He regretted the good old days when every lordling had instruments of torture in his manor, and dungeons, and, best, of all cannon. In ours we only had pitchforks and sticks, and a second-rate culverin which my Uncle John used to point—and point very well, in fact—and which was sufficient to keep at a respectful distance the military force of the district.

II

Old Mauprat was a treacherous animal of the carnivorous order, a cross between a lynx and a fox. Along with a copious and easy flow of language, he had a veneer of education which helped his cunning. He made a point of excessive politeness, and had great powers of persuasion, even with the objects of his vengeance. He knew how to entice them to his castle, where he would make them undergo frightful ill-treatment, for which, however, having no witnesses, they were unable to obtain redress by law. All his villainies bore the stamp of such consummate skill that the country came to view them with a sort of awe akin to respect. No one could ever catch him out of his den, though he issued forth often enough, and apparently without taking many precautions. In truth, he was a man with a genius for evil; and his sons, bound to him by no ties of affection, of which, indeed, they were incapable, yet acknowledged the sway of this superior evil genius, and gave him a uniform and ready obedience, in which there was something almost fanatic. He was their deliverer in all desperate cases; and when the weariness of confinement under our chilly vaults began to fill them with *ennui*, his mind, brutal even in jest, would cure them by arranging for their pleasure shows worthy of a den of thieves. Sometimes poor mendicant monks collecting alms would be terrified or tortured for their benefit; their beards would be burned off, or they would be lowered into a well and kept hanging between life and death until they had sung some foul song or uttered some blasphemy. Everybody knows the story of the notary who was allowed to enter in company with his four clerks, and whom they received with all the assiduity of pompous hospitality. My grandfather pretended to agree with a good grace to the execution of their warrant, and politely helped them to make an inventory of his furniture, of which the sale had been decreed. After this, when dinner was served and the king's men had taken their places at table, he said to the notary:

"Ah, mon Dieu! I was forgetting a poor hack of mine in the stable. It's a small matter. Still, you might be reprimanded for omitting it; and as I see that you are a worthy fellow I should be sorry to mislead you. Come with me and see it; it won't take us a moment."

The notary followed Mauprat unsuspectingly. Just as they were about to enter the stable together, Mauprat, who was leading the way, told him to put in his head only. The notary, anxious to show great consideration in the performance of his duties, and not to pry into things too closely, did as he was told. Then Mauprat suddenly pushed the door to and squeezed his neck so violently between it and the wall that the wretched man could not breathe. Deeming him sufficiently punished, Tristan opened the door again, and, asking pardon for his carelessness, with great civility offered the man his arm to take him back to dinner. This the notary did not consider it wise to refuse; but as soon as he re-entered the room where his colleagues were, he threw himself into a chair, and pointing to his livid face and mangled neck, demanded justice for the trap into which he had just been led. It was then that my grandfather, revelling in his rascally wit, went through a comedy scene of sublime audacity. He gravely reproached the notary with accusing him unjustly, and always addressing him kindly and with studied politeness, called the others to bear witness to his conduct, begging them to make allowances if his precarious position had forced him to give them such a poor reception, all the while doing the honours of the table in splendid style. The poor notary did not dare to press the matter and was compelled to dine, although half dead. His companions were so completely duped by Mauprat's assurance that they ate and drank merrily, treating the notary as a lunatic and a boor. They left Roche-Mauprat all drunk, singing the praises of their host, and laughing at the notary, who fell down dead upon the threshold of his house on dismounting from his horse.

The eight sons, the pride and strength of old Mauprat, all resembled him in physical vigour, brutality of manners, and, to some extent, in craftiness and jesting ill-nature. The truth is they were veritable brutes, capable of any evil, and completely dead to any noble thought or generous sentiment. Nevertheless, they were endowed with a sort of reckless, dashing courage which now and then seemed to have in it an element of grandeur. But it is time that I told you about myself, and gave you some idea of the development of my character in the thick of this filthy mire into which it had pleased God to plunge me, on leaving my cradle.

I should be wrong if, in order to gain your sympathy in these early years of my life, I asserted that I was born with a noble nature, a pure and incorruptible soul. As to this, I know nothing. Maybe there are no incorruptible souls. Maybe there are. That is what neither you nor any one will ever know. The great questions awaiting an answer are these: "Are our innate tendencies invincible? If not, can they be modified merely or wholly destroyed by education?" For myself, I would not dare to affirm. I am neither a metaphysician, nor a psychologist, nor a philosopher; but I have had a terrible life, gentlemen, and if I were a legislator, I would order that man to have his tongue torn out, or his head cut off, who dared to preach or write that the nature of individuals is unchangeable, and that it is no more possible to reform the character of a man than the appetite of a tiger. God has preserved me from believing this.

All I can tell you is that my mother instilled into me good principles, though, perhaps, I was not endowed by nature with her good qualities. Even with her I was of a violent disposition, but my violence was sullen and suppressed. I was blind and brutal in anger, nervous even to cowardice at the approach of danger, daring almost to foolhardiness when hand to hand with it—that is to say, at once timid and brave from my love of life. My obstinacy was revolting; yet my mother alone could conquer me; and without attempting to reason, for my mind developed very slowly, I used to obey her as if by a sort of magnetic necessity. This one guiding hand which I remember, and another woman's which I felt later, were and have been sufficient to lead me towards good. But I lost my mother before she had been able to teach me anything seriously; and when I was transplanted to Roche-Mauprat, my feeling for the evil done there was merely an instinctive aversion, feeble enough, perhaps, if fear had not been mingled with it.

But I thank Heaven from the bottom of my heart for the cruelties heaped upon me there, and above all for the hatred which my Uncle John conceived for me. My ill-fortune preserved me from indifference in the presence of evil, and my sufferings helped me to detest those who wrought it.

This John was certainly the most detestable of his race. Ever since a fall from his horse had maimed him, his evil temper had developed in proportion to his inability to do as much harm as his companions. Compelled to remain at home when the others set out on their expeditions, for he could not bestride a horse, he found his only chance of pleasure in those fruitless little attacks which the mounted police sometimes made on the castle, as if to ease their conscience. Then, intrenched behind a rampart of freestone which he had had built to suit himself, John, calmly seated near his culverin, would pick off a gentleman from time to time, and at once regain, as he said, his sleeping and eating power, which want of exercise had taken from him. And he would even climb up to his beloved platform without waiting for the excuse of an attack, and there, crouching down like a cat ready to spring, as soon as he saw any one appear in the distance without giving the signal, he would try his skill upon the target, and make the man retrace his steps. This he called sweeping the path clean.

As I was too young to accompany my uncles on their hunting and plundering expeditions, John naturally became my guardian and tutor—that is to say, my jailor and tormentor. I will not give you all the details of that infernal existence. For nearly ten years I endured cold, hunger, insults, the dungeon, and blows, according to the more or less savage caprices of this monster. His fierce hatred of me arose from the fact that he could not succeed in depraving me; my rugged, headstrong, and unsociable nature preserved me from his vile seductions. It is possible that I had not any strong tendencies to virtue; to hatred I luckily had. Rather than do the bidding of my tyrant I would have suffered a thousand deaths. And so I grew up without conceiving any affection for vice. However, my notions about society were so strange that my uncles' mode of life did not in itself cause me any repugnance. Seeing that I was brought up behind the walls of Roche-Mauprat, and that I lived in a state of perpetual siege, you will understand that I had precisely such ideas as any armed retainer in the barbarous ages of feudalism might have had. What, outside our den, was termed by other men assassinating, plundering, and torturing, I was taught to call fighting, conquering, and subduing. My sole knowledge of history consisted of an acquaintance with certain legends and ballads of chivalry which my grandfather used to repeat to me of an evening, when he had time to think of what he was pleased to call my education. Whenever

I asked him any question about the present time, he used to answer that times had sadly changed, that all Frenchmen had become traitors and felons, that they had frightened their kings, and that these, like cravens, had deserted the nobles, who in their turn had been cowardly enough to renounce their privileges and let laws be made for them by clodhoppers. I listened with surprise, almost with indignation, to this account of the age in which I lived, for me an age of shadows and mysteries. My grandfather had but vague ideas of chronology; not a book of any kind was to be found at Roche-Mauprat, except, I should say, the History of the Sons of Aymon, and a few chronicles of the same class brought by our servants from country fairs. Three names, and only three, stood clear in the chaos of my ignorance—Charlemagne, Louis XI, and Louis XIV; because my grandfather would frequently introduce these into dissertations on the unrecognised rights of the nobles. In truth, I was so ignorant that I scarcely knew the difference between a reign and a race; and I was by no means sure that my grandfather had not seen Charlemagne, for he spoke of him more frequently and more gladly than of any other man.

But, while my native energy led me to admire the exploits of my uncles, and filled me with a longing to share in them, the cold-blooded cruelty they perpetrated on returning from their expeditions, and the perfidious artifices by which they lured their dupes to the castle, in order to torture them to extort ransom, roused in me strange and painful emotions, which, now that I am speaking in all sincerity, it would be difficult for me to account for exactly. In the absence of all ordinary moral principles it might have been natural for me to accept the theory which I daily saw carried into practice, that makes it right; but the humiliation and suffering which my Uncle John inflicted on me in virtue of this theory, taught me to be dissatisfied with it. I could appreciate the right of the bravest, and I genuinely despised those who, with death in their power, yet chose life at the price of such ignominy as they had to bear at Roche-Mauprat. But I could only explain these insults and horrors heaped on prisoners, some of them women and mere children, as manifestations of bloodthirsty appetites. I do not know if I was sufficiently susceptible of a noble sentiment to be inspired with pity for the victim; but certain it is that I experienced that feeling of selfish commiseration which is common to all natures, and which, purified and ennobled, has become charity among civilized peoples. Under my coarse exterior my heart no doubt merely felt passing shocks of fear and disgust at the sight of punishments which I myself might have to endure any day at the caprice of my oppressors; especially as John, when he saw me turn pale at these frightful spectacles, had a habit of saying, in a mocking tone:

"That's what I'll do to you when you are disobedient."

All I know is that in presence of such iniquitous acts I experienced a horrible uneasiness; my blood curdled in my veins, my throat began to close, and I had to rush away, so as not to repeat the cries which pierced my ears. In time, however, I became somewhat hardened to these terrible impressions. The fibres of feeling grew tougher, and habit gave me power to hide what they termed my cowardice. I even felt ashamed of the signs of weakness I showed, and forced my face into the hyena smile which I saw on the faces of my kinsmen. But I could never prevent convulsive shudders from running through my limbs, and the coldness as of death from falling on my heart, at the recollection of these scenes of agony. The women, dragged half-willingly, half by force, under the roof of Roche-Mauprat, caused me inconceivable agitation. I began to feel the fires of youth kindling within me, and even to look with envy on this part of my uncles' spoil; but with these new-born desires were mingled inexpressible pangs. To all around me women were merely objects of contempt, and vainly did I try to separate this idea from that of the pleasure which was luring me. My mind was bewildered, and my irritated nerves imparted a violent and sickly strain to all my temptations. In other matters, I had as vile a disposition as my companions; if my heart was better than theirs, my manners were no less arrogant, and my jokes in no better taste. And here it may be well to give you an illustration of my youthful malice, especially as the results of these events have had an influence on the rest of my life.

III

Some three leagues from Roche-Mauprat, on your way to Fromental, you must have noticed an old tower standing by itself in the middle of the woods. It is famous for the tragic death of a prisoner about a century ago. The executioner, on his rounds, thought good to hang him without any further formality, merely to gratify an old Mauprat, his overlord.

At the time of which I am speaking Gazeau Tower was already deserted and falling into ruins. It was state property, and, more from negligence than kindness, the authorities had allowed a poor old fellow to take up his abode there. He was quite a character, used to live completely alone, and was known in the district as Gaffer Patience.

"Yes," I interrupted; "I have heard my nurse's grandmother speak of him; she believed he was a sorcerer."

Exactly so; and while we are at this point let me tell you what sort of a man this Patience really was, for I shall have to speak of him more than once in the course of my story. I had opportunities of studying him thoroughly.

Patience, then, was a rustic philosopher. Heaven had endowed him with a keen intellect, but he had had little education. By a sort of strange fatality, his brain had doggedly resisted the little instruction he might have received. For instance, he had been to the Carmelite's school at ——, and instead of showing any aptitude for work, he had played truant with a keener delight than any of his school-fellows. His was an eminently contemplative nature, kindly and indolent, but proud and almost savage in its love of independence; religious, yet opposed to all authority; somewhat captious, very suspicious, and inexorable with hypocrites. The observances of the cloister inspired him with but little awe; and as a result of once or twice speaking his mind too freely to the monks he was expelled from the school. From that time forth he was the sworn foe of what he called monkism, and declared openly for the cure of the Briantes, who was accused of being a Jansenist. In the instruction of Patience, however, the cure succeeded no better than the monks. The young peasant, endowed though he was with herculean strength and a great desire for knowledge, displayed an unconquerable aversion for every kind of work, whether physical or mental. He professed a sort of artless philosophy which the cure found it very difficult to argue against. There was, he said, no need for a man to work as long as he did not want money; and he was in no need of money as long as his wants were moderate. Patience practised what he preached: during the years when passions are so powerful he lived a life of austerity, drank nothing but water, never entered a tavern, and never joined in a dance. He was always very awkward and shy with women, who, it must be owned, found little to please in his eccentric character, stern face, and somewhat sarcastic wit. As if to avenge himself for this by showing his contempt, or to console himself by displaying his wisdom, he took a pleasure, like Diogenes of old, in decrying the vain pleasures of others; and if at times he was to be seen passing under the branches in the middle of the fetes, it was merely to throw out some shaft of scorn, a flash from his inexorable good sense. Sometimes, too, his uncompromising morality found expression in biting words, which left clouds of sadness or fear hanging over agitated consciences. This naturally gained him violent enemies; and the efforts of impotent hatred, helped by the feeling of awe which his eccentric behaviour produced, fastened upon him the reputation of a sorcerer.

When I said that Patience was lacking in education, I expressed myself badly. Longing for a knowledge of the sublime mysteries of Nature, his mind wished to soar to heaven on its first flight. From the very beginning, the Jansenist vicar was so perplexed and startled by the audacity of his pupil, he had to say so much to calm him into submission, he was obliged to sustain such assaults of bold questions and proud objections, that he had no leisure to teach him the alphabet; and at the end of ten years of studies, broken off and taken up at the bidding of a whim or on compulsion, Patience could not even read. It was only with great difficulty, after poring over a book for some two hours, that he deciphered a single page, and even then he did not grasp the meaning of most of the words expressing abstract ideas. Yet these abstract ideas were undoubtedly in him; you felt their presence while watching and listening to him; and the way in which he managed to embody them in homely phrase enlivened with a rude poetry was so marvellous, that one scarcely knew whether to feel astounded or amused.

Always serious, always positive himself, he scorned dalliance with any dialectic. A Stoic by nature and on principle, enthusiastic in the propagation of his doctrine of severance from false ideas, but resolute in the practice of resignation, he made many a breach in the poor cure's defences; and it was in these discussions, as he often told me in his last years, that he acquired his knowledge of philosophy. In order to make a stand against the battering-ram of natural logic, the worthy Jansenist was obliged to invoke the testimony of all the Fathers of the Church, and to oppose these, often even to corroborate them, with the teaching of all the sages and scholars of antiquity. Then Patience, his round eyes starting from his head (this was his own expression), lapsed into silence, and, delighted to learn without having the bother of studying, would ask for long explanations of the doctrines of these men, and for an account of their lives. Noticing this attention and this silence, his adversary would exult; but just as he thought he had convinced this rebellious soul, Patience, hearing the village clock strike midnight, would rise, take an affectionate leave of his host, and on the very threshold of the vicarage, would dismay the good man with some laconic and cutting comment that confounded Saint Jerome and Plato alike, Eusebius equally with Seneca, Tertullian no less than Aristotle.

The cure was not too ready to acknowledge the superiority of this untutored intellect. Still, he was quite astonished at passing so many winter evenings by his fireside with this peasant without feeling either bored or tired; and he would wonder how it was that the village schoolmaster, and even the prior of the convent, in spite of their Greek and Latin, appeared to him, the one a bore, the other a sophist, in all their discussions. Knowing the perfect purity of the peasant's life, he attributed the ascendency of his mind to the power of virtue and the charm it spreads over all things. Then, each evening, he would humbly accuse himself before God of not having disputed with his pupil from a sufficiently Christian point of view; he would confess to his guardian angel that pride in his own learning and joy at being listened to so devoutly had carried him somewhat beyond the bounds of religious instruction; that he had quoted profane writers too complacently; that he had even experienced a dangerous pleasure in roaming with his disciple through the fields of the past, plucking pagan flowers unsprinkled by the waters of baptism, flowers in whose fragrance a priest should not have found such delight.

On his side, Patience loved the cure dearly. He was his only friend, his only bond of union with society, his only bond of union, through the light of knowledge, with God. The peasant largely over-estimated his pastor's learning. He did not know that even the most enlightened men often draw wrong conclusions, or no conclusions at all, from the course of progress. Patience would have been spared great distress of mind if he could have seen for certain that his master was frequently mistaken and that it was the man, not the truth, that was at fault. Not knowing this, and finding the experience of the ages at variance with his innate sense of justice, he was continually a prey to agonizing reveries; and, living by himself, and wandering through the country at all hours of the day and night, wrapped in thoughts undreamed of by his fellows, he gave more and more credit to the tales of sorcery reported against him.

The convent did not like the pastor. A few monks whom Patience had unmasked hated Patience. Hence, both pastor and pupil were persecuted. The ignorant monks did not scruple to accuse the cure to his bishop of devoting himself to the occult sciences in concert with the magician Patience. A sort of religious war broke out in the village and neighbourhood. All who were not for the convent were for the cure, and *vice versa*. Patience scorned to take part in this struggle. One morning he went to see his friend, with tears in his eyes, and said to him:

"You are the one man in all the world that I love, and I will not have you persecuted on my account. Since, after you, I neither know nor care for a soul, I am going off to live in the woods, like the men of primitive times. I have inherited a field which brings me in fifty francs a year. It is the only land I have ever stirred with these hands, and half its wretched rent has gone to pay the tithe of labour I owe the seignior. I trust to die without ever doing duty as a beast of burden for others. And yet, should they remove you from your office, or rob you of your income, if you have a field that needs ploughing, only send me word, and you will see that these arms have not grown altogether stiff in their idleness."

It was in vain that the pastor opposed this resolve. Patience departed, carrying with him as his only belonging the coat he had on his back, and an abridgment of the teachings of Epictetus. For this book he had a great affection, and, thanks to much study of it, could read as many as three of its pages a day without unduly tiring himself. The rustic anchorite went into the desert to live. At first he built himself a hut of branches in a wood. Then, as wolves attacked him, he took refuge in one of the lower halls of Gazeau Tower, which he furnished luxuriously with a bed of moss, and some stumps of trees; wild roots, wild fruit, and goat's milk constituted a daily fare very little inferior to what he had had in the village. This is no exaggeration. You have to see the peasants in certain parts of Varenne to form an idea of the frugal diet on which a man can live and keep in good health. In the midst of these men of stoical habits all round him, Patience was still exceptional. Never had wine reddened his lips, and bread had seemed to him a superfluity. Besides, the doctrine of Pythagoras was not wholly displeasing to him; and in the rare interviews which he henceforth had with his friend he would declare that, without exactly believing in metempsychosis, and without making it a rule to eat vegetables only, he felt a secret joy at being able to live thus, and at having no further occasion to see death dealt out every day to innocent animals.

Patience had formed this curious resolution at the age of forty. He was sixty when I saw him for the first time, and he was then possessed of extraordinary physical vigour. In truth, he was in the habit of roaming about the country every year. However, in proportion as I tell you about my own life, I shall give you details of the hermit life of Patience.

At the time of which I am about to speak, the forest rangers, more from fear of his casting a spell over them than out of compassion, had finally ceased their persecutions, and given him full permission to live in Gazeau Tower, not, however, without warning him that it would probably fall about his head during the first gale of wind. To this Patience had replied philosophically that if he was destined to be crushed to death, the first tree in the forest would do the work quite as well as the walls of Gazeau Tower.

Before putting my actor Patience on the stage, and with many apologies for inflicting on you such a long preliminary biography, I have still to mention that during the twenty years of which I have spoken the cure's mind had bowed to a new power. He loved philosophy, and in spite of himself, dear man, could not prevent this love from embracing the philosophers too, even the least orthodox. The works of Jean Jacques Rousseau carried him away into new regions, in spite of all his efforts at resistance; and when one morning, when returning from a visit to some sick folk, he came across Patience gathering his dinner of herbs from the rocks of Crevant, he sat down near him on one of the druidical stones and made, without knowing it, the profession of faith of the Savoyard vicar. Patience drank more willingly of this poetic religion than of the ancient orthodoxy. The pleasure with which he listened to a summary of the new doctrines led the cure to arrange secret meetings with him in isolated parts of Varenne, where they agreed to come upon each other as if by chance. At these mysterious interviews the imagination of Patience, fresh and ardent from long solitude, was fired with all the magic of the thoughts and hopes which were then fermenting in France, from the court of Versailles to the most uninhabitable heath. He became enamoured of Jean Jacques, and made the cure read as much of him as he possibly could without neglecting his duties. Then he begged a copy of the *Contrat Social*, and hastened to Gazeau Tower to spell his way through it feverishly. At first the cure had given him of this manna only with a sparing hand, and while making him admire the lofty thoughts and noble sentiments of the philosopher, had thought to put him on his guard against the poison of anarchy. But all the old learning, all the happy texts of bygone days—in a word, all the theology of the worthy priest—was swept away like a fragile bridge by the torrent of wild eloquence and ungovernable enthusiasm which Patience had accumulated in his desert. The vicar had to give way and fall back terrified upon himself. There he discovered that the shrine of his own science was everywhere cracking and crumbling to ruin. The new sun which was rising on the political horizon and making havoc in so many minds, melted his own like a light snow under the first breath of spring. The sublime enthusiasm of Patience; the strange poetic life of the man which seemed to reveal him as one inspired; the romantic turn which their mysterious relations were taking (the ignoble persecutions of the convent making it noble to revolt)—all this so worked upon the priest that by 1770 he had already travelled far from Jansenism, and was vainly searching all the religious heresies for some spot on which he might rest before falling into the abyss of philosophy so often opened at his feet by Patience, so often hidden in vain by the exorcisms of Roman theology.

IV

After this account of the philosophical life of Patience, set forth by me now in manhood (continued Bernard, after a pause), it is not altogether easy to return to the very different impressions I received in boyhood on meeting the wizard of Gazeau Tower. I will make an effort, however, to reproduce my recollections faithfully.

It was one summer evening, as I was returning from bird-snaring with several peasant-boys, that I passed Gazeau Tower for the first time. My age was about thirteen, and I was bigger and stronger than any of my comrades; besides, I exercised over them, sternly enough, the authority I drew from my noble birth. In fact, the mixture of familiarity and etiquette in our intercourse was rather fantastic. Sometimes, when the excitement of sport or the fatigue of the day had greater powers over them than I, they used to have their own way; and I already knew how to yield at the right moment, as tyrants do, so as always to avoid the appearance of being compelled. However, I generally found a chance for revenge, and soon saw them trembling before the hated name of my family.

Well, night was coming on, and we were walking along gaily, whistling, knocking down crab-apples with stones, imitating the notes of birds, when the boy who was ahead suddenly stopped, and, coming back to us, declared that he was not going by the Gazeau Tower path, but would rather cut across the wood. This idea was favoured by two others. A third objected that we ran the risk of losing ourselves if we left the path, that night was near, and that there were plenty of wolves about.

"Come on, you funks!" I cried in a princely tone, pushing forward the guide; "follow the path, and have done with this nonsense."

"Not me," said the youngster. "I've just seen the sorcerer at his door saying magic words, and I don't want to have a fever all the year."

"Bah!" said another; "he doesn't do harm to everybody. He never hurts children; and, besides, we have only to pass by very quietly without saying anything to him. What do you suppose he'll do to us?"

"Oh, it would be all right if we were alone," answered the first; "but M. Bernard is here; we're sure to have a spell cast on us."

"What do you say, you fool?" I cried, doubling my fist.

"It's not my fault, my lord," replied the boy. "That old wretch doesn't like the gentry, and he has said he would be glad to see M. Tristan and all his sons hanging from the same bough."

"He said that, did he? Good!" I answered. "Come on, and you shall see. All who are my friends will follow; any one that leaves me is a coward."

Two of my companions, out of vanity, let themselves be drawn on. The others pretended to imitate them; but, after a few steps, they had all taken flight and disappeared into the copse. However, I went on proudly, escorted by my two acolytes. Little Sylvain, who was in front, took off his hat as soon as he saw Patience in the distance; and when we arrived opposite him, though the man was looking on the ground without appearing to notice us, he was seized with terror, and said, in a trembling voice:

"Good evening, Master Patience; a good night's rest to you."

The sorcerer, roused out of his reverie, started like a man waked from sleep; and I saw, not without a certain emotion, his weather-beaten face half covered with a thick gray beard. His big head was quite bald, and the bareness of his forehead only served to make his bushy eyebrows more prominent. Behind these his round deepset eyes seemed to flash like lightning at the end of summer behind the fading foliage. He was of small stature, but very broad-shouldered; in fact, built like a gladiator. The rags in which he was clad were defiantly filthy. His face was short and of a vulgar type, like that of Socrates; and if the fire of genius glowed in his strongly marked features, I certainly could not perceive it. He appeared to me a wild beast, an unclean animal. Filled with a sense of loathing, and determined to avenge the insult he had offered to my name, I put a stone in my sling, and without further ado hurled it at him with all my might.

At the moment the stone flew out, Patience was in the act of replying to the boy's greeting.

"Good evening, lads; God be with you!" he was saying when the stone whistled past his ear and struck a tame owl of which Patience had made a pet, and which at the approach of night was beginning to rouse itself in the ivy above the door.

The owl gave a piercing cry and fell bleeding at the feet of its master, who answered it with a roar of anger. For a few seconds he stood motionless with surprise and fury. Then suddenly, taking the palpitating victim by the feet, he lifted it up, and, coming towards us, cried in a voice of thunder:

"Which of you wretches threw that stone?"

The boy who had been walking behind, flew with the swiftness of the wind; but Sylvain, seized by the great hand of the sorcerer, fell upon his knees, swearing by the Holy Virgin and by Saint Solange, the patroness of Berry, that he was innocent of the death of the bird. I felt, I confess, a strong inclination to let him get out of the scrape as best he could, and make my escape into the thicket. I had expected to see a decrepit old juggler, not to fall into the hands of a robust enemy; but pride held me back.

"If you did this," said Patience to my trembling comrade, "I pity you; for you are a wicked child, and you will grow into a dishonest man. You have done a bad deed; you have made it your pleasure to cause pain to an old man who never did you any harm; and you have done this treacherously, like a coward, while feigning politeness and bidding him good-evening. You are a liar, a miscreant; you have robbed me of my only society, my only riches; you have taken delight in evil. God preserve you from living if you are going on in this way."

"Oh, Monsieur Patience!" cried the boy, clasping his hands; "do not curse me; do not bewitch me; do not give me any illness; it wasn't I! May God strike me dead if it was!"

"If it wasn't you, it was this one, then!" said Patience, seizing me by the coat-collar and shaking me like a young tree to be uprooted.

"Yes, I did it," I replied, haughtily; "and if you wish to know my name, learn that I am called Bernard Mauprat, and that a peasant who lays a hand on a nobleman deserves death."

"Death! You! You would put me to death, Mauprat!" cried the old man, petrified with surprise and indignation. "And what would God be, then, if a brat like you had a right to threaten a man of my age? Death! Ah, you are a genuine Mauprat, and you bite like your breed, cursed whelp! Such things as they talk of putting to death the very moment they are born! Death, my wolf-cub! Do you know it is yourself who deserves death, not for what you have just done, but for being the son of your father, and the nephew of your uncles? Ah! I am glad to hold a Mauprat in the hollow of my hand, and see whether a cur of a nobleman weighs as much as a Christian."

As he spoke he lifted me from the ground as he would have lifted a hare.

"Little one," he said to my comrade, "you can run home; you needn't be afraid. Patience rarely gets angry with his equals; and he always pardons his brothers, because his brothers are ignorant like himself, and know not what they do; but a Mauprat, look you, is a thing that knows how to read and write, and is only the viler for it all. Run away, then. But no; stay; I should like you once in your life to see a nobleman receive a thrashing from the hand of a peasant. And that is what you are going to see; and I ask you not to forget it, little one, and to tell your parents about it."

Livid, and gnashing my teeth with rage, I made desperate efforts to resist. Patience, with hideous calmness, bound me to a tree with an osier shoot. At the touch of his great horny hand I bent like a reed; and yet I was remarkably strong for my age. He fixed the owl to a branch above my head, and the bird's blood, as it fell on me drop by drop, caused me unspeakable horror; for though this was only the correction we administer to sporting dogs that worry game, my brain, bewildered by rage, despair, and my comrades' cries, began to imagine some frightful witchcraft. However, I really think I would rather have been metamorphosed into an owl at once than undergo the punishment he inflicted on me. In vain did I fling threats at him; in vain did I take terrible vows of vengeance; in vain did the peasant child throw himself on his knees again and supplicate:

"Monsieur Patience, for God's sake, for your own sake, don't harm him; the Mauprats will kill you."

He laughed, and shrugged his shoulders. Then, taking a handful of holly twigs, he flogged me in a manner, I must own, more humiliating than cruel; for no sooner did he see a few drops of my blood appear, than he stopped and threw down the rod. I even noticed a sudden softening of his features and voice, as if he were sorry for his severity.

"Mauprat," he said, crossing his arms on his breast and looking at me fixedly, "you have now been punished; you have now been insulted, my fine gentleman; that is enough for me. As you see, I might easily prevent you from ever harming me by stopping your breath with a touch of my finger, and burying you under the stone at my door. Who would think of coming to Gaffer Patience to look for this fine child of noble blood? But, as you may also see, I am not fond of vengeance; at the first cry of pain that escaped you, I stopped. No; I don't like to cause suffering; I'm not a Mauprat. Still, it was well for you to learn by experience what is to be a victim. May this disgust you of the hangman's trade, which had been handed down from father to son in your family. Good-evening! You can go now; I no longer bear you malice; the justice of God is satisfied. You can tell your uncles to put me on their gridiron; they will have a tough morsel to eat; and they will swallow flesh that will come to life again in their gullets and choke them."

Then he picked up the dead owl, and looking at it sadly:

"A peasant's child would not have done this," he said. "This is sport for gentle blood."

As he retired to his door he gave utterance to an exclamation which escaped him only on solemn occasions, and from which he derived his curious surname:

"Patience, patience!" he cried.

This, according to the gossips, was a cabalistic formula of his; and whenever he had been heard to pronounce it, some misfortune had happened to the individual who had offended him. Sylvain crossed himself to ward off the evil spirit. The terrible words resounded through the tower into which Patience had just withdrawn, then the door closed behind him with a bang.

My comrade was so eager to be off that he was within an ace of leaving me there bound to the tree. As soon as he had released me, he exclaimed:

"A sign of the cross! For God's sake, a sign of the cross! If you don't cross yourself you are bewitched; we shall be devoured by wolves as we go, or else we shall meet the great monster."

"Idiot!" I said; "I have something else to think about. Listen; if you are ever unlucky enough to tell a single soul of what has happened, I will strangle you."

"Alas! sir, what am I to do?" he replied with a mixture of innocence and malice. "The sorcerer said I was to tell my parents."

I raised my fist to strike him, but my strength failed. Choking with rage at the treatment I had just undergone, I fell down almost in a faint, and Sylvain seized the opportunity for flight.

When I came to I found myself alone. I did not know this part of Varenne; I had never been here before, and it was horribly wild. All through the day I had seen tracks of wolves and wild boars in the sand. And now night had come and I was still two leagues from Roche-Mauprat. The gate would be shut, the drawbridge up; and I should get a bullet through me if I tried to enter after nine o'clock. As I did not know the way, it was a hundred to one against my doing the two leagues in an hour. However, I would have preferred to die a thousand deaths rather than ask shelter of the man in Gazeau Tower, even had he granted it gracefully. My pride was bleeding more than my flesh.

I started off at a run, heedless of all risks. The path made a thousand turns; a thousand other paths kept crossing it. When I reached the plain I found myself in a pasture surrounded by hedges. There every trace of the path disappeared. I jumped the hedge at a venture, and fell into a field. The night was pitch-dark; even had it been day it would have been impossible to ascertain my way in the midst of little properties buried between high banks bristling with thorns. Finally I reached a heath, then some woods; and my fears, which had been somewhat subdued, now grew intense. Yes, I own I was a prey to mortal terrors. Trained to bravery, as a dog is to sport, I bore myself well enough before others. Spurred by vanity, indeed, I was foolishly bold when I had spectators; but left to myself, in the middle of the night, exhausted by toil and hunger, though with no longing for food, unhinged by the emotions I had just experienced, certain that my uncles would beat me when I returned, yet as anxious to return as if I were going to find paradise on earth at Roche-Mauprat, I wandered about until daybreak, suffering indescribable agonies. The howls of wolves, happily far off, more than once reached my ears and froze the blood in my veins; and, as if my position had not been perilous enough in reality, my overwrought imagination must needs add to it a thousand extravagant fantasies. Patience had the reputation of being a wolf-rearer. This, as you know, is a cabalistic speciality accredited in all countries. I kept on fancying, therefore, that I saw this devilish little gray-beard, escorted by his ravening pack, and himself in the form of a demi-wolf, pursing me through the woods. Several times when rabbits got up at my feet I almost fell backwards from the shock. And now, as I was certain that nobody could see, I made many a sign of the cross; for, while affecting incredulity, I was, of course, at heart filled with all the superstitions born of fear.

At last, at daybreak, I reached Roche-Mauprat. I waited in a moat until the gates were opened, and then slipped up to my room without being seen by anybody. As it was not altogether an unfailing tenderness that watched over me at Roche-Mauprat, my absence had not been noticed during the night. Meeting my Uncle John on the stairs, I led him to believe that I had just got up; and, as the artifice proved successful, I went off to the hayloft and slept for the rest of the day.

V

As I had nothing further to fear for myself, it would have been easy to take vengeance on my enemy. Everything was favourable. The words he had uttered against my family would have been sufficient without any mention of the outrage done to my own person, which, in truth, I hardly cared to make known. I had only to say a word, and in a quarter of an hour seven Mauprats would have been in the saddle, delighted at the opportunity of making an example of a man who paid them no dues. Such a man would have seemed to them good for nothing but hanging as a warning to others.

But even if things had not been likely to reach this pitch, I somehow felt an unconquerable aversion to asking eight men to avenge me on a single one. Just as I was about to ask them (for, in my anger, I had firmly resolved to do so), I was held back by some instinct for fair dealing to which I had hitherto been a stranger, and whose presence in myself I could hardly explain. Perhaps, too, the words of Patience had, unknown to myself, aroused in me a healthy sense of shame. Perhaps his righteous maledictions on the nobles had given me glimpses of the idea of justice. Perhaps, in short, what I had hitherto despised in myself as impulses of weakness and compassion, henceforth began dimly to take a more solemn and less contemptible shape.

Be that as it may, I kept silent. I contented myself with thrashing Sylvain as a punishment for having deserted me, and to impress upon him that he was not to breathe a word about my unfortunate adventure. The bitterness of the recollection was intensified by an incident which happened toward the end of autumn when I was out with him beating the woods for game. The poor boy was genuinely attached to me; for, my brutality notwithstanding, he always used to be at my heels the instant I was outside the castle. When any of his companions spoke ill of me, he would take up my cause, and declare that I was merely somewhat hasty and not really bad at heart. Ah, it is the gentle, resigned souls of the humble that keep up the pride and roughness of the great. Well, we were trying to trap larks when my sabot-shot page, who always hunted about ahead of me, came back, saying in his rude dialect:

"I can see the wolf-driver with the mole-catcher."

This announcement sent a shudder through all my limbs. However, the longing for revenge produced a reaction, and I marched straight on to meet the sorcerer. Perhaps, too, I felt somewhat reassured by the presence of his companion, who was a frequenter of Roche-Mauprat, and would be likely to show me respect and afford me assistance.

Marcasse, the mole-catcher, as he was called, professed to rid the dwellings and fields of the district of polecats, weasels, rats and other vermin. Nor did he confine his good offices to Berry; every year he went the round of La Marche, Nivernais, Limousin, and Saintonge, visiting, alone and on foot, all the places that had the good sense to appreciate his talents. He was well received everywhere, in the castle no less than in the cottage; for his was a trade that had been carried on successfully and honestly in his family for generations (indeed, his descendants still carry it on). Thus he had work and a home awaiting him for every day in the year. As regular in his round as the earth in her rotation, he would reappear on a given day at the very place where he had appeared the year before, and always with the same dog and with the same long sword.

This personage was as curious as the sorcerer Patience; perhaps more comic in his way than the sorcerer. He was a bilious, melancholy man, tall, lean, angular, full of languor, dignity, and deliberation in speech and action. So little did he like talking that he answered all questions in monosyllables; and yet he never failed to obey the laws of the most scrupulous politeness, and rarely said a word without raising his hand to the corner of his hat as a sign of respect and civility. Was he thus by nature, or, in his itinerant trade, had this wise reserve arisen from a fear of alienating some of his numerous clients by incautious chatter? No one knew. In all houses he was allowed a free hand; during the day he had the key of every granary; in the evening, a place at the fireside of every kitchen. He knew everything that happened; for his dreamy, absorbed air led people to talk freely in his presence; yet he had never been known to inform any household of the doings of another.

If you wish to know how I had become struck by this strange character, I may tell you that I had been a witness of my uncle's and grandfather's efforts to make him talk. They hoped to draw from him some information about the chateau of Saint-Severe, the home of a man they hated and envied, M. Hubert de Mauprat. Although Don Marcasse (they called him Don because he seemed to have the bearing and pride of a ruined hidalgo), although Don Marcasse, I say, had shown himself as incompressible here as elsewhere, the Coupe-Jarret Mauprats never failed to squeeze him a little more in the hope of extracting some details about the Casse-Tete Mauprats.

Nobody, then, could discover Marcasse's opinions about anything; it would have been simplest to suppose that he did not take the trouble to have any. Yet the attraction which Patience seemed to feel towards him—so great that he would accompany him on his travels for several weeks altogether—led one to believe that there was some witchery in the man's mysterious air, and that it was not solely the length of his sword and the skill of his dog which played such wonderful havoc with the moles and weasels. There were whispered rumours of the enchanted herbs that he employed to lure these suspicious animals from their holes into his nets. However, as people found themselves better off for his magic, no one dreamt of denouncing it as criminal.

I do not know if you have ever seen one of the rat-hunts. It is a curious sight, especially in a fodder-loft. The man and dog climbing up ladders and running along beams with marvellous assurance and agility, the dog sniffing every hole in the wall, playing the cat, crouching down and lying in wait until the game comes out for his master's rapier; the man thrusting through bundles of straw and putting the enemy to the sword—all this, when arranged and carried out with gravity and dignity by Don Marcasse, was, I assure you, a most singular and interesting performance.

When I saw this trusty fellow I felt equal to braving the sorcerer, and advanced boldly. Sylvain stared at me in admiration, and I noticed that Patience himself was not prepared for such audacity. I pretended to go up to Marcasse and speak to him, as though quite unconcerned about the presence of my enemy. Seeing this he gently thrust aside the mole-catcher, and, laying his heavy hand on my head, said very quietly:

"You have grown of late, my fine gentleman!"

The blood rushed to my face, and, drawing back scornfully, I answered:

"Take care what you are doing, clodhopper; you should remember that if you still have your two ears, it is to my kindness that you owe them."

"My two ears!" said Patience, with a bitter laugh.

Then making an allusion to the nickname of my family, he added:

"Perhaps you mean my two hamstrings? Patience, patience! The time, maybe, is not far distant when clodhoppers will rid the nobles of neither ears nor hamstrings, but of their heads and their purses."

"Silence, Master Patience!" said the mole-catcher solemnly; "these are not the words of a philosopher."

"You are quite right, quite right," replied the sorcerer; "and in truth, I don't know why I allow myself to argue with this lad. He might have had me made into pap by his uncles. I whipped him in the summer for playing me a stupid trick; and I don't know what happened to the family, but the Mauprats lost a fine chance of injuring a neighbour."

"Learn, peasant," I said, "that a nobleman always takes vengeance nobly. I did not want my wrongs avenged by people more powerful than yourself; but wait a couple of years; I promise I will hang you with my own hand on a certain tree that I shall easily recognise, not very far from the door of Gazeau Tower. If I don't I will renounce my birthright; if I spare you I will take the title of wolf-driver."

Patience smiled; then, suddenly becoming serious, he fixed on me that searching look which rendered his physiognomy so striking. Then turning to the weasel-hunter:

"It is strange," he said; "there must be something in blood. Take the vilest noble, and you will find that in certain things he has more spirit than the bravest of us. Ah! it is simple enough," he added, speaking to himself; "they are brought up like that, whilst we—we, they tell us, are born to obey. Patience!"

V

He was silent for an instant; then, rousing himself from his reverie, he said to me in a kindly though somewhat mocking tone:

"And so you want to hang me, Monseigneur Straw-Stalk? You will have to eat a lot of beef, then, for you are not yet tall enough to reach the branch which is to bear me; and before then . . . perhaps many things will happen that are not dreamt of in your little philosophy."

"Nonsense! Why talk nonsense?" said the mole-catcher, with a serious air; "come, make peace. Monseigneur Bernard, I ask pardon for Patience; he is an old man, a fool."

"No, no," said Patience; "I want him to hang me; he is right; this is merely my due; and, in fact, it may come more quickly than all the rest. You must not make too much haste to grow, monsieur; for I—well, I am making more haste to grow old than I would wish; and you who are so brave, you would not attack a man no longer able to defend himself."

"You didn't hesitate to use your strength against me!" I cried. "Confess, now; didn't you treat me brutally? Wasn't it a coward's work, that?"

"Oh, children, children!" he said. "See how the thing reasons! Out of the mouths of children cometh truth."

And he moved away dreamily, and muttering to himself as was his wont. Marcasse took off his hat to me and said in an impassive tone:

"He is wrong . . . live at peace . . . pardon . . . peace . . . farewell!"

They disappeared; and there ended my relations with Patience. I did not come in contact with him again until long afterward.

VI

I was fifteen when my grandfather died. At Roche-Mauprat his death caused no sorrow, but infinite consternation. He was the soul of every vice that reigned therein, and it is certain that he was more cruel, though less vile, than his sons. On his death the sort of glory which his audacity had won for us grew dim. His sons, hitherto held under firm control, became more and more drunken and debauched. Moreover, each day added some new peril to their expeditions.

Except for the few trusty vassals whom we treated well, and who were all devoted to us, we were becoming more and more isolated and resourceless. People had left the neighbouring country in consequence of our violent depredations. The terror that we inspired pushed back daily the bounds of the desert around us. In making our ventures we had to go farther afield, even to the borders of the plain. There we had not the upper hand; and my Uncle Laurence, the boldest of us all, was dangerously wounded in a skirmish. Other schemes had to be devised. John suggested them. One was that we should slip into the fairs under various disguises, and exercise our skill in thieving. From brigands we became pick-pockets, and our detested name sank lower and lower in infamy. We formed a fellowship with the most noisome characters our province concealed, and, by an exchange of rascally services, once again managed to avoid destitution.

I say we, for I was beginning to take a place in this band of cutthroats when my grandfather died. He had yielded to my entreaties and allowed me to join in some of the last expeditions he attempted. I shall make no apologies; but here, gentlemen, you behold a man who has followed the profession of a bandit. I feel no remorse at the recollection, no more than a soldier would feel at having served a campaign under orders from his general. I thought that I was still living in the middle ages. The laws of the land, with all their strength and wisdom, were to me words devoid of meaning. I felt brave and full of vigour; fighting was a joy. Truly, the results of our victories often made me blush; but, as they in no way profited myself, I washed my hands of them. Nay, I remember with pleasure that I helped more than one victim who had been knocked down to get up and escape.

This existence, with its movement, its dangers, and its fatigues, had a numbing effect on me. It took me away from any painful reflections which might have arisen in my mind. Besides, it freed me from the immediate tyranny of John. However, after the death of my grandfather, when our band degraded itself to exploits of a different nature, I fell back under his odious sway. I was by no means fitted for lying and fraud. I displayed not only aversion but also incapacity for this new industry. Consequently my uncle looked upon me as useless, and began to maltreat me again. They would have driven me away had they not been afraid that I might make my peace with society, and become a dangerous enemy to themselves. While they were in doubt as to whether it was wiser to feed me or to live in fear of me, they often thought (as I have since learned) of picking a quarrel with me, and forcing a fight in which I might be got rid of. This was John's suggestion. Antony, however, who retained more of Tristan's energy and love of fair play at home than any of his brothers, proved clearly that I did more good than harm. I was, he declared, a brave fighter, and there was no knowing when they might need an extra hand. I might also be shaped into a swindler. I was very young and very ignorant; but John, perhaps, would endeavour to win me over by kindness, and make my lot less wretched. Above all, he might enlighten me as to my true position, by explaining that I was an outcast from society, and could not return to it without being hanged immediately. Then, perhaps, my obstinacy and pride would give way, out of regard to my own well-being on the one hand, and from necessity on the other. At all events, they should try this before getting rid of me.

"For," said Antony to round off his homily, "we were ten Mauprats last year; our father is dead, and, if we kill Bernard, we shall only be eight."

This argument gained the day. They brought me forth from the species of dungeon in which I had languished for several months; they gave me new clothes; they exchanged my old gun for a beautiful carbine that I had always coveted; they explained to me my position in the world; they honoured me with the best wine at meals. I promised to reflect, and meanwhile, became rather more brutalized by inaction and drunkenness than I had been by brigandage.

However, my captivity had made such a terrible impression on me that I took a secret oath to dare any dangers that might assail me on the territories of the King of France, rather than endure a repetition of that hideous experience. Nothing but a miserable point of honour now kept me at Roche-Mauprat. It was evident that a storm was gathering over our heads. The peasants were discontented, in spite of all our efforts to attach them to us; doctrines of independence were secretly insinuating themselves into their midst; our most faithful retainers were growing tired of merely having their fill of bread and meat; they were demanding money, and we had none. We had received more than one serious summons to pay our fiscal dues to the state, and as our private creditors had joined hands with the crown officers and the recalcitrant peasants, everything was threatening us with a catastrophe like that which had just overtaken the Seigneur de Pleumartin in our province[1].

---

[1] The reputation which the Seigneur de Pleumartin has left behind him in the province will preserve the story of Mauprat from the reproach of exaggeration. Pen would refuse o trace the savage obscenities and refinements of cruelty which marked the life of this madman, and which perpetuated he traditions of feudal brigandage in Berry down to the ast days of the ancient monarchy. His chateau was besieged, nd after a stubborn resistance he was

My uncles had long thought of making common cause with this country squire in his marauding expeditions and his resistance to authority. However, just as Pleumartin, about to fall into the hands of his enemies, had given his word of honour that he would welcome us as friends and allies if we went to his assistance, we had heard of his defeat and tragic end. Thus we ourselves were now on our guard night and day. It was a question of either fleeing the country or bracing ourselves for a decisive struggle. Some counselled the former alternative; the others declared their resolve to follow the advice of their dying father and to find a grave under the ruins of the keep. Any suggestion of flight or compromise they denounced as contemptible cowardice. The fear, then, of incurring such a reproach, and perhaps in some measure an instinctive love of danger, still kept me back. However, my aversion to this odious existence was only lying dormant, ready to break out violently at any moment.

One evening, after a heavy supper, we remained at table, drinking and conversing—God knows in what words and on what subject! It was frightful weather. The rain, driven through the broken windows, was running in streams across the stone floor of the hall; and the old walls were trembling in the storm. The night wind was whistling through chinks in the roof and making the flames of our resin torches flicker weirdly. During the meal my uncles had rallied me very much on what they called my virtue; they had treated my shyness in the presence of women as a sign of continence; and it was especially in this matter that they urged me to evil by ridiculing my modesty. While parrying these coarse gibes and making thrusts in the same strain, I had been drinking enormously. Consequently, my wild imagination had become inflamed, and I boasted that I would be bolder and more successful with the first woman brought to Roche-Mauprat than any of my uncles. The challenge was accepted amid roars of laughter. Peals of thunder sent back an answer to the infernal merriment.

All at once the horn was heard at the portcullis. Everybody stopped talking. The blast just blown was the signal used by the Mauprats to summon each other or make themselves known. It was my Uncle Laurence, who had been absent all day and who was now asking to be let in. We had so little confidence in others that we acted as our own turnkeys in the fortress. John rose and took down the keys, but he stopped immediately on hearing a second blast of the horn. This meant that Laurence was bringing in a prize, and that we were to go and meet him. In the twinkling of an eye all the Mauprats were at the portcullis, torch in hand—except myself, whose indifference at this moment was profound, and whose legs were seriously conscious of wine.

"If it is a woman," cried Antony as he went out, "I swear by the soul of my father that she shall be handed over to you, my valiant young man, and we'll see if your courage comes up to your conceit."

I remained with my elbows on the table, sunk in an uncomfortable stupor.

---

taken and hanged. here are many people still living, nor yet very advanced in years, who knew the man.

VI

When the door opened again I saw a woman in a strange costume entering with a confident step. It required an effort to keep my mind from wandering, and to grasp what one of the Mauprats came and whispered to me. In the middle of a wolf-hunt, at which several of the nobles in the neighbourhood had been present with their wives, this young lady's horse had taken fright and bolted away from the rest of the field. When it had pulled up after a gallop of about a league, she had tried to find her way back; but, not knowing the Varenne district, where all the landmarks are so much alike, she had gone farther and farther astray. The storm and the advent of night had completed her perplexity. Laurence, happening to meet her, had offered to escort her to the chateau of Rochemaure, which, as a fact, was more than six leagues distant; but he had declared that it was quite near, and had pretended to be the gamekeeper there. She did not actually know the lady of Rochemaure, but being a distant connection of hers, she counted upon a welcome. Never having seen the face of a single Mauprat, and little dreaming that she was so near their haunt, she had followed her guide confidingly; and as she had never in her life caught a glimpse of Roche-Mauprat, whether in the distance or close at hand, she was led upon the scene of our orgies without having the least suspicion of the trap into which she had fallen.

When I rubbed my heavy eyes and beheld this woman, so young and so beautiful, with her expression of calm sincerity and of goodness, the like of which I had never seen on the brow of any other (for all those who had passed the portcullis of our abode were either insolent prostitutes or stupid victims), I could not but think I was dreaming.

Remembering how prominently fairies figured in my legends of chivalry, I almost fancied that Morgana or Urganda had come among us to administer justice; and, for the moment, I felt an inclination to throw myself on my knees and protest against any judgment which should confound me with my uncles. Antony, to whom Laurence had quickly given the cue, approached her with as much politeness as he had in his composition, and begged her to excuse his hunting costume, likewise that of his friends. They were all nephews or cousins of the lady of Rochemaure, whom they were now awaiting before sitting down to table. Being very religious, she was at present in the chapel, in pious conference with the chaplain. The air of simple confidence with which the stranger listened to these absurd lies went to my heart, but I had not a very clear idea of what I felt.

"Please," she said to my Uncle John, who was dancing attendance on her with the leer of a satyr, "please do not let me disturb this lady. I am so troubled about the anxiety I must be causing my father and my friends at the present moment, that I could not really stop here. All I ask is that she will be kind enough to lend me a fresh horse and a guide, so that I may return to the place where I presume my people may have gone to wait for me."

"Madame," replied John, with assurance, "it is impossible for you to start again in such weather as this; besides, if you did, that would only serve to delay the hour of rejoining those who are looking for you. Ten of our men, well mounted and provided with torches, shall set out this very moment in ten different directions and scour every corner of Varenne. Thus, in two hours at the most, your relatives will be certain to have news of you, and you will soon see them arriving here, where we will entertain them as best we can. Please, then, set your mind at rest, and take some cordial to restore you; for you must be wet through and quite exhausted."

"Were it not for the anxiety I feel," she answered with a smile, "I should be famished. I will try to eat something; but do not put yourselves to any inconvenience on my account. You have been far too good already."

Approaching the table, where I was still resting on my elbows, she took some fruit that was by my side without noticing me. I turned and stared at her insolently with a besotted expression. She returned my gaze haughtily—at least, so it appeared to me then. I have since learned that she did not even see me; for, while making a great effort to appear calm and to reply with an air of confidence to the offers of hospitality, she was at heart very much disturbed by the unexpected presence of so many strange men with their forbidding mien and rough garb. However, she did not suspect anything. I overheard one of the Mauprats near me saying to John:

"Good! It's all right; she is falling into the trap. Let us make her drink; then she will begin to talk."

"One moment," replied John; "watch her carefully; this is a serious matter; there is something better to be had out of this than a little passing pleasure. I am going to talk it over with the others; you will be sent for to give your opinion. Meanwhile keep an eye on Bernard."

"What is the matter?" I said abruptly, as I faced him. "Does not this girl belong to me? Did not Antony swear it by the soul of my grandfather?"

"Yes, confound it, that's true," said Antony, approaching our group, whilst the other Mauprats surrounded the lady. "Listen, Bernard; I will keep my word on one condition."

"What is that?"

"It is quite simple: that you won't within the next ten minutes tell this wench that she is not at old Rochemaure's."

"What do you take me for?" I answered, pulling my hat over my eyes. "Do you think that I am an idiot? Wait a minute; would you like me to go and get my grandmother's dress which is upstairs and pass myself off for this same lady of Rochemaure?"

"A splendid idea!" replied Laurence.

"But before anything is done," said John, "I want to speak to you all."

And making signs to the others, he drew them out of the hall. Just as they were going out I thought I noticed that John was trying to persuade Antony to keep watch over me. But Antony, with a firmness which I could not understand, insisted on following the rest. I was left alone with the stranger.

For a moment I remained bewildered, almost stupefied, and more embarrassed than pleased at the *tete-a-tete*. Then I endeavoured to think of some explanation of these mysterious things that were happening around me, and succeeded, as far as the fumes of the wine would allow me, in imagining something fairly probable, though, indeed, remote enough from the actual truth.

I thought I could account for everything I had just seen and heard by supposing, first, that the lady, quiet and richly dressed though she was, was one of those daughters of Bohemia that I had sometimes seen at fairs; secondly, that Laurence, having met her in the country, had brought her here to amuse the company; and, thirdly, that they had told her of my condition of swaggering drunkenness, and had prevailed on her to put my gallantry to the proof, whilst they were to watch me through the keyhole. My first movement, as soon as these ideas had taken possession of me, was to rise and go straight to the door. This I locked with a double turn and then bolted. When I had done this I returned to the lady, determined that I would not, at all events, give her cause to laugh at my bashfulness.

She was sitting close to the fire, and as she was occupied in drying her wet garments, leaning forward over the hearth, she had not taken any notice of what I was doing; but when I approached her the strange expression on my face caused her to start. I had made up my mind to kiss her, as a beginning; but, I know not by what miracle, as soon as she raised her eyes to mine, this familiarity became impossible. I only had sufficient courage to say:

"Upon my word, mademoiselle, you are a charming creature, and I love you—as true as my name is Bernard Mauprat."

"Bernard Mauprat!" she cried, springing up; "you are Bernard Mauprat, you? In that case, change your manner and learn to whom you are talking. Have they not told you?"

"No one has told me, but I can guess," I replied with a grin, while trying hard to trample down the feeling of respect with which her sudden pallor and imperious attitude inspired me.

"If you can guess," she said, "how is it possible that you allow yourself to speak to me in this way? But they were right when they said you were ill-mannered; and yet I always had a wish to meet you."

"Really!" I said, with the same hideous grin. "You! A princess of the king's highway, who have known so many men in your life? But let my lips meet your own, my sweet, and you shall see if I am not as nicely mannered as those uncles of mine whom you were listening to so willingly just now."

"Your uncles!" she cried, suddenly seizing her chair and placing it between us as if from some instinct of self-defence. "Oh, mon Dieu! mon Dieu! Then I am not at Madame de Rochemaure's?"

"Our name certainly begins in the same way, and we come of as good a rock as anybody."

"Roche-Mauprat!" she muttered, trembling from head to foot, like a hind when it hears the howl of wolves.

And her lips grew quite white. Her agony was manifest in every gesture. From an involuntary feeling of sympathy I shuddered myself, and I was on the point of changing my manner and language forthwith.

"What can there be in this to astound her so?" I asked myself. "Is she not merely acting a part? And even if the Mauprats are not hidden behind some wainscot listening to us, is she not sure to give them an account of everything that takes place? And yet she is trembling like an aspen leaf. But what if she is acting? I once saw an actress play Genevieve de Brabant, and she wept so that one might have been deceived."

I was in a state of great perplexity, and I cast harassed glances now at her, now at the doors, which I fancied every moment would be thrown wide open amid roars of laughter from my uncles.

This woman was beautiful as the day. I do not believe there has ever lived a woman as lovely as she. It is not I alone who say so; she has left a reputation for beauty which has not yet died out in her province. She was rather tall, slender, and remarkable for the easy grace of her movements. Her complexion was very fair, while her eyes were dark and her hair like ebony. Her glance and her smile showed a union of goodness and acuteness which it was almost impossible to conceive; it was as if Heaven had given her two souls, one wholly of intellect, the other wholly of feeling. She was naturally cheerful and brave—an angel, indeed, whom the sorrows of humanity had not yet dared to touch. She knew not what it was to suffer; she knew not what it was to distrust and dread. This, indeed, was the first trial of her life, and it was I, brute that I was, who made her undergo it. I took her for a gipsy, and she was an angel of purity.

She was my young cousin (or aunt, after the Breton fashion), Edmee de Mauprat, the daughter of M. Hubert, my great-uncle (again in the Breton fashion), known as the Chevalier—he who had sought release from the Order of Malta that he might marry, though already somewhat advanced in years. My cousin was the same age as myself; at least, there was a difference of only a few months between us. Both of us were now seventeen, and this was our first interview. She whom I ought to have protected at the peril of my life against the world was now standing before me trembling and terror-stricken, like a victim before the executioner.

She made a great effort, and approaching me as I walked about the hall deep in thought, she explained who she was, adding:

"It is impossible that you can be an infamous creature like all these brigands whom I have just seen, and of whose hideous life I have often heard. You are young; your mother was good and wise. My father wanted to adopt you and bring you up as his son. Even to-day he is still full of grief at not being able to draw you out of the abyss in which you lie. Have you not often received messages from him? Bernard, you and I are of the same family; think of the ties of blood; why would you insult me? Do they intend to assassinate me here or torture me? Why did they deceive me by saying that I was at Rochemaure? Why did they withdraw in this mysterious way? What are they preparing? What is going to happen?"

Her words were cut short by the report of a gun outside. A shot from the culverin replied to it, and the alarm trumpet shook the gloomy walls of the keep with its dismal note. Mademoiselle de Mauprat fell back into her chair. I remained where I was, wondering whether this was some new scene in the comedy they were enjoying at my expense. However, I resolved not to let the alarm cause me any uneasiness until I had certain proof that it was not a trick.

"Come, now," I said, going up to her again, "own that all this is a joke. You are not Mademoiselle de Mauprat at all; and you merely want to discover if I am an apprentice capable of making love."

"I swear by Christ," she answered, taking my hands in her own, which were cold as death, "that I am Edmee, your cousin, your prisoner—yes, and your friend; for I have always felt an interest in you; I have always implored my father not to cease his efforts for you. But listen, Bernard; they are fighting, and fighting with guns! It must be my father who has come to look for me, and they are going to kill him. Ah!" she cried, falling on her knees before me, "go and prevent that, Bernard! Tell your uncles to respect my father, the best of men, if you but knew! Tell them that, if they hate our family, if they must have blood, they may kill me! Let them tear my heart out; but let them respect my father . . ."

Some one outside called me in a violent voice.

"Where is the coward? Where is that wretched boy?" shouted my Uncle Laurence.

Then he shook the door; but I had fastened it so securely that it resisted all his furious blows.

"That miserable cur is amusing himself by making love while our throats are being cut! Bernard, the mounted police are attacking us! Your Uncle Louis had just been killed! Come and help us! For God's sake, come, Bernard!"

"May the devil take the lot of you," I cried, "and may you be killed yourself, if I believe a single word of all this. I am not such a fool as you imagine; the only cowards here are those who lie. Didn't I swear that the woman should be mine? I'm not going to give her up until I choose."

"To hell with you!" replied Laurence; "you are pretending . . ."

The shots rang out faster. Frightful cries were heard. Laurence left the door and ran in the direction of the noise. His eagerness proved him so much in earnest that I could no longer refuse to believe him. The thought that they would accuse me of cowardice overcame me. I advanced towards the door.

"O Bernard! O Monsieur de Mauprat!" cried Edmee, staggering after me; "let me go with you. I will throw myself at your uncles' feet; I will make them stop the fight; I will give them all I possess, my life, if they wish . . . if only they will spare my father."

"Wait a moment," I said, turning towards her; "I am by no means certain that this is not a joke at my expense. I have a suspicion that my uncles are there, behind that door, and that, while our whippers-in are firing off guns in the courtyard, they are waiting with a blanket to toss me. Now, either you are my cousin, or you are a . . . You must make me a solemn promise, and I will make you one in return. If you are one of these wandering charmers and I quit this room the dupe of your pretty acting, you must swear to be my mistress, and to allow none other near you until I have had my rights; otherwise, for my part, I swear that you shall be chastised, even as my spotted dog Flora was chastised this morning. If, on the other hand, you are Edmee, and I swear to intervene between your father and those who would kill him, what promise will you make me, what will you swear?"

"If you save my father," she cried, "I swear to you that I will marry you, I swear it."

"Ho! ho! indeed!" I said, emboldened by her enthusiasm, the sublimity of which I did not understand. "Give me a pledge, then, so that in any case I do not go out from here like a fool."

I took her in my arms and kissed her. She did not attempt to resist. Her cheeks were like ice. Mechanically she began to follow me as I moved to the door. I was obliged to push her back. I did so without roughness; but she fell as one in a faint. I began to grasp the gravity of my position; for there was nobody in the corridor and the tumult outside was becoming more and more alarming. I was about to run and get my weapons, when a last feeling of distrust, or it may have been another sentiment, prompted me to go back and double-lock the door of the hall where I was leaving Edmee. I put the key into my belt and hastened to the ramparts, armed with a gun, which I loaded as I ran.

It was simply an attack made by the mounted police, and had nothing whatever to do with Mademoiselle de Mauprat. A little while before our creditors had obtained a writ of arrest against us. The law officers, beaten and otherwise severely handled, had demanded of the King's advocate at the provincial court of Bourges another warrant of arrest. This the armed police were now doing their best to execute. They had hoped to effect an easy capture by means of a night surprise. But we were in a better state of defence than they had anticipated. Our men were brave and well armed; and then we were fighting for our very existence; we had the courage of despair, and this was an immense advantage. Our band amounted to twenty-four all told; theirs to more than fifty soldiers, in addition to a score or more of peasants, who were slinging stones from the flanks. These, however, did more harm to their allies than they did to us.

For half an hour the fighting was most desperate. At the end of this time the enemy had become so dismayed by our resistance that they fell back, and hostilities were suspended. However, they soon returned to the attack, and again were repulsed with loss. Hostilities were once more suspended. They then, for the third time, called upon us to surrender, promising that our lives should be spared. Antony Mauprat replied with an obscene jest. They remained undecided, but did not withdraw.

I had fought bravely; I had done what I called my duty. There was a long lull. It was impossible to judge the distance of the enemy, and we dared not fire at random into the darkness, for our ammunition was too precious. All my uncles remained riveted on the ramparts, in case of fresh attack. My Uncle Louis was dangerously wounded. Thoughts of my prisoner returned to my mind. At the beginning of the fight I had heard John Mauprat saying, that if our defeat seemed imminent, we must offer to hand her over to the enemy, on condition that they should raise the siege; that if they refused, we must hang her before their eyes. I had no longer any doubts about the truth of what she had told me. When victory appeared to declare for us they forgot the captive. But I noticed the crafty John quitting the culverin which he so loved to fire, and creeping away like a cat into the darkness. A feeling of ungovernable jealousy seized me. I threw down my gun and dashed after him, knife in hand, resolved, I believe, to stab him if he attempted to touch what I considered my booty. I saw him approach the door, try to open it, peer attentively through the keyhole, to assure himself that his prey had not escaped him. Suddenly shots were heard again. He sprang to his maimed feet with that marvellous agility of his, and limped off to the ramparts. For myself, hidden as I was by the darkness, I let him pass and did not follow. A passion other than the love of slaughter had just taken possession of me. A flash of jealousy had fired my senses. The smell of powder, the sight of blood, the noise, the danger, and the many bumpers of brandy we had passed round to keep up our strength had strangely heated my brain. I took the key from my belt and opened the door noisily. And now, as I stood before my captive again, I was no longer the suspicious and clumsy novice she had so easily moved to pity: I was the wild outlaw of Roche-Mauprat, a hundred times more dangerous than at first. She rushed towards me eagerly. I opened my arms to catch her; instead of being frightened she threw herself into them, exclaiming:

"Well! and my father?"

"Your father," I said, kissing her, "is not there. At the present moment there is no question either of him or of you. We have brought down a dozen gendarmes, that is all. Victory, as usual, is declaring for us. So, don't trouble yourself any more about your father; and I, I won't trouble myself further about the King's men. Let us live in peace and rejoice in love."

With these words I raised to my lips a goblet of wine which had been left on the table. But she took it out of my hands with an air of authority that made me all the bolder.

"Don't drink any more," she said; "think seriously of what you are saying. Is what you tell me true? Will you answer for it on your honour, on the soul of your mother?"

"Every word is true; I swear it by your pretty rosy lips," I replied, trying to kiss her again.

But she drew back in terror.

"Oh, mon Dieu!" she exclaimed, "he is drunk! Bernard! Bernard! remember what you promised; do not break your word. You have not forgotten, have you, that I am your kinswoman, your sister?"

"You are my mistress or my wife," I answered, still pursuing her.

"You are a contemptible creature!" she rejoined, repulsing me with her riding whip. "What have you done that I should be aught to you? Have you helped my father?"

"I swore to help him; and I would have helped him if he had been there; it is just the same, therefore, as if I really had. But, had he been there, and had I tried to save him and failed, do you know that for this treachery Roche-Mauprat could not have provided any instrument of torture cruel enough and slow enough to drag the life out of me inch by inch? For all I know, they may actually have heard my vow; I proclaimed it loudly enough. But what do I care? I set little store by a couple of days more or less of life. But I do set some store by your favour, my beau-beauty. I don't want to be the languishing knight that every one laughs at. Come, now, love me at once; or, my word, I will return to the fight, and if I am killed, so much the worse for you. You will no longer have a knight to help you, and you will still have seven Mauprats to keep at bay. I'm afraid you are not strong enough for that rough work, my pretty little love-bird."

These words, which I threw out at random, merely to distract her attention so that I might seize her hands or her waist, made a deep impression on her. She fled to the other end of the hall, and tried to force open the window; but her little hands could not even move the heavy leaden sash in the rusty ironwork. Her efforts made me laugh. She clasped her hands in terror, and remained motionless. Then all at once the expression of her face changed. She seemed to have resolved how to act, and came toward me smiling and with outstretched hand. So beautiful was she thus that a mist came over my eyes and for a moment I saw her not.

Ah, gentlemen, forgive my childishness. I must tell you how she was dressed. After that weird night she never wore that costume again, and yet I can remember it so exactly. It is a long, long time ago. But were I to live as long as I have already lived again, I should not forget a single detail, so much was I struck by it amid the tumult that was raging within me and without; amid the din of shots striking the ramparts, the lightning flashes ripping the sky, and the violent palpitations which sent my blood surging from my heart to my brain, and from my head to my breast.

Oh, how lovely she was! It seems as if her shade were even now passing before my eyes. Yes; I fancy I see her in the same dress, the riding-habit which used to be worn in those days. The skirt of it was of cloth and very full; round the waist was a red sash, while a waistcoat of pearl-gray satin, fastened with buttons, fitted closely to the figure; over this was a hunting-jacket, trimmed with lace, short and open in front; the hat, of gray felt, with a broad brim turned up in front, was crowned with half a dozen red feathers. The hair, which was not powdered, was drawn back from the face and fell down in two long plaits, like those of the Bernese women. Edmee's were so long that they almost reached the ground.

Her garb, to me so strangely fascinating, her youth and beauty, and the favour with which she now seemed to regard my pretensions, combined to make me mad with love and joy. I could imagine nothing more beautiful than a lovely woman yielding without coarse words, and without tears of shame. My first impulse was to take her in my arms; but, as if overcome by that irresistible longing to worship which characterizes a first love, even with the grossest of beings, I fell down before her and pressed her knees to my breast; and yet, on my own supposition, it was to a shameless wanton that this homage was paid. I was none the less nigh to swooning from bliss.

She took my head between her two beautiful hands, and exclaimed:

"Ah, I was right! I knew quite well that you were not one of those reprobates. You are going to save me, aren't you? Thank God! How I thank you, O God! Must we jump from the window? Oh, I am not afraid; come—come!"

I seemed as if awakened from a dream, and, I confess, the awakening was not a little painful.

"What does this mean?" I asked, as I rose to my feet. "Are you still jesting with me? Do you not know where you are? Do you think that I am a child?"

"I know that I am at Roche-Mauprat," she replied, turning pale again, "and that I shall be outraged and assassinated in a couple of hours, if meanwhile I do not succeed in inspiring you with some pity. But I shall succeed," she cried, falling at my feet in her turn; "you are not one of those men. You are too young to be a monster like them. I could see from your eyes that you pitied me. You will help me to escape, won't you, won't you, my dear heart?"

She took my hands and kissed them frenziedly, in the hope of moving me. I listened and looked at her with a sullen stupidity scarcely calculated to reassure her. My heart was naturally but little accessible to feelings of generosity and compassion, and at this moment a passion stronger than all the rest was keeping down the impulse she had striven to arouse. I devoured her with my eyes, and made no effort to understand her words. I only wished to discover whether I was pleasing to her, or whether she was trying to make use of me to effect her escape.

"I see that you are afraid," I said. "You are wrong to be afraid of me. I shall certainly not do you any harm. You are too pretty for me to think of anything but of caressing you."

"Yes; but your uncles will kill me," she cried; "you know they will. Surely you would not have me killed? Since you love me, save me; I will love you afterwards."

"Oh, yes; afterwards, afterwards," I answered, laughing with a silly, unbelieving air; "after you have had me hanged by those gendarmes to whom I have just given such a drubbing. Come, now; prove that you love me at once; I will save you afterwards. You see, I can talk about 'afterwards' too."

I pursued her round the room. Though she fled from me, she gave no signs of anger, and still appealed to me with soft words. In me the poor girl was husbanding her one hope, and was fearful of losing it. Ah, if I had only been able to realize what such a woman as she was, and what my own position meant! But I was unable then. I had but one fixed idea—the idea which a wolf may have on a like occasion.

At last, as my only answer to all her entreaties was, "Do you love me, or are you fooling me?" she saw what a brute she had to deal with, and, making up her mind accordingly, she came towards me, threw her arms round my neck, hid her face in my bosom, and let me kiss her hair. Then she put me gently from her, saying:

"Ah, mon Dieu! don't you see how I love you—how I could not help loving you from the very first moment I saw you? But don't you understand that I hate your uncles, and that I would be yours alone?"

"Yes," I replied, obstinately, "because you say to yourself: 'This is a booby whom I shall persuade to do anything I wish, by telling him that I love him; he will believe it, and I will take him away to be hanged.' Come; there is only one word which will serve if you love me."

She looked at me with an agonized air. I sought to press my lips to hers whenever her head was not turned away. I held her hands in mine. She was powerless now to do more than delay the hour of her defeat. Suddenly the colour rushed back to the pale face; she began to smile; and with an expression of angelic coquetry, she asked:

"And you—do you love me?"

From this moment the victory was hers. I no longer had power to will what I wished. The lynx in me was subdued; the man rose in its place; and I believe that my voice had a human ring, as I cried for the first time in my life:

"Yes, I love you! Yes, I love you!"

"Well, then," she said, distractedly, and in a caressing tone, "let us love each other and escape together."

"Yes, let us escape," I answered. "I loathe this house, and I loathe my uncles. I have long wanted to escape. And yet I shall only be hanged, you know."

"They won't hang you," she rejoined with a laugh; "my betrothed is a lieutenant-general."

"Your betrothed!" I cried, in a fresh fit of jealousy more violent than the first. "You are going to be married?"

"And why not?" she replied, watching me attentively.

I turned pale and clinched my teeth.

"In that case, . . ." I said, trying to carry her off in my arms.

"In that case," she answered, giving me a little tap on the cheek, "I see that you are jealous; but his must be a particular jealousy who at ten o'clock yearns for his mistress, only to hand her over at midnight to eight drunken men who will return her to him on the morrow as foul as the mud on the roads."

"Ah, you are right!" I exclaimed. "Go, then; go. I would defend you to the last drop of my blood; but I should be vanquished by numbers, and I should die with the knowledge that you were left to them. How horrible! I shudder to think of it. Come—you must go."

"Yes! yes, my angel!" she cried, kissing me passionately on the cheek.

These caresses, the first a woman had given me since my childhood, recalled, I know not how or why, my mother's last kiss, and, instead of pleasure, caused me profound sadness. I felt my eyes filling with tears. Noticing this, she kissed my tears, repeating the while:

"Save me! Save me!"

"And your marriage?" I asked. "Oh! listen. Swear that you will not marry before I die. You will not have to wait long; for my uncles administer sound justice and swift, as they say."

"You are not going to follow me, then?" she asked.

VI

"Follow you? No; it is as well to be hanged here for helping you to escape as to be hanged yonder for being a bandit. Here, at least, I avoid a twofold shame: I shall not be accounted an informer, and shall not be hanged in a public place."

"I will not leave you here," she cried, "though I die myself. Fly with me. You run no risk, believe me. Before God, I declare you are safe. Kill me, if I lie. But let us start—quickly. O God! I hear them singing. They are coming this way. Ah, if you will not defend me, kill me at once!"

She threw herself into my arms. Love and jealousy were gradually overpowering me. Indeed, I even thought seriously of killing her; and I kept my hand on my hunting-knife as long as I heard any noise or voices near the hall. They were exulting in their victory. I cursed Heaven for not giving it to our foes. I clasped Edmee to my breast, and we remained motionless in each other's arms, until a fresh report announced that the fight was beginning again. Then I pressed her passionately to my heart.

"You remind me," I said, "of a poor little dove which one day flew into my jacket to escape from a kite, and tried to hide itself in my bosom."

"And you did not give it up to the kite, did you?" asked Edmee.

"No, by all the devils! not any more than I shall give you up, you, the prettiest of all the birds in the woods, to these vile night-birds that are threatening you."

"But how shall we escape?" she cried, terror-stricken by the volleys they were firing.

"Easily," I said. "Follow me."

I seized a torch, and lifting a trap-door, I made her descend with me to the cellar. Thence we passed into a subterranean passage hollowed out of the rock. This, in bygone days had enabled the garrison, then more numerous, to venture upon an important move in case of an attack; some of the besieged would emerge into the open country on the side opposite the portcullis and fall on the rear of the besiegers, who were thus caught between two fires. But many years had passed since the garrison of Roche-Mauprat was large enough to be divided into two bodies; and besides, during the night it would have been folly to venture beyond the walls. We arrived, therefore, at the exit of the passage without meeting with any obstacle. But at the last moment I was seized with a fit of madness. I threw down my torch, and leaned against the door.

"You shall not go out from here," I said to the trembling Edmee, "without promising to be mine."

We were in darkness; the noise of the fight no longer reached us. Before any one could surprise us here we had ample time to escape. Everything was in my favour. Edmee was now at the mercy of my caprice. When she saw that the seductions of her beauty could no longer rouse me to ecstasy, she ceased to implore, and drew backward a few steps.

"Open the door," she said, "and go out first, or I will kill myself. See, I have your hunting-knife. You left it by the side of the trap-door. To return to your uncles you will have to walk through my blood."

Her resolute manner frightened me.

"Give me that knife," I said, "or, be the consequences what they may, I will take it from you by force."

"Do you think I am afraid to die?" she said calmly. "If this knife had only been in my hand yonder in the chateau, I should not have humbled myself before you."

"Confound it!" I cried, "you have deceived me. Your love is a sham. Begone! I despise you. I will not follow such as you."

At the same time I opened the door.

"I would not go without you," she cried; "and you—you would not have me go without dishonour. Which of us is the more generous?"

"You are mad," I said. "You have lied to me; and you do not know what to do to make a fool of me. However, you shall not go out from here without swearing that your marriage with the lieutenant-general or any other man shall not take place before you have been my mistress."

"Your mistress!" she said. "Are you dreaming? Could you not at least soften the insult by saying your wife?"

"That is what any one of my uncles would say in my place; because they would care only about your dowry. But I—I yearn for nothing but your beauty. Swear, then, that you will be mine first; afterwards you shall be free, on my honour. And if my jealousy prove so fierce that it may not be borne, well, since a man may not go from his word, I will blow my brains out."

"I swear," said Edmee, "to be no man's before being yours."

"That is not it. Swear to be mine before being any other's."

"It is the same thing," she answered. "Yes; I swear it."

"On the gospel? On the name of Christ? By the salvation of your soul? By the memory of your mother?"

"On the gospel; in the name of Christ; by the salvation of my soul; by the memory of my mother."

"Good."

"One moment," she rejoined; "I want you to swear that my promise and its fulfilment shall remain a secret; that my father shall never know it, or any person who might tell him."

"No one in the world shall hear it from me. Why should I want others to know, provided only that you keep your word?"

She made me repeat the formula of an oath. Then we hurried forth into the open, holding each other's hands as a sign of mutual trust.

But now our flight became dangerous. Edmee feared the besiegers almost as much as the besieged. We were fortunate enough not to meet any. Still, it was by no means easy to move quickly. The night was so dark that we were continually running against trees, and the ground was so slippery that we were unable to avoid falls. A sudden noise made us start; but, from the rattle of the chain fixed on its foot, I immediately recognised my grandfather's horse, an animal of an extraordinary age, but still strong and spirited. It was the very horse that had brought me to Roche-Mauprat ten years before. At present the only thing that would serve as a bridle was the rope round its neck. I passed this through its mouth, and I threw my jacket over the crupper and helped my companion to mount; I undid the chain, sprang on the animal's back, and urging it on desperately, made it set off at a gallop, happen what might. Luckily for us, it knew the paths better than I, and, as if by instinct, followed their windings without knocking against any trees. However, it frequently slipped, and in recovering itself, gave us such jolts that we should have lost our seats a thousand times (equipped as we were) had we not been hanging between life and death. In such a strait desperate ventures are best, and God protects those whom man pursues. We were congratulating ourselves on being out of danger, when all at once the horse struck against a stump, and catching his hoof in a root on the ground, fell down. Before we were up he had made off into the darkness, and I could hear him galloping farther and farther away. As we fell I had caught Edmee in my arms. She was unhurt. My own ankle, however, was sprained so severely that it was impossible for me to move a step. Edmee thought that my leg had been broken. I was inclined to think so myself, so great was the pain; but soon I thought no further either of my agony or my anxiety. Edmee's tender solicitude made me forget everything. It was in vain that I urged her to continue her flight without me. I pointed out that she could now escape alone; that we were some distance from the chateau; that day would soon be breaking; that she would be certain to find some house, and that everywhere the people would protect her against the Mauprats.

"I will not leave you," she persisted in answering. "You have devoted yourself to me; I will show the same devotion to you. We will both escape, or we will die together."

"I am not mistaken," I cried; "it is a light that I see between the branches. Edmee, there is a house yonder; go and knock at the door. You need not feel anxious about leaving me here; and you will find a guide to take you home."

"Whatever happens," she said, "I will not leave you; but I will try to find some one to help you."

"Yet, no," I said, "I will not let you knock at that door alone. That light, in the middle of the night, in a house situated in the heart of the woods, may be a lure."

I dragged myself as far as the door. It felt cold, as if of metal. The walls were covered with ivy.

"Who is there?" cried some one within, before we had knocked.

"We are saved!" cried Edmee; "it is Patience's voice."

"We are lost!" I said; "he and I are mortal enemies.

"Fear nothing," she said; "follow me. It was God that led us here."

"Yes, it was God that led you here, daughter of Heaven, morning star!" said Patience, opening the door; "and whoever is with you is welcome too at Gazeau Tower."

We entered under a surbased vault, in the middle of which hung an iron lamp. By the light of this dismal luminary and of a handful of brushwood which was blazing on the hearth we saw, not without surprise, that Gazeau Tower was exceptionally honoured with visitors. On one side the light fell upon the pale and serious face of a man in clerical garb. On the other, a broad-brimmed hat overshadowed a sort of olive-green cone terminating in a scanty beard; and on the wall could be seen the shadow of a nose so distinctly tapered that nothing in the world might compare with it except, perhaps, a long rapier lying across the knees of the personage in question, and a little dog's face which, from its pointed shape, might have been mistaken for that of a gigantic rat. In fact, it seemed as if a mysterious harmony reigned between these three salient points—the nose of Don Marcasse, his dog's snout, and the blade of his sword. He got up slowly and raised his hand to his hat. The Jansenist cure did the same. The dog thrust its head forward between its master's legs, and, silent like him, showed its teeth and put back its ears without barking.

"Quiet, Blaireau!" said Marcasse to it.

VII

No sooner had the cure recognised Edmee than he started back with an exclamation of surprise. But this was nothing to the stupefaction of Patience when he had examined my features by the light of the burning brand that served him as torch.

"The lamb in the company of the wolf!" he cried. "What has happened, then?"

"My friend," replied Edmee, putting, to my infinite astonishment, her little white hand into the sorcerer's big rough palm, "welcome him as you welcome me. I was a prisoner at Roche-Mauprat, and it was he who rescued me."

"May the sins of his fathers be forgiven him for this act!" said the cure.

Patience took me by the arm, without saying anything, and led me nearer the fire. They seated me on the only chair in the house, and the cure took upon himself the task of attending to my leg, while Edmee gave an account, up to a certain point, of our adventure. Then she asked for information about the hunt and about her father. Patience, however, could give her no news. He had heard the horn in the woods, and the firing at the wolves had disturbed his tranquility several times during the day. But since the storm broke over them the noise of the wind had drowned all other sounds, and he knew nothing of what was taking place in Varenne. Marcasse, meanwhile, had very nimbly climbed a ladder which served as an approach to the upper stories of the house, now that the staircase was broken. His dog followed him with marvellous skill. Soon they came down again, and we learned that a red light could be distinguished on the horizon in the direction of Roche-Mauprat. In spite of the loathing I had for this place and its owners, I could not repress a feeling very much like consternation on hearing that the hereditary manor which bore my own name had apparently been taken and set on fire. It meant disgrace, defeat; and this fire was as a seal of vassalage affixed to my arms by those I called clodhoppers and serfs. I sprang up from my chair, and had I not been held back by the violent pain in my foot, I believe I should have rushed out.

"What is the matter?" said Edmee, who was by my side at the time.

"The matter is," I answered abruptly, "that I must return yonder; for it is my duty to get killed rather than let my uncles parley with the rabble."

"The rabble!" cried Patience, addressing me for the first time since I arrived. "Who dares to talk of rabble here? I myself am of the rabble. It is my title, and I shall know how to make it respected."

"By Jove! Not by me," I said, pushing away the cure, who had made me sit down again.

"And yet it would not be for the first time," replied Patience, with a contemptuous smile.

"You remind me," I answered, "that we two have some old accounts to settle."

And heedless of the frightful agony caused by my sprain, I rose again, and with a backhander I sent Don Marcasse, who was endeavouring the play the cure's part of peacemaker, head over heels into the middle of the ashes. I did not mean him any harm, but my movements were somewhat rough, and the poor man was so frail that to my hand he was but as a weasel would have been to his own. Patience was standing before me with his arms crossed, in the attitude of a stoic phiphilosopher, but the fire was flashing in his eyes. Conscious of his position as my host, he was evidently waiting until I struck the first blow before attempting to crush me. I should not have kept him waiting long, had not Edmee, scorning the danger of interfering with a madman, seized my arm and said, in an authoritative tone:

"Sit down again, and be quiet; I command you."

So much boldness and confidence surprised and pleased me at the same time. The rights which she arrogated to herself over me were, in some measure, a sanction of those I claimed to have over her.

"You are right," I answered, sitting down.

And I added, with a glance at Patience:

"Some other time."

"Amen," he answered, shrugging his shoulders.

Marcasse had picked himself up with much composure, and shaking off the ashes with which he was covered, instead of finding fault with me, he tried, after his fashion to lecture Patience. This was in reality by no means easy to do; yet nothing could have been less irritating than that monosyllabic censure throwing out its little note in the thick of a quarrel like an echo in a storm.

"At your age," he said to his host; "not patient at all. Wholly to blame—yes—wrong—you!"

"How naughty you are!" Edmee said to me, putting her hand on my shoulder; "do not begin again, or I shall go away and leave you."

I willingly let myself be scolded by her; nor did I realize that during the last minutes we had exchanged parts. The moment we crossed the threshold of Gazeau Tower she had given evidence of that superiority over me which was really hers. This wild place, too, these strange witnesses, this fierce host, had already furnished a taste of the society into which I had entered, and whose fetters I was soon to feel.

"Come," she said, turning to Patience, "we do not understand each other here; and, for my part, I am devoured by anxiety about my poor father, who is no doubt searching for me, and wringing his hands at this very moment. My good Patience, do find me some means of rejoining him with this unfortunate boy, whom I dare not leave to your care, since you have not sufficient love for me to be patient and compassionate with him."

"What do you say?" said Patience, putting his hand to his brow as if waking from a dream. "Yes, you are right; I am an old brute, an old fool. Daughter of God, tell this boy, this nobleman, that I ask his pardon for the past, and that, for the present, my poor cell is at his disposal. Is that well said?"

"Yes, Patience," answered the cure. "Besides, everything may be managed. My horse is quiet and steady, and Mademoiselle de Mauprat can ride it, while you and Marcasse lead it by the bridle. For myself, I will remain here with our invalid. I promise to take good care of him and not to annoy him in any way. That will do, won't it, Monsieur Bernard? You don't bear me any ill-will, and you may be very sure that I am not your enemy."

"I know nothing about it," I answered; "it is as you please. Look after my cousin; take her home safely. For my own part, I need nothing and care for no one. A bundle of straw and a glass of wine, that is all I should like, if it were possible to have them."

"You shall have both," said Marcasse, handing me his flask, "but first of all here is something to cheer you up. I am going to the stable to get the horse ready."

"No, I will go myself," said Patience; "you see to the wants of this young man."

And he passed into another lower hall, which served as a stable for the cure's horse during the visits which the good priest paid him. They brought the animal through the room where we were; and Patience, after arranging the cure's cloak on the saddle, with fatherly care helped Edmee to mount.

"One moment," she said, before letting them lead her out. "Monsieur le Cure, will you promise me on the salvation of your soul not to leave my cousin before I return with my father to fetch him?"

"I promise solemnly," replied the cure.

"And you, Bernard," said Edmee, "will you give me your word of honour to wait for me here?"

"I can't say," I answered; "that will depend on the length of your absence and on my patience; but you know quite well, cousin, that we shall meet again, even if it be in hell; and for my part, the sooner the better."

By the light of the brand which Patience was holding to examine the horse's harness, I saw her beautiful face flush and then turn pale. Then she raised her eyes which had been lowered in sorrow, and looked at me fixedly with a strange expression.

"Are we ready to start?" said Marcasse, opening the door.

"Yes, forward," said Patience, taking the bridle. "Edmee, my child, take care to bend down while passing under the door."

"What is the matter, Blaireau?" said Marcasse, stopping on the threshold and thrusting out the point of his sword, gloriously rusted by the blood of the rodent tribe.

Blaireau did not stir, and if he had not been born dumb, as his master said, he would have barked. But he gave warning as usual by a sort of dry cough. This was his most emphatic sign of anger and uneasiness.

"There must be something down there," said Marcasse; and he boldly advanced into the darkness, after making a sign to the rider not to follow. The report of firearms made us all start. Edmee jumped down lightly from her horse, and I did not fail to notice that some impulse at once prompted her to come and stand behind my chair. Patience rushed out of the tower. The cure ran to the frightened horse, which was rearing and backing toward us. Blaireau managed to bark. I forgot my sprain, and in a single bound I was outside.

A man covered with wounds, and with the blood streaming from him, was lying across the doorway. It was my Uncle Laurence. He had been mortally wounded at the siege of Roche-Mauprat, and had come to die under our eyes. With him was his brother Leonard, who had just fired his last pistol shot at random, luckily without hitting any one. Patience's first impulse was to prepare to defend himself. On recognising Marcasse, however, the fugitives, far from showing themselves hostile, asked for shelter and help. As their situation was so desperate no one thought that assistance should be refused. The police were pursuing them. Roche-Mauprat was in flames; Louis and Peter had died fighting; Antony, John, and Walter had fled in another direction, and, perhaps, were already prisoners. No words would paint the horror of Laurence's last moments. His agony was brief but terrible. His blasphemy made the cure turn pale. Scarce had the door been shut and the dying man laid on the floor than the horrible death-rattle was heard. Leonard, who knew of no remedy but brandy, snatched Marcasse's flask out of my hand (not without swearing and scornfully reproaching me for my flight), forced open his brother's clinched teeth with the blade of his hunting-knife, and, in spite of our warning, poured half the flask down his throat. The wretched man bounded into the air, brandished his arms in desperate convulsions, drew himself up to his full height, and fell back stone dead upon the blood-stained floor. There was no time to offer up a prayer over the body, for the door resounded under the furious blows of our assailants.

"Open in the King's name!" cried several voices; "open to the police!"

"Help! help!" cried Leonard, seizing his knife and rushing towards the door. "Peasants, prove yourselves nobles! And you, Bernard, atone for your fault; wash out your shame; do not let a Mauprat fall into the hands of the gendarmes alive!"

Urged on by native courage and by pride, I was about to follow his example, when Patience rushed at him, and exerting his herculean strength, threw him to the ground. Putting one knee on his chest, he called to Marcasse to open the door. This was done before I could take my uncle's part against his terrible assailant. Six gendarmes at once rushed into the tower and, with their guns pointed, bade us move at our peril.

"Stay, gentlemen," said Patience, "don't harm any one. This is your prisoner. Had I been alone with him, I should either have defended him or helped him to escape; but there are honest people here who ought not to suffer for a knave; and I did not wish to expose them to a fight. Here is the Mauprat. Your duty, as you know, is to deliver him safe and sound into the hands of justice. This other is dead."

"Monsieur, surrender!" said the sergeant of the gendarmes, laying his hand on Leonard.

"Never shall a Mauprat drag his name into the dock of a police court," replied Leonard, with a sullen expression. "I surrender, but you will get nothing but my skin."

And he allowed himself to be placed in a chair without making any resistance.

But while they were preparing to bind him he said to the cure:

"Do me one last kindness, Father. Give me what is left in the flask; I am dying of thirst and exhaustion."

The good cure handed him the flask, which he emptied at a draught. His distorted face took on an expression of awful calm. He seemed absorbed, stunned, incapable of resistance. But as soon as they were engaged in binding his feet, he snatched a pistol from the belt of one of the gendarmes and blew his brains out.

This frightful spectacle completely unnerved me. Sunk in a dull stupor, no longer conscious of what was happening around me, I stood there as if turned to stone, and it was only after some minutes that I realized that I was the subject of a serious discussion between the police and my hosts. One of the gendarmes declared that he recognised me as a Hamstringer Mauprat. Patience declared that I was nothing but M. Hubert de Mauprat's gamekeeper, in charge of his daughter. Annoyed at the discussion, I was about to make myself known when I saw a ghost rise by my side. It was Edmee. She had taken refuge between the wall and the cure's poor frightened horse, which, with outstretched legs and eyes of fire, made her a sort of rampart with its body. She was as pale as death, and her lips were so compressed with horror that at first, in spite of desperate efforts to speak, she was unable to express herself otherwise than by signs. The sergeant, moved by her youth and her painful situation, waited with deference until she could manage to make herself understood. At last she persuaded them not to treat me as a prisoner, but to take me with her to her father's chateau, where she gave her word of honour that satisfactory explanations and guarantees would be furnished on my account. The cure and the other witnesses, having pledged their words to this, we set out all together, Edmee on the sergeant's horse, he on an animal belonging to one of his men, myself on the cure's, Patience and the cure afoot between us, the police on either side, and Marcasse in front, still impassive amid the general terror and consternation. Two of the gendarmes remained behind to guard the bodies and prepare a report.

VIII

We had travelled about a league through the woods. Wherever other paths had crossed our own, we had stopped to call aloud; for Edmee, convinced that her father would not return home without finding her, had implored her companions to help her to rejoin him. To this shouting the gendarmes had been very averse, as they were afraid of being discovered and attacked by bodies of the fugitives from Roche-Mauprat. On our way they informed us that this den had been captured at the third assault. Until then the assailants had husbanded their forces. The officer in command of the gendarmes was anxious to get possession of the keep without destroying it; and, above all, to take the defenders alive. This, however, was impossible on account of the desperate resistance they made. The besiegers suffered so severely in their second attempt that they found themselves compelled to adopt extreme measures or to retreat. They therefore set the outer buildings on fire, and in the ensuing assault put forth all their strength. Two Mauprats were killed while fighting on the ruins of their bastion; the other five disappeared. Six men were dispatched in pursuit of them in one direction, six in another. Traces of the fugitives had been discovered immediately, and the men who gave us these details had followed Laurence and Leonard so closely that several of their shots had hit the former only a short distance from Gazeau Tower. They had heard him cry that he was done for; and, as far as they could see, Leonard had carried him to the sorcerer's door. This Leonard was the only one of my uncles who deserved any pity, for he was the only one who might, perhaps, have been encouraged to a better kind of life. At times there was a touch of chivalry in his brigandage, and his savage heart was capable of affection. I was deeply moved, therefore, by his tragic death, and let myself be carried along mechanically, plunged in gloomy thoughts, and determined to end my days in the same manner should I ever be condemned to the disgrace he had scorned to endure.

All at once the sound of horns and the baying of hounds announced the approach of a party of huntsmen. While we, on our side, were answering with shouts, Patience ran to meet them. Edmee, longing to see her father again, and forgetting all the horrors of this bloody night, whipped up her horse and reached the hunters first. As soon as we came up with them, I saw Edmee in the arms of a tall man with a venerable face. He was richly dressed; his hunting-coat, with gold lace over all the seams, and the magnificent Norman horse, which a groom was holding behind him, so struck me that I thought I was in the presence of a prince. The signs of love which he was showing his daughter were so new to me that I was inclined to deem them exaggerated and unworthy of the dignity of a man. At the same time they filled me with a sort of brute jealousy; for it did not occur to my mind that a man so splendidly dressed could be my uncle. Edmee was speaking to him in a low voice, but with great animation. Their conversation lasted a few moments. At the end of it the old man came and embraced me cordially. Everything about these manners seemed so new to me, that I responded neither by word nor gesture to the protestations and caresses of which I was the object. A tall young man, with a handsome face, as elegantly dressed as M. Hubert, also came and shook my hand and proffered thanks; why, I could not understand. He next entered into a discussion with the gendarmes, and I gathered that he was the lieutenant-general of the province, and that he was ordering them to set me at liberty for the present, that I might accompany my uncle to his chateau, where he undertook to be responsible for me. The gendarmes then left us, for the chevalier and the lieutenant-general were sufficiently well escorted by their own men not to fear attack from any one. A fresh cause of astonishment for me was to see the chevalier bestowing marks of warm friendship on Patience and Marcasse. As for the cure, he was upon a footing of equality with these seigneurs. For some months he had been chaplain at the chateau of Saint-Severe, having previously been compelled to give up his living by the persecutions of the diocesan clergy.

All this tenderness of which Edmee was the object, this family affection so completely new to me, the genuinely cordial relations existing between respectful plebeians and kindly patricians—everything that I now saw and heard seemed like a dream. I looked on with a sensation that it was all unintelligible to me. However, soon after our caravan started my brain began to work; for I then saw the lieutenant-general (M. de la Marche) thrust his horse between Edmee's and my own, as if he had a right to be next to her. I remembered her telling me at Roche-Mauprat that he was her betrothed. Hatred and anger at once surged up within me, and I know not what absurdity I should have committed, had not Edmee, apparently divining the workings of my unruly soul, told him that she wanted to speak to me, and thus restored me to my place by her side.

"What have you to say to me?" I asked with more eagerness than politeness.

"Nothing," she answered in an undertone. "I shall have much to say later. Until then will you do everything I ask of you?"

"And why the devil should I do everything you ask of me, cousin?"

For a moment she hesitated to reply; then, making an effort, she said:

"Because it is thus that a man proves to a woman that he loves her."

"Do you believe that I don't love you?" I replied abruptly.

"How should I know?" she said.

This doubt astonished me very much, and I tried to combat it after my fashion.

"Are you not beautiful?" I said; "and am not I a young man? Perhaps you think I am too much of a boy to notice a woman's beauty; but now that my head is calm, and I am sad and quite serious, I can assure you that I am even more deeply in love with you than I thought. The more I look at you the more beautiful you seem. I did not think that a woman could be so lovely. I tell you I shall not sleep till . . ."

"Hold your tongue," she said sharply.

"Oh, I suppose you are afraid that man will hear me," I answered, pointing to M. de la Marche. "Have no fear; I know how to keep my word; and, as you are the daughter of a noble house, I hope you know how to keep yours."

She did not reply. We had reached a part of the road where it was only possible for two to walk abreast. The darkness was profound, and although the chevalier and the lieutenant-general were at our heels, I was going to make bold to put my arm round her waist, when she said to me, in a sad and weary voice:

"Cousin, forgive me for not talking to you. I'm afraid I did not quite understand what you said. I am so exhausted that I feel as if I were going to die. Luckily, we have reached home now. Promise me that you will love my father, that you will yield to all his wishes, that you will decide nothing without consulting me. Promise me this if you would have me believe in your friendship."

"Oh, my friendship? you are welcome not to believe in that," I answered; "but you must believe in my love. I promise everything you wish. And you, will you not promise me anything? Do, now, with a good grace."

"What can I promise that is not yours?" she said in a serious tone. "You saved my honour; my life belongs to you."

The first glimmerings of dawn were now beginning to light the horizon. We had reached the village of Saint-Severe, and soon afterward we entered the courtyard of the chateau. On dismounting from her horse Edmee fell into her father's arms; she was as pale as death. M. de la Marche uttered a cry, and helped to carry her away. She had fainted. The cure took charge of me. I was very uneasy about my fate. The natural distrust of the brigand sprang up again as soon as I ceased to be under the spell of her who had managed to lure me from my den. I was like a wounded wolf; I cast sullen glances about me, ready to rush at the first being who should stir my suspicions by a doubtful word or deed. I was taken into a splendid room, and a meal, prepared with a luxury far beyond anything I could have conceived, was immediately served. The cure displayed the kindest interest in me; and, having succeeded in reassuring me a little, he went to attend to his friend Patience. The disturbed state of my mind and my remnant of uneasiness were not proof against the generous appetite of youth. Had it not been for the respectful assiduity of a valet much better dressed than myself, who stood behind my chair, and whose politeness I could not help returning whenever he hastened to anticipate my wants, I should have made a terrific breakfast; as it was, the green coat and silk breeches embarrassed me considerably. It was much worse when, going down on his knees, he set about taking off my boots preparatory to putting me to bed. For the moment I thought he was playing a trick upon me, and came very near giving him a good blow on the head; but his manner was so serious as he went through this task that I sat and stared at him in amazement.

At first, at finding myself in bed without arms, and with people entering and leaving my room always on tip-toe, I again began to feel suspicious. I took advantage of a moment when I was alone to get out of bed and take from the table, which was only half cleared, the longest knife I could find. Feeling easier in my mind, I returned to bed and fell into a sound sleep, with the knife firmly clasped in my hand.

When I awoke again the rays of the setting sun, softened by my red damask curtains, were falling on my beautifully fine sheets and lighting up the golden pomegranates that adorned the corners of the bed. This bed was so handsome and soft that I felt inclined to make it my apologies for having slept in it. As I was about to get up I saw a kindly, venerable face looking through the half-drawn curtains and smiling. It was the Chevalier Hubert de Mauprat. He inquired anxiously about the state of my health. I endeavoured to be polite and to express my gratitude; but the language I used seemed so different from his that I was disconcerted and pained at my awkwardness without being able to realize why. To crown my misery, a movement that I made caused the knife which I had taken as bedfellow to fall at M. de Mauprat's feet. He picked it up, looked at it, and then at myself with extreme surprise. I turned as red as fire and stammered out I know not what. I expected he would reprove me for this insult to his hospitality. However, he was too polite to insist upon a more complete explanation. He quietly placed the knife on the mantel-piece and, returning to me, spoke as follows:

"Bernard, I now know that I owe to you the life that I hold dearest in the world. All my own life shall be devoted to giving you proofs of my gratitude and esteem. My daughter also is sacredly indebted to you. You need, then, have no anxiety about your future. I know what persecution and vengeance you exposed yourself to in coming to us; but I know, too, from what a frightful existence my friendship and devotion will be able to deliver you. You are an orphan, and I have no son. Will you have me for your father?"

I stared at the chevalier with wild eyes. I could not believe my ears. All feeling within me seemed paralyzed by astonishment and timidity. I was unable to answer a word. The chevalier himself evidently felt some astonishment; he had not expected to find a nature so brutishly ill-conditioned.

"Come," he said; "I hope that you will grow accustomed to us. At all events, shake hands, to show that you trust me. I will send up your servant; give him your orders; he is at your disposal. I have only one promise to exact from you, and that is that you will not go beyond the walls of the park until I have taken steps to make you safe from the pursuit of justice. At present it is possible that the charges which have been hanging over your uncles' heads might be made to fall on your own."

"My uncles!" I exclaimed, putting my hand to my brow. "Is this all a hideous dream? Where are they? What has become of Roche-Mauprat?"

"Roche-Mauprat," he answered, "has been saved from the flames. Only a few of the outer buildings have been destroyed; but I undertake to repair the house and to redeem your fief from the creditors who claim it. As to your uncles . . . you are probably the sole heir of a name that it behoves you to rehabilitate."

"The sole heir?" I cried. "Four Mauprats fell last night; but the other three . . ."

"The fifth, Walter, perished in his attempt to escape. His body was discovered this morning in the pond of Les Froids. Neither John nor Antony has been caught, but the horse belonging to one and a cloak of the other's, found near the spot where Walter's body was lying, seem to hint darkly that their fate was as his. Even if one of them manages to escape, he will never dare make himself known again, for there would be no hope for him. And since they have drawn down upon their heads the inevitable storm, it is best, both for themselves and for us, who unfortunately bear the same name, that they should have come to this tragic end—better to have fallen weapon in hand, than to have suffered an infamous death upon the gallows. Let us bow to what God has ordained for them. It is a stern judgment; seven men in the pride of youth and strength summoned in a single night to their terrible reckoning! . . . We must pray for them, Bernard, and by dint of good works try to make good the evil they have done, and remove the stains they have left on our escutcheon."

These concluding words summed up the chevalier's whole character. He was pious, just, and full of charity; but, with him, as with most nobles, the precepts of Christian humility were wont to fall before the pride of rank. He would gladly have had a poor man at his table, and on Good Friday, indeed, he used to wash the feet of twelve beggars; but he was none the less attached to all the prejudices of our caste. In trampling under foot the dignity of man, my cousins, he considered, had, as noblemen, been much more culpable than they would have been as plebeians. On the latter hypothesis, according to him, their crimes would not have been half so grave. For a long time I shared the conviction myself; it was in my blood, if I may use the expression. I lost it only in the stern lessons of my destiny.

He then confirmed what his daughter had told me. From my birth he had earnestly desired to undertake my education. But his brother Tristan had always stubbornly opposed this desire. There the chevalier's brow darkened.

"You do not know," he said, "how baneful have been the consequences of that simple wish of mine—baneful for me, and for you too. But that must remain wrapped in mystery—a hideous mystery, the blood of the Atridae. . . ."

He took my hand, and added, in a broken voice:

"Bernard, we are both of us victims of a vicious family. This is not the moment to pile up charges against those who in this very hour are standing before the terrible tribunal of God; but they have done me an irreparable wrong—they have broken my heart. The wrong they have done you shall be repaired—I swear it by the memory of your mother. They have deprived you of education; they have made you a partner in their brigandage; yet your soul has remained great and pure as was the soul of the angel who gave you birth. You will correct the mistakes which others made in your childhood; you will receive an education suitable to your rank. And then, Bernard, you will restore the honour of your family. You will, won't you? Promise me this, Bernard. It is the one thing I long for. I will throw myself at your knees if so I may win your confidence; and I shall win it, for Providence has destined you to be my son. Ah, once it was my dream that you should be more completely mine. If, when I made my second petition, they had granted you to my loving care, you would have been brought up with my daughter and you would certainly have become her husband. But God would not have it so.

You have now to begin your education, whereas hers is almost finished. She is of an age to marry; and, besides, her choice is already made. She loves M. de la Marche; in fact, their marriage is soon to take place. Probably she had told you."

I stammered out a few confused words. The affection and generous ideas of this noble man had moved me profoundly, and I was conscious of a new nature, as it were, awakening within me. But when he pronounced the name of his future son-in-law, all my savage instincts rose up again, and I felt that no principle of social loyalty would make me renounce my claim to her whom I regarded as my fairly won prize. I grew pale; I grew red; I gasped for breath. Luckily, we were interrupted by the Abbe Aubert (the Jansenist cure), who came to inquire how I was after my fall. Then for the first time the chevalier heard of my accident; an incident that had escaped him amid the press of so many more serious matters. He sent for his doctor at once, and I was overwhelmed with kind attentions, which seemed to me rather childish, but to which I submitted from a sense of gratitude.

I had not dared to ask the chevalier for any news of his daughter. With the abbe, however, I was bolder. He informed me that the length and uneasiness of her sleep were causing some anxiety; and the doctor, when he returned in the evening to dress my ankle, told me that she was very feverish, and that he was afraid she was going to have some serious illness.

For a few days, indeed, she was ill enough to cause anxiety. In the terrible experience she had gone through she had displayed great energy; but the reaction was correspondingly violent. For myself, I was also kept to my bed. I could not take a step without feeling considerable pain, and the doctor threatened that I should be laid up for several months if I did not submit to inaction for a few days. As I was otherwise in vigorous health, and had never been ill in my life, the change from any active habits to this sluggish captivity caused me indescribable *ennui*. Only those who have lived in the depths of woods, and experienced all the hardships of a rough life, can understand the kind of horror and despair I felt on finding myself shut up for more than a week between four silk curtains. The luxuriousness of my room, the gilding of my bed, the minute attentions of the lackeys, everything, even to the excellence of the food—trifles which I had somewhat appreciated the first day—became odious to me at the end of twenty-four hours. The chevalier paid me affectionate but short visits; for he was absorbed by the illness of his darling daughter. The abbe was all kindness. To neither did I dare confess how wretched I felt; but when I was alone I felt inclined to roar like a caged lion; and at night I had dreams in which the moss in the woods, the curtain of forest trees, and even the gloomy battlements of Roche-Mauprat, appeared to me like an earthly paradise. At other times, the tragic scenes that had accompanied and followed my escape were reproduced so vividly by my memory that, even when awake, I was a prey to a sort of delirium.

A visit from M. de la Marche stirred my ideas to still wilder disorder. He displayed the deepest interest in me, shook me by the hand again and again, and implored my friendship, vowed a dozen times that he would lay down his life for me, and made I don't know how many other protestations which I scarcely heard, for his voice was like a raging torrent in my ears, and if I had had my hunting-knife I believe I should have thrown myself upon him. My rough manners and sullen looks astonished him very much; but, the abbe having explained that my mind was disturbed by the terrible events which had happened in my family, he renewed his protestations, and took leave of me in the most affectionate and courteous manner.

This politeness which I found common to everybody, from the master of the house to the meanest of his servants, though it struck me with admiration, yet made me feel strangely ill at ease; for, even if it had not been inspired by good-will towards me, I could never have brought myself to understand that it might be something very different from real goodness. It bore so little resemblance to the facetious braggadocio of the Mauprats, that it seemed to me like an entirely new language, which I understood but could not speak.

However, I recovered the power of speech when the abbe announced that he was to have charge of my education, and began questioning me about my attainments. My ignorance was so far beyond anything he could have imagined that I was getting ashamed to lay it all bare; and, my savage pride getting the upper hand, I declared that I was a gentleman, and had no desire to become a clerk. His only answer was a burst of laughter, which offended me greatly. He tapped me quickly on the shoulder, with a good-natured smile, saying that I should change my mind in time, but that I was certainly a funny fellow. I was purple with rage when the chevalier entered. The abbe told him of our conversation and of my little speech. M. Hubert suppressed a smile.

"My boy," he said, in a kind tone, "I trust I may never do anything to annoy you, even from affection. Let us talk no more about work to-day. Before conceiving a taste for it you must first realize its necessity. Since you have a noble heart you can not but have a sound mind; the desire for knowledge will come to you of itself. And now to supper. I expect you are hungry. Do you like wine?"

"Much better than Latin," I replied.

"Come, abbe," he continued laughingly, "as a punishment for having played the pedant you must drink with us. Edmee is now quite out of danger. The doctor has said that Bernard can get up and walk a few steps. We will have supper served in this room."

The supper and wine were so good, indeed, that I was not long in getting tipsy, according to the Roche-Mauprat custom. I even saw they aided and abetted, in order to make me talk, and show at once what species of boor they had to deal with. My lack of education surpassed anything they had anticipated; but I suppose they augured well from my native powers; for, instead of giving me up, they laboured at the rough block with a zeal which showed at least that they were not without hope. As soon as I was able to leave my room I lost the feeling of *ennui*. The abbe was my inseparable companion through the whole first day. The length of the second was diminished by the hope they gave me of seeing Edmee on the morrow, and by the kindness I experienced from every one. I began to feel the charm of these gentle manners in proportion as I ceased to be astonished at them.

VIII

The never-failing goodness of the chevalier could not but overcome my boorishness; nay, more, it rapidly won my heart. This was the first affection of my life. It took up its abode in me side by side with a violent love for his daughter, nor did I even dream of pitting one of these feelings against the other. I was all yearning, all instinct, all desire. I had the passions of a man in the soul of a child.

IX

At last, one morning after breakfast, Mr. Hubert took me to see his daughter. When the door of her room was opened I felt almost suffocated by the warm-scented air which met me. The room itself was charming in its simplicity; the curtains and coverings of chintz, with a white ground. Large china vases filled with flowers exhaled a delicate perfume. African birds were sporting in a gilded cage, and singing their sweet little love songs. The carpet was softer to the feet than is the moss of the woods in the month of March. I was in such a state of agitation that my eyes grew more and more dim every moment. My feet caught in one another most awkwardly, and I kept stumbling against the furniture without being able to advance. Edmee was lying on a long white chair, carelessly fingering a mother-of-pearl fan. She seemed to me even more beautiful than before, yet so changed that a feeling of apprehension chilled me in the middle of my ecstasy. She held out her hand to me; I did not like to kiss it in the presence of her father. I could not hear what she was saying to me—I believe her words were full of affection. Then, as if overcome with fatigue, she let her head fall back on the pillow and closed her eyes.

"I have some work to do," said the chevalier to me. "Stay here with her; but do not make her talk too much, for she is still very weak."

This recommendation really seemed a sarcasm. Edmee was pretending to be sleepy, perhaps to conceal some of the embarrassment that weighed on her heart; and, as for myself, I felt so incapable of overcoming her reserve that it was in reality a kindness to counsel silence.

The chevalier opened a door at one end of the room and closed it after him; but, as I could hear him cough from time to time, I gathered that his study was separated from his daughter's room only by a wooden partition. Still, it was bliss to be alone with her for a few moments, as long as she appeared to be asleep. She did not see me, and I could gaze on her at will. So pale was she that she seemed as white as her muslin dressing-gown, or as her satin slippers with their trimming of swan's down. Her delicate, transparent hand was to my eyes like some unknown jewel. Never before had I realized what a woman was; beauty for me had hitherto meant youth and health, together with a sort of manly hardihood. Edmee, in her riding-habit, as I first beheld her, had in a measure displayed such beauty, and I had understood her better then. Now, as I studied her afresh, my very ideas, which were beginning to get a little light from without, all helped to make this second *tete-a-tete* very different from the first.

IX

But the strange, uneasy pleasure I experienced in gazing on her was disturbed by the arrival of a duenna, a certain Mademoiselle Leblanc, who performed the duties of lady's maid in Edmee's private apartments, and filled the post of companion in the drawing-room. Perhaps she had received orders from her mistress not to leave us. Certain it is that she took her place by the side of the invalid's chair in such a way as to present to my disappointed gaze her own long, meagre back, instead of Edmee's beautiful face. Then she took some work out of her pocket, and quietly began to knit. Meanwhile the birds continued to warble, the chevalier to cough, Edmee to sleep or to pretend to sleep, while I remained at the other end of the room with my head bent over the prints in a book that I was holding upside down.

After some time I became aware that Edmee was not asleep, and that she was talking to her attendant in a low voice. I fancied I noticed the latter glancing at me from time to time out of the corner of her eye in a somewhat stealthy manner. To escape the ordeal of such an examination, and also from an impulse of cunning, which was by no means foreign to my nature, I let my head fall on the book, and the book on the pier-table, and in this posture I remained as if buried in sleep or thought. Then, little by little, their voices grew louder, until I could hear what they were saying about me.

"It's all the same; you have certainly have chosen a funny sort of page, mademoiselle."

"A page, Leblanc! Why do you talk such nonsense? As if one had pages nowadays! You are always imagining we are still in my grandmother's time. I tell you he is my father's adopted son."

"M. le Chevalier is undoubtedly quite right to adopt a son; but where on earth did he fish up such a creature as that?"

I gave a side glance at them and saw that Edmee was laughing behind her fan. She was enjoying the chatter of this old maid, who was supposed to be a wag and allowed perfect freedom of speech. I was very much hurt to see my cousin was making fun of me.

"He looks like a bear, a badger, a wolf, a kite, anything rather than a man," continued Leblanc. "What hands! what legs! And now he has been cleaned up a little, he is nothing to what he was! You ought to have seen him the day he arrived with his smock and his leather gaiters; it was enough to take away one's breath."

"Do you think so?" answered Edmee. "For my part, I preferred him in his poacher's garb. It suited his face and figure better."

"He looked like a bandit. You could not have looked at him properly, mademoiselle."

"Oh! yes, I did."

The tone in which she pronounced these words, "Yes, I did," made me shudder; and somehow I again felt upon my lips the impress of the kiss she had given me at Roche-Mauprat.

"It would not be so bad if his hair were dressed properly," continued the duenna; "but, so far, no one had been able to persuade him to have it powdered. Saint-Jean told me that just as he was about to put the powder puff to his head he got up in a rage and said, 'Anything you like except that confounded flour. I want to be able to move my head about without coughing and sneezing.' Heavens, what a savage!"

"Yet, in reality, he is quite right. If fashion did not sanction the absurdity, everybody would perceive that it is both ugly and inconvenient. Look and see if it is not more becoming to have long black hair like his?"

"Long hair like that? What a mane. It is enough to frighten one."

"Besides, boys do not have their hair powdered, and he is still a boy."

"A boy? My stars! what a brat Boys? Why he would eat them for his breakfast; he's a regular ogre. But where does the hulking dog spring from? I suppose M. le Chevalier brought him here from behind some plough. What is his name again? . . . You did tell me his name, didn't you?"

"Yes, inquisitive; I told you he is called Bernard."

"Bernard! And nothing else?"

"Nothing, for the present. What are you looking at?"

"He is sleeping like a dormouse. Look at the booby. I was wondering whether he resembled M. le Chevalier. Perhaps it was a momentary error—a fit of forgetfulness with some milk-maid."

"Come, come, Leblanc; you are going too far . . ."

"Goodness gracious, mademoiselle, has not M. le Chevalier been young like any other man? And that does not prevent virtue coming on with years, does it?"

"Doubtless your own experience has shown you that this is possible. But listen: don't take upon yourself to make fun of this young man. It is possible that you have guessed right; but my father requires him to be treated as one of the family."

"Well, well; that must be pleasant for you, mademoiselle. As for myself, what does it matter to me? I have nothing to do with the gentleman."

"Ah, if you were thirty years younger."

"But did your father consult you, mademoiselle, before planting yon great brigand in your room?"

"Why ask such a question? Is there anywhere in the world a better father than mine?"

"But you are very good also. . . . There are many young ladies who would have been by no means pleased."

"And why, I should like to know? There is nothing disagreeable about the fellow. When he has been polished a little . . ."

"He will always be perfectly ugly."

"My dear Leblanc, he is far from ugly. You are too old; you are no longer a judge of young men."

Their conversation was interrupted by the chevalier, who came in to look for a book.

"Mademoiselle Leblanc is here, is she?" he said in a very quiet tone. "I thought you were alone with my son. Well, Edmee, have you had a talk with him? Did you tell him that you would be his sister? Are you pleased with her, Bernard?"

Such answers as I gave could compromise no one. As a rule, they consisted of four or five incoherent words crippled by shame. M. de Mauprat returned to his study, and I had sat down again, hoping that my cousin was going to send away her duenna and talk to me. But they exchanged a few words in a whisper; the duenna remained, and two mortal hours passed without my daring to stir from my chair. I believe Edmee really was asleep this time. When the bell rang for dinner her father came in again to fetch me, and before leaving her room he said to her again:

"Well, have you had a chat?"

"Yes, father, dear," she replied, with an assurance that astounded me.

My cousin's behaviour seemed to me to prove beyond doubt that she had merely been trifling with me, and that she was not afraid of my reproaches. And yet hope sprang up again when I remembered the strain in which she had spoken of me to Mademoiselle Leblanc. I even succeeded in persuading myself that she feared arousing her father's suspicions, and that she was now feigning complete indifference only to draw me the more surely to her arms as soon as the favourable moment had arrived. As it was impossible to ascertain the truth, I resigned myself to waiting. But days and nights passed without any explanation being sent, or any secret message bidding me be patient. She used to come down to the drawing-room for an hour in the morning; in the evening she was present at dinner, and then would play piquet or chess with her father. During all this time she was so well watched that I could not exchange a glance with her. For the rest of the day she remained in her own room—inaccessible. Noticing that I was chafing at the species of captivity in which I was compelled to live, the chevalier frequently said to me:

"Go and have a chat with Edmee. You can go to her room and tell her that I sent you."

But it was in vain that I knocked. No doubt they had heard me coming and had recognised me by my heavy shuffling step. The door was never opened to me. I grew desperate, furious.

Here I must interrupt the account of my personal impressions to tell you what was happening at this time in the luckless Mauprat family. John and Antony had really managed to escape, and though a very close search had been made for them, they had not as yet been captured. All their property was seized, and an order issued by the courts for the sale of the Roche-Mauprat fief. As it proved, however, a sale was unnecessary. M. Hubert de Mauprat put an end to the proceedings by coming forward as purchaser. The creditors were paid off, and the title-deeds of Roche-Mauprat passed into his hands.

The little garrison kept by the Mauprats, made up of adventurers of the lowest type, had met the same fate as their masters. As I have already said, the garrison had long been reduced to a few individuals. Two or three of these were killed, others took to flight; one only was captured. This man was tried and made to suffer for all. A serious question arose as to whether judgment should not also be given against John and Antony de Mauprat by default. There was apparently no doubt that they had fled; the pond in which Walter's body was found floating had been drained, yet no traces of the bodies had been discovered. The chevalier, however, for the sake of the name he bore, strove to prevent the disgrace of an ignominious sentence; as if such a sentence could have added aught to the horror of the name of Mauprat. He brought to bear all M. de la Marche's influence and his own (which was very real in the province, especially on account of his high moral character), to hush up the affair, and he succeeded. As for myself, though I had certainly had a hand in more than one of my uncles' robberies, there was no thought of discussing me even at the bar of public opinion. In the storm of anger that my uncles had aroused people were pleased to consider me simply as a young captive, a victim of their cruelty, and thoroughly well disposed towards everybody. Certainly, in his generous good nature and desire to rehabilitate the family, the chevalier greatly exaggerated my merits, and spread a report everywhere that I was an angel of sweetness and intelligence.

On the day that M. Hubert became purchaser of the estate he entered my room early in the morning accompanied by his daughter and the abbe. Showing me the documents which bore witness to his sacrifice (Roche-Mauprat was valued at about two hundred thousand francs), he declared that I was forthwith going to be put in possession not only of my share in the inheritance, which was by no means considerable, but also of half the revenue of the property. At the same time, he said, the whole estate, lands and produce, should be secured to me by his will on one condition, namely, that I would consent to receive an education suitable to my position.

The chevalier had made all these arrangements in the kindness of his heart and without ostentation, partly out of gratitude for the service he knew I had rendered Edmee, and partly from family pride; but he had not expected that I should prove so stubborn on the question of education. I cannot tell you the irritation I felt at this word "condition"; especially as I thought I detected in it signs of some plan that Edmee had formed to free herself from her promise to me.

"Uncle," I answered, after listening to all his magnificent offers in absolute silence, "I thank you for all you wish to do for me; but it is not right that I should avail myself of your kindness. I have no need of a fortune. A man like myself wants nothing but a little bread, a gun, a hound, and the first inn he comes to on the edge of the wood. Since you are good enough to act as my guardian pay me the income on my eighth of the fief and do not ask me to learn that Latin bosh. A man of birth is sufficiently well educated when he knows how to bring down a snipe and sign his name. I have no desire to be seigneur of Roche-Mauprat; it is enough to have been a slave there. You are most kind, and on my honour I love you; but I have very little love for conditions. I have never done anything from interested motives. I would rather remain an ignoramus than develop a pretty wit for another's dole. Moreover, I could never consent to make such a hole in my cousin's fortune; though I know perfectly well that she would willingly sacrifice a part of her dowry to obtain release from . . ."

Edmee, who until now had remained very pale and apparently heedless of my words, all at once cast a lightning glance at me and said with an air of unconcern:

"To obtain a release from what, may I ask, Bernard?"

I saw that, in spite of this show of courage, she was very much perturbed; for she broke her fan while shutting it. I answered her with a look in which the artless malice of the rustic must have been apparent:

"To obtain release, cousin, from a certain promise you made me at Roche-Mauprat."

She grew paler than ever, and on her face I could see an expression of terror, but ill-disguised by a smile of contempt.

"What was the promise you made him, Edmee?" asked the chevalier, turning towards her ingenuously.

At the same time the abbe pressed my arm furtively, and I understood that my cousin's confessor was in possession of the secret.

I shrugged my shoulders; their fears did me an injustice, though they roused my pity.

"She promised me," I replied, with a smile, "that she would always look upon me as a brother and a friend. Were not those your words, Edmee, and do you think it is possible to make them good by mere money?"

She rose as if filled with new life, and, holding out her hand to me, said in a voice full of emotion:

"You are right, Bernard; yours is a noble heart, and I should never forgive myself if I doubted it for a moment."

I caught sight of a tear on the edge of her eye-lid, and I pressed her hand somewhat too roughly, no doubt, for she could not restrain a little cry, followed, however, by a charming smile. The chevalier clasped me to his breast, and the abbe rocked about in his chair and exclaimed repeatedly:

"How beautiful! How noble! How very beautiful! Ah," he added, "that is something that cannot be learnt from books," turning to the chevalier. "God writes his words and breathes forth his spirit upon the hearts of the young."

"You will see," said the chevalier, deeply moved, "that this Mauprat will yet build up the honour of the family again. And now, my dear Bernard, I will say no more about business. I know how I ought to act, and you cannot prevent me from taking such steps as I shall think fit to insure the rehabilitation of my name by yourself. The only true rehabilitation is guaranteed by your noble sentiments; but there is still another which I know you will not refuse to attempt—the way to this lies through your talents and intelligence. You will make the effort out of love for us, I hope. However, we need not talk of this at present. I respect your proud spirit, and I gladly renew my offers without conditions. And now, abbe, I shall be glad if you will accompany me to the town to see my lawyer. The carriage is waiting. As for you, children, you can have lunch together. Come, Bernard, offer your arm to your cousin, or rather, to your sister. You must acquire some courtesy of manner, since in her case it will be but the expression of your heart."

"That is true, uncle," I answered, taking hold of Edmee's arm somewhat roughly to lead her downstairs.

I could feel her trembling; but the pink had returned to her cheeks, and a smile of affection was playing about her lips.

As soon as we were seated opposite each other at table our happy harmony was chilled in a very few moments. We both returned to our former state of embarrassment. Had we been alone I should have got out of the difficulty by one of those abrupt sallies which I knew how to force from myself when I grew too much ashamed of my bashfulness; but the presence of Saint-Jean, who was waiting upon us, condemned me to silence on the subject next to my heart. I decided, therefore, to talk about Patience. I asked her how it came to pass that she was on such good terms with him, and in what light I ought to look upon the pretended sorcerer. She gave me the main points in the history of the rustic philosopher, and explained that it was the Abbe Aubert who had taken her to Gazeau Tower. She had been much struck by the intelligence and wisdom of the stoic hermit, and used to derive great pleasure from conversation with him. On his side, Patience had conceived such a friendship for her that for some time he had relaxed his strict habits, and would frequently pay her a visit when he came to see the abbe.

As you may imagine, she had no little difficulty in making these explanations intelligible to me. I was very much surprised at the praise she bestowed on Patience, and at the sympathy she showed for his revolutionary ideas. This was the first time I had heard a peasant spoken of as a man. Besides, I had hitherto looked upon the sorcerer of Gazeau Tower as very much below the ordinary peasant, and here was Edmee praising him above most of the men she knew, and even siding with him against the nobles. From this I drew the comfortable conclusion that education was not so essential as the chevalier and the abbe would have me believe.

"I can scarcely read any better than Patience," I added, "and I only wish you found as much pleasure in my society as in his; but it hardly appears so, cousin, for since I came here . . ."

We were then leaving the table, and I was rejoicing at the prospect of being alone with her at last, so that I might talk more freely, when on going into the drawing-room we found M. de la Marche there. He had just arrived, and was in the act of entering by the opposite door. In my heart I wished him at the devil.

M. de la March was one of the fashionable young nobles of the day. Smitten with the new philosophy, devoted to Voltaire, a great admirer of Franklin, more well-meaning than intelligent, understanding the oracles less than he desired or pretended to understand them; a pretty poor logician, since he found his ideas much less excellent and his political hopes much less sweet on the day that the French nation took it into its head to realize them; for the rest, full of fine sentiments, believing himself much more sanguine and romantic than he was in reality; rather more faithful to the prejudices of caste and considerably more sensitive to the opinion of the world than he flattered and prided himself on being—

such was the man. His face was certainly handsome, but I found it excessively dull; for I had conceived the most ridiculous animosity for him. His polished manners seemed to me abjectly servile with Edmee. I should have blushed to imitate them, and yet my sole aim was to surpass him in the little services he rendered her. We went out into the park. This was very large, and through it ran the Indre, here merely a pretty stream. During our walk he made himself agreeable in a thousand ways; not a violet did he see but he must pluck it to offer to my cousin. But, when we arrived at the banks of the stream, we found that the plank which usually enabled one to cross at this particular spot had been broken and washed away by the storms of a few days before. Without asking permission, I immediately took Edmee in my arms, and quietly walked through the stream. The water came up to my waist, but I carried my cousin at arm's length so securely and skilfully that she did not wet a single ribbon. M. de la Marche, unwilling to appear more delicate than myself, did not hesitate to wet his fine clothes and follow me, though with some rather poor efforts the while to force a laugh. However, though he had not any burden to carry, he several times stumbled over the stones which covered the bed of the river, and rejoined us only with great difficulty. Edmee was far from laughing. I believe that this proof of my strength and daring, forced on her in spite of herself, terrified her as an evidence of the love she had stirred in me. She even appeared to be annoyed; and, as I set her down gently on the bank, said:

"Bernard, I must request you never to play such a prank again."

"That is all very well," I said; "you would not be angry if it were the other fellow."

"He would not think of doing such a thing," she replied.

"I quite believe it," I answered; "he would take very good care of that. Just look at the chap. . . . And I—I did not ruffle a hair of your head. He is very good at picking violets; but, take my word for it, in a case of danger, don't make him your first choice."

M. de la Marche paid me great compliments on this exploit. I had hoped that he would be jealous; he did not even appear to dream of it, but rather made merry over the pitiable state of his toilet. The day was excessively hot, and we were quite dry before the end of the walk. Edmee, however, remained sad and pensive. It seemed to me that she was making an effort to show me as much friendship as at luncheon. This affected me considerably; for I was not only enamoured of her—I loved her. I could not make the distinction then, but both feelings were in me—passion and tenderness.

The chevalier and the abbe returned in time for dinner. They conversed in a low voice with M. de la Marche about the settlement of my affairs, and, from the few words which I could not help overhearing, I gathered that they had just secured my future on the bright lines they had laid before me in the morning. I was too shy and proud to express my simple thanks. This generosity perplexed me; I could not understand it, and I almost suspected that it was a trap they were preparing to separate me from my cousin. I did not realize the advantage of a fortune.

Mine were not the wants of a civilized being; and the prejudices of rank were with me a point of honour, and by no means a social vanity. Seeing that they did not speak to me openly, I played the somewhat ungracious part of feigning complete ignorance.

Edmee grew more and more melancholy. I noticed that her eyes rested now on M. de la Marche, now on her father, with a vague uneasiness. Whenever I spoke to her, or even raised my voice in addressing others, she would start and then knit her brows slightly, as if my voice had caused her physical pain. She retired immediately after dinner. Her father followed her with evident anxiety.

"Have you not noticed," said the abbe, turning to M. de la Marche, as soon as they had left the room, "that Mademoiselle de Mauprat has very much changed of late?"

"She has grown thinner," answered the lieutenant-general; "but in my opinion she is only the more beautiful for that."

"Yes; but I fear she may be more seriously ill than she owns," replied the abbe. "Her temperament seems no less changed than her face; she has grown quite sad."

"Sad? Why, I don't think I ever saw her so gay as she was this morning; don't you agree with me, Monsieur Bernard? It was only after our walk that she complained of a slight headache."

"I assure you that she is really sad," rejoined the abbe. "Nowadays, when she is gay, her gaiety is excessive; at such a time there seems to be something strange and forced about her which is quite foreign to her usual manner. Then the next minute she relapses into a state of melancholy, which I never noticed before the famous night in the forest. You may be certain that night was a terrible experience."

"True, she was obliged to witness a frightful scene at Gazeau Tower," said M. de la Marche; "and then she must have been very much exhausted and frightened when her horse bolted from the field and galloped right through the forest. Yet her pluck is so remarkable that . . . What do you think, my dear Monsieur Bernard? When you met her in the forest, did she seem very frightened?"

"In the forest?" I said. "I did not meet her in the forest at all."

"No; it was in Varenne that you met her, wasn't it?"

The abbe hastened to intervene. . . . "By-the-bye, Monsieur Bernard, can you spare me a minute to talk over a little matter connected with your property at . . ."

Hereupon he drew me out of the drawing-room, and said in a low voice:

"There is no question of business; I only want to beg of you not to let a single soul, not even M. de la Marche, suspect that Mademoiselle de Mauprat was at Roche-Mauprat for the fraction of a second."

"And why?" I asked. "Was she not under my protection there? Did she not leave it pure, thanks to me? Must it not be well known to the neighbourhood that she passed two hours there?"

"At present no one knows," he answered. "At the very moment she left it, Roche-Mauprat fell before the attack of the police, and not one of its inmates will return from the grave or from exile to proclaim the fact. When you know the world better, you will understand how important it is for the reputation of a young lady that none should have reason to suppose that even a shadow of danger has fallen upon her honour. Meanwhile, I implore you, in the name of her father, in the name of the affection for her which you expressed this morning in so noble and touching a manner . . ."

"You are very clever, Monsieur l'Abbe," I said, interrupting him. "All your words have a hidden meaning which I can grasp perfectly well, clown as I am. Tell my cousin that she may set her mind at ease. I have nothing to say against her virtue, that is very certain; and I trust I am not capable of spoiling the marriage she desires. Tell her that I claim but one thing of her, the fulfilment of that promise of friendship which she made me at Roche-Mauprat."

"In your eyes, then, that promise has a peculiar solemnity?" said the abbe. "If so, what grounds for distrusting it have you?"

I looked at him fixedly, and as he appeared very much agitated, I took a pleasure in keeping him on the rack, hoping that he would repeat my words to Edmee.

"None," I answered. "Only I observe that you are afraid that M. de la Marche may break off the marriage, if he happens to hear of the adventure at Roche-Mauprat. If the gentleman is capable of suspecting Edmee, and of grossly insulting her on the eve of his wedding, it seems to me that there is one very simple means of mending matters."

"What would you suggest?"

"Why, to challenge him and kill him."

"I trust you will do all you can to spare the venerable M. Hubert the necessity of facing such a hideous danger."

"I will spare him this and many others by taking upon myself to avenge my cousin. In truth, this is my right, Monsieur l'Abbe. I know the duties of a gentleman quite as well as if I had learnt Latin. You may tell her this from me. Let her sleep in peace. I will keep silence, and if that is useless I will fight."

"But, Bernard," replied the abbe in a gentle, insinuating tone, "have you thought of your cousin's affection for M. de la Marche?"

"All the more reason that I should fight him," I cried, in a fit of anger.

And I turned my back on him abruptly.

The abbe retailed the whole of our conversation to the penitent. The part that the worthy priest had to play was very embarrassing. Under the seal of confession he had been intrusted with a secret to which in his conversations with me he could make only indirect allusions, to bring me to understand that my pertinacity was a crime, and that the only honourable course was to yield. He hoped too much of me. Virtue such as this was beyond my power, and equally beyond my understanding.

X

A few days passed in apparent calm. Edmee said she was unwell, and rarely quitted her room. M. de la Marche called nearly every day, his chateau being only a short distance off. My dislike for him grew stronger and stronger in spite of all the politeness he showed me. I understood nothing whatever of his dabblings in philosophy, and I opposed all his opinions with the grossest prejudices and expressions at my command. What consoled me in a measure for my secret sufferings was to see that he was no more admitted than myself to Edmee's rooms.

For a week the sole event of note was that Patience took up his abode in a hut near the chateau. Ever since the Abbe Aubert had found a refuge from ecclesiastical persecution under the chevalier's roof, he had no longer been obliged to arrange secret meetings with the hermit. He had, therefore, strongly urged him to give up his dwelling in the forest and to come nearer to himself. Patience had needed a great deal of persuasion. Long years of solitude had so attached him to his Gazeau Tower that he hesitated to desert it for the society of his friend. Besides, he declared that the abbe would assuredly be corrupted with commerce with the great; that soon, unknown to himself, he would come under the influence of the old ideas, and that his zeal for the sacred cause would grow cold. It is true that Edmee had won Patience's heart, and that, in offering him a little cottage belonging to her father situated in a picturesque ravine near the park gate, she had gone to work with such grace and delicacy that not even his techy pride could feel wounded. In fact, it was to conclude these important negotiations that the abbe had betaken himself to Gazeau Tower with Marcasse on that very evening when Edmee and myself sought shelter there. The terrible scene which followed our arrival put an end to any irresolution still left in Patience. Inclined to the Pythagorean doctrines, he had a horror of all bloodshed. The death of a deer drew tears from him, as from Shakespeare's Jacques; still less could he bear to contemplate the murder of a human being, and the instant that Gazeau Tower had served as the scene of two tragic deaths, it stood defiled in his eyes, and nothing could have induced him to pass another night there. He followed us to Sainte-Severe, and soon allowed his philosophical scruples to be overcome by Edmee's persuasive powers. The little cottage which he was prevailed on to accept was humble enough not to make him blush with shame at a too palpable compromise with civilization; and, though the solitude he found there was less perfect than at Gazeau Tower, the frequent visits of the abbe and of Edmee could hardly have given him a right to complain.

X

Here the narrator interrupted his story again to expatiate on the development of Mademoiselle de Mauprat's character.

Edmee, hidden away in her modest obscurity, was—and, believe me, I do not speak from bias—one of the most perfect women to be found in France. Had she desired or been compelled to make herself known to the world, she would assuredly have been famous and extolled beyond all her sex. But she found her happiness in her own family, and the sweetest simplicity crowned her mental powers and lofty virtues. She was ignorant of her worth, as I myself was at that time, when, brutelike, I saw only with the eyes of the body, and believed I loved her only because she was beautiful. It should be said, too, that her *fiance*, M. de la Marche, understood her but little better. He had developed the weakly mind with which he was endowed in the frigid school of Voltaire and Helvetius. Edmee had fired her vast intellect with the burning declamations of Jean Jacques. A day came when I could understand her—the day when M. de la Marche could have understood her would never have come.

Edmee, deprived of her mother from the very cradle, and left to her young devices by a father full of confidence and careless good nature, had shaped her character almost alone. The Abbe Aubert, who had confirmed her, had by no means forbidden her to read the philosophers by whom he himself had been lured from the paths of orthodoxy. Finding no one to oppose her ideas or even to discuss them—for her father, who idolized her, allowed himself to be led wherever she wished—Edmee had drawn support from two sources apparently very antagonistic: the philosophy which was preparing the downfall of Christianity, and Christianity which was proscribing the spirit of inquiry. To account for this contradiction, you must recall what I told you about the effect produced on the Abbe Aubert by the *Profession de Foi du Vicaire Savoyard.* Moreover, you must be aware that, in poetic souls, mysticism and doubt often reign side by side. Jean Jacques himself furnishes a striking example of this, and you know what sympathies he stirred among priests and nobles, even when he was chastising them so unmercifully. What miracles may not conviction work when helped by sublime eloquence! Edmee had drunk of this living fount with all the eagerness of an ardent soul. In her rare visits to Paris she had sought for spirits in sympathy with her own. There, however, she had found so many shades of opinion, so little harmony, and—despite the prevailing fashion—so many ineradicable prejudices, that she had returned with a yet deeper love to her solitude and her poetic reveries under the old oaks in the park. She would even then speak of her illusions, and—with a good sense beyond her years, perhaps, too, beyond her sex—she refused all opportunities of direct intercourse with the philosophers whose writings made up her intellectual life.

"I am somewhat of a Sybarite," she would say with a smile. "I would rather have a bouquet of roses arranged for me in a vase in the early morning, than go and gather them myself from out their thorns in the heat of the sun."

As a fact, this remark about her sybaritism was only a jest. Brought up in the country, she was strong, active, brave, and full of life. To all her charms of delicate beauty she united the energy of physical and moral health. She was the proud-spirited and fearless girl, no less than the sweet and affable mistress of the house. I often found her haughty and disdainful. Patience and the poor of the district never found her anything but modest and good-natured.

Edmee loved the poets almost as much as the transcendental philosophers. In her walks she always carried a book in her hand. One day when she had taken Tasso with her she met Patience, who, as was his wont, inquired minutely into both author and subject. Edmee thereupon had to give him an account of the Crusades. This was not the most difficult part of her task. Thanks to the stores of information derived from the abbe and to his prodigious memory for facts, Patience had a passable knowledge of the outlines of universal history. But what he had great trouble in grasping was the connection and difference between epic poetry and history. At first he was indignant at the inventions of the poets, and declared that such impostures ought never to have been allowed. Then, when he had realized that epic poetry, far from leading generations into error, only raised heroic deeds to vaster proportions and a more enduring glory, he asked how it was that all important events had not been sung by the bards, and why the history of man had not been embodied in a popular form capable of impressing itself on every mind without the help of letters. He begged Edmee to explain to him a stanza of *Jerusalem Delivered.* As he took a fancy to it, she read him a canto in French. A few days later she read him another, and soon Patience knew the whole poem. He rejoiced to hear that the heroic tale was popular in Italy; and, bringing together his recollections of it, endeavoured to give them an abridged form in rude prose, but he had no memory for words. Roused by his vivid impressions, he would call up a thousand mighty images before his eyes. He would give utterance to them in improvisations wherein his genius triumphed over the uncouthness of his language, but he could never repeat what he had once said. One would have had to take it down from his dictation, and even that would have been of no use to him; for, supposing he had managed to read it, his memory, accustomed to occupy itself solely with thoughts, had never been able to retain any fragment whatever in its precise words. And yet he was fond of quoting, and at times his language was almost biblical. Beyond, however, certain expressions that he loved, and a number of short sentences that he found means to make his own, he remembered nothing of the pages which had been read to him so often, and he always listened to them again with the same emotion as at first. It was a veritable pleasure to watch the effect of beautiful poetry on this powerful intellect. Little by little the abbe, Edmee, and subsequently I myself, managed to familiarize him with Homer and Dante. He was so struck by the various incidents in the *Divine Comedy* that he could give an analysis of the poem from beginning to end, without forgetting or misplacing the slightest detail in the journey, the encounters, and the emotions of the poet. There, however, his power ended. If he essayed to repeat some of the phrases which had so charmed him when they were read, he flung forth a mass of metaphors and images which savoured of delirium. This initiation into the wonders of poetry marked an epoch in the life of Patience. In the realm of fancy it supplied the action wanting to his real life. In his magic mirror he beheld gigantic combats between heroes ten cubits high; he understood love, which he himself had never known; he fought, he loved, he conquered; he enlightened nations, gave peace to the world, redressed the wrongs of mankind, and raised up temples to the mighty spirit of the universe. He saw in the starry firmament all the gods of Olympus, the fathers of primitive humanity. In the constellations he read the story of the golden age, and of the ages of brass; in the winter wind he heard the songs of Morven, and in the storm-clouds he bowed to the ghosts of Fingal and Comala.

"Before I knew the poets," he said towards the end of his life, "I was a man lacking in one of the senses. I could see plainly that this sense was necessary, since there were so many things calling for its operation. In my solitary walks at night I used to feel a strange uneasiness; I used to wonder why I could not sleep; why I should find such pleasure in gazing upon the stars that I could not tear myself from their presence; why my heart should suddenly beat with joy on seeing certain colours, or grow sad even to tears on hearing certain sounds. At times I was so alarmed on comparing my continual agitation with the indifference of other men of my class that I even began to imagine that I was mad. But I soon consoled myself with the reflection that such madness was sweet, and I would rather have ceased to exist than be cured of it. Now that I know these things have been thought beautiful in all times and by all intelligent beings, I understand what they are, and how they are useful to man. I find joy in the thought that there is not a flower, not a colour, not a breath of air, which has not absorbed the minds and stirred the hearts of other men till it has received a name sacred among all peoples. Since I have learnt that it is allowed to man, without degrading his reason, to people the universe and interpret it by his dreams, I live wholly in the contemplation of the universe; and when the sight of the misery and crime in the world bruises my heart and shakes my reason, I fall back upon my dreams. I say to myself that, since all men are united in their love of the works of God, some day they will also be united in their love of one another. I imagine that education grows more and more perfect from father to son. It may be that I am the first untutored man who has divined truths of which no glimpse was given him from without. It may be, too, that many others before myself have been perplexed by the workings of their hearts and brains and have died without ever finding an answer to the riddle." "Ah, we poor folk," added Patience, "we are never forbidden excess in labour, or in wine, or in any of the debauches which may destroy our minds. There are some people who pay dearly for the work of our arms, so that the poor, in their eagerness to satisfy the wants of their families, may work beyond their strength. There are taverns and other places more dangerous still, from which, so it is said, the government draws a good profit; and there are priests, too, who get up in their pulpits to tell us what we owe to the lord of our village, but never what the lord owes to us. Nowhere is there a school where they teach us our real rights; where they show us how to distinguish our true and decent wants from the shameful and fatal ones; where, in short, they tell us what we can and ought to think about when we have borne the burden and heat of the day for the profit of others, and are sitting in the evening at the door of our huts, gazing on the red stars as they come out on the horizon."

Thus would Patience reason; and, believe me, in translating his words into our conventional language, I am robbing them of all their grace, all their fire, and all their vigour. But who could repeat the exact words of Patience? His was a language used by none but himself; it was a mixture of the limited, though forcible, vocabulary of the peasants and of the boldest metaphors of the poets, whose poetic turns he would often make bolder still. To this mixed idiom his sympathetic mind gave order and logic. An incredible wealth of thought made up for the brevity of the phrases that clothed it. You should have seen how desperately his will and convictions strove to overcome the impotence of his language; any other than he would have failed to come out of the struggle with honour. And I assure you that any one capable of something more serious than laughing at his solecisms and audacities of phrase, would have found in this man material for the most important studies on the development of the human mind, and an incentive to the most tender admiration for primitive moral beauty.

When, subsequently, I came to understand Patience thoroughly, I found a bond of sympathy with him in my own exceptional destiny. Like him, I had been without education; like him, I had sought outside myself for an explanation of my being—just as one seeks the answer to a riddle. Thanks to the accidents of my birth and fortune, I had arrived at complete development, while Patience, to the hour of his death, remained groping in the darkness of an ignorance from which he neither would nor could emerge. To me, however, this was only an additional reason for recognising the superiority of that powerful nature which held its course more boldly by the feeble light of instinct, than I myself by all the brilliant lights of knowledge; and which, moreover, had not had a single evil inclination to subdue, while I had had all that a man may have.

At the time, however, at which I must take up my story, Patience was still, in my eyes, merely a grotesque character, an object of amusement for Edmee, and of kindly compassion for the Abbe Aubert. When they spoke to me about him in a serious tone, I no longer understood them, and I imagined they took this subject as a sort of text whereon to build a parable proving to me the advantages of education, the necessity of devoting myself to study early in life, and the futility of regrets in after years.

Yet this did not prevent me from prowling about the copses about his new abode, for I had seen Edmee crossing the park in that direction, and I hoped that if I took her by surprise as she was returning, I should get a conversation with her. But she was always accompanied by the abbe, and sometimes even by her father, and if she remained alone with the old peasant, he would escort her to the chateau afterwards. Frequently I have concealed myself in the foliage of a giant yew-tree, which spread out its monstrous shoots and drooping branches to within a few yards of the cottage, and have seen Edmee sitting at the door with a book in her hand while Patience was listening with his arms folded and his head sunk on his breast, as though he were overwhelmed by the effort of attention. At that time I imagined that Edmee was trying to teach him to read, and thought her mad to persist in attempting an impossible education. But how beautiful she seemed in the light of the setting sun, beneath the yellowing vine leaves that overhung the cottage door! I used to gaze on her and tell myself that she belonged to me, and vow never to yield to any force or persuasion which should endeavour to make me renounce my claim.

For some days my agony of mind had been intense. My only method of escaping from it had been to drink heavily at supper, so that I might be almost stupefied at the hour, for me so painful and so galling, when she would leave the drawing-room after kissing her father, giving her hand to M. de la Marche, and saying as she passed by me, "Good-night, Bernard," in a tone which seemed to say, "To-day has ended like yesterday, and to-morrow will end like to-day."

In vain would I go and sit in the arm-chair nearest her door, so that she could not pass without at least her dress brushing against me; this was all I ever got from her. I would not put out my hand to beg her own, for she might have given it with an air of unconcern, and I verily believe I should have crushed it in my anger.

Thanks to my large libations at supper, I generally succeeded in besotting myself, silently and sadly. I then used to sink into my favourite arm-chair and remain there, sullen and drowsy, until the fumes of the wine had passed away, and I could go and air my wild dreams and sinister plans in the park.

None seemed to notice this gross habit of mine. They showed me such kindness and indulgence in the family that they seemed afraid to express disapproval, however much I deserved it. Nevertheless, they were well aware of my shameful passion for wine, and the abbe informed Edmee of it. One evening at supper she looked at me fixedly several times and with a strange expression. I stared at her in return, hoping that she would say something to provoke me, but we got no further than an exchange of malevolent glances. On leaving the table she whispered to me very quickly, and in an imperious tone:

"Break yourself of this drinking, and pay attention to what the abbe has to say to you."

This order and tone of authority, so far from filling me with hope, seemed to me so revolting that all my timidity vanished in a moment. I waited for the hour when she usually went up to her room and, going out a little before her, took up my position on the stairs.

"Do you think," I said to her when she appeared, "that I am the dupe of your lies, and that I have not seen perfectly, during the month I have been here, without your speaking a word to me, that you are merely fooling me, as if I were a booby? You lied to me and now you despise me because I was honest enough to believe your word."

"Bernard," she said, in a cold tone, "this is neither the time nor the place for an explanation."

"Oh, I know well enough," I replied, "that, according to you, it will never be the time or the place. But I shall manage to find both, do not fear. You said that you loved me. You threw your arms about my neck and said, as you kissed me—yes, here, I can still feel your lips on my cheeks: 'Save me, and I swear on the gospel, on my honour, by the memory of my mother and your own, that I will be yours.' I can see through it; you said that because you were afraid that I should use my strength, and now you avoid me because you are afraid I shall claim my right. But you will gain nothing by it. I swear that you shall not trifle with me long."

"I will never be yours," she replied, with a coldness which was becoming more and more icy, "if you do not make some change in your language, and manners, and feelings. In your present state I certainly do not fear you. When you appeared to me good and generous, I might have yielded to you, half from fear and half from affection. But from the moment I cease to care for you, I also cease to be afraid of you. Improve your manners, improve your mind, and we will see."

"Very good," I said, "that is a promise I can understand. I will act on it, and if I cannot be happy, I will have my revenge."

"Take your revenge as much as you please," she said. "That will only make me despise you."

So saying, she drew from her bosom a piece of paper, and burnt it in the flame of her candle.

"What are you doing?" I exclaimed.

"I am burning a letter I had written to you," she answered. "I wanted to make you listen to reason, but it is quite useless; one cannot reason with brutes."

"Give me that letter at once," I cried, rushing at her to seize the burning paper.

But she withdrew it quickly and, fearlessly extinguishing it in her hand, threw the candle at my feet and fled in the darkness. I ran after her, but in vain. She was in her room before I could get there, and had slammed the door and drawn the bolts. I could hear the voice of Mademoiselle Leblanc asking her young mistress the cause of her fright.

"It is nothing," replied Edmee's trembling voice, "nothing but a joke."

I went into the garden, and strode up and down the walks at a furious rate. My anger gave place to the most profound melancholy. Edmee, proud and daring, seemed to me more desirable than ever. It is the nature of all desire to be excited and nourished by opposition. I felt that I had offended her, and that she did not love me, that perhaps she would never love me; and, without abandoning my criminal resolution to make her mine by force, I gave way to grief at the thought of her hatred of me. I went and leaned upon a gloomy old wall which happened to be near, and, burying my face in my hands, I broke into heart-rending sobs. My sturdy breast heaved convulsively, but tears would not bring the relief I longed for. I could have roared in my anguish, and I had to bite my handkerchief to prevent myself from yielding to the temptation. The weird noise of my stifled sobs attracted the attention of some one who was praying in the little chapel on the other side of the wall which I had chanced to lean against. A Gothic window, with its stone mullions surmounted by a trefoil, was exactly on a level with my head.

X

"Who is there?" asked some one, and I could distinguish a pale face in the slanting rays of the moon which was just rising.

It was Edmee. On recognising her I was about to move away, but she passed her beautiful arm between the mullions, and held me back by the collar of my jacket, saying:

"Why are you crying, Bernard?"

I yielded to her gentle violence, half ashamed at having betrayed my weakness, and half enchanted at finding that Edmee was not unmoved by it.

"What are you grieved at?" she continued. "What can draw such bitter tears from you?"

"You despise me; you hate me; and you ask why I am in pain, why I am angry!"

"It is anger, then, that makes you weep?" she said, drawing back her arm.

"Yes; anger or something else," I replied.

"But what else?" she asked.

"I can't say; probably grief, as you suggest. The truth is my life here is unbearable; my heart is breaking. I must leave you, Edmee, and go and live in the middle of the woods. I cannot stay here any longer."

"Why is life unbearable? Explain yourself, Bernard. Now is our opportunity for an explanation."

"Yes, with a wall between us. I can understand that you are not afraid of me now."

"And yet it seems to me that I am only showing an interest in you; and was I not as affectionate an hour ago when there was no wall between us?"

"I begin to see why you are fearless, Edmee; you always find some means of avoiding people, or of winning them over with pretty words. Ah, they were right when they told me that all women are false, and that I must love none of them."

"And who told you that? Your Uncle John, I suppose, or your Uncle Walter; or was it your grandfather, Tristan?"

"You can jeer—jeer at me as much as you like. It is not my fault that I was brought up by them. There were times, however, when they spoke the truth."

"Bernard, would you like me to tell you why they thought women false?"

"Yes, tell me."

"Because they were brutes and tyrants to creatures weaker than themselves. Whenever one makes one's self feared one runs the risk of being deceived. In your childhood, when John used to beat you, did you never try to escape his brutal punishment by disguising your little faults?"

"I did; that was my only resource."

"You can understand, then, that deception is, if not the right, at least the resource of the oppressed."

"I understand that I love you, and in that at any rate there can be no excuse for your deceiving me."

"And who says that I have deceived you?"

"But you have; you said you loved me; you did not love me."

"I loved you, because at a time when you were wavering between detestable principles and the impulses of a generous heart I saw that you were inclining towards justice and honesty. And I love you now, because I see that you are tri-triumphing over these vile principles, and that your evil inspirations are followed by tears of honest regret. This I say before God, with my hand on my heart, at a time when I can see your real self. There are other times when you appear to me so below yourself that I no longer recognise you and I think I no longer love you. It rests with you, Bernard, to free me from all doubts, either about you or myself."

"And what must I do?"

"You must amend your bad habits, open your ears to good counsel and your heart to the precepts of morality. You are a savage, Bernard; and, believe me, it is neither your awkwardness in making a bow, nor your inability to turn a compliment that shocks me. On the contrary, this roughness of manner would be a very great charm in my eyes, if only there were some great ideas and noble feelings beneath it. But your ideas and your feelings are like your manners, that is what I cannot endure. I know it is not your fault, and if I only saw you resolute to improve I should love you as much for your defects as for your qualities. Compassion brings affection in its train. But I do not love evil, I never loved it; and, if you cultivate it in yourself instead of uprooting it, I can never love you. Do you understand me?"

"No."

"What, no!"

"No, I say. I am not aware that there is any evil in me. If you are not displeased at the lack of grace in my legs, or the lack of whiteness in my hands, or the lack of elegance in my words, I fail to see what you find to hate in me. From my childhood I have had to listen to evil precepts, but I have not accepted them. I have never considered it permissible to do a bad deed; or, at least, I have never found it pleasurable. If I have done wrong, it is because I have been forced to do it. I have always detested my uncles and their ways. I do not like to see others suffer; I do not rob a fellow-creature; I despise money, of which they made a god at Roche-Mauprat; I know how to keep sober, and, though I am fond of wine, I would drink water all my life if, like my uncles, I had to shed blood to get a good supper. Yet I fought for them; yet I drank with them. How could I do otherwise? But now, when I am my own master, what harm am I doing? Does your abbe, who is always prating of virtue, take me for a murderer or a thief? Come, Edmee, confess now; you know well enough that I am an honest man; you do not really think me wicked; but I am displeasing to you because I am not clever, and you like M. de la Marche because he has a knack of making unmeaning speeches which I should blush to utter."

"And if, to be pleasing to me," she said with a smile, after listening most attentively, and without withdrawing her hand which I had taken through the bars, "if, in order to be preferred to M. de la Marche, it were necessary to acquire more wit, as you say, would you not try?"

"I don't know," I replied, after hesitating a moment; "perhaps I should be fool enough; for the power you have over me is more than I can understand; but it would be a sorry piece of cowardice and a great folly."

"Why, Bernard?"

"Because a woman who could love a man, not for his honest heart, but for his pretty wit, would be hardly worth the pains I should have to take; at least so it seems to me."

She remained silent in her turn, and then said to me as she pressed my hand:

"You have much more sense and wit than one might think. And since you force me to be quite frank with you, I will own that, as you now are and even should you never change, I have an esteem and an affection for you which will last as long as my life. Rest assured of that, Bernard, whatever I may say in a moment of anger. You know I have a quick temper—that runs in the family. The blood of the Mauprats will never flow as smoothly as other people's. Have a care for my pride, then, you know so well what pride is, and do not ever presume upon rights you have acquired. Affection cannot be commanded; it must be implored or inspired. Act so that I may always love you; never tell me that I am forced to love you."

"That is reasonable enough," I answered; "but why do you sometimes speak to me as if I were forced to obey you? Why, for instance, this evening did you *forbid* me to drink and *order* me to study?"

"Because if one cannot command affection which does not exist, one can at least command affection which does exist; and it is because I am sure yours exists that I commanded it."

"Good!" I cried, in a transport of joy; "I have a right then to order yours also, since you have told me that it certainly exists. . . . Edmee, I order you to kiss me."

"Let go, Bernard!" she cried; "you are breaking my arm. Look, you have scraped it against the bars."

"Why have you intrenched yourself against me?" I said, putting my lips to the little scratch I had made on her arm. "Ah, woe is me! Confound the bars! Edmee, if you would only bend your head down I should be able to kiss you . . . kiss you as my sister. Edmee, what are you afraid of?"

"My good Bernard," she replied, "in the world in which I live one does not kiss even a sister, and nowhere does one kiss in secret. I will kiss you every day before my father, if you like; but never here."

"You will never kiss me!" I cried, relapsing into my usual passion. "What of your promise? What of my rights?"

"If we marry," she said, in an embarrassed tone, "when you have received the education I implore you to receive, . . ."

"Death of my life! Is this a jest? Is there any question of marriage between us? None at all. I don't want your fortune, as I have told you."

"My fortune and yours are one," she replied. "Bernard, between near relations as we are, mine and thine are words without meaning. I should never suspect you of being mercenary. I know that you love me, that you will work to give me proof of this, and that a day will come when your love will no longer make me fear, because I shall be able to accept it in the face of heaven and earth."

"If that is your idea," I replied, completely drawn away from my wild passion by the new turn she was giving to my thoughts, "my position is very different; but, to tell you the truth, I must reflect on this; I had not realized that this was your meaning."

"And how should I have meant otherwise?" she answered. "Is not a woman dishonoured by giving herself to a man who is not her husband? I do not wish to dishonour myself; and, since you love me, you would not wish it either. You would not do me an irreparable wrong. If such were your intention you would be my deadliest enemy."

"Stay, Edmee, stay!" I answered. "I can tell you nothing about my intentions in regard to you, for I have never had any very definite. I have felt nothing but wild desires, nor have I ever thought of you without going mad. You wish me to marry you? But why—why?"

"Because a girl who respects herself cannot be any man's except with the thought, with the intention, with the certainty of being his forever. Do you not know that?"

"There are so many things I do not know or have never thought of."

"Education will teach you, Bernard, what you ought to think about the things which must concern you—about your position, your duties, your feelings. At present you see but dimly into your heart and conscience. And I, who am accustomed to question myself on all subjects and to discipline my life, how can I take for master a man governed by instinct and guided by chance?"

"For master! For husband! Yes, I understand that you cannot surrender your whole life to an animal such as myself . . . but that is what I have never asked of you. No, I tremble to think of it."

"And yet, Bernard, you must think of it. Think of it frequently, and when you have done so you will realize the necessity of following my advice, and of bringing your mind into harmony with the new life upon which you have entered since quitting Roche-Mauprat. When you have perceived this necessity you must tell me, and then we will make several necessary resolutions."

She withdrew her hand from mine quickly, and I fancy she bade me goodnight; but this I did not hear. I stood buried in my thoughts, and when I raised my head to speak to her she was no longer there. I went into the chapel, but she had returned to her room by an upper gallery which communicated with her apartments.

I went back into the garden, walked far into the park, and remained there all night. This conversation with Edmee had opened a new world to me. Hitherto I had not ceased to be the Roche-Mauprat man, nor had I ever contemplated that it was possible or desirable to cease to be so. Except for some habits which had changed with circumstances, I had never moved out of the narrow circle of my old thoughts. I felt annoyed that these new surroundings of mine should have any real power over me, and I secretly braced my will so that I should not be humbled. Such was my perseverance and strength of character that I believed nothing would ever have driven me from my intrenchment of obstinacy, had not Edmee's influence been brought to bear upon me. The vulgar comforts of life, the satisfactions of luxury, had no attraction for me beyond their novelty. Bodily repose was a burden to me, and the calm that reigned in this house, so full of order and silence, would have been unbearable, had not Edmee's presence and the tumult of my own desires communicated to it some of my disorder, and peopled it with some of my visions. Never for a single moment had I desired to become the head of this house, the possessor of this property; and it was with genuine pleasure that I had just heard Edmee do justice to my disinterestedness. The thought of coupling two ends so entirely distinct as my passion and my interests was still more repugnant to me. I roamed about the park a prey to a thousand doubts, and then wandered into the open country unconsciously. It was a glorious night. The full moon was pouring down floods of soft light upon the ploughed lands, all parched by the heat of the sun. Thirsty plants were straightening their bowed stems—each leaf seemed to be drinking in through all its pores all the dewy freshness of the night. I, too, began to feel a soothing influence at work. My heart was still beating violently, but regularly. I was filled with a vague hope; the image of Edmee floated before me on the paths through the meadows, and no longer stirred the wild agonies and frenzied desires which had been devouring me since the night I first beheld her.

I was crossing a spot where the green stretches of pasture were here and there broken by clumps of young trees. Huge oxen with almost white skins were lying in the short grass, motionless, as if plunged in peaceful thought. Hills sloped gently up to the horizon, and their velvety contours seemed to ripple in the bright rays of the moon. For the first time in my life I realized something of the voluptuous beauty and divine effluence of the night. I felt the magic touch of some unknown bliss. It seemed that for the first time in my life I was looking on moon and meadows and hills. I remembered hearing Edmee say that nothing our eyes can behold is more lovely than Nature; and I was astonished that I had never felt this before. Now and then I was on the point of throwing myself on my knees and praying to God: but I feared that I should not know how to speak to Him, and that I might offend Him by praying badly. Shall I confess to you a singular fancy that came upon me, a childish revelation, as it were, of poetic love from out of the chaos of my ignorance? The moon was lighting up everything so plainly that I could distinguish the tiniest flowers in the grass. A little meadow daisy seemed to me so beautiful with its golden calyx full of diamonds of dew and its white collaret fringed with purple, that I plucked it, and covered it with kisses, and cried in a sort of delirious intoxication:

"It is you, Edmee! Yes, it is you! Ah, you no longer shun me!"

But what was my confusion when, on rising, I found there had been a witness of my folly. Patience was standing before me.

I was so angry at having been surprised in such a fit of extravagance that, from a remnant of the Hamstringer instinct, I immediately felt for a knife in my belt;

but neither belt nor knife was there. My silk waistcoat with its pocket reminded me that I was doomed to cut no more throats. Patience smiled.

"Well, well! What is the matter?" said the anchorite, in a calm and kindly tone. "Do you imagine that I don't know perfectly well how things stand? I am not so simple but that I can reason; I am not so old but that I can see. Who is it that makes the branches of my yew shake whenever the holy maiden is sitting at my door? Who is it that follows us like a young wolf with measured steps through the copse when I take the lovely child to her father? And what harm is there in it? You are both young; you are both handsome; you are of the same family; and, if you chose, you might become a noble and honest man as she is a noble and honest girl."

All my wrath had vanished as I listened to Patience speaking of Edmee. I had such a vast longing to talk about her that I would even have been willing to have heard evil spoken of her, for the sole pleasure of hearing her name pronounced. I continued my walk by the side of Patience. The old man was tramping through the dew with bare feet. It should be mentioned, however, that his feet had long been unacquainted with any covering and had attained a degree of callosity that rendered them proof against anything. His only garments were a pair of blue canvas breeches which, in the absence of braces, hung loosely from his hips, and a coarse shirt. He could not endure any constraint in his clothes; and his skin, hardened by exposure, was sensitive to neither heat nor cold. Even when over eighty he was accustomed to go bareheaded in the broiling sun and with half-open shirt in the winter blasts. Since Edmee had seen to his wants he had attained a certain cleanliness. Nevertheless, in the disorder of his toilet and his hatred of everything that passed the bounds of the strictest necessity (though he could not have been charged with immodesty, which had always been odious to him), the cynic of the old days was still apparent. His beard was shining like silver. His bald skull was so polished that the moon was reflected in it as in water. He walked slowly, with his hands behind his back and his head raised, like a man who is surveying his empire. But most frequently his glances were thrown skywards, and he interrupted his conversation to point to the starry vault and exclaim:

"Look at that; look how beautiful it is!"

He is the only peasant I have ever known to admire the sky; or, at least, he is the only one I have ever seen who was conscious of his admiration.

"Why, Master Patience," I said to him, "do you think I might be an honest man if I chose? Do you think that I am not one already?"

"Oh, do not be angry," he answered. "Patience is privileged to say anything. Is he not the fool of the chateau?"

"On the contrary, Edmee maintains that you are its sage."

"Does the holy child of God say that? Well, if she believes so, I will try to act as a wise man, and give you some good advice, Master Bernard Mauprat. Will you accept it?"

"It seems to me that in this place every one takes upon himself to give advice. Never mind, I am listening."

X

"You are in love with your cousin, are you not?"

"You are very bold to ask such a question."

"It is not a question, it is a fact. Well, my advice is this: make your cousin love you, and become her husband."

"And why do you take this interest in me, Master Patience?"

"Because I know you deserve it."

"Who told you so? The abbe?"

"No."

"Edmee?"

"Partly. And yet she is certainly not very much in love with you. But it is your own fault."

"How so, Patience?"

"Because she wants you to become clever; and you—you would rather not. Oh, if I were only your age; yes, I, poor Patience; and if I were able, without feeling stifled, to shut myself up in a room for only two hours a day; and if all those I met were anxious to teach me; if they said to me, 'Patience, this is what was done yesterday; Patience, this is what will be done to-morrow.' But, enough! I have to find out everything myself, and there is so much that I shall die of old age before finding out a tenth part of what I should like to know. But, listen: I have yet another reason for wishing you to marry Edmee."

"What is that, good Monsieur Patience?"

"This La Marche is not the right man for her. I have told her so—yes, I have; and himself too, and the abbe, and everybody. He is not a man, that thing. He smells as sweet as a whole flower-garden; but I prefer the tiniest sprig of wild thyme."

"Faith! I have but little love for him myself. But if my cousin likes him, what then, Patience?"

"Your cousin does not like him. She thinks he is a good man; she thinks him genuine. She is mistaken; he deceives her, as he deceives everybody. Yes, I know: he is a man who has not any of this (and Patience put his hand to his heart). He is a man who is always proclaiming: 'In me behold the champion of virtue, the champion of the unfortunate, the champion of all the wise men and friends of the human race, etc., etc.' While I—Patience—I know that he lets poor folk die of hunger at the gates of his chateau. I know that if any one said to him, 'Give up your castle and eat black bread, give up your lands and become a soldier, and then there will be no more misery in the world, the human race—as you call it—will be saved,' his real self would answer, 'Thanks, I am lord of my lands, and I am not yet tired of my castle.' Oh! I know them so well, these sham paragons. How different with Edmee! You do not know that. You love her because she is as beautiful as the daisy in the meadows, while I—I love her because she is good as the moon that sheds light on all. She is a girl who gives away everything that she has; who would not wear a jewel, because with the gold in a ring a man could be kept alive for a year. And if she finds a foot-sore child by the road-side, she takes off her shoes and gives them to him, and goes on her way bare-footed. Then, look you, hers is a heart that never swerves. If to-morrow the village of Saint-Severe were to go to her in a body and say: 'Young lady, you have lived long enough in the lap of wealth, give us what you have, and take your turn at work'—'That is but fair, my good friends,' she would reply, and with a glad heart she would go and tend the flocks in the fields. Her mother was the same. I knew her mother when she was quite young, young as yourself; and I knew yours too. Oh, yes. She was a lady with a noble mind, charitable and just to all. And you take after her, they say."

"Alas, no," I answered, deeply touched by these words of Patience. "I know neither charity nor justice."

"You have not been able to practise them yet, but they are written in your heart. I can read them there. People call me a sorcerer, and so I am in a measure. I know a man directly I see him. Do you remember what you said to me one day on the heath at Valide? You were with Sylvain and I with Marcasse. You told me that an honest man avenges his wrongs himself. And, by-the-bye, Monsieur Mauprat, if you are not satisfied with the apologies I made you at Gazeau Tower, you may say so. See, there is no one near; and, old as I am, I have still a fist as good as yours. We can exchange a few healthy blows—that is Nature's way. And, though I do not approve of it, I never refuse satisfaction to any one who demands it. There are some men, I know, who would die of mortification if they did not have their revenge: and it has taken me—yes, the man you see before you—more than fifty years to forget an insult I once received . . . and even now, whenever I think of it, my hatred of the nobles springs up again, and I hold it as a crime to have let my heart forgive some of them."

"I am fully satisfied, Master Patience; and in truth I now feel nothing but affection for you."

"Ah, that comes of my scratching your back. Youth is ever generous. Come, Mauprat, take courage. Follow the abbe's advice; he is a good man. Try to please your cousin; she is a star in the firmament. Find out truth; love the people; hate those who hate them; be ready to sacrifice yourself for them. . . . Yes, one word more—listen. I know what I am saying—become the people's friend."

"Is the people, then, better than the nobility, Patience? Come now, honestly, since you are a wise man, tell me the truth."

"Ay, we are worth more than the nobles, because they trample us under foot, and we let them. But we shall not always bear this, perhaps. No; you will have to know it sooner or later, and I may as well tell you now. You see yonder stars? They will never change. Ten thousand years hence they will be in the same place and be giving forth as much light as to-day; but within the next hundred years, maybe within less, there will be many a change on this earth. Take the word of a man who has an eye for the truth of things, and does not let himself be led astray by the fine airs of the great. The poor have suffered enough; they will turn upon the rich, and their castles will fail and their lands be carved up. I shall not see it; but you will. There will be ten cottages in the place of this park, and ten families will live on its revenue. There will no longer be servants or masters, or villein or lord. Some nobles will cry aloud and yield only to force, as your uncles would do if they were alive, and as M. de la Marche will do in spite of all his fine talk. Others will sacrifice themselves generously, like Edmee, and like yourself, if you lis-listen to wisdom. And in that hour it will be well for Edmee that her husband is a man and not a mere fop. It will be well for Bernard Mauprat that he knows how to drive a plough or kill the game which the good God has sent to feed his family; for old Patience will then be lying under the grass in the churchyard, unable to return the services which Edmee has done him. Do not laugh at what I say, young man; it is the voice of God that is speaking. Look at the heavens. The stars live in peace, and nothing disturbs their eternal order. The great do not devour the small, and none fling themselves upon their neighbours. Now, a day will come when the same order will reign among men. The wicked will be swept away by the breath of the Lord. Strengthen your legs, Seigneur Mauprat, that you may stand firm to support Edmee. It is Patience that warns you; Patience who wishes you naught but good. But there will come others who wish you ill, and the good must make themselves strong."

We had reached Patience's cottage. He had stopped at the gate of his little inclosure, resting one hand on the cross-bar and waving the other as he spoke. His voice was full of passion, his eyes flashed fire, and his brow was bathed in sweat. There seemed to be some weird power in his words as in those of the prophets of old. The more than plebeian simplicity of his dress still further increased the pride of his gestures and the impressiveness of his voice. The French Revolution has shown since that in the ranks of the people there was no lack of eloquence or of pitiless logic; but what I saw at that moment was so novel, and made such an impression on me, that my unruly and unbridled imagination was carried away by the superstitious terrors of childhood. He held out his hand, and I responded with more of terror than affection. The sorcerer of Gazeau Tower hanging the bleeding owl above my head had just risen before my eyes again.

XI

When I awoke on the morrow in a state of exhaustion, all the incidents of the previous night appeared to me as a dream. I began to think that Edmee's suggestion of becoming my wife had been a perfidious trick to put off my hopes indefinitely; and, as to the sorcerer's words, I could not recall them without a feeling of profound humiliation. Still, they had produced their effect. My emotions had left traces which could never be effaced. I was no longer the man of the day before, and never again was I to be quite the man of Roche-Mauprat.

It was late, for not until morning had I attempted to make good my sleepless night. I was still in bed when I heard the hoofs of M. de la Marche's horse on the stones of the courtyard. Every day he used to come at this hour; every day he used to see Edmee at the same time as myself; and now, on this very day, this day when she had tried to persuade me to reckon on her hand, he was going to see her before me, and to give his soulless kiss to this hand that had been promised to myself. The thought of it stirred up all my doubts again. How could Edmee endure his attentions if she really meant to marry another man? Perhaps she dared not send him away; perhaps it was my duty to do so. I was ignorant of the ways of the world into which I was entering. Instinct counselled me to yield to my hasty impulses; and instinct spoke loudly.

I hastily dressed myself. I entered the drawing-room pale and agitated. Edmee was pale too. It was a cold, rainy morning. A fire was burning in the great fireplace. Lying back in an easy chair, she was warming her little feet and dozing. It was the same listless, almost lifeless, attitude of the days of her illness. M. de la Marche was reading the paper at the other end of the room. On seeing that Edmee was more affected than myself by the emotions of the previous night, I felt my anger cool, and, approaching her noiselessly, I sat down and gazed on her tenderly.

"Is that you, Bernard?" she asked without moving a limb, and with eyes still closed.

Her elbows were resting on the arms of her chair and her hands were gracefully crossed under her chin. At that period it was the fashion for women to have their arms half bare at all times. On one of Edmee's I noticed a little strip of court-plaster that made my heart beat. It was the slight scratch I had caused against the bars of the chapel window. I gently lifted the lace which fell over her elbow, and, emboldened by her drowsiness, pressed my lips to the darling wound. M. de la Marche could see me, and, in fact, did see me, as I intended he should. I was burning to have a quarrel with him. Edmee started and turned red; but immediately assuming an air of indolent playfulness, she said:

"Really, Bernard, you are as gallant this morning as a court abbe. Do you happen to have been composing a madrigal last night?"

I was peculiarly mortified at this jesting. However, paying her back in her own coin, I answered:

"Yes; I composed one yesterday evening at the chapel window; and if it is a poor thing, cousin, it is your fault."

"Say, rather, that it is the fault of your education," she replied, kindling.

And she was never more beautiful than when her natural pride and spirit were roused.

"My own opinion is that I am being very much over-educated," I answered; "and that if I gave more heed to my natural good sense you would not jeer at me so much."

"Really, it seems to me that you are indulging in a veritable war of wits with Bernard," said M. de la Marche, folding his paper carelessly and approaching us.

"I cry quits with her," I answered, annoyed at this impertinence. "Let her keep her wit for such as you."

I had risen to insult him, but he did not seem to notice it; and standing with his back to the fire he bent down towards Edmee and said, in a gentle and almost affectionate voice:

"What is the matter with him?" as if he were inquiring after the health of her little dog.

"How should I know?" she replied, in the same tone.

Then she rose and added:

"My head aches too much to remain here. Give me your arm and take me up to my room."

She went out, leaning upon his arm. I was left there stupefied.

I remained in the drawing-room, resolved to insult him as soon as he should return. But the abbe now entered, and soon afterward my Uncle Hubert. They began to talk on subjects which were quite strange to me (the subjects of their conversation were nearly always so). I did not know what to do to obtain revenge. I dared not betray myself in my uncle's presence. I was sensible to the respect I owed to him and to his hospitality. Never had I done such violence to myself at Roche-Mauprat. Yet, in spite of all efforts, my anger showed itself. I almost died at being obliged to wait for revenge. Several times the chevalier noticed the change in my features and asked in a kind tone if I were ill. M. de la Marche seemed neither to observe nor to guess anything. The abbe alone examined me attentively. More than once I caught his blue eyes anxiously fixed on me, those eyes in which natural penetration was always veiled by habitual shyness. The abbe did not like me. I could easily see that his kindly, cheerful manners grew cold in spite of himself as soon as he spoke to me; and I noticed, too, that his face would invariably assume a sad expression at my approach.

The constraint that I was enduring was so alien to my habits and so beyond my strength that I came nigh to fainting. To obtain relief I went and threw myself on the grass in the park. This was a refuge to me in all my troubles. These mighty oaks, this moss which had clung to their branches through the centuries, these pale, sweet-scented wild flowers, emblems of secret sorrow, these were the friends of my childhood, and these alone I had found the same in social as in savage life. I buried my face in my hands; and I never remember having suffered more in any of the calamities of my life, though some that I had to bear afterward were very real. On the whole I ought to have accounted myself lucky, on giving up the rough and perilous trade of a cut-throat, to find so many unexpected blessings—affection, devotion, riches, liberty, education, good precepts and good examples. But it is certain that, in order to pass from a given state to its opposite, though it be from evil to good, from grief to joy, from fatigue to repose, the soul of a man must suffer; in this hour of birth of a new destiny all the springs of his being are strained almost to breaking—even as at the approach of summer the sky is covered with dark clouds, and the earth, all a-tremble, seems about to be annihilated by the tempest.

At this moment my only thought was to devise some means of appeasing my hatred of M. de la Marche without betraying and without even arousing a suspicion of the mysterious bond which held Edmee in my power. Though nothing was less respected at Roche-Mauprat than the sanctity of an oath, yet the little reading I had had there—those ballads of chivalry of which I have already spoken—had filled me with an almost romantic love of good faith; and this was about the only virtue I had acquired there. My promise of secrecy to Edmee was therefore inviolable in my eyes.

"However," I said to myself, "I dare say I shall find some plausible pretext for throwing myself upon my enemy and strangling him."

To confess the truth, this was far from easy with a man who seemed bent on being all politeness and kindness.

Distracted by these thoughts, I forgot the dinner hour; and when I saw the sun sinking behind the turrets of the castle I realized too late that my absence must have been noticed, and that I could not appear without submitting to Edmee's searching questions, and to the abbe's cold, piercing gaze, which, though it always seemed to avoid mine, I would suddenly surprise in the act of sounding the very depths of my conscience.

I resolved not to return to the house till nightfall, and I threw myself upon the grass and tried to find rest for my aching head in sleep. I did fall asleep in fact. When I awoke the moon was rising in the heavens, which were still red with the glow of sunset. The noise which had aroused me was very slight; but there are some sounds which strike the heart before reaching the ear; and the subtlest emanations of love will at times pierce through the coarsest organization. Edmee's voice had just pronounced my name a short distance away, behind some foliage. At first I thought I had been dreaming; I remained where I was, held my breath and listened. It was she, on her way to the hermit's, in company with the abbe.

They had stopped in a covered walk five or six yards from me, and they were talking in low voices, but in those clear tones which, in an exchange of confidence, compels attention with peculiar solemnity.

"I fear," Edmee was saying, "that there will be trouble between him and M. de la Marche; perhaps something very serious—who knows? You do not understand Bernard."

"He must be got away from here, at all costs," answered the abbe. "You cannot live in this way, continually exposed to the brutality of a brigand."

"It cannot be called living. Since he set foot in the house I have not had a moment's peace of mind. Imprisoned in my room, or forced to seek the protection of my friends, I am almost afraid to move. It is as much as I dare to do to creep downstairs, and I never cross the corridor without sending Leblanc ahead as a scout. The poor woman, who has always found me so brave, now thinks I am mad. The suspense is horrible. I cannot sleep unless I first bolt the door. And look, abbe, I never walk about without a dagger, like the heroine of a Spanish ballad, neither more nor less."

"And if this wretch meets you and frightens you, you will plunge it into your bosom? Oh! that must not be. Edmee, we must find some means of changing a position which is no longer tenable. I take it that you do not wish to deprive him of your father's friendship by confessing to the latter the monstrous bargain you were forced to make with this bandit at Roche-Mauprat. But whatever may happen—ah! my poor little Edmee, I am not a bloodthirsty man, but twenty times a day I find myself deploring that my character of priest prevents me from challenging this creature, and ridding you of him forever."

This charitable regret, expressed so artlessly in my very ear, made me itch to reveal myself to them at once, were it only to put the abbe's warlike humour to the proof; but I was restrained by the hope that I should at last discover Edmee's real feelings and real intentions in regard to myself.

"Have no fear," she said, in a careless tone. "If he tries my patience too much, I shall not have the slightest hesitation in planting this blade in his cheek. I am quite sure that a little blood-letting will cool his ardour."

Then they drew a few steps nearer.

"Listen to me, Edmee," said the abbe, stopping again. "We cannot discuss this matter with Patience. Let us come to some decision before we put it aside. Your relations with Bernard are now drawing to a crisis. It seems to me, my child, that you are not doing all you ought to ward off the evils that may strike us; for everything that is painful to you will be painful to all of us, and will touch us to the bottom of our hearts."

"I am all attention, excellent friend," answered Edmee; "scold me, advise me, as you will."

So saying she leant back against the tree at the foot of which I was lying among the brushwood and long grass. I fancy she might have seen me, for I could see her distinctly. However, she little thought that I was gazing on her divine face, over which the night breeze was throwing, now the shadows of the rustling leaves, and now the pale diamonds that the moon showers down through the trees of the forest.

"My opinion, Edmee," answered the abbe, crossing his arms on his breast and striking his brow at intervals, "is that you do not take the right view of your situation. At times it distresses you to such an extent that you lose all hope and long to die—yes, my dear child, to such an extent that your health plainly suffers. At other times, and I must speak candidly at the risk of offending you a little, you view your perils with a levity and cheerfulness that astound me."

"That last reproach is delicately put, dear friend," she replied; "but allow me to justify myself. Your astonishment arises from the fact that you do not know the Mauprat race. It is a tameless, incorrigible race, from which naught but Head-breakers and Hamstringers may issue. Even in those who have been most polished by education there remains many a stubborn knot—a sovereign pride, a will of iron, a profound contempt for life. Look at my father. In spite of his adorable goodness, you see that he is sometimes so quick-tempered that he will smash his snuff-box on the table, when you get the better of him in some political argument, or when you win a game of chess. For myself, I am conscious that my veins are as full-blooded as if I had been born in the noble ranks of the people; and I do not believe that any Mauprat has ever shone at court for the charm of his manners. Since I was born brave, how would you have me set much store by life? And yet there are weak moments in which I get discouraged more than enough, and bemoan my fate like the true woman that I am. But, let some one offend me, or threaten me, and the blood of the strong surges through me again; and then, as I cannot crush my enemy, I fold my arms and smile with compassion at the idea that he should ever have hoped to frighten me. And do not look upon this as mere bombast, abbe. To-morrow, this evening perhaps, my words may turn to deeds. This little pearl-handled knife does not look like deeds of blood; still, it will be able to do its work, and ever since Don Marcasse (who knows what he is about) sharpened it, I have had it by me night and day, and my mind is made up. I have not a very strong fist, but it will no doubt manage to give myself a good stab with this knife, even as it manages to give my horse a cut with the whip. Well, that being so, my honour is safe; it is only my life, which hangs by a thread, which is at the mercy of a glass of wine, more or less, that M. Bernard may happen to drink one of these evenings; of some change meeting, or some exchange of looks between De la Marche and myself that he may fancy he has detected; a breath of air perhaps! What is to be done? Were I to grieve, would my tears wash away the past? We cannot tear out a single page of our lives; but we can throw the book into the fire. Though I should weep from night till morn, would that prevent Destiny from having, in a fit of ill-humour, taken me out hunting, sent me astray in the woods, and made me stumble across a Mauprat, who led me to his den, where I escaped dishonour and perhaps death only by binding my life forever to that of a savage who had none of my principles, and who probably (and who undoubtedly, I should say) never will have them? All this is a misfortune. I was in the full sunlight of a happy destiny; I was the pride and joy of my old father; I was about to marry a man I esteem and like; no sorrows, no fears had come near my path; I knew neither days fraught with danger nor nights bereft of sleep. Well, God did not wish such a beautiful life to continue; His will be done. There are days when the ruin of all my hopes seems to me so inevitable that I look upon myself as dead and my *fiance* as a widower. If it were not for my poor father, I should really laugh at it all; for I am so ill built for vexation and fears that during the short time I have known them they have already tired me of life."

"This courage is heroic, but it is also terrible," cried the abbe, in a broken voice. "It is almost a resolve to commit suicide, Edmee."

"Oh, I shall fight for my life," she answered, with warmth; "but I shall not stand haggling with it a moment if my honour does not come forth safe and sound from all these risks. No; I am not pious enough ever to accept a soiled life by way of penance for sins of which I never had a thought. If God deals so harshly with me that I have to choose between shame and death . . ."

"There can never be any shame for you, Edmee; a soul so chaste, so pure in intention . . ."

"Oh, don't talk of that, dear abbe! Perhaps I am not as good as you think; I am not very orthodox in religion—nor are you, abbe! I give little heed to the world; I have no love for it. I neither fear nor despise public opinion; it will never enter into my life. I am not very sure what principle of virtue would be strong enough to prevent me from falling, if the spirit of evil took me in hand. I have read *La Nouvelle Heloise*, and I shed many tears over it. But, because I am a Mauprat and have an unbending pride, I will never endure the tyranny of any man—the violence of a lover no more than a husband's blow; only a servile soul and a craven character may yield to force that which it refuses to entreaty. Sainte Solange, the beautiful shepherdess, let her head be cut off rather than submit to the seigneur's rights. And you know that from mother to daughter the Mauprats have been consecrated in baptism to the protection of the patron saint of Berry."

"Yes; I know that you are proud and resolute," said the abbe, "and because I respect you more than any woman in the world I want you to live, and be free, and make a marriage worthy of you, so that in the human family you may fill the part which beautiful souls still know how to make noble. Besides, you are necessary to your father; your death would hurry him to his grave, hearty and robust as the Mauprat still is. Put away these gloomy thoughts, then, and these violent resolutions. It is impossible. This adventure of Roche-Mauprat must be looked upon only as an evil dream. We both had a nightmare in those hours of horror; but it is time for us to awake; we cannot remain paralyzed with fear like children. You have only one course open to you, and that I have already pointed out."

"But, abbe, it is the one which I hold the most impossible of all. I have sworn by everything that is most sacred in the universe and the human heart."

"An oath extorted by threats and violence is binding on none; even human laws decree this. Divine laws, especially in a case of this nature, absolve the human conscience beyond a doubt. If you were orthodox, I would go to Rome—yes,

I would go on foot—to get you absolved from so rash a vow; but you are not a submissive child of the Pope, Edmee—nor am I."

"You wish me, then, to perjure myself?"

"Your soul would not be perjured."

"My soul would! I took an oath with a full knowledge of what I was doing and at a time when I might have killed myself on the spot; for in my hand I had a knife three times as large as this. But I wanted to live; above all, I wanted to see my father again and kiss him. To put an end to the agony which my disappearance must have caused him, I would have bartered more than my life, I would have bartered my immortal soul. Since then, too, as I told you last night, I have renewed my vow, and of my own free-will, moreover; for there was a wall between my amiable *fiance* and myself."

"How could you have been so imprudent, Edmee? Here again I fail to understand you."

"That I can quite believe, for I do not understand myself," said Edmee, with a peculiar expression.

"My dear child, you must open your hear to me freely. I am the only person here who can advise you, since I am the only one to whom you can tell everything under the seal of a friendship as sacred as the secrecy of Catholic confession can be. Answer me, then. You do not really look upon a marriage between yourself and Bernard Mauprat as possible?"

"How should that which is inevitable be impossible?" said Edmee. "There is nothing more possible than throwing one's self into the river; nothing more possible than surrendering one's self to misery and despair; nothing more possible, consequently, than marrying Bernard Mauprat."

"In any case I will not be the one to celebrate such an absurd and deplorable union," cried the abbe. "You, the wife and the slave of this Hamstringer! Edmee, you said just now that you would no more endure the violence of a lover than a husband's blow."

"You think the he would beat me?"

"If he did not kill you."

"Oh, no," she replied, in a resolute tone, with a wave of the knife, "I would kill him first. When Mauprat meets Mauprat . . .!"

"You can laugh, Edmee? O my God! you can laugh at the thought of such a match! But, even if this man had some affection and esteem for you, think how impossible it would be for you to have anything in common; think of the coarseness of his ideas, the vulgarity of his speech. The heart rises in disgust at the idea of such a union. Good God! In what language would you speak to him?"

Once more I was on the point of rising and falling on my panegyrist; but I overcame my rage. Edmee began to speak, and I was all ears again.

"I know very well that at the end of three or four days I should have nothing better to do than cut my own throat; but since sooner or later it must come to that, why should I not go forward to the inevitable hour? I confess that I shall be sorry to leave life. Not all those who have been to Roche-Mauprat have returned. I went there not to meet death, but to betroth myself to it. Well, then, I will go on to my wedding-day, and if Bernard is too odious, I will kill myself after the ball."

"Edmee, your head seems full of romantic notions at present," said the abbe, losing patience. "Thank God, your father will never consent to the marriage. He has given his word to M. de la March, and you too have given yours. This is the only promise that is valid."

"My father would consent—yes, with joy—to an arrangement which perpetuated his name and line directly. As to M. de la March, he will release me from any promise without my taking the trouble to ask him; as soon as he hears that I passed two hours at Roche-Mauprat there will be no need of any other explanation."

"He would be very unworthy of the esteem I feel for him, if he considered your good name tarnished by an unfortunate adventure from which you came out pure."

"Thanks to Bernard," said Edmee; "for after all I ought to be grateful to him; in spite of his reservations and conditions, he performed a great and inconceivable action, for a Hamstringer."

"God forbid that I should deny the good qualities which education may have developed in this young man; and it may still be possible, by approaching him on this better side of his, to make him listen to reason."

"And make him consent to be taught? Never. Even if he should show himself willing, he would no more be able than Patience. When the body is made for an animal life, the spirit can no longer submit to the laws of the intellect."

"I think so too; but that is not the point. I suggest that you should have an explanation with him, and make him understand that he is bound in honour to release you from your promise and resign himself to your marriage with M. de la Marche. Either he is a brute unworthy of the slightest esteem and consideration, or he will realize his crime and folly and yield honestly and with a good grace. Free me from the vow of secrecy to which I am bound; authorize me to deal plainly with him and I will guarantee success."

"And I—I will guarantee the contrary," said Edmee. "Besides, I could not consent to this. Whatever Bernard may be, I am anxious to come out of our duel with honour; and if I acted as you suggest, he would have cause to believe that up to the present I have been unworthily trifling with him."

"Well, there is only one means left, and that is to trust to the honour and discretion of M. de la Marche. Set before him the details of your position, and then let him give the verdict. You have a perfect right to intrust him with your secret, and you are quite sure of his honour. If he is coward enough to desert you in such a position, your remaining resource is to take shelter from Bernard's violence behind the iron bars of a convent. You can remain there a few years; you can make a show of taking the veil. The young man will forget you, and they will set you free again."

"Indeed, that is the only reasonable course to take, and I had already thought of it; but it is not yet time to make the move."

"Very true; you must first see the result of your confession to M. de la Marche. If, as I make no doubt, he is a man of mettle, he will take you under his protection, and then procure the removal of this Bernard, whether by persuasion or au-authority."

"What authority, abbe, if you please?"

"The authority which our customs allow one gentleman to exercise over his equal—honour and the sword."

"Oh, abbe! You too, then are a man with a thirst for blood. Well, that is precisely what I have hitherto tried to avoid, and what I will avoid, though it cost me my life and honour. I do not wish that there should be any fight between these two men."

"I understand: one of the two is very rightly dear to you. But evidently in this duel it is not M. de la Marche who would be in danger."

"Then it would be Bernard," cried Edmee. "Well, I should hate M. de la Marche, if he insisted on a duel with this poor boy, who only knows how to handle a stick or a sling. How can such ideas occur to you, abbe? You must really loathe this unfortunate Bernard. And fancy me getting my husband to cut his throat as a return for having saved my life at the risk of his own. No, no; I will not suffer any one either to challenge him, or humiliate him, or persecute him. He is my cousin; he is a Mauprat; he is almost a brother. I will not let him be driven out of this home. Rather I will go myself."

"These are very generous sentiments, Edmee," answered the abbe. "But with what warmth you express them! I stand confounded; and, if I were not afraid of offending you, I should confess that this solicitude for young Mauprat suggests to me a strange thought."

"Well, what is it, then?" said Edmee, with a certain brusqueness.

"If you insist, of course I will tell you: you seem to take a deeper interest in this young man than in M. de la Marche, and I could have wished to think otherwise."

"Which has the greater need of this interest, you bad Christian?" said Edmee with a smile. "Is it not the hardened sinner whose eyes have never looked upon the light?"

"But, come, Edmee! You love M. de la Marche, do you not? For Heaven's sake do not jest."

"If by love," she replied in a serious tone, "you mean a feeling of trust and friendship, I love M. de la Marche; but if you mean a feeling of compassion and solicitude, I love Bernard. It remains to be seen which of these two affections is the deeper. That is your concern, abbe. For my part, it troubles me but little; for I feel that there is only one being whom I love with passion, and that is my father; and only one thing that I love with enthusiasm, and that is my duty. Probably I shall regret the attentions and devotion of the lieutenant-general, and I shall share in the grief that I must soon cause him when I announce that I can never be his wife. This necessity, however, will by no means drive me to desperation, because

I know that M. de la Marche will quickly recover. . . . I am not joking, abbe; M. de la Marche is a man of no depth, and somewhat cold."

"If your love for him is no greater than this, so much the better. It makes one trial less among your many trials. Still, this indifference robs me of my last hope of seeing you rescued from Bernard Mauprat."

"Do not let this grieve you. Either Bernard will yield to friendship and loyalty and improve, or I shall escape him."

"But how?"

"By the gate of the convent—or of the graveyard."

As she uttered these words in a calm tone, Edmee shook back her long black hair, which had fallen over her shoulders and partly over her pale face.

"Come," she said, "God will help us. It is folly and impiety to doubt him in the hour of danger. Are we atheists, that we let ourselves be discouraged in this way? Let us go and see Patience. . . . He will bring forth some wise saw to ease our minds; he is the old oracle who solves all problems without understanding any."

They moved away, while I remained in a state of consternation.

Oh, how different was this night from the last! How vast a step I had just taken in life, no longer on the path of flowers but on the arid rocks! Now I understood all the odious reality of the part I had been playing. In the bottom of Edmee's heart I had just read the fear and disgust I inspired in her. Nothing could assuage my grief; for nothing now could arouse my anger. She had no affection for M. de la Marche; she was trifling neither with him nor with me; she had no affection for either of us. How could I have believed that her generous sympathy for me and her sublime devotion to her word were signs of love? How, in the hours when this presumptuous fancy left me, could I have believed that in order to resist my passion she must needs feel love for another? It had come to pass, then, that I had no longer any object on which to vent my rage; now it could result only in Edmee's flight or death? Her death! At the mere thought of it the blood ran cold in my veins, a weight fell on my heart, and I felt all the stings of remorse piercing it. This night of agony was for me the clearest call of Providence. At last I understood those laws of modesty and sacred liberty which my ignorance had hitherto outraged and blasphemed. They astonished me more than ever; but I could see them; their sanction was their own existence. Edmee's strong, sincere soul appeared before me like the stone of Sinai on which the finger of God has traced the immutable truth. Her virtue was not feigned; her knife was sharpened, ready to cut out the stain of my love. I was so terrified at having been in danger of seeing her die in my arms; I was so horrified at the gross insult I had offered her while seeking to overcome her resistance, that I began to devise all manner of impossible plans for righting the wrongs I had done, and restoring her peace of mind.

The only one which seemed beyond my powers was to tear myself away from her; for while these feelings of esteem and respect were springing up in me, my love was changing its nature, so to speak, and growing vaster and taking possession of all my being. Edmee appeared to me in a new light. She was no longer the lovely girl whose presence stirred a tumult in my senses; she was a young man of my own age, beautiful as a seraph, proud, courageous, inflexible in honour, generous, capable of that sublime friendship which once bound together brothers in arms, but with no passionate love except for Deity, like the paladins of old, who, braving a thousand dangers, marched to the Holy Land under their golden armour.

From this hour I felt my love descending from the wild storms of the brain into the healthy regions of the heart. Devotion seemed no longer an enigma to me. I resolved that on the very next morning I would give proof of my submission and affection. It was quite late when I returned to the chateau, tired out, dying of hunger, and exhausted by the emotions I had experienced. I entered the pantry, found a piece of bread, and began eating it, all moist with my tears. I was leaning against the stove in the dime light of a lamp that was almost out, when I suddenly saw Edmee enter. She took a few cherries from a chest and slowly approached the stove, pale and deep in thought. On seeing me she uttered a cry and let the cherries fall.

"Edmee," I said, "I implore you never to be afraid of me again. That is all I can say now; for I do not know how to explain myself; and yet I had resolved to say many things."

"You must tell me them some other time, cousin," she answered, trying to smile.

But she was unable to disguise the fear she felt at finding herself alone with me.

I did not try to detain her. I felt deeply pained and humiliated at her distrust of me, and I knew I had no right to complain. Yet never had any man stood in greater need of a word of encouragement.

Just as she was going out of the room I broke down altogether, and burst into tears, as on the previous night at the chapel window. Edmee stopped on the threshold and hesitated a moment. Then, yielding to the kindly impulses of her heart, she overcame her fears and returned towards me. Pausing a few yards from my chair, she said:

"Bernard, you are unhappy. Tell me; is it my fault?"

I was unable to reply; I was ashamed of my tears, but the more I tried to restrain them the more my breast heaved with sobs. With men as physically strong as I was, tears are generally convulsions; mine were like the pangs of death.

"Come now! Just tell me what is wrong," cried Edmee, with some of the bluntness of sisterly affection.

And she ventured to put her hand on my shoulder. She was looking at me with an expression of wistfulness, and a big tear was trickling down her cheek. I threw myself on my knees and tried to speak, but that was still impossible. I could do no more than mutter the word *to-morrow* several times.

"'To-morrow?' What of tomorrow?" said Edmee. "Do you not like being here? Do you want to go away?"

"I will go, if it will please you," I replied. "Tell me; do you wish never to see me again?"

"I do not wish that at all," she rejoined. "You will stop here, won't you."

XI

"It is for you to decide," I answered.

She looked at me in astonishment. I was still on my knees. She leant over the back of my chair.

"Yes; I am quite sure that you are good at heart," she said, as if she were answering some inner objection. "A Mauprat can be nothing by halves; and as soon as you have once known a good quarter of an hour, it is certain you ought to have a noble life before you."

"I will make it so," I answered.

"You mean it?" she said with unaffected joy.

"On my honour, Edmee, and on yours. Dare you give me your hand?"

"Certainly," she said.

She held out her hand to me; but she was still trembling.

"You have been forming good resolutions, then?" she said.

"I have been forming such resolutions," I replied, "that you will never have to reproach me again. And now, Edmee, when you return to your room, please do not bolt your door any more. You need no longer be afraid of me. Henceforth I shall only wish what you wish."

She again fixed on me a look of amazement. Then, after pressing my hand, she moved away, but turned round several times to look at me again, as if unable to believe in such a sudden conversion. At last, stopping in the doorway, she said to me in an affectionate tone:

"You, too, must go and get some rest. You look tired; and for the last two days you have seemed sad and very much altered. If you do not wish to make me anxious, you will take care of yourself, Bernard."

She gave me a sweet little nod. In her big eyes, already hollowed by suffering, there was an indefinable expression, in which distrust and hope, affection and wonder, were depicted alternately or at times all together.

"I will take care of myself; I will get some sleep; and I will not be sad any longer," I answered.

"And you will work?"

"And I will work—but, you, Edmee, will you forgive me for all the pain I have caused you? and will you try to like me a little?"

"I shall like you very much," she replied, "if you are always as you are this evening."

On the morrow, at daybreak, I went to the abbe's room. He was already up and reading.

"Monsieur Aubert," I said to him, "you have several times offered to give me lessons. I now come to request you to carry out your kind offer."

I had spent part of the night in preparing this opening speech and in deciding how I had best comport myself in the abbe's presence. Without really hating him, for I could quite see that he meant well and that he bore me ill-will only because of my faults, I felt very bitter towards him. Inwardly I recognised that I deserved all the bad things he had said about me to Edmee; but it seemed to me that he might have insisted somewhat more on the good side of mine to which he had given a merely passing word, and which could not have escaped the notice of a man so observant as himself. I had determined, therefore, to be very cold and very proud in my bearing towards him. To this end I judged with a certain show of logic, that I ought to display great docility as long as the lesson lasted, and that immediately afterwards I ought to leave him with a very curt expression of thanks. In a word, I wished to humiliate him in his post of tutor; for I was not unaware that he depended for his livelihood on my uncle, and that, unless he renounced this livelihood or showed himself ungrateful, he could not well refuse to undertake my education. My reasoning here was very good; but the spirit which prompted it was very bad; and subsequently I felt so much regret for my behaviour that I made him a sort of friendly confession with a request for absolution.

However, not to anticipate events, I will simply say that the first few days after my conversation afforded me an ample revenge for the prejudices, too well founded in many respects, which this man had against me. He would have deserved the title of "the just," assigned him by Patience, had not a habit of distrust interfered with his first impulses. The persecutions of which he had so long been the object had developed in him this instinctive feeling of fear, which remained with him all his life, and made trust in others always very difficult to him, though all the more flattering and touching perhaps when he accorded it. Since then I have observed this characteristic in many worthy priests. They generally have the spirit of charity, but not the feeling of friendship.

I wished to make him suffer, and I succeeded. Spite inspired me. I behaved as a nobleman might to an inferior. I preserved an excellent bearing, displayed great attention, much politeness, and an icy stiffness. I determined to give him no chance to make me blush at my ignorance, and, to this end, I acted so as to anticipate all his observations by accusing myself at once of knowing nothing, and by requesting him to teach me the very rudiments of things. When I had finished my first lesson I saw in his penetrating eyes, into which I had managed to penetrate myself, a desire to pass from this coldness to some sort of intimacy; but I carefully avoided making any response. He thought to disarm me by praising my attention and intelligence.

"You are troubling yourself unnecessarily, monsieur," I replied. "I stand in no need of encouragement. I have not the least faith in my intelligence, but of my attention I certainly am very sure; but since it is solely for my own good that I am doing my best to apply myself to this work, there is no reason why you should compliment me on it."

With these words I bowed to him and withdrew to my room, where I immediately did the French exercise that he had set me.

When I went down to luncheon, I saw that Edmee was already aware of the execution of the promise I had made the previous evening. She at once greeted me with outstretched hand, and frequently during luncheon called me her "dear cousin," till at last M. de la Marche's face, which was usually expressionless, expressed surprise or something very near it. I was hoping that he would take the opportunity to demand an explanation of my insulting words of the previous day; and although I had resolved to discuss the matter in a spirit of great moderation, I felt very much hurt at the care which he took to avoid it. This indifference to an insult that I had offered implied a sort of contempt, which annoyed me very much; but the fear of displeasing Edmee gave me strength to restrain myself.

Incredible as it may seem, my resolve to supplant him was not for one moment shaken by this humiliating apprenticeship which I had now to serve before I could manage to obtain the most elementary notions of things in general. Any other than I, filled like myself with remorse for wrongs committed, would have found no surer method of repairing them than by going away, and restoring to Edmee her perfect independence and absolute peace of mind. This was the only method which did not occur to me; or if it did, it was rejected with scorn, as a sign of apostasy. Stubbornness, allied to temerity, ran through my veins with the blood of the Mauprats. No sooner had I imagined a means of winning her whom I loved than I embraced it with audacity; and I think it would not have been otherwise even had her confidences to the abbe in the park shown me that her love was given to my rival. Such assurance on the part of a young man who, at the age of seventeen, was taking his first lesson in French grammar, and who, moreover, had a very exaggerated notion of the length and difficulty of the studies necessary to put him on a level with M. de la March, showed, you must allow, a certain moral force.

I do not know if I was happily endowed in the matter of intelligence. The abbe assured me that I was; but, for my own part, I think that my rapid progress was due to nothing but my courage. This was such as to make me presume too much on my physical powers. The abbe had told me that, with a strong will, any one of my age could master all the rules of the language within a month. At the end of the month I expressed myself with facility and wrote correctly. Edmee had a sort of occult influence over my studies; at her wish I was not taught Latin; for she declared that I was too old to devote several years to a fancy branch of learning, and that the essential thing was to shape my heart and understanding with ideas, rather than to adorn my mind with words.

Of an evening, under pretext of wishing to read some favourite book again, she read aloud, alternately with the abbe, passages from Condillac, Fenelon, Bernardin de Saint-Pierre, Jean Jacques, and even from Montaigne and Montesquieu. These passages, it is true, were chosen beforehand and adapted to my powers. I understood them fairly well, and I secretly wondered at this; for if during the day I opened these same books at random, I found myself brought to a standstill at every line. With the superstition natural to young lovers, I willingly imagined that in passing through Edmee's mouth the authors acquired a magic clearness, and that by some miracle my mind expanded at the sound of her voice. However, Edmee was careful to disguise the interest she took in teaching me herself. There is no doubt that she was mistaken in thinking that she ought not to betray her solicitude: it would only have roused me to still greater efforts in my work. But in this, imbued as she was with the teachings of *Emile*, she was merely putting into practice the theories of her favourite philosopher.

As it was, I spared myself but little; for my courage would not admit of any forethought. Consequently I was soon obliged to stop. The change of air, of diet, and of habits, my lucubrations, the want of vigorous exercise, my intense application, in a word, the terrible revolution which my nature had to stir up against itself in order to pass from the state of a man of the woods to that of an intelligent being, brought on a kind of brain fever which made me almost mad for some weeks, then an idiot for some days, and finally disappeared, leaving me a mere wreck physically, with a mind completely severed from the past, but sternly braced to meet the future.

One night, when I was at the most critical stage of my illness, during a lucid interval, I caught sight of Edmee in my room. At first I thought I was dreaming. The night-light was casting an unsteady glimmer over the room. Near me was a pale form lying motionless on an easy chair. I could distinguish some long black tresses falling loosely over a white dress. I sat up, weak though I was and scarcely able to move, and tried to get out of bed. Patience, however, suddenly appeared by the bedside and gently stopped me. Saint-Jean was sleeping in another arm-chair. Every night there used to be two men watching me thus, ready to hold me down by force whenever I became violent during my delirium. Frequently the abbe was one; sometimes the worthy Marcasse, who, before leaving Berry to go on his annual round through the neighbouring province, had returned to have a farewell hunt in the outhouses of the chateau, and who kindly offered to relieve the servants in their painful task of keeping watch over me.

As I was wholly unconscious of my illness, it was but natural that the unexpected presence of the hermit in my room should cause me considerable astonishment, and throw me into a state of great agitation. My attacks had been so violent that evening that I had no strength left. I abandoned myself, therefore, to my melancholy ravings, and, taking the good man's hand, I asked him if it was really Edmee's corpse that he had placed in the arm-chair by my bedside.

"It is Edmee's living self," he answered, in a low voice; "but she is still asleep, my dear monsieur, and we must not wake her. If there is anything you would like, I am here to attend to you, and right gladly I do it."

"My good Patience, you are deceiving me," I said; "she is dead, and so am I, and you have come to bury us. But you must put us in the same coffin, do you hear? for we are betrothed. Where is her ring? Take it off and put it on my finger; our wedding-night has come."

He tried in vain to dispel this hallucination. I held to my belief that Edmee was dead, and declared that I should never be quiet in my shroud until I had been given my wife's ring. Edmee, who had sat up with me for several nights, was so exhausted that our voices did not awaken her. Besides, I was speaking in a whisper, like Patience, with that instinctive tendency to imitate which is met with only in children or idiots. I persisted in my fancy, and Patience, who was afraid that it might turn into madness, went and very carefully removed a cornelian ring from one of Edmee's fingers and put it on mine. As soon as I felt it there, I carried it to my lips; and then with my arms crossed on my breast, in the manner of a corpse in a coffin, I fell into a deep sleep.

On the morrow when they tried to take the ring from me I resisted violently, and they abandoned the attempt. I fell asleep again and the abbe removed it during my sleep. But when I opened my eyes I noticed the theft, and once more began to rave. Edmee, who was in the room, ran to me at once and pressed the ring over my finger, at the same time rebuking the abbe. I immediately grew calm, and gazing, on her with lack-lustre eyes, said:

"Is it not true that you are my wife in death as in life?"

"Certainly," she replied. "Set your mind at rest."

"Eternity is long," I said, "and I should like to spend it in recalling your caresses. But I send my thoughts back in vain; they bring me no remembrance of your love."

She leant over and gave me a kiss.

"Edmee, that is very wrong," said the abbe; "such remedies turn to poison."

"Let me do as I like, abbe," she replied, with evident impatience, sitting down near my bed; "I must ask you to let me do as I please."

I fell asleep with one of my hands in hers, repeating at intervals:

"How sweet it is in the grave! Are we not fortunate to be dead?"

During my convalescence Edmee was much more reserved, but no less attentive. I told her my dreams and learnt from her how far my recollections were of real events. Without her testimony I should always have believed that I had dreamt everything. I implored her to let me keep the ring, and she consented. I ought to have added, to show my gratitude for all her goodness, that I should keep it as a pledge of friendship, and not as a sign of our engagement; but such a renunciation was beyond me.

One day I asked for news of M. de la Marche. It was only to Patience that I dared to put this question.

"Gone," he answered.

"What! Gone?" I replied. "For long?"

"Forever, please God! I don't know anything about it, for I ask no questions; but I happened to be in the garden when he took leave of her, and it was all as cold as a December night. Still, *au revoir* was said on both sides, but though Edmee's manner was kind and honest as it always is, the other had the face of a farmer when he sees frosts in April. Mauprat, Mauprat, they tell me that you have become a great student and a genuine good fellow. Remember what I told you; when you are old there will probably no longer be any titles or estate. Perhaps you will be called 'Father' Mauprat, as I am called 'Father' Patience, though I have never been either a priest or a father of a family."

"Well, what are you driving at?"

"Remember what I once told you," he repeated. "There are many ways of being a sorcerer, and one may read the future without being a servant of the devil. For my part, I give my consent to your marriage with your cousin. Continue to behave decently. You are a wise man now, and can read fluently from any book set before you. What more do you want? There are so many books here that the sweat runs from my brow at the very sight of them; it seems as if I were again starting the old torment of not being able to learn to read. But you have soon cured yourself. If M. Hubert were willing to take my advice, he would fix the wedding for the next Martinmas."

"That is enough, Patience!" I said. "This is a painful subject with me; my cousin does not love me."

"I tell you she does. You lie in your throat, as the nobles say. I know well enough how she nursed you; and Marcasse from the housetop happened to look through her window and saw her on her knees in the middle of the room at five o'clock in the morning the day that you were so ill."

These imprudent assertions of Patience, Edmee's tender cares, the departure of M. de la Marche, and, more than anything else, the weakness of my brain, enabled me to believe what I wished; but in proportion as I regained my strength Edmee withdrew further and further within the bounds of calm and discreet friendship. Never did man recover his health with less pleasure than I mine; for each day made Edmee's visits shorter; and when I was able to leave my room I had merely a few hours a day near her, as before my illness. With marvellous skill she had given me proof of the tenderest affection without ever allowing herself to be drawn into a fresh explanation concerning our mysterious betrothal. If I had not yet sufficient greatness of soul to renounce my rights, I had at least developed enough honour not to refer to them; and I found myself on exactly the same terms with her as at the time when I had fallen ill. M. de la Marche was in Paris; but according to her he had been summoned thither by his military duties and ought to return at the end of the winter on which we were entering. Nothing that the chevalier or the abbe said tended to show that there had been a quarrel between Edmee and him. They rarely spoke of the lieutenant-general, but when they had to speak of him they did so naturally and without any signs of repugnance. I was again filled with my old doubts, and could find no remedy for them except in the kingdom of my own will. "I will force her to prefer me," I would say to myself as I raised my eyes from my book and watched Edmee's great, inscrutable eyes calmly fixed on the letters which her father occasionally received from M. de la Marche, and which he would hand to her as soon as he had read them. I buried myself in my work again. For a long time I suffered from frightful pains in the head, but I overcame them stoically. Edmee again began the course of studies which she had indirectly laid down for my winter evenings. Once more I astonished the abbe by my aptitude and the rapidity of my conquests. The kindness he had shown me during my illness had disarmed me; and although I was still unable to feel any genuine affection for him, knowing well that he was of little service to me with my cousin, I gave him proof of much more confidence and respect than in the past. His talks were as useful to me as my reading. I was allowed to accompany him in his walks in the park and in his philosophical visits to Patience's snow-covered hut. This gave me an opportunity of seeing Edmee more frequently and for longer periods. My behaviour was such that all her mistrust vanished, and she no longer feared to be alone with me. On such occasions, however, I had but little scope for displaying my heroism; for the abbe, whose vigilance nothing could lull to sleep, was always at our heels. This supervision no longer annoyed me; on the contrary, I was pleased at it; for, in spite of all my resolutions, the storms of passion would still sweep my senses into a mysterious disorder; and once or twice when I found myself alone with Edmee I left her abruptly and went away, so that she might not perceive my agitation.

Our life, then, was apparently calm and peaceful, and for some time it was so in reality; but soon I disturbed it more than ever by a vice which education developed in me, and which had hitherto been hidden under coarser but less fatal vices. This vice, the bane of my new period of life, was vanity.

In spite of their theories, the abbe and my cousin made the mistake of showing too much pleasure at my rapid progress. They had so little expected perseverance from me that they gave all the credit to my exceptional abilities. Perhaps, too, in the marked success of the philosophical ideas they had applied to my education they saw something of a triumph for themselves. Certain it is, I was not loath to let myself be persuaded that I had great intellectual powers, and that I was a man very much above the average. My dear instructors were soon to gather the sad fruit of their imprudence, and it was already too late to check the flight of my immoderate conceit.

Perhaps, too, this abominable trait in my character, kept under by the bad treatment I had endured in childhood, was now merely revealing its existence. There is reason to believe that we carry within us from our earliest years the seeds of those virtues and vices which are in time made to bear fruit by the action of our environment. As for myself, I had not yet found anything whereon my vanity could feed; for on what could I have prided myself at the beginning of my acquaintance with Edmee? But no sooner was food forthcoming than suffering vanity rose up in triumph, and filled me with as much presumption as previously it had inspired me with bashfulness and boorish reserve. I was, moreover, as delighted at being able at last to express my thoughts with ease as a young falcon fresh from the nest trying its wings for the first time. Consequently, I became as talkative as I had been silent. The others were too indulgent to my prattle. I had not sense enough to see that they were merely listening to me as they would to a spoilt child. I thought myself a man, and what is more, a remarkable man. I grew arrogant and superlatively ridiculous.

My uncle, the chevalier, who had not taken any part in my education, and who only smiled with fatherly good-nature at the first steps I took in my new career, was the first to notice the false direction in which I was advancing. He found it unbecoming that I should raise my voice as loudly as his own, and mentioned the matter to Edmee. With great sweetness she warned me of this, and, lest I should feel annoyed at her speaking of it, told me that I was quite right in my argument, but that her father was now too old to be converted to new ideas, and that I ought to sacrifice my enthusiastic affirmations to his patriarchal dignity. I promised not to repeat the offence; and I did not keep my word.

The fact is, the chevalier was imbued with many prejudices. Considering the days in which he lived, he had received a very good education for a country nobleman; but the century had moved more rapidly than he. Edmee, ardent and romantic; the abbe, full of sentiment and systems, had moved even more rapidly than the century; and if the vast gulf which lay between them and the patriarch was scarcely perceptible, this was owing to the respect which they rightly felt for him, and to the love he had for his daughter. I rushed forward at full speed, as you may imagine, into Edmee's ideas, but I had not, like herself, sufficient delicacy of feeling to maintain a becoming reticence. The violence of my character found an outlet in politics and philosophy, and I tasted unspeakable pleasure in those heated disputes which at that time in France, not only at all public meetings but also in the bosoms of families, were preluding the tempests of the Revolution. I doubt if there was a single house, from palace to hovel, which had not its orator—rugged, fiery, absolute, and ready to descend into the parliamentary arena. I was the orator of the chateau of Sainte-Severe, and my worthy uncle, accustomed to a resemblance of authority over those about him, which prevented him from seeing the real revolt of their minds, could ill endure such candid opposition as mine. He was proud and hot-tempered, and, moreover, had a difficulty in expressing himself which increased his natural impatience, and made him feel annoyed with himself. He would give a furious kick to the burning logs on the hearth; he would smash his eye-glasses into a thousand pieces; scatter clouds of snuff about the floor, and shout so violently as to make the lofty ceilings of his mansion ring with his resonant voice. All this, I regret to say, amused me immensely; and with some sentence but newly spelt out from my books I loved to destroy the frail scaffolding of ideas which had served him all his life. This was great folly and very foolish pride on my part; but my love of opposition and my desire to display intellectually the energy which was wanting in my physical life were continually carrying me away. In vain would Edmee cough, as a hint that I should say no more, and make an effort to save her father's *amour propre* by bringing forward some argument in his favour, though against her own judgement; the lukewarmness of her help, and my apparent submission to her only irritated my adversary more and more.

"Let him have his say," he would cry; "Edmee, you must not interfere; I want to beat him on all points. If you continually interrupt us, I shall never be able to make him see his absurdity."

And then the squall would blow stronger from both sides, until at last the chevalier, seriously offended, would walk out of the room, and go and vent his ill-humour on his huntsman or his hounds.

What most contributed to the recurrence of these unseemly wrangles and to the growth of my ridiculous obstinacy was my uncle's extreme goodness and the rapidity of his recovery. At the end of an hour he had entirely forgotten my rudeness and his own irritation. He would speak to me as usual and inquire into all my wishes and all my wants with that fatherly solicitude which always kept him in a benevolent mood. This incomparable man could never had slept had he not, before going to bed, embraced all his family, and atoned, either by a word or a kindly glance, for any ebullitions of temper which the meanest of his servants might have had to bear during the day. Such goodness ought to have disarmed me and closed my mouth forever. Each evening I vowed that it should; but each morning I returned, as the Scriptures say, to my vomit again.

Edmee suffered more and more every day from this development of my character. She cast about for means to cure it. If there was never *fiancee* stronger-minded and more reserved than she, never was there mother more tender. After many discussions with the abbe she resolved to persuade her father to change the routine of our life somewhat, and to remove our establishment to Paris for the last weeks of the carnival. Our long stay in the country; the isolation which the position of Sainte-Severe and the bad state of the roads had left us since the beginning of winter; the monotony of our daily life—all tended to foster our wearisome quibbling. My character was being more and more spoilt by it; and though it afforded my uncle even greater pleasure than myself, his health suffered as a result, and the childish passions daily aroused were no doubt hastening his decay. The abbe was suffering from *ennui*; Edmee was depressed. Whether in consequence of our mode of life or owing to causes unknown to the rest, it was her wish to go, and we went; for her father was uneasy about her melancholy, and sought only to do as she desired. I jumped for joy at the thought of seeing Paris; and while Edmee was flattering herself that intercourse with the world would refine the grossness of my pedantry, I was dreaming of a triumphal progress through the world which had been held up to such scorn by our philosophers. We started on our journey one fine morning in March; the chevalier with his daughter and Mademoiselle Leblanc in one post-chaise; myself in another with the abbe, who could ill conceal his delight at the thought of seeing the capital for the first time in him life; and my valet Saint-Jean, who, lest he should forget his customary politeness, made profound bows to every individual we passed.

XII

Old Bernard, tired from talking so long, had promised to resume his story on the morrow. At the appointed hour we called upon him to keep his word; and he continued thus:

This visit marked a new phase in my life. At Sainte-Severe I had been absorbed in my love and my work. I had concentrated all my energies upon these two points. No sooner had I arrived at Paris than a thick curtain seemed to fall before my eyes, and, for several days, as I could not understand anything, I felt astonished at nothing. I formed a very exaggerated estimate of the passing actors who appeared upon the scene; but I formed no less exaggerated an estimate of the ease with which I should soon rival these imaginary powers. My enterprising and presumptuous nature saw challenges everywhere and obstacles nowhere.

Though I was in the same house as my uncle and cousin, my room was on a separate floor, and henceforth I spent the greater part of my time with the abbe. I was far from being dazed by the material advantages of my position; but in proportion as I realized how precarious or painful were the positions of many others, the more conscious I became of the comfort of my own. I appreciated the excellent character of my tutor, and the respect my lackey showed me no longer seemed objectionable. With the freedom that I enjoyed, and the unlimited money at my command, and the restless energy of youth, it is astonishing that I did not fall into some excess, were it only gambling, which might well have appealed to my combative instincts. It was my own ignorance of everything that prevented this; it made me extremely suspicious, and the abbe, who was very observant, and held himself responsible for my actions, managed most cleverly to work upon my haughty reserve. He increased it in regard to such things as might have done me harm, and dispelled it in contrary cases. Moreover, he was careful to provide me with sufficient reasonable distractions, which while they could not take the place of the joys of love, served at least to lessen the smart of its wounds. As to temptations to debauchery, I felt none. I had too much pride to yearn for any woman in which I had not seen, as in Edmee, the first of her sex.

We used all to meet at dinner, and as a rule we paid visits in the evening. By observing the world from a corner of a drawing-room, I learnt more of it in a few days than I should have done in a whole year from guesses and inquiries. I doubt whether I should ever have understood society, if I had always been obliged to view it from a certain distance. My brain refused to form a clear image of the ideas which occupied the brains of others. But as soon as I found myself in the midst of this chaos, the confused mass was compelled to fall into some sort of order and reveal a large part of its elements. This path which led me into life was not without charms for me, I remember, at its beginning. Amid all the conflicting interests of the surrounding world I had nothing to ask for, aim at, or argue about. Fortune had taken me by the hand. One fine morning she had lifted me out of an abyss and put me down on a bed of roses and made me a young gentleman. The eagerness of others was for me but an amusing spectacle. My heart was interested in the future only on one mysterious point, the love which I felt for Edmee.

My illness, far from robbing me of my physical vigour, had but increased it. I was no longer the heavy, sleepy animal, fatigued by digestion and stupefied by weariness. I felt the vibrations of all my fibres filling my soul with unknown harmonies; and I was astonished to discover within myself faculties of which I had never suspected the use. My good kinfolk were delighted at this, though apparently not surprised. They had allowed themselves to augur so well of me from the beginning that it seemed as if they had been accustomed all their lives to the trade of civilizing barbarians.

The nervous system which had just been developed in me, and which made me pay for the pleasures and advantages it brought by keen and constant sufferings during the rest of my life, had rendered me specially sensitive to impressions from without; and this quickness to feel the effect of external things was helped by an organic vigour such as is only found among animals or savages. I was astounded at the decay of the faculties in other people. These men in spectacles, these women with their sense of smell deadened by snuff, these premature graybeards, deaf and gouty before their time, were painful to behold. To me society seemed like a vast hospital; and when with my robust constitution I found myself in the midst of these weaklings, it seemed to me that with a puff of my breath I could have blown them into the air as if they had been so much thistle-down.

This unfortunately led me into the error of yielding to that rather stupid kind of pride which makes a man presume upon his natural gifts. For a long time it induced me to neglect their real improvement, as if this were a work of supererogation. The idea that gradually grew up in me of the worthlessness of my fellows prevented me from rising above those whom I henceforth looked upon as my inferiors. I did not realize that society is made up of so many elements of little value in themselves, but so skilfully and solidly put together that before adding the least extraneous particle a man must be a qualified artificer. I did not know that in this society there is no resting-place between the role of the great artist and that of the good workman. Now, I was neither one nor the other, and, if the truth must be told, all my ideas have never succeeded in lifting me out of the ordinary ruck; all my strength has only enabled me with much difficulty to do as others do.

In a few weeks, then, I passed from an excess of admiration to an excess of contempt for society. As soon as I understood the workings of its springs they seemed to me so miserably regulated by a feeble generation that the hopes of my mentors, unknown to themselves, were doomed to disappointment. Instead of realizing my own inferiority and endeavouring to efface myself in the crowd, I imagined that I could give proof of my superiority whenever I wished; and I fed on fancies which I blush to recall. If I did not show myself egregiously ridiculous, it was thanks to the very excess of this vanity which feared to stultify itself before others.

At that time Paris presented a spectacle which I shall not attempt to set before you, because no doubt you have often eagerly studied it in the excellent pictures which have been painted by eye-witnesses in the form of general history or private memoirs. Besides, such a picture would exceed the limits of my story, for I promised to tell you only the cardinal events in my moral and philosophical development. In order to give you some idea of the workings of my mind at this period it will suffice to mention that the War of Independence was breaking out in America; that Voltaire was receiving his apotheosis in Paris; that Franklin, the prophet of a new political religion, was sowing the seed of liberty in the very heart of the Court of France; while Lafayette was secretly preparing his romantic expedition. The majority of young patricians were being carried away either by fashion, or the love of change, or the pleasure inherent in all opposition which is not dangerous.

Opposition took a graver form and called for more serious work in the case of the old nobles, and among the members of the parliaments. The spirit of the League was alive again in the ranks of these ancient patricians and these haughty magistrates, who for form's sake were still supporting the tottering monarchy with one arm, while with the other they gave considerable help to the invasions of philosophy. The privileged classes of society were zealously lending a hand to the imminent destruction of their privileges by complaining that these had been curtailed by the kings. They were bringing up their children in constitutional principles, because they imagined they were going to found a new monarchy in which the people would help them to regain their old position above the throne; and it is for this reason that the greatest admiration for Voltaire and the most ardent sympathies with Franklin were openly expressed in the most famous salons in Paris.

So unusual and, if it must be said, so unnatural a movement of the human mind had infused fresh life into the vestiges of the Court of Louis XIV, and replaced the customary coldness and stiffness by a sort of quarrelsome vivacity. It had also introduced certain serious forms into the frivolous manners of the regency, and lent them an appearance of depth. The pure but colourless life of Louis XVI counted for nothing, and influenced nobody. Never had there been such serious chatter, so many flimsy maxims, such an affectation of wisdom, so much inconsistency between words and deeds as might have been found at this period among the so-called enlightened classes.

It was necessary to remind you of this in order that you might understand the admiration which I had at first for a world apparently so disinterested, so courageous, so eager in the pursuit of truth, and likewise the disgust which I was soon to feel for so much affectation and levity, for such an abuse of the most hallowed words and the most sacred convictions. For my own part, I was perfectly sincere;

and I founded my philosophic fervour (that recently discovered sentiment of liberty which was then called the cult of reason) on the broad base of an inflexible logic. I was young and of a good constitution, the first condition perhaps of a healthy mind; my reading, though not extensive, was solid, for I had been fed on food easy of digestion. The little I knew served to show me, therefore, that others either knew nothing at all, or were giving themselves the lie.

At the commencement of our stay in Paris the chevalier had but few visitors. The friend and contemporary of Turgot and several other distinguished men, he had not mixed with the gilded youth of his day, but had lived soberly in the country after loyally serving in the wars. His circle of friends, therefore, was composed of a few grave gentlemen of the long robe, several old soldiers, and a few nobles from his own province, both old and young, who, thanks to a respectable fortune, were able, like himself, to come and spend the winter in Paris. He had, moreover, kept up a slight intercourse with a more brilliant set, among whom Edmee's beauty and refined manners were noticed as soon as she appeared. Being an only daughter, and passably rich, she was sought after by various important matrons, those procuresses of quality who have always a few young proteges whom they wish to clear from debt at the expense of some family in the provinces. And then, when it became known that she was engaged to M. de la Marche, the almost ruined scion of a very illustrious family, she was still more kindly received, until by degrees the little salon which she had chosen for her father's old friends became too small for the wits by quality and profession, and the grand ladies with a turn for philosophy who wished to know the young Quakeress, the Rose of Berry (such were the names given her by a certain fashionable woman).

This rapid success in a world in which she had hitherto been unknown by no mean dazzled Edmee; and the control which she possessed over herself was so great that, in spite of all the anxiety with which I watched her slightest movement, I could never discover if she felt flattered at causing such a stir. But what I could perceive was the admirable good sense manifested in everything she did and everything she said. Her manner, at once ingenuous and reserved, and a certain blending of unconstraint with modest pride, made her shine even among the women who were the most admired and the most skilled in attracting attention. And this is the place to mention that at first I was extremely shocked at the tone and bearing of these women, whom everybody extolled; to me they seemed ridiculous in their studied posings, and their grand society manners looked very much like insufferable effrontery. Yes, I, so intrepid at heart, and but lately so coarse in my manners, felt ill at ease and abashed in their presence; and it needed all Edmee's reproaches and remonstrances to prevent me from displaying a profound contempt for this meretriciousness of glances, of toilets, and allurements which was known in society as allowable coquetry, as the charming desire to please, as amiability, and as grace. The abbe was of my opinion. When the guests had gone we members of the family used to gather round the fireside for a short while before separating. It is at such a time that one feels an impulse to bring together one's scattered impressions and communicate them to some sympathetic being.

The abbe, then, would break the same lances as myself with my uncle and cousin. The chevalier, who was an ardent admirer of the fair sex, of which he had had but little experience, used to take upon himself, like a true French knight, to defend all the beauties that we were attacking so unmercifully. He would laughingly accuse the abbe of arguing about women as the fox in the fable argued about the grapes. For myself, I used to improve under the abbe's criticisms; this was an emphatic way of letting Edmee know how much I preferred her to all others. She, however, appeared to be more scandalized than flattered, and seriously reproved me for the tendency to malevolence which had its origin, she said, in my inordinate pride.

It is true that after generously undertaking the defence of the persons in question, she would come over to our opinion as soon as, Rousseau in hand, we told her that the women in Paris society had cavalier manners and a way of looking a man in the face which must needs be intolerable in the eyes of a sage. When once Rousseau had delivered judgment, Edmee would object no further; she was ready to admit with him that the greatest charm of a woman is the intelligent and modest attention she gives to serious discussions, and I always used to remind her of the comparison of a superior woman to a beautiful child with its great eyes full of feeling and sweetness and delicacy, with its shy questionings and its objections full of sense. I hoped that she would recognise herself in this portrait upon the text, and, enlarging the portrait:

"A really superior woman," I said, looking at her earnestly, "is one who knows enough to prevent her from asking a ridiculous or unseasonable question, or from ever measuring swords with men of merit. Such a woman knows when to be silent, especially with the fools whom she could laugh at, or the ignorant whom she could humiliate. She is indulgent towards absurdities because she does not yearn to display her knowledge, and she is observant of whatsoever is good, because she desires to improve herself. Her great object is to understand, not to instruct. The great art (since it is recognised that art is required even in the commerce of words) is not to pit against one another two arrogant opponents, eager to parade their learning and to amuse the company by discussing questions the solution of which no one troubles about, but to illumine every unprofitable disputation by bringing in the help of all who can throw a little light on the points at issue. This is a talent of which I can see no signs among the hostesses who are so cried up. In their houses I always find two fashionable barristers, and a thunderstruck audience, in which no one dares to be judge. The only art these ladies have is to make the man of genius ridiculous, and the ordinary man dumb and inert. One comes away from such houses saying, 'Those were fine speeches,' and nothing more."

I really think that I was in the right here; but I cannot forget that my chief cause of anger against these women arose from the fact that they paid no attention to people, however able they might think themselves, unless they happened to be famous—the *people* being myself, as you may easily imagine. On the other hand, now that I look back on those days without prejudice and without any sense of wounded vanity, I am certain that these women had a way of fawning on public favourites which was much more like childish conceit than sincere admiration or candid sympathy. They became editors, as it were, of the conversation, listening with all their might and making peremptory signals to the audience to listen to every triviality issuing from an illustrious mouth; while they would suppress a yawn and drum with their fans at all remarks, however excellent, as soon as they were unsigned by a fashionable name. I am ignorant of the airs of the intellectual women of the nineteenth century; nay, I do not know if the race still exists. Thirty years have passed since I mixed in society; but, as to the past, you may believe what I tell you. There were five or six of these women who were absolutely odious to me. One of them had some wit, and scattered her epigrams right and left. These were at once hawked about in all drawing-rooms, and I had to listen to them twenty times in a single day. Another had read Montesquieu, and gave lessons in law to the oldest magistrates. A third used to play the harp execrably, but it was agreed that her arms were the most beautiful in France, and we had to endure the harsh scraping of her nails over the strings so that she might have an opportunity of removing her gloves like a coy little girl. What can I say of the others, except that they vied with one another in all those affectations and fatuous insincerities, by which all the men childishly allowed themselves to be duped. One alone was really pretty, said nothing, and gave pleasure by her very lack of artificiality. To her I might have been favourably inclined because of her ignorance, had she not gloried in this, and tried to emphasize her difference from the others by a piquant ingenuousness. One day I discovered that she had plenty of wit, and straightway I abhorred her.

Edmee alone preserved all the freshness of sincerity and all the distinction of natural grace. Sitting on a sofa by the side of M. de Malesherbes, she was for me the same being that I had gazed on so many times in the light of the setting sun, as she sat on the stone seat at the door of Patience's cottage.

XIII

You will readily believe that all the homage paid to my cousin fanned into fresh flames the jealousy which had been smouldering in my breast. Since the day when, in obedience to her command, I began to devote myself to work, I could hardly say whether I had dared to count on her promise that she would become my wife as soon as I was able to understand her ideas and feelings. To me, indeed, it seemed that the time for this had already arrived; for it is certain that I understood Edmee, better perhaps than any of the men who were paying their addresses to her in prose and verse. I had firmly resolved not to presume upon the oath extorted from her at Roche-Mauprat; yet, when I remembered her last promise, freely given at the chapel window, and the inferences which I could have drawn from her conversation with the abbe which I had overheard in the parlour at Sainte-Severe; when I remembered her earnestness in preventing me from going away and in directing my education; the motherly attentions she had lavished on me during my illness—did not all these things give me, if not some right, at least some reason to hope? It is true that her friendship would become icy as soon as my passion betrayed itself in words or looks; it is true that since the first day I saw her I had not advanced a single step towards close affection; it is also true that M. de la Marche frequently came to the house, and that she always showed him as much friendship as myself, though with less familiarity and more respect in it, a distinction which was naturally due to the difference in our characters and our ages, and did not indicate any preference for one or the other. It was possible, therefore, to attribute her promise to the prompting of her conscience; the interest which she took in my studies to her worship of human dignity as it stood rehabilitated by philosophy; her quiet and continued affection for M. de la March to a profound regret, kept in subjection by the strength and wisdom of her mind. These perplexities I felt very acutely. The hope of compelling her love by submission and devotion had sustained me; but this hope was beginning to grow weak; for though, as all allowed, I had made prodigious efforts and extraordinary progress, Edmee's regard for me had been very far from increasing in the same proportion. She had not shown any astonishment at what she called my lofty intellect; she had always believed in it; she had praised it unreasonably. But she was not blind to the faults in my character, to the vices of my soul. She had reproached me with these with an inexorable sweetness, with a patience calculated to drive me to despair; for she seemed to have made up her mind that, whatever the future might bring, she would never love me more and never less.

XIII

Meanwhile all were paying court to her and none were accepted. It had, indeed, been given out that she was engaged to M. de la Marche, but no one understood any better than myself the indefinite postponement of the marriage. People came to the conclusion that she was seeking a pretext to get rid of him, and they could find no ground for her repugnance except by supposing that she had conceived a great passion for myself. My strange history had caused some stir; the women examined me with curiosity; the men seemed interested in me and showed me a sort of respect which I affected to despise, but to which, however, I was far from insensible. And, since nothing finds credence in the world until it is embellished with some fiction, people strangely exaggerated my wit, my capabilities and my learning; but, as soon as they had seen M. de la Marche and myself in Edmee's company, all their inferences were annihilated by the composure and ease of our manners. To both of us Edmee was the same in public as in private; M. de la Marche, a soulless puppet, was perfectly drilled in conventional manners; and myself, a prey to divers passions, but inscrutable by reason of my pride and also, I must confess, of my pretensions to the sublimity of the *American manner*. I should tell you that I had been fortunate enough to be introduced to Franklin as a sincere devotee of liberty. Sir Arthur Lee had honoured me with a certain kindness and some excellent advice; consequently my head was somewhat turned, even as the heads of those whom I railed at so bitterly were turned, and to such an extent that this little vainglory brought sorely needed relief to my agonies of mind. Perhaps you will shrug your shoulders when I own that I took the greatest pleasure in the world in leaving my hair unpowdered, in wearing big shoes, and appearing everywhere in a dark-coloured coat, of aggressively simple cut and stiffly neat—in a word, in aping, as far as was then permissible without being mistaken for a regular plebeian, the dress and ways of the Bonhomme Richard! I was nineteen, and I was living in an age when every one affected a part—that is my only excuse.

I might plead also that my too indulgent and too simple tutor openly approved of my conduct; that my Uncle Hubert, though he occasionally laughed at me, let me do as I wished, and that Edmee said absolutely nothing about this ridiculous affectation, and appeared never to notice it.

Meanwhile spring had returned; we were going back to the country; the salons were being gradually deserted. For myself, I was still in the same state of uncertainty. I noticed one day that M. de la Marche seemed anxious to find an opportunity of speaking to Edmee in private. At first I found pleasure in making him suffer, and did not stir from my chair. However, I thought I detected on Edmee's brow that slight frown which I knew so well, and after a silent dialogue with myself I went out of the room, resolving to observe the results of this *tete-a-tete*, and to learn my fate, whatever it might be.

At the end of an hour I returned to the drawing-room. My uncle was there; M. de la Marche was staying to dinner; Edmee seemed meditative but not melancholy; the abbe's eyes were putting questions to her which she did not understand, or did not wish to understand.

M. de la Marche accompanied my uncle to the Comedie Francaise. Edmee said that she had some letters to write and requested permission to remain at home. I followed the count and the chevalier, but after the first act I made my escape and returned to the house. Edmee had given orders that she was not to be disturbed; but I did not consider that this applied to myself; the servants thought it quite natural that I should behave as the son of the house. I entered the drawing-room, fearful lest Edmee should have retired to her bed-room; for there I could not have followed her. She was sitting near the fire and amusing herself by pulling out the petals of the blue and white asters which I had gathered during a walk to the tomb of Jean Jacques Rousseau. These flowers brought back to me a night of ecstasy, under the clear moonlight, the only hours of happiness, perhaps, that I could mention in all my life.

"Back already?" she said, without any change of attitude.

"Already is an unkind word," I replied. "Would you like me to retire to my room, Edmee?"

"By no means; you are not disturbing me at all; but you would have derived more profit from seeing *Merope* than from listening to my conversation this evening; for I warn you that I feel a complete idiot."

"So much the better, cousin; I shall not feel humiliated this evening, since for the first time we shall be upon a footing of equality. But, might I ask you why you so despise my asters? I thought that you would probably keep them as a souvenir."

"Of Rousseau?" she asked with a malicious little smile, and without raising her eyes to mine.

"Naturally that was my meaning," I answered.

"I am playing a most interesting game," she said; "do not interrupt me."

"I know it," I said. "All the children in Varenne play it, and there is not a lass but believes in the decree of fate that it revels. Would you like me to read your thoughts as you pull out these petals four by four?"

"Come, then, O mighty magician!"

"A little, that is how some one loves you; much, that is how you love him; passionately, that is how another loves you; not at all, thus do you love this other."

"And might I inquire, Sir Oracle," replied Edmee, whose face became more serious, "who some one and another may be? I suspect that you are like the Pythonesses of old; you do not know the meaning of your auguries yourself."

"Could you not guess mine, Edmee?"

"I will try to interpret the riddle, if you will promise that afterward you will do what the Sphinx did when vanquished by OEdipus."

"Oh, Edmee," I cried; "think how long I have been running my head against walls on account of you and your interpretations. And yet you have not guessed right a single time."

"Oh, good heavens! I have," she said, throwing the bouquet on to the mantelpiece. "You shall see. I love M. de la Marche a little, and I love you much. He loves me passionately, and you love me not at all. That is the truth."

XIII

"I forgive you this malicious interpretation with all my heart for the sake of the word 'much,'" I replied.

I tried to take her hands. She drew them away quickly, though, in fact, she had no need to fear; for had she given me them, I merely intended to press them in brotherly fashion; but this appearance of distrust aroused memories which were dangerous for me. I fancy she showed a great deal of coquetry that evening in her expression and manners; and, until then, I had never seen the least inclination toward it. I felt my courage rising, though I could not explain why; and I ventured on some pointed remarks about her interview with M. de la Marche. She made no effort to deny my interpretations, and began to laugh when I told her that she ought to thank me for my exquisite politeness in retiring as soon as I saw her knit her brow.

Her supercilious levity was beginning to irritate me a little, when a servant entered and handed her a letter, saying that some one was waiting for an answer.

"Go to my writing-table and cut a pen for me, please," she said to me.

With an air of unconcern she broke the seal and ran through the letter, while I, quite ignorant of the contents, began preparing her writing materials.

For some time the crow-quill had been cut ready for use; for some time the paper with its coloured vignette had been waiting by the side of the amber writing-case; yet Edmee paid no attention to them and made no attempt to use them. The letter lay open in her lap; her feet were on the fire-dogs, her elbows on the arm of her chair in her favourite attitude of meditation. She was completely absorbed. I spoke to her softly; she did not hear me. I thought that she had forgotten the letter and had fallen asleep. After a quarter of an hour the servant came back and said that the messenger wished to know if there was any answer.

"Certainly," she replied; "ask him to wait."

She read the letter again with the closest attention, and began to write slowly; then she threw her reply into the fire, pushed away the arm-chair with her foot, walked round the room a few times, and suddenly stopped in front of me and looked at me in a cold, hard manner.

"Edmee," I cried, springing to me feet, "what is the matter, and how does that letter which is worrying you so much concern myself?"

"What is that to you?" she replied.

"What is that to me?" I cried. "And what is the air I breathe to me? and what is the blood that flows in my veins? Ask me that, if you like, but do not ask how one of your words or one of your glances can concern me; for you know very well that my life depends on them."

"Do not talk nonsense now, Bernard," she answered, returning to her arm-chair in a distracted manner. "There is a time for everything."

"Edmee, Edmee! do not play with the sleeping lion, do not stir up the fire which is smouldering in the ashes."

She shrugged her shoulders, and began to write with great rapidity. Her face was flushed, and from time to time she passed her fingers through the long hair which fell in ringlets over her shoulders. She was dangerously beautiful in her agitation; she looked as if in love—but with whom? Doubtless with him to whom she was writing. I began to feel the fires of jealousy. I walked out of the room abruptly and crossed the hall. I looked at the man who had brought the letter; he was in M. de la Marche's livery. I had no further doubts; this, however, only increased my rage. I returned to the drawing-room and threw open the door violently. Edmee did not even turn her head; she continued writing. I sat down opposite her, and stared at her with flashing eyes. She did not deign to raise her own to mine. I even fancied that I noticed on her ruby lips the dawn of a smile which seemed an insult to my agony. At last she finished her letter and sealed it. I rose and walked towards her, feeling strongly tempted to snatch it from her hands. I had learnt to control myself somewhat better than of old; but I realized how, with passionate souls, a single instant may destroy the labours of many days.

"Edmee," I said to her, in a bitter tone, and with a frightful grimace that was intended to be a sarcastic smile, "would you like me to hand this letter to M. de la Marche's lackey, and at the same time tell him in a whisper at what time his master may come to the tryst?"

"It seems to me," she replied, with a calmness that exasperated me, "that it was possible to mention the time in my letter, and that there is no need to inform a servant of it."

"Edmee, you ought to be a little more considerate of me," I cried.

"That doesn't trouble me the least in the world," she replied.

And throwing me the letter she had received across the table she went out to give the answer to the messenger herself. I do not know whether she had told me to read this letter; but I do know that the impulse which urged me to do so was irresistible. It ran somewhat as follows:

"Edmee, I have at last discovered the fatal secret which, according to you, sets an impassable barrier in the way of our union. Bernard loves you; his agitation this morning betrayed him. But you do not love him, I am sure . . . that would be impossible! You would have told me frankly. The obstacle, then, must be elsewhere. Forgive me! It has come to my knowledge that you spent two hours in the brigand's den. Unhappy girl! your misfortune, your prudence, your sublime delicacy make you still nobler in my eyes. And why did you not confide to me at once the misfortune of which you were a victim? I could have eased your sorrow and my own by a word. I could have helped you to hide your secret. I could have wept with you; or, rather, I could have wiped out the odious recollection by displaying an attachment proof against anything. But there is no need to despair; there is still time to say this word, and I do so now: Edmee, I love you more than ever; more than ever I am resolved to offer you my name; will you deign to accept it?"

This note was signed Adhemar de la Marche.

I had scarcely finished reading it when Edmee returned, and came towards the fire-place with an anxious look, as if she had forgotten some precious object. I handed her the letter that I had just read; but she took it absently, and, stooping over the hearth with an air of relief, eagerly seized a crumpled piece of paper which the flames had merely scorched. This was the first answer she had written to M. de la Marche's note, the one she had not judged fit to send.

"Edmee," I said, throwing myself on my knees, "let me see that letter. Whatever if may be, I will submit to the decree dictated by your first impulse."

"You really would?" she asked, with an indefinable expression. "Supposing I loved M. de la Marche, and that I was making a great sacrifice for your sake in refusing him, would you be generous enough to release me from my word?"

I hesitated for a moment. A cold sweat broke out all over me. I looked her full in the face; but her eyes were inscrutable and betrayed no hint of her thoughts. If I had fancied that she really loved me and that she was putting my virtue to the test, I should perhaps have played the hero; but I was afraid of some trap. My passion overmastered me. I felt that I had not the strength to renounce my claim with a good grace; and hypocrisy was repugnant to me. I rose to my feet, trembling with rage.

"You love him!" I cried. "Confess that you love him!"

"And if I did," she answered, putting the letter in her pocket, "where would be the crime?"

"The crime would be that hitherto you have lied in telling me that you did not love him."

"Hitherto is saying a good deal," she rejoined, looking at me fixedly; "we have not discussed the matter since last year. At that time it was possible that I did not love Adhemar very much, and at present it might be possible that I loved him more than you. If I compare the conduct of both to-day I see on the one hand a man without proper pride and without delicacy, presuming upon a promise which my heart perhaps has never ratified; on the other I see an admirable friend whose sublime devotion is ready to brave all prejudices; who—believing that I bear the smirch of an indelible shame—is none the less prepared to cover the blot with his protection."

"What! this wretch believes that I have done violence to you, and yet does not challenge me to a duel?"

"That is not what he believes, Bernard. He knows that you rescued me from Roche-Mauprat; but he thinks that you helped me too late, and that I was the victim of the other brigands."

"And he wants to marry you, Edmee? Either the man's devotion is sublime, as you say, or he is deeper in debt than you think."

"How dare you say that?" said Edmee angrily. "Such an odious explanation of generous conduct can proceed only from an unfeeling soul or a perverse mind. Be silent, unless you wish me to hate you."

"Say that you hate me, Edmee; say so without fear; I know it."

"Without fear! You should know likewise that I have not yet done you the honour to fear you. However, tell me this: without inquiring into what I intend to do, can you understand that you ought to give me my liberty, and abandon your barbarous rights?"

"I understand nothing except that I love you madly, and that these nails of mine shall tear out the heart of any man who tries to win you from me. I know that I shall force you to love me, and that, if I do not succeed, I will at any rate not let you belong to another while I am alive. The man will have to walk over my body riddled with wounds and bleeding from every pore, ere he can put the wedding-ring on your finger; with my last breath, too, I will dishonour you by proclaiming that you are my mistress, and thus cloud the joy of any man who may triumph over me; and if I can stab you as I die, I will, so that in the tomb, at least, you may be my wife. That is what I purpose doing, Edmee. And now, practise all your arts on me; lead me on from trap to trap; rule me with your admirable diplomacy. I may be duped a hundred times because of my ignorance, but have I not sworn by the name of Mauprat?"

"Mauprat the Hamstringer!" she added with freezing irony.

And she turned to go out.

I was about to seize her arm when the bell rang; it was the abbe who had returned. As soon as he appeared Edmee shook hands with him, and retired to her room without saying a single word to me.

The good abbe, noticing my agitation, questioned me with that assurance which his claims on my affections were henceforth to give him. The present matter, however, was the only one on which we had never had an explanation. In vain had he sought to introduce it. He had not given me a single lesson in history without leading up to some famous love affairs and drawing from them an example or a precept of moderation or generosity; but he had not succeeded in making me breathe a word on this subject. I could not bring myself to forgive him altogether for having done me an ill turn with Edmee. I even had a suspicion that he was still injuring my cause; and I therefore put myself on guard against all the arguments of his philosophy and all the seductions of his friendship. On this special evening I was more unassailable than ever. I left him ill at ease and depressed, and went and threw myself on my bed, where I buried my head in the clothes so as to stifle the customary sobs, those pitiless conquerors of my pride and my rage.

XIV

The next day I was in a state of gloomy despair; Edmee was icily cold; M. de la Marche did not come. I fancied I had seen the abbe going to call on him, and subsequently telling Edmee the result of their interview. However, they betrayed no signs of agitation, and I had to endure my suspense in silence. I could not get a minute with Edmee alone. In the morning I went on foot to M. de la Marche's house. What I intended saying to him I do not know; my state of exasperation was such that it drove me to act without either object or plan. Having learnt that he had left Paris, I returned. I found my uncle very depressed. On seeing me he frowned, and, after forcing himself to exchange a few meaningless words with me, left me to the abbe, who tried to draw me on to speak, but succeeded no better than the night before. For several days I sought an opportunity of speaking with Edmee, but she always managed to avoid it. Preparations were being made for the return to Sainte-Severe; she seemed neither sorry nor pleased at the prospect. I determined to slip a note between the page of her book asking for an interview. Within five minutes I received the following reply:

"An interview would lead to nothing. You are persisting in your boorish behaviour; I shall persevere in what I believe to be the path of integrity. An upright conscience cannot go from its word. I had sworn never to be any man's but yours. I shall not marry, for I did not swear that I would be yours whatever might happen. If you continue to be unworthy of my esteem I shall take steps to remain free. My poor father is sinking into the grave; a convent shall be my refuge when the only tie which binds me to the world is broken."

I had fulfilled all the conditions imposed by Edmee, and now, it seemed, her only return was an order that I should break them. I thus found myself in the same position as on the day of her conversation with the abbe.

I passed the remainder of the day shut up in my room. All through the night I walked up and down in violent agitation. I made no effort to sleep. I will not tell you the thoughts that passed through my mind; they were not unworthy of an honest man. At daybreak I was at Lafayette's house. He procured me the necessary papers for leaving France. He told me to go and await him in Spain, whence he was going to sail for the United States. I returned to our house to get the clothes and money indispensable to the humblest of travellers. I left a note for my uncle, so that he might not feel uneasy at my absence; this I promised to explain very soon in a long letter. I begged him to refrain from passing sentence on me until it arrived, and assured him that I should never forget all his goodness.

I left before any one in the house was up; for I was afraid that my resolution might be shaken at the least sign of friendship, and I felt that I could no longer impose upon a too generous affection. I could not, however, pass Edmee's door without pressing my lips to the lock. Then, hiding my head in my hands, I rushed away like a madman, and scarcely stopped until I had reached the other side of the Pyrenees. There I took a short rest, and wrote to Edmee that, as far as concerned myself, she was free; that I would not thwart a single wish of hers; but that it was impossible for me to be a witness of my rival's triumph. I felt firmly convinced that she loved him; and I resolved to crush out my own love. I was promising more than I could perform; but these first manifestations of wounded pride gave me confidence in myself. I also wrote to my uncle to tell him I should not hold myself worthy of the boundless affection he had bestowed on me until I had won my spurs as a knight. I confided to him my hopes of a soldier's fame and fortune with all the candour of conceit; and since I felt sure that Edmee would read this letter I feigned unclouded delight and an ardour that knew no regrets; I did not know whether my uncle was aware of the real cause of my departure; but my pride could not bring itself to confess. It was the same with the abbe, to whom I likewise wrote a letter full of gratitude and affection. I ended by begging my uncle to put himself to no expense on my account over the gloomy keep at Roche-Mauprat, assuring him that I could never bring myself to live there. I urged him to consider the fief as his daughter's property, and only asked that he would be good enough to advance me my share of the income for two or three years, so that I might pay the expenses of my own outfit, and thus prevent my devotion to the American cause from being a burden to the noble Lafayette.

My conduct and my letters apparently gave satisfaction. Soon after I reached the coast of Spain I received from my uncle a letter full of kindly exhortations, and of mild censure for my abrupt departure. He gave me a father's blessing, and declared on his honour that the fief of Roche-Mauprat would never be accepted by Edmee, and sent me a considerable sum of money exclusive of the income due me in the future. The abbe expressed the same mild censure, together with still warmer exhortations. It was easy to see that he preferred Edmee's tranquility to my happiness, and that he was full of genuine joy at my departure. Nevertheless he had a liking for me, and his friendship showed itself touchingly through the cruel satisfaction that was mingled with it. He expressed envy of my lot; proclaimed his enthusiasm for the cause of independence; and declared that he himself had more than once felt tempted to throw off the cassock and take up the musket. All this, however, was mere boyish affectation; his timid, gentle nature always kept him the priest under the mask of the philosopher.

Between these two letters I found a little note without any address, which seemed as if it had been slipped in as an after-thought. I was not slow to see that it was from the one person in the world who was of real interest to me. Yet I had not the courage to open it. I walked up and down the sandy beach, turning over this little piece of paper in my hands, fearful that by reading it I might destroy the kind of desperate calm my resolution had given me. Above all, I dreaded lest it might contain expressions of thanks and enthusiastic joy, behind which I should have divined the rapture of contented love for another.

"What can she be writing to me about?" I said to myself. "Why does she write at all? I do not want her pity, still less her gratitude."

I felt tempted to throw this fateful little note into the sea. Once, indeed I held it out over the waves, but I immediately pressed it to my bosom, and kept it hidden there a few moments as if I had been a believer in that second sight preached by the advocates of magnetism, who assert that they can read with the organs of feeling and thought as well as with their eyes.

At last I resolved to break the seal. The words I read were these:

"You have done well, Bernard; but I give you no thanks, as your absence will cause me more suffering than I can tell. Still, go wherever honour and love of truth call you; you will always be followed by my good wishes and prayers. Return when your mission is accomplished; you will find me neither married nor in a convent."

In this note she had inclosed the cornelian ring she had given me during my illness and which I had returned on leaving Paris. I had a little gold box made to hold this ring and note, and I wore it near my heart as a talisman. Lafayette, who had been arrested in France by order of the Government, which was opposed to his expedition, soon came and joined us after escaping from prison. I had had time to make my preparations, and I sailed full of melancholy, ambition, and hope.

You will not expect me to give an account of the American war. Once again I will separate my existence from the events of history as I relate my own adventures. Here, however, I shall suppress even my personal adventures; in my memory these form a special chapter in which Edmee plays the part of a Madonna, constantly invoked but invisible. I cannot think that you would be the least interested in listening to a portion of my narrative from which this angelic figure, the only one worthy of your attention, firstly by reason of her own worth, and then from her influence on myself, was entirely absent. I will only state that from the humble position which I gladly accepted in the beginning in Washington's army, I rose regularly but rapidly to the rank of officer. My military education did not take long. Into this, as into everything that I have undertaken during my life, I put my whole soul, and through the pertinacity of my will I overcame all obstacles.

I won the confidence of my illustrious chiefs. My excellent constitution fitted me well for the hardships of war; my old brigand habits too were of immense service to me; I endured reverses with a calmness beyond the reach of most of the young Frenchmen who had embarked with me, however brilliant their courage might otherwise have been. My own was cool and tenacious, to the great surprise of our allies, who more than once doubted my origin, on seeing how quickly I made myself at home in the forests, and how often my cunning and suspiciousness made me a match for the savages who sometimes harassed our manoeuvres.

In the midst of my labours and frequent changes of place I was fortunate enough to be able to cultivate my mind through my intimacy with a young man of merit whom Providence sent me as a companion and friend. Love of the natural sciences had decided him to join our expedition, and he never failed to show himself a good soldier; but it was easy to see that political sympathy had played only a secondary part in his decision. He had no desire for promotion, no aptitude for strategic studies. His herbarium and his zoological occupations engaged his thoughts much more than the successes of the war and the triumph of liberty. He fought too well, when occasion arose, to ever deserve the reproach of lukewarmness; but up to the eve of a fight and from the morrow he seemed to have forgotten that he was engaged in anything beyond a scientific expedition into the wilds of the New World. His trunk was always full, not of money and valuables, but of natural history specimens; and while we were lying on the grass on the alert for the least noise which might reveal the approach of the enemy, he would be absorbed in the analysis of some plant or insect. He was an admirable young man, as pure, as an angel, as unselfish as a stoic, as patient as a savant, and withal cheerful and affectionate. When we were in danger of being surprised, he could think and talk of nothing but the precious pebbles and the invaluable bits of grass that he had collected and classified; and yet were one of us wounded, he would nurse him with a kindness and zeal that none could surpass.

One day he noticed my gold box as I was putting it in my bosom, and he immediately begged me to let him have it, to keep a few flies' legs and grasshoppers' wings which he would have defended with the last drop of his blood. It needed all the reverence I had for the relics of my love to resist the demands of friendship. All he could obtain from me was permission to hide away a very pretty little plant in my precious box. This plant, which he declared he was the first to discover, was allowed a home by the side of my *fiancee's* ring and note only on condition that it should be called Edmunda sylvestris; to this he consented. He had given the name of Samuel Adams to a beautiful wild apple-tree; he had christened some industrious bee or other Franklin; and nothing pleased him more than to associate some honoured name with his ingenious observations.

The attachment I felt for him was all the more genuine from its being my first friendship with a man of my own age. The pleasure which I derived from this intimacy gave me a new insight into life, and revealed capacities and needs of the soul of which I had hitherto been ignorant. As I could never wholly break away from that love of chivalry which had been implanted in me in early childhood, it pleased me to look upon him as my "brother in arms," and I expressed a wish that he would give me this special title too, to the exclusion of every other intimate friend. He caught at the idea with a gladness of heart that showed me how lively was the sympathy between us. He declared that I was a born naturalist, because I was so fitted for a roving life and rough expeditions. Sometimes he would reproach me with absent-mindedness, and scold me seriously for carelessly stepping upon interesting plants, but he would assert that I was endowed with a sense of method, and that some day I might invent, not a theory of nature, but an excellent system of classification. His prophecy was never fulfilled, but his encouragement aroused a taste for study in me, and prevented my mind from being wholly paralyzed by camp life. To me he was as a messenger from heaven; without him I should perhaps have become, if not the Hamstringer of Roche-Mauprat, at all events the savage of Varenne again. His teachings revived in me the consciousness of intellectual life. He enlarged my ideas and also ennobled my instincts; for, though his marvellous integrity and his modest disposition prevented him from throwing himself into philosophical discussions, he had an innate love of justice, and he judged all questions of sentiment and morality with unerring wisdom. He acquired an ascendency over me which the abbe had never been able to acquire, owing to the attitude of mutual distrust in which we had been placed from the beginning. He revealed to me the wonders of a large part of the physical world, but what he taught me of chiefest value was to learn to know myself, and to ponder over my own impressions. I succeeded in controlling my impulses up to a certain point. I could never subdue my pride and violent temper. A man cannot change the essence of his nature, but he can guide his divers faculties towards a right path; he can almost succeed in turning his faults to account—and this, indeed, is the great secret and the great problem of education.

The conversations with my friend Arthur led me into such a train of thought that from my recollections of Edmee's conduct I came to deduce logically the motives which must have inspired it. I found her noble and generous, especially in those matters which, owing to my distorted vision and false judgment, had caused me most pain. I did not love her the more for this—that would have been impossible—but I succeeded in understanding why I loved her with an unconquerable love in spite of all she had made me suffer. This sacred fire burned in my soul without growing dim for one instant during the whole six years of our separation. In spite of the rich vitality which pulsed through my veins; in spite of the promptings of an external nature full of voluptuousness; in spite of the bad examples and numerous opportunities which tempted mortal weakness in the freedom of a roving, military life, I call God to witness that I preserved my robe of innocence undefiled, and that I never felt the kiss of a woman. Arthur, whose calmer organization was less susceptible to temptation, and who, moreover, was almost entirely engrossed in intellectual labour, did not always practise the same austerity; nay, he frequently advised me not to run the risk of an exceptional life, contrary to the demands of Nature. When I confided to him that a master-passion removed all weaknesses from my path and made a fall impossible, he ceased to reason against what he called my fanaticism (this was a word very much in vogue and applied indiscriminately to almost everything). I observed, indeed, that he had a more profound esteem for me, I may even say a sort of respect which did not express itself in words, but which was revealed by a thousand little signs of compliance and deference.

One day, when he was speaking of the great power exercised by gentleness of manners in alliance with a resolute will, citing both good and bad examples from the history of men, especially the gentleness of the apostles and the hypocrisy of the priests of all religions, it came into my mind to ask him if, with my headstrong nature and hasty temper, I should ever be able to exercise any influence on my fellows. When I used this last word I was, of course, thinking only of Edmee. Arthur replied that the influence which I exercised would be other than that of studied gentleness.

"Your influence," he said, "will be due to your natural goodness of heart. Warmth of soul, ardour and perseverance in affection, these are what are needed in family life, and these qualities make our defects loved even by those who have to suffer from them most. We should endeavour, therefore, to master ourselves out of love for those who love us; but to propose to one's self a system of moderation in the most intimate concerns of love and friendship would, in my opinion, be a childish task, a work of egotism which would kill all affection, in ourselves first, and soon afterwards in the others. I was speaking of studied moderation only in the exercise of authority over the masses. Now, should your ambition ever . . ."

"You believe, then," I said, without listening to the last part of his speech, "that, such as I am, I might make a woman happy and force her to love me, in spite of all my faults and the harm they cause?"

"O lovelorn brain!" he exclaimed. "How difficult it is to distract your thoughts! . . . Well, if you wish to know, Bernard, I will tell you what I think of your love-affair. The person you love so ardently loves you, unless she is incapable of love or quite bereft of judgment."

I assured him that she was as much above all other women as the lion is above the squirrel, the cedar above the hyssop, and with the help of metaphors I succeeded in convincing him. Then he persuaded me to tell him a few details, in order, as he said, that he might judge of my position with regard to Edmee. I opened my heart without reserve, and told him my history from beginning to end. At this time we were on the outskirts of a beautiful forest in the last rays of the setting sun. The park at Sainte-Severe, with its fine lordly oaks which had never known the insult of an axe, came into my thoughts as I gazed on these trees of the wilds, exempt from all human care, towering out above our heads in their might and primitive grace. The glowing horizon reminded me of the evening visits to Patience's hut, and Edmee sitting under the golden vine-leaves, and the notes of the merry parrots brought back to me the warbling of the beautiful exotic birds she used to keep in her room. I wept as I thought of the land of my birth so far away, of the broad ocean between us which had swallowed so many pilgrims in the hour of their return to their native shores. I also thought of the prospects of fortune, of the dangers of war, and for the first time I felt the fear of death; for Arthur, pressing my hand in his, assured me that I was loved, and that in each act of harshness or distrust he found but a new proof of affection.

"My boy," he said, "cannot you see that if she did not want to marry you, she would have found a hundred ways of ridding herself of your pretensions forever? And if she had not felt an inexhaustible affection for you, would she have taken so much trouble, and imposed so many sacrifices upon herself to raise you from the abject condition in which she found you, and make you worthy of her? Well, you are always dreaming of the mighty deeds of the knight-errants of old: cannot you see that you are a noble knight condemned by your lady to rude trials for having failed in the laws of gallantry, for having demanded in an imperious tone the love which ought to be sued for on bended knee?"

He then entered into a detailed examination of my misdeeds, and found that the chastisement was severe but just. Afterwards he discussed the probabilities of the future, and very sensibly advised me to submit until she thought right to pardon me.

"But," I said, "is there no shame in a man ripened, as I am now, by reflection, and roughly tried by war, submitting like a child to the caprices of a woman?"

"No," replied Arthur, "there is no shame in that; and the conduct of this woman is not dictated by caprice. One can win nothing but honour in repairing any evil one has done; and how few men are capable of it! It is only just that offended modesty should claim its rights and its natural independence. You have behaved like Albion; do not be astonished that Edmee behaves like Philadelphia. She will not yield, except on condition of a glorious peace, and she is right."

He wished to know how she had treated me during the two years we had been in America. I showed him the few short letters I had received from her. He was struck by the good sense and perfect integrity which seemed manifested in their lofty tone and manly precision. In them Edmee had made me no promise, nor had she even encouraged me by holding out any direct hopes; but she had displayed a lively desire for my return, and had spoken of the happiness we should all enjoy when, as we sat around the fire, I should while away the evenings at the chateau with accounts of my wonderful adventures; and she had not hesitated to tell me that, together with her father, I was the one object of her solicitude in life. Yet, in spite of this never-failing tenderness, a terrible suspicion harassed me. In these short letters from my cousin, as in those from her father and in the long, florid and affectionate epistles from the Abbe Aubert, they never gave me any news of the events which might be, and ought to be, taking place in the family. Each spoke of his or her own self and never mentioned the others; or at most they only spoke of the chevalier's attacks of the gout. It was as though an agreement had been made between the three that none should talk about the occupations and state of mind of the other two.

"Shed light and ease my mind on this matter if you can," I said to Arthur. "There are moments when I fancy that Edmee must be married, and that they have agreed not to inform me until I return, and what is to prevent this, in fact? Is it probable that she likes me enough to live a life of solitude out of love for me, when this very love, in obedience to the dictation of a cold reason and an austere conscience, can resign itself to seeing my absence indefinitely prolonged with the war? I have duties to perform here, no doubt; honour demands that I should defend my flag until the day of the triumph or the irreparable defeat of the cause I serve; but I feel that Edmee is dearer to me than these empty honours, and that to see her but one hour sooner I would leave my name to the ridicule or the curses of the world."

"This last thought," replied Arthur, with a smile, "is suggested to you by the violence of your passion; but you would not act as you say, even if the opportunity occurred. When we are grappling with a single one of our faculties we fancy the others annihilated; but let some extraneous shock arouse them, and we realize that our soul draws its life from several sources at the same time. You are not insensible to fame, Bernard; and if Edmee invited you to abandon it you would perceive that it was dearer to you than you thought. You have ardent republican convictions, and Edmee herself was the first to inspire you with them. What, then, would you think of her, and, indeed, what sort of woman would she be, if she said to you to-day, 'There is something more important than the religion I preached to you and the gods I revealed; something more august and more sacred, and that is my own good pleasure'? Bernard, your love is full of contradictory desires. Inconsistency, moreover, is the mark of all human loves. Men imagine that a woman can have no separate existence of her own, and that she must always be wrapped up in them; and yet the only woman they love deeply is she whose character seems to raise her above the weakness and indolence of her sex. You see how all the settlers in this country dispose of the beauty of their slaves, but they have no love for them, however beautiful they may be; and if by chance they become genuinely attached to one of them, their first care is to set her free. Until then they do not think that they are dealing with a human being. A spirit of independence, the conception of virtue, a love of duty, all these privileges of lofty souls are essential, therefore, in the woman who is to be one's companion through life; and the more your mistress gives proof of strength and patience, the more you cherish her, in spite of what you may have to suffer. You must learn, then, to distinguish love from desire; desire wishes to break through the very impediments by which it is attracted, and it dies amid the ruins of the virtue it has vanquished; love wishes to live, and in order to do that, it would fain see the object of its worship long defended by that wall of adamant whose strength and splendour mean true worth and true beauty."

In this way would Arthur explain to me the mysterious springs of my passion, and throw the light of his wisdom upon the stormy abyss of my soul. Sometimes he used to add:

"If Heaven had granted me the woman I have now and then dreamed of, I think I should have succeeded in making a noble and generous passion of my love; but science has asked for too much of my time. I have not had leisure to look for my ideal; and if perchance it has crossed my path, I have not been able either to study it or recognise it. You have been fortunate, Bernard, but then, you do not sound the deeps of natural history; one man cannot have everything."

As to my suspicions about Edmee's marriage, he rejected them with contempt as morbid fancies. To him, indeed, Edmee's silence showed an admirable delicacy of feeling and conduct.

"A vain person," he said, "would take care to let you know all the sacrifices she had made on your account, and would enumerate the titles and qualities of the suitors she had refused. Edmee, however, has too noble a soul, too serious a mind, to enter into these futile details. She looks upon your covenant as inviolable, and does not imitate those weak consciences which are always talking of their victories, and making a merit of doing that in which true strength finds no difficulty. She is so faithful by nature that she never imagines that any one can suspect her of being otherwise."

These talks poured healing balm on my wounds. When at last France openly declared herself an ally of America, I received a piece of news from the abbe that entirely set my mind at ease on one point. He wrote to me that I should probably meet an old friend again in the New World; the Count de la Marche had been given command of a regiment, and was setting out for the United States.

"And between ourselves," added the abbe, "it is quite time that he made a position for himself. This young man, though modest and steady, has always been weak enough to yield to the prejudices of noble birth. He has been ashamed of his poverty, and has tried to hide it as one hides a leprosy. The result is that his efforts to prevent others from seeing the progress of his ruin, have now ruined him completely. Society attributes the rupture between Edmee and him to these reverses of fortune; and people even go so far as to say that he was but little in love with her person, and very much with her dowry. I cannot bring myself to credit him with contemptible views; and I can only think that he is suffering those mortifications which arise from a false estimate of the value of the good things of this world. If you happen to meet him, Edmee wishes you to show him some friendship, and to let him know how great an interest she has always taken in him. Your excellent cousin's conduct in this matter, as in all others, has been full of kindness and dignity."

XV

One the eve of M. de la Marche's departure, and after the abbe's letter had been sent, a little incident had happened in Varenne which, when I heard of it in America, caused me considerable surprise and pleasure. Moreover, it is linked in a remarkable manner with the most important events of my life, as you will see later.

Although rather seriously wounded in the unfortunate affair of Savannah, I was actively engaged in Virginia, under General Greene, in collecting the remains of the army commanded by Gates, whom I considered a much greater hero than his more fortunate rival, Washington. We had just learnt of the landing of M. de Ternay's squadron, and the depression which had fallen on us at this period of reverses and distress was beginning to vanish before the prospect of re-enforcements. These, as a fact, were less considerable than we had expected. I was strolling through the woods with Arthur, a short distance from the camp, and we were taking advantage of this short respite to have a talk about other matters than Cornwallis and the infamous Arnold. Long saddened by the sight of the woes of the American nation, by the fear of seeing injustice and cupidity triumphing over the cause of the people, we were seeking relief in a measure of gaiety. When I had an hour's leisure I used to escape from my stern toils to the oasis of my own thoughts in the family at Sainte-Severe. At such a time I was wont to tell my kind friend Arthur some of the comic incidents of my entry into life after leaving Roche-Mauprat. At one time I would give him a description of the costume in which I first appeared; at another I would describe Mademoiselle Leblanc's contempt and loathing for my person, and her recommendation to her friend Saint-Jean never to approach within arms' length of me. As I thought of these amusing individuals, the face of the solemn hidalgo, Marcasse, somehow arose in my memory, and I began to give a faithful and detailed picture of the dress, and bearing, and conversation of this enigmatic personage. Not that Marcasse was actually as comic as he appeared to be in my imagination; but at twenty a man is only a boy, especially when he is a soldier and has just escaped great dangers, and so is filled with careless pride at the conquest of his own life. Arthur would laugh right heartily as he listened to me, declaring that he would give his whole collection of specimens for such a curious animal as I had just described. The pleasure he derived from my childish chatter increased my vivacity, and I do not know whether I should have been able to resist the temptation to exaggerate my uncle's peculiarities, when suddenly at a turn in our path we found ourselves in the presence of a tall man, poorly dressed, and terribly haggard, who was walking towards us with a serious pensive expression, and carrying in his hand a long naked sword, the point of which was peacefully lowered to the ground. This individual bore such a strong resemblance to the one I had just described to Arthur, struck by the parallel, burst into uncontrollable laughter, and moving aside to make way for Marcasse's double, threw himself upon the grass in a convulsive fit of coughing.

For myself, I was far from laughing; for nothing that has a supernatural air about it fails to produce a vivid impression even on the man most accustomed to dangers. With staring eyes and outstretched arms we drew near to each other, myself and he, not the shade of Marcasse, but the venerable person himself, in flesh and blood, of the hidalgo mole-catcher.

Petrified with astonishment when I saw what I had taken for his ghost slowly carry his hand to the corner of his hat and raise it without bending the fraction of an inch, I started back a yard or two; and this movement, which Arthur thought was a joke on my part, only increased his merriment. The weasel-hunter was by no means disconcerted; perhaps in his judicial gravity he was thinking that this was the usual way to greet people on the other side of the ocean.

But Arthur's laughter almost proved infectious when Marcasse said to me with incomparable gravity:

"Monsieur Bernard, I have had the honour of searching for you for a long time."

"For a long time, in truth, my good Marcasse," I replied, as I shook my old friend's hand with delight. "But, tell me by what strange power I have been lucky enough to draw you hither. In the old days you passed for a sorcerer; is it possible that I have become one too without knowing it?"

"I will explain all that, my dear general," answered Marcasse, who was apparently dazzled by my captain's uniform. "If you will allow me to accompany you I will tell you many things—many things!"

On hearing Marcasse repeat his words in a low voice, as if furnishing an echo for himself, a habit which only a minute before I was in the act of imitating, Arthur burst out laughing again. Marcasse turned toward him and after surveying him intently bowed with imperturbable gravity. Arthur, suddenly recovering his serious mood, rose and, with comic dignity, bowed in return almost to the ground.

We returned to the camp together. On the way Marcasse told me his story in that brief style of his, which, as it forced his hearer to ask a thousand wearisome questions, far from simplifying his narrative, made it extraordinarily complicated. It afforded Arthur great amusement; but as you would not derive the same pleasure from listening to an exact reproduction of this interminable dialogue, I will limit myself to telling you how Marcasse had come to leave his country and his friends, in order to give the American cause the help of his sword.

M. de la Marche happened to be setting out for America at the very time when Marcasse came to his castle in Berry for a week, to make his annual round among the beams and joists in the barns. The inmates of the chateau, in their excitement at the count's departure, indulged in wonderful commentaries on that far country, so full of dangers and marvels, from which, according to the village wiseacres, no man ever returned without a vast fortune, and so many gold and silver ingots that he needed ten ships to carry them all. Now, under his icy exterior, Don Marcasse, like some hyperborean volcano, concealed a glowing imagination, a passionate love of the marvellous. Accustomed to live in a state of equilibrium on narrow beams in evidently loftier regions than other men, and not insensible to the glory of astounding the bystanders every day by the calm daring of his acrobatic movements, he let himself be fired by these pictures of Eldorado; and his dreams were the more extravagant because, as usual, he unbosomed himself to no one. M. de la Marche, therefore, was very much surprised when, on the eve of his departure, Marcasse presented himself, and proposed to accompany him to America as his valet. In vain did M. de la Marche remind him that he was very old to abandon his calling and run the risks of a new kind of life. Marcasse displayed so much firmness that in the end he gained his point. Various reasons led M. de la Marche to consent to the strange request. He had resolved to take with him a servant older still than the weasel-hunter, a man who was accompanying him only with great reluctance. But this man enjoyed his entire confidence, a favour which M. de la Marche was very slow to grant, since he was only able to keep up the outward show of a man of quality, and wished to be served faithfully, and with economy and prudence. He knew, however, that Marcasse was scrupulously honest, and even singularly unselfish; for there was something of Don Quixote in the man's soul as well as in his appearance. He had found in some ruins a sort of treasure-trove, that is to say, an earthenware jar containing a sum of about ten thousand francs in old gold and silver coins; and not only had he handed it over to the owner of the ruins, whom he might easily have deceived, but further he had refused to accept any reward, declaring emphatically in his abbreviated jargon, "honesty would die selling itself."

Marcasse's economy, his discretion, his punctuality, seemed likely to make him a valuable man, if he could be trained to put these qualities at the service of others. The one thing to be feared was that he might not be able to accustom himself to his loss of independence. However, M. de la Marche thought that, before M. de Ternay's squadron sailed, he would have time to test his new squire sufficiently.

On his side, Marcasse felt many regrets at taking leave of his friends and home; for if he had "friends everywhere and everywhere a native place," as he said, in allusion to his wandering life, he still had a very marked preference for Varenne; and of all his castles (for he was accustomed to call every place he stopped at "his"), the chateau of Sainte-Severe was the only one which he arrived at with pleasure and left with regret. One day, when he had missed his footing on the roof and had rather a serious fall, Edmee, then still a child, had won his heart by the tears she had shed over this accident, and the artless attentions she had shown him. And ever since Patience had come to dwell on the edge of the park, Marcasse had felt still more attracted toward Sainte-Severe; for in Patience Marcasse had found his Orestes. Marcasse did not always understand Patience; but

Patience was the only man who thoroughly understood Marcasse, and who knew how much chivalrous honesty and noble courage lay hidden beneath that odd exterior. Humbly bowing to the hermit's intellectual superiority, the weasel-hunter would stop respectfully whenever the poetic frenzy took possession of Patience and made his words unintelligible. At such a time Marcasse would refrain from questions and ill-timed remarks with touching gentleness; would lower his eyes, and nodding his head from time to time as if he understood and approved, would, at least, afford his friend the innocent pleasure of being listened to without contradiction.

Marcasse, however, had understood enough to make him embrace republican ideas and share in those romantic hopes of universal levelling and a return to the golden age, which had been so ardently fostered by old Patience. Having frequently heard his friend say that these doctrines were to be cultivated with prudence (a precept, however, to which Patience gave but little heed himself), the hidalgo, inclined to reticence both by habit and inclination, never spoke of his philosophy; but he proved himself a more efficacious propagandist by carrying about from castle to cottage, and from house to farm, those little cheap editions of *La Science du Bonhomme Richard*, and other small treatises on popular patriotism, which, according to the Jesuits, a secret society of Voltairian philosophers, devoted to the diabolical practice of freemasonry, circulated gratis among the lower classes.

Thus in Marcasse's sudden resolution there was as much revolutionary enthusiasm as love of adventure. For a long time the dormouse and polecat had seemed to him overfeeble enemies for his restless valour, even as the granary floor seemed to afford too narrow a field. Every day he read the papers of the previous day in the servants' hall of the houses he visited; and it appeared to him that this war in America, which was hailed as the awakening of the spirit of justice and liberty in the New World, ought to produce a revolution in France. It is true he had a very literal notion of the way in which ideas were to cross the seas and take possession of the minds of our continent. In his dreams he used to see an army of victorious Americans disembarking from numberless ships, and bringing the olive branch of peace and the horn of plenty to the French nation. In these same dreams he beheld himself at the head of a legion of heroes returning to Varenne as a warrior, a legislator, a rival of Washington, suppressing abuses, cutting down enormous fortunes, assigning to each proletarian a suitable share, and, in the midst of his far-reaching and vigorous measures, protecting the good and fair-dealing nobles, and assuring an honourable existence to them. Needless to say, the distress inseparable from all great political crises never entered into Marcasse's mind, and not a single drop of blood sullied the romantic picture which Patience had unrolled before his eyes.

From these sublime hopes to the role of valet to M. de la Marche was a far cry; but Marcasse could reach his goal by no other way. The ranks of the army corps destined for America had long been filled, and it was only in the character of a passenger attached to the expedition that he could take his place on one of the merchant ships that followed the expedition. He had questioned the abbe on these points without revealing his plans. His departure quite staggered all the inhabitants of Varenne.

No sooner had he set foot on the shores of the States than he felt an irresistible inclination to take his big hat and his big sword and go off all alone through the woods, as he had been accustomed to do in his own country. His conscience, however, prevented him from quitting his master after having pledged himself to serve him. He had calculated that fortune would help him, and fortune did. The war proved much more bloody and vigorous than had been expected, and M. de la Marche feared, though wrongly, that he might be impeded by the poor health of his gaunt squire. Having a suspicion, too, of the man's desire for liberty, he offered him a sum of money and some letters of recommendation, to enable him to join the American troops as a volunteer. Marcasse, knowing the state of his master's fortune, refused the money, and only accepted the letters; and then set off with as light a step as the nimblest weasels that he had ever killed.

His intention was to make for Philadelphia; but, through a chance occurrence which I need not relate, he learnt that I was in the South, and, rightly calculating that he would obtain both advice and help from me, he had set out to find me, alone, on foot, through unknown countries almost uninhabited and often full of danger of all kinds. His clothes alone had suffered; his yellow face had not changed its tint, and he was no more surprised at his latest exploit than if he had merely covered the distance from Sainte-Severe to Gazeau Tower.

The only fresh habit that I noticed in him, was that he would turn round from time to time, and look behind him, as if he had felt inclined to call some one; then immediately after he would smile and sigh almost at the same instant. I could not resist a desire to ask him the cause of his uneasiness.

"Alas!" he replied, "habit can't get rid of; a poor dog! good dog! Always saying, 'Here Blaireau! Blaireau, here!'"

"I understand," I said, "Blaireau is dead, and you cannot accustom yourself to the idea that you will never see him at your heels again."

"Dead!" he exclaimed, with an expression of horror. "No, thank God! Friend Patience, great friend! Blaireau quite well off, but sad like his master; his master alone!"

"If Blaireau is with Patience," said Arthur, "he is well off, as you say; for Patience wants nothing. Patience will love him because he loves his master, and you are certain to see your good friend and faithful dog again."

Marcasse turned his eyes upon the individual who seemed to be so well acquainted with his life; but, feeling sure that he had never seen him before, he acted as he was wont to do when he did not understand; he raised his hat and bowed respectfully.

On my immediate recommendation Marcasse was enrolled in my company and, a little while afterward, was made a sergeant. The worthy man went through the whole campaign with me, and went through it bravely; and in 1782, when I rejoined Rochambeau's army to fight under the French flag, he followed me, as he was anxious to share my lot until the end. In the early days I looked upon him rather as an amusement than a companion; but his excellent conduct and calm fearlessness soon won for him the esteem of all, and I had reason to be proud of my *protege*. Arthur also conceived a great friendship for him; and, when off duty, he accompanied us in all our walks, carrying the naturalist's box and running the snakes through with his sword.

But when I tried to make him speak of my cousin, he by no means satisfied me. Whether he did not understand how eager I felt to learn all the details of the life she was leading far away from me, or whether in this matter he was obeying one of those inviolable laws which governed his conscience, I could never obtain from him any clear solution of the doubts which harassed me. Quite early he told me that there was no question of her marriage with any one; but, accustomed though I was to his vague manner of expressing himself, I imagined he seemed embarrassed in making this assertion and had the air of a man who had sworn to keep a secret. Honour forbade me to insist to such an extent as to let him see my hopes, and so there always remained between us a painful point which I tried to avoid touching upon, but to which, in spite of myself, I was continually returning. As long as Arthur was near me, I retained my reason, and interpreted Edmee's letters in the most loyal way; but when I was unfortunate enough to be separated from him, my sufferings revived, and my stay in America became more irksome to me every day.

Our separation took place when I left the American army to fight under the command of the French general. Arthur was an American; and, moreover, he was only waiting for the end of the war to retire from the service, and settle in Boston with Dr. Cooper, who loved him as his son, and who had undertaken to get him appointed principal librarian to the library of the Philadelphia Society. This was all the reward Arthur desired for his labours.

The events which filled my last years in America belong to history. It was with a truly personal delight that I hailed the peace which proclaimed the United States a free nation. I had begun to chafe at my long absence from France; my passion had been growing ever greater, and left no room for the intoxication of military glory. Before my departure I went to take leave of Arthur. Then I sailed with the worthy Marcasse, divided between sorrow at parting from my only friend, and joy at the prospect of once more seeing my only love. The squadron to which my ship belonged experienced many vicissitudes during the passage, and several times I gave up all hope of ever kneeling before Edmee under the great oaks of Sainte-Severe. At last, after a final storm off the coast of France, I set foot on the shores of Brittany, and fell into the arms of my poor sergeant, who had borne our common misfortunes, if not with greater physical courage, at least with a calmer spirit, and we mingled our tears.

XVI

We set out from Brest without sending any letter to announce our coming.

When we arrived near Varenne we alighted from the post-chaise and, ordering the driver to proceed by the longest road to Saint-Severe, took a short cut through the woods. As soon as I saw the trees in the park raising their venerable heads above the copses like a solemn phalanx of druids in the middle of a prostrate multitude, my heart began to beat so violently that I was forced to stop.

"Well," said Marcasse, turning round with an almost stern expression, as if he would have reproached me for my weakness.

But a moment later I saw that his own face, too, was betraying unexpected emotion. A plaintive whining and a bushy tail brushing against his legs had made him start. He uttered a loud cry on seeing Blaireau. The poor animal had scented his master from afar, and had rushed forward with all the speed of his first youth to roll at his feet. For a moment we thought he was going to die there, for he remained motionless and convulsed, as it were, under Marcasse's caressing hand; then suddenly he sprang up, as if struck with an idea worthy of a man, and set off with the speed of lightning in the direction of Patience's hut.

"Yes, go and tell my friend, good dog!" exclaimed Marcasse; "a better friend than you would be more than man."

He turned towards me, and I saw two big tears trickling down the cheeks of the impassive hidalgo.

We hastened our steps till we reached the hut. It had undergone striking improvements; a pretty rustic garden, inclosed by a quickset hedge with a bank of stones behind, extended round the little house. The approach to this was no longer a rough little path, but a handsome walk, on either side of which splendid vegetables stretched out in regular rows, like an army in marching order. The van was composed of a battalion of cabbages; carrots and lettuces formed the main body; and along the hedge some modest sorrel brought up the rear. Beautiful apple-trees, already well grown, spread their verdant shade above these plants; while pear-trees, alternately standards and espaliers, with borders of thyme and sage kissing the feet of sunflowers and gilliflowers, convicted Patience of a strange return to ideas of social order, and even to a taste for luxuries.

The change was so remarkable that I thought I should no longer find Patience in the cottage. A strange feeling of uneasiness began to come over me; my fear almost turned into certainty when I saw two young men from the village occupied in trimming the espaliers. Our passage had lasted more than four months, and it must have been quite six months since we had had any news of the hermit. Marcasse, however, seemed to feel no fear; Blaireau had told him plainly that Patience was alive, and the footmarks of the little dog, freshly printed in the sand of the walk, showed the direction in which he had gone. Notwithstanding, I was so afraid of seeing a cloud come over the joy of this day, that I did not dare to question the gardeners about Patience. Silently I followed the hidalgo, whose eyes grew full of tears as they gazed upon this new Eden, and whose prudent mouth let no sound escape save the word "change," which he repeated several times.

At last I grew impatient; the walk seemed interminable, though very short in reality, and I began to run, my heart beating wildly.

"Perhaps Edmee," I said to myself, "is here!"

However, she was not there, and I could only hear the voice of the hermit saying:

"Now, then! What is the matter? Has the poor dog gone mad? Down, Blaireau! You would never have worried your master in this way. This is what comes of being too kind!"

"Blaireau is not mad!" I exclaimed, as I entered. "Have you grown deaf to the approach of a friend, Master Patience?"

Patience, who was in the act of counting a pile of money, let it fall on the table and came towards me with the old cordiality. I embraced him heartily; he was surprised and touched at my joy. Then he examined me from head to foot, and seemed to be wondering at the change in my appearance, when Marcasse arrived at the door.

Then a sublime expression came over Patience's face, and lifting his strong arms to heaven, he exclaimed:

"The words of the canticle! Now let me depart in peace; for mine eyes have seen him I yearned for."

The hidalgo said nothing; he raised his hat as usual; then sitting down he turned pale and shut his eyes. His dog jumped up on his knees and displayed his affection by attempts at little cries which changed into a series of sneezes (you remember that he was born dumb). Trembling with old age and delight, he stretched out his pointed nose towards the long nose of his master; but his master did not respond with the customary "Down, Blaireau!"

Marcasse had fainted.

This loving soul, no more able than Blaireau to express itself in words, had sunk beneath the weight of his own happiness. Patience ran and fetched him a large mug of wine of the district, in its second year—that is to say, the oldest and best possible. He made him swallow a few drops; its strength revived him. The hidalgo excused his weakness on the score of fatigue and the heat. He would not or could not assign it to its real sense. There are souls who die out, after burning with unsurpassable moral beauty and grandeur, without ever having found a way, and even without ever having felt the need, of revealing themselves to others.

When Patience, who was as demonstrative as his friend was the contrary, had recovered from his first transports, he turned to me and said:

"Now, my young officer, I see that you have no wish to remain here long. Let us make haste, then, to the place you are burning to reach. There is some one who will be much surprised and much delighted, you may take my word."

We entered the park, and while crossing it, Patience explained the change which had come over his habitation and his life.

"For myself," he said to me, "you see that I have not changed. The same appearance, the same ways; and if I offered you some wine just now, that does not prevent me from drinking water myself. But I have money, and land, and workmen—yes, I have. Well, all this is in spite of myself, as you will see. Some three years ago Mademoiselle Edmee spoke of the difficulty she had in bestowing alms so as to do real good. The abbe was as unskilful as herself. People would impose on them every day and use their money for bad ends; whereas proud and hard-working day-labourers might be in a state of real distress without any one being able to discover the fact. She was afraid that if she inquired into their wants they might take it as an insult; and when worthless fellows appealed to her she preferred being their dupe to erring against charity. In this manner she used to give away a great deal of money and do very little good. I then made her understand how money was the thing that was the least necessary to the necessitous. I explained that men were really unfortunate, not when they were unable to dress better than their fellows, or go to the tavern on Sundays, or display at high-mass a spotlessly white stocking with a red garter above the knee, or talk about 'My mare, my cow, my vine, my barn, etc.,' but rather when they were afflicted with poor health and a bad season, when they could not protect themselves against the cold, and heat and sickness, against the pangs of hunger and thirst. I told her, then, not to judge of the strength and health of peasants by myself, but to go in person and inquire into their illnesses and their wants.

"These folk are not philosophers," I said; "they have their little vanities, they are fond of finery, spend the little they earn on cutting a figure, and have not foresight enough to deprive themselves of a passing pleasure in order to lay by something against a day of real need. In short, they do not know how to use their money; they tell you they are in debt, and, though that may be true, it is not true that they will use the money you give them to pay what they owe. They take no thought of the morrow; they will agree to as high a rate of interest as may be asked, and with your money they will buy a hemp-field or a set of furniture so as to astonish their neighbours and make them jealous. Meanwhile their debts go on increasing year by year, and in the end they have to sell their hemp-field and their furniture, because the creditor, who is always one of themselves, calls for repayment or for more interest than they can furnish. Everything goes; the principal takes all their capital, just as the interest has taken all their income. Then you grow old and can work no longer; your children abandon you, because you have brought them up badly, and because they have the same passions and the same vanities as yourself. All you can do is to take a wallet and go from door to door to beg your bread, because you are used to bread and would die if you had to live on roots like the sorcerer Patience, that outcast of Nature, whom everybody hates and despises because he has not become a beggar.

"The beggar, moreover, is hardly worse off than the day-labourer; probably he is better off. He is no longer troubled with pride, whether estimable or foolish; he has no longer to suffer. The folks in his part of the country are good to him; there is not a beggar that wants for a bed or supper as he goes his round. The peasants load him with bits of bread, to such an extent that he has enough to feed both poultry and pigs in the little hovel where he has left a child and an old mother to look after his animals. Every week he returns there and spends two or three days, doing nothing except counting the pennies that have been given him. These poor coins often serve to satisfy the superfluous wants which idleness breeds. A peasant rarely takes snuff; many beggars cannot do without it; they ask for it more eagerly than for bread. So the beggar is no more to be pitied than the labourer; but he is corrupt and debauched, when he is not a scoundrel and a brute, which, in truth, is seldom enough.

"'This, then, is what ought to be done,' I said to Edmee; 'and the abbe tells me that this is also the idea of your philosophers. You who are always ready to help the unfortunate, should give without consulting the special fancies of the man who asks, but only after ascertaining his real wants.'

"Edmee objected that it would be impossible for her to obtain the necessary information; that she would have to give her whole time to it, and neglect the chevalier, who is growing old and can no longer read anything without his daughter's eyes and head. The abbe was too fond of improving his mind from the writings of the wise to have time for anything else.

"'That is what comes of all this study of virtue!' I said to her; 'it makes a man forget to be virtuous.'

"'You are quite right,' answered Edmee; 'but what is to be done?'

"I promised to think it over; and this is how I went to work. Instead of taking my walks as usual in the direction of the woods, I paid a visit every day to the small holdings. It cost me a great effort; I like to be alone; and everywhere I had shunned my fellow-men for so many years that I had lost touch with them. However, this was a duty and I did it. I went to various houses, and by way of conversation, first of all over hedges, and then inside the houses themselves, I made inquiries as to those points which I wanted to learn. At first they gave me a welcome such as they would give to a lost dog in time of drought; and with a vexation I could scarce conceal I noticed the hatred and distrust on all their faces. Though I had not cared to live among other men, I still had an affection for them; I knew that they were unfortunate rather than vicious; I had spent all my time in lamenting their woes and railing against those that caused them; and when for the first time I saw a possibility of doing something for some of them, these very men shut their doors the very moment they caught sight of me in the distance, and their children (those pretty children that I love so much!) would hide themselves in ditches so as to escape the fever which, it was said, I could give with a glance. However, as Edmee's friendship for me was well known, they did not dare to repulse me openly, and I succeeded in getting the information we wanted. Whenever I told her of any distress she at once supplied a remedy. One house was full of cracks; and while the daughter was wearing an apron of cotton-cloth at four francs an ell, the rain was falling on the grandmother's bed and the little children's cradles. The roof and walls were repaired; we supplied the materials and paid the workmen; but no more money for gaudy aprons. In another case, an old woman had been reduced to beggary because she had listened too well to her heart, and given all she had to her children, who had turned her out of doors, or made her life so unbearable that she preferred to be a tramp. We took up the old woman's cause, and threatened that we would bring the matter before the courts at our own expense. Thus we obtained for her a pension, to which we added when it was not sufficient. We induced several old persons who were in a similar position to combine and live together under the same roof. We chose one as head, and gave him a little capital, and as he was an industrious and methodical man, he turned it to such profit that his children came and made their peace with him, and asked to be allowed to help in his establishment.

"We did many other things besides; I need not give you details, as you will see them yourself. I say 'we,' because, though I did not wish to be concerned in anything beyond what I had already done, I was gradually drawn on and obliged to do more and more, to concern myself with many things, and finally with everything. In short, it is I who make the investigations, superintend the works, and conduct all negotiations. Mademoiselle Edmee wished me to keep a sum of money by me, so that I might dispose of it without consulting her first. This I have never allowed myself to do; and, moreover, she has never once opposed any of my ideas. But all this, you know, has meant much work and many worries. Ever since the people realized that I was a little Turgot they have grovelled before me, and that has pained me not a little. And so I have various friends that I don't care for, and various enemies that I could well do without. The sham poor owe me a grudge because I do not let myself be duped by them; and there are perverse and worthless people who think one is always doing too much for others, and never enough for them. With all this bustle and all these bickerings, I can no longer take my walk during the night, and my sleep during the day. I am now Monsieur Patience, and no longer the sorcerer of Gazeau Tower; but alas! I am a hermit no more; and, believe me, I would wish with all my heart that I could have been born selfish, so that I might throw off my harness, and return to my savage life and my liberty."

When Patience had given us this account of his work we complimented him on it; but we ventured to express a doubt about his pretended self-sacrifice; this magnificent garden seemed to indicate a compromise with "those superfluous necessities," the use of which by others he had always deplored.

"That?" he said, waving his arm in the direction of his inclosure. "That does not concern me; they made it against my wishes; but, as they were worthy folk and my refusal would have grieved them, I was obliged to allow it. You must know that, if I have stirred ingratitude in many hearts, I have also made a few happy ones grateful. So, two or three families to whom I had done some service, tried all possible means to give me pleasure in return; and, as I refused everything, they thought they would give me a surprise. Once I had to pay a visit to Berthenoux for several days, on some confidential business which had been entrusted to me; for people have come to imagine me a very clever man, so easy is it to pass from one extreme to another. On my return I found this garden, marked out, planted and inclosed as you see it. In vain did I get angry, and explain that I did not want to work, that I was too old, and that the pleasure of eating a little more fruit was not worth the trouble that this garden was going to cost me; they finished it without heeding what I said, and declared that I need not trouble in the least, because they would undertake to cultivate it for me. And, indeed, for the last two years the good folk have not failed to come, now one and now another, and give such time in each season as was necessary to keep it in perfect order. Besides, though I have altered nothing in my own ways of living, the produce of this garden has been very useful; during the winter I was able to feed several poor people with my vegetables; while my fruit has served to win the affection of the little children, who no longer cry out 'wolf' when they see me, but have grown bold enough to come and kiss the sorcerer. Other people have forced me to accept presents of wine, and now and then of white bread, and cheeses of cow's milk. All these things, however, only enable me to be polite to the village elders when they come and report the deserving cases of the place, so that I may make them known at the castle. These honours have not turned my head, as you see; nay, more, I may say that when I have done about all that I have to do, I shall leave the cares of greatness behind me, and return to my philosopher's life, perhaps to Gazeau Tower—who knows?"

We were now at the end of our walk. As I set foot on the steps of the chateau, I was suddenly filled with a feeling of devoutness; I clasped my hands and called upon Heaven in a sort of terror. A vague, indefinable fear arose in me; I imagined all manner of things that might hinder my happiness. I hesitated to cross the threshold of the house; then I rushed forward. A mist came over my eyes, a buzzing filled my ears. I met Saint-Jean, who, not recognising me, gave a loud cry and threw himself in my path to prevent me from entering without being announced. I pushed him aside, and he sank down astounded on one of the hall chairs while I hastened to the door of the drawing-room. But, just as I was about to throw it open, I was seized with a new fear and checked myself; then I opened it so timidly that Edmee, who was occupied at some embroidery on a frame, did not raise her eyes, thinking that in this slight noise she recognised the respectful Saint-Jean. The chevalier was asleep and did not wake. This old man, tall and thin like all the Mauprats, was sitting with his head sunk on his breast; and his pale, wrinkled face, which seemed already wrapped in the torpor of the grave, resembled one of those angular heads in carved oak which adorned the back of his big arm-chair. His feet were stretched out in front of a fire of dried vine-branches, although the sun was warm and a bright ray was falling on his white head and making it shine like silver. And how could I describe to you my feelings on beholding Edmee?

She was bending over her tapestry and glancing from time to time at her father to notice his slightest movements. But what patience and resignation were revealed in her whole attitude! Edmee was not fond of needlework; her mind was too vigorous to attach much importance to the effect of one shade by the side of another shade, and to the regularity of one stitch laid against another stitch. Besides, the blood flowed swiftly in her veins, and when her mind was not absorbed in intellectual work she needed exercise in the open air. But ever since her father, a prey to the infirmities of old age, had been almost unable to leave his arm-chair, she had refused to leave him for a single moment; and, since she could not always be reading and working her mind, she had felt the necessity of taking up some of those feminine occupations which, as she said, "are the amusements of captivity." She had conquered her nature then in truly heroic fashion. In one of those secret struggles which often take place under our eyes without our suspecting the issue involved, she had done more than subdue her nature, she had even changed the circulation of her blood. I found her thinner; and her complexion had lost that first freshness of youth which, like the bloom that the breath of morning spreads over fruit, disappears at the slightest shock from without, although it may have been respected by the heat of the sun. Yet in this premature paleness and in this somewhat unhealthy thinness there seemed to be an indefinable charm; her eyes, more sunken, but inscrutable as ever, showed less pride and more melancholy than of old; her mouth had become more mobile, and her smile was more delicate and less contemptuous. When she spoke to me, I seemed to behold two persons in her, the old and the new; and I found that, so far from having lost her beauty, she had attained ideal perfection. Still, I remember several persons at that time used to declare that she had "changed very much," which with them meant that she had greatly deteriorated. Beauty, however, is like a temple in which the profane see naught but the external magnificence. The divine mystery of the artist's thought reveals itself only to profound sympathy, and the inspiration in each detail of the sublime work remains unseen by the eyes of the vulgar. One of your modern authors, I fancy, has said this in other words and much better. As for myself, at no moment in her life did I find Edmee less beautiful than at any other. Even in the hours of suffering, when beauty in its material sense seems obliterated, hers but assumed a divine form in my eyes, and in her face I beheld the splendour of a new moral beauty. However, I am but indifferently endowed with artistic feeling, and had I been a painter, I could not have created more than a single type, that which filled my whole soul; for in the course of my long life only one woman has seemed to me really beautiful; and that woman was Edmee.

For a few seconds I stood looking at her, so touchingly pale, sad yet calm, a living image of filial piety, of power in thrall to affection. Then I rushed forward and fell at her feet without being able to say a word. She uttered no cry, no exclamation of surprise, but took my head in her two arms and held it for some time pressed to her bosom. In this strong pressure, in this silent joy I recognised the blood of my race, I felt the touch of a sister. The good chevalier, who had waked with a start, stared at us in astonishment, his body bent forward and his elbow resting on his knee; then he said:

"Well, well! What is the meaning of this?"

He could not see my face, hidden as it was in Edmee's breast. She pushed me towards him; and the old man clasped me in his feeble arms with a burst of generous affection that gave him back for a moment the vigour of youth.

I leave you to imagine the questions with which I was overwhelmed, and the attentions that were lavished on me. Edmee was a veritable mother to me. Her unaffected kindness and confidence savoured so much of heaven that throughout the day I could not think of her otherwise than if I had really been her son.

I was very much touched at the pleasure they took in preparing a big surprise for the abbe; I saw in this a sure proof of the delight he would feel at my return. They made me hide under Edmee's frame, and covered me with the large green cloth that was generally thrown over her work. The abbe sat down quite close to me, and I gave a shout and seized him by the legs. This was a little practical joke that I used to play on him in the old days. When, throwing aside the frame, and sending the balls of wool rolling over the floor, I came out from my hiding-place, the expression of terror and delight on his face was most quaint.

But I will spare you all these family scenes to which my memory goes back too readily.

XVII

An immense change had taken place in me during the course of six years. I had become a man very much like other men; my instincts had managed to bring themselves into harmony with my affections, my intuitions with my reason. This social education had been carried on quite naturally; all I had to do was to accept the lessons of experience and the counsels of friendship. I was far from being a learned man; but I had developed a power of acquiring solid learning very rapidly. My notions of things in general were as clear as could be obtained at that time. Since then I know that real progress has been made in human knowledge; I have watched it from afar and have never thought of denying it. And as I notice that not all men of my age show themselves as reasonable, it pleases me to think that I was put on a fairly right road early in life, since I have never stopped in the blind alley of errors and prejudices.

The progress I had made intellectually seemed to satisfy Edmee.

"I am not astonished at it," she said. "I could see it in your letters; but I rejoice at it with a mother's pride."

My good uncle was no longer strong enough to engage in the old stormy discussions; and I really think that if he had retained his strength he would have been somewhat grieved to find that I was no longer the indefatigable opponent who had formerly irritated him so persistently. He even made a few attempts at contradiction to test me; but at this time I should have considered it a crime to have gratified him. He showed a little temper at this, and seemed to think that I treated him too much as an old man. To console him I turned the conversation to the history of the past, to the years through which he himself had lived, and questioned him on many points wherein his experience served him better than my knowledge. In this way I obtained many healthy notions for the guidance of my own conduct, and at the same time I fully satisfied his legitimate *amour propre*. He now conceived a friendship for me from genuine sympathy, just as formerly he had adopted me from natural generosity and family pride. He did not disguise from me that his great desire, before falling into the sleep that knows no waking, was to see me married to Edmee; and when I told him that this was the one thought of my life, the one wish of my soul, he said:

"I know, I know. Everything depends on her, and I think she can no longer have any reasons for hesitation. . . . At all events," he added, after a moment's silence and with a touch of peevishness, "I cannot see any that she could allege at present."

XVII

From these words, the first he had ever uttered on the subject which most interested me, I concluded that he himself had long been favourable to my suit, and that the obstacle, if one still existed, lay with Edmee. My uncle's last remark implied a doubt which I dared not try to clear up, and which caused me great uneasiness. Edmee's sensitive pride inspired me with such awe, her unspeakable goodness filled me with such respect that I dared not ask her point-blank to decide my fate. I made up my mind to act as if I entertained no other hope than that she would always let me be her brother and friend.

An event which long remained inexplicable afforded some distraction to my thoughts for a few days. At first I had refused to go and take possession of Roche-Mauprat.

"You really must," my uncle had said, "go and see the improvements I have made in your property, the lands which have been brought under cultivation, the cattle that I have put on each of your metayer-farms. Now is the time for you to see how your affairs stand, and show your tenants that you take an interest in their work. Otherwise, on my death, everything will go from bad to worse and you will be obliged to let it, which may bring you in a larger income, perhaps, but will diminish the value of the property. I am too old now to go and manage your estate. For the last two years I have been unable to leave off this miserable dressing-gown; the abbe does not understand anything about it; Edmee has an excellent head; but she cannot bring herself to go to that place; she says she would be too much afraid, which is mere childishness."

"I know that I ought to display more courage," I replied; "and yet, uncle, what you are asking me to do is for me the most difficult thing in the world. I have not set foot on that accursed soil since the day I left it, bearing Edmee away from her captors. It is as if you were driving me out of heaven to send me on a visit to hell."

The chevalier shrugged his shoulders; the abbe implored me to bring myself to do as he wished, as the reluctance I showed was a veritable disappointment to my uncle. I consented, and with a determination to conquer myself, I took leave of Edmee for two days. The abbe wanted to accompany me, to drive away the gloomy thoughts which would no doubt besiege me; but I had scruples about taking him from Edmee even for this short time; I knew how necessary he was to her. Tied as she was to the chevalier's arm-chair, her life was so serious, so retired, that the least change was acutely felt. Each year had increased her isolation, and it had become almost complete since the chevalier's failing health had driven from his table those happy children of wine, songs, and witticisms. He had been a great sportsman; and Saint Hubert's Day, which fell on his birthday, had formerly brought all the nobility of the province to his house. Year after year the courtyards had resounded with the howls of the pack; year after year the stables had held their two long rows of spirited horses in their glistening stalls; year after year the sound of the horn had echoed through the great woods around, or sent out its blast under the windows of the big hall at each toast of the brilliant company. But those glorious days had long disappeared; the chevalier had given up hunting; and the hope of obtaining his daughter's hand no longer brought round his arm-chair young men, who were bored by his old age, his attacks of gout, and the stories which he would repeat in the evening without remembering that he had already told them in the morning. Edmee's obstinate refusals and the dismissal of M. de la Marche had caused great astonishment, and given rise to many conjectures among the curious. One young man who was in love with her, and had been rejected like the rest, was impelled by a stupid and cowardly conceit to avenge himself on the only woman of his own class who, according to him, had dared to repulse him. Having discovered that Edmee had been carried off by the Hamstringers, he spread a report that she had spent a night of wild debauch at Roche-Mauprat. At best, he only deigned to concede that she had yielded only to violence. Edmee commanded too much respect and esteem to be accused of having shown complaisance to the brigands; but she soon passed for having been a victim of their brutality. Marked with an indelible stain, she was no longer sought in marriage by any one. My absence only served to confirm this opinion. I had saved her from death, it was said, but not from shame, and it was impossible for me to make her my wife; I was in love with her, and had fled lest I should yield to the temptation to marry her. All this seemed so probable that it would have been difficult to make the public accept the true version. They were the less ready to accept it from the fact that Edmee had been unwilling to put an end to the evil reports by giving her hand to a man she could not love. Such, then, were the causes of her isolation; it was not until later that I fully understood them. But I could see the austerity of the chevalier's home and Edmee's melancholy calm, and I was afraid to drop even a dry leaf in the sleeping waters. Thus I begged the abbe to remain with them until my return. I took no one with me except my faithful sergeant Marcasse. Edmee had declared that he must not leave me, and had arranged that henceforth he was to share Patience's elegant hut and administrative life.

I arrived at Roche-Mauprat one foggy evening in the early days of autumn; the sun was hidden, and all Nature was wrapped in silence and mist. The plains were deserted; the air alone seemed alive with the noise of great flocks of birds of passage; cranes were drawing their gigantic triangles across the sky, and storks at an immeasurable height were filling the clouds with mournful cries, which fell upon the saddened country like the dirge of parting summer. For the first time in the year I felt a chilliness in the air. I think that all men are filled with an involuntary sadness at the approach of the inclement season. In the first hoar-frosts there is something which bids man remember the approaching dissolution of his own being.

My companion and I had traversed woods and heaths without saying a single word; we had made a long *detour* to avoid Gazeau Tower, which I felt I could not bear to look upon again. The sun was sinking in shrouds of gray when we passed the portcullis at Roche-Mauprat. This portcullis was broken; the drawbridge was never raised, and the only things that crossed it now were peaceful flocks and their careless shepherds. The fosses were half-filled, and the bluish osiers were already spreading out their flexible branches over the shallow waters; nettles were growing at the foot of the crumbling towers, and the traces of the fire seemed still fresh upon the walls. The farm buildings had all been repaired; and the court, full of cattle and poultry and sheep-dogs and agricultural implements, contrasted strangely with the gloomy inclosure in which I still seemed to see the red flames of the besiegers shooting up, and the black blood of the Mauprats flowing.

I was received with the quiet and somewhat chilly hospitality of the peasants of Berry. They did not lay themselves out to please me, but they let me want for nothing. Quarters were found for me in the only one of the old wings which had not been damaged in the siege, or subsequently abandoned to the ravages of time. The massive architecture of the body of the building dated from the tenth century; the door was smaller than the windows, and the windows themselves gave so little light that we had to take candles to find our way, although the sun had hardly set. The building had been restored provisionally to serve as an occasional lodging for the new seigneur or his stewards. My Uncle Hubert had often been there to see to my interests so long as his strength had allowed him; and they showed me to the room which he had reserved for himself, and which had therefore been known as the master's room. The best things that had been saved from the old furniture had been placed there; and, as it was cold and damp, in spite of all the trouble they had taken to make it habitable, the tenant's servant preceded me with a firebrand in one hand and a fagot in the other.

Blinded by the smoke which she scattered round me in clouds, and deceived by the new entrance which they had made in another part of the courtyard, and by certain corridors which they had walled up to save the trouble of looking after them, I reached the room without recognising anything; indeed, I could not have said in what part of the old buildings I was, to such an extent had the new appearance of the courtyard upset my recollections, and so little had my mind in its gloom and agitation been impressed by surrounding objects.

While the servant was lighting the fire, I threw myself into a chair, and, burying my head in my hands, fell into a melancholy train of thought. My position, however, was not without a certain charm; for the past naturally appears in an embellished or softened form to the minds of young men, those presumptuous masters of the future. When, by dint of blowing the brand, the servant had filled the room with dense smoke, she went off to fetch some embers and left me alone. Marcasse had remained in the stable to attend to our horses. Blaireau had followed me; lying down by the hearth, he glanced at me from time to time with a dissatisfied air, as if to ask me the reason of such wretched lodging and such a poor fire.

Suddenly, as I cast my eyes round the room, old memories seemed to awaken in me. The fire, after making the green wood hiss, sent a flame up the chimney, and the whole room was illumined with a bright though unsteady light, which gave all the objects a weird, ambiguous appearance. Blaireau rose, turned his back to the fire and sat down between my legs, as if he thought that something strange and unexpected was going to happen.

I then realized that this place was none other than my grandfather Tristan's bed-room, afterward occupied for several years by his eldest son, the detestable John, my cruelest oppressor, the most crafty and cowardly of the Hamstringers. I was filled with a sense of terror and disgust on recognising the furniture, even the very bed with twisted posts on which my grandfather had given up his blackened soul to God, amid all the torments of a lingering death agony. The arm-chair which I was sitting in was the one in which John the Crooked (as he was pleased to call himself in his facetious days) used to sit and think out his villainies or issue his odious orders. At this moment I thought I saw the ghosts of all the Mauprats passing before me, with their bloody hands and their eyes dulled with wine. I got up and was about to yield to the horror I felt by taking to flight, when suddenly I saw a figure rise up in front of me, so distinct, so recognisable, so different in its vivid reality from the chimeras that had just besieged me, that I fell back in my chair, all bathed in a cold sweat. Standing by the bed was John Mauprat. He had just got out, for he was holding the half-opened curtain in his hand. He seemed to me the same as formerly, only he was still thinner, and paler and more hideous. His head was shaved, and his body wrapped in a dark winding-sheet. He gave me a hellish glance; a smile full of hate and contempt played on his thin, shrivelled lips. He stood motionless with his gleaming eyes fixed on me, and seemed as if about to speak. In that instant I was convinced that what I was looking on was a living being, a man of flesh and blood; it seems incredible, therefore, that I should have felt paralyzed by such childish fear. But it would be idle for me to deny it, nor have I ever yet been able to find an explanation; I was riveted to the ground with fear. The man's glance petrified me; I could not utter a sound. Blaireau rushed at him; then he waved the folds of his funeral garment, like a shroud all foul with the dampness of the tomb, and I fainted.

When I recovered consciousness Marcasse was by my side, anxiously endeavouring to lift me. I was lying on the ground rigid as a corpse. It was with a great difficulty that I collected my thoughts; but, as soon as I could stand upright, I seized Marcasse and hurriedly dragged him out of the accursed room. I had several narrow escapes of falling as I hastened down the winding stairs, and it was only on breathing the evening air in the courtyard, and smelling the healthy odour of the stables, that I recovered the use of my reason.

I did not hesitate to look upon what had just happened as an hallucination. I had given proof of my courage in war in the presence of my worthy sergeant; I did not blush, therefore, to confess the truth to him. I answered his questions frankly, and I described my horrible vision with such minute details that he, too, was impressed with the reality of it, and, as he walked about with me in the courtyard, kept repeating with a thoughtful air:

"Singular, singular! Astonishing!"

"No, it is not astonishing," I said, when I felt that I had quite recovered. "I experienced a most painful sensation on my way here; for several days I had struggled to overcome my aversion to seeing Roche-Mauprat again. Last night I had a nightmare, and I felt so exhausted and depressed this morning that, if I had not been afraid of offending my uncle, I should have postponed this disagreeable visit. As we entered the place, I felt a chill come over me; there seemed to be a weight on my chest, and I could not breathe. Probably, too, the pungent smoke that filled the room disturbed my brain. Again, after all the hardships and dangers of our terrible voyage, from which we have hardly recovered, either of us, is it astonishing that my nerves gave way at the first painful emotion?"

"Tell me," replied Marcasse, who was still pondering the matter, "did you notice Blaireau at the moment? What did Blaireau do?"

"I thought I saw Blaireau rush at the phantom at the moment when it disappeared; but I suppose I dreamt that like the rest."

"Hum!" said the sergeant. "When I entered, Blaireau was wildly excited. He kept coming to you, sniffing, whining in his way, running to the bed, scratching the wall, coming to me, running to you. Strange, that! Astonishing, captain, astonishing, that!"

After a silence of a few moments:

"Devil don't return!" he exclaimed, shaking his head. "Dead never return; besides, why dead, John? Not dead! Still two Mauprats! Who knows? Where the devil? Dead don't return; and my master—mad? Never. Ill? No."

After this colloquy the sergeant went and fetched a light, drew his faithful sword from the scabbard, whistled Blaireau, and bravely seized the rope which served as a balustrade for the staircase, requesting me to remain below. Great as was my repugnance to entering the room again, I did not hesitate to follow Marcasse, in spite of his recommendation. Our first care was to examine the bed; but while we had been talking in the courtyard the servant had brought clean sheets, had made the bed, and was now smoothing the blankets.

"Who has been sleeping there?" asked Marcasse, with his usual caution.

"Nobody," she replied, "except M. le Chevalier or M. l'Abbe Aubert, in the days when they used to come."

"But yesterday, or to-day, I mean?" said Marcasse.

"Oh! yesterday and to-day, nobody, sir; for it is quite two years since M. le Chevalier came here; and as for M. l'Abbe, he never sleeps here, now that he comes alone. He arrives in the morning, has lunch with us, and goes back in the evening."

"But the bed was disarranged," said Marcasse, looking at her attentively.

"Oh, well! that may be, sir," she replied. "I do not know how they left it the last time some one slept here; I did not pay any attention to that as I put on the sheets; all I know is that M. Bernard's cloak was lying on the top."

"My cloak?" I exclaimed. "It was left in the stable."

"And mine, too," said Marcasse. "I have just folded both together and put them on the corn-bin."

"You must have had two, then," replied the servant; "for I am sure I took one off the bed. It was a black cloak, not new."

Mine, as a fact, was lined with red and trimmed with gold lace. Marcasse's was light gray. It could not, therefore, have been one of our cloaks brought up for a moment by the man and then taken back to the stable.

"But, what did you do with it?" said the sergeant.

"My word, sir," replied the fat girl, "I put it there, over the arm-chair. You must have taken it while I went to get a candle. I can't see it now."

We searched the room thoroughly; the cloak was not to be found. We pretended that we needed it, not denying that it was ours. The servant unmade the bed in our presence, and then went and asked the man what he had done with it. Nothing could be found either in the bed or in the room; the man had not been upstairs. All the farm-folk were in a state of excitement, fearing that some one might be accused of theft. We inquired if a stranger had not come to Roche-Mauprat, and if he was not still there. When we ascertained that these good people had neither housed or seen any one, we reassured them about the lost cloak by saying that Marcasse had accidentally folded it with the two others. Then we shut ourselves in the room, in order to explore it at our ease; for it was now almost evident that what I had seen was by no means a ghost, but John Mauprat himself, or a man very like him, whom I had mistaken for John.

Marcasse having aroused Blaireau by voice and gesture, watched all his movements.

"Set your mind at rest," he said with pride; "the old dog has not forgotten his old trade. If there is a hole, a hole as big as your hand, have no fear. Now, old dog! Have no fear."

Blaireau, indeed, after sniffing everywhere, persisted in scratching the wall where I had seen the apparition; he would start back every time his pointed nose came to a certain spot in the wainscotting; then, wagging his bushy tail with a satisfied air, he would return to his master as if to tell him to concentrate his attention on this spot. The sergeant then began to examine the wall and the woodwork; he tried to insinuate his sword into some crack; there was no sign of an opening. Still, a door might have been there, for the flowers carved on the woodwork would hide a skilfully constructed sliding panel. The essential thing was to find the spring that made this panel work; but that was impossible in spite of all the efforts we made for two long hours. In vain did we try to shake the panel; it gave forth the same sound as the others. They were all sonorous, showing that the wainscot was not in immediate contact with the masonry. Still, there might be a gap of only a few inches between them. At last Marcasse, perspiring profusely, stopped, and said to me:

"This is very stupid; if we searched all night we should not find a spring if there is none; and however hard we hammered, we could not break in the door if there happened to be big iron bars behind it, as I have sometimes seen in other old country-houses."

"The axe might help us to find a passage," I said, "if there is one; but why, simply because your dog scratches the wall, persist in believing that John Mauprat, or the man who resembles him, could not have come in and gone out by the door?"

"Come in, if you like," replied Marcasse, "but gone out—no, on my honour! For, as the servant came down I was on the staircase brushing my boots. As soon as I heard something fall here, I rushed up quickly three stairs at a time, and found that it was you—like a corpse, stretched out on the floor, very ill; no one inside nor outside, on my honour!

"In that case, then, I must have dreamt of my fiend of an uncle, and the servant must have dreamt of the black cloak; for it is pretty certain that there is no secret door here; and even if there were one, and all the Mauprats, living and dead, knew the secret of it, what were that to us? Do we belong to the police that we should hunt out these wretched creatures? And if by chance we found them hidden somewhere, should we not help them to escape, rather than hand them over to justice? We are armed; we need not be afraid that they will assassinate us to-night; and if they amuse themselves by frightening us, my word, woe betide them! I have no eye for either relatives or friends when I am startled in my sleep. So come, let us attack the omelette that these good people my tenants are preparing for us; for if we continue knocking and scratching the walls they will think we are mad."

Marcasse yielded from a sense of duty rather than from conviction. He seemed to attach great importance to the discovery of this mystery, and to be far from easy in his mind. He was unwilling to let me remain alone in the haunted room, and pretended that I might fall ill again and have a fit.

"Oh, this time," I said, "I shall not play the coward. The cloak has cured me of my fear of ghosts; and I should not advise any one to meddle with me."

The hildago was obliged to leave me alone. I loaded my pistols and put them on the table within reach of my hand; but these precautions were a pure waste of time; nothing disturbed the silence of the room, and the heavy red silk curtains, with their coat of arms at the corners in tarnished silver, were not stirred by the slightest breath. Marcasse returned and, delighted at finding me as cheerful as he had left me, began preparing our supper with as much care as if we had come to Roche-Mauprat for the sole purpose of making a good meal. He made jokes about the capon which was still singing on the spit, and about the wine which was so like a brush in the throat. His good humour increased when the tenant appeared, bringing a few bottles of excellent Madeira, which had been left with him by the chevalier, who liked to drink a glass or two before setting foot in the stirrup. In return we invited the worthy man to sup with us, as the least tedious way of discussing business matters.

"Good," he said; "it will be like old times when the peasants used to eat at the table of the seigneurs of Roche-Mauprat. You are doing the same, Monsieur Bernard, you are quite right."

"Yes, sir," I replied very coldly; "only I behave thus with those who owe me money, not those to whom I owe it."

This reply, and the word "sir," frightened him so much that he was at great pains to excuse himself from sitting down to table. However, I insisted, as I wished to give him the measure of my character at once. I treated him as a man I was raising to my own level, not as one to whom I wished to descend. I forced him to be cleanly in his jokes, but allowed him to be free and facetious within the limits of decent mirth. He was a frank, jovial man. I questioned him minutely to discover if he was not in league with the phantom who was in the habit of leaving his cloak upon the bed. This, however, seemed far from probable; the man evidently had such an aversion for the Hamstringers, that, had not a regard for my relationship held him back, he would have been only too glad to have given them such a dressing in my presence as they deserved. But I could not allow him any license on this point; so I requested him to give me an account of my property, which he did with intelligence, accuracy, and honesty.

As he withdrew I noticed that the Madeira had had considerable effect on him; he seemed to have no control over his legs, which kept catching in the furniture; and yet he had been in sufficient possession of his faculties to reason correctly. I have always observed that wine acts much more powerfully on the muscles of peasants than on their nerves; that they rarely lose their heads, and that, on the contrary, stimulants produce in them a bliss unknown to us; the pleasure they derive from drunkenness is quite different from ours and very superior to our febrile exaltation.

When Marcasse and I found ourselves alone, though we were not drunk, we realized that the wine had filled us with gaiety and light-heartedness which we should not have felt at Roche-Mauprat, even without the adventure of the ghost. Accustomed as we were to speak our thoughts freely, we confessed mutually, and agreed that we were much better prepared than before supper to receive all the bogies of Varenne.

This word "bogey" reminded me of the adventure which had brought me into far from friendly contact with Patience at the age of thirteen. Marcasse knew about it already, but he knew very little of my character at that time, and I amused myself by telling him of my wild rush across the fields after being thrashed by the sorcerer.

"This makes me think," I concluded by saying, "that I have an imagination which easily gets overexcited, and that I am not above fear of the supernatural. Thus the apparition just now . . ."

"No matter, no matter," said Marcasse, looking at the priming of my pistols, and putting them on the table by my bed. "Do not forget that all the Hamstringers are not dead; that, if John is in this world, he will do harm until he is under the ground, and trebly locked in hell."

The wine was loosening the hidalgo's tongue; on those rare occasions when he allowed himself to depart from his usual sobriety, he was not wanting in wit. He was unwilling to leave me, and made a bed for himself by the side of mine. My nerves were excited by the incidents of the day, and I allowed myself, therefore, to speak of Edmee, not in such a way as to deserve the shadow of a reproach from her if she had heard my words, but more freely than I might have spoken with a man who was as yet my inferior and not my friend, as he became later. I could not say exactly how much I confessed to him of my sorrows and hopes and anxieties; but those confidences had a disastrous effect, as you will soon see.

We fell asleep while we were talking, with Blaireau at his master's feet, the hidalgo's sword across his knees near the dog, the light between us, my pistols ready to hand, my hunting-knife under my pillow, and the bolts shot. Nothing disturbed our repose. When the sun awakened us the cocks were crowing merrily in the courtyard, and the labourers were cracking their rustic jokes as they yoked the oxen under our windows.

"All the same there is something at the bottom of it."

Such was Marcasse's first remark as he opened his eyes, and took up the conversation where he had dropped it the night before.

"Did you see or hear anything during the night?" I asked.

"Nothing at all," he replied. "All the same, Blaireau has been disturbed in his sleep; for my sword has fallen down; and then, we found no explanation of what happened here."

"Let who will explain it," I answered. "I shall certainly not trouble myself."

"Wrong, wrong; you are wrong!"

"That may be, my good sergeant; but I do not like this room at all, and it seems to me so ugly by daylight, that I feel that I must get far away from it, and breathe some pure air."

"Well, I will go with you; but I shall return. I do not want to leave this to chance. I know what John Mauprat is capable of; you don't."

"I do not wish to know; and if there is any danger here for myself or my friends, I do not wish you to return."

Marcasse shook his head and said nothing. We went round the farm once more before departing. Marcasse was very much struck with a certain incident to which I should have paid but little attention. The farmer wished to introduce me to his wife, but she could not be persuaded to see me, and went and hid herself in the hemp-field. I attributed this to the shyness of youth.

"Fine youth, my word!" said Marcasse; "youth like mine fifty years old and more! There is something beneath it, something beneath, I tell you."

"What the devil can there be?"

"Hum! She was very friendly with John Mauprat in her day. She found his crooked legs to her liking. I know about it; yes, I know many other things, too; many things—you may take my word!"

"You shall tell me them the next time we come; and that will not be so soon; for my affairs are going on much better than if I interfered with them; and I should not like to get into the habit of drinking Madeira to prevent myself from being frightened at my own shadow. And now, Marcasse, I must ask you as a favour not to tell any one what has happened. Everybody has not your respect for your captain."

"The man who does not respect my captain is an idiot," answered the hidalgo, in a tone of authority; "but, if you order me, I will say nothing."

He kept his word. I would not on any account have had Edmee's mind disturbed by this stupid tale. However, I could not prevent Marcasse from carrying out his design; early the following morning he disappeared, and I learnt from Patience that he had returned to Roche-Mauprat under the pretence of having forgotten something.

XVIII

While Marcasse was devoting himself to serious investigations, I was spending days of delight and agony in Edmee's presence. Her behaviour, so constant and devoted, and yet in many respects so reserved, threw me into continual alternations of joy and grief. One day while I was taking a walk the chevalier had a long conversation with her. I happened to return when their discussion had reached its most animated stage. As soon as I appeared, my uncle said to me:

"Here, Bernard; come and tell Edmee that you love her; that you will make her happy; that you have got rid of your old faults. Do something to get yourself accepted; for things cannot go on as they are. Our position with our neighbours is unbearable; and before I go down to the grave I should like to see my daughter's honour cleared from stain, and to feel sure that some stupid caprice of hers will not cast her into a convent, when she ought to be filling that position in society to which she is entitled, and which I have worked all my life to win for her. Come, Bernard, at her feet, lad! Have the wit to say something that will persuade her! Otherwise I shall think—God forgive me!—that it is you that do not love her and do not honestly wish to marry her."

"I! Great heavens!" I exclaimed. "Not wish to marry her—when for seven years I have had no other thought; when that is the one wish of my heart, and the only happiness my mind can conceive!"

Then I poured forth all the thoughts that the sincerest passion could suggest. She listened to me in silence, and without withdrawing her hands, which I covered with kisses. But there was a serious expression in her eyes, and the tone of her voice made me tremble when, after reflecting a few moments, she said:

"Father, you should not doubt my word; I have promised to marry Bernard; I promised him, and I promised you; it is certain, therefore, that I shall marry him."

Then she added, after a fresh pause, and in a still severe tone:

"But if, father, you believe that you are on the brink of the grave, what sort of heart do you suppose I can have, that you bid me think only of myself, and put on my wedding-dress in the hour of mourning for you? If, on the contrary, you are, as I believe, still full of vigour, in spite of your sufferings, and destined to enjoy the love of your family for many a long year yet, why do you urge me so imperiously to cut short the time I have requested? Is not the question important enough to demand my most serious reflection? A contract which is to bind me for the rest of my life, and on which depends, I do not say my happiness, for that I would gladly sacrifice to your least wish, but the peace of my conscience and the dignity of my conduct (since no woman can be sufficiently sure of herself to answer for a future which has been fettered against her will), does not such a contract bid me weigh all its risks and all its advantages for several years at least?"

"Good God!" said the chevalier. "Have you not been weighing all this for the last seven years? You ought to have arrived at some conclusion about your cousin by now. If you are willing to marry him, marry him; but if not, for God's sake say so, and let another man come forward."

"Father," replied Edmee, somewhat coldly, "I shall marry none but him."

"'None but him' is all very well," said the chevalier, tapping the logs with the tongs; "but that does not necessarily mean that you will marry him."

"Yes, I will marry him, father," answered Edmee. "I could have wished to be free a few months more; but since you are displeased at all these delays, I am ready to obey your orders, as you know."

"Parbleu! that is a pretty way of consenting," exclaimed my uncle, "and no doubt most gratifying to your cousin! By Jove! Bernard, I have lived many years in this world, but I must own that I can't understand these women yet, and it is very probable that I shall die without ever having understood them."

"Uncle," I said, "I can quite understand my cousin's aversion for me; it is only what I deserve. I have done all I could to atone for my errors. But, is it altogether in her power to forget a past which has doubtless caused her too much pain? However, if she does not forgive me, I will imitate her severity: I will not forgive myself. Abandoning all hope in this world, I will tear myself away from her and you, and chasten myself with a punishment worse than death."

"That's it! Go on! There's an end of everything!" said the chevalier, throwing the tongs into the fire. "That is just what you have been aiming at, I suppose, Edmee?"

I had moved a few steps towards the door; I was suffering intensely. Edmee ran after me, took me by the arm, and brought me back towards her father.

"It is cruel and most ungrateful of you to say that," she said. "Does it show a modest spirit and generous heart, to forget a friendship, a devotion, I may even venture to say, a fidelity of seven years, because I ask to prove you for a few months more? And even if my affection for you should never be as deep as yours for me, is what I have hitherto shown you of so little account that you despise it and reject it, because you are vexed at not inspiring me with precisely as much as you think you are entitled to? You know at this rate a woman would have no right to feel affection. However, tell me, is it your wish to punish me for having been a mother to you by leaving me altogether, or to make some return only on condition that I become your slave?"

"No, Edmee, no," I replied, with my heart breaking and my eyes full of tears, as I raised her hand to my lips; "I feel that you have done far more for me than I deserved; I feel that it would be idle to think of tearing myself from your presence; but can you account it a crime in me to suffer by your side? In any case it is so involuntary, so inevitable a crime, that it must needs escape all your reproaches and all my own remorse. But let us talk of this no more. It is all I can do. Grant me your friendship still; I shall hope to show myself always worthy of you in the future."

"Come, kiss each other," said the chevalier, much affected, "and never separate. Bernard, however capricious Edmee may seem, never abandon her, if you would deserve the blessing of your foster-father. Though you should never be her husband, always be a brother to her. Remember, my lad, that she will soon be alone in the world, and that I shall die in sorrow if I do not carry with me to the grave a conviction that a support and a defender still remains to her. Remember, too, that it is on your account, on account of a vow, which her inclination, perhaps, would reject, but which her conscience respects, that she is thus forsaken and slandered . . ."

The chevalier burst into tears, and in a moment all the sorrows of the unfortunate family were revealed to me.

"Enough, enough!" I cried, falling at their feet. "All this is too cruel. I should be the meanest wretch on earth if I had need to be reminded of my misdeeds and my duties. Let me weep at your knees; let me atone for the wrong I have done you by eternal grief, by eternal renunciation. Why not have driven me away when I did the wrong? Why not, uncle, have blown out my brains with your pistol, as if I had been a wild beast? What have I done to be spared, I who repaid your kindness with the ruin of your honour? No, no; I can see that Edmee ought not to marry me; that would be accepting the shame of the insult I have drawn upon her. All I ask is to be allowed to remain here; I will never see her face, if she makes this a condition; but I will lie at her door like a faithful dog and tear to pieces the first man who dares to present himself otherwise than on his knees; and if some day an honest man, more fortunate than myself, shows himself worthy of her love, far from opposing him, I will intrust to him the dear and sacred task of protecting and vindicating her. I will be but a friend, a brother to her, and when I see that they are happy together, I will go far away from them and die in peace."

My sobs choked me; the chevalier pressed his daughter and myself to his heart, and we mingled our tears, swearing to him that we would never leave each other, either during his life or after his death.

"Still, do not give up all hope of marrying her," whispered the chevalier to me a few moments later, when we were somewhat calmer. "She has strange whims; but nothing will persuade me to believe that she does not love you. She does not want to explain matters yet. Woman's will is God's will."

"And Edmee's will is my will," I replied.

A few days after this scene, which brought the calmness of death into my soul in place of the tumult of life, I was strolling in the park with the abbe.

"I must tell you," he said, "of an adventure which befell me yesterday. There is a touch of romance in it. I had been for a walk in the woods of Briantes, and had made my way down to the spring of Fougeres. It was as warm, you remember, as in the middle of summer; and our beautiful plants, in their autumn red, seemed more beautiful than ever as they stretched their delicate tracery over the stream. The trees have very little foliage left; but the carpet of dried leaves one walks upon gives forth a sound which to me is full of charm. The satiny trunks of the birches and young oaks are covered with moss and creepers of all shades of brown, and tender green, and red and fawn, which spread out into delicate stars and rosettes, and maps of all countries, wherein the imagination can behold new worlds in miniature. I kept gazing lovingly on these marvels of grace and delicacy, these arabesques in which infinite variety is combined with unfailing regularity, and as I remembered with pleasure that you are not, like the vulgar, blind to these adorable coquetries of nature, I gathered a few with the greatest care, even bringing away the bark of the tree on which they had taken root, in order not to destroy the perfection of their designs. I made a little collection, which I left at Patience's as I passed; we will go and see them, if you like. But, on our way, I must tell you what happened to me as I approached the spring. I was walking upon the wet stones with my head down, guided by the slight noise of the clear little jet of water which bursts from the heart of the mossy rock. I was about to sit down on the stone which forms a natural seat at the side of it, when I saw that the place was already occupied by a good friar whose pale, haggard face was half-hidden by his cowl of coarse cloth. He seemed much frightened at my arrival; I did my best to reassure him by declaring that my intention was not to disturb him, but merely to put my lips to the little bark channel which the woodcutters have fixed to the rock to enable one to drink more easily.

"'Oh, holy priest,' he said to me in the humblest tone, 'why are you not the prophet whose rod could smite the founts of grace? and why cannot my soul, like this rock, give forth a stream of tears?'

"Struck by the manner in which this monk expressed himself, by his sad air, by his thoughtful attitude in this poetic spot, which has often made me dream of the meeting of the Saviour and the woman of Samaria, I allowed myself to be drawn into a more intimate conversation. I learnt from the monk that he was a Trappist, and that he was making a penitential tour.

"'Ask neither my name nor whence I come,' he said. 'I belong to an illustrious family who would blush to know that I am still alive. Besides, on entering the Trappist order, we abjure all pride in the past; we make ourselves like new-born children; we become dead to the world that we may live again in Jesus Christ. But of this be sure: you behold in me one of the most striking examples of the miraculous power of grace; and if I could make known to you the tale of my religious life, of my terrors, my remorse, and my expiations, you would certainly be touched by it. But of what avail the indulgence and compassion of man, if the pity of God will not deign to absolve me?'

"You know," continued the abbe, "that I do not like monks, that I distrust their humility and abhor their lives of inaction. But this man spoke in so sad and kindly a manner; he was so filled with a sense of his duty; he seemed so ill, so emaciated by asceticism, so truly penitent, that he won my heart. In his looks and in his talk were bright flashes which betrayed a powerful intellect, indefatigable energy, and indomitable perseverance. We spent two whole hours together, and I was so moved by what he said that on leaving him I expressed a wish to see him again before he left this neighbourhood. He had found a lodging for the night at the Goulets farm, and I tried in vain to persuade him to accompany me to the chateau. He told me that he had a companion he could not leave.

"'But, since you are so sympathetic,' he said, 'I shall esteem it a pleasure to meet you here to-morrow towards sunset; perhaps I may even venture to ask a favour of you; you can be of service to me in an important matter which I have to arrange in this neighbourhood; more than this I cannot tell you at the present moment.'

"I assured him that he could reckon on me, and that I should only be too happy to oblige a man such as himself."

"And the result is, I suppose, that you are waiting impatiently for the hour of your appointment?" I said to the abbe.

"I am," he replied; "and my new acquaintance has so many attractions for me that, if I were not afraid of abusing the confidence he has placed in me, I should take Edmee to the spring of Fougeres."

"I fancy," I replied, "that Edmee has something better to do than to listen to the declamations of your monk, who perhaps, after all, is only a knave, like so many others to whom you have given money blindly. You will forgive me, I know, abbe; but you are not a good physiognomist, and you are rather apt to form a good or bad opinion of people for no reason except that your own romantic nature happens to feel kindly or timidly disposed towards them."

The abbe smiled and pretended that I said this because I bore him a grudge; he again asserted his belief in the Trappist's piety, and then went back to botany. We passed some time at Patience's, examining the collection of plants; and as my one desire was to escape from my own thoughts, I left the hut with the abbe and accompanied him as far as the wood where he was to meet the monk. In proportion as we drew near to the place the abbe seemed to lose more and more of his eagerness of the previous evening, and even expressed a fear that he had gone too far. This hesitation, following so quickly upon enthusiasm, was very characteristic of the abbe's mobile, loving, timid nature, with its strange union of the most contrary impulses, and I again began to rally him with all the freedom of friendship.

"Come, then," he said, "I should like to be satisfied about this; you must see him. You can study his face for a few minutes, and then leave us together, since I have promised to listen to his secrets."

As I had nothing better to do I followed the abbe; but as soon as we reached a spot overlooking the shady rocks whence the water issues, I stopped and examined the monk through the branches of a clump of ash-trees. Seated immediately beneath us by the side of the spring, he had his eyes turned inquiringly on the angle of the path by which he expected the abbe to arrive; but he did not think of looking at the place where we were, and we could examine him at our ease without being seen by him.

No sooner had I caught sight of him than, with a bitter laugh, I took the abbe by the arm, drew him back a short distance, and, not without considerable agitation, said to him:

"My dear abbe, in bygone years did you never catch sight of the face of my uncle, John de Mauprat?"

"Never, as far as I know," replied the abbe, quite amazed. "But what are you driving at?"

"Only this, my friend; you have made a pretty find here; this good and venerable Trappist, in whom you see so much grace and candour, and contrition, and intelligence, is none other than John de Mauprat, the Hamstringer."

"You must be mad!" cried the abbe, starting back. "John de Mauprat died a long time ago."

"John Mauprat is not dead, nor perhaps Antony Mauprat either; and my surprise is less than yours only because I have already met one of these two ghosts. That he has become a monk, and is repenting for his sins, is very possible; but alas! it is by no means impossible that he has disguised himself in order to carry out some evil design, and I advise you to be on your guard."

The abbe was so frightened that he no longer wanted to keep his appointment. I suggested that it would be well to learn what the old sinner was aiming at. But, as I knew the abbe's weak character, and feared that my Uncle John would manage to win his heart by his lying confessions and wheedle him into some false step, I made up my mind to hide in a thicket whence I could see and hear everything.

But things did not happen as I had expected. The Trappist, instead of playing the politician, immediately made known his real name to the abbe. He declared that he was full of contrition, and that, as his conscience would not allow him to make the monk's habit a refuge from punishment (he had really been a Trappist for several years), he was about to put himself into the hands of justice, that he might atone in a striking way for the crimes with which he was polluted. This man, endowed as he was with conspicuous abilities, had acquired a mystic eloquence in the cloister. He spoke with so much grace and persuasiveness that I was fascinated no less than the abbe. It was in vain that the latter attempted to combat a resolution which appeared to him insane; John Mauprat showed the most unflinching devotion to his religious ideas. He declared that, having committed the crimes of the old barbarous paganism, he could not ransom his soul save by a public expiation worthy of the early Christians.

"It is possible," he said, "to be a coward with God as well as with man, and in the silence of my vigils I hear a terrible voice answering to my tears: 'Miserable craven, it is the fear of man that has thrown you upon the bosom of God, and if you had not feared temporal death, you would never have thought of life eternal!'

"Then I realize that what I most dread is not God's wrath, but the rope and the hangman that await me among my fellows. Well, it is time to end this sense of secret shame; not until the day when men crush me beneath their abuse and punishment shall I fell absolved and restored in the sight of Heaven; then only shall I account myself worthy to say to Jesus my Saviour: 'Give ear to me, innocent victim, Thou who heardest the penitent thief; give ear to a sullied but contrite victim, who has shared in the glory of Thy martyrdom and been ransomed by Thy blood!'"

"If you persist in your enthusiastic design," said the abbe, after unsuccessfully bringing forward all possible objections, "you must at least let me know in what way you thought I could be of service to you."

"I cannot act in this matter," replied the Trappist, "without the consent of a young man who will soon be the last of the Mauprats; for the chevalier has not many days to wait before he will receive the heavenly reward due to his virtues; and as for myself, I cannot avoid the punishment I am about to seek, except by falling back into the endless night of the cloister. I speak of Bernard Mauprat; I will not call him my nephew, for if he heard me he would blush to think that he bore this shameful title. I heard of his return from America, and this news decided me to undertake the journey at the painful end of which you now behold me."

It seemed to me that while he was saying this he kept casting side-glances towards the clump of trees where I was, as if he had guessed my presence there. Perhaps the movement of some branches had betrayed me.

"May I ask," said the abbe, "what you now have in common with this young man? Are you not afraid that, embittered by the harsh treatment formerly lavished on him at Roche-Mauprat, he may refuse to see you?"

"I am certain that he will refuse; for I know the hatred that he still has for me," said the Trappist, once more looking towards the spot where I was. "But I hope that you will persuade him to grant me an interview; for you are a good and generous man, Monsieur l'Abbe. You promised to oblige me; and, besides, you are young Mauprat's friend, and you will be able to make him understand that his interests are at stake and the honour of his name."

"How so?" answered the abbe. "No doubt he will be far from pleased to see you appear before the courts to answer for crimes which have since been effaced in the gloom of the cloister. He will certainly wish you to forego this public expiation. How can you hope that he will consent?"

"I have hope, because God is good and great; because His grace is mighty; because it will touch the heart of him who shall deign to hear the prayer of a soul which is truly penitent and deeply convinced; because my eternal salvation is in the hands of this young man, and he cannot wish to avenge himself on me beyond the grave. Moreover, I must die at peace with those I have injured; I must fall at the feet of Bernard Mauprat and obtain his forgiveness of my sins. My tears will move him, or, if his unrelenting soul despises them, I shall at least have fulfilled an imperious duty."

Seeing that he was speaking with a firm conviction that he was being heard by me, I was filled with disgust; I thought I could detect the deceit and cowardice that lay beneath this vile hypocrisy. I moved away and waited for the abbe some distance off. He soon rejoined me; the interview had ended by a mutual promise to meet again soon. The abbe had undertaken to convey the Trappist's words to me, while the latter had threatened in the most honeyed tone in the world to come and see me if I refused his request. The abbe and I agreed to consult together, without informing the chevalier or Edmee, that we might not disquiet them unnecessarily. The Trappist had gone to stay at La Chatre, at the Carmelite convent; this had thoroughly aroused the abbe's suspicions, in spite of his first enthusiasm at the penitence of the sinner. The Carmelites had persecuted him in his youth, and in the end the prior had driven him to secularize himself. The prior was still alive, old but implacable; infirm, and withdrawn from the world, but strong in his hatred, and his passion for intrigue. The abbe could not hear his name without shuddering, and he begged me to act prudently in this affair.

"Although John Mauprat," he said, "is under the bane of the law, and you are at the summit of honour and prosperity, do not despise the weakness of your enemy. Who knows what cunning and hatred may do? They can usurp the place of the just and cast him out on the dung-heap; they can fasten their crimes on others and sully the robe of innocence with their vileness. Maybe you have not yet finished with the Mauprats."

The poor abbe did not know that there was so much truth in his words.

XIX

After thoroughly reflecting on the Trappist's probable intentions, I decided that I ought to grant him the interview he had requested. In any case, John Mauprat could not hope to impose upon me, and I wished to do all in my power to prevent him from pestering my great-uncle's last days with his intrigues. Accordingly, the very next day I betook myself to the town, where I arrived towards the end of Vespers. I rang, not without emotion, at the door of the Carmelites.

The retreat chosen by the Trappist was of those innumerable mendicant societies which France supported at that time. Though its rules were ostensibly most austere, this monastery was rich and devoted to pleasure. In that age of scepticism the small number of the monks was entirely out of proportion to the wealth of the establishment which had been founded for them; and the friars who roamed about the vast monasteries in the most remote parts of the provinces led the easiest and idlest lives they had ever known, in the lap of luxury, and entirely freed from the control of opinion, which always loses its power when man isolates himself. But this isolation, the mother of the "amiable vices," as they used to phrase it, was dear only to the more ignorant. The leaders were a prey to the painful dreams of an ambition which had been nurtured in obscurity and embittered by inaction. To do something, even in the most limited sphere and with the help of the feeblest machinery; to do something at all costs—such was the one fixed idea of the priors and abbes.

The prior of the Carmelites whom I was about to see was the personification of this restless impotence. Bound to his great arm-chair by the gout, he offered a strange contrast to the venerable chevalier, pale and unable to move like himself, but noble and patriarchal in his affliction. The prior was short, stout, and very petulant. The upper part of his body was all activity; he would turn his head rapidly from side to side; he would brandish his arms while giving orders. He was sparing of words, and his muffled voice seemed to lend a mysterious meaning to the most trivial things. In short, one-half of his person seemed to be incessantly striving to drag along the other, like the bewitched man in the Arabian Nights, whose robe hid a body that was marble up to the waist.

He received me with exaggerated attention, got angry because they did not bring me a chair quickly enough, stretched out his fat, flabby hand to draw this chair quite close to his own, and made a sign to a tall, bearded satyr, whom he called the Brother Treasurer, to go out; then, after overwhelming me with questions about my journey, and my return, and my health, and my family, while his keen restless little eyes were darting glances at me from under eyelids swollen and heavy from intemperance, he came to the point.

"I know, my dear child," he said, "what brings you here; you wish to pay your respects to your holy relative, to the Trappist, that model of faith and holiness whom God has sent to us to serve as an example to the world, and reveal to all the miraculous power of grace."

"Prior," I answered, "I am not a good enough Christian to judge of the miracle you mention. Let devout souls give thanks to Heaven for it. For myself, I have come here because M. Jean de Mauprat desires to inform me, as he has said, of plans which concern myself, and to which I am ready to listen. If you will allow me to go and see him——"

"I did not want him to see you before myself, young man," exclaimed the prior, with an affectation of frankness, at the same time seizing my hands in his, at the touch of which I could not repress a feeling of disgust. "I have a favour to ask of you in the name of charity, in the name of the blood which flows in your veins . . ."

I withdrew one of my hands, and the prior, noticing my expression of displeasure, immediately changed his tone with admirable skill.

"You are a man of the world, I know. You have a grudge against him who once was Jean de Mauprat, and who to-day is the humble Brother Jean Nepomucene. But if the precepts of our divine Master, Jesus Christ, cannot persuade you to pity, there are considerations of public propriety and of family pride which must make you share my fears and assist my efforts. You know the pious but rash resolution which Brother John has formed; you ought to assist me in dissuading him from it, and you will do so, I make no doubt."

"Possibly, sir," I replied very coldly; "but might I ask to what my family is indebted for the interest you are good enough to take in its affairs?"

"To that spirit of charity which animates all the followers of Christ," answered the monk, with very well assumed dignity.

Fortified with this pretext, on the strength of which the clergy have always taken upon themselves to meddle in all family secrets, it was not difficult for him to put an end to my questions; and, though he could not destroy the suspicions which I felt at heart, he succeeded in proving to my ears that I ought to be grateful to him for the care which he had taken of the honour of my name. I wanted to find out what he was driving at; it was as I had foreseen. My Uncle John claimed from me his share in the fief of Roche-Mauprat; and the prior was deputed to make me understand that I had to choose between paying a considerable sum of money (for he spoke of the interest accruing through the seven years of possession, besides a seventh part of the whole estate) and the insane step he intended taking, the scandal of which could not fail to hasten the chevalier's death and cause me, perhaps, "strange personal embarrassments." All this was hinted with consummate skill under the cover of the most Christian solicitude for my own welfare, the most fervent admiration for the Trappist's zeal, and the most sincere anxiety about the results of this "firm resolve." Finally, it was made evident that John Mauprat was not coming to ask me for the means of existence, but that I should have to humbly beseech him to accept the half of my possessions, if I wished to prevent him from dragging my name and probably my person to the felon's dock.

I tried a final objection.

"If," I said, "this resolve of Brother Nepomucene, as you call him, is as fixed as you say; if the only one care he has in the world is for his own salvation, will you explain to me how the attractions of temporal wealth can possibly turn him from it? There seems to be a contradiction in this which I fail to understand."

The prior was somewhat embarrassed by the piercing glance I turned on him, but he immediately started on one of those exhibitions of simplicity which are the supreme resource of rogues:

"Mon Dieu! my dear son," he exclaimed, "you do not know, then, the immense consolation a pious soul can derive from the possession of worldly wealth? Just as perishable riches must be despised when they represent vain pleasures, even so must they be resolutely defended by the upright man when they afford him the means of doing good. I will not hide from you that if I were the holy Trappist I would not yield my rights to any one; I would found a religious society for the propagation of the faith and the distribution of alms with the wealth which, in the hands of a brilliant young nobleman like yourself, is only squandered on horses and dogs. The Church teaches us that by great sacrifices and rich offerings we may cleanse our souls of the blackest sins. Brother Nepomucene, a prey to holy fear, believes that a public expiation is necessary for his salvation. Like a devout martyr, he wishes to satisfy the implacable justice of men with blood. But how much sweeter for you (and safer, at the same time) to see him raise some holy altar to the glory of God, and hide in the blessed peace of the cloister the baleful lustre of the name he has already abjured! He is so much swayed by the spirit of his order, he has conceived such a love for self-denial, for humility and poverty, that it will need all my efforts and much help from on high to make him agree to this change of expiations."

"It is you, then, prior, who from sheer goodness of heart are undertaking to alter this fatal resolution? I admire your zeal, and I thank you for it; but I do not think there will be any need of all these negotiations. M. Jean de Mauprat claims his share of the inheritance; nothing can be more just. Even should the law refuse all civil rights to a man who owed his safety only to flight (a point which I will pass over), my relative may rest assured that there would never be the least dispute between us on this ground, if I were the absolute possessor of any fortune whatever. But you are doubtless aware that I owe the enjoyment of this fortune only to the kindness of my great-uncle, the Chevalier Hubert de Mauprat; that he had enough to do to pay the debts of the family, which amounted to more than the total value of the estate; that I can alienate nothing without his permission, and that, in reality, I am merely the depositary of a fortune which I have not yet accepted."

The prior stared at me in astonishment, as if dazed by an unexpected blow. Then he smiled with a crafty expression, and said:

"Very good! It appears that I have been mistaken, and that I must apply to M. Hubert de Mauprat. I will do so; for I make no doubt that he will be very grateful to me for saving his family from a scandal which may have very good results for one of his relatives in the next world, but which, for a certainty, will have very bad ones for another relation in the present world."

"I understand, sir," I replied. "This is a threat. I will answer in the same strain: If M. Jean de Mauprat ventures to importune my uncle and cousin, it is with me that he will have to deal; and it will not be before the courts that I shall summon him to answer for certain outrages which I have by no means forgotten. Tell him that I shall grant no pardon to the Trappist penitent unless he remains faithful to the role he has adopted. If M. Jean de Mauprat is without resources, and he asks my help, I may, out of the income I receive, furnish him with the means of living humbly and decently, according to the spirit of the vows he has taken; but if ecclesiastical ambition has taken possession of his mind, and he thinks, by stupid, childish threats, to intimidate my uncle to such an extent that he will be able to extort from him the wherewithal to satisfy his new tastes, let him undeceive himself—tell him so from me. The old man's peace of mind and his daughter's future have only myself as guardian, and I shall manage to guard them, though it be at the risk of my life and my honour."

"And yet honour and life are of some importance at your age," replied the abbe, visibly irritated, but feigning a suaver manner than ever. "Who knows into what folly religious fervour may lead the Trappist? For, between ourselves be it said, my child—you see, I am a man of moderation—I knew the world in my youth, and I do not approve of these violent resolves, which are more often dictated by pride than piety. For instance, I have consented to temper the austerity of our rules; my friars look well-fed, and they wear shirts. Rest assured, my good sir, I am far from approving of your uncle's design, and I shall do all that is possible to hinder it. Yet, if he still persists, how will my efforts profit you? He has obtained his superior's permission, and may, after all, yield to his fatal inspiration. You may be seriously compromised by an affair of this kind; for, although reports say that you are a worthy young gentleman, though you have abjured the errors of the past, and though, perhaps, your soul has always hated iniquity, you have certainly been involved in many misdeeds which human laws condemn and punish. Who can tell into what involuntary revelations Brother Nepomucene may find himself drawn if he sets in motion the machinery of criminal proceedings? Can he set it in motion against himself without at the same time setting it in motion against you? Believe me, I wish for peace—I am a kindly man."

"Yes, a very kindly man, father," I answered, in a tone of irony. "I see that perfectly. But do not let this matter cause you needless anxiety; for there is one very clear argument which must reassure both of us. If a veritable religious impulse urges Brother John the Trappist to make a public reparation, it will be easy to make him understand that he ought to hesitate before he drags another than himself into the abyss; the spirit of Christ forbids him to do this. But, if the truth is, as I presume, that M. Jean de Mauprat has not the least wish to hand himself over to justice, his threats are but little calculated to terrify me, and I shall take steps to prevent them from making more stir than is desirable."

"So that is the only answer I am to give him?" asked the prior, darting a vindictive glance at me.

"Yes, sir," I replied; "unless he would prefer to come here and receive the answer from my own mouth. I came with a determination to conquer the disgust which his presence arouses in me; and I am astonished that, after expressing so much eagerness to see me, he should remain in the background when I arrive."

"Sir," answered the prior, with ridiculous majesty, "my duty is to see that the peace of our Lord reigns in this holy place. I must, therefore, set myself against any interview which might lead to violent explanations . . ."

"You are much too easily frightened, sir," I replied. "There is nothing to arouse passion in this matter. However, as it was not I who called for these explanations, and as I came here out of pure compliance, I most willingly refrain from pushing them further, and I thank you for having been good enough to act as intermediary."

With that, I made a profound bow and retired.

XX

I gave an account of this interview to the abbe, who was waiting for me at Patience's. He was entirely of my own opinion; he thought, like myself, that the prior, so far from endeavouring to turn the Trappist from his pretended designs, was trying with all his power to frighten me, in the hope that I should be brought to make considerable sacrifices of money. In his eyes it was clear that this old man, faithful to the monkish spirit, wished to put into the hands of a clerical Mauprat the fruit of the labours and thrift of a lay Mauprat.

"That is the indelible mark of the Catholic clergy," he said. "They cannot live without waging war on the families around them, and being ever on the watch for opportunities to spoil them. They look upon this wealth as their property, and upon all ways of recovering it as lawful. It is not as easy as you think to protect one's self against this smooth-faced brigandage. Monks have stubborn appetites and ingenious minds. Act with caution and be prepared for anything. You can never induce a Trappist to show fight. Under the shelter of his hood, with head bowed and hands crossed, he will accept the cruelest outrages; and, knowing quite well that you will not assassinate him, he will hardly fear you. Again, you do not know what justice can become in man's hands, and how a criminal trial is conducted and decided when one of the parties will not stick at any kind of bribery and intimidation. The Church is powerful, the law grandiloquent. The words 'honesty' and 'integrity' have for centuries been ringing against the hardened walls of courts of justice; but that has not prevented judges from being false or verdicts from being iniquitous. Have a care; have a care! The Trappist may start the cowled pack on his own track and throw them off by disappearing at the right point and leading them on yours. Remember that you have wounded many an *amour propre* by disappointing the pretensions of the dowry-hunters. One of the most incensed of them, and at the same time one of the most malicious, is a near relative of a magistrate who is all-powerful in the province. De la Marche has given up the gown for the sword; but among his old colleagues he may have left some one who would like to do you an ill-turn. I am sorry you were not able to join him in America, and get on good terms with him. Do not shrug your shoulders; you may kill a dozen of them, and things will go from bad to worse. They will avenge themselves; not on your life, perhaps, for they know that you hold that cheap, but on your honour; and your great-uncle will die of grief. In short—"

"My dear abbe," I said, interrupting him, "you have a habit of seeing everything black at the first glance, when you do not happen to see the sun in the middle of the night. Now let me tell you some things which ought to drive out these gloomy presentiments. I know John Mauprat of old; he is a signal impostor, and, moreover, the rankest of cowards. He will sink into the earth at the sight of me, and as soon as I speak I will make him confess that he is neither Trappist, nor monk, nor saint. All this is a mere sharper's trick. In the old days I have heard him making plans which prevent me from being astonished at his impudence now; so I have but little fear of him."

"There you are wrong," replied the abbe. "You should always fear a coward, because he strikes from behind while you are expecting him in front. If John Mauprat were not a Trappist, if the papers he showed me were lies, the prior of the Carmelites is too shrewd and cautious to have let himself be deceived. Never would he have espoused the cause of a layman, and never would he mistake a layman for one of his own cloth. However, we must make inquiries; I will write to the superior of the Trappist monastery at once, but I am certain he will confirm what I know already. It is even possible that John Mauprat is a genuine devotee. Nothing becomes such a character better than certain shades of the Catholic spirit. The inquisition is the soul of the Church, and the inquisition should smile on John Mauprat. I firmly believe that he would give himself up to the sword of justice solely for the pleasure of compassing your ruin with his own, and that the desire to found a monastery with your money is a sudden inspiration, the honour of which belongs entirely to the prior of the Carmelites . . ."

"That is hardly probable, my dear abbe," I said. "Besides, where can these discussions lead us? Let us act. Let us keep the chevalier in sight, so that the unclean beast may not come and poison the calm of his last days. Write to the Trappist superior; I will offer the creature a pension, and when he comes, let us carefully watch his slightest movements. My sergeant, Marcasse, is an admirable bloodhound. Let us put him on the track, and if he can manage to tell us in vulgar speech what he has seen and heard, we shall soon know everything that is happening in the province."

Chatting thus, we arrived at the chateau towards the close of day. As I entered the silent building, I was seized with a fond, childish uneasiness, such as may come upon a mother when she leaves her babe a moment. The eternal security which nothing had ever disturbed within the bounds of the old sacred walls, the decrepitude of the servants, the way in which the doors always stood open, so that beggars would sometimes enter the drawing-room without meeting any one and without giving umbrage—the whole atmosphere of peace and trust and isolation—formed a strange contrast to the thoughts of strife, and the cares with which John's return and the prior's threats had filled my mind for some hours. I quickened my pace, and, seized with an involuntary trembling, I crossed the billiard-room. At that moment I thought I saw a dark shadow pass under the windows of the ground floor, glide through the jasmines, and disappear in the twilight. I threw open the door of the drawing-room and stood still. There was not a sound, not a movement. I was going to look for Edmee in her father's room, when I thought I saw something white moving near the chimney-corner where the chevalier always sat.

"Edmee! Is that you?" I exclaimed.

No one answered. My brow was covered with a cold sweat and my knees were trembling. Ashamed of this strange weakness, I rushed towards the hearth, repeating Edmee's name in agonized tones.

"Have you come at last, Bernard?" she replied, in a trembling voice.

I seized her in my arms. She was kneeling beside her father's arm-chair and pressing to her lips the old man's icy hands.

"Great God!" I cried, when by the dim light in the room I could distinguish the chevalier's livid face. "Is our father dead?"

"Perhaps," she said, in a stifled voice; "perhaps he has only fainted, please God! But, a light, for Heaven's sake! Ring the bell! He has only been in this state for a moment."

I rang in all haste. The abbe now came in, and fortunately we succeeded in bringing my uncle back to life.

But when he opened his eyes, his mind seemed to be struggling against the impressions of a fearful dream.

"Has he gone? Has the vile phantom gone?" he repeated several times. "Ho, there, Saint-Jean! My pistols! Now, my men! Throw the fellow out of the window!"

I began to suspect the truth.

"What has happened?" I said the Edmee, in a low tone. "Who has been here in my absence?"

"If I told you," answered Edmee, "you would hardly believe it. You would think my father and I were mad. But I will tell you everything presently; let us attend to him."

With her soft words and loving attentions she succeeded in calming the old man. We carried him to his room, and he fell into a quiet sleep. When Edmee had gently withdrawn her hand from his and lowered the wadded curtain over his head, she joined the abbe and myself, and told us that a quarter of an hour before we returned a mendicant friar had entered the drawing-room, where, as usual, she was embroidering near her father, who had fallen asleep. Feeling no surprise at an incident which frequently happened, she had risen to get her purse from the mantel-piece, at the same time addressing a few words to the monk. But just as she was turning round to offer him an alms the chevalier had awakened with a start, and eyeing the monk from head to foot, had cried in a tone half of anger and half of fear:

"What the devil are you doing here in that garb?"

Thereupon Edmee had looked at the monk's face and had recognised . . .

"A man you would never dream of," she said; "the frightful John Mauprat. I had only seen him a single hour in my life, but that repulsive face has never left my memory, and I have never had the slightest attack of fever without seeing it again. I could not repress a cry.

"'Do not be afraid,' he said, with a hideous smile. 'I come here not as an enemy, but as a supplicant.'

"And he went down on his knees so near my father, that, not knowing what he might do, I rushed between them, and hastily pushed back the arm-chair to the wall. Then the monk, speaking in a mournful tone, which was rendered still more terrifying by the approach of night, began to pour out some lamentable rigmarole of a confession, and ended by asking pardon for his crimes, and declaring that he was already covered by the black veil which parricides wear when they go to the scaffold.

"'This wretched creature has gone mad,' said my father, pulling the bell-rope.

"But Saint-Jean is deaf, and he did not come. So we had to sit in unspeakable agony and listen to the strange talk of the man who calls himself a Trappist and declares that he had come to give himself up to justice in expiation of his transgressions. Before doing so, he wished to implore my father's forgiveness and his last blessing. While saying this he was moving forward on his knees, and speaking with an intense passion. In the sound of this voice, uttering words of extravagant humility, there seemed to be insult and a menace. As he continued moving nearer to my father, and as the idea of the foul caresses which he apparently wished to lavish on him filled me with disgust, I ordered him in a somewhat imperious tone to rise and speak becomingly. My father angrily ordered him to say no more and depart; and as at this moment he cried, 'No, you must let me clasp your knees!' I pushed him back to prevent him from touching my father. I shudder to think that my glove has touched that unclean gown. He turned towards me, and, though he still feigned penitence and humility, I could see rage gleaming in his eyes. My father made a violent effort to get up, and in fact he got up, as if by a miracle; but the next instant he fell back fainting in his chair. Then steps were heard in the billiard-room, and the monk rushed out by the glass door with the speed of lightning. It was then that you found me half-dead and frozen with terror at the feet of my prostate father."

"The abominable coward has lost no time, you see, abbe," I cried. "His aim was to frighten the chevalier and Edmee, and he has succeeded; but he reckoned without me, and I swear that—though he should have to be treated in the Roche-Mauprat fashion—if he ever dares to come here again——"

"That is enough, Bernard," said Edmee. "You make me shudder. Speak seriously, and tell me what all this means."

When I had informed her of what had happened to the abbe and myself, she blamed us for not warning her.

"Had I known," she said, "what to expect I should not have been frightened, and I could have taken care never to be left alone in the house with my father, and Saint-Jean, who is hardly more active. Now, however, I am no longer afraid; I shall be on my guard. But the best thing, Bernard dear, is to avoid all contact with this loathsome man, and to make him as liberal an allowance as possible to get rid of him. The abbe is right; he may prove formidable. He knows that our kinship with him must always prevent us from summoning the law to protect us against his persecutions; and though he cannot injure us as seriously as he flatters himself, he can at least cause us a thousand annoyances, which I am reluctant to face. Throw him gold and let him take himself off. But do not leave me again, Bernard; you see you have become absolutely necessary to me; brood no more over the wrong you pretend to have done me."

I pressed her hand in mine, and vowed never to leave her, though she herself should order me, until this Trappist had freed the country from his presence.

The abbe undertook the negotiations with the monastery. He went into the town the following day, carrying from me a special message to the Trappist that I would throw him out of the window if he ever took it into his head to appear at Sainte-Severe again. At the same time I proposed to supply him with money, even liberally, on condition that he would immediately withdraw to his convent or to any other secular or religious retreat he might choose, and that he would never again set foot in Berry.

The prior received the abbe with all the signs of profound contempt and holy aversion for his state of heresy. Far from attempting to wheedle him like myself, he told him that he wished to have nothing to do with this business, that he washed his hands of it, and that he would confine himself to conveying the decisions on both sides, and affording a refuge to Brother Nepomucene, partly out of Christian charity, and partly to edify his monks by the example of a truly devout man. According to him, Brother Nepomucene would be the second of that name placed in the front rank of the heavenly host by virtue of the canons of the Church.

The next day the abbe was summoned to the convent by a special messenger, and had an interview with the Trappist. To his great surprise, he found that the enemy had changed his tactics. He indignantly refused help of any sort, declaring that his vow of poverty and humility would not allow it; and he strongly blamed his dear host, the prior, for daring to suggest, without his consent, an exchange of things eternal for things temporal. On other matters he refused to explain his views, and took refuge in ambiguous and bombastic replies. God would inspire him, he said, and at the approaching festival of the Virgin, at the august and sublime hour of holy communion, he expected to hear the voice of Jesus speaking to his heart and announcing the line of conduct he ought to follow. The abbe was afraid of betraying uneasiness, if he insisted on probing this "Christian mystery," so he returned with this answer, which was least of all calculated to reassure me. He did not appear again either at the castle or in the neighbourhood, and kept himself so closely shut up in the convent that few people ever saw his face. However, it soon became known, and the prior was most active in spreading the news, that John Mauprat had been converted to the most zealous and exemplary piety, and was now staying at the Carmelite convent for a term, as a penitent from La Trappe. Every day they reported some fresh virtuous trait, some new act of austerity of this holy personage. Devotees, with a thirst for the marvellous, came to see him, and brought him a thousand little presents, which he obstinately refused. At times he would hide so well that people said he had returned to his monastery; but just as we were congratulating ourselves on getting rid of him, we would hear that he had recently inflicted some terrible mortifications on himself in sackcloth and ashes; or else that he had gone barefooted on a pilgrimage into some of the wildest and most desolate parts of Varenne. People went so far as to say that he could work miracles. If the prior had not been cured of his gout, that was because, in a spirit of true penitence, he did not wish to be cured.

This state of uncertainty lasted almost two months.

XXI

These days, passed in Edmee's presence, were for me days of delight, yet of suffering. To see her at all hours, without fear of being indiscreet, since she herself would summon me to her side, to read to her, talk with her on all subjects, share the loving attentions she bestowed on her father, enter into half her life exactly as if we had been brother and sister—this was great happiness, no doubt, but it was a dangerous happiness, and again the volcano kindled in my breast. A few confused words, a few troubled glances betrayed me. Edmee was by no means blind, but she was impenetrable; her dark and searching eyes, fixed on me as on her father, with the solicitude of an absorbing affection, would at times suddenly grow cold, just as the violence of my passion was ready to break out. Her countenance would then express nothing but patient curiosity and an unswerving resolve to read to the bottom of my soul without letting me see even the surface of her own.

My sufferings, though acute, were dear to me at first; it pleased me to think that I was secretly offering them to Edmee as an expiation of my past faults. I hoped that she would perceive this and be satisfied with me. She saw it, and said nothing. My agony grew more intense; but still some days passed before I lost all power to hide it. I say days, because whoever has loved a woman, and has been much alone with her, yet always kept in check by her severity, must have found days like centuries. How full life seemed and yet how consuming! What languor and unrest! What tenderness and rage! It was as though the hours were years; and at this very day, if I did not bring in dates to rectify the error of my memory, I could easily persuade myself that these two months filled half my life.

Perhaps, too, I should like to persuade myself of this, in order to find some excuse for the foolish and culpable conduct into which I fell in spite of all the good resolutions which I had but lately formed. The relapse was so sudden and complete that I should still blush at the thought, if I had not cruelly atoned for it, as you will soon see.

After a night of agony, I wrote her an insane letter which came nigh to producing terrible consequences for me; it was somewhat as follows:

"You do not love me, Edmee; you will never love me. I know this; I ask for nothing, I hope for nothing. I would only remain near you and consecrate my life to your service and defence. To be useful to you I will do all that my strength will allow; but I shall suffer, and, however I try to hide it, you will see it; and perhaps you will attribute to wrong causes the sadness I may not be able to suppress with uniform heroism. You pained me deeply yesterday, when you advised me to go out a little 'to distract my thoughts.' To distract my thoughts from you, Edmee! What bitter mockery! Do not be cruel, sister; for then you become my haughty betrothed of evil days again . . . and, in spite of myself, I again become the brigand whom you used to hate. . . . Ah, if you knew how unhappy I am! In me there are two men who are incessantly waging a war to the death. It is to be hoped that the brigand will fall; but he defends himself step by step, and he cries aloud because he feels himself covered with wounds and mortally stricken. If you knew, Edmee, if you only knew what struggles, what conflicts, rend my bosom; what tears of blood my heart distils; and what passions often rage in that part of my nature which the rebel angels rule! There are nights when I suffer so much that in the delirium of my dreams I seem to be plunging a dagger into your heart, and thus, by some sombre magic, to be forcing you to love me as I love you. When I awake, in a cold sweat, bewildered, beside myself, I feel tempted to go and kill you, so as to destroy the cause of my anguish. If I refrain from this, it is because I fear that I should love you dead with as much passion and tenacity as if you were alive. I am afraid of being restrained, governed, swayed by your image as I am by your person. Then, again, a man cannot destroy the being he loves and fears; for when she has ceased to exist on earth she still exists in himself. It is the lover's soul which serves as a coffin for his mistress and which forever preserves her burning remains, that it may feed on them without ever consuming them. But, great Heaven! what is this tumult in my thoughts? You see, Edmee, to what an extent my mind is sick; take pity on me, then. Bear with me, let me be sad, never doubt my devotion. I am often mad, but I worship you always. A word, a look from you, will always recall me to a sense of duty, and this duty will be sweet when you deign to remind me of it. As I write to you, Edmee, the sky is full of clouds that are darker and heavier than lead; the thunder is rumbling, and doleful ghosts of purgatory seem to be floating in the glare of the lightning. The weight of the storm lies on my soul; my bewildered mind quivers like the flashes which leap from the firmament. It seems as if my whole being were about to burst like the tempest. Ah, could I but lift up to you a voice like unto its voice! Had I the power to lay bare the agonies and passions which rend me within! Often, when a storm has been sweeping over the great oaks above, you have told me that you enjoy gazing upon the fury of the one and the resistance of the other. This, you say, is a battle of mighty forces; and in the din in the air you fancy you can detect the curses of the north wind and the mournful cries of the venerable branches. Which suffers the more, Edmee, the tree which resists, or the wind which exhausts itself in the attack? Is it not always the wind that yields and falls? And then the sky, grieved at the defeat of her noble son, sheds a flood of tears upon the earth. You love these wild images, Edmee; and whenever you behold strength vanquished by resistance you smile cruelly, and there is a look in your inscrutable eyes that seems to insult my misery. Well, you have cast me to the ground, and, though shattered, I still suffer; yes, learn this, since you wish to know it, since you are merciless enough to question me and to feign compassion. I suffer, and I no longer try to remove the foot which the proud conqueror has placed on my broken heart."

The rest of this letter, which was very long, very rambling and absurd from beginning to end, was in the same strain. It was not the first time that I had written to Edmee, though I lived under the same roof, and never left her except during the hours of rest. My passion possessed me to such a degree that I was irresistibly drawn to encroach upon my sleep in order to write to her, I could never feel that I had talked enough about her, that I had sufficiently renewed my promises of submission—a submission in which I was constantly failing. The present letter, however, was more daring and more passionate than any of the others. Perhaps, in some mysterious way, it was written under the influence of the storm which was rending the heavens while I, bent over my table, with moist brow and dry, burning hand, drew this frenzied picture of my sufferings. A great calm, akin to despair, seemed to come over me as I threw myself upon my bed after going down to the drawing-room and slipping my letter into Edmee's work-basket. Day was breaking, and the horizon showed heavy with the dark wings of the storm, which was flying to other regions. The trees, laden with rain, were tossing under the breeze, which was still blowing freshly. Profoundly sad, but blindly resigned to my suffering, I fell asleep with a sense of relief, as if I had made a sacrifice of my life and hopes. Apparently Edmee did not find my letter, for she gave me no answer. She generally replied verbally, and these letters of mine were a means of drawing from her those professions of sisterly friendship with which I had perforce to be satisfied, and which, at least, poured soothing balm into my wound. I ought to have known that this time my letter must either lead to a decisive explanation, or be passed over in silence. I suspected the abbe of having taken it and thrown it into the fire; I accused Edmee of scorn and cruelty; nevertheless, I held my tongue.

The next day the weather was quite settled again. My uncle went for a drive, and during the course of it told us that he should not like to die without having had one last great fox-hunt. He was passionately devoted to this sport, and his health had so far improved that he again began to show a slight inclination for pleasure and exercise. Seated in a very light, narrow *berline*, drawn by strong mules, so that he might move rapidly over the sandy paths in our woods, he had already followed one or two little hunts which we had arranged for his amusement. Since the Trappist's visit, the chevalier had entered, as it were, upon a fresh term of life. Endowed with strength and pertinacity, like all his race, it seemed as if he had been decaying for want of excitement, for the slightest demand on his energy immediately set his stagnant blood in motion. As he was very much pleased with this idea of a hunt, Edmee undertook to organize, with my help, a general battue and to join in the sport herself. One of the greatest delights of the good old man was to see her on horseback, as she boldly pranced around his carriage and offered him all the flowering sprigs which she plucked from the bushes she passed. It was arranged that I should ride with her, and that the abbe should accompany the chevalier in the carriage. All the gamekeepers, foresters, huntsmen, and even poachers of Varenne were invited to this family function. A splendid meal was prepared with many goose-pies and much local wine. Marcasse, whom I had made my manager at Roche-Mauprat, and who had a considerable knowledge of the art of fox-hunting, spent two whole days in stopping up the earths. A few young farmers in the neighbourhood, interested in the battue and able to give useful advice, graciously offered to join the party; and, last of all, Patience, in spite of his aversion for the destruction of innocent animals, consented to follow the hunt as a spectator. On the appointed day, which opened warm and cloudless on our happy plans and my own implacable destiny, some fifty individuals met with horns, horses, and hounds. At the end we were to play havoc with the rabbits, of which there were too many on the estate. It would be easy to destroy them wholesale by falling back upon that part of the forest which had not been beaten during the hunt. Each man therefore armed himself with a carbine, and my uncle also took one, to shoot from his carriage, which he could still do with much skill.

Edmee was mounted on a very spirited Limousin mare, which she amused herself by exciting and quieting with a touching coquetry to please her old father. For the first two hours she hardly left the carriage at all, and the chevalier, now full of new life, gazed on her with smiles and tears of love. Just as in the daily rotation of our globe, ere passing into night, we take leave of the radiant orb which is going to reign over another hemisphere, even so did the old man find some consolation for his death in the thought that the youth and vigour and beauty of his daughter were surviving him for another generation.

When the hunt was in full swing, Edmee, who certainly inherited some of the martial spirit of the family, and the calmness of whose soul could not always restrain the impetuosity of her blood, yielded to her father's repeated signs—for his great desire now was to see her gallop—and went after the field, which was already a little distance ahead.

"Follow her! follow her!" cried the chevalier, who had no sooner seen her galloping off than his fond paternal vanity had given place to uneasiness.

I did not need to be told twice; and digging my spurs into my horse's flanks, I rejoined Edmee in a cross-path which she had taken to come up with the hunt. I shuddered as I saw her bending like a reed under the branches, while her horse, which she was still urging on, carried her between the trees with the rapidity of lightning.

"For God's sake, Edmee," I cried, "do not ride so fast! You will be killed!"

"Let me have a gallop," she said gaily. "My father has allowed me. You must not interfere; I shall rap you on the knuckles if you try to stop my horse."

"At least let me follow you, then," I said, keeping close to her. "Your father wished it; and I shall at least be there to kill myself if anything happens to you."

Why I was filled with these gloomy forebodings I do not know, for I had often seen Edmee galloping through the woods. I was in a peculiar state; the heat of noon seemed mounting to my brain, and my nerves were strangely excited. I had eaten no breakfast, as I had felt somewhat out of sorts in the morning, and, to sustain myself, had swallowed several cups of coffee mixed with rum. At first I experienced a horrible sense of fear; then, after a few minutes, the fear gave way to an inexpressible feeling of love and delight. The excitement of the gallop became so intense that I imagined my only object was to pursue Edmee. To see her flying before me, as light as her own black mare, whose feet were speeding noiselessly over the moss, one might have taken her for a fairy who had suddenly appeared in this lonely spot to disturb the mind of man and lure him away to her treacherous haunts. I forgot the hunt and everything else. I saw nothing but Edmee; then a mist fell upon my eyes, and I could see her no more. Still, I galloped on; I was in a state of silent frenzy, when she suddenly stopped.

"What are we doing?" she said. "I cannot hear the hunt any longer, and here is the river in front. We have come too far to the left."

"No, no, Edmee," I answered, without knowing in the least what I was saying. "Another gallop and we shall be there."

"How red you are!" she said. "But how shall we cross the river?"

"Since there is a road, there must be a ford," I replied. "Come on! come on!"

I was filled with an insane desire to go on galloping, I believe my idea was to plunge deeper and deeper into the forest with her; but this idea was wrapped in a haze, and when I tried to pierce it, I was conscious of nothing but a wild throbbing of my breast and temples.

Edmee made a gesture of impatience.

"These woods are accursed!" she said. "I am always losing my way in them."

No doubt she was thinking of the fatal day when she had been carried far from another hunt and brought to Roche-Mauprat. I thought of it too, and the ideas that came into my mind produced a sort of dizziness. I followed her mechanically towards the river. Suddenly I realized that she was on the other bank. I was filled with rage on seeing that her horse was cleverer and braver than my own. Before I could get the animal to take the ford, which was rather a nasty one, Edmee was a long way ahead of me again. I dug my spurs into its sides till the blood streamed from them. At last, after being nearly thrown several times, I reached the other bank, and, blind with rage, started in pursuit of Edmee. I overtook her, and seizing the mare's bridle, I exclaimed:

"Stop, Edmee, I say! You shall not go any farther."

At the same time I shook the reins so violently that her horse reared. She lost her balance, and, to avoid falling, jumped lightly to the ground between our two animals, at the risk of being hurt. I was on the ground almost as soon as herself. I at once pushed the horses away. Edmee's, which was very quiet, stopped and began to browse. Mine bolted out of sight. All this was the affair of an instant.

I had caught Edmee in my arms; she freed herself and said, in a sharp tone:

"You are very brutal, Bernard; and I hate these ways of yours. What is the matter with you?"

Perplexed and confused, I told her that I thought her mare was bolting, and that I was afraid some accident might happen to her if she allowed herself to be carried away by the excitement of the ride.

"And to save me," she replied, "you make me fall, at the risk of killing me! Really, that was most considerate of you."

"Let me help you to mount again," I said.

And without waiting for her permission, I took her in my arms and lifted her off the ground.

"You know very well that I do not mount in this way!" she exclaimed, now quite irritated. "Leave me alone; I don't want your help."

But I was no longer in a state to obey her. I was losing my head; my arms were tightening around her waist, and it was in vain that I endeavoured to take them away. My lips touched her bosom in spite of myself. She grew pale with anger.

"Oh, how unfortunate I am!" I said, with my eyes full of tears; "how unfortunate I am to be always offending you, and to be hated more and more in proportion as my love for you grows greater!"

Edmee was of an imperious and violent nature. Her character, hardened by trials, had every year developed greater strength. She was no longer the trembling girl making a parade of courage, but in reality more ingenuous than bold, whom I had clasped in my arms at Roche-Mauprat. She was now a proud, fearless woman, who would have let herself be killed rather than give the slightest countenance to an audacious hope. Besides, she was now the woman who knows that she is passionately loved and is conscious of her power. She repulsed me, therefore, with scorn; and as I followed her distractedly, she raised her whip and threatened to leave a mark of ignominy on my face if I dared to touch even her stirrup.

I fell on my knees and begged her not to leave me thus without forgiving me. She was already in her saddle, and, as she looked round for the way back, she exclaimed:

"That was the one thing wanting—to behold this hateful spot again! Do you see where we are?"

I looked in my turn, and saw that we were on the edge of the forest, quite close to the shady little pond at Gazeau. A few yards from us, through the trees which had grown denser since Patience left, I perceived the door of the tower, opening like a big black mouth behind the green foliage.

I was seized with a fresh dizziness. A terrible struggle was taking place between two instincts. Who shall explain the mysterious workings of man's brain when his soul is grappling with the senses, and one part of his being is striving to strangle the other? In an organization like mine, such a conflict, believe me, was bound to be terrible; and do not imagine that the will makes but a feeble resistance in natures carried away by passion; it is idiotic to say to a man who lies spent with such struggles, "You ought to have conquered yourself."

XXII

How shall I describe to you what I felt at the unexpected sight of Gazeau Tower? I had seen it but twice in my life; each time I had taken part in a painfully stirring scene there. Yet these scenes were as naught beside the one awaiting me on this third encounter; there must be a curse on certain places.

I fancied I could still see the blood of the two Mauprats sprinkled on the shattered door. Their life of crime and their tragic end made me shudder at the violent instincts which I felt in myself. I was filled with a horror of my own feelings, and I understood why Edmee did not love me. But, as if yonder deplorable blood had power to stir a fatal sympathy, I felt the wild strength of my passion increasing in proportion as my will made greater efforts to subdue it. I had trampled down all other passions; scarcely a trace of them remained in me. I was sober; if not gentle and patient, I was at least capable of affection and sympathy; I had a profound sense of the laws of honour, and the highest respect for the dignity of others. Love, however, was still the most formidable of my enemies; for it was inseparably connected with all that I had acquired of morality and delicacy; it was the tie that bound the old man to the new, an indissoluble tie, which made it almost impossible for me to find the golden mean between reason and passion.

Standing before Edmee, who was about to leave me behind and on foot; furious at seeing her escape me for the last time (since after the insult I had just offered her she would doubtless never run the risk of being alone with me again), I gazed on her with a terrible expression. I was livid; my fists were clinched. I had but to resolve, and the slightest exertion of my strength would have snatched her from her horse, thrown her to the ground and left her at the mercy of my desires. I had but to let my old savage instincts reign for a second and I could have slaked, extinguished the fires which had been consuming me for seven years. Never did Edmee know the danger her honour ran in that minute of agony, and never have I ceased to feel remorse for it; but God alone shall be my Judge, for I triumphed, and this was the last evil thought of my life. In this thought, moreover, lay the whole of my crime; the rest was the work of fate.

Filled with fear, I suddenly turned my back on her and, wringing my hands in despair, hastened away by the path which had brought me thither. I cared little where I went; I only knew that I had to tear myself away from perilous temptations. It was a broiling day; the odour of the woods seemed intoxicating; the mere ght of them was stirring up the instincts of my old savage life; I had to flee or

With an imperious gesture, Edmee ordered me to depart from her presence.

The idea that any danger could possibly threaten her except from myself naturally did not come into my head or her own. I plunged into the forest. I had not gone more than thirty paces when I heard the report of a gun from the spot where I had left Edmee. I stopped, petrified with horror; why, I know not; for in the middle of a battue the report of a gun was by no means extraordinary; but my soul was so sorrowful that it seemed ready to find fresh woe in everything. I was about to retrace my steps and rejoin Edmee at the risk of offending her still more when I thought I heard the moaning of a human being in the direction of Gazeau Tower. I rushed forward, and then fell upon my knees, as if stunned by emotion. It took me some minutes to recover; my brain seemed full of doleful sights and sounds; I could no longer distinguish between illusion and reality; though the sun was shining brightly I began to grope my way among the trees. All of a sudden I found myself face to face with the abbe; he was anxiously looking for Edmee. The chevalier had driven to a certain spot to watch the field pass, and not seeing his daughter, had been filled with apprehension. The abbe had plunged into the forest at once, and, soon finding the tracks of our horses, had come to see what had happened to us. He had heard the gun, but had thought nothing of it. Seeing me pale and apparently dazed, with my hair disarranged, and without either horse or gun (I had let mine fall on the spot where I had half fainted, and had not thought of picking it up), he was as terrified as myself; nor did he know any more than I for what reason.

"Edmee!" he said to me, "where is Edmee?"

I made a rambling reply. He was so alarmed at seeing me in such a state that he felt secretly convinced I had committed some crime, as he subsequently confessed to me.

"Wretched boy!" he said, shaking me vigorously by the arm to bring me to my senses. "Be calm; collect your thoughts, I implore you! . . ."

I did not understand a word, but I led him towards the fatal spot; and there—a sight never to be forgotten—Edmee was lying on the ground rigid and bathed in blood. Her mare was quietly grazing a few yards away. Patience was standing by her side with his arms crossed on his breast, his face livid, and his heart so full that he was unable to answer a word to the abbe's cries and sobs. For myself, I could not understand what was taking place. I fancy that my brain, already bewildered by my previous emotions, must have been completely paralyzed. I sat down on the ground by Edmee's side. She had been shot in the breast in two places. I gazed on her lifeless eyes in a state of absolute stupor.

"Take away that creature," said Patience to the abbe, casting a look of contempt on me. "His perverse nature is what it always was."

"Edmee, Edmee!" cried the abbe, throwing himself upon the grass and endeavouring to stanch the blood with his handkerchief.

"Dead, dead!" said Patience. "And there is the murderer! She said so as she gave up her pure soul to God; and Patience will avenge her! It is very hard; but it must be so! It is God's will, since I alone was here to learn the truth."

"Horrible, horrible!" exclaimed the abbe.

I heard the sound of this last word, and with a smile I repeated it like an echo.

Some huntsmen now appeared. Edmee was carried away. I believe that I caught sight of her father walking without help. However, I should not dare to affirm that this was not a mere extravagant vision (for I had no definite consciousness of anything, and these awful moments have left in my mind nothing but vague memories, as of a dream), had I not been assured that the chevalier got out of the carriage without any help, walked about, and acted with as much presence of mind as a young man. On the following day he fell into a state of absolute dotage and insensibility, and never rose from his arm-chair again.

But what happened to myself? I do not know. When I recovered my reason, I found that I was in another part of the forest near a little waterfall, to the murmur of which I was listening mechanically with a sort of vague delight. Blaireau was asleep at my feet, while his master, leaning against a tree, was watching me attentively. The setting sun was sending shafts of ruddy gold between the slender stems of the young ash-trees; the wild flowers seemed to be smiling at me; and birds were warbling sweet melodies. It was one of the most beautiful days of the year.

"What a gorgeous evening!" I said to Marcasse. "This spot is as beautiful as an American forest. Well, old friend, what are you doing there? You ought to have awakened me sooner. I have had such hideous dreams."

Marcasse came and knelt down beside me; two streams of tears were running down his withered, sallow cheeks. On his face, usually so impassive, there was an ineffable expression of pity and sorrow and affection.

"Poor master!" he said, "delirium, head bad, that's all. Great misfortune! But fidelity not changed. Always with you; if need be, ready to die with you."

His tears and words filled me with sadness; but this was owing to an instinctive sympathy enhanced by the weak state of my nerves, for I did not remember a thing. I threw myself into his arms and wept like himself; he pressed me to his bosom, as a father might his son. I was fully conscious that some frightful misfortune had overtaken me, but I was afraid to learn what it was, and nothing in the world would have induced me to ask him.

He took me by the arm and led me through the forest. I let myself be taken like a child. Then a fresh sense of weariness came over me, and he was obliged to let me sit down again for half an hour. At last he lifted me up and succeeded in leading me to Roche-Mauprat, where we arrived very late. I do not know what happened to me during the night. Marcasse told me subsequently that I had been very delirious. He took upon himself to send to the nearest village for a barber, who bled me early in the morning, and a few minutes later I recovered my reason.

But what a frightful service they seemed to have done me. Dead! Dead! Dead! This was the only word I could utter. I did nothing but groan and toss about on my bed. I wanted to get up and run to Sainte-Severe. My poor sergeant would throw himself at my feet, or plant himself in front of the door to prevent me. To keep me back, he would tell me various things which I did not in the least understand. However, his manifest solicitude for me and my own feeling of exhaustion made me yield, though I could not explain his conduct. In one of these struggles my vein opened again, and I returned to bed before Marcasse noticed it. Gradually I sank into a deep swoon, and I was almost dead when, seeing my blue lips and purple cheeks, he took it into his head to lift up the bed-clothes, and found me lying in a pool of blood.

However, this was the most fortunate thing that could have happened to me. For several days I remained in a state of prostration in which there was but little difference between my waking and sleeping hours. Thanks to this, I understood nothing, and therefore did not suffer.

One morning, having managed to make me take a little nourishment, and noticing that with my strength my melancholy and anxiety were returning, Marcasse announced, with a simple, genuine delight, that Edmee was not dead, and that they did not despair of saving her. These words fell upon me like a thunderbolt; for I was still under the impression that this frightful adventure was a delusion of my delirium. I began to shout and to brandish my arms in a terrible manner. Marcasse fell on his knees by my bed and implored me to be calm, and a score of times he repeated the following words, which to me were like the meaningless words one hears in dreams:

"You did not do it on purpose; I know well enough. No, you did not do it on purpose. It was an accident; a gun going off in your hand by chance."

"Come, now, what do you mean?" I exclaimed impatiently. "What gun? What accident? What have I to do with it?"

"Don't you know, then, sir, how she was hit?"

I passed my hands over my brow as if to bring back to my mind the energy of life, and as I had no clear recollection of the mysterious event which had unhinged it, I thought that I was mad, and remained silent and dismayed, fearful lest any word should escape to betray the loss of my faculties.

At last, little by little, I collected my thoughts. I asked for some wine, as I felt weak; and no sooner had I drunk a few drops than all the scenes of the fatal day unrolled themselves before me as if by magic. I even remembered the words that I had heard Patience utter immediately after the event. It was as if they had been graven in that part of the memory which preserves the sound of words, even when the other part which treasures up their sense is asleep. For one more moment I was uncertain; I wondered if my gun could have gone off in my hands just as I was leaving Edmee. I distinctly remembered firing it at a pewit an hour before, for Edmee had wanted to examine the bird's plumage. Further, when I heard the shot which had hit her, my gun was in my hands, and I had not thrown it down until a few seconds later, so it could not have been this weapon which had gone off on falling. Besides, even granting a fatality which was incredible, I was much too far from Edmee at that moment to have shot her. Finally, I had not a single bullet on me throughout the day; and it was impossible for my gun to have been loaded, unknown to myself, since I had not unslung it after killing the pewit.

Quite convinced, therefore, that I was not the cause of the hideous accident, it remained to me to find an explanation of this crushing catastrophe. To me it was perfectly simple; some booby with a gun, I thought, must have caught sight of Edmee's horse through the branches and mistaken it for a wild beast; and I did not dream of accusing any one of a deliberate attempt at murder. I discovered, however, that I was accused myself. I drew the truth from Marcasse. He informed me that the chevalier and all the people who took part in the hunt had attributed the misfortune to a pure accident, their opinion being that, to my great sorrow, my gun had gone off when my horse threw me, for it was believed that I had been thrown. This was practically the view they all took. In the few words that Edmee had been able to utter she seemed to confirm the supposition. Only one person accused me, and that was Patience; but he had accused me before none but his two friends, Marcasse and the Abbe Aubert, and then only after pledging them to secrecy.

"There is no need," added Marcasse, "for me to tell you that the abbe maintains an absolute silence, and refuses to believe that you are guilty. As for myself, I swear to you that I shall never—"

"Stop! stop!" I said. "Do not tell me even that; it would imply that some one in the world might actually believe it. But Edmee said something extraordinary to Patience just as she was dying; for she is dead; it is useless for you to try to deceive me. She is dead, and I shall never see her again."

"She is not dead!" cried Marcasse.

And his solemn oaths convinced me, for I knew that he would have tried in vain to lie; his simple soul would have risen in revolt against his charitable intentions. As for Edmee's words, he frankly refused to repeat them; from which I gathered that their testimony seemed overwhelming. Thereupon I dragged myself out of bed, and stubbornly resisted all Marcasse's efforts to keep me back; I had the farmer's horse saddled and started off at a gallop. I staggered into the drawing-room without meeting any one except Saint-Jean, who uttered a cry of terror on seeing me, and rushed off without answering my questions.

The drawing-room was empty. Edmee's embroidery frame, buried under the green cloth, which her hand, perchance, would never lift again, seemed to me like a bier under its pall. My uncle's big arm-chair was no longer in the chimney-corner. My portrait, which I had had painted in Philadelphia and had sent over during the American war, had been taken down from the wall. These were signs of death and malediction.

I left this room with all haste and went upstairs with the courage of innocence, but with despair in my soul. I walked straight to Edmee's room, knocked, and entered at once. Mademoiselle Leblanc was coming towards the door; she gave a loud scream and ran away, hiding her face in her hands as if she had seen a wild beast. Who, then, could have been spreading hideous reports about me? Had the abbe been disloyal enough to do so? I learnt later that Edmee, though generous and unshaken in her lucid moments, had openly accused me in her delirium.

I approached her bed and, half delirious myself, forgetting that my sudden appearance might be a deathblow to her, I pulled the curtains aside with an eager hand and gazed on her. Never have I seen more marvellous beauty. Her big dark eyes had grown half as large again; they were shining with an extraordinary brilliancy, though without any expression, like diamonds. Her drawn, colourless cheeks, and her lips, as white as her cheeks, gave her the appearance of a beautiful marble head. She looked at me fixedly, with as little emotion as if she had been looking at a picture or a piece of furniture; then, turning her face slightly towards the wall, she said, with a mysterious smile:

"This is the flower they call *Edmea sylvestris*."

I fell upon my knees; I took her hand; I covered it with kisses; I broke into sobs. But she gave no heed; her hand remained in mine icy and still, like a piece of alabaster.

XXIII

The abbe came in and greeted me in a cold and sombre manner. Then he made a sign to me, and drawing me away from the bed, said:

"You must be mad! Return at once; and if you are wise, you will remain away. It is the only thing left for you to do."

"And since when," I cried, flying into a passion, "have you had the right to drive me out of the bosom of my family?"

"Alas! you have no longer a family," he answered, with an accent of sorrow that somewhat disarmed me. "What were once father and daughter are now naught but two phantoms, whose souls are already dead and whose bodies soon will be. Show some respect for the last days of those who loved you."

"And how can I show my respect and grief by quitting them?" I replied, quite crushed.

"On this point," said the abbe, "I neither wish nor ought to say anything; for you know that your presence here is an act of rashness and a profanation. Go away. When they are no more (and the day cannot be far distant), if you have any claims to this house, you may return, and you will certainly not find me here to contest them or affirm them. Meanwhile, as I have no knowledge of these claims, I believe I may take upon myself to see that some respect is paid to the last hours of these two holy people."

"Wretched man!" I said, "I do not know what prevents me from tearing you to pieces! What abominable impulse urges you to be everlastingly turning the dagger in my breast? Are you afraid that I may survive this blow? Cannot you see that three coffins will be taken out together from this house? do you imagine that I have come here for aught but a farewell look and a farewell blessing?"

"You might say a farewell pardon," replied the abbe, in a bitter tone, and with a gesture of merciless condemnation.

"What I say is that you are mad!" I cried, "and that if you were not a priest, this hand of mine should crush the life out of you for daring to speak to me in this way."

"I have but little fear of you, sir," he rejoined. "To take my life would be doing me a great service; but I am sorry that your threats and anger should lend weight to the charges under which you lie. If I saw that you were moved to penitence, I would weep with you; but your assurance fills me with loathing. Hitherto, I had seen in you nothing worse than a raging lunatic; to-day I seem to see a scoundrel. Begone, sir!"

XXIII

I fell into an arm-chair, choking with rage and anguish. For a moment I hoped that I was about to die. Edmee was dying by my side, and before me was a judge so firmly convinced of my guilt that his usual gentle, timid nature had become harsh and pitiless. The imminent loss of her I loved was hurrying me into a longing for death. Yet the horrible charge hanging over me began to rouse my energies. I did not believe that such an accusation could stand for a single instant against the voice of truth. I imagined that one word from me, one look, would be sufficient to make it fall to the ground; but I felt so dazed, so deeply wounded, that this means of defence was denied me. The more grievously the disgrace of such a suspicion weighed upon my mind, the more clearly I realized that it is almost impossible for a man to defend himself successfully when his only weapon is the pride of slandered innocence.

I sat there overwhelmed, unable to utter a word. It seemed as if a dome of lead were weighing on my skull. Suddenly the door opened and Mademoiselle Leblanc approached me stiffly; in a tone full of hatred she informed me that some one outside wished to speak to me. I went out mechanically, and found Patience waiting with his arms folded, in his most dignified attitude, and with an expression on his face which would have compelled both respect and fear if I had been guilty.

"Monsieur de Mauprat," he said, "I must request you to grant me a private interview. Will you kindly follow me to my cottage?"

"Yes, I will," I replied. "I am ready to endure any humiliation, if only I can learn what is wanted of me and why you are all pleased to insult the most unfortunate of men. Lead the way, Patience, and go quickly; I am eager to return here."

Patience walked in front of me with an impassive air. When we arrived at his little dwelling, we found my poor sergeant, who had just arrived likewise. Not finding any horse on which he could follow me, and not wishing to quit me, he had come on foot, and so quickly that he was bathed in perspiration. Nevertheless, the moment he saw us he sprang up full of life from the bench on which he had thrown himself under the bower of vine-branches, and came to meet us.

"Patience!" he cried, in a dramatic style which would have made me smile had it been possible for me to display a glimmer of mirth at such a moment. "Old fool! . . . Slanderer at your age? . . . Fie, sir! . . . Ruined by good fortune . . . you are . . . yes."

Patience, impassive as ever, shrugged his shoulders and said to his friend:

"Marcasse, you do not know what you are saying. Go and rest awhile at the bottom of the orchard. This matter does not concern you. I want to speak to your master alone. I wish you to go," he added, taking him by the arm; and there was a touch of authority in his manner to which the sergeant, in spite of his ticklish prided, yielded from instinct and habit.

As soon as we were alone Patience proceeded to the point; he began by a series of questions to which I resolved to submit, so that I might the more quickly obtain some light on the state of affairs around me.

"Will you kindly inform me, monsieur," he said, "what you purpose doing now?"

"I purpose remaining with my family," I answered, "as long as I have a family; and when this family is no more, what I shall do concerns no one."

"But, sir," replied Patience, "if you were told that you could not remain under the same roof with them without causing the death of one or the other, would you persist in staying?"

"If I were convinced that this was so," I rejoined, "I would not appear in their presence. I would remain at their door and await the last day of their life, or the first day of their renewed health, and again implore a love I have not yet ceased to deserve."

"Ah, we have come to this!" said Patience, with a smile of contempt. "I should not have believed it. However, I am very glad; it makes matters clearer."

"What do you mean?" I cried. "Speak, you wretch! Explain yourself!"

"You are the only wretch here," he answered coldly, at the same time sitting down on the one stool in the cottage, while I remained standing before him.

I wanted to draw an explanation from him, at all costs. I restrained my feelings; I even humbled myself so far as to say that I should be ready to accept advice, if he would consent to tell me the words that Edmee had uttered immediately after the event, and those which she had repeated in her hours of delirium.

"That I will not," replied Patience sternly; "you are not worthy to hear any words from that mouth, and I shall certainly never repeat them to you. Why do you want to know them? Do you hope to hide anything from men hereafter? God saw you; for Him there are no secrets. Leave this place; stay at Roche-Mauprat; keep quiet there; and when your uncle is dead and your affairs are settled, leave this part of the country. If you take my advice, you will leave it this very day. I do not want to put the law on your track, unless your actions force me. But others besides myself, if they are not certain of the truth, have at least a suspicion of it. Before two days have passed a chance word said in public, the indiscretion of some servant, may awaken the attention of justice, and from that point to the scaffold, when a man is guilty, is but a single step. I used not to hate you; I even had a liking for you; take this advice, then, which you say you are ready to follow. Go away at once, or remain in hiding and ready for flight. I do not desire your ruin; Edmee would not desire it either—so—do you understand?"

"You must be insane to think that I could listen to such advice. I, hide myself! or flee like a murderer! You can't dream of that! Come on! come on! I defy the whole of you! I know not what fury and hatred are fretting you and uniting you all against me; I know not why you want to keep me from seeing my uncle and cousin; but I despise your follies. My place is here; I shall not quit it except by order of my cousin or uncle; and this order, too, I must take from their own lips; I cannot allow sentence to be brought me by any outsider. So, thanks for your wisdom, Monsieur Patience; in this case my own will suffice. I am your humble servant, sir."

I was preparing to leave the cottage when he rushed in front of me, and for a moment I saw that he was ready to use force to detain me. In spite of his advanced age, in spite of my height and strength, he might still have been a match, perhaps more than a match, for me in a struggle of this kind. Short, bent, broad-shouldered, he was a Hercules.

He stopped, however, just as he was about to lay hands on me, and, seized with one of those fits of deep tenderness to which he was subject in his moments of greatest passion, he gazed at me with eyes of pity, and said, in a gentle tone:

"My poor boy! you whom I loved as a son (for I looked upon you as Edmee's brother), do not hasten to your ruin. I beseech you in the name of her whom you have murdered, and whom you still love—I can see it—but whom you may never behold again. Believe me, but yesterday your family was a proud vessel, whose helm was in your hands; to-day it is a drifting wreck, without either sail or pilot—left to be handled by cabinboys, as friend Marcasse says. Well, my poor mariner, do not persist in drowning yourself; I am throwing you a rope; take it—a day more, and it may be too late. Remember that if the law gets hold of you, the man who is trying to save you to-day, to-morrow will be obliged to appear against you and condemn you. Do not compel me to do a thing the very thought of which brings tears to my eyes. Bernard, you have been loved, my lad; even to-day you may live on the past."

I burst into tears, and the sergeant, who returned at this moment, began to weep also; he implored me to go back to Roche-Mauprat; but I soon recovered and, thrusting them both away, said:

"I know that both of you are excellent men, and both most generous; you must have some love for me too, since, though you believe me blackened with a hideous crime, you can still think of saving my life. But have no fears on my account, good friends; I am innocent of this crime, and my one wish is that the matter may be fully investigated, so that I may be acquitted—yes, this is inevitable, I owe it to my family to live until my honour has been freed from stain. Then, if I am condemned to see my cousin die, as I have no one in the world to love but her, I will blow my brains out. Why, then, should I be downcast? I set little store by my life. May God make the last hours of her whom I shall certainly not survive painless and peaceful—that is all I ask of Him."

Patience shook his head with a gloomy, dissatisfied expression. He was so convinced of my crime that all my denials only served to alienate his pity. Marcasse still loved me, though he thought I was guilty. I had no one in the world to answer for my innocence, except myself.

"If you persist on returning to the chateau," exclaimed Patience, "you must swear before you leave that you will not enter your cousin's room, or your uncle's, without the abbe's permission."

"What I swear is that I am innocent," I replied, "and that I will allow no man to saddle me with a crime. Back, both of you! Let me pass! Patience, if you consider it your duty to denounce me, go and do so. All that I ask is that I may not be condemned without a hearing; I prefer the bar of justice to that of mere opinion."

I rushed out of the cottage and returned to the chateau. However, not wishing to make a scandal before the servants, and knowing quite well that they could not hide Edmee's real condition from me, I went and shut myself up in the room I usually occupied.

But in the evening, just as I was leaving it to get news of the two patients, Mademoiselle Leblanc again told me that some one wished to speak with me outside. I noticed that her face betrayed a sense of joy as well as fear. I concluded that they had come to arrest me, and I suspected (rightly, as it transpired) that Mademoiselle Leblanc had denounced me. I went to the window, and saw some of the mounted police in the courtyard.

"Good," I said; "let my destiny take its course."

But, before quitting, perhaps forever, this house in which I was leaving my soul, I wished to see Edmee again for the last time. I walked straight to her room. Mademoiselle Leblanc tried to throw herself in front of the door; I pushed her aside so roughly that she fell, and, I believe, hurt herself slightly. She immediately filled the house with her cries; and later, in the trial, made a great pother about what she was pleased to call an attempt to murder her. I at once entered Edmee's room; there I found the abbe and the doctor. I listened in silence to what the latter was saying. I learnt that the wounds in themselves were not mortal, that they would not even be very serious, had not a violent disturbance in the brain complicated the evil and made him fear tetanus. This frightful word fell upon me like a death sentence. In America I had seen many men die of this terrible malady, the result of wounds received in the war. I approached the bed. The abbe was so alarmed that he did not think of preventing me. I took Edmee's hand, cold and lifeless, as ever. I kissed it a last time, and, without saying a single word to the others, went and gave myself up to the police.

XXIV

I was immediately thrown into prison at La Chatre. The public prosecutor for the district of Issoudun took in hand this case of the attempted murder of Mademoiselle de Mauprat, and obtained permission to have a monitory published on the morrow. He went to the village of Sainte-Severe, and then to the farms in the neighbourhood of the Curat woods, where the event had happened, and took the depositions of more than thirty witnesses. Then, eight days after I had been arrested, the writ of arrest was issued. If my mind had been less distracted, or if some one had interested himself in me, this breach of the law and many others that occurred during the trial might have been adduced as powerful arguments in my favour. They would at least have shown that the proceedings were inspired by some secret hatred. In the whole course of the affair an invisible hand directed everything with pitiless haste and severity.

The first examination had produced but a single indictment against me; this came from Mademoiselle Leblanc. The men who had taken part in the hunt declared that they knew nothing, and had no reason to regard the occurrence as a deliberate attempt at murder. Mademoiselle Leblanc, however, who had an old grudge against me for certain jokes I had ventured to make at her expense, and who, moreover, had been suborned, as I learned afterward, declared that Edmee, on recovering from her first swoon, at a time when she was quite calm and in full possession of her reason, had confided to her, under a pledge of secrecy, that she had been insulted, threatened, dragged from her horse, and finally shot by me. This wicked old maid, putting together the various revelations that Edmee had made in her delirium, had, cleverly enough, composed a connected narrative, and added to it all the embellishments that hatred could suggest. Distorting the incoherent words and vague impressions of her mistress, she declared upon oath that Edmee had seen me point the barrel of my carbine at her, with the words, "As I swore, you shall die by my hand."

Saint-Jean, who was examined the same day, declared that he knew nothing beyond what Mademoiselle Leblanc had told him that evening, and his deposition was very similar to hers. He was honest enough, but dull and narrow-minded. From love of exactness, he omitted no trifling detail which might be interpreted against me. He asserted that I had always been subject to pains in the head, during which I lost my senses; that several times previously, when my nerves were disordered, I had spoken of blood and murder to some individual whom I always fancied I could see; and, finally, that my temper was so violent that I was "capable of throwing the first thing that came to hand at any one's head, though as a fact I had never, to his knowledge, committed any excess of this kind." Such are the depositions that frequently decide life and death in criminal cases.

Patience could not be found on the day of this inquiry. The abbe declared that his ideas on the occurrence were so vague that he would undergo all the penalties inflicted on recalcitrant witnesses rather than express his opinion before fuller investigations had been made. He requested the public prosecutor to give him time, promising on his honour that he would not resist the demands of justice, and representing that at the end of a few days, by inquiring into certain things, he would probably arrive at a conviction of some sort; in this event he undertook to speak plainly, either for or against me. This delay was granted.

Marcasse simply said that if I had inflicted the wounds on Mademoiselle de Mauprat, about which he was beginning to feel very doubtful, I had at least inflicted them unintentionally; on this he was prepared to stake his honour and his life.

Such was the result of the first inquiry. It was resumed at various times during the following days, and several false witnesses swore that they had seen me shoot Mademoiselle de Mauprat, after vainly endeavouring to make her yield to my wishes.

One of the most baneful instruments of ancient criminal procedure was what was known as the monitory; this was a notice from the pulpit, given out by the bishop and repeated by all vicars to their parishioners, ordering them to make inquiries about the crime in question, and to reveal all the facts which might come to their knowledge. This was merely a modified form of the inquisitorial principle which reigned more openly in other countries. In the majority of cases, the monitory, which had, as a fact, been instituted in order to encourage informers in the name of religion, was a marvel of ridiculous atrocity; it frequently set forth the crime and all the imaginary circumstances the plaintiffs were eager to prove; it was, in short, the publication of a ready-made case, which gave the first knave that came a chance of earning some money by making a lying deposition in favour of the highest bidder. The inevitable effect of the monitory, when it was drawn up with a bias, was to arouse public hatred against the accused. The devout especially, receiving their opinions ready-made from the clergy, pursued the victim without mercy. This is what happened in my own case; but here the clergy of the province were playing a further secret part which almost decided my fate.

The case was taken to the assizes at the court of Bourges, and proceedings began in a very few days.

You can imagine the gloomy despair with which I was filled. Edmee's condition was growing more and more serious; her mind was completely unhinged. I felt no anxiety as to the result of the trial; I never imagined it was possible to convict me of a crime I had not committed; but what were honour and life to me, if Edmee were never to regain the power of recognising my innocence? I looked upon her as already dead, and as having cursed me dying! So I was inflexibly resolved to kill myself immediately after receiving my sentence, whatever it might be. Until then I felt that it was my duty to live, and to do what might be necessary for the triumph of truth; but I was plunged in such a state of stupor that I did not even think of ascertaining what was to be done. Had it not been for the cleverness and zeal of my counsel, and the sublime devotion of Marcasse, my listlessness would have left me to the most terrible fate.

Marcasse spent all his time in expeditions on my behalf. In the evening he would come and throw himself on a bundle of straw at the foot of my trunkle bed, and, after giving me news of Edmee and the chevalier, whom he went to see every day, he would tell me the results of his proceedings. I used to grasp his hand affectionately; but I was generally so absorbed by the news he had just given me of Edmee, that I never heard anything further.

This prison of La Chatre had formerly been the stronghold of the Elevains of Lombaud, the seigneurs of the province. Nothing was left of it but a formidable square tower at the top of a ravine where the Indre forms a narrow, winding valley, rich with the most beautiful vegetation. The weather was magnificent. My room, situated at the top of the tower, received the rays of the rising sun, which cast the long, thin shadows of a triple row of poplars as far as the eye could see. Never did landscape more smiling, fresh, and pastoral offer itself to the eyes of a prisoner. But how could I find pleasure in it? Words of death and contumely came to me in every breeze that blew through the wall-flowers growing in the crannies. Every rustic sound, every tune on the pipe that rose to my room, seemed to contain an insult or to proclaim profound contempt for my sorrow. There was nothing, even to the bleating of the flocks, which did not appear to me an expression of neglect or indifference.

For some time Marcasse had had one fixed idea, namely, that Edmee had been shot by John Mauprat. It was possible; but as there was no evidence to support the conjecture, I at once ordered him not to make known his suspicions. It was not for me to clear myself at the expense of others. Although John Mauprat was capable of anything, it was possible that he had never thought of committing this crime; and as I had not heard him spoken of for more than six weeks, it seemed to me that it would have been cowardly to accuse him. I clung to the belief that one of the men in the battue had fired at Edmee by mistake, and that a feeling of fear and shame prevented him from confessing his misadventure. Marcasse had the courage to go and see all those who had taken part in the hunt, and, with such eloquence as Heaven had granted him, implored them not to fear the penalty for unintentional murder, and not to allow an innocent man to be accused in their stead. All these efforts were fruitless; from none of the huntsmen did my poor friend obtain a reply which left him any nearer a solution of the mystery that surrounded us.

On being transferred to Bourges, I was thrown into the castle which had belonged to the old dukes of Berry; this was henceforth to be my prison. It was a great grief to me to be separated from my faithful sergeant. He would have been allowed to follow me, but he had a presentiment that he would soon be arrested at the suggestion of my enemies (for he persisted in believing that I was the victim of a plot), and thus be unable to serve me any more. He wished, therefore, to lose no time, and to continue his investigations as long as they "should not have seized his person."

Two days after my removal to Bourges, Marcasse produced a document which had been drawn up at his instance by two notaries of La Chatre. It contained the depositions of ten witnesses to the effect that for some days before the attempted assassination, a mendicant friar had been prowling about Varenne; that he had appeared in different places very close together; and, notably, that he had slept at Notre-Dame de Poligny the night before the event. Marcasse maintained that this monk was John Mauprat. Two women declared that they had thought they recognised him either as John or Walter Mauprat, who closely resembled him. But Walter had been found drowned the day after the capture of the keep; and the whole town of La Chatre, on the day when Edmee was shot, had seen the Trappist engaged with the Carmelite prior from morning till night in conducting the procession and services for the pilgrimage of Vaudevant. These depositions, therefore, so far from being favourable to me, produced a very bad effect, and threw odium on my defence. The Trappist conclusively proved his alibi, and the prior of the Carmelites helped him to spread a report that I was a worthless villain. This was a time of triumph for John Mauprat; he proclaimed aloud that he had come to deliver himself up to his natural judges to suffer punishment for his crimes in the past; but no one could think of prosecuting such a holy man. The fanaticism that he inspired in our eminently devout province was such that no magistrate would have dared to brave public opinion by proceeding against him. In his own depositions, Marcasse gave an account of the mysterious and inexplicable appearance of the Trappist at Roche-Mauprat, the steps he had taken to obtain an interview with M. Hubert and his daughter, his insolence in entering and terrifying them in their drawing-room, and the efforts the Carmelite prior had made to obtain considerable sums of money from me on behalf of this individual. All these depositions were treated as fairy tales, for Marcasse admitted that he had not seen the Trappist in any of the places mentioned, and neither the chevalier nor his daughter was able to give evidence. It is true that my answers to the various questions put to me confirmed Marcasse's statements; but as I declared in all sincerity that for some two months the Trappist had given me no cause for uneasiness or displeasure, and as I refused to attribute the murder to him, it seemed for some days as if he would be forever reinstated in public opinion. My lack of animosity against him did not, however, diminish that which my judges showed against me. They made use of the arbitrary powers which magistrates had in bygone days, especially in remote parts of the provinces, and they paralyzed all my lawyer's efforts by a fierce haste. Several legal personages, whose names I will not mention, indulged, even publicly, in a strain of invective against me which ought to have excluded them from any court dealing with questions of human dignity and morality. They intrigued to induce me to confess, and almost went so far as to promise me a favourable verdict if I at least acknowledged that I had wounded Mademoiselle de Mauprat accidently. The scorn with which I met these overtures alienated them altogether. A stranger to all intrigue, at a time when justice and truth could not triumph except by intrigue, I was a victim of two redoubtable enemies, the Church and the Law; the former I had offended in the person of the Carmelite prior; and the latter hated me because, of the suitors whom Edmee had repulsed, the most spiteful was a man closely related to the chief magistrate.

Nevertheless, a few honest men to whom I was almost unknown, took an interest in my case on account of the efforts of others to make my name odious. One of them, a Monsieur E——, who was not without influence, for he was the brother of the sheriff of the province and acquainted with all the deputies, rendered me a service by the excellent suggestions he made for throwing light on this complicated affair.

Patience, convinced as he was of my guilt, might have served my enemies without wishing to do so; but he would not. He had resumed his roaming life in the woods, and, though he did not hide, could never be found. Marcasse was very uneasy about his intentions and could not understand his conduct at all. The police were furious to find that an old man was making a fool of them, and that without going beyond a radius of a few leagues. I fancy that the old fellow, with his habits and constitution, could have lived for years in Varenne without falling into their hands, and, moreover, without feeling that longing to surrender which a sense of *ennui* and the horror of solitude so frequently arouse, even in great criminals.

XXV

The day of the public trial came. I went to face it quite calmly; but the sight of the crowd filled me with a profound melancholy. No support, no sympathy for me there! It seemed to me that on such an occasion I might at least have looked for that show of respect to which the unfortunate and friendless are entitled. Yet, on all the faces around I saw nothing but a brutal and insolent curiosity. Girls of the lower classes talked loudly of my looks and my youth. A large number of women belonging to the nobility or moneyed classes displayed their brilliant dresses in the galleries, as if they had come to some *fete*. A great many monks showed their shaven crowns in the middle of the populace, which they were inciting against me; from their crowded ranks I could frequently catch the words "brigand," "ungodly," and "wild beast." The men of fashion in the district were lolling on the seats of honour, and discussing my passion in the language of the gutter. I saw and heard everything with that tranquility which springs from a profound disgust of life; even as a traveller who has come to the end of his journey, may look with indifference and weariness on the eager bustle of those who are setting off for a more distant goal.

The trial began with that emphatic solemnity which at all times has been associated with the exercise of judicial power. My examination was short, in spite of the innumerable questions that were asked me about my whole life. My answers singularly disappointed the expectations of public curiosity, and shortened the trial considerably. I confined myself to three principal replies, the substance of which I never changed. Firstly, to all questions concerning my childhood and education, I replied that I had not come into the defendant's dock to accuse others. Secondly, to those bearing on Edmee, the nature of my feeling for her, and my relations with her, I replied that Mademoiselle de Mauprat's worth and reputation could not permit even the simplest question as to the nature of her relations with any man whatever; and that, as to my feelings for her, I was accountable for them to no one. Thirdly, to those which were designed to make me confess my pretended crime, I replied that I was not even the unwilling author of the accident. In brief answers I gave some details of the events immediately preceding it; but, feeling that I owed it to Edmee as much as to myself to be silent about the tumultuous impulses that had stirred me, I explained the scene which had resulted in my quitting her, as being due to a fall from my horse; and that I had been found some distance from her body was, I said, because I had deemed it advisable to run after my horse, so that I might again escort her. Unfortunately all this was not very clear, and, naturally, could not be. My horse had gone off in the direction opposite to that which I said; and the bewildered state in which I had been found before I knew of the accident, was not sufficiently explained by a fall from my horse. They questioned me especially about the gallop I had had with my cousin through the wood, instead of following the hunt as we had intended; they would not believe that we had gone astray, guided altogether by chance. It was impossible, they said, to look upon chance as a reasonable being, armed with a gun, waiting for Edmee at Gazeau Tower at an appointed time, in order to shoot her the moment I turned my back for five minutes. They pretended that I must have taken her to this out-of-the-way spot either by craft or force to outrage her; and that I had tried to kill her either from rage at not succeeding, or from fear of being discovered and punished for my crime.

Then all the witnesses for and against me were heard. It is true that among the former Marcasse was the only one who could really be considered as a witness for the defence. The rest merely affirmed that a "monk bearing a resemblance to the Mauprats" had been roaming about Varenne at the period in question, and that he had even appeared to hide himself on the evening of the event. Since then he had not been seen. These depositions, which I had not solicited, and which I declared had not been taken at my request, caused me considerable astonishment; for among the witnesses who made them I saw some of the most honest folk in the country. However, they had no weight except in the eyes of Monsieur E——, the magistrate, who was really interested in discovering the truth. He interposed, and asked me how it was that M. Jean de Mauprat had not been summoned to confront these witnesses, seeing that he had taken the trouble to put in his affidavit to prove an alibi. This objection was received with a murmur of indignation. There were not a few people, however, who by no means looked upon John Mauprat as a saint; but they took no interest in myself, and had merely come to the trial as to a play.

The enthusiasm of the bigots reached a climax when the Trappist suddenly stood up in the crowd. Throwing back his cowl in a theatrical manner, he boldly approached the bar, declaring that he was a miserable sinner worthy of all scorn, but on this occasion, when it was the duty of every one to strive for truth, he considered it incumbent on him to set an example of simple candour by voluntarily offering himself for any examination which might shed light on the judges' minds. These words were greeted with applause. The Trappist was admitted to the witness-box, and confronted with the witnesses, who all declared, without any hesitation, that the monk they had seen wore the same habit as this man, and that there was a family likeness, a sort of distant resemblance between the two; but that it was not the same person—on this point they had not the least doubt.

The result of this incident was a fresh triumph for the Trappist. No one seemed to notice that, as the witnesses had displayed so much candour, it was difficult to believe that they had not really seen another Trappist. At this moment I remembered that, at the time of the abbe's first interview with John Mauprat at the spring at Fougeres, the latter had let fall a few words about a friar of the same order who was travelling with him, and had passed the night at the Goulets farm. I thought it advisable to mention this fact to my counsel. He discussed it in a low voice with the abbe, who was sitting among the witnesses. The latter remembered the circumstance quite clearly, but was unable to add any further details.

When it came to the abbe's turn to give evidence he looked at me with an expression of agony; his eyes filled with tears, and he answered the formal questions with difficulty, and in an almost inaudible voice. He made a great effort to master himself, and finally he gave his evidence in these words:

"I was driving in the woods when M. le Chevalier Hubert de Mauprat requested me to alight, and see what had become of his daughter, Edmee, who had been missing from the field long enough to cause him uneasiness. I ran for some distance, and when I was about thirty yards from Gazeau Tower I found M. Bernard de Mauprat in a state of great agitation. I had just heard a gun fired. I noticed that he was no longer carrying his carbine; he had thrown it down (discharged, as has been proved), a few yards away. We both hastened to Mademoiselle de Mauprat, whom we found lying on the ground with two bullets in her. Another man had reached her before us and was standing near her at this moment. He alone can make known the words he heard from her lips. She was unconscious when I saw her."

"But you heard the exact words from this individual," said the president; "for rumour has it that there is a close friendship between yourself and the learned peasant known as Patience."

The abbe hesitated, and asked if the laws of conscience were not in this case at variance with the laws of the land; and if the judges had a right to ask a man to reveal a secret intrusted to his honour, and to make him break his word.

"You have taken an oath here in the name of Christ to tell the truth, the whole truth," was the reply. "It is for you to judge whether this oath is not more solemn than any you may have made previously."

"But, if I had received this secret under the seal of the confessional," said the abbe, "you certainly would not urge me to reveal it."

"I believe, Monsieur l'Abbe," said the president, "that it is some time since you confessed any one."

At this unbecoming remark I noticed an expression of mirth on John Mauprat's face—a fiendish mirth, which brought back to me the man as I knew him of old, convulsed with laughter at the sight of suffering and tears.

The annoyance which the abbe felt at this personal attack gave him the courage which might otherwise have been wanting. He remained for a few moments with downcast eyes. They thought that he was humiliated; but, as soon as he raised his head, they saw his eyes flashing with the malicious obstinacy of the priest.

"All things considered," he said, in the most gentle tone, "I think that my conscience bids me keep this secret; I shall keep it."

"Aubert," said the King's advocate, angrily, "you are apparently unaware of the penalties which the law inflicts on witnesses who behave as you are doing."

"I am aware of them," replied the abbe, in a still milder tone.

"Doubtless, then, you do not intend to defy them?"

"I will undergo them if necessary," rejoined the abbe, with an imperceptible smile of pride, and such a dignified bearing that all the women were touched.

Women are excellent judges of things that are delicately beautiful.

"Very good," replied the public prosecutor. "Do you intend to persist in this course of silence?"

"Perhaps," replied the abbe.

"Will you tell us whether, during the days that followed this attempt to murder Mademoiselle de Mauprat, you were in a position to hear the words she uttered, either during her delirium or during her lucid intervals?"

"I can give you no information on that point," answered the abbe. "It would be against my inclinations, and, moreover, in my eyes, an outrage on propriety, to repeat words which, in the case of delirium, could prove absolutely nothing, and, if uttered in a lucid moment, could only have been the outpouring of a genuinely filial affection."

"Very good," said the King's advocate, rising. "We shall call upon the Court to deliberate on your refusal of evidence, taking this incident in connection with the main question."

"And I," said the president, "in virtue of my discretionary power, do order that Aubert be meanwhile arrested and taken to prison."

The abbe allowed himself to be led away with unaffected calmness. The spectators were filled with respect, and a profound silence reigned in court, in spite of the bitter efforts of the monks and cures, who continued to revile the heretic in an undertone.

When the various witnesses had been heard (and I must say that those who had been suborned played their part very feebly in public), to crown all, Mademoiselle Leblanc appeared. I was surprised to find the old maid so bitter against me and able to turn her hatred to such account. In truth, the weapons she could bring against me were only too powerful. In virtue of the right which domestics claim to listen at doors and overhear family secrets, this skilled misinterpreter and prolific liar had learnt and shaped to her own purposes most of the facts in my life which could be utilized for my ruin. She related how, seven years before, I had arrived at the chateau of Sainte-Severe with Mademoiselle de Mauprat, whom I had rescued from the roughness and wickedness of my uncles.

"And let that be said," she added, turning toward John Mauprat with a polite bow, "without any reference to the holy man in this court, who was once a great sinner, and is now a great saint. But at what a price," she continued, facing the judges again, "had this miserable bandit saved my dear mistress! He had dishonoured her, gentlemen; and, throughout the days that followed, the poor young lady had abandoned herself to grief and shame on account of the violence which had been done her, for which nothing could bring consolation. Too proud to breath her misfortune to a single soul, and too honest to deceive any man, she broke off her engagement with M. de la Marche, whom she loved passionately, and who returned her passion. She refused every offer of marriage that was made her, and all from a sense of honour, for in reality she hated M. Bernard. At first she wanted to kill herself; indeed, she had one of her father's little hunting-knives sharpened and (M. Marcasse can tell you the same, if he chooses to remember) she would certainly have killed herself, if I had not thrown this knife into the well belonging to the house. She had to think, too, of defending herself against the night attacks of her persecutor; and, as long as she had this knife, she always used to put it under her pillow; every night she would bolt the door of her room; and frequently I have seen her rush back, pale and ready to faint, quite out of breath, like a person who has just been pursued and had a great fright. When this gentleman began to receive some education, and learn good manners, mademoiselle, seeing that she could never have any other husband, since he was always talking of killing any man who dared to present himself, hoped he would get rid of his fierceness, and was most kind and good to him. She even nursed him during his illness; not that she liked and esteemed him as much as M. Marcasse was pleased to say in his version; but she was always afraid that in his delirium he might reveal, either to the servants or her father, the secret of the injury he had done her. This her modesty and pride made her most anxious to conceal, as all the ladies present will readily understand. When the family went to Paris for the winter of '77, M. Bernard became jealous and tyrannical and threatened so frequently to kill M. de la Marche that mademoiselle was obliged to send the latter away. After that she had some violent scenes with Bernard, and declared that she did not and never would love him. In his rage and grief—for it cannot be denied that he was enamoured of her in his tigerish fashion—he went off to America, and during the six years he spent there his letters seemed to show that he had much improved. By the time he returned, mademoiselle had made up her mind to be an old maid, and had become quite calm again. And M. Bernard, too, seemed to have grown into a fairly good young gentleman. However, through seeing her every day and everlastingly leaning over the back of her arm-chair, or winding her skeins of wool and whispering to her while her father was asleep, he fell so deeply in love again that he lost his head. I do not wish to be too hard on him, poor creature! and I fancy his right place is in the asylum rather than on the scaffold. He used to shout and groan all night long; and the letters he wrote her were so stupid that she used to smile as she read them and then put them in her pocket without answering them. Here is one of these letters that I found upon her when I undressed her after the horrible deed; a bullet has gone through it, and it is stained with blood, but enough may still be read to show that monsieur frequently intended to kill mademoiselle."

So saying, she put down on the table a sheet of paper half burnt and half covered with blood, which sent a shudder through the spectators—genuine with some of them, mere affectation with many others.

Before this letter was read, she finished her deposition, and ended it with some assertions which perplexed me considerably; for I could no longer distinguish the boundary between truth and perfidy.

"Ever since her accident," she said, "mademoiselle has been hovering between life and death. She will certainly never recover, whatever the doctors may declare. I venture to say that these gentlemen, who only see the patient at certain hours, do not understand her illness as well as I, who have never left her for a single night. They pretend that her wounds are going on well and that her head is deranged; whereas I say that her wounds are going on badly, and that her head is better than they say. Mademoiselle very rarely talks irrationally, and if by chance she does, it is in the presence of these gentlemen, who confuse and frighten her. She then makes such efforts not to appear mad that she actually becomes so; but as soon as they leave her alone with me or Saint-Jean or Monsieur l'Abbe, who could quite well have told you how things are, if he had wished, she becomes calm again, and sweet and sensible as usual. She says that she could almost die of pain, although to the doctors she pretends that she is scarcely suffering at all. And then she speaks of her murderer with the generosity that becomes a Christian; a hundred times a day she will say:

"'May God pardon him in the next life as I pardon him in this! After all, a man must be very fond of a woman to kill her! I was wrong not to marry him; perhaps he would have made me happy. I drove him to despair and he has avenged himself on me. Dear Leblanc, take care never to betray the secret I have told you. A single indiscreet word might send him to the scaffold, and that would be the death of my father.'

"The poor young lady is far from imagining that things have come to this pass; that I have been summoned by the law and my religion to make known what I would rather conceal; and that, instead of going out to get an apparatus for her shower-baths, I have come here to confess the truth. The only thing that consoles me is that it will be easy to hide all this from M. le Chevalier, who has no more sense now than a babe just born. For myself, I have done my duty; may God be my judge!"

After speaking thus with perfect self-possession and great volubility, Mademoiselle Leblanc sat down again amid a murmur of approbation, and they proceeded to read the letter which had been found on Edmee.

It was, indeed, the one I had written to her only a few days before the fatal day. They handed it to me; I could not help pressing my lips to the stains of Edmee's blood. Then, after glancing at the writing, I returned the letter, and declared quite calmly that it was written by me.

The reading of this letter was my *coup de grace*. Fate, who seems ingenious in injuring her victims, had obtained (and perhaps some famous hand had contributed to the mutilation) that the passages expressing my obedience and respect should be destroyed. Certain poetic touches which might have furnished an explanation of, and an excuse for, my wild ramblings, were illegible. What showed plain to every eye, and carried conviction to every mind, were the lines that remained intact, the lines that bore witness to the violence of my passion and the vehemence of my frenzy. They were such phrases as these: "Sometimes I feel inclined to rise in the middle of the night and go and kill you! I should have done this a hundred times, if I had been sure that I should love you no more after your death. Be considerate; for there are two men in me, and sometimes the brigand of old lords it over the new man, etc." A smile of triumph played about my enemies' mouths. My supporters were demoralized, and even my poor sergeant looked at me in despair. The public had already condemned me.

This incident afforded the King's advocate a fine chance of thundering forth a pompous address, in which he described me as an incurable blackguard, as an accursed branch of an accursed stock, as an example of the fatality of evil instincts. Then, after exerting himself to hold me up as an object of horror and fear, he endeavoured, in order to give himself an air of impartiality and generosity, to arouse the compassion of the judges in my favour; he proceeded to show that I was not responsible for my actions; that my mind had been perverted in early childhood by foul sights and vile principles, and was not sound, nor ever could have been, whatever the origin and growth of my passions. At last, after going through a course of philosophy and rhetoric, to the great delight of the audience, he demanded that I should be condemned to privation of civil rights and imprisonment for life.

Though my counsel was a man of spirit and intelligence, the letter had so taken him by surprise, the people in court were so unfavourably disposed towards me, and the judges, as they listened to him, so frequently showed signs of incredulity and impatience (an unseemly habit which appears to be the heritage of the magisterial benches of this country), that his defence was tame. All that he seemed justified in demanding with any vigour was a further inquiry. He complained that all the formalities had not been fulfilled; that sufficient light had not been thrown on certain points in the case; that it would be showing too much haste to give a verdict when several circumstances were still wrapped in mystery. He demanded that the doctors should be called to express an opinion as to the possibility of taking Mademoiselle de Mauprat's evidence. He pointed out that the most important, in fact the only important, testimony was that of Patience, and that Patience might appear any day and prove me innocent. Finally, he demanded that they should order a search to be made for the mendicant friar whose resemblance to the Mauprats had not yet been explained, and had been sworn to by trustworthy witnesses. In his opinion it was essential to discover what had become of Antony Mauprat, and to call upon the Trappist for information on this point. He complained bitterly that they had deprived him of all means of defence by refusing any delay; and he had the courage to assert that some evil passions must be responsible for such blind haste as had marked the conduct of this trial. On this the president called him to order. Then the King's advocate replied triumphantly that all formalities had been fulfilled; that the court was sufficiently enlightened; that a search for the mendicant friar would be a piece of folly and in bad taste, since John Mauprat had proved his last brother's death, which had taken place several years before. The court retired to deliberate; at the end of half an hour they came back with a verdict condemning me to death.

XXVI

Although the haste with which the trial had been conducted and the severity of the sentence were iniquitous, and filled those who were most bitter against me with amazement, I received the blow with supreme indifference; I no longer felt an interest in anything on earth. I commended my soul and the vindication of my memory to God. I said to myself that if Edmee died I should find her again in a better world; that if she survived me and recovered her reason, she would one day succeed in discovering the truth, and that then I should live in her heart as a dear and tender memory. Irritable as I am, and always inclined to violence in the case of anything that is an obstacle or an offence to me, I am astonished at the philosophical resignation and the proud calm I have shown on the momentous occasions of life, and above all on this one.

It was two o'clock in the morning. The case had lasted for fourteen hours. A silence as of death reigned over the court, which was as full and as attentive as at the beginning, so fond are mortals of anything in the nature of a show. That offered by the criminal court at this moment was somewhat dismal. Those men in red robes, as pale and stern and implacable as the Council of Ten at Venice; those ghosts of women decked with flowers, who, by the dim light of the tapers, looked like mere reflections of life hovering in the galleries above the priests of death; the muskets of the guard glittering in the gloom in the back of the court; the heart-broken attitude of my poor sergeant, who had fallen at my feet; the silent but vast delight of the Trappist, still standing unwearied near the bar; the mournful note of some convent bell in the neighbourhood beginning to ring for matins amid the silence of the assembly—was not all this enough to touch the nerves of the wives of the farmers-general and to send a thrill through the brawny breasts of the tanners in the body of the court?

Suddenly, just as the court was about to disperse, a figure like that of the traditional peasant of the Danube—squat, rugged, barefooted, with a long beard, dishevelled hair, a broad, grave brow, and a stern, commanding glance—rose in the midst of the flickering reflections by which the hall was half lighted, and standing erect before the bar, said in a deep, striking voice:

"I, Jean le Houx, known as Patience, oppose this judgment as iniquitous in substance and illegal in form. I demand that it be revised, so that I may give my evidence, which is necessary, may be of sovereign importance, and should have been waited for."

"If you had anything to say," cried the King's advocate, in a passion, "why did you not present yourself when you were summoned. You are imposing on the court by pretending that you have important evidence to give."

"And you," answered Patience, more slowly and in an even deeper tone than before, "you are imposing on the public by pretending that I have not. You know well enough that I must have."

"Remember where you are, witness, and to whom you are speaking."

"I know too well, and I shall not say too much. I hereby declare that I have some important things to say, and that I should have said them at the right time, if you had not done violence to the time. I wish to say them, and I shall; and, believe me, it is better that I should make them known while it is still possible to revise these proceedings. It is even better for the judges than the prisoner; for the one comes to life again in honour, as soon as the others die in infamy."

"Witness," said the irritated magistrate, "the virulence and impertinence of your language will be prejudicial rather than advantageous to the prisoner."

"And who says that I am favourable to the prisoner?" said Patience in a voice of thunder. "What do you know about me? What if it pleases me to change an illegal and worthless verdict into one which is legal and irrevocable?"

"But how can you reconcile this desire to see the laws respected," said the magistrate, genuinely moved by Patience's powerful personality, "with your own breach of them in not appearing when summoned by the public prosecutor?"

"I did not wish to appear."

"Severe penalties may be inflicted on those whose wishes are not in harmony with the laws of the land."

"Possibly."

"Have you come here to-day with the intention of submitting to them?"

"I have come to see that you respect them."

"I warn you that, if you do not change your tone, I shall have you taken off to prison."

"And I warn you that, if you love justice and serve God, you will listen to me and suspend the execution of this sentence. It is not for him who brings truth to humble himself before those who should be seeking it. But you who are listening to me now, you men of the people, whom I will not accuse the great of wishing to dupe, you whose voice is called 'the voice of God,' side with me; embrace the cause of truth, that truth which is in danger of being stifled under false outward shows, or else is about to triumph by unfair means. Go down on your knees, you men of the people, my brothers, my children; pray, implore, require that justice be done and anger repressed. It is your duty, it is your right, and to your own interest; for it is you who are insulted and threatened when laws are violated."

Patience spoke with so much warmth, and his sincerity was so strikingly manifest, that a thrill of sympathy ran through the whole audience. At that time, philosophy was too fashionable with the young men of quality for these not to be among the first to respond to an appeal, though addressed to others than themselves. They rose with chivalrous enthusiasm and turned round to the people, who, carried away by their noble example, rose likewise. There was a wild uproar, and one and all, conscious of their dignity and power, cast away personal prejudices in order to combine for their common rights. Thus, a noble impetuosity and a true word are sometimes sufficient to bring back the masses who have long been led astray by sophism.

A respite was granted, and I was led back to my prison amid the applause of the people. Marcasse followed me. Patience disappeared without giving me a chance to thank him.

The revision of the sentence could not be made without an order from the high court. For my own part, before the verdict was given I had resolved to make no appeal to this court of cassation of the old jurisprudence. But Patience's bearing and words had had as much effect on my mind as on the minds of the spectators. The spirit of resistance and the sense of human dignity, dulled in me and paralyzed, as it were, by grief, suddenly awoke again, and in this hour I realized that man is not made for that selfish concentration of despair which is known as resignation or stoicism. No man can cease to have a regard for his own honour without at the same time ceasing to feel the respect due to the principle of honour. If it is grand to sacrifice personal glory and life to the mysterious decrees of conscience, it is cowardly to abandon both to the fury of an unjust persecution. I felt that I had risen in my own estimation, and I passed the rest of this momentous night in devising means of vindicating myself, with as much persistence as I had previously displayed in abandoning myself to fate. With this feeling of energy I could feel hope springing up anew. Edmee, perhaps, was neither mad nor mortally wounded. She might acquit me; she might recover.

"Who knows?" I said to myself. "Perhaps she has already done me justice. Perhaps it was she who sent Patience to my rescue. Undoubtedly I shall best please her by taking courage again, and not letting myself be crushed by a set of knaves."

But how was I to obtain this order from the high court? It needed a special mandate from the King; who would procure this? Who would cut short those odious delays which the law can introduce at will into the very cases that it has previously hurried on with blind precipitation? Who would prevent my enemies from injuring me and paralyzing all my efforts? In a word, who would fight for me? The abbe alone could have taken up my cause; but he was already in prison on my account. His generous behaviour in the trial had proved that he was still my friend, but his zeal was now fettered. And what could Marcasse do, hampered by his humble birth and enigmatical language? Evening came, and I fell asleep in the hope that help would be sent from on high; for I had prayed to God with my whole soul. A few hours of sleep refreshed me; I was aroused by the noise of bolts being drawn at the other side of my door. O God of goodness! what was my delight on seeing Arthur, my brother in arms, my other self, the man from whom I had had no secret for six long years! I wept like a child on receiving this mark of love from Providence. Arthur did not believe me guilty! Scientific matters connected with the library at Philadelphia had taken him to Paris, where he had heard of this sad affair in which I was implicated. He had broken a lance with all who attacked me, and had not lost a moment in coming to offer help or consolation.

In a transport of joy I poured out my soul to him, and then explained how he could assist me. He wanted to take the coach for Paris that very evening; but I implored him to go to Sainte-Severe first of all to get news of Edmee. Four mortal days had passed since I had received any; and, moreover, Marcasse had never given me such exact details as I could have wished.

"Ease your mind," said Arthur. "I will undertake to bring you the truth. I am a pretty good surgeon; and I have a practised eye. I shall be able to give you some idea of what you have to hope or fear. From Sainte-Severe I shall go straight to Paris."

Two days later I received a long letter from him giving full details about Edmee.

Her condition was extraordinary. She did not speak, nor did she appear to be in pain as long as nothing happened to excite her nerves; but on the first word which stirred up recollections of her troubles she would be seized with convulsions. Her moral isolation formed the greatest obstacle to recovery. Physically she wanted for nothing; she had two good doctors and a most devoted nurse. Mademoiselle Leblanc likewise was very zealous in her attentions, though this dangerous woman often gave her pain by untimely remarks and indiscreet questions. Furthermore, Arthur assured me that, if ever Edmee had thought me guilty and had expressed an opinion on this point, it must have been in some previous phase of her illness; for, during the last fortnight at least, she had been in a state of complete torpor. She would frequently doze, but without quite falling asleep; she could take liquid food and jellies, nor did she ever complain. When her doctors questioned her about her sufferings she answered by careless signs and always negatively; and she would never give any indication that she remembered the affections which had filled her life. Her love for her father, however, that feeling which had always been so deep and powerful in her, was not extinct; she would often shed copious tears; but at such a time she seemed to be deaf to all sounds; in vain would they try to make her understand that her father was not dead, as she appeared to believe. With a gesture of entreaty she would beg them to stop, not the noise (for that did not seem to strike her ear), but the bustle that was going on around her; then, hiding her face in her hands, lying back in her arm-chair and bringing her knees up almost to her breast, she would apparently give way to inconsolable despair. This silent grief, which could no longer control itself and no longer wished to be controlled; this powerful will, which had once been able to quell the most violent storms, and now going adrift on a dead sea and in an unruffled calm—this, said Arthur, was the most painful spectacle he had ever beheld. Edmee seemed to wish to have done with life. Mademoiselle Leblanc, in order to test her and arouse her, had brutally taken upon herself to announce that her father was dead; she had replied by a sign that she knew. A few hours later the doctors had tried to make her understand that he was alive; she had replied by another sign that she did not believe them. They had wheeled the chevalier's arm-chair into her room; they had brought father and daughter face to face and the two had not recognised each other. Only, after a few moments, Edmee, taking her father for a ghost, had uttered piercing cries, and had been seized with convulsions that had opened one of her wounds again, and made the doctors tremble for her life. Since then, they had taken care to keep the two apart, and never to breathe a word about the chevalier in Edmee's presence. She had taken Arthur for one of the doctors of the district and had received him with the same sweetness and the same indifference as the others. He had not dared to speak to her about me; but he extorted me not to despair. There was nothing in Edmee's condition that time and rest could not triumph over; there was but little fever left; none of her vital organs were really affected; her wounds were almost healed; and it did not seem as if her brain were in such an excited condition that it would be permanently deranged. The weak state of her mind, and the prostration of all the other organs could not, according to Arthur, long withstand the vitality of youth and the recuperative power of an admirable constitution. Finally, he advised me to think of myself; I might help towards her recovery, and I might again find happiness in her affection and esteem.

In a fortnight Arthur returned from Paris with an order from the King for the revision of my sentence. Fresh witnesses were heard. Patience did not appear; but I received a note from him containing these words in a shapeless hand, "You are not guilty, so don't despair." The doctors declared that Mademoiselle de Mauprat might be examined without danger, but that her answers would have no meaning. She was now in better health. She had recognised her father, and at present would never leave him; but she could understand nothing that was not connected with him. She seemed to derive great pleasure from tending him like a child, and, on his side, the chevalier would now and then recognise his beloved daughter; but his vital powers were visibly decaying. They questioned him in one of his lucid moments. He replied that his daughter had, indeed, fallen from her horse while hunting, and that she had torn her breast on the stump of a tree, but that not a soul had fired at her, even by mistake, and that only a madman could possibly believe her cousin capable of such a crime. This was all the information they could draw from him. When they asked him what he thought of his nephew's absence, he answered that his nephew was still in the house, and that he saw him every day. Was it that, in his devotion to the good name of a family—alas! so compromised—he thought to defeat the aims of justice by childish lies? This is a point I was never able to ascertain. As for Edmee, it was impossible to examine her. At the first question that was asked her, she shrugged her shoulders and made a sign that she did not wish to be bothered. As the public prosecutor insisted and became more explicit, she stared at him and seemed to be making an effort to understand. He pronounced my name, she gave a loud cry and fainted. He had to abandon all thoughts of taking her evidence. However, Arthur did not despair. On the contrary, the account of this scene made him think that Edmee's mental faculties might be about to take a favourable turn. He immediately returned to Sainte-Severe, where he remained several days without writing to me, which caused me great anxiety.

When the abbe was questioned again, he persisted in his calm, laconic refusal to give evidence.

My judges, seeing that the information promised by Patience was not forthcoming, hurried on the revision of the trial, and, by another exhibition of haste, gave another proof of their animosity. The appointed day arrived. I was devoured by anxiety. Arthur had written me to keep up my courage, in as laconic a style as Patience. My counsel had been unable to obtain any fresh evidence in my favour. I could see clearly that he was beginning to believe me guilty. All he hoped for was to obtain a further delay.

XXVII

There were even more people present than at the first trial. The guard were forced back to the doors of the court, and the crowd occupied every available space, even to the windows of the mansion of Jacques Coeur, the town-hall of the present day. I was much agitated this time, though I had strength and pride enough not to let it be seen. I was now interested in the success of my case, and, as it seemed as if my hopes were not to be realized, I experienced an indescribable feeling of uneasiness, a sort of suppressed rage, a bitter hatred of these men who would not open their eyes to my innocence, and even of God who seemed to have deserted me.

In this state of agitation I had to make such violent efforts to appear calm that I scarcely noticed what was happening around me. I recovered sufficient presence of mind when my fresh examination took place to answer in the same terms as at the first trial. Then a black veil seemed to fall over my head, an iron ring gripped my brow; the sockets of my eyes went icily cold; I could see nothing but myself, hear nothing but vague, unintelligible sounds. I do not know what actually took place; I do not know if any one announced the apparition which suddenly appeared before me. I only remember that a door opened behind the judges, and that Arthur came forward leading a veiled woman, that he took off her veil after making her sit down in a big arm-chair which the ushers eagerly wheeled toward her, and that a cry of admiration rang through the hall when Edmee's pale, sublime beauty was revealed.

At this moment I forgot the crowd, and the judges, and my cause, and the whole universe. I believe that no human power could have withstood my wild rush. I dashed like a thunderbolt into the middle of the inclosure and, falling at Edmee's feet, I showered kisses on her knees. I have been told that this act won over the public, and that nearly all the ladies burst into tears. The young dandies did not venture to laugh; the judges were affected; and for a moment truth was completely triumphant.

Edmee looked at me for some time. Her face was as expressionless as the face of death. It did not seem as if she could ever recognise me. The spectators were waiting in profound silence for her to show some sign of hatred or affection for me. All at once she burst into tears, threw her arms around my neck, and then lost consciousness. Arthur had her carried out immediately; he had some trouble in making me return to my place. I could not remember where I was or the issues that were at stake; I clung to Edmee's dress, and only wanted to follow her. Arthur addressed the court and requested that the doctors who had examined Edmee in the morning might again pronounce upon the state of her health. He likewise demanded that she should be recalled to give evidence, and to be confronted with me as soon as she recovered from the attack.

"This attack is not serious," he said. "Mademoiselle de Mauprat has had several of the same kind during the last few days and on her way here. After each her mental faculties have taken a more and more favourable turn."

"Go and attend to the invalid," said the president. "She shall be recalled in two hours, if you think she will have recovered from her swoon by then. Meanwhile the court will hear the witness on whose demand the first sentence was not carried out."

Arthur withdrew and Patience was introduced. He was dressed quite neatly; but, after saying a few words, he declared that it would be impossible to continue unless they allowed him to take off his coat. This borrowed finery so embarrassed him and seemed so heavy that he was perspiring profusely. No sooner did the president make a sign of consent, accompanied by a smile of scorn, than he threw to the ground this badge of civilization. Then, after carefully pulling down his shirt-sleeves over his sinewy arms, he spoke almost as follows:

"I will speak the truth, the whole truth. I take the oath for the second time; for I have to speak of things that seem contradictory, things that I cannot explain to myself. I swear before God and man that I will say what I know, and as I know it, without being influenced for or against any one."

He lifted his big hand and turned round towards the people with a simple confidence, as if to say, "You can all see that I am taking an oath, and you know that I am to be trusted." This confidence of his was not ill-founded. Since the incident in the first trial the public mind had been much occupied about this extraordinary man, who had spoken before the court with so much daring, and harangued the people in presence of the judges. His conduct had filled all the democrats and *Philadelphians* with great curiosity and sympathy. The works of Beaumarchais were very fashionable among the upper classes, and this will explain how it was that Patience, though opposed to all the authorities in the province, yet found himself supported and applauded by every man who prided himself on his intelligence. They all thought they saw in him Figaro under a new form. The fame of his private virtues had spread; for you remember that during my stay in America, Patience had made himself known among the people of Varenne and had exchanged his sorcerer's reputation for that of a public benefactor. They had given him the title of the *great judge*, because he was always ready to intervene in disputes, and would always settle to the satisfaction of both sides with admirable good-nature and tact.

This time he spoke in a high, penetrating voice. It was a rich voice of wide compass. His gestures were quiet or animated, according to the circumstances, but always dignified and impressive; the expression on his short, Socratic face was never anything but fine. He had all the qualities of an orator; but there was no vanity in his display of them. He spoke in the plain, concise style that he had been obliged to acquire in his recent intercourse with men, in discussions about their practical interests.

"When Mademoiselle de Mauprat was shot," he said, "I was not more than a dozen paces from her; but the brushwood at that spot is so thick that I could not see more than two paces in front of me. They had persuaded me to take part in the hunt; but it gave me but little pleasure. Finding myself near Gazeau Tower, where I lived for some twenty years, I felt an inclination to see my old cell again, and I was bearing down upon it at a great pace when I heard a shot. That did not frighten me in the least; it seemed but natural that there should be some gun fired during a battue. But when I got through the thicket, that is today, some two minutes later, I found Edmee—excuse me, I generally call her by this name; I am, so to speak, a sort of foster-father to her—I found Edmee on her knees upon the ground, wounded as you have been told, and still holding the bridle of her horse, which was rearing. She did not know whether she was seriously or slightly wounded, but she had her other hand on her breast, and she was saying:

"'Bernard, this is hideous! I should never have thought that you would kill me. Bernard, where are you? Come and see me die. This will kill father!'

"As she said this she let go the horse's bridle and fell to the ground. I rushed towards her.

"'Ah, you saw it, Patience?' she said. 'Do not speak about it; do not tell my father . . .'

"She threw out her arms, and her body became rigid. I thought that she was dead. She spoke no more until night, after they had extracted the bullets from her breast."

"Did you then see Bernard de Mauprat?"

"I saw him on the spot where the deed was done, just as Edmee lost consciousness and seemed to be giving up her soul; he seemed to be out of his mind. I thought that he was overwhelmed with remorse. I spoke to him sternly, and treated him as a murderer. He made no reply, but sat down on the ground by his cousin's side. He remained there in a dazed condition, even a long time after they had taken her away. No one thought of accusing him. The people thought that he had had a fall, because they saw his horse trotting by the side of the pond; they believed that his carbine had gone off as he fell. The Abbe Aubert was the only one who heard me accuse M. Bernard of having murdered his cousin. During the days that followed, Edmee spoke occasionally, but it was not always in my presence; besides, at this time she was nearly always delirious. I maintain that she told nobody (and least of all Mademoiselle Leblanc) what had passed between herself and M. de Mauprat before the gun was fired. Nor did she confide this to me any more than others. On the rare occasions when she was in possession of her senses she would say in answer to our questions, that Bernard had certainly not done it on purpose, and several times during the first three days she even asked to see him. However, when she was delirious she would sometimes cry, 'Bernard! Bernard! You have committed a great crime. You have killed my father!'

"That was her idea; she used really to think that her father was dead; and she thought so for a long time. Very little, therefore, of what she said is to be taken seriously. The words that Mademoiselle Leblanc has put into her mouth are false. After three days she ceased to talk intelligibly, and at the end of a week she ceased to speak altogether. When she recovered her reason, about a week ago, she sent away Mademoiselle Leblanc, which would clearly show that she had some ground for disliking her maid. That is what I have to say against M. de Mauprat. It rested entirely with myself to keep silent; but having other things to say yet, I wished to make known the whole truth."

Patience paused awhile; the public and the judges themselves, who were beginning to take an interest in me and lose the bitterness of their prejudices, were apparently thunderstruck at hearing evidence so different from what they expected.

Patience continued as follows:

"For several weeks I remained convinced of Bernard's guilt. But I was pondering over the matter the while; I frequently said to myself that a man as good and clever as Bernard, a man for whom Edmee felt so much esteem, and whom M. le Chevalier loved like a son, a man, in short, so deeply imbued with the spirit of justice and truth, could not between one day and the next turn into a scoundrel. Then the idea came into my head that, after all, it might have been some other Mauprat who fired the shot. I do not speak of the one who has become a Trappist," he added, looking among the audience for Jean de Mauprat, who, however was not there; "I speak of the man whose death has never been proved, although the court thought fit to overlook this, and to accept M. Jean de Mauprat's word."

"Witness," said the president, "I must remind you that you are not here to serve as counsel for the prisoner, or to criticise the decisions of this court. You must confine yourself to a statement of facts, and not express your opinion on the question at issue."

"Very well," replied Patience. "I must, however, explain why I did not wish to appear at the first trial, seeing that the only evidence I had was against M. Bernard, and that I could not trust that evidence myself."

"You are not asked to explain this at present. Please keep to your evidence."

"One moment. I have my honour to defend; I have to explain my own conduct, if you please."

"You are not the prisoner; you are not here to plead your own cause. If the court thinks right to prosecute you for contempt you can see to your own defence; but there is no question of that now."

"I beg your pardon. The question is for me to let the court see whether I am an honest man or a false witness. It would seem that this has something to do with the case; the prisoner's life depends on it; the court cannot consider that a matter of indifference."

"Proceed," said the King's advocate, "and try to remember the respect you owe to the court."

"I have no wish to offend the court," replied Patience. "I would merely observe that a man may refuse to submit to the orders of the court from conscientious motives which the court can legally condemn, but which each judge, personally, can understand and excuse. I say, then, that I could not persuade myself of Bernard de Mauprat's guilt; my ears alone knew of it; this was not enough for me. Pardon me, gentlemen, I, too, am a judge. Make inquiries about me; in my village they call me 'the great judge.' When my fellow-villagers ask me to decide some tavern dispute or the boundary of some field, I do not so much listen to their opinions as my own. In judging a man one must take account of more than a single little act. Many previous ones will help to show the truth or falsity of the last that is imputed to him. Thus, being unable to believe that Bernard was a murderer, and having heard more than a dozen people, whom I consider incapable of giving false evidence, testify to the fact that a monk 'bearing a resemblance to the Mauprats' had been prowling about the country, and having myself seen this monk's back and habit as he was passing through Pouligny on the morning of the event, I wished to discover if he was in Varenne; and I learnt that he was still there; that is to say, after leaving it, he had returned about the time of the trial last month. And, what is more, I learnt that he was acquainted with John Mauprat. Who can this monk be? I asked myself; why does the very sight of him frighten all the people in the country? What is he doing in Varenne? If he belongs to the Carmelite convent, why does he not wear their habit? If he is of the same order as John, why is he not staying with him at the Carmelites? If he is collecting money, why, after making a collection in one place, does he not move on to another, instead of returning and bothering people who have given him money only the day before? If he is a Trappist and does not want to stay with the Carmelites like the other, why does he not go back to his own convent? What is this wandering monk? And how does John Mauprat, who has told several people that he does not know him, know him so well that they lunch together from time to time in a tavern at Crevant? I made up my mind, then, to give evidence, though it might, in a measure, do harm to M. Bernard, so as to be able to say what I am now saying, even if it should be of no use. But as you never allow witnesses sufficient time to try to verify what they have reason to believe, I started off immediately for my woods, where I live like the foxes, with a determination not to quit them until I had discovered what this monk was doing in the country. So I put myself on his track and I have discovered who he is; he is the murderer of Edmee de Mauprat; his name is Antony Mauprat."

This revelation caused a great stir on the bench and among the public. Every one looked around for John Mauprat, whose face was nowhere to be seen.

"What proof have you of this?" said the president.

"I am about to tell you," replied Patience. "Having learnt from the landlady at Crevant, to whom I have occasionally been of some assistance, that the two Trappists used to lunch at her tavern from time to time, as I have said, I went and took up my abode about half a league from here, in a hermitage known as Le Trou aux Fades, situated in the middle of the woods and open to the first comer, furniture and all. It is a cave in the rock, containing a seat in the shape of a big stone and nothing else. I lived there for a couple of days on roots and bits of bread that they occasionally brought me from the tavern. It is against my principles to live in a tavern. On the third day the landlady's little boy came and informed me that the two monks were about to sit down to a meal. I hastened back, and hid myself in a cellar which opens into the garden. The door of this cellar is quite close to the apple-tree under which these gentlemen were taking luncheon in the open air. John was sober; the other was eating like a Carmelite and drinking like a Franciscan. I could hear and see everything at my ease.

"'There must be an end of this,' Antony was saying—I easily recognised the man when I saw him drink and heard him swear—'I am tired of playing this game for you. Hide me away with the Carmelites or I shall make a row.'

"'And what row can you make that will not bring you to the gallows, you clumsy fool!' answered John. 'It is very certain that you will not set foot inside the monastery. I don't want to find myself mixed up in a criminal trial; for they would discover what you are in an hour or two.'

"'And why, I should like to know? You make them all believe that you are a saint!'

"'Because I know how to behave like a saint; whereas you—you behave like a fool. Why, you can't stop swearing for an hour, and you would be breaking all the mugs after dinner!'

"'I say, Nepomucene,' rejoined the other, 'do you fancy that you would get off scot-free if I were caught and tried?'

"'Why not?' answered the Trappist. 'I had no hand in your folly, nor did I advise anything of this kind.'

"'Ha! ha! my fine apostle!' cried Antony, throwing himself back in his chair in a fit of laughter. 'You are glad enough about it, now that it is done. You were always a coward; and had it not been for me you would never have thought of anything better than getting yourself made a Trappist, to ape devotion and afterward get absolution for the past, so as to have a right to draw a little money from the "Headbreakers" of Sainte-Severe. By Jove! a mighty fine ambition, to give up the ghost under a monk's cowl after leading a pretty poor life and only tasting half its sweets, let alone hiding like a mole! Come, now; when they have hung my pretty Bernard, and the lovely Edmonde is dead, and when the old neck-breaker has given back his big bones to the earth; when we have inherited all that pretty fortune yonder; you will own that we have done a capital stroke of business—three at a blow! It would cost me rather too much to play the saint, seeing that convent ways are not quite my ways, and that I don't know how to wear the habit; so I shall throw the cowl to the winds, and content myself with building a chapel at Roche-Mauprat and taking the sacrament four times a year.'

"'Everything you have done in this matter is stupid and infamous.'

"'Bless my soul! Don't talk of infamy, my sweet brother, or I shall make you swallow this bottle whole.'

"'I say that it is a piece of folly, and if it succeeds you ought to burn a fine candle to the Virgin. If it does not succeed, I wash my hands of the whole business, do you hear? After I had been in hiding in the secret passage in the keep, and had heard Bernard telling his valet after supper that he was going out of his mind on account of the beautiful Edmee, I happened to throw out a suggestion that there might be a chance here of doing a good stroke of business; and like a fool you took the matter seriously, and, without consulting me or waiting for a favourable moment, you went and did a deed that should have been thought over and properly planned.'

"'A favourable moment, chicken-heart that you are! How the deuce was I to get one? "Opportunity makes the thief." I find myself surprised by the hunt in the middle of the forest; I go and hide in that cursed Gazeau Tower; I see my turtle-doves coming; I overhear a conversation that might make one die of laughing, and see Bernard blubbering and the girl playing the haughty beauty; Bernard goes off like an idiot without showing himself a man; I find on me—God knows how—a rascally pistol already loaded. Bang! . . .'

"'Hold your tongue, you wild brute!' said the other, quite frightened. 'Do you think a tavern is the proper place to talk of these things? Keep that tongue quiet, you wretched creature, or I will never see you again.'

"'And yet you will have to see me, sweet brother mine, when I go and ring the bell at the gate of the Carmelite monastery.'

"'If you come I will denounce you.'

"'You will not denounce me, for I know too much about you.'

"'I am not afraid. I have given proofs of my repentance; I have expiated my sins.'

"'Hypocrite!'

"'Come, now, hold your tongue, you madman!' said the other. 'I must leave you. There is some money.'

"'That all?'

"'What do you expect from a monk? Do you imagine that I am rich?'

"'Your Carmelites are; and you can do what you like with them.'

"'I might give you more, but I would rather not. As soon as you got a couple of louis you would be off for a debauch, and make enough row to betray yourself.'

"'And if you want me to quit this part of the country for some time, what do you suppose I am to travel with?'

"'Three times already I have given you enough to take you away, haven't I? And each time you have come back, after drinking it all in the first place of ill-fame on the frontier of the province! Your impudence sickens me, after the evidence given against you, when the police are on the watch, when Bernard is appealing for a fresh trial. You may be caught at any moment!'

"'That is for you to see to, brother. You can lead the Carmelites by the nose; and the Carmelites can lead the bishop, through some little peccadillo, I suppose, done together on the quiet in the convent after supper . . .'"

Here the president interrupted Patience.

"Witness," he said, "I call you to order. You are outraging a prelate's virtue by daring to retail such a conversation."

"By no means," replied Patience. "I am merely reporting a drunkard's and a murderer's invectives against the prelate. They do not concern me in the least; and every one here knows what value to put upon them; but, if you wish, I will say no more on this point. The discussion lasted for some time longer. The real Trappist wanted to make the sham Trappist leave the country, and the latter persisted in remaining, declaring that, if he were not on the spot, his brother would have him arrested immediately after Bernard's head had been cut off, so that he might have the whole inheritance to himself. John, driven to extremities, seriously threatened to denounce him and hand him over to justice.

"'Enough!' replied Antony. 'You will take good care not to do that, I know; for, if Bernard is acquitted, good-bye to the inheritance!'

"Then they separated. The real Trappist went away looking very anxious; the other fell asleep, with his elbows on the table. I left my hiding-place to take steps for his arrest. It was just then that the police, who had been on my track for some time to force me to come and give evidence, collared me. In vain did I point to the monk as Edmee's murderer; they would not believe me, and said they had no warrant against him. I wanted to arouse the village, but they prevented me from speaking. They brought me here, from station to station, as if I had been a deserter, and for the last week I have been in the cells and no one has deigned to heed my protests. They would not even let me see M. Bernard's lawyer, or inform him that I was in prison; it was only just now that the jailer came, and told me that I must put on my coat and appear in court. I do not know whether all this is according to the law; but one thing is certain, namely, that the murderer might have been arrested and has not been; nor will he be, unless you secure the person of John Mauprat to prevent him from warning, I do not say his accomplice, but his *protege*. I state on oath that, from all I have heard, John Mauprat is above any suspicion of complicity. As to the act of allowing an innocent man to be handed over to the rigour of the law, and of endeavouring to save a guilty man by going so far as to give false evidence, and produce false documents to prove his death . . ."

Patience, noticing that the president was again about to interrupt him, hastened to end his testimony by saying:

"As to that, gentlemen, it is for you, not for me, to judge him."

XXVIII

After this important evidence the trial was suspended for a few minutes. When the judges returned Edmee was brought back into the court. Pale and weak, scarcely able to drag herself to the arm-chair which was reserved for her, she nevertheless displayed considerable mental vigour and presence of mind.

"Do you think you can answer the questions which will be put to you without unduly exciting yourself?" asked the president.

"I hope so, sir," she replied. "It is true that I have recently been seriously ill, and that it is only within the last few days that I have recovered my memory; but I believe I have completely recovered it, and my mind feels quite clear."

"Your name?"

"Solange-Edmonde de Mauprat; *Edmea sylvestris*," she added in an undertone.

I shuddered. As she said these unseasonable words her eyes had assumed a strange expression. I feared that her mind was going to wander still further. My counsel was also alarmed and looked at me inquiringly. No one but myself had understood these two words which Edmee had been in the habit of frequently repeating during the first and last days of her illness. Happily this was the last sign of any disturbance in her faculties. She shook her beautiful head, as if to drive out any troublesome ideas; and, the president having asked her for an explanation of these unintelligible words, she replied with sweetness and dignity:

"It is nothing, sir. Please continue my examination."

"Your age, mademoiselle?"

"Twenty-four."

"Are you related to the prisoner?"

"He is my second cousin, and my father's grand-nephew."

"Do you swear to speak the truth, the whole truth?"

"Yes, sir."

"Raise your hand."

Edmee turned towards Arthur with a sad smile. He took off her glove, and helped to raise her arm, which hung nerveless and powerless by her side. I felt big tears rolling down my cheeks.

With delicacy and simplicity Edmee related how she and I had lost our way in the woods; how I, under the impression that her horse had bolted, had unseated her in my eager anxiety to stop the animal; how a slight altercation had ensued, after which, with a little feminine temper, foolish enough, she had wished to mount her mare again without help; how she had even spoken unkindly to me, not meaning a word of what she said, for she loved me like a brother; how, deeply hurt by her harshness, I had moved away a few yards to obey her; and how, just as she was about to follow me, grieved herself at our childish quarrel, she had felt a violent shock in her breast, and had fallen almost without hearing any report. It was impossible for her to say in which direction she was looking, or from which side the shot had come.

"That is all that happened," she added. "Of all people I am least able to explain this occurrence. In my soul and conscience I can only attribute it to the carelessness of one of the hunting party, who is afraid to confess. Laws are so severe. And it is so difficult to prove the truth."

"So, mademoiselle, you do not think that your cousin was the author of this attempt?"

"No, sir, certainly not! I am no longer delirious, and I should not have let myself be brought before you if I had felt that my mind was at all weak."

"Apparently, then, you consider that a state of mental aberration was responsible for the revelations you made to Patience, to Mademoiselle Leblanc, your companion, and also, perhaps, to Abbe Aubert."

"I made no revelations," she replied emphatically, "either to the worthy Patience, the venerable abbe, or my servant Leblanc. If the meaningless words we utter in a state of delirium are to be called 'revelations,' all the people who frighten us in our dreams would have to be condemned to death. How could I have revealed facts of which I never had any knowledge?"

"But at the time you received the wound, and fell from your horse, you said: 'Bernard, Bernard! I should never have thought that you would kill me!'"

"I do not remember having said so; and, even if I did, I cannot conceive that any one would attach much importance to the impressions of a person who had suddenly been struck to the ground, and whose mind was annihilated, as it were. All that I know is that Bernard de Mauprat would lay down his life for my father or myself; which does not make it very probable that he wanted to murder me. Great God! what would be his object?"

In order to embarrass Edmee, the president now utilized all the arguments which could be drawn from Mademoiselle Leblanc's evidence. As a fact, they were calculated to cause her not a little confusion. Edmee, who was at first somewhat astonished to find that the law was in possession of so many details which she believed were unknown to others, regained her courage and pride, however, when they suggested, in those brutally chaste terms which are used by the law in such a case, that she had been a victim of my violence at Roche-Mauprat. Her spirit thoroughly roused, she proceeded to defend my character and her own honour, and declared that, considering how I had been brought up, I had behaved much more honourably than might have been expected. But she still had to explain all her life from this point onward, the breaking off of her engagement with M. de la Marche, her frequent quarrels with myself, my sudden departure for America, her refusal of all offers of marriage.

"All these questions are abominable," she said, rising suddenly, her physical strength having returned with the exercise of her mental powers. "You ask me to give an account of my inmost feelings; you would sound the mysteries of my soul; you put my modesty on the rack; you would take to yourself rights that belong only to God. I declare to you that, if my own life were now at stake and not another's, you should not extract a word more from me. However, to save the life of the meanest of men I would overcome my repugnance; much more, therefore, will I do for him who is now at the bar. Know then—since you force me to a confession which is painful to the pride and reserve of my sex—that everything which to you seems inexplicable in my conduct, everything which you attribute to Bernard's persecutions and my own resentment, to his threats and my terror, finds its justification in one word: I love him!"

On uttering this word, the red blood in her cheeks, and in the ringing tone of the proudest and most passionate soul that ever existed, Edmee sat down again and buried her face in her hands. At this moment I was so transported that I could not help crying out:

"Let them take me to the scaffold now; I am king of all the earth!"

"To the scaffold! You!" said Edmee, rising again. "Let them rather take me. Is it your fault, poor boy, if for seven years I have hidden from you the secret of my affections; if I did not wish you to know it until you were the first of men in wisdom and intelligence as you are already the first in greatness of heart? You are paying dearly for my ambition, since it has been interpreted as scorn and hatred. You have good reason to hate me, since my pride has brought you to the felon's dock. But I will wash away your shame by a signal reparation; though they send you to the scaffold, you shall go there with the title of my husband."

"Your generosity is carrying you too far, Edmee de Mauprat," said the president. "It would seem that, in order to save your relative, you are accusing yourself of coquetry and unkindness; for, how otherwise do you explain the fact that you exasperated this young man's passion by refusing him for seven years?"

"Perhaps, sir," replied Edmee archly, "the court is not competent to judge this matter. Many women think it no great crime to show a little coquetry with the man they love. Perhaps we have a right to this when we have sacrificed all other men to him. After all, it is a very natural and very innocent ambition to make the man of one's choice feel that one is a soul of some price, that one is worth wooing, and worth a long effort. True, if this coquetry resulted in the condemnation of one's lover to death, one would speedily correct one's self of it. But, naturally, gentlemen, you would not think of atoning for my cruelty by offering the poor young man such a consolation as this."

After saying these words in an animated, ironical tone, Edmee burst into tears. This nervous sensibility which brought to the front all the qualities of her soul and mind, tenderness, courage, delicacy, pride, modesty, gave her face at the same time an expression so varied, so winning in all its moods, that the grave, sombre assembly of judges let fall the brazen cuirass of impassive integrity and the leaden cope of hypocritical virtue. If Edmee had not triumphantly defended me by her confession, she had at least roused the greatest interest in my favour. A man who is loved by a beautiful woman carries with him a talisman that makes him invulnerable; all feel that his life is of greater value than other lives.

Edmee still had to submit to many questions; she set in their proper light the facts which had been misrepresented by Mademoiselle Leblanc. True, she spared me considerably; but with admirable skill she managed to elude certain questions, and so escaped the necessity of either lying or condemning me. She generously took upon herself the blame for all my offences, and pretended that, if we had had various quarrels, it was because she herself took a secret pleasure in them; because they revealed the depth of my love; that she had let me go to America to put my virtue to the proof, thinking that the campaign would not last more than a year, as was then supposed; that afterwards she had considered me in honour bound to submit to the indefinite prolongation, but that she had suffered more than myself from my absence; finally, she quite remembered the letter which had been found upon her, and, taking it up, she gave the mutilated passages with astonishing accuracy, and at the same time called the clerk to follow as she deciphered the words which were half obliterated.

"This letter was so far from being a threatening letter," she said, "and the impression it left on me was so far from filling me with fear or aversion, that it was found on my heart, where I had been carrying it for a week, though I had not even let Bernard know that I had received it."

"But you have not yet explained," said the president, "how it was that seven years ago, when your cousin first came to live in your house, you armed yourself with a knife which you used to put under your pillow every night, after having it sharpened as if to defend yourself in case of need."

"In my family," she answered with a blush, "we have a somewhat romantic temperament and a very proud spirit. It is true that I frequently thought of killing myself, because I felt an unconquerable affection for my cousin springing up in me. Believing myself bound by indissoluble ties to M. de la Marche. I would have died rather than break my word, or marry any other than Bernard. Subsequently M. de la Marche freed me from my promise with much delicacy and loyalty, and I no longer thought of dying."

Edmee now withdrew, followed by all eyes and by a murmur of approbation. No sooner had she passed out of the hall than she fainted again; but this attack was without any grave consequences, and left no traces after a few days.

I was so bewildered, so intoxicated by what she had just said, that henceforth I could scarcely see what was taking place around me. Wholly wrapped up in thoughts of my love, I nevertheless could not cast aside all doubts; for, if Edmee had been silent about some of my actions, it was also possible that she had exaggerated her affection for me in the hope of extenuating my faults. I could not bring myself to think that she had loved me before my departure for America, and, above all, from the very beginning of my stay at Sainte-Severe. This was the one thought that filled my mind; I did not even remember anything further about the case or the object of my trial. It seemed to me that the sole question at issue in this chill Areopagus was this: Is he loved, or is he not? For me, victory or defeat, life or death, hung on that, and that alone.

I was roused from these reveries by the voice of Abbe Aubert. He was thin and wasted, but seemed perfectly calm; he had been kept in solitary confinement and had suffered all the hardships of prison life with the resignation of a martyr. In spite, however, of all precautions, the clever Marcasse, who could work his way anywhere like a ferret, had managed to convey to him a letter from Arthur, to which Edmee had added a few words. Authorized by this letter to say everything, he made a statement similar to that made by Patience, and owned that Edmee's first words after the occurrence had made him believe me guilty; but that subsequently, seeing the patient's mental condition, and remembering my irreproachable behaviour for more than six years, and obtaining a little new light from the preceding trial and the public rumours about the possible existence of Antony Mauprat, he had felt too convinced of my innocence to be willing to give evidence which might injure me. If he gave his evidence now, it was because he thought that further investigations might have enlightened the court, and that his words would not have the serious consequences they might have had a month before.

Questioned as to Edmee's feelings for me, he completely destroyed all Mademoiselle Leblanc's inventions, and declared that not only did Edmee love me ardently, but that she had felt an affection for me from the very first day we met. This he affirmed on oath, though emphasizing my past misdeeds somewhat more than Edmee had done. He owned that at first he had frequently feared that my cousin would be foolish enough to marry me, but that he had never had any fear for her life, since he had always seen her reduce me to submission by a single word or a mere look, even in my most boorish days.

The continuation of the trial was postponed to await the results of the warrants issued for the arrest of the assassin. People compared my trial to that of Calas, and the comparison had no sooner become a general topic of conversation than my judges, finding themselves exposed to a thousand shafts, realized very vividly that hatred and prejudice are bad counsellors and dangerous guides. The sheriff of the province declared himself the champion of my cause and Edmee's knight, and he himself escorted her back to her father. He set all the police agog. They acted with vigour and arrested John Mauprat. When he found himself a prisoner and threatened, he betrayed his brother, and declared that they might find him any night at Roche-Mauprat, hiding in a secret chamber which the tenant's wife helped him to reach, without her husband's knowledge.

They took the Trappist to Roche-Mauprat under a good escort, so that he might show them this secret chamber, which, in spite of his genius for exploring walls and timber-work, the old pole-cat hunter and mole-catcher Marcasse had never managed to reach. They took me there, likewise, so that I might help to find this room or passage leading to it, in case the Trappist should repent of his present sincere intentions. Once again, then, I revisited this abhorred manor with the ancient chief of the brigands transformed into a Trappist. He showed himself so humble and cringing in my presence, he made so light of his brother's life, and expressed such abject submission that I was filled with disgust, and after a few moments begged him not to speak to me any more. Keeping in touch with the mounted police outside, we began our search for the secret chamber. At first John had pretended that he knew of its existence, without knowing its exact location now that three-quarters of the keep had been destroyed. When he saw me, however, he remembered that I had surprised him in my room, and that he had disappeared through the wall. He resigned himself, therefore, to taking us to it, and showing us the secret; this was very curious; but I will not amuse myself by giving you an account of it. The secret chamber was opened; no one was there. Yet the expedition had been made with despatch and secrecy. It did not appear probable that John had had time to warn his brother. The keep was surrounded by the police and all the doors were well guarded. The night was dark, and our invasion had filled all the inmates of the farm with terror. The tenant had no idea what we were looking for, but his wife's agitation and anxiety seemed a sure sign that Antony was still in the keep. She had not sufficient presence of mind to assume a reassured air after we had explored the first room, and that made Marcasse think that there must be a second. Did the Trappist know of this, and was he pretending ignorance? He played his part so well that we were all deceived. We set to work to explore all the nooks and corners of the ruins again. There was one large tower standing apart from the other buildings; it did not seem as if this could offer any one a refuge. The staircase had completely fallen in at the time of the fire, and there could not be found a ladder long enough to reach the top story; even the farmer's ladders tied together with ropes were too short. This top story seemed to be in a state of good preservation and to contain a room lighted by two loopholes. Marcasse, after examining the thickness of the wall, affirmed that there might be a staircase inside, such as might be found in many an old tower. But where was the exit? Perhaps it was connected with some subterranean passage. Would the assassin dare to issue from his retreat as long as we were there? If, in spite of the darkness of the night and the silence of our proceedings, he had got wind of our presence, would he venture into the open as long as we continued on the watch at all points?

"That is not probable," said Marcasse. "We must devise some speedy means of getting up there; and I see one."

He pointed to a beam at a frightful height, all blackened by the fire, and running from the tower over a space of some twenty feet to the garrets of the nearest building. At the end of this beam there was a large gap in the wall of the tower caused by the falling-in of the adjoining parts. In his explorations, indeed, Marcasse had fancied that he could see the steps of a narrow staircase through this gap. The wall, moreover, was quite thick enough to contain one. The molecatcher had never cared to risk his life on this beam; not that he was afraid of its narrowness or its height; he was accustomed to these perilous "crossings," as he called them; but the beam had been partly consumed by the fire and was so thin in the middle that it was impossible to say whether it would bear the weight of a man, even were he as slender and diaphanous as the worthy sergeant. Up to the present nothing had happened here of sufficient importance for him to risk his life in the experiment. Now, however, the case was different. Marcasse did not hesitate. I was not near him when he formed his plan; I should have dissuaded him from it at all costs. I was not aware of it until he had already reached the middle of the beam, the spot where the burnt wood was perhaps nothing more than charcoal. How shall I describe to you what I felt when I beheld my faithful friend in mid-air, gravely walking toward his goal? Blaireau was trotting in front of him as calmly as in the old days when it was a question of hunting through bundles of hay in search of stoats and dormice. Day was breaking, and the hildalgo's slim outline and his modest yet stately bearing could be clearly seen against the gray sky. I put my hands to my face; I seemed to hear the fatal beam cracking; I stifled a cry of terror lest I should unnerve him at this solemn and critical moment. But I could not suppress this cry, or help raising my head when I heard two shots fired from the tower. Marcasse's hat fell at the first shot; the second grazed his shoulder. He stopped a moment.

"Not touched!" he shouted at us.

And making a rush he was quickly across the aerial bridge. He got into the tower through the gap and darted up the stairs, crying:

"Follow me, my lads! The beam will bear."

Immediately five other bold and active men who had accompanied him got astride upon the beam, and with the help of their hands reached the other end one by one. When the first of them arrived in the garret whither Antony Mauprat had fled, he found him grappling with Marcasse, who, quite carried away by his triumph and forgetting that it was not a question of killing an enemy but of capturing him, set about lunging at him with his long rapier as if he had been a weasel. But the sham Trappist was a formidable enemy. He had snatched the sword from the sergeant's hands, hurled him to the ground, and would have strangled him had not a gendarme thrown himself on him from behind. With his prodigious strength he held his own against the first three assailants; but, with the help of the other two, they succeeded in overcoming him. When he saw that he was caught he made no further resistance and let his hands be bound together. They brought him down the stairs, which were found to lead to the bottom of a dry well in the middle of the tower. Antony was in the habit of leaving and entering by means of a ladder which the farmer's wife held for him and immediately afterwards withdrew. In a transport of delight I threw myself into my sergeant's arms.

"A mere trifle," he said; "enjoyed it. I found that my foot was still sure and my head cool. Ha! ha! old sergeant," he added, looking at his leg, "old hidalgo, old mole-catcher, after this they won't make so many jokes about your calves!"

XXIX

If Anthony Mauprat had been a man of mettle he might have done me a bad turn by declaring that he had been a witness of my attempt to assassinate Edmee. As he had reasons for hiding himself before this last crime, he could have explained why he had kept out of sight, and why he had been silent about the occurrences at Gazeau Tower. I had nothing in my favour except Patience's evidence. Would this have been sufficient to procure my acquittal? The evidence of so many others was against me, even that given by my friends, and by Edmee, who could not deny my violent temper and the possibility of such a crime.

But Antony, in words the most insolent of all the "Hamstringers," was the most cowardly in deeds. He no sooner found himself in the hands of justice than he confessed everything, even before knowing that his brother had thrown him over.

At his trial there were some scandalous scenes, in which the two brothers accused each other in a loathsome way. The Trappist, whose rage was kept in check by his hypocrisy, coldly abandoned the ruffian to his fate, and denied that he had ever advised him to commit the crime. The other, driven to desperation, accused him of the most horrible deeds, including the poisoning of my mother, and Edmee's mother, who had both died of violent inflammation of the intestines within a short time of each other. John Mauprat, he declared, used to be very skilful in the art of preparing poisons and would introduce himself into houses under various disguises to mix them with the food. He affirmed that, on the day that Edmee had been brought to Roche-Mauprat, John had called together all his brothers to discuss plans for making away with this heiress to a considerable fortune, a fortune which he had striven to obtain by crime, since he had tried to destroy the effects of the Chevalier Hubert's marriage. My mother's life, too, had been the price paid for the latter's wish to adopt his brother's child. All the Mauprats had been in favour of making away with Edmee and myself simultaneously, and John was actually preparing the poison when the police happened to turn aside their hideous designs by attacking the castle. John denied the charges with pretended horror, saying humbly that he had committed quite enough mortal sins of debauchery and irreligion without having these added to his list. As it was difficult to take Antony's word for them without further investigation; as this investigation was almost impossible, and as the clergy were too powerful and too much interested in preventing a scandal to allow it, John Mauprat was acquitted on the charge of complicity and merely sent back to the Trappist monastery; the archbishop forbade him ever to set foot in the diocese again, and, moreover, sent a request to his superiors that they would never allow him to leave the convent. He died there a few years later in all the terrors of a fanatic penitence very much akin to insanity.

It is probable that, as a result of feigning remorse in order to find favour among his fellows, he had at last, after the failure of his plans, and under the terrible asceticism of his order, actually experienced the horrors and agonies of a bad conscience and tardy repentance. The fear of hell is the only creed of vile souls.

No sooner was I acquitted and set at liberty, with my character completely cleared, than I hastened to Edmee. I arrived in time to witness my great-uncle's last moments. Towards the end, though his mind remained a blank as to past events, the memory of his heart returned. He recognised me, clasped me to his breast, blessed me at the same time as Edmee, and put my hand into his daughter's. After we had paid the last tribute of affection to our excellent and noble kinsman, whom we were as grieved to lose as if we had not long foreseen and expected his death, we left the province for some time, so as not to witness the execution of Antony, who was condemned to be broken on the wheel. The two false witnesses who had accused me were flogged, branded, and expelled from the jurisdiction of the court. Mademoiselle Leblanc, who could not exactly be accused of giving false evidence, since hers had consisted of mere inferences from facts, avoided the public displeasure by going to another province. Here she lived in sufficient luxury to make us suspect that she had been paid considerable sums to bring about my ruin.

Edmee and I would not consent to be separated, even temporarily, from our good friends, my sole defenders, Marcasse, Patience, Arthur, and the Abbe Aubert. We all travelled in the same carriage; the first two, being accustomed to the open air, were only too glad to sit outside; but we treated them on a footing of perfect equality. From that day forth they never sat at any table but our own. Some persons had the bad taste to express astonishment at this; we let them talk. There are circumstances that obliterate all distinctions, real or imaginary, of rank and education.

We paid a visit to Switzerland. Arthur considered this was essential to the complete restoration of Edmee's health. The delicate, thoughtful attentions of this devoted friend, and the loving efforts we made to minister to her happiness, combined into the beautiful spectacle of the mountains to drive away her melancholy and efface the recollection of the troublous times through which we had just passed. On Patience's poetic nature Switzerland had quite a magic effect. He would frequently fall into such a state of ecstasy that we were entranced and terrified at the same time. He felt strongly tempted to build himself a chalet in the heart of some valley and spend the rest of his life there in contemplation of Nature; but his affection for us made him abandon this project. As for Marcasse, he declared subsequently that, despite all the pleasure he had derived from our society, he looked upon this visit as the most unlucky event of his life. At the inn at Martigny, on our return journey, Blaireau, whose digestion had been impaired by age, fell a victim to the excess of hospitality shown him in the kitchen. The sergeant said not a word, but gazed on him awhile with heavy eye, and then went and buried him under the most beautiful rose-tree in the garden; nor did he speak of his loss until more than a year later.

During our journey Edmee was for me a veritable angel of kindness and tender thought; abandoning herself henceforth to all the inspirations of her heart, and no longer feeling any distrust of me, or perhaps thinking that I deserved some compensation for all my sufferings, she repeatedly confirmed the celestial assurances of love which she had given in public, when she lifted up her voice to proclaim my innocence. A few reservations that had struck me in her evidence, and a recollection of the damning words that had fallen from her lips when Patience found her shot, continued, I must confess, to cause me pain for some time longer. I thought, rightly perhaps, that Edmee had made a great effort to believe in my innocence before Patience had given his evidence. But on this point she always spoke most unwillingly and with a certain amount of reserve. However, one day she quite healed my wound by saying with her charming abruptness:

"And if I loved you enough to absolve you in my own heart, and defend you in public at the cost of a lie, what would you say to that?"

A point on which I felt no less concern was to know how far I might believe in the love which she declared she had had for me from the very beginning of our acquaintance. Here she betrayed a little confusion, as if, in her invincible pride, she regretted having revealed a secret she had so jealously guarded. It was the abbe who undertook to confess for her. He assured me that at that time he had frequently scolded Edmee for her affection for "the young savage." As an objection to this, I told him of the conversation between Edmee and himself which I had overheard one evening in the park. This I repeated with that great accuracy of memory I possess. However, he replied:

"That very evening, if you had followed us a little further under the trees, you might have overheard a dispute that would have completely reassured you, and have explained how, from being repugnant (I may almost say odious) to me, as you then were, you became at first endurable, and gradually very dear."

"You must tell me," I exclaimed, "who worked the miracle."

"One word will explain it," he answered; "Edmee loved you. When she had confessed this to me, she covered her face with her hands and remained for a moment as if overwhelmed with shame and vexation; then suddenly she raised her head and exclaimed:

"'Well, since you wish to know the absolute truth, I love him! Yes, I love him! I am smitten with him, as you say. It is not my fault; why should I blush at it? I cannot help it; it is the work of fate. I have never loved M. de la Marche; I merely feel a friendship for him. For Bernard I have a very different feeling—a feeling so strong, so varied, so full of unrest, of hatred, of fear, of pity, of anger, of tenderness, that I understand nothing about it, and no longer try to understand anything.'"

"'Oh, woman, woman!' I exclaimed, clasping my hands in bewilderment, 'thou art a mystery, an abyss, and he who thinks to know thee is totally mad!'

"'As many times as you like, abbe,' she answered, with a firmness in which there were signs of annoyance and confusion, 'it is all the same to me. On this point I have lectured myself more than you have lectured all your flocks in your whole life. I know that Bernard is a bear, a badger, as Mademoiselle Leblanc calls him, a savage, a boor, and anything else you like. There is nothing more shaggy, more prickly, more cunning, more malicious than Bernard. He is an animal who scarcely knows how to sign his name; he is a coarse brute who thinks he can break me in like one of the jades of Varenne. But he makes a great mistake; I will die rather than ever be his, unless he becomes civilized enough to marry me. But one might as well expect a miracle. I try to improve him, without daring to hope. However, whether he forces me to kill myself or to turn nun, whether he remains as he is or becomes worse, it will be none the less true that I love him. My dear abbe, you know that it must be costing me something to make this confession; and, when my affection for you brings me as a penitent to your feet and to your bosom, you should not humiliate me by your expressions of surprise and your exorcisms! Consider the matter now; examine, discuss, decide! Consider the matter now; examine, discuss, decide! The evil is—I love him. The symptoms are—I think of none but him, I see none but him; and I could eat no dinner this evening because he had not come back. I find him handsomer than any man in the world. When he says that he loves me, I can see, I can feel that it is true; I feel displeased, and at the same time delighted. M. de la Marche seems insipid and prim since I have known Bernard. Bernard alone seems as proud, as passionate, as bold as myself—and as weak as myself; for he cries like a child when I vex him, and here I am crying, too, as I think of him.'"

"Dear abbe," I said, throwing myself on his neck, "let me embrace you till I have crushed your life out for remembering all this."

"The abbe is drawing the long bow," said Edmee archly.

"What!" I exclaimed, pressing her hands as if I would break them. "You have made me suffer for seven years, and now you repent a few words that console me . . ."

"In any case do not regret the past," she said. "Ah, with you such as you were in those days, we should have been ruined if I had not been able to think and decide for both of us. Good God! what would have become of us by now? You would have had far more to suffer from my sternness and pride; for you would have offended me from the very first day of our union, and I should have had to punish you by running away or killing myself, or killing you—for we are given to killing in our family; it is a natural habit. One thing is certain, and that is that you would have been a detestable husband; you would have made me blush for your ignorance; you would have wanted to rule me, and we should have fallen foul of each other; that would have driven my father to despair, and, as you know, my father had to be considered before everything. I might, perhaps, have risked my own fate lightly enough, if I had been alone in the world, for I have a strain of rashness in my nature; but it was essential that my father should remain happy, and tranquil, and respected. He had brought me up in happiness and independence, and I should never have forgiven myself if I had deprived his old age of the blessings he had lavished on my whole life. Do not think that I am full of virtues and noble qualities, as the abbe pretends; I love, that is all; but I love strongly, exclusively, steadfastly. I sacrificed you to my father, my poor Bernard; and Heaven, who would have cursed us if I had sacrificed my father, rewards us today by giving us to each other, tried and not found wanting. As you grew greater in my eyes I felt that I could wait, because I knew I had to love you long, and I was not afraid of seeing my passion vanish before it was satisfied, as do the passions of feeble souls. We were two exceptional characters; our loves had to be heroic; the beaten track would have led both of us to ruin."

XXX

We returned to Sainte-Severe at the expiration of Edmee's period of mourning. This was the time that had been fixed for our marriage. When we had quitted the province where we had both experienced so many bitter mortifications and such grievous trials, we had imagined that we should never feel any inclination to return. Yet, so powerful are the recollections of childhood and the ties of family life that, even in the heart of an enchanted land which could not arouse painful memories, we had quickly begun to regret our gloomy, wild Varenne, and sighed for the old oaks in the park. We returned, then, with a sense of profound yet solemn joy. Edmee's first care was to gather the beautiful flowers in the garden and to kneel by her father's grave and arrange them on it. We kissed the hallowed ground, and there made a vow to strive unceasingly to leave a name as worthy of respect and veneration as his. He had frequently carried this ambition to the verge of weakness, but it was a noble weakness, a sacred vanity.

Our marriage was celebrated in the village chapel, and the festivities were confined to the family; none but Arthur, the abbe, Marcasse, and Patience sat down to our modest banquet. What need had we of the outside world to behold our happiness? They might have believed, perhaps, that they were doing us an honour by covering the blots on our escutcheon with their august presence. We were enough to be happy and merry among ourselves. Our hearts were filled with as much affection as they could hold. We were too proud to ask more from any one, too pleased with one another to yearn for greater pleasure. Patience returned to his sober, retired life, resumed the duties of "great judge" and "treasurer" on certain days of the week. Marcasse remained with me until his death, which happened towards the end of the French Revolution. I trust I did my best to repay his fidelity by an unreserved friendship and an intimacy that nothing could disturb.

Arthur, who had sacrificed a year of his life to us, could not bring himself to abjure the love of his country, and his desire to contribute to its progress by offering it the fruits of his learning and the results of his investigations; he returned to Philadelphia, where I paid him a visit after I was left a widower.

I will not describe my years of happiness with my noble wife; such years beggar description. One could not resign one's self to living after losing them, if one did not make strenuous efforts to avoid recalling them too often. She gave me six children; four of these are still alive, and all honourably settled in life. I have lived for them, in obedience to Edmee's dying command. You must forgive me for not speaking further of this loss, which I suffered only ten years ago. I feel it now as keenly as on the first day, and I do not seek to find consolation for it, but to make myself worthy of rejoining the holy comrade of my life in a better world after I have completed my period of probation in this. She was the only woman I ever loved; never did any other win a glance from me or know the pressure of my hand. Such is my nature; what I love I love eternally, in the past, in the present, in the future.

The storms of the Revolution did not destroy our existence, nor did the passions it aroused disturb the harmony of our private life. We gladly gave up a large part of our property to the Republic, looking upon it, indeed, as a just sacrifice. The abbe, terrified by the bloodshed, occasionally abjured this political faith, when the necessities of the hour were too much for the strength of his soul. He was the Girondin of the family.

With no less sensibility, Edmee had greater courage; a woman and compassionate, she sympathized profoundly with the sufferings of all classes. She bewailed the misfortune of her age; but she never failed to appreciate the greatness of its holy fanaticism. She remained faithful to her ideas of absolute equality. At a time when the acts of the Mountain were irritating the abbe, and driving him to despair, she generously sacrificed her own patriotic enthusiasm; and her delicacy would never let her mention in his presence certain names that made him shudder, names for which she herself had a sort of passionate veneration, the like of which I have never seen in any woman.

As for myself, I can truthfully say that it was she who educated me; during the whole course of my life I had the profoundest respect for her judgment and rectitude. When, in my enthusiasm, I was filled with a longing to play a part as a leader of the people, she held me back by showing how my name would destroy any influence I might have; since they would distrust me, and imagine my aim was to use them as an instrument for recovering my rank. When the enemy was at the gates of France, she sent me to serve as a volunteer; when the Republic was overthrown, and a military career came to be merely a means of gratifying ambition, she recalled me, and said:

"You must never leave me again."

Patience played a great part in the Revolution. He was unanimously chosen as judge of his district. His integrity, his impartiality between castle and cottage, his firmness and wisdom will never be forgotten in Varenne.

During the war I was instrumental in saving M. de la Marche's life, and helping him to escape to a foreign country.

Such, I believe, said old Mauprat, are all the events of my life in which Edmee played a part. The rest of it is not worth the telling. If there is anything helpful in my story, try to profit by it, young fellows. Hope to be blessed with a frank counsellor, a severe friend; and love not the man who flatters, but the man who reproves. Do not believe too much in phrenology; for I have the murderer's bump largely developed, and, as Edmee used to say with grim humour, "killing comes natural" to our family. Do not believe in fate, or, at least, never advise any one to tamely submit to it. Such is the moral of my story.

XXX

After this old Bernard gave us a good supper, and continued conversing with us for the rest of the evening without showing any signs of discomposure or fatigue. As we begged him to develop what he called the moral of his story a little further, he proceeded to a few general considerations which impressed me with their soundness and good sense.

I spoke of phrenology, he said, not with the object of criticising a system which has its good side, in so far as it tends to complete the series of physiological observations that aim at increasing our knowledge of man; I used the word phrenology because the only fatality that we believe in nowadays is that created by our own instincts. I do not believe that phrenology is more fatalistic than any other system of this kind; and Lavater, who was also accused of fatalism in his time, was the most Christian man the Gospel has ever formed.

Do not believe in any absolute and inevitable fate; and yet acknowledge, in a measure, that we are moulded by instincts, our faculties, the impressions of our infancy, the surroundings of our earliest childhood—in short, by all that outside world which has presided over the development of our soul. Admit that we are not always absolutely free to choose between good and evil, if you would be indulgent towards the guilty—that is to say, just even as Heaven is just; for there is infinite mercy in God's judgments; otherwise His justice would be imperfect.

What I am saying now is not very orthodox, but, take my word for it, it is Christian, because it is true. Man is not born wicked; neither is he born good, as is maintained by Jean Jacques Rousseau, my beloved Edmee's old master. Man is born with more or less of passions, with more or less power to satisfy them, with more or less capacity for turning them to a good or bad account in society. But education can and must find a remedy for everything; that is the great problem to be solved, to discover the education best suited to each individual. If it seems necessary that education should be general and in common, does it follow that it ought to be the same for all? I quite believe that if I had been sent to school when I was ten, I should have become a civilized being earlier; but would any one have thought of correcting my violent passions, and of teaching me how to conquer them as Edmee did? I doubt it. Every man needs to be loved before he can be worth anything; but each in a different way; one with never-failing indulgence, another with unflinching severity. Meanwhile, until some one solves the problem of making education common to all, and yet appropriate to each, try to improve one another.

Do you ask me how? My answer will be brief: by loving one another truly. It is in this way—for the manners of a people mould their laws—that you will succeed in suppressing the most odious and impious of all laws, the *lex talionis*, capital punishment, which is nothing else than the consecration of the principle of fatality, seeing that it supposes the culprit incorrigible and Heaven implacable.

MADAME DELMARE DISCOVERS NOUN'S BODY

Terror nailed her to the spot; but the stream flowed on, slowly drawing a body from the reeds among which it had caught, and bringing it toward Madame Delmare.

INDIANA

TRANSLATED INTO ENGLISH BY G. BURNHAM IVES

WITH SIX PHOTOGRAVURES AFTER PAINTINGS BY ORESTE CORTAZZO

INTRODUCTION

I wrote *Indiana* during the autumn of 1831. It was my first novel; I wrote it without any fixed plan, having no theory of art or philosophy in my mind. I was at the age when one writes with one's instincts, and when reflection serves only to confirm our natural tendencies. Some people chose to see in the book a deliberate argument against marriage. I was not so ambitious, and I was surprised to the last degree at all the fine things that the critics found to say concerning my subversive purposes. Criticism is far too acute; that is what will cause its death. It never passes judgment ingenuously. It looks for noon at four o'clock, as the old women say, and must cause much suffering to artists who care more for its decrees than they ought to do.

Under all régimes and in all times there has been a race of critics, who, in contempt of their own talent, have fancied that it was their duty to ply the trade of denouncers, of purveyors to the prosecuting attorney's office; extraordinary functions for men of letters to assume with regard to their confrères! The rigorous measures of government against the press never satisfy these savage critics. They would have them directed not only against works but against persons as well, and, if their advice were followed, some of us would be forbidden to write anything whatsoever.

At the time that I wrote *Indiana*, the cry of Saint Simonism was raised on every pretext. Later they shouted all sorts of other things. Even now certain writers are forbidden to open their mouths, under pain of seeing the police agents of certain newspapers pounce upon their work and hale them before the police of the constituted powers. If a writer puts noble sentiments in the mouth of a mechanic, it is an attack on the bourgeoisie; if a girl who has gone astray is rehabilitated after expiating her sin, it is an attack on virtuous women; if an impostor assumes titles of nobility, it is an attack on the patrician caste; if a bully plays the swashbuckling soldier, it is an insult to the army; if a woman is maltreated by her husband, it is an argument in favor of promiscuous love. And so with everything. Kindly brethren, devout and generous critics! What a pity that no one thinks of creating a petty court of literary inquisition in which you should be the torturers! Would you be satisfied to tear the books to pieces and burn them at a slow fire, and could you not, by your urgent representations, obtain permission to give a little taste of the rack to those writers who presume to have other gods than yours?

Thank God, I have forgotten the names of those who tried to discourage me at my first appearance, and who, being unable to say that my first attempt had fallen completely flat, tried to distort it into an incendiary proclamation against the repose of society. I did not expect so much honor, and I consider that I owe to those critics the thanks which the hare proffered the frogs, imagining from their alarm that he was entitled to deem himself a very thunderbolt of war.

GEORGE SAND.

Nohant, May, 1852.

PREFACE TO THE EDITION OF 1832

If certain pages of this book should incur the serious reproach of tending toward novel beliefs, if unbending judges shall consider their tone imprudent and perilous, I should be obliged to reply to the criticism that it does too much honor to a work of no importance; that, in order to attack the great questions of social order, one must either be conscious of great strength of purpose or pride one's self upon great talent, and that such presumption is altogether foreign to a very simple tale, in which the author has invented almost nothing. If, in the course of his task, he has happened to set forth the lamentations extorted from his characters by the social malady with which they were assailed; if he has not shrunk from recording their aspirations after a happier existence, let the blame be laid upon society for its inequalities, upon destiny for its caprices! The author is merely a mirror which reflects them, a machine which reverses their tracing, and he has no reason for self-reproach if the impression is exact, if the reflection is true.

Consider further that the narrator has not taken for text or devise a few shrieks of suffering and wrath scattered through the drama of human life. He does not claim to conceal serious instruction beneath the exterior form of a tale; it is not his aim to lend a hand in constructing the edifice which a doubtful future is preparing for us and to give a sly kick at that of the past which is crumbling away. He knows too well that we live in an epoch of moral deterioration, wherein the reason of mankind has need of curtains to soften the too bright glare which dazzles it. If he had felt sufficiently learned to write a genuinely useful book, he would have toned down the truth, instead of presenting it in its crude tints and with its startling effects. That book would have performed the functions of blue spectacles for weak eyes.

He does not abandon the idea of performing that honorable and laudable task some day; but, being still a young man, he simply tells you to-day what he has seen, not presuming to draw his conclusions concerning the great controversy between the future and the past, which perhaps no man of the present generation is especially competent to do. Too conscientious to conceal his doubts from you, but too timid to transform them into certainties, he relies upon your reflections and abstains from weaving into the woof of his narrative preconceived opinions, judgments all formed. He plies with exactitude his trade of narrator. He will tell you everything, even painful truths; but, if you should wrap him in the philosopher's robe, you would find that he was exceedingly confused, simple story-teller that he is, whose mission is to amuse and not to instruct.

Even were he more mature and more skilful, he would not dare to lay his hand upon the great sores of dying civilization. One must be so sure of being able to cure them when one ventures to probe them! He would much prefer to arouse your interest in old discarded beliefs, in old-fashioned, vanished forms of devotion, to employing his talent, if he had any, in blasting overturned altars. He knows, however, that, in these charitable times, a timorous conscience is despised by public opinion as hypocritical reserve, just as, in the arts, a timid bearing is sneered at as an absurd mannerism; but he knows also that there is honor, if not profit, in defending lost causes.

To him who should misunderstand the spirit of this book, such a profession of faith would sound like an anachronism. The narrator hopes that few auditors, after listening to his tale to the end, will deny the *moral* to be derived from the facts, a moral which triumphs there as in all human affairs; it seemed to him, when he wrote the last line, that his conscience was clear. He flattered himself, in a word, that he had described social miseries without too much bitterness, human passions without too much passion. He placed the mute under his strings when they echoed too loudly; he tried to stifle certain notes of the soul which should remain mute, certain voices of the heart which cannot be awakened without danger.

Perhaps you will do him justice if you agree that the being who tries to free himself from his lawful curb is represented as very wretched indeed, and the heart that rebels against the decrees of its destiny as in sore distress. If he has not given the best imaginable rôle to that one of his characters who represents *the law*, if that one who represents *opinion* is even less cheerful, you will see a third representing *illusion*, who cruelly thwarts the vain hopes and enterprises of passion. Lately, you will see that, although he has not strewn rose-leaves on the ground where the law pens up our desires like a sheep's appetite, he has scattered thistles along the roads which lead us away from it.

These facts, it seems to me, are sufficient to protect this book from the reproach of immorality; but, if you absolutely insist that a novel should end like one of Marmontel's tales, you will perhaps chide me on account of the last pages; you will think that I have done wrong in not casting into misery and destitution the character who has transgressed the laws of mankind through two volumes. In this regard, the author will reply that before being moral he chose to be true; he will say again, that, feeling that he was too new to the trade to compose a philosophical treatise on the manner of enduring life, he has restricted himself to telling you the story of *Indiana*, a story of the human heart, with its weaknesses, its passions, its rights and its wrongs, its good qualities and its evil qualities.

Indiana, if you insist upon an explanation of every thing in the book, is a type; she is woman, the feeble being whose mission it is to represent *passions* repressed, or, if you prefer, suppressed by *the law*; she is desire at odds with necessity; she is love dashing her head blindly against all the obstacles of civilization. But the serpent wears out his teeth and breaks them in trying to gnaw a file; the powers of the soul become exhausted in trying to struggle against the positive facts of life. That is the conclusion you may draw from this tale, and it was in that light that it was told to him who transmits it to you.

But despite these protestations the narrator anticipates reproaches. Some upright souls, some honest men's consciences will be alarmed perhaps to see virtue so harsh, reason so downcast, opinion so unjust. He is dismayed at the prospect; for the thing that an author should fear more than anything in the world is the alienating from his works the confidence of good men, the awakening of an ominous sympathy in embittered souls, the inflaming of the sores, already too painful, which are made by the social yoke upon impatient and rebellious necks.

The success which is based upon an unworthy appeal to the passions of the age is the easiest to win, the least honorable to strive for. The historian of *Indiana* denies that he has ever dreamed of it; if he thought that he had reached that result, he would destroy his book, even though he felt for it the artless fatherly affection which swaddles the rickety offspring of these days of literary abortions.

But he hopes to justify himself by stating that he thought it better to enforce his principles by real examples than by poetic fancies. He believes that his tale, with the depressing atmosphere of frankness that envelopes it, may make an impression upon young and ardent brains. They will find it difficult to distrust a historian who forces his way brutally through the midst of facts, elbowing right and left, with no more regard for one camp than for the other. To make a cause odious or absurd is to persecute it, not to combat it. It may be that the whole art of the novelist consists in interesting the culprits whom he wishes to redeem, the wretched whom he wishes to cure, in their own story.

It would be giving overmuch importance to a work that is destined doubtless to attract very little notice, to seek to protect it against every sort of accusation. Therefore the author surrenders unconditionally to the critics; a single charge seems to him too serious to accept, and that is the charge that he has written a dangerous book. He would prefer to remain in a humble position forever to building his reputation upon a ruined conscience. He will add a word therefore to repel the blame which he most dreads.

Raymon, you will say, is society; egoism is substituted for morality and reason. Raymon, the author will reply, is the false reason, the false morality by which society is governed; he is the man of honor as the world understands the phrase, because the world does not examine closely enough to see everything. The good man you have beside Raymon; and you will not say that he is the enemy of order; for he sacrifices his happiness, he loses all thought of self before all questions of social order.

Then you will say that virtue is not rewarded with sufficient blowing of trumpets. Alas! the answer is that we no longer witness the triumph of virtue elsewhere than at the boulevard theatres. The author will tell you that he has undertaken to exhibit society to you, not as virtuous, but as necessary, and that honor has become as difficult as heroism in these days of moral degeneration. Do you think that this truth will cause great souls to loathe honor? I think just the opposite.

PREFACE TO THE EDITION OF 1842

In allowing the foregoing pages to be reprinted, I do not mean to imply that they form a clear and complete summary of the beliefs which I hold to-day concerning the rights of society over individuals. I do it simply because I regard opinions freely put forth in the past as something sacred, which we should neither retract nor cry down nor attempt to interpret as our fancy directs. But to-day, having advanced on life's highway and watched the horizon broaden around me, I deem it my duty to tell the reader what I think of my book.

When I wrote *Indiana*, I was young; I acted in obedience to feelings of great strength and sincerity which overflowed thereafter in a series of novels, almost all of which were based on the same idea: the ill-defined relations between the sexes, attributable to the constitution of our society. These novels were all more or less inveighed against by the critics, as making unwise assaults upon the institution of marriage. *Indiana*, notwithstanding the narrowness of its scope and the ingenuous uncertainty of its grasp, did not escape the indignation of several self-styled serious minds, whom I was strongly disposed at that time to believe upon their simple statement and to listen to with docility. But, although my reasoning powers were developed hardly enough to write upon so grave a subject, I was not so much of a child that I could not pass judgment in my turn on the thoughts of those persons who passed judgment on mine. However simple-minded a man accused of crime may be and however shrewd the magistrate, the accused has enough common-sense to know whether the magistrate's sentence is equitable or inequitable, wise or absurd.

Certain journalists of our day who set themselves up as representatives and guardians of public morals–I know not by virtue of what mission they act, since I know not by what faith they are commissioned–pronounced judgment pitilessly against my poor tale, and, by representing it as an argument against social order, gave it an importance and a sort of echo which it would not otherwise have obtained. They thereby imposed a very serious and weighty rôle upon a young author hardly initiated in the most elementary social ideas, whose whole literary and philosophical baggage consisted of a little imagination, courage and love of the truth. Sensitive to the reproofs and almost grateful for the lessons which they were pleased to administer, he examined the arguments which arraigned the moral character of his thoughts before the bar of public opinion, and, by virtue of that examination, which he conducted entirely without pride, he gradually acquired convictions which were mere feelings at the outset of his career and which to-day are fundamental principles.

During ten years of investigations, of scruples, and of irresolution, often painful but always sincere, shunning the rôle of pedagogue which some attributed to me to make me ridiculous, abhorring the imputation of pride and spleen with which others pursued me to make me odious, proceeding according to the measure of my artistic faculties, to seek the synthesis of life by analyzing it, I related facts which have sometimes been acknowledged to be plausible, and drew characters which have often been described as having been studied with care. I restricted myself to that, striving to establish my own conviction rather than to shake other people's, and saying to myself that, if I were mistaken, society would find no lack of loud voices to overturn my arguments and to repair by judicious answers the evil that my imprudent questions might have done. Numerous voices did, in fact, arise to put the public on its guard against the dangerous writer, but, as for the judicious answers, the public and the author are still awaiting them.

A long while after I wrote the preface to *Indiana* under the influence of a remnant of respect for constituted society, I was still seeking to solve this insoluble problem: *the method of reconciling the welfare and the dignity of individuals oppressed by that same society without modifying society itself.* Leaning over the victims and mingling his tears with theirs, making himself their interpreter with his readers, but, like a prudent advocate, not striving overmuch to palliate the wrong-doing of his clients, and addressing himself to the clemency of the judges rather than to their austerity, the novelist is really the advocate of the abstract beings who represent our passions and our sufferings before the tribunal of superior force and the jury of public opinion. It is a task which has a gravity of its own beneath its trivial exterior, and a task which it is exceedingly difficult to confine to its true path, pestered as you are at every step by those who accuse you of being too serious in respect to form and by those who accuse you of being too frivolous in respect to substance.

I do not flatter myself that I performed this task skilfully; but I am sure that I attempted it in all seriousness, amid inward hesitations wherein my conscience, sometimes dismayed by its ignorance of its rights, sometimes inspired by a heart enamored of justice and truth, marched forward to its goal, without swerving too far from the straight road and without too many backward steps.

To enlighten the public as to this inward struggle by a series of prefaces and discussions would have been a puerile method, wherein the vanity of talking about one's self would have taken too much space to suit me. I could but abstain from it as well as from touching too hastily upon the points which were still obscure in my mind. Conservators called me too bold, innovators too timid. I confess that I had respect and sympathy for the past and the future alike, and in the battle I found no peace of mind until the day when I fully realized that the one should not be the violation and the annihilation of the other, but its continuation and development.

After this novitiate of ten years, being initiated at last in broader ideas which I derived not from myself but from the philosophical progress which had taken place around me–and particularly from a few vast intellects which I religiously questioned, and, generally speaking, from the spectacle of the sufferings of my fellowmen,–I realized at last that, although I may have done well to distrust myself and to hesitate to put forth my views at the epoch of ignorance and inexperience when I wrote *Indiana*, my present duty is to congratulate myself on the bold utterances to which I allowed myself to be impelled then and afterwards; bold utterances for which I have been reproached so bitterly, and which would have been bolder still had I known how legitimate and honest and sacred they were.

To-day therefore, having re-read the first novel of my youth with as much severity and impartiality as if it were the work of another person, on the eve of giving it a publicity which it has not yet derived from the popular edition, having resolved beforehand not to retract–one should never retract what was said or done in good faith–but to condemn myself if I should discover that my former tendencies were mistaken or dangerous, I find myself so entirely in accord with myself with respect to the sentiment which dictated *Indiana* and which would dictate it now if I had that story to tell to-day for the first time, that I have not chosen to change anything in it save a few ungrammatical sentences and some inappropriate words. Doubtless many more of the same sort remain, and the literary merits of my writings I submit without reserve to the animadversions of the critics; I gladly accord to them all the competence in that regard which I myself lack. That there is an incontestable mass of talent in the daily press of the present day, I do not deny and I delight to acknowledge it. But that there are many philosophers and moralists in this array of polished writers, I do positively deny, with due respect to those who have condemned me, and who will condemn me again on the first opportunity, from their lofty plane of morality and philosophy.

I repeat then, I wrote *Indiana*, and I was justified in writing it; I yielded to an overpowering instinct of outcry and rebellion which God had implanted in me, God who makes nothing that is not of some use, even the most insignificant creatures, and who interposes in the most trivial as well as in great causes. But what am I saying? is this cause that I am defending so very trivial, pray? It is the cause of half of the human race, nay, of the whole human race; for the unhappiness of woman involves that of man, as that of the slave involves that of the master, and I strove to demonstrate it in *Indiana*. Some persons said that I was pleading the cause of an individual; as if, even assuming that I was inspired by personal feeling, I was the only unhappy mortal in this peaceful and radiant human race! So many cries of pain and sympathy answered mine that I know now what to think concerning the supreme felicity of my fellowman.

I do not think that I have ever written anything under the influence of a selfish passion; I have never even thought of avoiding it. They who have read me without prejudice understand that I wrote *Indiana* with a feeling, not deliberately reasoned out, to be sure, but a deep and genuine feeling that the laws which still govern woman's existence in wedlock, in the family and in society are unjust and barbarous. I had not to write a treatise on jurisprudence but to fight against public opinion; for it is that which postpones or advances social reforms. The war will be long and bitter; but I am neither the first nor the last nor the only champion of so noble a cause, and I will defend it so long as the breath of life remains in my body.

This feeling which inspired me at the beginning I reasoned out and developed as it was combated and reproved. Unjust and malevolent critics taught me much more than I should have discovered in the calm of impunity. For this reason therefore I offer thanks to the bungling judges who enlightened me. The motives that inspired their judgments cast a bright light upon my mind and enveloped my conscience in a sense of profound security. A sincere mind turns everything to advantage, and facts that would discourage vanity redouble the ardor of genuine devotion.

Let no one look upon the reproof which, from the depths of a heart that is to-day serious and tranquil, I have just addressed to the majority of journalists of my time, as implying even a suggestion of protest against the right of censorship with which public morality invests the French press. That criticism often ill performs and ill comprehends its mission in the society of the present day, is evident to all; but that the mission is in itself providential and sacred, no one can deny unless he be an atheist in the matter of progress, unless he be an enemy of the truth, a blasphemer of the future and an unworthy child of France! Liberty of thought, liberty to write and to speak, blessed conquest of the human mind! What are the petty sufferings and the fleeting cares engendered by thy errors or abuses compared to the infinite blessings which thou hast in store for the world!

PART FIRST

I

On a certain cool, rainy evening in autumn, in a small château in Brie, three pensive individuals were gravely occupied in watching the wood burn on the hearth and the hands of the clock move slowly around the dial. Two of these silent guests seemed to give way unreservedly to the vague ennui that weighed upon them; but the third gave signs of open rebellion: he fidgeted about on his seat, stifled half audibly divers melancholy yawns, and tapped the snapping sticks with tongs, with a manifest intention of resisting the common enemy.

This person, who was much older than the other two, was the master of the house, Colonel Delmare, an old warrior on half-pay, once a very handsome man, now over-corpulent, with a bald head, gray moustache and awe-inspiring eye; an excellent master before whom everybody trembled, wife, servants, horses and dogs.

At last he left his chair, evidently vexed because he did not know how to break the silence, and began to walk heavily up and down the whole length of the salon, without laying aside for an instant the rigidity which characterizes all the movements of an ex-soldier, resting his weight on his loins and turning the whole body at once, with the unfailing self-satisfaction peculiar to the man of show and the model officer.

But the glorious days had passed, when Lieutenant Delmare inhaled triumph with the air of the camps; the retired officer, forgotten now by an ungrateful country, was condemned to undergo all the consequences of marriage. He was the husband of a young and pretty wife, the proprietor of a commodious manor with its appurtenances, and, furthermore, a manufacturer who had been fortunate in his undertakings; in consequence whereof the colonel was ill-humored, especially on the evening in question; for it was very damp, and the colonel had rheumatism.

He paced gravely up and down his old salon, furnished in the style of Louis XV., halting sometimes before a door surmounted by nude Cupids in fresco, who led in chains of flowers well-bred fawns and good-natured wild boars; sometimes before a panel overladen with paltry, over-elaborated sculpture, whose tortuous vagaries and endless intertwining the eye would have wearied itself to no purpose in attempting to follow. But these vague and fleeting distractions did not prevent the colonel, whenever he turned about, from casting a keen and searching glance at the two companions of his silent vigil, resting upon them alternately that watchful eye which for three years past had been standing guard over a fragile and priceless treasure, his wife.

For his wife was nineteen years of age; and if you had seen her buried under the mantel of that huge fire-place of white marble inlaid with burnished copper; if you had seen her, slender, pale, depressed, with her elbow resting on her knee, a mere child in that ancient household, beside that old husband, like a flower of yesterday that had bloomed in a gothic vase, you would have pitied Colonel Delmare's wife, and the colonel even more perhaps than his wife.

The third occupant of this lonely house was also sitting under the same mantel, at the other end of the burning log. He was a man in all the strength and all the bloom of youth, whose glowing cheeks, abundant golden hair and full whiskers presented a striking contrast to the grizzly hair, weather-beaten complexion and harsh countenance of the master of the house; but the least *artistic* of men would none the less have preferred Monsieur Delmare's harsh and stern expression to the younger man's regular but insipid features. The bloated face carved in relief on the sheet of iron that formed the back of the fire-place, with its eye fixed constantly on the burning logs, was less monotonous perhaps than the pink and white fair-haired character in this narrative, absorbed in like contemplation. However, his strong and supple figure, the clean-cut outline of his brown eyebrows, the polished whiteness of his forehead, the tranquil expression of his limpid eyes, the beauty of his hands, and even the rigorously correct elegance of his hunting costume, would have caused him to be considered a very comely *cavalier* in the eyes of any woman who had conceived a passion for the so-called *philosophic* tastes of another century. But perhaps Monsieur Delmare's young and timid wife had never as yet examined a man with her eyes; perhaps there was an entire absence of sympathy between that pale and unhappy woman and that sound sleeper and hearty eater. Certain it is that the conjugal Argus wearied his hawklike eye without detecting a glance, a breath, a palpitation, between these two very dissimilar beings. Thereupon, being assured that he had not the slightest pretext for jealousy to occupy his mind, he relapsed into a state of depression more profound than before, and abruptly plunged his hands into his pockets.

The only cheerful and attractive face in the group was that of a beautiful hunting dog, of the large breed of pointers, whose head was resting on the knees of the younger man. She was remarkable by reason of her long body, her powerful hairy legs, her muzzle, slender as a fox's, and her intelligent face, covered with disheveled hair, through which two great tawny eyes shone like topazes. Those dog's eyes, so fierce and threatening during the chase, had at that moment an indefinable expression of affectionate melancholy; and when her master, the object of that instinctive love, sometimes so superior to the deliberate affection of man, ran his fingers through the beautiful creature's silky silver locks, her eyes sparkled with pleasure, while her long tail swept the hearth in regular cadence, and scattered the ashes over the inlaid floor.

It was a fitting subject for Rembrandt's brush, that interior, dimly lighted by the fire on the hearth. At intervals fugitive white gleams lighted up the room and the faces, then, changing to the red tint of the embers, gradually died away; the gloom of the salon varying as the fitful gleams grew more or less dull. Each time that Monsieur Delmare passed in front of the fire, he suddenly appeared, like a ghost, then vanished in the mysterious depths of the salon. Strips of gilding stood forth in the light now and then on the oval frames, adorned with wreaths and medallions and fillets of wood, on furniture, inlaid with ebony and copper, and even on the jagged cornices of the wainscoting. But when a brand went out, resigning its brilliancy to some other blazing point, the objects which had been in the light a moment before withdrew into the shadow, and other projections stood forth from the obscurity. Thus one could have grasped in due time all the details of the picture, from the console supported by three huge gilded tritons, to the frescoed ceiling, representing a sky studded with stars and clouds, and to the heavy hangings of crimson damask, with long tassels, which shimmered like satin, their ample folds seeming to sway back and forth as they reflected the flickering light.

One would have said, from the immobility of the two figures in bold relief before the fire, that they feared to disturb the immobility of the scene; that they had been turned to stone where they sat, like the heroes of a fairy tale, and that the slightest word or movement would bring the walls of an imaginary city crumbling about their ears. And the dark-browed master, who alone broke the silence and the shadow with his regular tread, seemed a magician who held them under a spell.

At last the dog, having obtained a smile from her master, yielded to the magnetic power which the eye of man exerts over that of the lower animals. She uttered a low whine of timid affection and placed her fore paws on her beloved's shoulders with inimitable ease and grace of movement.

"Down, Ophelia, down!"

And the young man reproved the docile creature sternly in English, whereupon she crawled toward Madame Delmare, shamefaced and repentant, as if to implore her protection. But Madame Delmare did not emerge from her reverie, and allowed Ophelia's head to rest on her two white hands, as they lay clasped on her knee, without bestowing a caress upon her.

"Has that dog taken up her quarters in the salon for good?" said the colonel, secretly well-pleased to find a pretext for an outburst of ill-humor, to pass the time. "Be off to your kennel, Ophelia! Come, out with you, you stupid beast!"

If anyone had been watching Madame Delmare closely he could have divined, in that trivial and commonplace incident of her private life, the painful secret of her whole existence. An imperceptible shudder ran over her body, and her hands, in which she unconsciously held the favorite animal's head, closed nervously around her rough, hairy neck, as if to detain her and protect her. Whereupon Monsieur Delmare, drawing his hunting-crop from the pocket of his jacket, walked with a threatening air toward poor Ophelia, who crouched at his feet, closing her eyes, and whining with grief and fear in anticipation. Madame Delmare became even paler than usual; her bosom heaved convulsively, and, turning her great blue eyes upon her husband with an indescribable expression of terror, she said:

"In pity's name, monsieur, do not kill her!"

These few words gave the colonel a shock. A feeling of chagrin took the place of his angry impulse.

"That, madame, is a reproof which I understand very well," he said, "and which you have never spared me since that day that I killed your spaniel in a moment of passion while hunting. He was a great loss, was he not? A dog that was forever forcing the hunting and rushing after the game! Whose patience would he not have exhausted? Indeed, you were not nearly so fond of him until he was dead; before that you paid little attention to him; but now that he gives you a pretext for blaming me–"

"Have I ever reproached you?" said Madame Delmare in the gentle tone which we adopt from a generous impulse with those we love, and from self-esteem with those whom we do not love.

"I did not say that you had," rejoined the colonel in a half-paternal, half-conjugal tone; "but the tears of some women contain bitterer reproaches than the fiercest imprecations of others. *Morbleu!* madame, you know perfectly well that I hate to see people weeping about me."

"I do not think that you ever see me weep."

"Even so! don't I constantly see you with red eyes? On my word, that's even worse!"

During this conjugal colloquy the young man had risen and put Ophelia out of the room with the greatest tranquillity; then he returned to his seat opposite Madame Delmare after lighting a candle and placing it on the chimney-piece.

This act, dictated purely by chance, exerted a sudden influence upon Monsieur Delmare's frame of mind. As soon as the light of the candle, which was more uniform and steadier than that of the fire, fell upon his wife, he observed the symptoms of suffering and general prostration which were manifest that evening in her whole person: in her weary attitude, in the long brown hair falling over her emaciated cheeks and in the purple rings beneath her dull, inflamed eyes. He took several turns up and down the room, then returned to his wife and, suddenly changing his tone:

"How do you feel to-day, Indiana?" he said, with the stupidity of a man whose heart and temperament are rarely in accord.

"About as usual, thank you," she replied, with no sign of surprise or displeasure.

"'As usual' is no answer at all, or rather it's a woman's answer; a Norman answer, that means neither yes nor no, neither well nor ill."

"Very good; I am neither well nor ill."

"I say that you lie," he retorted with renewed roughness; "I know that you are not well; you have told Sir Ralph here that you are not. Tell me, isn't that the truth? Did she not tell you so, Monsieur Ralph?"

"She did," replied the phlegmatic individual addressed, paying no heed to the reproachful glance which Indiana bestowed upon him.

At that moment, a fourth person entered the room: it was the factotum of the household, formerly a sergeant in Monsieur Delmare's regiment.

I

He explained briefly to Monsieur Delmare that he had his reasons for believing that charcoal thieves had been in the park the last few nights at the same hour, and that he had come to ask for a gun to take with him in making his nightly round before locking the gates. Monsieur Delmare, scenting powder in the adventure, at once took down his fowling-piece, gave Lelièvre another, and started to leave the room.

"What!" said Madame Delmare in dismay, "you would kill a poor peasant on account of a few bags of charcoal?"

"I will shoot down like a dog," retorted Delmare, irritated by this remonstrance, "any man whom I find prowling around my premises at night. If you knew the law, madame, you would know that it authorizes me to do it."

"It is a horrible law," said Indiana, warmly. But she quickly repressed this impulse and added in a lower tone: "But your rheumatism? You forget that it rains, and that you will suffer for it to-morrow if you go out tonight."

"You are terribly afraid that you will have to nurse your old husband," replied Delmare, impatiently opening the door.

And he left the room, still muttering about his age and his wife.

II

The two personages whom we have mentioned, Indiana Delmare and Sir Ralph, or, if you prefer, Monsieur Rodolphe Brown, continued to face each other, as calm and cold as if the husband were standing between them. The Englishman had no idea of justifying himself, and Madame Delmare realized that she had no serious grounds for reproaching him, for he had spoken with no evil intention. At last, making an effort, she broke the silence and upbraided him mildly.

"That was not well done of you, my dear Ralph," she said. "I had forbidden you to repeat the words that I let slip in a moment of pain, and Monsieur Delmare is the last person in the world whom I should want told of my trouble."

"I can't understand you, my dear," Sir Ralph replied; "you are ill and you refuse to take care of yourself. I had to choose between the chance of losing you and the necessity of letting your husband know."

"Yes," said Madame Delmare, with a sad smile, "and you decided to *notify the authorities."*

"You are wrong, you are wrong, on my word, to allow yourself to inveigh so against the colonel; he is a man of honor, a worthy man."

"And who says that he's not, Sir Ralph?"

"Why, you do, without meaning to. Your depression, your ailing condition, and, as he himself observes, your red eyes, tell everybody every hour in the day that you are not happy."

"Hush, Sir Ralph, you go too far. I have never given you permission to find out so much."

"I anger you, I see; but what would you have! I am not clever; I am not acquainted with the subtle distinctions of your language, and then, too, I resemble your husband in many ways. Like him I am utterly in the dark as to what a man must say to a woman, either in English or in French, to console her. Another man would have conveyed to your mind, without putting it in words, the idea that I have just expressed so awkwardly; he would have had the art to insinuate himself into your confidence without allowing you to detect his progress, and perhaps he would have succeeded in affording some relief to your heart, which puts fetters on itself and locks itself up before me. This is not the first time that I have noticed how much more influence words have upon women than ideas, especially in France. Women more than–"

"Oh! you have a profound contempt for women, my dear Ralph. I am alone here against two of you, so I must make up my mind never to be right."

II

"Put us in the wrong, my dear cousin, by recovering your health, your good spirits, your bloom, your animation of the old days; remember Ile Bourbon and that delightful retreat of ours, Bernica, and our happy childhood, and our friendship, which is as old as you are yourself."

"I remember my father, too," said Indiana, dwelling sadly upon the words and placing her hand in Sir Ralph's.

They relapsed into profound silence.

"Indiana," said Ralph, after a pause, "happiness is always within our reach. Often one has only to put out his hand to grasp it. What do you lack? You have modest competence, which is preferable to great wealth, an excellent husband, who loves you with all his heart, and, I dare to assert, a sincere and devoted friend."

Madame Delmare pressed Sir Ralph's hand faintly; but she did not change her attitude; her head still hung forward on her breast and her tear-dimmed eyes were fixed on the magic effects produced by the embers.

"Your depression, my dear friend," continued Sir Ralph, "is due purely to physical causes; which one of us can escape disappointment, vexation? Look below you and you will see people who envy you, and with good reason. Man is so constituted that he always aspires to what he has not."

I spare you a multitude of other commonplaces which the excellent Sir Ralph put forth in a tone as monotonous and sluggish as his thoughts. It was not that Sir Ralph was a fool, but he was altogether out of his element. He lacked neither common sense nor shrewdness; but the role of consoler of women was, as he himself acknowledged, beyond his capacity. And this man had so little comprehension of another's grief, that with the best possible disposition to furnish a remedy, he could not touch it without inflaming it. He was so conscious of his awkwardness that he rarely ventured to take notice of his friend's sorrows; and on this occasion he made superhuman efforts to perform what he considered the most painful duty of friendship.

When he saw that Madame Delmare was obliged to make an effort to listen to him, he held his peace, and naught could be heard save the innumerable little voices whispering in the burning wood, the plaintive song of the log as it becomes heated and swells, the crackling of the bark as it curls before breaking, and the faint phosphorescent explosions of the alburnum, which emits a bluish flame. From time to time the baying of a dog mingled with the whistling of the wind through the cracks of the door and the beating of the rain against the windowpanes. That evening was one of the saddest that Madame Delmare had yet passed in her little manor-house in Brie.

"Moreover, an indefinable vague feeling of suspense weighed upon that impressionable soul and its delicate fibres. Weak creatures live on alarms and presentiments. Madame Delmare had all the superstitions of a nervous, sickly Creole; certain nocturnal sounds, certain phases of the moon were to her unfailing presages of specific events, of impending misfortunes, and the night spoke to that dreamy, melancholy creature a language full of mysteries and phantoms which she alone could understand and translate according to her fears and her sufferings.

"You will say again that I am mad," she said, withdrawing her hand, which Sir Ralph still held, "but some disaster, I don't know what, is preparing to fall upon us. Some danger is impending over someone–myself, no doubt–but, look you, Ralph, I feel intensely agitated, as at the approach of a great crisis in my destiny. I am afraid," she added, with a shudder, "I feel faint."

And her lips became as white as her cheeks. Sir Ralph, terrified, not by Madame Delmare's presentiments, which he looked upon as symptoms of extreme mental exhaustion, but by her deathly pallor, pulled the bell-rope violently to summon assistance. No one came, and as Indiana grew weaker and weaker, Sir Ralph, more alarmed in proportion, moved her away from the fire, deposited her in a reclining chair, and ran through the house at random, calling the servants, looking for water or salts, finding nothing, breaking all the bell-ropes, losing his way in the labyrinth of dark rooms, and wringing his hands with impatience and anger against himself.

At last it occurred to him to open the glass door that lead into the park, and to call alternately Lelièvre and Noun, Madame Delmare's Creole maid.

A few moments later Noun appeared from one of the dark paths in the park, and hastily inquired if Madame Delmare were worse than usual.

"She is really ill," replied Sir Ralph.

They returned to the salon and devoted themselves to the task of restoring the unconscious Madame Delmare, one with all the ardor of useless and awkward zeal, the other with the skill and efficacy of womanly affection.

Noun was Madame Delmare's foster-sister; the two young women had been brought up together and loved each other dearly. Noun was tall and strong, glowing with health, active, alert, overflowing with ardent, passionate creole blood; and she far outshone with her resplendent beauty the frail and pallid charms of Madame Delmare; but the tenderness of their hearts and the strength of their attachment killed every feeling of feminine rivalry.

When Madame Delmare recovered consciousness, the first thing that she observed was the unusual expression of her maid's features, the damp and disordered condition of her hair and the excitement which was manifest in her every movement.

"Courage, my poor child," she said kindly; "my illness is more disastrous to you than to myself. Why, Noun, you are the one to take care of yourself; you are growing thin and weeping as if it were not your destiny to live; dear Noun, live is so bright and fair before you!"

Noun pressed Madame Delmare's hand to her lips effusively, and said, in a sort of frenzy, glancing wildly about the room:

"*Mon Dieu!* madame, do you know why Monsieur Delmare is in the park?"

"Why?" echoed Indiana, losing instantly the faint flush that had reappeared on her cheeks. "Wait a moment–I don't know–You frighten me! What is the matter, pray?"

II

"Monsieur Delmare declares that there are thieves in the park," replied Noun in a broken voice. "He is making the rounds with Lelièvre, both armed with guns."

"Well?" said Indiana, apparently expecting some shocking news.

"Why, madame," rejoined Noun, clasping her hands frantically, "isn't it horrible to think that they are going to kill a man?"

"Kill a man!" cried Madame Delmare, springing to her feet with the terrified credulity of a child frightened by it's nurse's tales.

"Ah! yes, they will kill him," said Noun, stifling her sobs.

"These two women are mad," thought Sir Ralph, who was watching this strange scene with a bewildered air. "Indeed," he added mentally, "all women are."

"But why do you say that, Noun," continued Madame Delmare; "do you believe that there are any thieves there?"

"Oh! if they were really thieves! but some poor peasant perhaps, who has come to pick up a handful of wood for his family!"

"Yes, that would be ghastly, as you say! But it is not probable; right at the entrance to Fontainebleau forest, when it is so easy to steal wood there, nobody would take the risk of a park enclosed by walls. Bah! Monsieur Delmare won't find anybody in the park, so don't you be afraid."

But Noun was not listening; she walked from the window to her mistress's chair, her ears strained to catch the slightest sound; she seemed torn between the longing to run after Monsieur Delmare and the desire to remain with the invalid.

Her anxiety seemed so strange, so uncalled-for to Monsieur Brown, that he laid aside his customary mildness of manner, and said, grasping her arm roughly:

"Have you lost your wits altogether? don't you see that you frighten your mistress and that your absurd alarms have a disastrous effect upon her?"

Noun did not hear him; she had turned her eyes upon her mistress, who had just started on her chair as if the concussion of the air had imparted an electric shock to her senses. Almost at the same instant the report of a gun shook the windows of the salon, and Noun fell upon her knees.

"What miserable woman's terrors!" cried Sir Ralph, worn out by their emotion; "in a moment a dead rabbit will be brought to you in triumph, and you will laugh at yourselves."

"No, Ralph," said Madame Delmare, walking with a firm step toward the door, "I tell you that human blood has been shed."

Noun uttered a piercing shriek and fell upon her face.

The next moment they heard Lelièvre's voice in the park: "He's there! he's there! Well aimed, my colonel! the brigand is down!"

Sir Ralph began to be excited. He followed Madame Delmare. A few moments later a man covered with blood and giving no sign of life was brought under the peristyle.

"Not so much noise! less shrieking!" said the colonel with rough gayety to the terrified servants who crowded around the wounded man; "this is only a joke; my gun was loaded with nothing but salt. Indeed I don't think I touched him; he fell from fright."

"But what about this blood, monsieur?" said Madame Delmare in a profoundly reproachful tone, "was it fear that caused it to flow?"

"Why are you here, madame?" cried Monsieur Delmare, "what are you doing here?"

"I have come to repair the harm that you have done, as it is my duty to do," replied Madame Delmare coldly.

She walked up to the wounded man with a courage of which no one of the persons present had as yet felt capable, and held a light to his face. Thereupon, instead of the plebeian features and garments which they expected to see, they discovered a young man with noble features and fashionably dressed, albeit in hunting costume. He had a trifling wound on one hand, but his torn clothes and his swoon indicated a serious fall.

"I should say as much!" said Lelièvre; "he fell from a height of twenty feet. He was just putting his leg over the wall when the colonel fired, and a few grains of small shot or salt in the right hand prevented his getting a hold. The fact is, I saw him fall, and when he got to the bottom he wasn't thinking much about running away, poor devil!"

"Would any one believe," said one of the female servants, "that a man so nicely dressed would amuse himself by stealing?"

"And his pockets are full money!" said another, who had unbuttoned the supposed thief's waistcoat.

"It is very strange," said the colonel, gazing, not without emotion, at the man stretched out before him. "If the man is dead it's not my fault; examine his hand, madame, and see if you can find a particle of lead in it."

"I prefer to believe you, monsieur," replied Madame Delmare, who, with a self-possession and moral courage of which no one would have deemed her capable, was closely scrutinizing his pulse and the arteries of his neck. "Certainly," she added, "he is not dead, and he requires speedy attention. The man hasn't the appearance of a thief and perhaps he deserves our care; even if he does not deserve it, our duty calls upon us women to care for him none the less."

Thereupon Madame Delmare ordered the wounded man to be carried to the billiard room, which was nearest. A mattress was placed on several chairs, and Indiana, assisted by her women, busied herself in dressing the wounded hand, while Sir Ralph, who had some surgical knowledge, drew a large quantity of blood from him.

Meanwhile, the colonel, much embarrassed, found himself in the position of a man who has shown more ill-temper than he intended to show. He felt the necessity of justifying himself in the eyes of the others, or rather of making them justify him in his own eyes. So he had remained under the peristyle, surrounded by his servants, and indulging with them in the excited, prolix and perfectly useless disquisitions which are always forthcoming after the event. Lelièvre had already

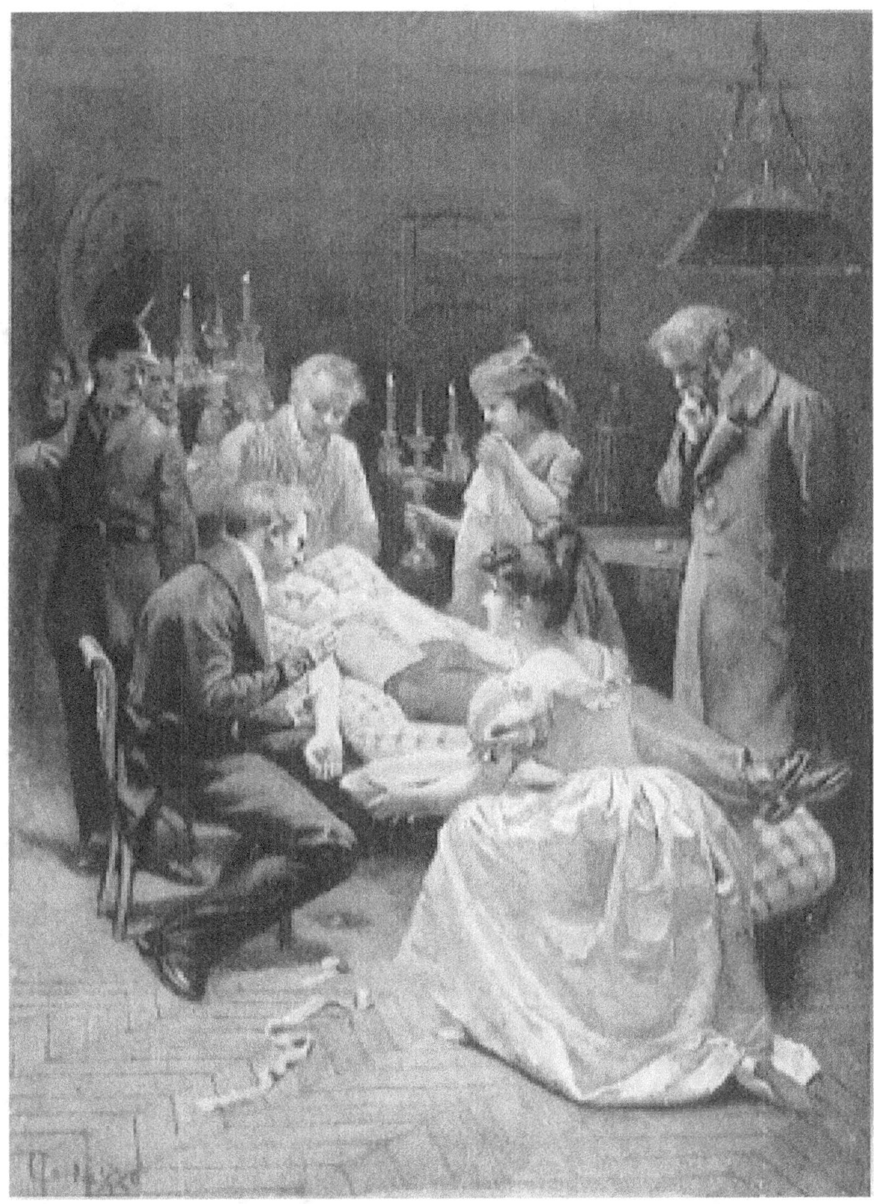

MADAME DELMARE DRESSES DE RAMIÈRE'S WOUNDS

A mattress was placed on several chairs, and Indiana, assisted by her women, busied herself in dressing the wounded hand, while Sir Ralph, who had some surgical knowledge, drew a large quantity of blood from him. Copyright 1900 by G. Barrie & Son

explained twenty times, with the most minute details, the shot, the fall and its results, while the colonel, who had recovered his good nature among his own people, according to his custom after giving way to his anger, impeached the purposes of a man who entered private property in the night-time over a wall. Every one agreed with the master, when the gardener, quietly leading him aside, assured him that the thief was the living image of a young land-owner who had recently settled in the neighborhood, and whom he had seen talking with Mademoiselle Noun three days before at the rustic fête at Rubelles.

This information gave a different turn to Monsieur Delmare's ideas; on his ample forehead, bald and glistening, appeared a huge swollen vein, which was always the precursor of the tempest.

"Morbleu!" he said, clenching his fists, "Madame Delmare takes a deal of interest in this puppy, who sneaks into my park over the wall!"

And he entered the billiard room, pale and trembling with wrath.

III

"You may be reassured, monsieur," said Indiana; "the man you killed will be quite well in a few days; at least we hope so, although he is not yet able to talk."

"That's not the question, madame," said the colonel, in a voice that trembled with suppressed passion; "I insist upon knowing the name of this interesting patient of yours, and how it came about that he mistook the wall of my park for the avenue to my house."

"I have absolutely no idea," replied Madame Delmare with such a cold and haughty air that her redoubtable spouse was bewildered for an instant.

But his jealous suspicions soon regained the upper hand.

"I shall find out, madame," he said in an undertone; "you may be sure that I shall find out."

Thereupon, as Madame Delmare pretended not to notice his rage and continued her attentions to the wounded man, he left the room, in order not to explode before the women, and recalled the gardener.

"What is the name of the man who, you say, resembles our prowler?"

"Monsieur de Ramière. It is he who has just bought Monsieur de Cercy's little English house."

"What sort of man is he? a nobleman, a fop, a fine gentleman?"

"A fine gentleman, monsieur; noble, I think."

"Undoubtedly," rejoined the colonel with emphasis. "Monsieur de Ramière! Tell me Louis," he added, lowering his voice, "have you ever seen this fop prowling about here?"

"Last night, monsieur," Louis replied, with an embarrassed air, "I certainly saw–as to its being a fop, I can't say, but it was a man, sure enough."

"And you saw him?"

"As plainly as I see you, under the windows of the orangery."

"And you didn't fall upon him with the handle of your shovel?"

"I was just going to do it, monsieur; but I saw a woman meet him. At that moment I said to myself: 'Perhaps it's monsieur and madame, who have taken a fancy to walk a bit before daybreak;' and I went back to bed. But this morning I heard Lelièvre talking about a thief whose tracks he had seen in the park, and I said to myself: 'There's something under this.' "

"And why didn't you tell me immediately, stupid?"

"*Dame!* monsieur, there are some things in life that are *so delicate!* "

"I understand–you presume to have doubts. You are a fool; if you ever have another insolent idea of this sort I'll cut off your ears. I know very well who the thief is and why he came into the garden. I have put all these questions to you simply to find out what care you take of your orangery. Remember that I have some rare plants there that madame sets great store by, and that there are collectors who are insane enough to rob their neighbors' hothouses; it was I whom you saw last night with Madame Delmare."

And the poor colonel walked away, more tormented, more exasperated than before, leaving his gardener far from convinced that there are horticulturists fanatical enough to risk a bullet in order to purloin a shoot or a cutting.

Monsieur Delmare returned to the billiard-room and, paying no heed to the symptoms of returning consciousness which the wounded man displayed at last, he was preparing to search the pockets of his jacket which lay on a chair, when he put out his hand and said in a faint voice:

"You wish to know who I am, monsieur, but it is useless. I will tell you when we are alone. Until then spare me the embarrassment of making myself known in my present disagreeable and absurd position."

"It is a great pity in truth!" retorted the colonel sourly; "but I confess that I hardly appreciate it. However, as I trust that we shall meet again, and alone, I consent to defer an acquaintance until then. Meanwhile will you kindly tell me where I shall have you taken."

"To the public house in the nearest village, if you please."

"But monsieur is no condition to be moved, is he, Ralph?" said Madame Delmare hastily.

"Monsieur's condition affects you far too much, madame," said the colonel. "Leave the room, all of you," he said to the women in attendance. "Monsieur feels better, and he will find strength now to explain his presence on my premises."

"Yes, monsieur," rejoined the wounded man, "and I beg all those who have been kind enough to bestow any care upon me to listen to my acknowledgement of my misconduct. I feel that is of much importance that there should be no misunderstanding here of my motives, and it is of importance to myself that I should not be deemed what I am not. Let me tell you than what rascally scheme brought me to your park. You have installed, monsieur, by methods of extreme simplicity, known to you alone, a factory which is immeasurably superior to all similar factories in the province, both in respect to its processes and its product. My brother owns a very similar establishment in the south of France, but the cost of running it is enormous. His business was approaching shipwreck when I learned of the success of your venture; whereupon I determined to come and ask you to give me advice on certain points,–a generous service which could not possibly injure your own interests, as my brother's output is of an entirely different nature from yours. But the gate of your English garden was rigorously closed to me; and when I asked for an interview with you, I was told that you would not even allow me to look over your establishment. Repelled by these discourteous refusals, I determined to save my brother's life and honor even at the peril of my own; I entered your premises at night by scaling the wall, and tried to obtain entrance to the factory in order to determine the machinery. I had determined to hide in a corner; to bribe your workmen, to steal your secret,–in a word, to enable an honest man to profit by it without injuring you. Such was my crime. Now, monsieur, if you demand any other reparation than that which you have just taken, I am ready to offer it to you as soon as I am strong enough; indeed, I may perhaps demand it."

"I think that we should cry quits, monsieur," replied the colonel, half relieved form great anxiety. "Take notice, all of you, of the explanation monsieur has given me. I am over-avenged, assuming that I require any revenge. Go now and leave us to discuss my profitable business operations."

The servants left the room; but they alone were deceived by this reconciliation. The wounded man, weakened by his long speech, was not capable of appreciating the tone of the colonel's last words. He fell back into Madame Delmare's arms and lost consciousness a second time. She leaned over him, not deigning to raise her eyes to her angry husband, and the two strikingly contrasted faces of Monsieur Delmare and Monsieur Brown, the one pale and distorted by anger, the other calm and expressionless as usual, questioned each other in silence.

Monsieur Delmare did not need to say a word to make himself understood; however he drew Sir Ralph aside and said, crushing his fingers in his grasp:

"This is an admirably woven intrigue, my friend. I am delighted, perfectly delighted with this young fellow's quick wit, which enabled him to save my honor in the eyes of my servants. But, *mordieu!* he shall pay dear for the insult, which I feel in the depths of my heart. And that woman nursing him, who pretends not to know him! Ah! how true it is that cunning is inborn in those creatures!"

Sir Ralph, utterly nonplussed, walked methodically up and down the room three times. At his first turn he drew the conclusion: *improbable;* at the second: *impossible;* at the third: *proven.* Then, returning with his impassive face to the colonel, he pointed to Noun, who was standing behind the wounded man, wringing her hands, with haggard eyes and livid cheeks, in the immobility of despair, terror and misery.

A real discovery carries with it such a power of swift and overwhelming conviction, that the colonel was more impressed by Sir Ralph's emphatic gesture than he would have been by the most persuasive eloquence. Doubtless Sir Ralph had more than one means of striking the right scent; he recalled the fact that Noun was in the park when he called her, her wet hair, her damp, muddy shoes, which testified to a strange fancy for walking abroad in the rain–trivial details which had made but slight impression on him at the time that Madame Delmare fainted, but which recurred to his memory now. Then, too, the extraordinary terror she had manifested, her convulsive agitation, and the cry she had uttered when she heard the shot.

Monsieur Delmare did not require all this evidence; being more penetrating because he had more interest in the matter, he had only to look at the girl's face to see that she alone was guilty. But his wife's assiduity in ministering to the hero of this amorous adventure became more and more distasteful to him.

"Leave us, Indiana," he said. "It is late and you are not well. Noun will remain with monsieur to take care of him during the night, and to-morrow, if he is better, we will see about having him taken home."

There was nothing to say in reply to this unexpected complaisance. Madame Delmare, who was so determined in her resistance to her husband's violence, always yielded to his milder moods. She requested Sir Ralph to remain a little longer with the patient, and withdrew to her bedroom.

Not without ulterior motives had the colonel arranged things thus. An hour later, when everybody had gone to bed and the house was still, he stole softly into the room where Monsieur de Ramière lay, and, hiding behind a curtain, was speedily convinced, by the young man's conversation with the lady's-maid, that an amorous intrigue between the two was in progress. The young creole's unusual beauty had created a sensation at the rustic balls in the neighborhood. She had not lacked offers of homage, even from members of some of the finest families of the province. More than one handsome officer of lancers, in garrison at Melun, had put himself out to please her; but Noun was still to have her first love affair, and only one of her suitors had succeed in pleasing her: Monsieur de Ramière.

Colonel Delmare was by no means desirous of following the development of their liaison; so he retired as soon as he had made sure that his wife had not for an instant occupied the thoughts of the Almaviva of this adventure. He heard enough of it, however, to realize the difference between the love of poor Noun, who threw herself into the affair with all the vehemence of her passionate nature, and that of the well-born youth, who yielded to the impulse of a day without abjuring the right to resume his reason on the morrow.

When Madame Delmare awoke she found Noun beside her bed, embarrassed and downcast. But she had ingenuously given credence to Monsieur de Ramière's explanation, the more readily as persons interested in Monsieur Delmare's line of trade had previously tried to surprise the secrets of the Delmare factory, by stratagem or by fraud. She attributed her companion's embarrassment therefore to the excitement and fatigue of the night, and Noun took courage when she saw the colonel calmly enter his wife's room and discuss the affair of the previous evening with her as a perfectly natural occurrence.

In the morning Sir Ralph had satisfied himself as to the patient's condition. The fall, although a severe one, had had no serious result; the wound in the hand had already closed; Monsieur de Ramière had expressed a desire to be taken to Melun, and he had distributed the contents of his purse among the servants to induce them to keep quiet concerning his adventure, in order, he said, that his mother, who lived within a few leagues, might not be alarmed. Thus the story became known very slowly, and in several different versions. Certain information concerning the English factory of Monsieur de Ramière, the brother, added weight to the fiction the intruder had happily improvised. The colonel and Sir Ralph had the delicacy to keep Noun's secret, without even letting her know that they knew it; and the Delmare family soon ceased to give any thought to the incident.

IV

You will find it difficult to believe perhaps that Monsieur de Ramière, a young man of brilliant intellect, considerable talents and many estimable qualities, accustomed to salon triumphs and to adventures in perfumed boudoirs, had conceived a very durable passion for the housekeeper in the household of a small manufacturer in Brie. And yet Monsieur de Ramière was neither fop nor libertine. We have said that he was intelligent–that is to say, he appreciated the advantages of birth at their real value. He was a man of high principle when he argued with himself; but vehement passions often carried him beyond the bounds of his theories. At such times he was incapable of reflection, or he avoided appearing before the tribunal of his conscience: he went astray, as if without his own knowledge, and the man of yesterday strove to deceive him of to-morrow. Unfortunately the most salient feature in his character was not his principles, which he possessed in common with many other white-gloved philosophers and which no more preserved him from inconsistency than they preserve them; but his passions, which no principles could stifle, and which made of him a man apart in that degenerate society where it is so difficult to depart from the beaten path without appearing ridiculous. Raymon had the art of being often culpable without arousing hatred, often eccentric without being offensive; indeed he sometimes succeeded in arousing the pity of people who had the most reason to complain of him. There are men who are humored thus by every one who approaches them. Sometimes an attractive face and animated speech make up the sum total of their sensibility. We do not presume to judge Monsieur Raymon de Ramière so harshly, nor to draw his portrait before exhibiting him in action. We are examining him now at a distance, like the multitude who pass him in the street.

Monsieur de Ramière was in love with the young creole with the great black eyes, who had aroused the admiration of the whole province at the fête of Rubelles; but he was in love and nothing more. He had made her acquaintance because he had nothing else to do, perhaps, and success had kindled his desires; he had obtained more than he asked, and on the day that he triumphed over that easily vanquished heart he returned home dismayed by his victory, and said to himself, striking his forehead:

"God grant that she doesn't love me!"

Thus it was not until after he had accepted all the proofs of her love that he began to suspect the existence of that love. Then he repented, but it was too late; he must either resign himself to what the future might have in store, or retreat like a coward toward the past. Raymon did not hesitate; he allowed himself to be loved, he loved in return for gratitude; he scaled the walls of the Delmare estate from the love of danger; he had a terrible fall from awkwardness; and he was so touched by his lovely mistress's grief that he deemed himself justified thenceforth in his own eyes in continuing to dig the pit into which she was destined to fall.

When he had recovered, winter had no storms, darkness no perils, remorse no stings which could deter him from passing through the corner of the forest to meet the young creole and swear to her that he had never loved any other woman; that he preferred her to the queens of society, and a thousand other exaggerations which will always be fashionable with poor and credulous maidens. In January Madame Delmare went to Paris with her husband; Sir Ralph Brown, their excellent neighbor, betook himself to his own estate, and Noun, being left in charge of her master's country house, was able to absent herself on various pretexts. It was unfortunate for her, and this facility of intercourse with her lover greatly abridged the ephemeral happiness which she was destined to enjoy. The forest with its poetic shadows, its arabesques of hoar-frost, its moonlight effects, the mysterious going and coming by the little gate, the furtive departure in the morning when Noun's little feet, as she accompanied him to the gate, left their prints on the snow in the park–all these accessories of an amorous intrigue served to prolong Monsieur de Ramière's intoxication. Noun, in white *déshablilé*, with her long black hair for ornament, was a lady, a queen, a fairy; when he saw her come forth from that red brick castle, a heavy, square structure of the time of the Regency, with a semi-feudal aspect, he could easily fancy her a châtelaine of the Middle Ages, and in the summer-house filled with rare flowers, where she made him drunk with the seductions of youth and passion, he readily forgot all that he was destined to remember later.

But when Noun, disdaining precautions and defying danger in her turn, came to him at his home, with her white apron and neckerchief coquettishly arranged according to the fashion of her country, she was nothing more than a maid and a maid in the service of a pretty woman–a circumstance that always makes a soubrette seem like a makeshift. And yet Noun was very lovely, it was in that dress that he had first seen her at that village fête where he had forced his way through the crowd of curious bystanders, and had enjoyed the petty triumph of carrying her off from a score of rivals. Noun would lovingly remind him of that day; she did not know, poor child, that Raymon's love did not date back so far, and that her day of pride had been only a day of vanity to him. And then the courage with which she sacrificed her reputation to him–that courage which should have made him love her all the more–displeased Monsieur de Ramière. The wife of a peer of France who should sacrifice herself so recklessly would be a priceless conquest; but a lady's maid! That which is heroism in the one becomes brazen-faced effrontery in the other. With the one a world of jealous rivals envies you; with the other a rabble of scandalized flunkeys condemns you. The lady of quality sacrifices twenty previous lovers to you; the lady's maid sacrifices only a husband that she might have had.

What can you expect? Raymon was a man of fashionable morals, of elegant manners, of poetic passion. In his eyes a grisette was not a woman, and Noun, by virtue of a beauty of the first order, had taken him by surprise on a day of popular merrymaking. All this was not Raymon's fault; he had been reared to shine in society, all his thoughts had been directed toward an exalted goal, all his faculties had been moulded to enjoy princely good fortune, and the ardor of his blood had led him into bourgeois amours against his will. He had done all that he possibly could do to prolong his enjoyment, but he had failed; what could he do now? Ideas extravagant in generosity had passed through his brain; on the days when he was most in love with his mistress he had thought seriously of raising her to his level, of legitimizing their union. Yes, upon my honor, he had thought of it; but love, which legitimizes everything, was growing weaker now; it was passing away with the perils of the intrigue and the piquant charm of mystery. Marriage was no longer possible; and note this: Raymon reasoned very cogently and altogether in his mistress's favor.

If he had really loved her, he could, by sacrificing to her his future, his family and his reputation, still have found happiness, and, consequently, have made her happy; for love is a contract no less than marriage. But, his ardor having cooled as he felt that it had, what future could he create for her? Should he marry her and display day after day a gloomy face, a cold heart, a comfortless home? Should he marry her and make her odious to her family, contemptible in the eyes of her equals, and a laughing-stock to her servants; take the risk of introducing her in a social circle where she would feel that she was out of place; where humiliation would kill her; and, lastly, overwhelm her with remorse by forcing her to realize all the trials she had brought upon her lover?

No, you will agree with him that it was impossible, that it would not have been generous, that a man cannot contend thus with society, and that such heroic virtue resembles Don Quixote breaking his lance against a windmill; an iron courage which a breath of wind scatters; the chivalry of another age which arouses the pitying contempt of this age.

Having thus weighed all the arguments, Monsieur de Ramière concluded that it would be better to break that unfortunate bond. Noun's visits were beginning to be painful to him. His mother, who had gone to Paris for the winter, would not fail to hear of the little scandal before long. Even now she was surprised at his frequent visits to Cercy, their country estate, and at his passing whole weeks there. He had, to be sure, alleged as a pretext, an important piece of work which he was finishing away from the noise of the city; but that pretext was beginning to be worn out. It grieved Raymon to deceive so kind a mother, to deprive her for so long a time of his filial attentions; and–how shall I tell you?–he left Cercy and did not return.

Noun wept and waited, and as the days and weeks passed, unhappy creature that she was, she ventured so far as to write. Poor girl! that was the last stroke. A letter from a lady's maid! Yet she had taken satin-finished paper and perfumed wax from Madame Delmare's desk, and her style from her heart. But the spelling!

Do you know how much energy a syllable more or less adds to or detracts from the sentiments? Alas! the poor half-civilized girl from Ile Bourbon did not know even that there were rules for the use of the language. She believed that she wrote and spoke as correctly as her mistress, and when she found that Raymon did not return she said to herself:

"And yet my letter was well adapted to bring him."

That letter Raymon lacked the courage to read to the end. It was a masterpiece of ingenious and graceful passion; it is doubtful if Virginia wrote Paul a more charming one after she left her native land. But Monsieur de Ramière made haste to throw it in the fire, fearful lest he should blush for himself. Once more, what do you expect? This is a prejudice of education, and self-love is a part of love just as self-interest is a part of friendship.

Monsieur de Ramière's absence had been noticed in society; that is much to say of a man, in respect to this society of ours where all men resemble another. One may be a man of intelligence and still care for society, just as one may be a fool and despise it. Raymon liked it, and he was justified in his liking, for he was a favorite and was much sought after; and that multitude of indifferent or sneering masks assumed for him attentive and interested smiles. Unfortunate men may be misanthropes, but those persons of whom one is fond are rarely ungrateful; at least so Raymon thought. He was grateful for the slightest manifestations of attachment, desirous of universal esteem, proud of having a large number of friends.

In this society, whose prejudices are absolute, everything had succeeded in his case, even his faults; and when he sought the cause of this universal affection which had always encompassed him, he found it in himself, in his longing to obtain it, in the joy it caused him, in the hearty kindliness which he dealt out lavishly without exhausting it.

He owed it in some measure to his mother too, whose superior intelligence, sparkling conversation and private virtues made her an exceptional woman. It was from her that he inherited those excellent principles which always led him back to the right path and prevented him, despite the impetuosity of his twenty-five years, from ever forfeiting his claim to public esteem. Moreover, people were more indulgent to him than to others because his mother had the knack of apologizing for him while blaming him, of commanding indulgence when she seemed to implore it. She was one of those women who had lived through different epochs so utterly dissimilar that their minds become as flexible as their destinies; who have grown rich on experience of misfortune; who have escaped the scaffolds of '93, the vices of the Directory, the vanities of the Empire and the enmities of the Restoration; rare women, whose kind is dying out.

It was at a ball at the Spanish ambassador's that Raymon reappeared in society.

"Monsieur de Ramière, if I am not mistaken," said a pretty woman to her neighbor.

"He is a comet who appears at irregular intervals," was the reply. "It is centuries since any one heard of the pretty fellow."

The lady who spoke thus was a middle-aged foreigner. Her companion blushed slightly.

"He's very good-looking, is he not, madame?" she said.

"Charming, on my word," replied the old Sicilian.

"You are talking about the hero of the eclectic salons, the dark-eyed Raymon, I'll be bound," said a dashing colonel of the guard.

"He has a fine head to study," rejoined the younger woman.

"And what pleases you even more, I dare say," said the colonel, "a wicked head."

The young woman was his wife.

"Why a wicked head?" queried the Sicilian.

"Full of genuine Southern passions, madame, worthy of the bright sunlight of Palermo."

Two or three young women put forward their flower-laden heads to hear what the colonel was saying.

"He made ravages in the garrison last year, I promise you," he continued. "We fellows shall be obliged to pick a quarrel with him, in order to get rid of him."

"If he's a Lovelace, so much the worse for him," said a young lady with a satirical cast of countenance; "I can't endure men whom everybody loves."

The ultramontane countess waited until the colonel had walked away, when she tapped Mademoiselle de Nangy's fingers lightly with her fan and said:

"Don't speak so; you don't know here what to think of a man who wants to be liked."

"Do you think, pray, that all they have to do is to want it?" said the damsel with the long sardonic eyes.

"Mademoiselle," said the colonel, coming up again to invite her to dance; "take care that the charming Raymon does not overhear you."

Mademoiselle de Nangy laughed; but during the rest of the evening the pretty group of which she was one dared not mention Monsieur de Ramière's name again.

V

Monsieur de Ramière wandered amid the undulating waves of that gayly-dressed crowd without distaste and without ennui.

Nevertheless, he was fighting against a feeling of chagrin. On returning to his own sphere he had a species of remorse, of shame for all the wild ideas which a misplaced attachment had suggested to him. He looked at the women so brilliantly beautiful in the bright light; he listened to their refined and clever conversation; he heard their talents highly praised; and in those marvellous specimens of their sex, those almost royal costumes, those exquisitely appropriate remarks, he found on all sides an implied reproach for having been untrue to his destiny. But, despite this species of mental bewilderment, Raymon suffered from more genuine remorse; for his intentions were always kind and considerate to the last degree, and a woman's tears broke his heart, hardened as it was.

The honors of the evening were universally accorded to a young woman whose name no one knew, and who enjoyed the privilege of monopolizing attention because her appearance in society was a novelty. The simplicity of her costume alone would have sufficed to make her a distinguished figure amid the diamonds, feathers and flowers in which the other women were arrayed. Strings of pearls woven into her black hair were her only jewels. The lustreless white of her necklace, her crêpe dress and her bare shoulders blended at a little distance, and the heated atmosphere of the apartments had barely succeeded in bringing to her cheeks a faint flush of as delicate a shade as that of a Bengal rose blooming on the snow. She was a tiny, dainty, slender creature; a salon type of beauty to which the bright light of the candles gave a fairylike touch, and which a sunbeam would have dimmed. When she danced she was so light that a breath would have whisked her away; but in her lightness there was no animation, no pleasure. When she was seated she bent forward as if her too flexible body lacked strength to support itself, and when she spoke she smiled sadly. Fantastic tales were at the very height of their vogue at this period. Accordingly, those who were learned in that line compared this young woman to a fascinating apparition evoked by sorcery, which would fade away and vanish like a dream when the first flush of dawn appeared on the horizon.

Meanwhile they crowded about her to invite her to dance.

"Make haste," said a dandy of a romantic turn to one of his friends; "the cock will crow soon, and even now your partner's feet have ceased to touch the floor. I'll wager that you can't feel her hand in yours."

"Pray look at Monsieur de Ramière's dark, strongly-marked face," said an *artistic* lady to her neighbor. "Contrast him with that pale, slender young woman, and see if the *solid* tone of the one doesn't make an admirable foil for the *delicate* tone of the other."

"That young woman," said a woman who knew everybody and who played the part of an almanac at social functions, "is the daughter of that old fool, De Carvajal, who tried to play Joséphin, and who died ruined at Ile Bourbon. This lovely exotic flower has made a foolish marriage, I believe; but her aunt stands well at court."

Raymon had drawn near the fair Indian. A peculiar emotion seized him every time that he looked at her; he had seen that pale, sad face; perhaps in some dream, but at all events he had seen it, and his eyes rested upon it with the delight we all feel on seeing once more a charming vision which we thought that we had lost forever.

Raymon's gaze disturbed her who was the object of it; she was awkward and shy, like a person unaccustomed to society, and the sensation that she caused seemed to embarrass rather than to please her. Raymon made the circuit of the salon, succeeded finally in learning that her name was Madame Delmare, and went and asked her to dance.

"You do not remember me," he said, when they were alone in the midst of the crowd; "but I have not been able to forget you, madame. And yet I saw you for an instant only, through a cloud; but in that instant you seemed so kind, so compassionate."

Madame Delmare started.

"Oh! yes, monsieur," she said, quickly, "it is you! I recognized you , too."

Then she blushed and seemed to fear that she had offended the proprieties. She looked around as if to see whether anyone had heard her. Her timidity enhanced her natural charm, and Raymon was touched to the heart by the tone of that creole voice, slightly husky, but so sweet that it seemed made to pray or to bless.

"I was afraid," he said, "that I should never have an opportunity to thank you. I could not call upon you and I knew that you went but little into society. I feared, also, that if I made your acquaintance I should come in contact with Monsieur Delmare, and our previous relations could not fail to make that contact disagreeable. How glad I am for this moment, which enables me to pay the debt of my heart!"

"It would be much pleasanter for me," said she, "if Monsieur Delmare also could enjoy it; and if you knew him better you would know that he is as kind as he is brusque. You would forgive him for having been your involuntary assailant, for his heart certainly bled more freely than your wound."

"Let us not talk of Monsieur Delmare, madame; I forgive him with all my heart. I injured him and he took the law into his own hands. I have nothing more to do but to forget; but as to you, madame, who lavished such delicate and generous attentions upon me, I choose to remember all my life your treatment of me, your pure features, your angelic gentleness, and these hands which poured balm upon my wounds and which I dared not kiss."

While he spoke Raymon held Madame Delmare's hand, to be prepared to walk through their figure in the contra-dance. He pressed that hand gently in his, and all the young woman's blood rushed to her heart.

When he led Madame Delmare back to her seat, her aunt, Madame de Carvajal, had gone; the crowd was thinning. Raymon sat down beside her. He had that ease of manner which a wide experience of affairs of the heart imparts; it is the violence of our desires, the precipitate haste of our love, that makes us stupid when we are with women. The man who has rubbed the edge off his emotions a little is more anxious to please than to love. Nevertheless Monsieur de Ramière felt more deeply moved in the presence of that simple, unspoiled woman than he had ever been. Perhaps this swift impression was due to his memory of the night he had passed at her house; but it is certain that, while he talked to her with animation, his heart did not lead his mouth astray. However, the habit he had acquired with other women gave to his words a power of persuasion to which the untutored Indiana yielded, not understanding that it had not all been invented expressly for her.

In general–and women are well aware of it–a man who talks wittily of love is only moderately in love. Raymon was an exception; he expressed passion artistically and felt it ardently. But it was not passion that rendered him eloquent, it was eloquence that made him passionate. He knew that he had a weakness for women, and he would become eloquent in order to seduce a woman and fall in love with her while seducing her. It was sentiment of the sort dealt in by advocates and preachers, who weep hot tears when they perspire freely. He sometimes fell in with women who were shrewd enough to distrust these heated improvisations; but he had committed what are called follies for love's sake: he had run away with a girl of noble birth; he had compromised women of very high station; he had had three sensational duels; he had displayed to a crowded evening party, to a whole theatre full of spectators, the bewilderment of his heart and the disarray of his thoughts. A man who does all this without fear of ridicule or of curses, and who succeeds in avoiding both, is safe from all assault; he can take any risk and hope for anything. Thus the most skilfully constructed defences yielded to the consideration that Raymon was madly in love when he meddled with love at all. A man capable of making a fool of himself for love is a rare prodigy in society, and one that women do not disdain.

I do not know how it happened, but when he escorted Madame de Carvajal and Madame Delmare to their carriage he succeeded in putting Indiana's little hand to his lips. Never before had a man's furtive, burning kiss breathed upon that woman's fingers, although she was born in a fiery climate and was nineteen years old; nineteen years of Ile Bourbon, which are equivalent to twenty-five in our country.

Ill and nervous as she was, that kiss almost extorted a shriek from her, and she had to be assisted into the carriage. Raymon had never come in contact with such a delicate organization. Noun, the creole, was in robust health, and Parisian women do not faint when their hands are kissed.

"If I should see her twice," he said to himself as he walked away, "I should lose my head over her."

The next morning he had completely forgotten Noun.

All that he knew about her was that she belonged to Madame Delmare. The pale-faced Indiana engrossed all his thoughts, filled all his dreams. When Raymon began to feel the shafts of love he was in the habit of seeking to distract his thoughts, not in order to stifle the budding passion, but, on the contrary, to drive away the reasoning power that urged him to weigh its consequences. Of an ardent temperament, he pursued his object hotly. He had not the power to quell the tempests which arose in his bosom, nor to rekindle them when he felt that they were dying away and vanishing.

He succeeded the next day in learning that Monsieur Delmare had gone to Brussels on a business trip, and had left his wife in charge of Madame de Carvajal, of whom he was not at all fond, but who was Madame Delmare's only relative. He, an upstart soldier, belonged to a poor and obscure family, of which he seemed to be ashamed, simply because he repeated so often that he was not ashamed of it. But, although he passed his life reproaching his wife for alleged scorn of him which she did not entertain, he was conscious that he ought not to compel her to live on terms of intimacy with his uneducated kindred. Moreover, despite his dislike for Madame de Carvajal, he could not refuse to treat her with great deference for these reasons.

Madame de Carvajal, who was descended from a noble Spanish family, was one of those women who cannot make up their minds to be of no account in the world. In the days when Napoleon ruled Europe she had burned incense to the glory of Napoleon, and with her husband and brother-in-law had joined the party of the Joséphinos; but her husband had lost his life at the fall of the conqueror's short-lived dynasty, and Indiana's father had taken refuge in the French colonies. Thereupon Madame Carvajal, being a clever and active person, had repaired to Paris, and there, by some fortunate speculations on the Bourse, had built up for herself a new competence on the ruins of her past splendors. By dint of shrewd wit, intrigues and piety she had also obtained some favor at Court, and her establishment, while it was no means brilliant, was one of the most respectable of all those presided over by protégés of the Civil List.

When Indiana arrived in France after her father's death, as the bride of Colonel Delmare, Madame de Carvajal was but moderately pleased by so paltry an alliance. Nevertheless she saw that Monsieur Delmare, whose good sense and activity in business were worth a dowry, prospered with his slender capital; and she purchased for Indiana the little château of Lagny and the factory connected with it. In two years, thanks to Monsieur Delmare's technical knowledge and certain funds advanced by Sir Rodolphe Brown, his wife's cousin by marriage, the colonel's affairs took a fortunate turn; he began to pay off his debts, and Madame de Carvajal, in whose eyes fortune was the first recommendation, manifested much affection for her niece and promised her the remnant of her wealth. Indiana, who was devoid of ambition, was devotedly kind and attentive to her aunt from gratitude, not from self-interest; but there was at least as much of one as of the other in the colonel's manoeuvres. He was a man of iron in the matter of his political opinions; he would listen to no argument concerning the unassailable glory of his great emperor, and he upheld that glory with the blind obstinacy of a child of sixty years. He was obliged therefore to put forth all his patience to refrain from breaking out again and again in Madame de Carvajal's salon, where the Restoration was lauded to the skies. What Delmare suffered at the hands of five or six pious old women is beyond description. His vexation on this account was in part the cause of his frequent ill-humor against his wife.

So much for Madame de Carvajal; we return now to Monsieur de Ramière. At the end of three days he had learned all these domestic details, so actively had he followed up everything likely to put him in the way of an intimate acquaintance with the Delmare family. He learned that by acquiring Madame de Carvajal's favor he could obtain opportunities of meeting Indiana. On the evening of the third day he procured an introduction to the aunt.

In her salon there were four or five barbarians solemnly playing *reversi*, and two or three young men of family, as utterly vapid as it is allowable for a man to be who has sixteen quarterings of nobility. Indiana was at work patiently filling in the background of a piece of embroidery on her aunt's frame. She was leaning over her work, apparently absorbed by that mechanical operation, and, it may be, well pleased to escape in this way the dull chatter of her neighbors. For aught I know, behind the long black hair that fell over the flowers of her embroidery, she was reviewing in her mind the emotions of that fleeting instant which had opened the door of a new life to her, when the servant's voice, announcing several new arrivals, made it necessary for her to rise. She did so mechanically, for she had paid no heed to the names, and barely lifted her eyes from her embroidery; but a voice at her side made her start as if she had received an electric shock, and she was obliged to lean on her worktable to avoid falling.

VI

Raymon was not prepared for that silent salon, peopled only by a few taciturn guests. It was impossible to utter a word which was not heard in every corner of the room. The dowagers who were playing cards seemed to be there for the sole purpose of embarrassing the conversation of the younger guests, and Raymon fancied that he could read on their stern features the secret satisfaction which old age takes in avenging itself by blocking other people's pleasure. He had counted upon a less constrained, tenderer interview than that of the ball, and it was just the opposite. This unexpected difficulty gave greater intensity to his desires, more fire to his glances, more animation and vivacity to the roundabout remarks he addressed to Madame Delmare. The poor child was altogether unused to this style of attack. She could not possibly defend herself, because nothing was asked of her; but she was forced to listen to the proffer of an ardent heart, to learn how dearly she was loved, and to allow herself to be encompassed by all the perils of seduction without making any resistance. Her embarrassment increased with Raymon's boldness. Madame de Carvajal, who made some reasonably well-founded claims to wit, and to whom Monsieur de Ramière's wit had been highly praised, left the card-table to challenge him to a refined discussion concerning love, into which she introduced much Spanish heat and German metaphysics. Raymon eagerly accepted the challenge, and, on the pretext of answering the aunt, said to the niece all that she would have refused to hear. The poor young wife, without a protector and exposed to so lively and skilful an assault on all sides, could not muster strength to take part in that thorny discussion. In vain did her aunt, who was anxious to exhibit her to advantage, call upon her to testify to the truth of certain subtle theories of sentiment; she confessed blushingly that she knew nothing about such things, and Raymon, intoxicated with joy to see her cheeks flush and her bosom heave, swore inwardly that he would teach her.

Indiana slept less that night than she had done for the last two or three nights; as we have said, she had never been in love, and her heart had long been ripe for a sentiment which none of the men she had met hitherto had succeeded in arousing. She had been brought up by a father of an eccentric and violent character, and had never known the happiness which is derived from the affection of another person. Monsieur de Carvajal, drunk with political passions, consumed by ambitious regrets, had become the most cruel planter and the most disagreeable neighbor in the colonies; his daughter had suffered keenly from his detestable humor. But, by dint of watching the constant tableau of the evils of slavery, of enduring the weariness of solitude and dependence, she had acquired a superficial patience, proof against every trial, an adorable kindliness toward her inferiors, but also an iron will and an incalculable power of resistance to everything that that tended to oppress her. By marrying Delmare she simply changed masters; by coming to live at Lagny, she changed her prison and the locus of her solitude. She did not love her husband, perhaps for the very reason that she was told that it was her duty to love him, and that it had become with her a sort of second nature, a principle of conduct, a law of conscience, to resist mentally every sort of moral constraint. No one had attempted to point out to her any other law than that of blind obedience.

Brought up in the desert, neglected by her father, surrounded by slaves, to whom she could offer no other assistance or encouragement than her compassion and her tears, she had accustomed herself to say: "A day will come when everything in my life will be changed, when I shall do good to others, when some one will love me, when I shall give my whole heart to the man who gives me his; meanwhile, I will suffer in silence and keep my love as a reward for him who shall set me free." This liberator, this Messiah had not come; Indiana was still awaiting him. She no longer dared, it is true, to confess to herself her whole thought. She had realized under the clipped hedge-rows of Lagny that thought itself was more fettered there than under the wild palms of Ile Bourbon; and when she caught herself saying, as she used to say: "A day will come–a man will come"–she forced that rash longing back to the depths of her heart, and said to herself; "Death alone will bring that day!"

And so she was dying. A strange malady was consuming her youth. She was without strength and unable to sleep. The doctors looked in vain for any discoverable disorder, for none existed; all her faculties were failing away in equal degree, all her organs were gradually degenerating; her heart was burning at a slow fire, her eyes were losing their lustre, the circulation of her blood was governed entirely by excitement and fever; a few months more and the poor captive bird would surely die. But, whatever the extent of her resignation and her discouragement, the need remained the same. That silent, broken heart was still calling involuntarily to some generous youthful heart to revivify it. The being whom she had loved most dearly hitherto was Noun, the cheery and brave companion of her tedious solitude; and the man who had manifested the greatest liking for her was her phlegmatic cousin Sir Ralph. What food for the all-consuming activity of her thoughts–a poor girl, ignorant and neglected like herself, and an Englishman whose only passion was fox-hunting!

Madame Delmare was genuinely unhappy, and the first time that she felt the burning breath of a young and passionate man enter her frigid atmosphere, the first time that a tender and caressing word delighted her ear, and quivering lips left a mark as of a red-hot iron on her hand, she thought neither of the duties that had been laid upon her, nor of the prudence that had been enjoined upon her, nor of the future that had been predicted for her; she remembered only the hateful past, her long suffering, her despotic masters. Nor did it occur to her that the man before her might be false or fickle. She saw him as she wished him to be, as she had dreamed of him, and Raymon could easily have deceived her if he had not been sincere.

But how could he fail to be sincere with so lovely and loving a woman? What other had ever laid bare her heart to him with such candor and ingenuousness? With what other had he been able to look forward to a future so captivating and so secure? Was she not born to love him, this slave who simply awaited a sign to break her chains, a word to follow him? Evidently heaven had made for Raymon this melancholy child of Ile Bourbon, whom no one had ever loved, and who but for him must have died.

Nevertheless a feeling of terror succeeded this all-pervading, feverish joy in Madame Delmare's heart. She thought of her quick-tempered, keen-eyed, vindictive husband, and she was afraid,–not for herself, for she was inured to threats, but for the man who was about to undertake a battle to the death with her tyrant. She knew so little of society that she transformed her life into a tragic romance; a timid creature, who dared not love for fear of endangering her lover's life, she gave no thought to the danger of destroying herself.

This'then was the secret of her resistance, the motive of her virtue. She made up her mind on the following day to avoid Monsieur de Ramière. That very evening there was a ball at the house of one of the leading bankers of Paris. Madame de Carvajal, who, being an old woman with no ties of affection, was very fond of society, proposed to attend with Indiana; but Raymon was to be there and Indiana determined not to go. To avoid her aunt's persecution, Madame Delmare, who was never able to resist except in action, pretended to assent to the plan; she allowed herself to be dressed and waited until Madame de Carvajal was ready; then she changed her ball dress for a robe de chambre, seated herself in front of the fire and resolutely awaited the conflict. When the old Spaniard, as rigid and gorgeous as a portrait by Van Dyck, came to call her, Indiana declared that she was not well and did not feel that she could go out. In vain did her aunt urge her to make an effort.

"I would be only too glad to go," she said, "but you see that I can hardly stand. I should be only a trouble to you to-night. Go to the ball without me, dear aunt; I shall enjoy the thought of your pleasure."

"Go without you!" said Madame de Carvajal, who was sorely distressed at the idea of having made an elaborate toilet to no purpose, and who shrank from the horrors of a solitary evening. "Why, what business have I in society, an old woman whom no one speaks to except to be near you? What will become of me without my niece's lovely eyes to give me value?"

"Your wit will fill the gap, my dear aunt," said Indiana.

The Marquise de Carvajal, who only wanted to be urged, set off at last. Whereupon, Indiana hid her face in her hands and began to weep; for she had made a great sacrifice and believed that she had already blasted the attractive prospect of the day before.

But Raymon would not have it so. The first thing that he saw at the ball was the old marchioness's haughty aigrette. In vain did he look for Indiana's white dress and black hair in her vicinity. He drew near and heard her say in an undertone to another lady:

"My niece is ill; or rather," she added, to justify her own presence at the ball, "it's a mere girlish whim. She wanted to be left alone in the salon with a book in her hand, like a sentimental beauty."

"Can it be that she is avoiding me?" thought Raymon.

He left the ball at once. He hurried to the marchioness's house, entered without speaking to the concierge, and asked the first servant that he saw, who was half asleep in the antechamber, for Madame Delmare.

"Madame Delmare is ill."

"I know it. I have come at Madame de Carvajal's request to see how she is."

"I will tell madame."

"It is not necessary. Madame Delmare will receive me."

And Raymon entered the salon unannounced. All the other servants had retired. A melancholy silence reigned in the deserted apartments. A single lamp, covered with its green silk shade, lighted the main salon dimly. Indiana's back was turned to the door; she was completely hidden in the depths of a huge easy-chair, sadly watching the burning logs, as on the evening when Raymon entered the park of Lagny over the wall; sadder now, for her former undefined sufferings, aimless desires had given place to a fleeting joy, a gleam of happiness that was not for her.

Raymon, his feet encased in dancing shoes, approached noiselessly over the soft, heavy carpet. He saw that she was weeping, and, when she turned her head, she found him at her feet, taking forcible possession of her hands, which she struggled in vain to withdraw from his clasp. Then, I agree, she was overjoyed beyond words to find that her scheme of resistance had failed. She felt that she passionately loved this man who paid no heed to obstacles and who had brought happiness to her in spite of her efforts. She blessed heaven for rejecting her sacrifice, and, instead of scolding Raymon, she was very near thanking him .

As for him, he knew already that she loved him. He needed not to see the joy that shone through her tears to realize that he was master, and that he could venture. He gave her no time to question him, but, changing rôles with her, vouchsafing no explanation of his unlooked-for presence, and no apology intended to make him seem less guilty than he was, he said:

"You are weeping, Indiana. Why do you weep? I insist upon knowing."

She started when he called her by her name; but there was additional joy in the surprise which that audacity caused her.

"Why do you ask?" she said. "I must not tell you."

"Well, I know, Indiana. I know your whole history, your whole life. Nothing that concerns you is unknown to me, because nothing that concerns you is indifferent to me. I resolved to know everything about you, and I have learned nothing that was not revealed to me during the brief moment that I passed under your roof, when I was brought, all crushed and bleeding, to your feet, and your husband was angry to see you, so lovely and so kind, support me with your soft arms and pour balm upon my wounds with your sweet breath. He was jealous? oh! I can readily understand it; I should have been, in his place, Indiana; or rather in his place, I would kill myself; for to be your husband, madame, to possess you, to hold you in his arms, and not to deserve you, not to win your heart, is to be the most miserable or the most dastardly of men!"

"O heaven! hush," she cried, putting her hand over his mouth; "hush! for you make me guilty. Why do you speak to me of him? why seek to teach me to curse him? If he should hear you! But I have said no evil of him; I have not authorized you to commit this crime! I do not hate him; I esteem him, I love him!"

"Say rather that you are horribly afraid of him; for the despot has broken your spirit, and fear has sat at your bedside ever since you became that man's prey. You, Indiana, profaned by the touch of that boor, whose iron hand has bowed your head and ruined your life! Poor child! so young and so lovely, to have suffered so horribly! for you cannot deceive me, Indiana, who look at you with other eyes than those of the common herd; I know all the secrets of your destiny, and you cannot hope to hide the truth from me. Let those who look at you because you are lovely say, when they notice your pallor and your melancholy: 'She is ill;'–well and good; but I, who follow you with my heart, whose whole soul encompasses you with solicitude and love, I am well aware what your disease is. I know that if God willed it so, if he had given you to me, unlucky wretch that I am, who deserve to have my head broken for having come so late, you would not be ill. On my life I swear, Indiana, I would have loved you so that you would have loved me the same and that you would have blessed the chain that bound us. I would have carried you in my arms to prevent your feet from being wounded; I would have warmed them with my breath. I would have held you against my breast to save you from suffering. I would have given all my blood to make up your lack of it, and if you had lost sleep with me, I would have passed the night saying soft words to you, smiling on you to restore your courage, weeping the while to see you suffer. When sleep had breathed upon your silken eyelids, I would have brushed them with my lips to close them more softly, and I would have watched over you, kneeling by your bed. I would have forced the air to caress you gently, golden dreams to throw flowers to you. I would have kissed noiselessly your lovely tresses, I would have counted with ecstatic joy the palpitations of your breast, and, at your awakening, Indiana, you would have found me at your feet, guarding you like a jealous master, waiting upon you as a slave, watching for your first smile, seizing upon your first thought, your first glance, your first kiss."

"Enough! enough!" said Indiana, agitated and quivering with emotion, "you make me faint."

And yet, if people died of happiness, Indiana would have died at that moment.

"Do not speak so to me," she said–"to me who am destined never to be happy; do not depict heaven upon earth to me who am doomed to die."

"To die!" cried Raymon vehemently, seizing her in his arms; "you, die! Indiana! die before you have lived–before you have loved! No, you shall not die; I will not let you die, for my life is bound to yours henceforth. You are the woman of whom I dreamed, the purity that I adored, the chimera that always fled from me, the bright star that shone before me and said to me: 'Go forward in this life of wretchedness and heaven will send one of its angels to bear you company.' You were always destined for me; your soul was always betrothed to mine, Indiana! Men and their iron laws have disposed of you; they have snatched from me the mate God would have chosen for me, if God did not sometimes forget his promises. But what do we care for men and laws if I love you still in another's arms, if you can still love me, accursed and unhappy as I am in having lost you! I tell you, Indiana, you belong to me; you are the half of my heart, which has long been struggling to join the other half. When you dreamed of a friend on Ile Bourbon, you dreamed of me; when, at the word husband, a sweet thrill of fear and hope passed through your heart, it was because I was destined to be your husband. Do you not recognize me? Does not it seem to you that we must have met twenty years ago? Did I not recognize you, my angel, when you stanched my blood with your veil, when you placed your hand on my dying heart to bring back its heat and its life? Ah! I remember distinctly enough. When I opened my eyes I said to myself: 'There she is! she has been like that in all my dreams–pale, melancholy and kind-hearted. She is my own; it is she who is destined to fill my cup with unknown joys.' And the physical life which returned to me then was your work. For we were brought together by no commonplace circumstances, you see; it was neither chance nor caprice, but fatality, death, which opened the gates of this new life to me. It was your husband–your master–who, guided by his destiny, brought me all bleeding in his arms and threw me at your feet, saying: 'Here is something for you!' And now nothing can part us."

"Yes, he can part us!" hastily interposed Madame Delmare, who, carried away by her lover's transports, had listened to him in ecstasy. "Alas! alas! you do not know him; he is a man who knows nothing of pardon–a man who cannot be deceived; He will kill you, Raymon!"

She hid her face in his bosom, sobbing. Raymon embraced her passionately.

"Let him come!" he cried; "let him come and snatch this moment of happiness from me! I defy him! Stay here, Indiana–here against my heart; let it be your refuge and your protection. Love me and I shall be invulnerable. You know that it is not in that man's power to kill me; I have already been exposed defenceless to his blows. But you, my good angel, were hovering over me, and your wings protected me. Have no fear, I say, we shall find a way to turn aside his wrath; and now I am not even afraid for you, for I shall be at hand. And when this master of yours attempts to oppress you, I will protect you against him. I will rescue you, if necessary, from his cruel laws. Would you like me to kill him? Tell me that you love me, and I will be his executioner if you sentence him to death."

"Hush! hush! you make me shudder! If you wish to kill some one, kill me; for I have lived one whole day and I ask nothing more."

"Die, then, but let it be of happiness!" cried Raymon, pressing his lips to Indiana's.

But the storm was too severe for so fragile a plant; she turned pale, put her hand to her heart and swooned.

At first Raymon thought that his caresses would call her blood back into her icy veins; but in vain did he cover her hand with kisses; in vain did he call her by the sweetest names. It was not a premeditated swoon of the sort we so often see. Madame Delmare had been seriously ill for a long time, and was subject to nervous paroxysms which sometimes lasted whole hours. Raymon, in desperation, was reduced to the necessity of calling for help. He rang; a maid appeared; but the phial that she held escaped from her hands, and a cry from her throat, when she recognized Raymon. He, recovering instantly all his self-possession, put his mouth to her ear.

"Hush, Noun! I knew that you were here and I came to see you. I did not expect to see your mistress, who was, as I supposed, at the ball. When I came in I frightened her and she fainted. Be prudent; I am going away."

Raymon fled, leaving each of the two women in possession of a secret which was destined to carry despair to the heart of the other.

VII

The next morning Raymon, on waking, received a second letter from Noun. He did not toss this one disdainfully aside; on the contrary, he opened it eagerly: it might have something to say of Madame Delmare. So, in fact, it did; but in what an embarrassing position this complication of intrigues placed Raymon! It had become impossible to conceal the girl's secret. Already suffering and terror had thinned her cheeks. Madame Delmare observed her ailing condition, but was unable to discover its cause. Noun dreaded the colonel's severity, but she dreaded her mistress's gentleness even more. She was very sure that she would obtain forgiveness, but she would die of shame and grief in being forced to make the confession. What would become of her if Raymon were not careful to protect her from the humiliations that were certain to overwhelm her! He must give some thought to her, or she would throw herself at Madame Delmare's feet and tell her the whole story.

The fear of this result had a powerful effect upon Monsieur de Ramière. His first thought was to separate Noun from her mistress.

"Be very careful not to speak without my consent," he wrote in reply. "Try and be in Lagny this evening. I will be there."

On his way thither he reflected as to the course he had better pursue. Noun had common sense enough not to expect a reparation–that was out of the question. She had never dared to utter the word marriage, and because she was discreet and generous, Raymon deemed himself less guilty. He said to himself that he had not deceived her, and that Noun must have foreseen what her fate must be. The cause of Raymon's embarrassment was not any hesitation about offering the poor girl half of his fortune; he was ready to enrich her, to take all the care her that the most sensitive delicacy could suggest. What made his position so painful was the necessity of telling her that he no longer loved her; for he did not know how to dissemble. Although his conduct at this crisis seems two-faced and treacherous, his heart was sincere, and had always been. He had loved Noun with his senses; he loved Madame Delmare with all his heart. Thus far he had lied to neither. His aim now was to avoid beginning to lie, and Raymon felt equally incapable of deceiving Noun and of dealing her the fatal blow. He must make a choice between a cowardly and a barbarous act. Raymon was very unhappy. He had come to no decision when he reached the gate of Lagny park.

Noun, for her part, had not expected so prompt a reply, and had recovered a little hope.

"He still loves me," she said to herself, "he doesn't mean to abandon me. He had forgotten me a little, that's not to be wondered at; in Paris, in the midst of merry-making, with all the women in love with him, as they are sure to be, he has allowed himself to be led away from the poor creole for a few moments. Alas! who am I that he should sacrifice to me all those great ladies who are much lovelier and richer than I am? Who knows," she said to herself artlessly, "perhaps the Queen of France is in love with him!"

By dint of meditating upon the seductions which luxurious surroundings probably exerted on her lover, Noun thought of a scheme for making herself more agreeable to him. She arrayed herself in her mistress's clothes, lighted a great fire in the room that Madame Delmare occupied at Lagny, decorated the mantel with the loveliest flowers she could find in the greenhouse, prepared a collation of fruit and choice wines, in a word resorted to all the dainty devices of the boudoir, of which she had never thought before; and when she looked at herself in a great mirror, she did herself no more than justice in deciding that she was fairer than the flowers with which she had sought to embellish her charms.

"He has often told me," she said to herself, "that I needed no ornaments to make me lovely, and that no woman at court, in all the splendor of her diamonds, was worth one of my smiles. And yet those same women that he used to despise fill thoughts now. Come, I must be cheerful, I must seem lively and happy; perhaps I shall reconquer to-night all the love I once aroused in him."

Raymon, having left his horse at a charcoal-burner's cabin in the forest, entered the park, to which he had a key. This time he did not run the risk of being taken for a thief; for almost all the servants had gone with their masters, he had taken the gardener into his confidence, and he knew all the approaches to Lagney as well as those to his own estate.

It was a cold night; the trees in the park were enveloped in a dense mist, and Raymon could hardly distinguish their black trunks through the white mist which swathed them in diaphanous robes. He wandered some time through the winding paths before he found the door of the summer-house where Noun awaited him. She was wrapped in a pelisse with the hood thrown over her head.

"We cannot stay here," she said, "it is too cold. Follow me and do not speak."

Raymon felt an extreme reluctance to enter Madame Delmare's house as the lover of her maid. However, he could not but comply; Noun was walking lightly away in front of him, and this interview was to be the last.

She led him across the courtyard, quieted the dogs, opened the doors noiselessly, and, taking his hand, guided him in silence through the dark corridors; at last she ushered him into a circular room, furnished simply but with refinement, where flowering orange-bushes exhaled their sweet perfume; transparent wax candles were burning in the candelabra.

Noun had strewn the floor with the petals of Bengal roses, the divan was covered with violets, a subtle warmth entered at every pore, and the glasses gleamed on the table amid the fruit, whose ruddy cheeks were daintily blended with green moss.

VII

Dazzled by the sudden transition from darkness to brilliant light, Raymon stood for a moment bewildered; but it was not long ere he realized where he was. The exquisite taste and chaste simplicity which characterized the furniture; the love stories and books of travel scattered over the mahogany shelves; the embroidery frame covered with a bright, pretty piece of work, the diversion of hours of patient melancholy; the harp whose strings seemed still to quiver with strains of love and longing; the engravings representing the pastoral attachment of Paul and Virginie, the peaks of Ile Bourbon and the blue shores of Saint-Paul; and, above all, the little bed half-hidden behind its muslin curtains, as white and modest as a maiden's bed, and over the headboard, by way of consecrated boxwood, a bit of palm, taken perhaps from some tree in her native island, on the day of her departure;–all these revealed the presence of Madame Delmare, and Raymon was seized with a strange thrill as he thought that the cloak-enveloped woman who had led him thither might be Indiana herself. This extravagant supposition seemed to be confirmed when he saw, in the mirror opposite, a white figure, the phantom of a woman entering a ball-room and laying aside her cloak, to appear, radiant and half-nude, in the dazzling light. But it was only a momentary error–Indiana would have concealed her charms more carefully; her modest bosom would have been visible only through the triple gauze veil of her corsage; she would perhaps have dressed her hair with natural camellias, but they would not have frisked about on her head in such seductive disorder; she might have encased her feet in satin shoes, but her chaste gown would not have betrayed thus shamelessly the mysteries of her shapely legs.

Taller and more powerfully built than her mistress, Noun was dressed, not clothed in her finery. She was graceful but lacked nobility of bearing; she was lovely with the loveliness of women, not of fairies; she invited pleasure and gave no promise of sublime bliss.

Raymon, after scrutinizing her in the mirror without turning his head, turned his eyes upon everything that was calculated to give forth a purer reflection of Indiana–the musical instruments, the paintings, the narrow, maidenly bed. He was intoxicated by the vague perfume her presence had left behind in that sanctuary; he shuddered with desire as he thought of the day when Indiana herself should throw open its delights to him; and Noun, standing behind him with her arms folded, gazed ecstatically at him, fancying that he was overwhelmed with delight at the sight of all the pains she had taken to please him.

But he broke the silence at last.

"I thank you," he said, "for all the preparations you have made for me; I thank you especially for bringing me here, but I have enjoyed this pleasant surprise long enough. Let us leave this room; we are not in our proper place here, and I must have some respect for Madame Delmare, even in her absence."

"That is very cruel," said Noun, who did not understand him, but remarked his cold and displeased manner; "it is very hard to have had such hopes of pleasing you and to see that you spurn me."

"No, dear Noun, I shall never spurn you; I came here to have a serious talk with you and to show you the deep affection that I owe you. I am grateful for your desire to please me; but I loved you better adorned by your youth and your natural charms than in this borrowed finery."

Noun half understood and wept.

"I am a miserable creature," she said; "I hate myself, for I no longer please you. I should have foreseen that you would not love me long, being, as I am, a poor, uneducated girl. I do not reproach you for anything. I knew well enough that you would not marry me; but if you would have kept on loving me, I would have sacrificed everything without a regret, endured everything without complaining. Alas! I am ruined! I am dishonored! perhaps I shall be turned out-of-doors. I am going to give life to a creature who will be even more unfortunate than I am, and no one will pity me. Everyone will feel that he has a right to trample on me. But I would joyfully submit to all that, if you still loved me."

Noun talked thus a long while. Perhaps she did not repeat the same words, but she said the same things, and said them a hundred times more eloquently than I can say them. Where are we to look for the secret of eloquence which suddenly reveals itself to an ignorant, inexperienced mind in the crisis of a genuine passion and a profound sorrow? At such times words have a greater value than in all the other scenes of life; at such times trivial words become sublime by reason of the sentiment that dictates them and the accent with which they are spoken. At such times the woman of the lowest rank, abandoning herself to the frenzy of her emotions, becomes more pathetic and more convincing than her to whom education has taught moderation and reserve.

Raymon was flattered to find that he had inspired so generous an attachment, and gratitude, compassion, perhaps a little vanity, rekindled love for a moment.

Noun was suffocated by her tears; she had torn the flowers from her hair which fell in disorder over her broad and dazzling shoulders. If Madame Delmare had not had her slavery and her sufferings to heighten her charms, Noun would have surpassed her immeasurably in beauty at that moment; she was resplendent with grief and love. Raymon was vanquished; he drew her into his arms, made her sit beside him on the sofa, moved the little decanter-laden table nearer to them, and poured a few drops of orange-flower water in a silver cup for her. Comforted by this mark of interest far more than by the calming potion, Noun wiped away her tears and threw herself at Raymon's feet.

"Do love me," she said, passionately embracing his knees; "tell me that you still love me and I shall be cured, I shall be saved. Kiss me as you used to, and I will not regret having ruined myself to give you a few days of pleasure."

She threw her cool, brown arms about him, she covered him with her long hair; her great black eyes emitted a burning languor and betrayed that ardor of the blood, that purely oriental lust which is capable of triumphing over all the efforts of the will, all the chaste delicacy of the thought. Raymon forgot everything–his resolutions, his new love and his surroundings. He returned Noun's delirious caresses. He moistened his lips at the same cup, and the heady wines which were close at hand completed the dethronement of their reason.

Little by little a vague and shadowy memory of Indiana was blended with Raymon's drunkenness. The two glass panels which repeated Noun's image *ad infinitum* seemed to be peopled by a thousand phantoms. He gazed into the depths of that multiple reflection, looking for a slenderer figure there, and it seemed to him that he could distinguish, in the last hazy and confused shadow of Noun's image the graceful and willowy form of Madame Delmare.

Noun, herself bewildered by the strong liquors which she knew not how to use, no longer noticed her lover's strange remarks. If she had not been as drunk as he, she would have understood that in his wildest flights Raymon was thinking of another woman. She would have seen him kiss the scarf and the ribbons Indiana had worn, inhale the perfume which reminded him of her, crumple in his burning hands the tissue that had covered her breast; but Noun appropriated all these transports to herself, when Raymon saw naught of her but Indiana's dress. If he kissed her black hair, he fancied that he was kissing Indiana's black hair. It was Indiana whom he saw in the fumes of the punch which Noun's hand had lighted; it was she who smiled upon him and beckoned him from behind those white muslin curtains; and it was she of whom he dreamed upon that chaste and spotless bed, when, yielding to the influence of love and wine, he led thither his dishevelled creole.

When Raymon woke, a sort of half light was shining through the cracks of the shutters, and he lay a long while without moving, absorbed by a vague feeling of surprise and gazing at the room in which he was and the bed in which he had slept, as if they were a vision of his slumber. Everything in Madame Delmare's chamber had been put in order. Noun, who had fallen asleep the sovereign mistress of that place, had waked in the morning a lady's-maid once more. She had taken away the flowers and put the remains of the collation out of sight; the furniture was all in place, nothing suggested the amorous debauch of the night, and Indiana's chamber had resumed its innocent and virtuous aspect.

Overwhelmed with shame, he rose and attempted to leave the room, but he was locked in; the window was thirty feet from the ground, and he must needs remain in that remorse-laden atmosphere, like Ixion on his wheel. Thereupon he fell on his knees with his face toward that disarranged, tumbled bed which made him blush.

"O Indiana!" he cried, wringing his hands, "how I have outraged you! Can you ever forgive me for such infamous conduct? Even if you should forgive me, I can never forgive myself. Resist me now, my gentle, trustful Indiana; for you do not know the baseness and brutality of the man to whom you would surrender the treasures of your innocence! Repulse me, trample on me, for I have not respected the sanctuary of your sacred modesty; I have befuddled myself with your wine like a footman, sitting beside your maid; I have sullied your spotless robe with my accursed breath, and your chaste girdle with my infamous kisses on another's breast; I have not shrunk from poisoning the repose of your lonely nights, and from shedding, even upon this bed, which your husband himself respected, the influences of seduction and adultery! What safety will you find henceforth behind these curtains whose mysteries I have not shrunk from profaning? What impure dreams, what bitter and consuming thoughts will cling fast to your brain and wither it! What phantoms of vice and shamelessness will crawl upon the virginal linen of your couch! And your sleep, pure as a child's–what chaste divinity will care to protect it now? Have I not put to flight the angel who guarded your pillow? Have I not thrown your alcove open to the demon of lust? Have I not sold him your soul? And will not the insane passion which consumes the vitals of this lascivious creole cling to yours, like Dejanira's robe and gnaw at them! Oh! miserable wretch! miserable, guilty wretch that I am! if only I could wash away with my blood the stain I have left on this couch!"

And Raymon sprinkled it with his tears.

At that moment Noun returned, in her neckerchief and apron; she fancied, when she saw Raymon kneeling, that he was praying. She did not know that society people do not pray. She stood waiting in silence, until he should deign to notice her presence.

Raymon, when he saw her, had a feeling of embarrassment and irritation, but without the courage to scold her, without the strength to say a friendly word to her.

"Why did you lock me in this room?" he said at last. "Do you forget that it is broad daylight and that I cannot go out without compromising you openly?"

"So you're not to go out," said Noun caressingly. "The house is deserted and no one can see you; the gardener never comes to this part of the building to which I alone have the keys. You must stay with me all day; you are my prisoner."

This arrangement drove Raymon to despair; he had no other feeling for his mistress than a sort of aversion. However, he could do nothing but submit, and it may be that, notwithstanding what he suffered in that room, an invincible attraction detained him there.

When Noun left him to go and find something for breakfast, he set about examining by daylight all those dumb witnesses of Indiana's solitude. He opened her books, turned the leaves of her albums, then closed them precipitately; for he still shrank from committing a profanation and violating some feminine mystery. At last he began to pace the room and noticed, on the wooden panel opposite Madame Delmare's bed, a large picture, richly framed and covered with a double thickness of gauze.

Perhaps it was Indiana's portrait. Raymon, in his eagerness to see it, forgot his scruples, stepped on a chair, removed the pins, and was amazed to see a full-length portrait of a handsome young man.

VIII

"It seems to me that I know that face," he said to Noun, struggling to assume an indifferent attitude.

"Fi! monsieur," said the girl, as she placed on a table the tray that she brought containing the breakfast; "it is not right to try and find out my mistress's secrets."

This remark made Raymon turn pale.

"Secrets!" he said. "If this is a secret, it has been confided to you, Noun, and you were doubly guilty in bringing me to this room."

"Oh! no, it's not a secret," said Noun with a smile; "for Monsieur Delmare himself assisted in hanging Sir Ralph's portrait on that panel. As if madame could have any secrets with a husband so jealous!"

"Sir Ralph, you say? Who is Sir Ralph?"

"Sir Rodolphe Brown, madame's cousin, her playmate in childhood, and my own, too, I might say; he is such a good man!"

Raymon scrutinized the picture with surprise and some uneasiness.

We have said that Sir Ralph was an extremely comely person, physically; with a red and white complexion and abundant hair, a tall figure, always perfectly dressed, and capable, if not of turning a romantic brain, of satisfying the vanity of an unromantic one. The peaceable baronet was represented in hunting costume, about as we saw him in the first chapter of this narrative, and surrounded by his dogs, the beautiful pointer Ophelia in the foreground, because of the fine silver-gray tone of her silky coat and the purity of her Scotch blood. Sir Ralph had a hunting-horn in one hand and in the other the rein of a superb, dapple-gray English hunter, who filled almost the whole background of the picture. It was an admirably executed portrait, a genuine family picture with all its perfection of detail, all its puerile niceties of resemblance, all its bourgeois minutiæ a picture to make a nurse weep, dogs bark and a tailor faint with joy. There was but one thing on earth more insignificant than the portrait, and that was the original.

Nevertheless it kindled a violent flame of wrath in Raymon.

"Upon my word!" he said to himself, "this dapper young Englishman enjoys the privilege of being admitted to Madame Delmare's most secret apartment! His vapid face is always here, looking coldly on at the most private acts of her life! He watches her, guards her, follows her every movement, possesses her every hour in the day! At night he watches her asleep and surprises the secret of her dreams; in the morning, when she comes forth, all white and quivering, from her bed, he sees the dainty bare foot that steps lightly on the carpet; and when she dresses with all precaution–when she believes that she is quite alone, hidden from every eye–that insolent face is there, feasting on her charms! That man, all booted and spurred, presides over her toilet. Is this gauze usually spread over the picture?" he asked the maid.

"Always," she replied, "when madame is absent. But don't take the trouble to replace it, for madame is coming in a few days."

"In that case, Noun, you would do well to tell her that the expression of the face is very impertinent. If I had been in Monsieur Delmare's place I wouldn't have consented to leave it here unless I had cut out the eyes. But that's just like the stupid jealousy of the ordinary husband! They imagine everything and understand nothing."

"For heaven's sake, what have you against good Monsieur Brown's face?" said Noun, as she made her mistress's bed; "he is such an excellent master! I used not to care much for him, because I always heard madame say that he was selfish; but ever since the day that he took care of you–"

"True," Raymon interrupted her, "it was he who helped me that day; I remember him perfectly now. But I owe his interest only to Madame Delmare's prayers."

"Because she is so kind-hearted," said poor Noun. "Who could help being kind-hearted after living with her?"

When Noun spoke of Madame Delmare, Raymon listened with an interest of which she had no suspicion.

The day passed quietly enough, but Noun dared not lead the conversation to her real object. At last, toward evening, she made an effort and compelled him to declare his intentions.

Raymon had no other intention than to rid himself of a dangerous witness and of a woman whom he no longer loved. But he proposed to assure her future, and in fear and trembling he made her the most liberal offers.

It was a bitter affront to the poor girl; she tore her hair, and would have beaten her head against the wall if Raymon had not put forth all his strength to hold her. Thereupon, employing all the resources of language and intellect with which nature had endowed him, he made her understand that it was not for her, but for the child she was to bring into the world, that he desired to make provision.

"It is my duty," he said; "I hand the funds over to you as the child's heritage, and you would fail in your duty to him if a false sense of delicacy should lead you to reject them."

Noun became calmer and wiped her eyes.

"Very well," she said, "I will accept the money if you will promise to keep on loving me; for, just by doing your duty to the child, you will not do it to the mother. Your gift will keep him alive, but your indifference will kill me. Can't you take me into your service? I am not exacting; I don't aspire to all that another woman in my place might have had the skill to obtain. But let me be your servant. Obtain a place for me in your mother's family. She will be satisfied with me, I give you my word; and, even if you don't love me, I shall at least see you."

"What you ask is impossible, my dear Noun. In your present condition you cannot think of entering anyone's service; and to deceive my mother–to play upon her confidence in me–would be a base act to which I shall never consent. Go to Lyon or Bordeaux; I will undertake to see to it that you want for nothing until such time as you can show yourself again. Then I will obtain a place for you with some one of my acquaintances–at Paris, if you wish, if you insist upon being near me–but as to living under the same roof, that is impossible."

"Impossible!" echoed Noun, wringing her hands in a passion of grief. "I see that you despise me–that you blush for me. But no, I will not go away, alone and degraded, to die abandoned in some distant city where you will forget me. What do I care for my reputation? Your love is what I wanted to retain."

"Noun, if you fear that I am deceiving you, come with me. The same carriage shall take us to whatever place you choose. I will go with you anywhere, except to Paris or to my mother's, and I will bestow upon you all the care and attention that I owe you."

"Yes, to abandon me on the day after you have put me down, a useless burden, in some foreign land!" she rejoined, smiling bitterly. "No, monsieur, no, I will stay here; I do not choose to lose everything at once. I should sacrifice, by following you, the person whom I loved best in the world before I knew you; but I am not anxious enough to conceal my dishonor to sacrifice both my love and my friendship. I will go and throw myself at Madame Delmare's feet; I will tell her all, and she will forgive me, I know, for she is kind and she loves me. We were born on almost the same day, and she is my foster-sister. We have never been separated, and she will not want me to leave her. She will weep with me; she will take care of me, and she will love my child–my poor child! Who knows! she has not the good fortune to be a mother; perhaps she will bring it up as her own! Ah! I was mad to think of leaving her, for she is the only person on earth who will take pity on me!"

This determination plunged Raymon in horrible perplexity; but suddenly the rumbling of a carriage was heard in the courtyard. Noun, in dismay, ran to the window.

"It's Madame Delmare!" she cried; "go instantly!"

In that moment of excitement the key to the secret staircase could not be found. Noun took Raymon's arm and hurriedly pulled him into the hall; but they were not half way to the stairs when they heard footsteps in the same passage; they heard Madame Delmare's voice ten steps in front of them, and a candle carried by a servant who attended her cast its flickering light almost on their terrified faces. Noun had barely time to retrace her steps, still pulling Raymon after her, and to return with him to the bedroom.

A dressing room, with a glass door, might afford a place of refuge for a few moments; but there was no way of locking the door, and it was possible that Madame Delmare might go to the dressing-room at once. To avoid being detected instantly, Raymon was obliged to rush into the alcove and hide behind the curtains. It was not probable that Madame Delmare would retire at once, and meanwhile Noun might find an opportunity to help him to escape.

Indiana busted into the room tossed her hat on the bed and kissed Noun with the familiarity of a sister. There was so little light in the room that she did not notice her companion's emotion.

"You expected me, did you?" she said, going to the fire; "how did you know I was coming?–Monsieur Delmare," she added, not waiting for a reply, "will be here to-morrow. I started at once on receiving his letter. I have certain reasons for receiving him here and not in Paris. I will tell you what they are. But, in heaven's name, why don't you speak to me? you don't seem so glad to see me as usual."

"I am low-spirited," said Noun, kneeling by her mistress to remove her shoes. "I have something to tell you, too, but later; come to the salon now."

"God forbid! what an idea! it's deathly cold there!"

"No, there's a good fire."

"You are dreaming! I just came through it."

"But your supper is waiting for you."

"I don't want any supper; besides, there is nothing ready. Go and get my boa, I left it in the carriage."

"In a moment."

"Why not now? Go, I say, go!"

As she spoke, she pushed Noun toward the door with a playful air; and the maid, seeing that she must be bold and self-possessed, went out for a few moments. But she had no sooner left the room than Madame Delmare threw the bolt and removed her cloak, placing it on the bed beside her hat. As she did it, she went so near to Raymon, that he instinctively stepped back, and the bed, which apparently rested on well-oiled castors, moved with a slight noise. Madame Delmare was surprised but not frightened, for it was quite possible that she had herself moved the bed; she stretched forth her neck, drew the curtain aside and revealed a man's head outlined against the wall in the half-light cast by the fire on the hearth.

In her terror she uttered a shriek and rushed to the mantel to seize the bell-cord and summon help. Raymon would have preferred to be taken for a thief again than to be recognized in that situation. But if he did not make himself known, Madame Delmare would call her servants and compromise her own reputation. He place his trust in the love he had inspired in her, and, rushing to her, tried to stop her shrieks and to keep her away from the bell-cord, saying to her in an undertone, for fear of being heard by Noun, who was probably not far away:

"It is I, Indiana; look at me and forgive me! Indiana! forgive an unhappy wretch whose reason you have led astray, and who could not make up his mind to give you back to your husband until he had seen you once more."

And while he held Indiana in his arms, no less in the hope of moving her than to keep her from ringing, Noun was knocking at the door in an agony of apprehension. Madame Delmare, extricating herself from Raymon's arms, ran and opened the door, then sank into a chair.

Pale as death and almost fainting, Noun threw herself against the door to prevent the servants, who were running hither and thither, from interrupting this strange scene; paler than her mistress, with trembling knees and her back glued to the door, she awaited her fate.

Raymon felt that with due address he might still deceive both women at once.

"Madame," he said, falling on his knees before Indiana, "my presence here must seem to you an outrageous insult; here at your feet I implore your forgiveness. Grant me an interview of a few moments and I will explain–"

"Hush, monsieur, and leave this house," cried Madame Delmare, recovering all the dignity befitting her situation; "leave this house openly. Open the door, Noun, and allow monsieur to go, so that all my servants may see him and that the disgrace of such a proceeding may fall upon him."

Noun, believing that she was detected, threw herself on her knees by Raymon's side. Madame Delmare looked at her in amazement, but said nothing.

Raymon tried to take her hand; but she indignantly withdrew it. Flushed with anger, she rose and pointed to the door.

"Go, I tell you!" she said; "go, for your conduct is despicable. So these are the means you chose to employ! you, monsieur, hiding in my bedroom, like a thief! It seems that it is a habit of yours to introduce yourself into families in this way! and this is the pure attachment that you offered me the night before last! This is the way you were to protect me, respect me and defend me! This is the way you worship me! You see a woman who has nursed you with her hands, who, to restore you to life, defied her husband's anger; you deceive her by a pretence of gratitude, you promise her a love worthy of her, and as a reward for her attentions, as the price of her credulity, you seek to surprise her in her sleep and to hasten your triumph by indescribable infamy! You bribe her maid, you almost creep into her bed, like a lover already favored; you do not shrink from admitting her servants to the secret of an intimacy that does not exist. Go, monsieur; you have taken pains to undeceive me very quickly! Go, I say! do not remain another moment under my roof! And you, wretched girl, who have so little regard for your mistress's honor–you deserve to be dismissed. Stand away from that door, I tell you!"

Noun, half dead with surprise and despair, gazed fixedly at Raymon as if to ask him for an explanation of this incredible mystery. Then, with a wild gleam in her eyes, hardly able to stand, she dragged herself to Indiana and seized her arm fiercely.

"What was that you said?" she cried, her teeth clenched with rage; "this man loved you?"

""Eh! you must have known that he did!" said Madame Delmare, pushing her away contemptuously and with all her strength; "you must have known what reasons a man has for hiding behind a woman's curtains. Ah! Noun," she added, noticing the girl's evident despair, "it was a dastardly thing, and one of which I would never have believed you to be capable; you consented to sell her honor who had such perfect faith in yours!"

Madame Delmare was shedding tears, tears of indignation as well as of grief. Raymon had never seen her so lovely; but he hardly dared look at her, for her haughty air, the air of an insulted woman, forced him to lower his eyes. He was terror-stricken, too, petrified by Noun's presence. If he had been alone with Madame Delmare, he might perhaps have been able to soften her. But Noun's expression was terrifying; her features were distorted by rage and hatred.

A knock at the door startled them all three. Noun rushed forward once more to keep out intruders; but Madame Delmare, pushing her aside imperatively, motioned to Raymon to withdraw to the corner of the room. Then, with the self-possession which made her so remarkable at critical moments, she wrapped herself in a shawl, partly opened the door herself, and asked the servant who had knocked what he had to say to her.

"Monsieur Rodolphe Brown is here," was the reply; "he wishes to know if madame will receive him."

"Say to Monsieur Rodolphe Brown that I am delighted that he has come and that I will join him at once. Make a fire in the salon and bid them prepare some supper. One moment! Go and get the key to the small park."

The servant retired. Madame Delmare remained at the door, holding it open, not deigning to listen to Noun and imperiously enjoining silence on Raymon.

The servant returned in a few moments. Madame Delmare, still holding the door open between him and Monsieur de Ramière, took the key from him, bade him hurry up the supper, and, as soon as he had gone, turned to Raymon.

"The arrival of my cousin, Sir Rodolphe Brown," she said, "saves you from the public scandal which I intended to inflict on you; he is a man of honor, who would eagerly assume the duty of defending me; but as I should be very sorry to expose a man like him to danger at the hands of such a man as you, I will allow you to go without scandal. Noun, who admitted you, will find a way to let you out. Go!"

"We shall meet again, madame," replied Raymon with an attempt at self-assurance; "and although I am culpable, you will perhaps regret the harshness with which you treat me now."

"I trust, monsieur, that we shall never meet again," she rejoined.

And still standing at the door, not deigning to bow, she watched him depart with his miserable and trembling accomplice.

When he was alone with Noun in the obscurity of the park, Raymon expected reproaches from her; but she did not speak to him. She led him to the gate of the small park, and, when he tried to take her hand, she had already vanished. He called her in a low voice, for he was anxious to learn his fate; but she did not reply, and the gardener, suddenly appearing, said to him:

"Come, monsieur, you must be off; madame is here and you may be discovered."

VIII

Raymon took his departure with death in his heart; but in his despair at having offended Madame Delmare he almost forgot Noun and thought of nothing but possible methods of appeasing her mistress; for it was a part of his nature to be irritated by obstacles and never to cling passionately except to things that were well-nigh desperate.

At night, when Madame Delmare, after supping silently with Sir Ralph, withdrew to her own apartments, Noun did not come, as usual, to undress her; she rang for her to no purpose, and when she had concluded that the girl was resolved not to obey, she locked her door and went to bed. But she passed a horrible night, and, as soon as the day broke, went down into the park. She was feverish and agitated; she longed to feel the cold enter her body and allay the fire that consumed her breast. The day before, at that hour, she was happy, abandoning herself to the novel sensations of that intoxicating love. What a ghastly disillusionment in twenty-four hours! First of all, the news of her husband's return several days earlier than she expected; those four or five days which she had hoped to pass in Paris were to her a whole lifetime of never-ending bliss, a dream of love never to be interrupted by awakening; but in the morning she had to abandon the hope, to resume the yoke, and to go to meet her master in order that he might not meet Raymon at Madame de Carvajal's; for Indiana thought that it would be impossible for her to deceive her husband if he should see her in Raymon's presence. And then this Raymon, whom she loved as a god–it was by him of all men that she was thus basely insulted! And lastly, her life-long companion, the young creole whom she loved so dearly, suddenly proved to be unworthy of her confidence and her esteem!

Madame Delmare had wept all night long. She sank upon the turf, still whitened by the morning rime, on the bank of the little stream that flowed through the park. It was late in March and nature was beginning to awake; the morning, although cold, was not devoid of beauty; patches of mist still rested on the water like a floating scarf, and the birds were trying their first songs of love and springtime.

Indiana felt as if relieved of a heavy weight, and a wave of religious feeling overflowed her soul.

"God willed it so," she said to herself; "in His providence he has given me a harsh lesson, but it is fortunate for me. That man would perhaps have led me into vice, he would have ruined me; whereas now the vileness of his sentiments is revealed to me, and I shall be on my guard against the tempestuous and detestable passion that fermented in his breast. I will love my husband! I will try to love him! At all events I will be submissive to him, I will make him happy by never annoying him, I will avoid whatever can possibly arouse his jealousy; for now I know what to think of the false eloquence that men know how to lavish on us. I shall be fortunate, perhaps, if God will take pity on my sorrows and send death to me soon."

The clatter of the mill-wheel that started the machinery in Monsieur Delmare's factory made itself heard behind the willows on the other bank. The river, rushing through the newly opened gates, began to boil and bubble on the surface; and, as Madame Delmare followed with a melancholy eye the swift rush of the stream, she saw floating among the reeds something like a bundle of cloth which the current strove to hurry along in its train. She rose, leaned over the bank and distinctly saw a woman's clothes,–clothes that she knew too well. Terror nailed her to the spot; but the stream flowed on, slowly drawing a body from the reeds among which it had caught, and bringing it toward Madame Delmare.

A piercing shriek attracted the workmen from the factory to the spot; Madame Delmare had fainted on the bank, and Noun's body was floating in the water at her feet.

PART SECOND

IX

Two months have passed. Nothing is changed at Lagny, in that house to which I introduced you one winter evening, except that all about its red brick walls with their frame of gray stone and its slated roofs yellowed by venerable moss, the springtime is in its bloom. The family is scattered here and there, enjoying the mild and fragrant evening air; the setting sun gilds the windowpanes and the roar of the factory mingles with the various noises of the farm. Monsieur Delmare is seated on the steps, gun in hand, practising at shooting swallows on the wing. Indiana, at her embroidery frame near the window of the salon, leans forward now and then to watch with a sad face the colonel's cruel amusement in the courtyard. Ophelia leaps about and barks, indignant at a style of hunting so contrary to her habits; and Sir Ralph, astride the stone railing, is smoking a cigar and, as usual, looking on impassively at other people's pleasure or vexation.

"Indiana," cried the colonel, laying aside his gun, "do for heaven's sake put your work away; you tire yourself out as if you were paid so much an hour."

"It is still broad daylight," Madame Delmare replied.

"No matter; come to the window, I have something to tell you."

Indiana obeyed, and the colonel, drawing near the window, which was almost on a level with the ground, said to her with as near an approach to playfulness of manner as an old and jealous husband can manage:

"As you have worked hard to-day and as you are very good, I am going to tell you something that will please you."

Madame Delmare struggled hard to smile; her smile would have driven a more sensitive man than the colonel to despair.

"You will be pleased to know," he continued, "that I have invited one of your humble adorers to breakfast with you to-morrow, to divert you. You will ask me which one; for you have a very pretty collection of them, you flirt!"

"Perhaps it's our dear old curé?" said Madame Delmare, whose melancholy was enhanced by her husband's gayety.

"Oh! no, indeed!"

"Then it must be the mayor of Chailly or the old notary from Fontainebleau."

"Oh! the craft of women! You know very well that it would be none of those people. Come, Ralph, tell madame the name she has on the tip of her tongue but doesn't choose to pronounce herself."

"You need not go through so much preparation to announce a visit from Monsieur de Ramière," said Sir Ralph, tranquilly, as he threw away his cigar; "I suppose that it's a matter of perfect indifference to her."

Madame Delmare felt the blood rush to her cheeks; she made a pretence of looking for something in the salon, then returned to the window with as calm a manner as she could command.

"I fancy that this is a jest," she said, trembling in every limb.

"On the contrary I am perfectly serious; you will see him here at eleven o'clock to-morrow."

"What! the man who stole into your premises to obtain unfair possession of your invention, and whom you almost killed as a criminal! You must both be very pacific to forget such grievances!"

"You set me the example, dearest, by receiving him very graciously at your aunt's, where he called on you."

Indiana turned pale.

"I do not by any means appropriate that call," she said earnestly, "and I am so little flattered by it that, if I were in your place, I would not receive him."

"You women are all false and cunning just for the pleasure of being so. You danced with him during one whole ball, I was told."

"You were misinformed."

"Why, it was your aunt herself who told me! However, you need not defend yourself so warmly; I have no fault to find, as your aunt desired and assisted to bring about this reconciliation between us. Monsieur de Ramière has been seeking it for a long while. He has rendered me some very valuable services with respect to my business, and he has done it without ostentation and almost without my knowledge; so, as I am not so savage as you say, and also as I do not choose to be under obligations to a stranger, I determined to make myself square with him."

"How so?"

"By making a friend of him; by going to Cercy this morning with Sir Ralph. We found his mother there, who seems a delightful woman; and the house is furnished with refinement and comfort, but without ostentation and without a trace of the pride that attaches to venerable names. After all, this Ramière's a good fellow, and I have invited him to come and breakfast with us and inspect the factory. I hear favorable accounts of his brother, and I have made sure that he cannot injure me by adopting the same methods that I use; so I prefer that that family should profit by them rather than any other. You see no secrets are kept very long, and mine will soon be like a stage secret if progress in manufacturing continues at the present rate."

"For my part," said Sir Ralph, "I have always disapproved of this secrecy, as you know; a good citizen's discovery belongs to his country as much as to himself, and if I–"

"*Parbleu!* that is just like you, Sir Ralph, with your practical philanthropy! You will make me think that your fortune doesn't belong to you, and that, if the nation takes a fancy to it to-morrow, you are ready to exchange your fifty thousand francs a year for a wallet and staff! It looks well for a *buck* like you, who are as fond of the comforts of life as a sultan, to preach contempt of wealth!"

"What I say," rejoined Sir Ralph, "is not meant to be philanthropic at all; my point is that selfishness properly understood leads us to do good to others to prevent them injuring us. I am selfish myself, as everybody knows. I have accustomed myself not to blush for it, and, after analyzing all the virtues, I find personal interest at the foundation of them all. Love and devotion, which are two apparently generous passions, are perhaps the most selfish passions that exist; nor is patriotism less so, my word for it. I care little for men; but not for anything in the world would I undertake to prove it to them, my fear of them is inversely proportional to my esteem for them. We are both selfish therefore but I admit it, whereas you deny it."

A discussion arose between them wherein each sought by all the arguments of selfishness to demonstrate the selfishness of the others. Madame Delmare took advantage of it to retire to her room and to abandon herself to all the reflections to which news so entirely unexpected naturally gave birth.

It will be well not only to admit you to the secret of her thoughts, but also to enlighten you as to the situation of the various persons whom Noun's death had affected in greater or less degree.

It is almost proven, so far as the reader and I myself are concerned, that that unfortunate creature threw herself into the stream through despair, in one of those moments of frenzy when extreme resolutions are most easily formed. But, as she evidently did not return to the house after leaving Raymon–as no one had met her and had an opportunity to divine her purpose–there was no indication of suicide to throw light upon the mystery of her death.

Two persons were in a position to attribute it with moral certainty to her own act–Monsieur de Ramière and the gardener of Lagny. The grief of the former was concealed beneath a pretence of illness; the terror and remorse of the other enjoined silence upon him. This man who, from cupidity, had connived at the intercourse of the lovers throughout the winter, was the only person who had been in a position to remark the young creole's secret misery. Justly fearing the reproaches of his employers and the criticisms of his equals, he held his peace in his own interest; and when Monsieur Delmare, who had some suspicions after the discovery of this intrigue, questioned him as to the lengths to which it had been carried during his absence, he boldly denied that it had continued at all. Some people in the neighborhood–a very lonely neighborhood, by the way–had noticed Noun walking toward Crecy at unreasonable hours; but apparently there had been no relations between her and Monsieur de Ramière since the end of January, and her death occurred on the 28th of March. So far as appeared, her death was attributable to chance; as she was walking through the park at nightfall, she might have been deceived by the dense fog that had prevailed for several days, have lost her way and missed the English bridge over the stream, which was quite narrow but had very steep banks and was swollen by recent rains.

Although Sir Ralph, who was more observant than his reflections indicated, had found in his private thoughts grounds for strong suspicion of Monsieur de Ramière, he communicated them to no one, regarding as useless and cruel any reproachful words addressed to a man who was so unfortunate as to have such a source of remorse in his life. He even succeeded in convincing the colonel, who expressed in his presence some suspicions in that regard, that it was most urgent, in Madame Delmare's delicate condition, to continue to conceal from her the possible causes of her old playmate's suicide. So it was with the poor girl's death as with her love affair. There was a tacit agreement never to mention it before Indiana, and ere long it ceased to be talked about at all.

But these precautions were of no avail, for Madame Delmare had her own reasons for suspecting a part of the truth; the bitter reproaches she had heaped on the unhappy girl on that fatal evening seemed to her a sufficient explanation of her sudden resolution. So it was that, at the ghastly moment when she discovered the dead bqdy floating in the water, Indiana's repose, already so disturbed, and her heart, already so sad, had received the final blow; her lingering disease was progressing actively; and this woman, young and perhaps strong, refusing to be cured, concealing her sufferings from her husband's undiscerning and far from delicate affection, sank voluntarily beneath the burden of sorrow and discouragement.

"Woe is me!" she cried as she entered her room, after learning of Raymon's impending visit. "A curse on that man, who has entered this house only to bring despair and death! O God! why dost Thou permit him to come between Thee and me, to take command of my destiny at his pleasure, so that he has only to put out his hand and say: 'She is mine! I will derange her reason, I will bring desolation into her life; and if she resists me I will spread mourning around her, I will encompass her with remorse, regrets and alarms!' O God! it is not fair that a poor woman should be so persecuted!"

She wept bitterly; for the thought of Raymon revived the memory of Noun, more vivid and heartrending than ever.

"Poor Noun! my poor playmate! my countrywoman, my only friend!" she exclaimed sorrowfully; "that man is your murderer. Unhappy child! his influence was fatal to you as to me! You loved me so dearly, you were the only one who could divine my sorrows and mitigate them by your artless gayety! Woe to me who have lost you! Was it for this that I brought you from so far away! By what wiles did that man surprise your good faith and induce you to do such a despicable thing? Ah! he must have deceived you shamefully, and you did not realize your error until you saw my indignation! I was too harsh, Noun; I was so harsh that I was downright cruel; I drove you to despair, I killed you! Poor girl! why did you not wait a few hours until the wind had blown away my resentment like a wisp of straw! Why did you not come and weep on my bosom and say: 'I was deceived; I acted without knowing what I was doing, but you know well enough that I respect you and love you!'–I would have taken you in my arms, we would have wept together, and you would not be dead. Dead! dead so young and so lovely and so full of life! Dead at nineteen and such a ghastly death!"

While thus weeping for her companion, Indiana, unknown to herself, wept also for her three days of illusion, the loveliest days of her life, the only days when she had really lived; for during those three days she had loved with a passion which Raymon, had he been the most presumptuous of men, could never have imagined. But the blinder and more violent that love had been, the more keenly had she felt the insult she had received; the first love of a heart like hers contains so much modesty and sensitive delicacy!

And yet Indiana had yielded to a burst of shame and anger rather than to a well-matured determination. I have no doubt that Raymon would have obtained his pardon had he been allowed a few more minutes in which to plead for it. But fate had defeated his love and his address, and Madame Delmare honestly believed now that she hated him.

X

For his part, it was neither in a spirit of bravado nor because of the injury to his self-esteem that he aspired more ardently than ever to Madame Delmare's love and forgiveness. He believed that they were unattainable, and no other woman's love, no other earthly joy seemed to him their equivalent. Such was his nature. An insatiable craving for action and excitement consumed his life. He loved society with its laws and its fetters, because it offered him material for combat and resistance; and if he had a horror of license and debauchery, it was because they promised insipid and easily obtained pleasure.

Do not believe, however, that he was insensible to Noun's ruin. In the first impulse, he conceived a horror of himself and loaded his pistols with a very real purpose of blowing out his brains; but a praiseworthy feeling stayed his hand. What would become of his mother, his aged, feeble mother, the poor woman whose life had been so agitated and so sorrowful, who lived only for him, her only treasure, her only hope? Must he break her heart, shorten the few years that still remained to her? No, surely not. The best way to redeem his wrongdoing was to devote himself thenceforth solely to his mother, and it was with that purpose in mind that he returned to her at Paris, and put forth all his energies to make her forget his desertion of her during a large part of the winter.

Raymon exerted an incredible influence over everybody about him; for, take him for all in all, with his faults and his youthful escapades, he was above the average of society men. We have not as yet told you upon what his reputation for wit and talent was based, because it was aside from the events we had to describe; but it is time to inform you that this Raymon, whose weaknesses you have followed and whose frivolity you have censured, is one of the men who have had the most control and influence over your thoughts, whatever your opinions to-day may be. You have devoured his political pamphlets, and, while reading the newspapers of the period, you have often been captivated by the irresistible charm of his style and the grace of his courteous and worldly logic.

I am speaking of a time already far away, in these days when time is no longer reckoned by centuries, nor even by reigns, but by ministries. I am speaking of the Martignac year, of that epoch of repose and doubt, interjected in the middle of a political era, not like a treaty of peace, but like an armistice; of those fifteen months of the reign of doctrines, which had such a strange influence on principles and on morals, and which may perhaps have paved the way for the extraordinary result of our latest revolution.

X

It was in those days that men saw the blooming of certain youthful talents, unfortunate in that they were born in a period of transition and of compromise; for they paid their tribute to the conciliatory and wavering tendencies of the time. Never, so far as I know, was knowledge of mere words and ignorance, or pretended ignorance, of things carried so far. It was the reign of restrictions, and it is beyond my power to say who made the fullest use of them, short-gowned Jesuits or long-gowned lawyers. Political moderation had become a part of the national character, like courteous manners, and it was the same with the first variety of courtesy as with the second: it served as a mask for secret antipathies, and taught them how to fight without scandal and publicity. We must say, however, in defence of the young men of that period, that they were often towed like light skiffs in the wake of great ships, with no very clear idea of where they were being taken, proud and happy to be cleaving the waves and swelling out their new sails.

Placed by his birth and his wealth among the partisans of absolute royalty, Raymon made a sacrifice to the *youthful* ideas of his time by clinging religiously to the Charter; at all events that was what he thought that he was doing and what he exerted himself to prove. But conventions that have fallen into desuetude are subject to interpretation, and the Charter of Louis XVIII was already in the same plight as the Gospel of Jesus Christ; it was simply a text upon which everybody practised his powers of eloquence, and a speech thereon created a precedent no more than a sermon. A period of luxurious living and indolence, when civilization lay sleeping on the brink of a bottomless abyss, eager to enjoy its last pleasures.

Raymon had taken his stand upon the line between abuse of power and abuse of licence, a shifting ground upon which good men still sought, but in vain, a shelter from the tempest that was brewing. To him, as to many other experienced minds, the rôle of conscientious statesman still seemed possible. A manifest error at a time when people pretended to defer to the voice of reason only to stifle it the more surely on every side. Being without political passions, Raymon fancied that he was without interests to promote; but he was mistaken, for society, constituted as it then was, was agreeable and advantageous to him; it could not be disturbed without a diminution in the sum total of his well-being, and that perfect contentment with one's social position, which communicates itself to the thought, is a wonderful promoter of moderation. Who is so ungrateful to Providence as to reproach it for the misfortunes of other people, if it has only smiles and benefactions for him? How was it possible to persuade those young supporters of the constitutional monarchy that the constitution was already antiquated, that it weighed heavily on the social body and fatigued it, while they found its burdens light and reaped only its advantages?

Nothing is so easy and so common as to deceive one's self when one does not lack wit and is familiar with all the niceties of the language. Language is a prostitute queen who descends and rises to all rôles, disguises herself, arrays herself in fine apparel, hides her head and effaces herself; an advocate who has an answer for everything, who has always foreseen everything, and who assumes a thousand forms in order to be right. The most honorable of men is he who thinks best and acts best, but the most powerful is he who is best able to talk and write.

As his wealth relieved him from the necessity of writing for money, Raymon wrote from a liking for it, and–he said it with perfect good faith–from a sense of duty. The rare faculty that he possessed, of refuting positive truth by sheer talent, had made him an invaluable man to the ministry, whom he served much better by his impartial criticism than did its creatures by their blind devotion; and even more invaluable to that fashionable young society which was quite willing to abjure the absurdities of its former privileges, but wished at the same time to retain the benefit of its present advantageous position.

They were in very truth men of great talent who still supported society, tottering on the brink of the precipice, and who, being themselves suspended between two reefs, struggled calmly and with perfect self-possession against the harsh reality that was on the point of engulfing them. To succeed in such wise as to create a conviction against every sort of probability and to keep that conviction alive for some time among men of no convictions, is the art which most impresses and surpasses the understanding of an uncultivated, vulgar mind which has studied none but commonplace truths.

Thus Raymon had no sooner returned to that society, which was his element and his home, than he felt its vital and exciting influences. The petty love affairs that had engrossed him vanished for a moment in the face of broader and more brilliant interests. He carried into these the same boldness of attack, the same ardor; and when he saw that he was more eagerly sought than ever by all the most distinguished people in Paris, he felt that he loved life more than ever. Was he to be blamed for forgetting a secret remorse while reaping the reward he had merited for services rendered his country? He felt life overflowing through every pore of his young heart, his active brain, his whole vigorous and buoyant being, he felt that destiny was making him happy in spite of himself; and he would crave forgiveness of an indignant ghost that came sometimes and bewailed her fate in his dreams, for having sought in the affection of the living a protection against the terrors of the grave.

But he had no sooner returned to life, as it were, than he felt, as in the past, the need of mingling thoughts of love and plans of intrigue with his political meditations, his dreams of ambition and philosophy. I say ambition, not meaning ambition for honor and wealth, for which he had no use, but for reputation and aristocratic popularity.

He had at first despaired of ever seeing Madame Delmare again after the tragic ending of his double intrigue. But, as he measured the extent of his loss, as he brooded over the thought of the treasure that had escaped him, he conceived the hope of grasping it once more, and, at the same time he regained determination and confidence. He calculated the obstacles he should encounter, and realized that the most difficult to overcome at the outset would come from Indiana herself; therefore he must use the husband to protect him from the attack. This was not a new idea, but it was sure; jealous husbands are particularly well adapted to this service.

A fortnight after he had conceived this idea, Raymon was on the way to Lagny, where he was expected to breakfast. You will not require me to describe to you in detail the shrewdly proffered services by which he had succeeded in making himself agreeable to Monsieur Delmare; I prefer, as I am describing the features of the characters in this tale, to draw a hasty sketch of the colonel for you.

Do you know what they call an *honest man* in the provinces? He is a man who does not encroach on his neighbor's field; who does not demand from his debtors a sou more than they owe him; who raises his hat to every person who bows to him; who does not ravish maidens in the public roads; who sets fire to no other man's barn; who does not rob wayfarers at the corner of his park. Provided that he religiously respects the lives and purses of his fellow-citizens, nothing more is demanded of him. He may beat his wife, maltreat his servants, ruin his children, and it is nobody's business. Society punishes only those acts which are injurious to it; private life is beyond its jurisdiction.

Such was Monsieur Delmare's theory of morals. He had never studied any other social contract than this: *Every man is master in his own house*. He treated all affairs of the heart as feminine puerilities, sentimental subtleties. Being a man devoid of wit, of tact and of education, he enjoyed greater consideration than a man obtains by dint of talent and amiability. He had broad shoulders and a strong wrist; he handled the sword and the sabre perfectly, and was exceedingly quick to take offence. As he did not always understand a joke, he was constantly haunted by the idea that people were making fun of him. Being incapable of suitable repartee, he had but one way of defending himself: to enforce silence by threats. His favorite epigrams always turned upon cow-hidings to be administered and affairs of honor to be settled; wherefore the province always prefixed to his name the epithet *brave*, because military valor apparently consists in having broad shoulders and long moustaches, in swearing fiercely, and in putting one's hand to the sword on the slightest pretext.

God forbid that I should believe that camp life makes all men brutes! but I may be permitted to believe that one must have a large stock of tact and discretion to resist the habit of passive and brutal domination. If you have served in the army, you are familiar with what the troops call *skin-breeches*, and will agree that there are large numbers of them among the remains of the old imperial cohorts. Those men who, when brought together and urged forward by a powerful hand, performed such magnificent exploits, towered like giants amid the smoke of the battle-field; but, having returned to civil life, the heroes became mere soldiers once more, bold, vulgar fellows who reasoned like machines; and it was fortunate if they did not behave in society as in conquered territory. It was the fault of the age rather than theirs. Ingenuous minds, they had faith in the adulation of victory, and allowed themselves to be persuaded that they were great patriots because they defended their country–some against their will, others for money and honors. But how did they defend it, those tens of thousands of men who blindly embraced the error of a single man, and who, after saving their country, basely destroyed it? And again, if a soldier's devotion to his captain seems to you a great and noble thing, well and good, so it does to me; but I call that fidelity, not patriotism. I congratulate the conquerors of Spain, I do not thank them. As for the honor of the French name, I by no means understand that method of safeguarding it among neighbors, and I find it difficult to believe that the Emperor's generals were very deeply engrossed by it at that deplorable stage of our glory; but I know that we are forbidden to discuss these matters impartially; I hold my peace, posterity will pass judgment on them.

Monsieur Delmare had all the good qualities and all the failings of these men. He was innocent to childishness concerning certain refinements of the point of honor, yet he was very well able to conduct his affairs to the best possible end without disturbing himself as to the good or evil which might result therefrom to others. His whole conscience was the law; his whole moral code was his rights under the law. His was one of those rigid, unbending probities which never borrow for fear of not returning, and never lend for fear of not recovering. He was the honest man who neither takes nor gives aught; who would rather die than steal a bundle of sticks in the king's forest, but would kill you without ceremony for picking up a twig in his. He was useful to himself alone, harmful to nobody. He took part in nothing that was going on about him, lest he might be compelled to do somebody a favor. But, when he deemed himself in honor bound to do it, no one could go about it with more energy and zeal and a more chivalrous spirit. At once trustful as a child and suspicious as a despot, he would believe a false oath and distrust a sincere promise. As in the military profession, form was everything with him. Public opinion governed him so exclusively that common sense and argument counted for nothing in his decisions, and when he said: "Such things are done," he thought that he had stated an irrefutable argument.

Thus it will be seen that his nature was most antipathetic to his wife's, his heart entirely unfitted to understand her, his mind entirely incapable of appreciating her. And yet it is certain that slavery had engendered in her woman's heart a sort of virtuous and unspoken aversion which was not always just. Madame Delmare doubted her husband's heart overmuch; he was only harsh and she deemed him cruel. There was more roughness than anger in his outbreaks, more vulgarity than impertinence in his manners. Nature had not made him evil-minded: he had moments of compassion which led him to repentance, and in his repentance he was almost sensitive. It was camp life that had raised brutality to a principle in him. With a less refined, less gentle wife he would have been as gentle as a tame wolf; but this woman was disheartened with her fate; she did not take the trouble to try to make it happier.

XI

As he alighted from his tilbury in the courtyard at Lagny, Raymon's heart failed him. So he was once more to enter that house which recalled such awful memories! His arguments, being in accord with his passions, might enable him to overcome the impulses of his heart, but not to stifle them, and at that moment the sensation of remorse was as keen as that of desire.

The first person who came forward to meet him was Sir Ralph Brown, and when he spied him in his everlasting hunting costume, flanked by his hounds and sober as a Scotch laird, he fancied that the portrait he had seen in Madame Delmare's chamber was walking before his eyes. A few moments later the colonel appeared, and the breakfast was served without Indiana. As he passed through the vestibule, by the door of the billiard room, and recognized the places he had previously seen under such different circumstances, Raymon was so distressed that he could hardly remember why he had come there now.

"Is Madame Delmare really not coming down?" the colonel asked his factotum Lelièvre, with some asperity.

"Madame slept badly," replied Lelièvre, "and Mademoiselle Noun–that devil of a name keeps coming to my tongue!–Mademoiselle Fanny, I mean, just told me that madame is lying down now."

"How does it happen then that I just saw her at her window? Fanny is mistaken. Go and tell madame that breakfast is served; or stay–Sir Ralph, my dear kinsman, be pleased to go up and see for yourself if your cousin is really ill."

While the unfortunate name that the servant had mentioned from habit caused Raymon's nerves a painful thrill, the colonel's expedient caused him a strange sensation of jealous anger.

"In her bedroom!" he thought. "He doesn't confine himself to hanging the man's portrait there, but sends him there in person. This Englishman has privileges here which the husband himself seems to be afraid to claim."

"Don't let that surprise you," said Monsieur Delmare, as if he had divined Raymon's reflections; "Monsieur Brown is the family physician; and then he's our cousin too, a fine fellow whom we love with all our hearts."

Ralph remained absent ten minutes. Raymon was distraught, ill at ease. He did not eat and kept looking at the door. At last the Englishman reappeared.

"Indiana is really ill," he said, "I told her to go back to bed."

He took his seat tranquilly and ate with a robust appetite. The colonel did likewise.

"This is evidently a pretext to avoid seeing me," thought Raymon. "These two men don't suspect it, and the husband is more displeased than worried about his wife's condition. Good! my affairs are progressing more favorably than I hoped."

This resistance rearoused his determination and Noun's image vanished from the dismal hangings, which, at the beginning, had congealed his blood with terror. Soon he saw nothing but Madame Delmare's slender form. In the salon he sat at her embroidery frame, examined the flowers she was making–talking all the while and feigning deep interest–handled all the silks, inhaled the perfume her tiny fingers had left upon them. He had seen the same piece of work before, in Indiana's bedroom; then it was hardly begun, now it was covered with flowers that had bloomed beneath the breath of fever, watered by her daily tears. Raymon felt the tears coming to his own eyes, and, by virtue of some unexplained sympathy, sadly raising his eyes to the horizon, at which Indiana was in the habit of gazing in melancholy mood, he saw in the distance the white walls of Cercy standing out against a background of dark hills.

The colonel's voice roused him with a start.

"Well, my excellent neighbor," he said, "it is time for me to pay my debt to you and keep my promises. The factory is in full swing and the hands are all at work. Here are paper and pencils, so that you can take notes."

Raymon followed the colonel, inspected the factory with an eager, interested air, made comments which proved that chemistry and mechanics were equally familiar to him, listened with incredible patience to Monsieur Delmare's endless dissertations, coincided with some of his ideas, combated some others, and in every respect so conducted himself as to persuade his guide that he took an absorbing interest in these things, whereas he was hardly thinking of them and all his thoughts were directed toward Madame Delmare.

It was a fact that he was familiar with every branch of knowledge, that no invention was without interest for him; moreover he was forwarding the interests of his brother, who had really embarked his whole fortune in a similar enterprise, although of much greater extent. Monsieur Delmare's technical knowledge, his only claim to superiority, pointed out to him at that moment the best method of taking advantage of this interview.

Sir Ralph, who was a poor business man but a very shrewd politician, suggested during the inspection of the factory some economical considerations of considerable importance. The workmen, being anxious to display their skill to an expert, surpassed themselves in deftness and activity. Raymon looked at everything, heard everything, answered everything, and thought of nothing but the love affair that brought him to that place.

When they had exhausted the subject of machinery the discussion fell upon the volume and force of the stream. They went out and climbed upon the dam, bidding the overseer raise the gates and mark the different depths.

"Monsieur," said the man, addressing Monsieur Delmare, who fixed the maximum at fifteen feet, "I beg pardon, but we had it seventeen once this year."

"When was that? You are mistaken," said the colonel.

XI

"Excuse me, monsieur, it was on the eve of your return from Belgium, the very night Mademoiselle Noun was found drowned; what I say is proved by the fact that the body passed over that dike yonder and did not stop until it got here, just where monsieur is standing."

Speaking thus, with much animation, the man pointed to where Raymon stood. The unhappy young man turned pale as death; he cast a horrified glance at the water flowing at his feet; it seemed to him that the livid face was reflected in it, that the body was still floating there; he had an attack of vertigo and would have fallen into the river had not Monsieur Brown caught his arm and pulled him away.

"Very good," said the colonel, who noticed nothing, and who gave so little thought to Noun that he did not suspect Raymon's emotion; "but that was an extraordinary instance, and the average depth of the water is– But what the devil's the matter with you two?" he inquired, suddenly interrupting himself.

"Nothing," replied Sir Ralph; "as I turned I trod on monsieur's foot; I am distressed, for I must have hurt him terribly."

Sir Ralph made this reply in so calm and natural a tone that Raymon was convinced that he thought he was telling the truth. A few courteous words were exchanged and the conversation resumed its course.

Raymon left Lagny a few hours later without seeing Madame Delmare. It was better than he hoped; he had feared that he should find her calm and indifferent.

However he repeated his visit with no better success. That time the colonel was alone; Raymon put forth all the resources of his wit to captivate him, and shrewdly descended to innumerable little acts of condescension–praised Napoléon, whom he did not like, deplored the indifference of the government, which left the illustrious remnant of the Grande Armée in oblivion and something like contempt, carried opposition tenets as far as his opinions would permit him to go, and selected from his various beliefs those which were likely to flatter Monsieur Delmare's. He even provided himself with a character different from his real one, in order to attract his confidence. He transformed himself into a *bon vivant*, a "hail fellow well met," a careless good-for-naught.

"What if that fellow should ever make a conquest of my wife!" said the colonel to himself as he watched him drive away.

Then he began to chuckle inwardly and to think that Raymon was a *charming fellow.*

Madame de Ramière was at Cercy at this time: Raymon extolled Madame Delmare's charms and wit to her, and without urging her to call upon her, had the art to suggest the thought.

"I believe she is the only one of my neighbors whom I do not know," she said; "and as I am a new arrival in the neighborhood it is my place to begin. We will go to Lagny together next week."

The appointed day arrived.

"She cannot avoid me now," thought Raymon.

In truth Madame Delmare could not escape the necessity of receiving him, for when she saw an elderly woman she did not know step from the carriage, she went out on the stoop herself to meet her. At the same moment she recognized Raymon in the man who accompanied her; but she realized that he must have deceived his mother to induce her to take that step, and her displeasure on that ac-account gave her strength to be dignified and calm. She received Madame de Ramière with a mixture of respect and affability; but her coldness to Raymon was so absolutely glacial that he felt that he could not long endure it. He was not accustomed to disdain and his pride took fire at being unable to conquer with a glance those who were prepossessed against him. Thereupon, deciding upon his course like a man who cared nothing for a woman's whim, he asked permission to join Monsieur Delmare in the park and left the two women together.

Little by little, vanquished by the charm which a superior intellect, combined with a noble and generous heart, is capable of exerting even in its least intimate relations, Indiana became affable, affectionate and almost playful with Madame de Ramière. She had never known her mother, and Madame de Carvajal, despite her presents and her words of praise, was far from being a mother to her; so she felt a sort of fascination of the heart with Raymon's mother.

When he joined her as she was stepping into her carriage he saw Indiana put to her lips the hand that Madame de Ramière offered her. Poor Indiana felt the need of having some one to cling to. Everything that offered a prospect of interest and of companionship in her lonely and unhappy life was welcomed by her with the keenest delight; and then she said to herself that Madame de Ramière would preserve her from the snare into which Raymon sought to lure her.

"I will throw myself into this good woman's arms," she was thinking already, "and, if necessary, I will tell her everything. I will implore her to save me from her son, and her prudence will stand guard over him and over me."

Such was not Raymon's reasoning.

"Dear mother!" he said to himself, as he drove back with her to Cercy, "her charm and her goodness of heart perform miracles. What do I not owe to them already! my education, my success in life, my standing in society. I lacked nothing but the happiness of owing to her the heart of such a woman as Indiana."

Raymon, as we see, loved his mother because of his need of her and of the well-being he owed to her; so do all children love their mothers.

A few days later Raymon received an invitation to pass three days at Bellerive, a beautiful country seat owned by Sir Ralph Brown, between Cercy and Lagny, where it was proposed, in concert with the best hunters of the neighborhood, to destroy a part of the game that was devouring the owner's woods and gardens. Raymon liked neither Sir Ralph nor hunting, but Madame Delmare did the honors of her cousin's house on great occasions, and the hope of meeting her soon decided Raymon to accept the invitation.

The fact was that Sir Ralph did not expect Madame Delmare on this occasion; she had excused herself on the ground of her wretched health. But the colonel, who took umbrage when his wife sought diversion on her own account, took still greater umbrage when she declined such diversions as he chose to allow her.

XI

"Do you want to make the whole province think that I keep you under lock and key?" he said to her. "You make me appear like a jealous husband; it's an absurd role and one that I do not propose to play any longer. Besides, what does this lack of courtesy to your cousin mean? Does it become you, when we owe to his friendship the establishment and prosperity of our business, to refuse him such a service? You are necessary to him and you hesitate! I cannot understand your whims. All the people whom I don't like are sure of a hearty welcome from you; but those whom I esteem are unfortunate enough not to please you."

"That reproach has very little application to the present case, I should say," replied Madame Delmare. "I love my cousin like a brother, and my affection for him was of long standing when yours began."

"Oh! yes, yes, more of your fine words; but I know that you don't find him sentimental enough, the poor devil! you call him selfish because he doesn't like novels and doesn't cry over the death of a dog. However, he's not the only one. How did you receive Monsieur de Ramière? a charming young fellow, on my word! Madame de Carvajal introduces him to you and you receive him with the greatest affability; but I have the ill-luck to think well of him and you pronounce him unendurable, and when he calls upon you, you go to bed! Are you trying to make me appear a perfect boor? It is time for this to come to an end and for you to begin to live like other people."

Raymon deemed it inadvisable, in view of his plans, to show too much eagerness; threats of indifference are successful with almost all women who think that they are loved. But the hunting had been in progress since morning when he reached Sir Ralph's, and Madame Delmare was not expected until dinner time. He employed the interval in preparing a plan of action.

It occurred to him that he must find some method of justifying his conduct, for the critical moment was at hand. He had two days before him and he determined to apportion the time thus: the rest of the day that was nearly ended to make an impression, the next day to persuade and the following day to be happy. He even consulted his watch and calculated almost to an hour the time when his enterprise would succeed or fail.

XII

He had been two hours in the salon when he heard Madame Delmare's sweet and slightly husky voice in the adjoining room. By dint of reflecting on his scheme of seduction he had become as passionately interested as an author in his subject or a lawyer in his cause, and the emotion that he felt at the sight of Indiana may be compared to that of an actor thoroughly imbued with the spirit of his role who finds himself in the presence of the principal character of the drama and can no longer distinguish artificial stage effects from reality.

She was so changed that a feeling of sincere compassion found its way into Raymon's being, amid the nervous tremors of his brain. Unhappiness and illness had left such deep traces on her face that she was hardly pretty, and that he felt that there was more glory than pleasure to be gained by the conquest. But he owed it to himself to restore this woman to life and happiness.

Seeing how pale and sad she was, he judged that he had no very strong will to contend against. Was it possible that such a frail envelope could conceal great power of moral resistance?

He reflected that it was necessary first of all to interest her in herself, to frighten her concerning her depression and her failing health, in order the more easily to open her mind to the desire and the hope of a better destiny.

"Indiana!" he began, with secret assurance perfectly concealed beneath an air of profound melancholy, "to think that I should find you in such a condition as this! I did not dream that this moment to which I have looked forward so long, which I have sought so eagerly, would cause me such horrible pain!"

Madame Delmare hardly anticipated this language; she expected to surprise Raymon in the attitude of a confused and shrinking culprit; and lo! instead of accusing himself–of telling her of his grief and repentance–his sorrow and pity were all for her! She must be sorely cast down and broken in spirit to inspire compassion in a man who should have implored hers!

A French woman–a woman of the world–would not have lost her head at such a delicate juncture; but Indiana had no tact; possessed neither the skill nor the power of dissimulation necessary to preserve the advantage of her position. His words brought before her eyes the whole picture of her sufferings and tears glistened on the edge of her eyelids.

"I am ill, in truth," she said, as she seated herself, feebly and wearily, in the chair Raymon offered her; "I feel that I am very ill, and, in your presence, monsieur, I have the right to complain."

XII

Raymon had not hoped to progress so fast. He seized the opportunity by the hair, as the saying is, and, taking possession of a hand which felt cold and dry in his, he replied:

"Indiana! do not say that; do not say that I am the cause of your illness, for you make me mad with grief and joy."

"And joy!" she repeated, fixing upon him her great blue eyes overflowing with melancholy and amazement.

"I should have said hope; for, if I have caused you unhappiness, madame, I can perhaps bring it to an end. Say a word," he added, kneeling beside her on a cushion that had fallen from the divan, "ask me for my blood, my life!"

"Oh! hush!" said Indiana bitterly, withdrawing her hand; "you made a shameful misuse of promises before; try to repair the evil you have done!"

"I intend to do it; I will do it!" he cried, trying to take her hand again.

"It is too late," she said. "Give me back my companion, my sister; give me back Noun, my only friend!"

A cold shiver ran through Raymon's veins. This time he had no need to encourage her emotion; there are emotions which awake unbidden, mighty and terrible, without the aid of art.

"She knows all," he thought, "and she has judged me."

Nothing could be more humiliating to him than to be reproached for his crime by the woman who had been his innocent accomplice; nothing more bitter than to see Noun's rival lamenting her death.

"Yes, monsieur," said Indiana, raising her face, down which the tears were streaming, "you were the cause–"

But she paused when she observed Raymon's pallor. It must have been most alarming, for he had never suffered so keenly.

Thereupon all the kindness of her heart and all the involuntary emotion which he aroused in her resumed their sway over Madame Delmare.

"Forgive me!" she said in dismay; "I hurt you terribly; I have suffered so myself! Sit down and let us talk of something else."

This sudden manifestation of her sweet and generous nature rendered Raymon's emotion deeper than ever. He sobbed aloud; he put Indiana's hand to his lips and covered it with tears and kisses. It was the first time that he had been able to weep since Noun's death, and it was Indiana who relieved his breast of that terrible weight.

"Oh! since you, who never knew her, weep for her so freely," she said; "since you regret so bitterly the injury you have done me, I dare not reproach you any more. Let us weep for her together, monsieur, so that, from her place in heaven, she may see us and forgive us."

Raymon's forehead was wet with cold perspiration. If the words *you who never knew her* had delivered him from painful anxiety, this appeal to his victim's memory, in Indiana's innocent mouth, terrified him with a superstitious terror. Sorely distressed, he rose and walked feverishly to a window and leaned on the sill to breathe the fresh air. Indiana remained in her chair, silent and deeply moved. She felt a sort of secret joy on seeing Raymon weep like a child and display the weakness of a woman.

"He is naturally kind," she murmured to herself; "he is fond of me; his heart is warm and generous. He did wrong, but his repentance expiates his fault, and I ought to have forgiven him sooner."

She gazed at him with a softened expression; her confidence in him had returned. She mistook the remorse of the guilty man for the repentance of love.

"Do not weep any more," she said, rising and walking up to him; "it was I who killed her; I alone am guilty. This remorse will sadden my whole life. I gave way to an impulse of suspicion and anger; I humiliated her, wounded her to the heart. I vented upon her all my spleen against you; it was you alone who had offended me, and I punished my poor friend for it. I was very hard to her!"

"And to me," said Raymon, suddenly forgetting the past to think only of the present.

Madame Delmare blushed.

"I should not perhaps have reproached you for the cruel loss I sustained on that awful night," she said; "but I cannot forget the imprudence of your conduct toward me. The lack of delicacy in your romantic and culpable project wounded me very deeply. I believed then that you loved me!–and you did not even respect me!"

Raymon recovered his strength, his determination, his love, his hopes; the sinister presentiment, which had made his blood run cold, vanished like a nightmare. He awoke once more, young, ardent, overflowing with desire, with passion, and with hopes for the future.

"I am guilty if you hate me," he said, vehemently, throwing himself at her feet; "but, if you love me, I am not guilty–I never have been. Tell me, Indiana, do you love me?"

"Do you deserve it?" she asked.

"If, in order to deserve it," said Raymon, "I must love you to adoration–"

"Listen to me," she said, abandoning her hands to him and fastening upon him her great eyes, swimming in tears, wherein a sombre flame gleamed at intervals. "Do you know what it is to love a woman like me? No, you do not know. You thought that it was merely a matter of gratifying the caprice of a day. You judged my heart by all the surfeited hearts over which you have hitherto exerted your ephemeral domination. You do not know that I have never loved as yet and that I will not give my untouched virgin heart in exchange for a ruined, withered heart, my enthusiastic love for a lukewarm love, my whole life for one brief day!"

"Madame, I love you passionately; my heart too is young and ardent, and, if it is not worthy of yours, no man's heart will ever be. I know how you must be loved; I have not waited until this day to find out. Do I not know your life? did I not describe it to you at the ball, the first time that I ever had the privilege of speaking to you? Did I not read the whole history of your heart in the first one of your glances that ever fell upon me? And with what did I fall in love, think you? with your beauty alone? Ah! that is surely enough to drive an older and less passionate man to frenzy; but for my part, if I adore that gracious and charming envelope, it is because it encloses a pure and divine soul, it is because a celestial fire quickens it, and because I see in you not a woman simply, but an angel."

"I know that you possess the art of praising; but do not hope to move my vanity. I have no need of homage, but of affection. I must be loved without a rival, without reserve and forever; you must be ready to sacrifice everything to me, fortune, reputation, duty, business, principles, family–everything, monsieur, because I shall place the same absolute devotion in my scale, and I wish them to balance. You see that you cannot love me like that!"

It was not the first time that Raymon had seen a woman take love seriously, although such cases are rare, luckily for society; but he knew that promises of love do not bind the honor, again luckily for society. Sometimes too the women who had demanded from him these solemn pledges had been the first to break them. He did not take fright therefore at Madame Delmare's demands, or rather he gave no thought either to the past or the future. He was borne along by the irresistible fascination of that frail, passionate woman, so weak in body, so resolute in heart and mind. She was so beautiful, so animated, so imposing as she dictated her laws to him, that he remained as if fascinated at her knees.

"I swear," he said, "that I will be yours body and soul; I devote my life, I consecrate my blood to you, I place my will at your service; take everything, do as you will with my fortune, my honor, my conscience, my thoughts, my whole being."

"Hush! "said Indiana hastily, "here is my cousin."

As she spoke the phlegmatic Sir Ralph Brown entered the room with his usual tranquil air, expressing great surprise and pleasure to see his cousin, whom he had not hoped to see. Then he asked permission to kiss her by way of manifesting his gratitude, and, leaning over her with methodical moderation, he kissed her on the lips, according to the custom among children in his country.

Raymon turned pale with anger and Ralph had no sooner left the room to give some order, than he went to Indiana and tried to remove all trace of that impertinent kiss. But Madame Delmare calmly pushed him away.

"Remember," she said, "that you owe much reparation if you wish me to believe in you."

Raymon did not understand the delicacy of this rebuff; he saw in it nothing but a rebuff and he was angry with Sir Ralph. Shortly after he noticed that, when Sir Ralph spoke to Indiana in an undertone, he used the more familiar form of address, and he was on the verge of mistaking the reserve which custom imposed upon Sir Ralph at other times, for the precaution of a favored lover. But he blushed for his insulting suspicions as soon as he met the young woman's pure glance.

That evening Raymon displayed his intellectual powers. There was a large company and people listened to him; he could not escape the prominence which his talents gave him. He talked, and if Indiana had been vain she would have had her first taste of happiness in listening to him. But on the contrary her simple, straightforward mind took fright at Raymon's superiority; she struggled against the magic power which he exerted over all about him, a sort of magnetic influence which heaven, or hell, accords to certain men–a partial and ephemeral royalty, so real that no mediocre mind can escape its ascendancy, so fleeting that no trace of it remains after them, and that when they die we are amazed at the sensation they made during their lives.

There were many times when Indiana was fascinated by such a brilliant display; but she at once said to herself sadly that she was eager for happiness, not for glory. She asked herself in dismay if this man, for whom life had so many different aspects, so many absorbing interests, could devote his whole mind to her, sacrifice all his ambitions to her. And while he defended step by step, with such courage and skill, such ardor and self-possession, doctrines purely speculative and interests entirely foreign to their love, she was terrified to see that she was of so little account in his life while he was everything in hers. She said to herself in terror that she was to him a three days' fancy and that he had been to her the dream of a whole life.

When he offered her his arm as they were leaving the salon, he whispered a few words of love in her ear; but she answered sadly:

"You have a great mind!"

Raymon understood the reproof and passed the whole of the following day at Madame Delmare's feet. The other guests, being engrossed by their hunting, left them entirely to themselves.

Raymon was eloquent; Indiana had such a craving to believe, that half of his eloquence was wasted. Women of France, you do not know what a creole is; you would undoubtedly have yielded less readily to conviction, for you are not the ones to be deceived or betrayed!

XIII

When Sir Ralph returned from hunting and as usual felt Madame Delmare's pulse, Raymon, who was watching him closely, detected an almost imperceptible expression of surprise and pleasure on his placid features. And then, in obedience to some mysterious secret impulse, the two men looked at each other, and Sir Ralph's light eyes, fastened like an owl's upon Raymon's black ones, forced them to look down. During the rest of the day the baronet's manner toward Madame Delmare, beneath his apparent imperturbability, was keenly observant, indicative of something which might be called interest or solicitude if his face had been capable of reflecting a decided sentiment. But Raymon exerted himself in vain to discover if fear or hope were uppermost in his thoughts; Ralph was impenetrable.

Suddenly, as he stood a few steps behind Madame Delmare's chair, he heard her cousin say to her in an undertone:

"You would do well, cousin, to go out in the saddle to-morrow."

"Why, I have no horse just now, as you know," she said.

"We will find one for you. Will you hunt with us?"

Madame Delmare resorted to various pretexts to escape. Raymon understood that she preferred to remain with him, but he thought at the same time that her cousin seemed to display extraordinary persistence in preventing her from doing so. So he left the persons with whom he was talking, walked up to her and joined Sir Ralph in urging her to go. He had a feeling of bitter resentment against this importunate chaperon, and determined to tire out his watchfulness.

"If you will agree to follow the hunt," he said to Indiana, "you will embolden me to follow your example, Madame. I care little for hunting; but to have the privilege of being your esquire–"

"In that case I will go," replied Indiana, heedlessly.

She exchanged a meaning glance with Raymon; but, swift as it was, Sir Ralph caught it on the wing, and Raymon was unable, during the rest of the evening, to glance at her or address her without encountering Monsieur Brown's eyes or ears.

A feeling of aversion, almost of jealousy, arose in his heart. By what right did this cousin, this friend of the family, assume to act as a school-master with the woman whom *he* loved! He swore that Sir Ralph should repent, and he sought an opportunity to insult him without compromising Madame Delmare; but that was impossible. Sir Ralph did the honors of his establishment with a cold and dignified courtesy which offered no handle for an epigram or a contradiction.

The next morning, before the rising-bell had rung, Raymon was surprised to see his host's solemn face enter his room. There was something even stiffer than usual in his manner, and Raymon felt his heart beat fast with longing and impatience at the prospect of a challenge. But he came simply to talk about a horse which Raymon had brought to Bellerive and had expressed a desire to sell. The bargain was concluded in five minutes; Sir Ralph made no objection to the price but produced a *rouleau* of gold from his pocket and counted down the amount on the mantel with a coolness of manner that was altogether extraordinary, not deigning to pay any heed to Raymon's remonstrances concerning such scrupulous promptness. As he was leaving the room, he turned back to say:

"Monsieur, the horse belongs to me from this morning!"

At that Raymon fancied that he could detect a purpose to prevent him from hunting, and he observed dryly that he did not propose to follow the hunt on foot.

"Monsieur," replied Sir Ralph, with a slight trace of affectation, "I am too well versed in the laws of hospitality."

And he withdrew.

On going down into the courtyard Raymon saw Madame Delmare in her riding-habit, playing merrily with Ophelia, who was tearing her handkerchief. Her cheeks had taken on a faint rosy tinge, her eyes shone with a brilliancy that had long been absent from them. She had already recovered her beauty; her curly black hair escaped from beneath her little hat, in which she was charming; and the cloth habit buttoned to the chin outlined her slender, graceful figure. The principal charm of the Creoles, to my mind, consists in the fact that the excessive delicacy of their features and their proportions enables them to retain for a long while the daintiness of childhood. Indiana, in her gay and laughing mood, seemed to be no more than fourteen.

Raymon, impressed by her charms, felt a thrill of triumph and paid her the least insipid compliment he could invent upon her beauty.

"You were anxious about my health," she said to him in an undertone; "do you not see that I long to live?"

He could not reply otherwise than by a happy, grateful glance. Sir Ralph himself brought his cousin her horse; Raymon recognized the one he had just sold.

"What!" said Madame Delmare in amazement, for she had seen him trying the animal the day before in the courtyard, "is Monsieur de Ramière so polite as to lend me his horse?"

"Did you not admire the creature's beauty and docility yesterday?" said Sir Ralph; "he is yours from this moment. I am sorry, my dear, that I couldn't have given him to you sooner."

"You are growing facetious, cousin," said Madame Delmare; "I do not understand this joke at all. Whom am I to thank–Monsieur de Ramière, who consents to lend me his horse, or you, who perhaps asked him for it?"

"You must thank your cousin," said Monsieur Delmare, "who bought this horse for you and makes you a present of him."

XIII

"Is it really true, my dear Ralph?" said Madame Delmare, patting the pretty creature with the delight of a girl at receiving her first jewels.

"Didn't we agree that I should give you a horse in exchange for the piece of embroidery you are doing for me? Come, mount him, have no fear. I have studied his disposition, and I tried him only this morning."

Indiana threw her arms around Sir Ralph's neck, then leaped upon Raymon's horse and fearlessly made him prance.

This whole domestic scene took place in a corner of the courtyard before Raymon's eyes. He was conscious of a paroxysm of violent anger when the simple and trustful affection of those two displayed itself before him; passionately in love as he was and with less than a whole day in which to have Indiana to himself.

"How happy I am!" she said, calling him to her side on the avenue. "It seems my dear Ralph divined what gift would be most precious to me. And aren't you happy too, Raymon, to see the horse you have ridden pass into my hands? Oh I how I will love him and care for him! What do you call him? Tell me; for I prefer not to take away the name you gave him."

"If there is a happy man here," rejoined Raymon, "it should be your cousin, who gives you presents and whom you kiss so heartily."

"Are you really jealous of our friendship and of those loud smacks?" she said with a laugh.

"Jealous? perhaps so, Indiana; I am not sure. But when that red-cheeked young cousin puts his lips to yours, when he takes you in his arms to seat you on the horse that he *gives* you and I *sell* you, I confess that I suffer. No, madame, I am not happy to see you the mistress of the horse I loved. I can understand that one might be happy in giving him to you; but to play the tradesman in order to provide another with the means of making himself agreeable to you, is a very cleverly managed humiliation on Sir Ralph's part. If I did not believe that all this cunning was quite involuntary, I would like to be revenged on him."

"Oh! fie! this jealousy is not becoming to you! How can our commonplace intimacy arouse any feeling in you, in you who should be, so far as I am concerned, outside of the common life of mankind and should create for me a world of enchantment–in you of all men! I am displeased with you already, Raymon; I perceive that there is something like wounded self-esteem in this angry feeling displayed toward this poor cousin. It seems to me that you are more jealous of the lukewarm preference which I display for him in public than of the exclusive affection which I might secretly entertain for another."

"Forgive me, forgive me, Indiana, I am wrong! I am not worthy of you, angel of goodness and gentleness! but I confess that I have suffered cruelly because of the right that man has seemed to assume."

"He assume rights, Raymon! Do you not know what sacred gratitude binds us to him? do you not know that his mother was my mother's sister? that we were born in the same valley; that in our early years he was my protector; that he was my mainstay, my only teacher, my only companion at Ile Bourbon; that he has followed me everywhere; that he left the country which I left, to come and live where I lived; in a word, that he is the only being who loves me and who takes any interest in my life?"

"Curse him! all that you tell me, Indiana, inflames the wound. So he loves you very dearly, does this Englishman, eh? Do you know how I love you?"

"Oh! let us not compare the two. If an attachment of the same nature made you rivals, I should owe the preference to the one of longer standing. But have no fear, Raymon, that I shall ever ask you to love me as Ralph loves me."

"Tell me about the man, I beg you; for who can penetrate his stone mask?"

"Must I do the honors for my cousin?" she said with a smile. "I confess that I do not altogether like the idea of describing him; I love him so dearly that I would like to flatter him; as he is, I am afraid that you will not find him a very noble figure. Do try to help me; come, how does he seem to you?"

"His face–forgive me if I wound you–indicates absolute nonentity; but there are signs of good sense and education in his conversation when he deigns to speak; but he speaks so hesitatingly, so coldly, that no one profits by his knowledge, his delivery is so depressing and tiresome. And then there is something commonplace and dull in his thoughts which is not redeemed by measured purity of expression. I think that his is a mind imbued with all the ideas that have been suggested to him, but too apathetic and too mediocre to have any of his own. He is just the sort of man that one must be to be looked upon in society as a serious-minded person. His gravity forms three-fourths of his merit, his indifference the rest."

"There is some truth in your portrait," said Indiana, "but there is prejudice too. You boldly solve doubts which I should not dare to solve, although I have known Ralph ever since I was born. It is true that his great defect consists in looking frequently through the eyes of others; but that is not the fault of his mind but of his education. You think that, without education, he would have been an absolute nonentity; I think that he would have been less so than he is. I must tell you one fact in his life which will help to explain his character. He was unfortunate to have a brother whom his parents openly preferred to him; this brother had all the brilliant qualities that he lacks. He learned easily, he had a taste for all the arts, he fairly sparkled with wit; his face, while less regular than Ralph's, was more expressive. He was affectionate, zealous, active, in a word, he was lovable. Ralph, on the contrary, was awkward, melancholy, undemonstrative; he loved solitude, learned slowly and did not make a display of what little knowledge he possessed. When his parents saw how different he was from his older brother, they maltreated him; they did worse than that: they humiliated him. Thereupon, child as he was, his character became gloomy and pensive and an unconquerable timidity paralyzed all his faculties. They had succeeded in inspiring in him self-aversion and self-contempt; he became discouraged with life, and, at the age of fifteen, he was attacked by the spleen, a malady that is wholly physical under the foggy sky of England, wholly mental under the revivifying sky of Ile Bourbon. He has often told me that one day he left the house with a determination to throw himself into the sea; but as he sat on the shore collecting his thoughts, as he was on the point of carrying out his plan, he saw me coming toward him in the arms of the negress who had been my nurse. I was then five years old. I was pretty, they say, and I manifested a predilection for my taciturn cousin which nobody shared. To be sure, he was attentive and kind to me in a way I was not accustomed to in my father's house. As we were both unhappy, we understood each other even then. He taught me his father's language, and I lisped mine to him. This blending of Spanish and English may be said to express Ralph's character. When I threw my arms around his neck, I saw that he was weeping, and, without knowing why, I began to weep too. Thereupon he pressed me to his heart and, so he told me afterward, made a vow to live for me, a neglected if not hated child, to whom his friendship would at all events be a kindness and his life of some benefit. Thus I was the first and only tie in his sad life. After that day we were hardly ever apart; we passed our days leading a free and healthy life in the solitude of the mountains. But perhaps these tales of our childhood bore you, and you would prefer to join the hunt and have a gallop."

"Foolish girl," said Raymon, seizing the bridle of Madame Delmare's horse.

"Very well, I will go on," said she. "Edmond Brown, Ralph's older brother, died at the age of twenty; his mother also died of grief, and his father was inconsolable. Ralph would have been glad to mitigate his sorrow, but the coldness with which Monsieur Brown greeted his first attempts increased his natural timidity. He passed whole hours in melancholy silence beside that heartbroken old man, not daring to proffer a word or a caress, he was so afraid that his consolation would seem misplaced or trivial. His father accused him of lack of feeling, and Edmond's death left Ralph more wretched and more misunderstood than ever. I was his only consolation."

"I cannot pity him, whatever you may do," Raymon interrupted; "but there is one thing in his life and yours that I cannot understand: it is that you never married."

"I can give you a very good reason for that," she replied. "When I reached a marriageable age, Ralph, who was ten years older than I–an enormous difference in our climate, where the childhood of girls is so brief–Ralph, I say, was already married."

"Is Sir Ralph a widower? I never heard anyone mention his wife."

"Never mention her to him. She was young and rich and lovely, but she had been in love with Edmond–she had been betrothed to him; and when, in order to serve family interests and family sentiment, she was made to marry Ralph, she did not so much as try to conceal her aversion for him. He was obliged to go to England with her, and when he returned to Ile Bourbon after his wife's death, I was married to Monsieur Delmare and just about to start for Europe. Ralph tried to live alone, but solitude aggravated his misery. Although he has never mentioned Mistress Ralph Brown to me, I have every reason to believe that he was even more unhappy in his married life than he had been in his father's house, and that his natural melancholy was increased by recent and painful memories. He was attacked with the spleen again; whereupon he sold his coffee plantation and came to France to settle down. His manner of introducing himself to my husband was original, and would have made me laugh if my good Ralph's attachment had not touched me deeply. 'Monsieur,' he said, 'I love your wife; it was I who brought her up; I look upon her as my sister and even more as my daughter. She is my only remaining relative and the only person to whom I am attached. Allow me to establish myself near you and let us three pass our lives together. They say that you are a little jealous of your wife, but they say also that you are a man of honor and uprightness. When I tell you that I have never had any other than brotherly love for her, and that I shall never have, you can regard me with as little anxiety as if I were really your brother-in-law. Isn't it so, monsieur?' Monsieur Delmare, who is very proud of his reputation for soldierly frankness, greeted this outspoken declaration with a sort of ostentatious confidence. But several months of careful watching were necessary before that confidence became as genuine as he boasted that it was. Now it is as impregnable as Ralph's steadfast and pacific heart."

"Are you perfectly sure, Indiana," said Raymon, "that Sir Ralph is not deceiving himself the least bit in the world when he swears that he never loved you?"

"1 was twelve years old when he left Ile Bourbon to go with his wife to England; I was sixteen when he returned to find me married, and he manifested more joy than sorrow. Now, Ralph is really an old man."

"At twenty-nine?"

"Don't laugh at what I say. His face is young, but his heart is worn out by suffering, and he no longer loves anybody, in order to avoid suffering."

"Not even you?"

"Not even me. His friendship is simply a matter of habit; it was generous in the old days when he took upon himself to protect and educate my childhood, and then I loved him as he loves me to-day because of the need I had of him. To-day my whole heart is bent upon paying my debt to him, and my life is passed in trying to beautify and enliven his. But, when I was a child, I loved him with the instinct rather than with the heart, and he, now that he is a man, loves me less with the heart than with the instinct. I am necessary to him because I am almost alone in loving him; and to-day, as Monsieur Delmare manifests some attachment to him, he is almost as fond of him as of me. His protection, formerly so fearless in face of my father's despotism, has become lukewarm and cautious in face of my husband's. He never reproaches himself because I suffer, provided that I am near him. He does not ask himself if I am unhappy; it is enough for him to see that I am alive. He does not choose to lend me a support, which, while it would make my lot less cruel, would disturb his serenity by making trouble between him and Monsieur Delmare. By dint of hearing himself say again and again that his heart is dry, he has persuaded himself that it is true, and his heart has withered in the inaction in which he has allowed it to fall asleep from distrust. He is a man whom the affection of another person might have developed; but it was withdrawn from him and he shrivelled up. Now he asserts that happiness consists in repose, pleasure, in the comforts of life. He asks no questions about cares that he has not. I must say the word: Ralph is selfish."

"Very good, so much the better," said Raymon; "I am no longer afraid of him; indeed I will love him if you wish."

"Yes, love him, Raymon," she replied; "he will appreciate it; and, so far as we are concerned, let us never trouble ourselves to explain why people love us, but how they love us. Happy the man who can be loved, no matter for what reason!"

"What you say, Indiana," replied Raymon, grasping her slender, willowy form, "is the lament of a sad and solitary heart; but, in my case, I want you to know both why and how, especially why."

"To give me happiness, is it not?" she said, with a sad but passionate glance.

"To give you my life," said Raymon, brushing Indiana's floating hair with his lips.

A blast upon the horn near by warned them to be on their guard; it was Sir Ralph, who saw them or did not see them.

XIV

Raymon was amazed at what seemed to take place in Indiana's being as soon as the hounds were away. Her eyes gleamed, her cheeks flushed, the dilation of her nostrils betrayed an indefinable thrill of fear or pleasure, and suddenly, driving her spurs into her horse's side, she left him and galloped after Ralph. Raymon did not know that hunting was the only passion that Ralph and Indiana had in common. Nor did he suspect that in that frail and apparently timid woman there abode a more than masculine courage, that sort of delirious intrepidity which sometimes manifests itself like a nervous paroxysm in the feeblest creatures. Women rarely have the physical courage which consists in offering the resistance of inertia to pain or danger; but they often have the moral courage which attains its climax in peril or suffering. Indiana's delicate fibres delighted above all things in the tumult, the rapid movement and the excitement of the chase, that miniature image of war with its fatigues, its stratagems, its calculations, its hazards and its battles. Her dull, ennui-laden life needed this excitement; at such times she seemed to wake from a lethargy and to expend in one day all the energy that she had left to ferment uselessly in her blood for a whole year.

Raymon was terrified to see her ride away so fast, abandoning herself fearlessly to the impetuous spirit of a horse that she hardly knew, rushing him through the thickets, avoiding with amazing skill the branches that lashed at her face as they sprang back, leaping ditches without hesitation, venturing confidently on clayey, slippery ground, heedless of the risk of breaking her slender limbs, but eager to be first on the smoking scent of the boar. So much determination alarmed him and nearly disgusted him with Madame Delmare. Men, especially lovers, are addicted to the innocent fatuity of preferring to protect weakness rather than to admire courage in womankind. Shall I confess it? Raymon was terrified at the promise of high spirit and tenacity in love which such intrepidity seemed to afford. It was not like the resignation of poor Noun, who preferred to drown herself rather than to contend against her misfortunes.

"If there's as much vigor and excitement in her tenderness as there is in her diversions," he thought; "if her will clings to me, fierce and palpitating, as her caprice clings to that boar's quarters, why society will impose no fetters on her, the law will havc no forcc; my destiny will have to succumb and I shall have to sacrifice my future to her present."

XIV

THE BOAR HUNT

Raymond was terrified to see her ride away so fast, abandoning herself fearlessly to the impetuous spirit of a horse that she hardly knew, rushing him through the thickets, avoiding with amazing skill the branches that lashed at her face as they sprang back, leaping ditches without hesitation, venturing confidently on clayey, slippery ground, heedless of the risk of breaking her slender limbs, but eager to be first on the smoking scent of the boar. *Copyright 1900 by G. Barrie & Son*

Cries of terror and distress, among which he could distinguish Madame Delmare's voice, roused Raymon from these reflections. He anxiously urged his horse forward and was soon overtaken by Ralph, who asked him if he had heard the outcries.

At that moment several terrified whippers-in rode up to them, crying out confusedly that the boar had charged and overthrown Madame Delmare. Other huntsmen, in still greater dismay, appeared, calling for Sir Ralph whose surgical skill was required by the injured person.

"It's of no use," said a late arrival. "There is no hope, your help will be too late."

In that moment of horror, Raymon's eyes fell upon the pale, gloomy features of Monsieur Brown. He did not cry out, he did not foam at the mouth, he did not wring his hands; he simply took out his hunting-knife and with a *sang-froid* truly English was preparing to cut his own throat, when Raymon snatched the weapon from him and hurried him in the direction from which the cries came.

Ralph felt as if he were waking from a dream when he saw Madame Delmare rush to meet him and urge him forward to the assistance of her husband, who lay on the ground, apparently lifeless. Sir Ralph made haste to bleed him; for he had speedily satisfied himself that he was not dead; but his leg was broken and he was taken to the château.

As for Madame Delmare, in the confusion her name had been substituted by accident for that of her husband, or perhaps Ralph and Raymon had erroneously thought that they heard the name in which they were most interested.

Indiana was uninjured, but her fright and consternation had almost taken away her power of locomotion. Raymon supported her in his arms and was reconciled to her womanly heart when he saw how deeply affected she was by the misfortune of a husband whom she had much to forgive before pitying him.

Sir Ralph had already recovered his accustomed tranquillity; but an extraordinary pallor revealed the violent shock he had experienced; he had nearly lost one of the two human beings whom he loved.

Raymon, who alone, in that moment of confusion and excitement, had retained sufficient presence of mind to understand what he saw, had been able to judge of Ralph's affection for his cousin, and how little it was balanced by his feeling for the colonel. This observation, which positively contradicted Indiana's opinion, did not depart from Raymon's memory as it did from that of the other witnesses of the scene

However Raymon never mentioned to Madame Delmare the attempted suicide of which he had been a witness. In this ungenerous reserve there was a suggestion of selfishness and bad temper which you will forgive perhaps in view of the amorous jealousy which was responsible for it.

After six weeks the colonel was with much difficulty removed to Lagny; but it was more than six months thereafter before he could walk; for before the fractured femur was fairly reduced he had an acute attack of rheumatism in the injured leg, which condemned him to excruciating pain and absolute immobility.

XIV

His wife lavished the most loving attentions upon him; she never left his bedside and endured without a complaint his bitter fault-finding humor, his soldier-like testiness and his invalid's injustice.

Despite the ennui of such a depressing life, her health became robust and flourishing once more and happiness took up its abode in her heart. Raymon loved her, he really loved her. He came every day ; he was discouraged by no difficulty in the way of seeing her, he bore with the infirmities of her husband, her cousin's coldness, the constraint of their interviews. A glance from him filled Indiana's heart with joy for a whole day. She no longer thought of complaining of life; her heart was full, her youthful nature had ample employment, her moral force had something to feed upon.

The colonel gradually came to feel very friendly to Raymon. He was simple enough to believe that his neighbor's assiduity in calling upon him was a proof of the interest he took in his health. Madame de Ramière also came occasionally, to sanction the liaison by her presence, and Indiana became warmly and passionately attached to Raymon's mother. At last the wife's lover became the husband's friend.

As a result of being thus constantly thrown together, Raymon and Ralph perforce became intimate in a certain sense; they called each other "my dear fellow," they shook hands morning and night. If either of them desired to ask a slight favor of the other, the regular form was this: "I count upon your friendship," etc. And when they spoke of each other they said: "He is a friend of mine.

But, although they were both as frank and outspoken as a man can be in the world, they were not at all fond of each other. They differed essentially in their opinions on every subject; they had no likes or dislikes in common; and, although they both loved Madame Delmare, they loved her in such a different way that that sentiment divided them instead of bringing them together. They found a singular pleasure in contradicting each other and in disturbing each other's equanimity as much as possible by reproaches which were none the less sharp and bitter because they took the form of generalities.

Their principal and most frequent controversies began with politics and ended with morals. It was in the evening, when they were all assembled around Monsieur Delmare's easy-chair, that discussions arose on the most trivial pretexts. They always maintained the external courtesy which philosophy imposed on the one and social custom on the other: but they sometimes said to each other, under the thin veil of allusions, some very harsh things, which amused the colonel; for he was naturally bellicose and quarrelsome and loved disputes in default of battles.

For my part, I believe that a man's political opinion is the whole man. Tell me what your heart and your head are and I will tell you your political opinions. In whatever rank or political party chance may have placed us at our birth, our character prevails sooner or later over the prejudice or artificial beliefs of education. You will call that a very sweeping statement perhaps; but how could I persuade myself to augur well of a mind that clings to certain theories which a generous spirit rejects? Show me a man who maintains the usefulness of capital punishment, and, however conscientious and enlightened he may be, I defy you ever to establish any sympathetic connection between him and me. If such a man attempts to instruct me as to facts which I do not know, he will never succeed; for it will not be in my power to give him my confidence.

Ralph and Raymon differed on all points, and, yet, before they knew each other, they had no clearly defined opinions. But, as soon as they were at odds, each of them maintained the contrary of what the other advanced, and in that way they would form for themselves an absolute, unassailable conviction. Raymon was on all occasions the champion of existing society, Ralph attacked its structure at every point.

The explanation was simple: Raymon was happy and treated with the utmost consideration, Ralph had known nothing of life but its evils and its bitterness; one found everything very satisfactory, the other was dissatisfied with everything. Men and things had maltreated Ralph and heaped benefits upon Raymon; and, like two children, they referred everything to themselves, setting themselves up as a court of last resort in regard to the great questions of social order, although they were equally incompetent.

Thus Ralph always upheld his visionary scheme of a republic from which he proposed to exclude all abuses, all prejudices, all injustice; a scheme founded entirely upon the hope of a new race of men. Raymon upheld his doctrine of an hereditary monarchy, preferring, he said, to endure abuses, prejudice and injustice, to seeing scaffolds erected and innocent blood shed.

The colonel was almost always on Ralph's side at the beginning of the discussion. He hated the Bourbons and imparted to all his opinions all the animosity of his sentiments. But soon Raymon would adroitly bring him over to his side by proving to him that the monarchy was in principle much nearer the Empire than the Republic. Ralph was so lacking in the power of persuasion, he was so sincere, so bungling, the poor baronet! his frankness was so unpolished, his logic so dull, his principles so rigid! He spared no one, he softened no harsh truth.

"*Parbleu!* " he would say to the colonel, when that worthy cursed England's intervention, "what in heaven's name have you, a man of some common sense and reasoning power, I suppose, to complain of because a whole nation fought fairly against you?"

"Fairly?" Delmare would repeat the word, grinding his teeth together and brandishing his crutch.

"Let us leave political questions to be decided by the powers concerned," Sir Ralph would say, "as we have adopted a form of government which forbids us to discuss our interests ourselves. If a nation is responsible for the faults of its legislature, what one can you find that is guiltier than yours?"

"And so I say, monsieur, shame upon France, which abandoned Napoléon and submitted to a king proclaimed by the bayonets of foreigners!" the colonel would exclaim.

"For my part, I do not say shame upon France," Sir Ralph would rejoin, "but woe to her! I pity her because she was so weak and so diseased, on the day she was purged of her tyrant, that she was compelled to accept your rag of a constitutional Charter, a mere shred of liberty which you are beginning to respect now that you must throw it aside and conquer your liberty over again."

Thereupon Raymon would pick up the gauntlet that Sir Ralph threw down. A knight of the Charter, he chose to be a knight of liberty as well, and he proved to Ralph with marvelous skill that one was the expression of the other; that, if he shattered the Charter he overturned his own idol. In vain would the baronet struggle in the unsound arguments in which Monsieur de Ramière entangled him; with admirable force he would argue that a greater extension of the suffrage would infallibly lead to the excesses of '93, and that the nation was not yet ripe for liberty, which is not the same as license. And when Sir Ralph declared that it was absurd to attempt to confine a constitution within a certain number of articles, that what was sufficient at first would eventually become insufficient, supporting his argument by the example of the convalescent, whose needs increased every day, Raymon would reply to all these commonplaces expressed with difficulty by Monsieur Brown that the Charter was not an immovable circle, that it would stretch with the necessities of France, attributing to it an elasticity which, he said, would afford later a means of satisfying the demands of the nation, but which in fact satisfied only those of the crown.

As to Delmare, he had not advanced a step since 1815. He was a stationary mortal, as full of prejudices and as obstinate as the émigrés at Coblentz, the never-failing subjects of his implacable irony. He was like an old child and had failed utterly to comprehend the great drama of the downfall of Napoléon. He had seen naught but the fortune of war in that crisis when the power of public opinion triumphed. He was forever talking of treason and of selling the country, as if a whole nation could betray a single man, as if France would have allowed herself to be sold by a few generals! He accused the Bourbons of tyranny and sighed for the glorious days of the Empire, when arms were lacking to till the soil and families were without bread. He declaimed against Franchet's police and extolled Fouché's. He was still at the day after Waterloo.

It was really a curious thing to listen to the sentimental idiocies of Delmare and Monsieur de Ramière, philanthropic dreamers both, one under the sword of Napoléon, the other under the sceptre of Saint-Louis; Monsieur Delmare planted at the foot of the Pyramids, Raymon seated under the monarchic shadow of the oak of Vincennes. Their Utopias, which clashed at first, became reconciled in due time: Raymon limed the colonel with his chivalrous sentiments; for one concession he exacted ten, and he accustomed him little by little to the spectacle of twenty-five years of victory ascending in a spiral column under the folds of the white flag. If Ralph had not constantly cast his abrupt, rough observations into the centre of Monsieur de Ramierè's flowery rhetoric, he would infallibly have won Delmare over to the throne of 1815; but Ralph irritated his self-esteem, and the bungling outspokenness with which the Englishman strove to shake his convictions served only to anchor him more firmly in his imperialism. Thus all Monsieur de Ramière's efforts were wasted; Ralph trod heavily upon the flowers of his eloquence and the colonel returned with renewed enthusiasm to his tri-color. He swore that he would shake off the dust from it some fine day, that he would spit on the lilies and restore the Duc de Reichstadt to the throne of *his fathers;* he would begin anew the conquest of the world; and he always concluded by lamenting the disgrace that rested upon France, the rheumatism that glued him to his chair and the ingratitude of the Bourbons to the old moustaches whom the sun of the desert had burned and who had swarmed over the ice-floes of the Moskowa.

"My poor fellow!" Ralph would say, "for heaven's sake be fair; you complain because the Restoration did not pay for services rendered the Empire and because it did reimburse its *émigrés.* Tell me, if Napoléon could come to life again to-morrow in all his power, would you like it if he should withdraw his favor from you and bestow it on the partisans of legitimacy? Every one for himself and his own; these are business discussions, disputes concerning private interests, which have little interest for France, now that you are almost all as incapacitated as the *voltigeurs* of the emigration, and that, whether gouty, married or sulking, you are all equally useless to her. However, she must support you all, and you see who can complain the loudest of her. When the day of the Republic dawns, she will clear her skirts of all your demands, and it will be no more than justice."

These trivial but self-evident observations offended the colonel like so many personal affronts; and Ralph who, with all his good sense, did not realize that the pettiness of spirit of a man whom he esteemed could go so far, fell into the habit of irritating him without mercy.

Before Raymon's arrival there had been a tacit agreement between the two to avoid every subject of controversy in which there might be some clashing and wounding of delicate sensibilities. But Raymon brought into their conversation all the subtleties of the language, all the petty artifices of civilization. He taught them that people can say anything to one another, indulge in all sorts of reproaches and shield themselves behind the pretext of legitimate discussion. He introduced among them the habit of disputation, then tolerated in the salons, because the vindictive passions of the Hundred Days had finally become appeased, had assumed divers milder shades. But the colonel had retained all the vehemence of his passions, and Ralph made a sad mistake in thinking that it was possible for him to listen to reason. Monsieur Delmare became daily more sour toward him and drew nearer to Raymon, who, without making too extensive concessions, knew how to assume an appearance of graciousness in order to spare the other's self-esteem.

It is a great imprudence to introduce politics as a pastime in the domestic circle. If there exist to-day any peaceful and happy families, I advise them to subscribe to no newspaper; not to read a single line of the budget, to bury themselves in the depth of their country estates as in an oasis, and to draw between themselves and the rest of society a line that none may pass; for, if they allow the echoes of our disputes to meet their ears, it is all over with their union and their repose. It is hard to imagine how much gall and bitterness political differences cause between near kindred. Most of the time they simply afford them an opportunity for reproaching one another for defects of character, mental obliquities and vices of the heart.

They would not dare to call one another knave, imbecile, ambitious villain or poltroon. They express the same idea by such names as *jesuit, royalist, revolutionist* and *trimmer.* These are different words, but the insult is the same, and all the more stinging because they may pursue and attack one another in this fashion without restraint, without mercy. There is an end to all mutual toleration of failings, all charitable spirit, all generous and delicate reserve; nothing is overlooked, everything is attributed to political feeling, and beneath that mask hatred and vengeance are freely exhaled. O ye blessed dwellers in the country, if there still be any country in France, shun, shun politics, and read the *Peau d'Ane* by your firesides! But the contagion is so great that there is no retreat obscure enough, no solitude profound enough to hide and shelter the man who would find a refuge for his amiable heart from the tempests of our civil dissensions.

In vain had the little château in Brie defended itself for years against this ill-omened invasion; it lost in time its heedlessness, its active domestic life, its long evenings of silence and meditation. Noisy disputes awoke its slumbering echoes; bitter and threatening words terrified the faded cherubs who had smiled amid the dust of the hangings for a hundred years past. The excitements of present-day life found their way into that ancient dwelling, and all those old-fashioned splendors, all those relics of a period of pleasure and frivolity saw with dismay the advent of an epoch of doubt and declamation, represented by three men who shut themselves up together every day to quarrel from morning till night.

XV

Despite these never-ending dissensions, Madame Delmare clung with the confidence of her years to the hope of a happy future. It was her first happiness; and her ardent imagination, her rich young heart, were able to supply it with all that it lacked. She was ingenious in creating keen and pure joys for herself–in bestowing upon herself the complement of the precarious favors of her destiny. Raymon loved her. In truth he did not lie when he told her that she was the only love of his life; he had never loved so innocently nor so long. With her he forgot everything but her. The world and politics were blotted out by the thought of her; he enjoyed the domestic life, the being treated like one of the family, as she treated him. He admired her patience and her strength of will; he wondered at the contrast between her mind and her character; he wondered especially that, after importing so much solemnity into their first compact, she was so unexacting, satisfied with such furtive and infrequent joys, and that she trusted him so blindly and so absolutely. But love was a novel and generous passion in her heart, and a thousand noble and delicate sentiments were included in it and gave it a force which Raymon could not understand.

For his own part, he was annoyed at first by the constant presence of the husband or the cousin. He had intended that this love should be like all his previous loves, but Indiana soon compelled him to rise to her level. The resignation with which she endured the constant surveillance, the happy air with which she glanced at him by stealth, her eyes which spoke to him in eloquent though silent language, her sublime smile when a sudden allusion in conversation brought their hearts nearer together–these soon became keen pleasures which Raymon craved and appreciated, thanks to the refinement of his mind and the culture of education.

What a difference between that chaste creature who seemed not to contemplate the possibility of a *dénoûment* to her love and all those other women who were intent only upon hastening it while pretending to shun it! When Raymon happened to be alone with her, Indiana's cheeks did not turn a deeper red, nor did she avert her eyes in confusion. No, her tranquil, limpid eyes were always fixed upon him in ecstasy; an angelic smile played always about her lips, as ruddy as a little girl's who has known no kisses but her mother's. When he saw her so trustful, so passionate, so pure, living solely with the heart and not realizing that her lover's heart was in torment when he was at her feet, Raymon dared not be a man, lest he should seem to her inferior to her dreams of him, and, through self-love, he became as virtuous as she.

XV

Madame Delmare, ignorant as a genuine creole, had never dreamed hitherto of considering the momentous questions that were now discussed before her every day. She had been brought up by Sir Ralph, who had a poor opinion of the intelligence and reasoning power of womankind, and who had confined himself to imparting some positive information likely to be of immediate use. Thus she had a very shadowy idea of the world's history, and any serious discussion bored her to death. But when she heard Raymon apply to those dry subjects all the charm of his wit, all the poesy of his language, she listened and tried to understand; then she ventured timidly to ask ingenuous questions which a girl of ten brought up according to worldly ideas would readily have answered. Raymon took pleasure in enlightening that virgin mind which seemed destined to open to receive his principles; but, despite the power he exerted over her untrained, artless mind, his sophisms sometimes encountered resistance from her.

Indiana opposed to the interests of civilization, when raised to the dignity of principles of action, the straightforward ideas and simple laws of good sense and humanity; her arguments were characterized by an unpolished freedom which sometimes embarrassed Raymon and always charmed him by its childlike originality. He applied himself as to a task of serious importance to the attempt to bring her around gradually to his principles, to his beliefs. He would have been proud to dominate her conscientious and naturally enlightened convictions but he had some difficulty in attaining his end. Ralph's generous theories, his unbending hatred of the vices of society, his keen impatience for the reign of other laws and other morals were sentiments to which Indiana's unhappy memories responded. But Raymon suddenly unhorsed his adversary by demonstrating that this aversion for the present was the work of selfishness; he described with much warmth his own attachments, his devotion to the royal family, which he had the art to clothe with all the heroism of a perilous loyalty, his respect for the persecuted faith of his fathers, his religious sentiments, which were not the fruit of reasoning, he said, but to which he clung by instinct and from necessity. And the joy of loving one's fellow-creatures, of being bound to the present generation by all the ties of honor and philanthropy; the pleasure of serving one's country by repelling dangerous innovations, by maintaining domestic peace, by giving, if need be, all one's blood to save the shedding of one drop of that of the lowest of one's countrymen! he depicted all these attractive Utopian visions with so much art and charm that Indiana submitted to be led on to the feeling that she must love and respect all that Raymon loved and respected. It was fairly proved that Ralph was an egotist; when he maintained a generous idea, they smiled; it was clear that at such times his heart and his mind were in contradiction. Was it not better to believe Raymon, who had such a big, warm, expansive heart?

There were moments, however, when Raymon almost forgot his love to think only of his antipathy. When he was with Madame Delmare, he could see nobody but Sir Ralph, who presumed, with his rough, cool common sense, to attack him, a man of superior talents, who had overthrown such doughty adversaries! He was humiliated to find himself engaged with so paltry an adversary, and thereupon would overwhelm him with the weight of his eloquence; he would bring into play all the resources of his talent, and Ralph, bewildered, slow in collecting his ideas, slower still in expressing them, would be made painfully conscious of his weakness.

At such moments it seemed to Indiana that Raymon's thoughts were altogether diverted from her; she had spasms of anxiety and terror as she reflected that perhaps all those noble and high-sounding sentiments so eloquently declaimed were simply the pompous scaffolding of words, the ironical harangue of the lawyer, listening to himself and practising the comedy which is to take by surprise the good-nature of the tribunal. She was especially fearful when, as her eyes met his, she fancied that she saw gleaming in them, not the pleasure of having been understood by her, but the triumphant self-satisfaction of having made a fine argument. She was afraid at such times, and her thoughts turned to Ralph, the egotist, to whom they had perhaps been unjust; but Ralph was not tactful enough to say anything to prolong this uncertainty, and Raymon was very skilful in removing it.

Thus there was but one really perturbed existence, but one really ruined happiness in that domestic circle: the existence and happiness of Sir Ralph Brown, a man born to misfortune, for whom life had displayed no brilliant aspects, no intense, heart-filling joys; a victim of great but secret unhappiness, who complained to no one and whom no one pitied; a truly accursed destiny, in the poetic sense without thrilling adventures; a commonplace, bourgeois, melancholy destiny, which no friendship had sweetened, no love charmed, which was endured in silence, with the heroism which the love of life and the need of hoping give; a lonely mortal who had had a father and mother like everybody else, a brother, a wife, a son, a friend, and who had reaped no benefit, retained nothing of all those ties; a stranger in life who went his way melancholy and indifferent, having not even that exalted consciousness of his misfortune which enables one to find some fascination in sorrow.

Despite his strength of character, he sometimes felt discouraged with virtue. He hated Raymon, and it was in his power to drive him from Lagny with a word; but he did not say it, because he had one belief, a single one, which was stronger than Raymon's countless beliefs. It was neither the church, nor the monarchy, nor society, nor reputation, nor the law, which dictated his sacrifices and his courage–it was his conscience.

He had lived so alone that he had not accustomed himself to rely upon others; but he had learned, in his isolation, to know himself. He had made a friend of his own heart; by dint of self-communion, of asking himself the cause of the unjust acts of others, he had assured himself that he had not earned them by any vice; he had ceased to be irritated by them, because he set little store by his own personality, which he knew to be insipid and commonplace. He understood the indifference of which he was the object, and he had chosen his course with regard to it; but his heart told him that he was capable of feeling all that he did not inspire, and, while he was disposed to forgive everything in others, he had decided to tolerate nothing in himself. This wholly inward life, these wholly private sensations gave him all the outward appearance of a selfish man; indeed nothing resembles selfishness more closely than self-respect.

However, as it often happens that, because we attempt to do too much good, we do much less than enough, it happened that Sir Ralph made a great mistake from over-scrupulousness and caused Madame Delmare an irreparable injury from dread of burdening his own conscience with a cause of reproach. That mistake was his failure to enlighten her as to the real reasons of Noun's death. Had he done so she would doubtless have reflected on the perils of her love for Raymon; but we shall see later why Monsieur Brown dared not inform his cousin and what painful scruples led him to keep silence on so momentous a question. When he decided to break his silence it was too late; Raymon had had time to establish his empire.

An unforeseen event occurred to cloud the future prospects of the colonel and his wife; a business house in Belgium, upon which all the prosperity of the Delmare establishment depended, had suddenly failed, and the colonel, who had hardly recovered his health, started in hot haste for Antwerp.

He was still so weak and ill that his wife wished to accompany him; but Monsieur Delmare, being threatened with complete ruin and resolved to honor all his obligations, feared that his journey would then seem too much like a flight; so he determined to leave his wife at Lagny as a pledge of his return. He even declined the company of Sir Ralph and begged him to remain and stand by Madame Delmare in case of any trouble on the part of anxious or over-eager creditors.

At this painful crisis Indiana was alarmed at nothing save the possibility of having to leave Lagny and be separated from Raymon; but he comforted her by convincing her that the colonel would surely go to Paris. Moreover he gave her his word that he would follow her, on some pretext or other, wherever she might go, and the credulous creature deemed herself almost happy in a misfortune which enabled her to put Raymon's love to the test. As for him, a vague hope, a persistent, importunate thought had absorbed his mind ever since he had heard of this event: he was to be alone with Indiana at last, the first time for six months. She had never seemed to attempt to avoid a tête-à-tête, and although he was in no haste to triumph over a love whose ingenuous chastity had for him the attraction of novelty, he was beginning to feel that his honor was involved in bringing it to some conclusion. He honorably repelled any malicious insinuation concerning his relations with Madame Delmare; he declared very modestly that there was nothing more than a placid and pleasant friendship between them; but not for anything in the world would he have admitted, even to his best friend, that he had been passionately in love for six months and had as yet obtained no fruit of that love.

He was somewhat disappointed in his anticipations when he saw that Sir Ralph seemed determined to replace Monsieur Delmare so far as surveillance was concerned, that he appeared at Lagny in the morning and did not return to Bellerive until night; indeed, as their road was the same for some distance, Ralph, with an intolerable affectation of courtesy, insisted upon timing his departure by Raymon's. This constraint soon became intensely disagreeable to Monsieur de

Ramière, and Madame Delmare fancied that she could detect in it not only a suspicion insulting to herself, but a purpose to assume despotic control over her conduct.

Raymon dared not request a secret interview; whenever he had made the attempt, Madame Delmare had reminded him of certain conditions agreed upon between them. Meanwhile a week had passed since the colonel's departure; he might return very soon; the present opportunity must be turned to advantage. To allow Sir Ralph the victory would be a disgrace to Raymon. One morning he slipped this letter into Madame Delmare's hand:

"Indiana! do you not love me as I love you? My angel! I am unhappy and you do not see it. I am sad, anxious concerning your future, not my own; for, wherever you may be, there I shall live and die. But the thought of poverty alarms me on your account; ill and frail as you are, my poor child, how will you endure privation? You have a rich and generous cousin: your husband will perhaps accept at his hands what he will refuse at mine. Ralph will ameliorate your lot, and I shall be able to do nothing for you!

"Be sure, be sure, my dear love, that I have reason to be depressed and disappointed. You are heroic, you laugh at everything, you insist that I must not grieve. Ah! how I crave your gentle words, your sweet glances, to sustain my courage! But, by a monstrous fatality, these days that I hoped to pass freely at your feet, have brought me nothing but a constraint that grows ever more galling.

"Say a word, Indiana, so that we may be alone at least an hour, that I may weep upon your white hands and tell you all that I suffer, and that a word from you may console and comfort me.

"And then, Indiana, I have a childish caprice, a genuine lover's caprice. I would like to enter your room. Oh! don't be frightened, my gentle creole! It is my bounden duty not only to respect you, but to fear you; that is the very reason why I would like to enter your room, to kneel in that place where you were so angry with me, and where, bold as I am, I dared not look at you. I would like to prostrate myself there, to pass a meditative, happy hour there; I would crave no other favor, Indiana, than that you should place your hand on my heart and cleanse it of its crime, pacify it if it beats too rapidly, and give it your confidence once more if you find me worthy of you at last. Yes! I would like to prove to you that now I am worthy, that I know you through and through, that I worship you with an adoration as pure and holy as ever maiden conceived for her Madonna! I would like to be sure that you no longer fear me, that you esteem me as much as I revere you; I would like to live an hour as angels live, with my head upon your heart. Tell me, Indiana, may I? One hour–the first, perhaps the last!

"It is time to forgive me, Indiana, to give me back your confidence, so cruelly snatched from me, so dearly redeemed. Are you not satisfied with me? Have I not passed six months behind your chair, confining my desires to a glance at your snow-white neck through the curls of your black hair, as you leaned over your work, to a breath of the perfume which emanates from you and which the air from the window at which you sit brings faintly to my nostrils? Does not such submission deserve the reward of a kiss? a sister's kiss, if you will, a kiss on the forehead? I will remain true to our agreements, I swear it. I will ask for nothing. But, cruel one, will you grant me nothing? Are you afraid of yourself?"

Madame Delmare went to her room to read this letter; she replied to it instantly, and handed him the reply with a key to the park-gate, which he knew too well.

"I afraid of you, Raymon? Oh! no, not now. I know too well that you love me, I am too blissfully happy in the belief that you love me. Come then, for I am not afraid of myself either; if I loved you less, perhaps I should be less calm; but I love you with a love of which you yourself have no idea. Go away early, so that Ralph may suspect nothing. Return at midnight; you are familiar with the park and the house; here is the key of the small gate; lock it after you."

This ingenuous, generous confidence made Raymon blush. He had tried to inspire it, with the purpose of abusing it; he had counted on the darkness, the opportunity, the danger. If Indiana had shown any fear, she was lost; but she was perfectly calm; she placed her trust in his good faith; he swore that he would give her no cause to repent. But the important point was to pass a night in her bedroom, in order not to be a fool in his own eyes, in order to defeat Ralph's prudence, and to be able to laugh at him in his sleeve. That was a personal gratification which he craved.

XVI

But Ralph was really intolerable on this particular evening; he had never been more stupid and dull and tiresome. He could say nothing apropos, and, to cap the climax of his loutishness, he gave no sign of taking his leave even when the evening was far advanced. Madame Delmare began to be ill at ease; she glanced alternately at the clock, which had struck eleven–at the door, which had creaked in the wind–and at the expressionless face of her cousin, who sat opposite her in front of the fire, placidly watching the blaze without seeming to suspect that his presence was distasteful.

But Sir Ralph's tranquil mask, his petrified features, concealed at that moment a profound and painful mental agitation. He was a man whom nothing escaped because he observed everything with perfect self-possession. He had not been deceived by Raymon's pretended departure; he perceived very plainly Madame Delmare's anxiety at that moment. He suffered more than she did herself, and he moved irresolutely between the impulse to give her a salutary warning and the fear of giving way to feelings which he disavowed; at last his cousin's interest carried the day, and he summoned all his moral courage in order to break the silence.

"That reminds me," he said abruptly, following out the line of thought with which his mind was busy, "that it was just a year ago to-day that you and I sat in this chimney-corner as we are sitting now. The clock marked almost the same hour; the weather was cold and threatening as it is to-night. You were ill, and were disturbed by melancholy ideas; a fact that almost makes me believe in the truth of presentiments."

"What can he be coming to?" thought Madame Delmare, gazing at her cousin with mingled surprise and uneasiness.

"Do you remember, Indiana," he continued, "that you felt even less well than usual that night? Why, I can remember your words as if I had just heard them. 'You will call me insane,' you said, 'but some danger is hovering about us and threatening some one of us–threatening me, I have no doubt,' you added; 'I feel intensely agitated, as if some great crisis in my destiny were at hand–I am afraid!' Those are your very words."

"I am no longer ill," said Indiana, who had suddenly turned as pale as at the time of which Sir Ralph spoke; "I no longer believe in such foolish terrors."

"But I believe in them," he rejoined, "for you were a true prophet that night, Indiana; a great danger did threaten us–a disastrous influence surrounded this peaceful abode."

"*Mon Dieu!* I do not understand you!"

"You soon will understand me, my poor girl. That was the evening that Raymon de Ramière was brought here. Do you remember in what condition?"

Ralph paused a few seconds, but dared not look at his cousin. As she made no reply, he continued:

"I was told to bring him back to life and I did so, as much to satisfy you as to obey the instincts of humanity; but, in truth, Indiana, it was a great misfortune that I saved that man's life! It was I who did all the harm."

"I don't know what you mean by harm!" rejoined Indiana, dryly.

She was deeply moved in advance by the explanation which she foresaw.

"I mean that unfortunate creature's death," said Ralph. "But for him she would still be alive; but for his fatal love the lovely, honest girl who loved you so dearly would still be at your side."

Thus far Madame Delmare did not understand. She was exasperated beyond measure by the strange and cruel method which her cousin adopted to reproach her for her attachment to Monsieur de Ramière.

"Enough of this," she said, rising.

But Ralph apparently took no notice of her remark.

"What always astonished me," he continued, "was that you never guessed the real motive that led Monsieur de Ramière to scale the walls."

A suspicion darted through Indiana's mind; her legs trembled under her, and she resumed her seat.

Ralph had buried the knife in her breast and made a ghastly wound. He no sooner saw the effect of his work than he hated himself for it; he thought only of the injury he had inflicted on the person whom he loved best in all the world; he felt that his heart was breaking. He would have wept bitterly if he could have wept; but the poor fellow had not the gift of tears; he had naught of that which eloquently translates the language of the heart. The external coolness with which he performed the cruel operation gave him the air of an executioner in Indiana's eyes.

"This is the first time," she said bitterly, "that I have known your antipathy for Monsieur de Ramière to lead you to employ weapons that are unworthy of you; but I do not see how it assists your vengeance to stain the memory of a person who was dear to me, and whom her melancholy end should have made sacred to us. I have asked you no questions, Sir Ralph; I do not know what you refer to. With your permission I will listen to no more."

She rose and left Monsieur Brown bewildered and crushed.

He had foreseen that he could not enlighten Madame Delmare except at his own expense. His conscience had told him that he must speak, whatever the result might be, and he had done it with all the abruptness of method, all the awkwardness of execution of which he was capable. What he had not fully appreciated was the violence of a remedy so long delayed.

He left Lagny in despair and wandered through the forest in a sort of frenzy.

It was midnight; Raymon was at the park gate. He opened it, but as he opened it he felt his brow grow chill. For what purpose had he come to this rendezvous? He had made divers virtuous resolutions, but would he be amply rewarded by a chaste interview, by a sisterly kiss, for the torture he was undergoing at that moment? For, if you remember under what circumstances he had previously passed through those garden paths, stealthily, at night, you will understand that it required a certain degree of moral courage to go in search of pleasure along such a road and amid such memories.

Late in October the climate of the suburbs of Paris becomes damp and foggy, especially at night and in the neighborhood of streams. Chance decreed that the fog should be as dense on this night as on certain other nights in the preceding spring. Raymon felt his way along the mist-enveloped trees. He passed a summerhouse which contained a fine collection of geraniums in winter. He glanced at the door, and his heart beat fast at the extravagant idea that it might open and give egress to a woman wrapped in a pelisse. Raymon smiled at this superstitious weakness and went his way. Nevertheless the cold seized him, and he felt an unpleasant tightness at his throat as he approached the stream.

He had to cross it to reach the flower-garden, and the only means of crossing in that vicinity was a narrow wooden bridge. The fog became more dismal than ever over the river-bed, and Raymon clung to the railing of the bridge in order not to go astray among the reeds that grew along the banks. The moon was just rising, and, as it strove to pierce the vapors, cast an uncertain light on the plants which the wind and the current moved to and fro. In the breeze which rustled the leaves and ruffled the surface of the water there was a sort of wailing sound like human words half-spoken. There was a faint sob close beside Raymon and a sudden movement among the reeds; it was a curlew flying away at his approach. The cry of that shore-bird closely resembles the moaning of an abandoned child; and when it comes up from among the reeds you would say that it was the last effort of a drowning man. Perhaps you will consider that Raymon was very weak and cowardly; his teeth chattered and he nearly fell; but he soon realized the absurdity of his terror and crossed the bridge.

He was half-way across when a human figure appeared in front of him, at the end of the rail, as if waiting for him to approach. Raymon's ideas became confused; his bewildered brain had not the strength to reason. He retraced his steps and hid among the trees, gazing with a fixed, terrified stare at that ill-defined apparition which remained in the same place, as vague and uncertain as the river mist and the trembling rays of the moon. He was beginning to believe that in his mental preoccupation he had been deceived, and that what he took for a human form was only a tree-trunk or the stalk of a shrub, when he distinctly saw it move and walk toward him.

At that moment, had not his legs absolutely refused to act, he would have fled in as great a panic as the child who passes a cemetery at night and fancies that he hears mysterious steps running after him on the tips of the blades of grass. But he felt as if he were paralyzed, and, to support himself, threw his arms around the trunk of the willow behind which he was hidden. The next moment Sir Ralph, wrapped in a light cloak which gave him the aspect of a phantom at three yards, passed very close to him and took the path by which he had just come.

"Bungling spy!" thought Raymon, as he saw him looking for his footprints. "I will escape your cowardly surveillance, and while you are mounting guard here I will be enjoying myself yonder."

He crossed the bridge as lightly as a bird, and with the confidence of a lover. His terrors were at an end; Noun had never existed; real life was awakening all about him; Indiana awaited him yonder; and Ralph was on sentry-go to keep him from entering.

"Watch closely," said Raymon, gayly, as he saw him in the distance going in the opposite direction. "Watch for me, dear Sir Rodolphe Brown; protect my good fortune, O my officious friend; and, if the dogs are restless, if the servants wake, pacify them, keep them quiet by saying: 'It is I who am watching, sleep in peace.'"

Scruples, remorse, virtue were at an end for Raymon; he had paid dearly enough for the hour that was striking. His blood that had frozen in his veins flowed now toward his brain with maddening violence. A moment ago the pallid terrors of death, dismal visions of the tomb; now the impetuous realities of love, the keen joys of life. Raymon felt as bold and full of animation as in the morning, when an ugly dream has enveloped us in its shroud and suddenly a merry sunbeam awakens and revivifies us.

"Poor Ralph!" he thought as he ascended the secret staircase with a bold, light step, "you would have it so!"

PART THIRD

XVII

On leaving Sir Ralph, Madame Delmare had locked herself into her room, and a thousand tempestuous thoughts had invaded her mind. It was not the first time that a vague suspicion had cast its ominous light upon the fragile edifice of her happiness. Monsieur Delmare had previously let slip in conversation some of those indelicate jests which pass for compliments. He had complimented Raymon on his knightly triumphs in a way to give the cue to ears that knew naught of the incident. Every time that Madame Delmare had spoken to the gardener, Noun's name had been injected, as if by an unavoidable necessity, into the most trivial details, and then Monsieur de Ramière's had always glided in by virtue of some mysterious junction of ideas which seemed to have taken possession of the man's brain and to beset him in spite of himself. Madame Delmare had been struck by his strange and bungling questions. He became confused in his speech on the slightest pretext; he seemed to be oppressed by a burden of remorse which he betrayed while struggling to conceal it. At other times Indiana had found in Raymon's own confusion those indications which she did not seek, but which forced themselves upon her. One circumstance in particular would have enlightened her further, if she had not closed her mind to all distrust. They had found on Noun's finger a very handsome ring which Madame Delmare had noticed some time before her death and which the girl claimed to have found. Since her death Madame Delmare had always worn that pledge of sorrow, and she had often noticed that Raymon changed color when he took her hand to put it to his lips. Once he had begged her never to mention Noun to him because he looked upon himself as the cause of her death; and when she sought to banish that painful thought by taking all the blame to herself, he had replied:

"No, my poor Indiana, do not accuse yourself; you have no idea how guilty I am."

Those words, uttered in a bitter, gloomy tone, had alarmed Madame Delmare. She had not dared to insist, and, now that she was beginning to understand all these fragments of discoveries, she had not the courage to fix her thoughts upon them and put them together.

She opened her window, and, as she looked out upon the calm night, upon the moon so pale and lovely behind the silvery vapors on the horizon, as she remembered that Raymon was coming, that he was perhaps in the park even now, and thought of all the joy she had anticipated in that hour of love and mystery, she cursed Ralph who with a word had poisoned her hope and destroyed her repose forever. She even felt that she hated him, the unhappy man who had been a father to her and who had sacrificed his future for her; for his future was Indiana's friendship; that was his only treasure, and he resigned himself to the certainty of forfeiting it in order to save her.

Indiana could not read in the depths of his heart, nor had she been able to fathom Raymon's. She was unjust, not from ingratitude, but from ignorance. Being under the influence of a strong passion she could not but feel strongly the blow that had been dealt her. For an instant she laid the whole crime upon Ralph, preferring to accuse him rather than to suspect Raymon.

And then she had so little time to collect her thoughts, and make up her mind: Raymon was coming. Perhaps it was he whom she had seen for some minutes wandering about the little bridge. How much more intense would her aversion for Ralph have been at that moment, if she could have recognized him in that vague figure, which constantly appeared and disappeared in the mist, and which, like a spirit stationed at the gate of the Elysian Fields, sought to keep the guilty man from entering!

Suddenly there came to her mind one of those strange, half-formed ideas, which only restless and unhappy persons are capable of conceiving. She risked her whole destiny upon a strange and delicate test against which Raymon could not be on his guard. She had hardly completed her mysterious preparations when she heard Raymon's footsteps on the secret stairway. She ran and unlocked the door, then returned to her chair, so agitated that she felt that she was on the point of falling; but, as in all the great crises of her life, she retained a remarkable clearness of perception and great strength of mind.

Raymon was still pale and breathless when he opened the door; impatient to see the light, to grasp reality once more. Indiana's back was turned to him, she was wrapped in a fur-lined pelisse. By a strange chance it was the same that Noun wore when she went to meet him in the park at their last rendezvous. I do not know if you remember that at that time Raymon had had for an instant the untenable idea that that woman shrouded in her cloak was Madame Delmare. Now, when he saw once more the same apparition sitting inert in a chair, with her head on her breast, by the light of a pale, flickering lamp, on the same spot where so many memories awaited him, in that room which he had not entered since the darkest night in his life and which was full to overflowing of his remorse, he involuntarily recoiled and remained in the doorway, his terrified gaze fixed upon that motionless figure, and trembling like a coward, lest, when it turned, it should display the livid features of a drowned woman.

Madame Delmare had no suspicion of the effect she produced upon Raymon. She had wound about her head a handkerchief of India silk, tied carelessly in true creole style; it was Noun's usual headdress. Raymon, fairly overcome by terror, nearly fell backward, thinking that his superstitious fancies were realized. But, recognizing the woman he had come to seduce, he forgot the one whom he had seduced and walked toward her. Her face wore a grave, meditative expression:

she gazed earnestly at him, but with close attention rather than affection, and did not make a motion to draw him to her side more quickly.

Raymon, surprised by this reception, attributed it to some scruple of chastity, to some girlish impulse of delicacy or constraint. He knelt at her feet, saying:

"Are you afraid of me, my beloved?" But at that moment he noticed that Madame Delmare held something in her hands to which she seemed to direct his attention with a playful affectation of gravity. He looked more closely and saw a mass of black hair, of varying lengths, which seemed to have been cut in haste, and which Indiana was smoothing with her hand.

"Do you recognize it?" she asked, fastening upon him her limpid eyes, in which there was a peculiar, penetrating gleam.

Raymon hesitated, looked again at the handkerchief about her head, and thought that he understood.

"Naughty girl!" he said, taking the hair in his hand, "why did you cut it off? It was so beautiful, and I loved it so dearly!"

"You asked me yesterday," she said with the shadow of a smile, "if I would sacrifice it to you."

"O Indiana!" cried Raymon, "you know well that you will be lovelier than ever to me henceforth. Give it to me. I do not choose to regret the absence from your head of that glorious hair which I admired every day, and which now I can kiss every day without restraint. Give it to me, so that it may never leave me."

But as he gathered up in his hand that luxuriant mass of which some locks reached to the floor, Raymon fancied that it had a dry, rough feeling which his fingers had never noticed in the silken tresses over Indiana's forehead. He was conscious, also, of an indefinable nervous thrill, it felt so cold and dead, as if it had been cut a long time, and seemed to have lost its perfumed moisture and vital warmth. Then he looked at it again, and sought in vain the blue gleam which made Indiana's hair resemble the blue-black wing of the crow; this was of an Ethiopian black, of an Indian texture, of a lifeless heaviness.

Indiana's bright piercing eyes followed Raymon's. He turned them involuntarily upon an open ebony casket from which several locks of the same hair protruded.

"This is not yours," he said, untying the kerchief which concealed Madame Delmare's hair.

It was untouched, and fell over her shoulders in all its splendor. But she made a gesture as if to push him away and said, still pointing to the hair:

"Don't you recognize this? Did you never admire, never caress it? Has the damp night air robbed it of all its fragrance? Have you not a thought, a tear for her who wore this ring?"

Raymon sank upon a chair; Noun's locks fell from his trembling hand. So much painful excitement had exhausted him. He was a man of choleric temper, whose blood flowed rapidly, whose nerves were easily and deeply irritated. He shivered from head to foot and fell in a swoon on the floor.

When he came to himself, Madame Delmare was on her knees beside him, weeping copiously and asking his forgiveness; but Raymon no longer loved her.

"You have inflicted a horrible wound on me," he said; "a wound which it is not in your power to cure. You will never restore the confidence I had in your heart; that is evident to me. You have shown me how vindictive and cruel your heart can be. Poor Noun! poor unhappy girl! It was she whom I treated badly, not you; it was she who had the right to avenge herself, and she did not. She took her own life in order to leave me the future. She sacrificed herself to my repose. You are not the woman to have done as much, madame ! Give me her hair; it is mine–it belongs to me ; it is all that remains to me of the only woman who ever loved me truly. Unhappy Noun! you were worthy of a better love! And you, madame, dare to reproach me with her death; you, whom I loved so well that I forgot her–that I defied the ghastly torture of remorse; you who, on the faith of a kiss, have led me across that river–across that bridge–alone, with terror at my side, pursued by the infernal illusions of my crime! And when you discover with what a frantic passion I love you, you bury your woman's nails in my heart, seeking there another drop of blood which may still be made to flow for you! Ah! when I spurned so devoted a love to take up with so savage a passion as yours, I was no less mad than guilty."

Madame Delmare did not reply. Pale and motionless, with dishevelled hair and staring eyes, she moved Raymon to pity. He took her hand.

"And yet," he said, "this love I feel for you is so blind that, in spite of myself, I can still forget the past and the present–the sin that blasted my life and the crime you have just committed. So love me, and I will forgive you."

Madame Delmare's despair rekindled desire and pride in her lover's heart. When he saw how dismayed she was at the thought of losing his love–how humble before him, how resigned to accept his decrees for the future by way of atonement for the past–he remembered what his intentions had been when he eluded Ralph's vigilance, and he realized all the advantages of his position. He pretended to be absorbed in a melancholy, sombre reverie for some moments; he hardly responded to Indiana's tears and caresses. He waited until her heart should break and overflow in sobs, until she should realize all the horrors of desertion–until she should have exhausted all her strength in heart-rending emotion; and then, when he saw her at his feet, fainting, utterly worn out, awaiting death at a word from him, he seized her in his arms with convulsive passion and strained her to his heart. She yielded like a weak child; she abandoned her lips to him unresistingly. She was almost dead.

But suddenly, as if waking from a dream, she snatched herself away from his burning caresses, rushed to the end of the room where Sir Ralph's portrait hung on the panel; and, as if she would place herself under the protection of that grave personage with the unruffled brow and tranquil lips, she shrank back against the portrait, wild-eyed, quivering from head to foot, in the clutches of a strange fear. It was this that made Raymon think that she had been deeply moved in his arms–that she was afraid of herself–that she was his. He ran to her; drew her by force from her retreat, and told her that he had come with the purpose of keeping his promises, but that her cruel treatment of him had absolved him from his oath.

"I am no longer either your slave or your ally," he said. "I am simply the man who loves you madly and who has you in his arms, a wicked, capricious, cruel, mad creature, but lovely and adored. With sweet, confiding words you might have cooled my blood. Had you been as calm and generous as yesterday, you would have made me mild and submissive as usual. But you have kindled all my passions, overturned all my ideas. You have made me unhappy, cowardly, ill, frantic, desperate, one after another. You must make me happy now, or I feel that I can no longer believe in you–that I can no longer love you or bless you. Forgive me, Indiana, forgive me! If I frighten you it is your own fault; you have made me suffer so that I have lost my reason!"

Indiana trembled in every limb. She knew so little of life that she believed resistance to be impossible; she was ready to concede from fear what she would refuse from love; but, as she struggled feebly in Raymon's arms, she said, in desperation:

"So you are capable of using force with me?"

Raymon paused, impressed with this moral resistance, which survived physical resistance. He hastily pushed her away.

"Never!" he cried: "I would rather die than possess you except by your own will!"

He threw himself on his knees, and all that the mind can supply in place of the heart, all the poesy that the imagination can impart to the ardor of the blood, he expressed in a fervent and dangerous entreaty. And when he saw that she did not surrender, he yielded to necessity and reproached her with not loving him; a commonplace expedient which he despised and which made him smile, with a feeling of something like shame at having to do with a woman so innocent as not to smile at it herself.

That reproach went to Indiana's heart more swiftly than all the exclamations with which Raymon had embellished his discourse.

But suddenly she remembered.

"Raymon," she said, "the other, who loved you so dearly–of whom we were speaking just now–she refused you nothing, I suppose?"

"Nothing!" exclaimed Raymon, annoyed by this inopportune reminder. "Instead of reminding me of her so continually, you would do well to make me forget how dearly she loved me!"

"Listen!" rejoined Indiana, thoughtfully and gravely; "have a little courage, for I must say something more. Perhaps you have not been as guilty towards me as I thought. It would be sweet to me to be able to forgive you for what I considered a mortal insult. Tell me then–when I surprised you here–for whom did you come? for her or for me?"

Raymon hesitated; then, as he thought that the truth would soon be known to Madame Delmare, that perhaps she knew it already, he answered:

"For her."

"Well, I prefer it so," she said sadly; "I prefer an infidelity to an insult. Be frank to the end, Raymon. How long had you been in my room when I came? Remember that Ralph knows all, and that, if I chose to question him–"

"There is no need of Sir Ralph's testimony, madame. I had been here since the night before."

"And you had passed the night in this room. Your silence is a sufficient answer."

They both remained silent for some moments; then Indiana rose and was about to continue, when a sharp knock at the door checked the flow of the blood in her veins. Neither she nor Raymon dared to breathe.

A paper was slipped under the door. It was a leaf from a note-book on which these words were scrawled in pencil, almost illegibly:

"Your husband is here.
"RALPH."

XVIII

"This is a wretchedly devised falsehood," said Raymon, as soon as the sound of Ralph's footsteps had died away. "Sir Ralph needs a lesson, and I will administer it in such shape–"

"I forbid it," said Indiana, in a cold, determined tone: "my husband is here: Ralph never lied. You and I are lost. There was a time when the thought would have frozen me with horror; to-day it matters little to me!"

"Very well!" said Raymon, seizing her in his arms excitedly, "since death encompasses us, be mine! Forgive everything, and let your last word in this supreme moment be a word of love, my last breath a breath of joy."

"This moment of terror and courage might have been the sweetest moment in my life," she said, "but you have spoiled it for me."

There was a rumbling of wheels in the farmyard, and the bell at the gate of the château was rung by a strong and impatient hand.

"I know that ring," said Indiana, watchful and cool. "Ralph did not lie; but you have time to escape; go!"

"I will not," cried Raymon; "I suspect some despicable treachery and you shall not be the only victim. I will remain and my breast shall protect you–"

"There is no treachery–listen–the servants are stirring and the gate will be opened directly. Go: the trees in the garden will conceal you, and the moon is not fairly out yet. Not a word more, but go!"

Raymon was compelled to obey; but she accompanied him to the foot of the stairs and cast a searching glance about the flower-garden. All was silent and calm. She stood a long while on the last stair, listening with terror to the grinding of his footsteps on the gravel, entirely oblivious of her husband's arrival. What cared she for his suspicions and his anger, provided that Raymon was out of danger?

As for him he crossed the stream and hurried swiftly through the park. He reached the small gate and, in his excitement, had some difficulty in opening it. He was no sooner in the road than Sir Ralph appeared in front of him and said with as much *sang-froid* as if he were accosting him at a party:

"Be good enough to let me have that key. If there should be a search for it, it would be less inconvenient for it to be found in my hands."

Raymon would have preferred the most deadly insult to this satirical generosity.

"I am not the man to forget a well-meant service," said he; "I am the man to avenge an insult and to punish treachery."

Sir Ralph changed neither his tone nor his expression.

"I want none of your gratitude," he rejoined, "and I await your vengeance tranquilly; but this is no time to talk. There is your path–think of Madame Delmare's good name."

And he disappeared.

This night of agitation had overturned Raymon's brain so completely that he would readily have believed in witchcraft at that moment. He reached Cercy at daybreak and went to bed with a raging fever.

As for Madame Delmare, she did the honors of the breakfast table for her husband and cousin with much calmness and dignity. She had not as yet reflected upon her situation; she was absolutely under the influence of instinct, which enjoined *sang-froid* and presence of mind upon her. The colonel was gloomy and thoughtful, but it was his business alone that preoccupied him, and no jealous suspicion found a place in his thoughts.

Toward evening Raymon mustered courage to think about his love; but that love had diminished materially. He loved obstacles; but he hated to be bored and he foresaw that he should be bored times without number now that Indiana had the right to reproach him. However, he remembered at last that his honor demanded that he should inquire for her, and he sent his servant to prowl around Lagny and find out what was going on there. The servant brought him the following letter which Madame Delmare herself had handed him:

"I hoped last night that I should lose either my reason or my life. Unhappily for me I have retained both; but I will not complain, I have deserved the suffering that I am undergoing; I chose to live this tempestuous life; it would be cowardly to recoil to-day. I do not know whether you are guilty, I do not want to know. We will never return to that subject, will we? It causes us both too much suffering: so let this be the last time it is mentioned between us.

"You said one thing at which I felt a cruel joy. Poor Noun! from your place in heaven forgive me! you no longer suffer, you no longer love, perhaps you pity me! You told me, Raymon, that you sacrificed that unhappy girl to me, that you loved me better than her. Oh! do not take it back; you said it, and I feel so strongly the need to believe it that I do believe it. And yet your conduct last night, your entreaties, your wild outbreaks, might well have made me doubt it. I forgave you on account of the mental disturbance under which you were laboring; but now you have had time to reflect, to become yourself once more; tell me, will you renounce loving me in that way? I, who love you with my heart, have believed hitherto that I could arouse in you a love as pure as my own. And then I had not thought very much about the future; I had not looked ahead very far, and I had not taken alarm at the thought that the day might come when, conquered by your devotion, I should sacrifice to you my scruples and my repugnance. But to-day, it can no longer be the same; I can see in the future only a ghastly parallel between myself and Noun! Oh! the thought of being loved no more than she was! If I believed it! And yet she was lovelier than I, far lovelier! Why did you prefer me? You must have loved me differently and better,–That is what I wanted you to say. Will you give up being my lover in the way that you have been? In that case I can still esteem you, believe in your remorse, your sincerity, your love; if not, think of me no more, you will never see me again. I shall die of it perhaps, but I would rather die than descend so low as to be your mistress."

Raymon was sorely embarrassed as to how he should reply. This pride offended him; he had never supposed hitherto that a woman who had thrown herself into his arms could resist him thus outspokenly and give reasons for her resistance.

"She does not love me," he said to himself; "her heart is dry, she is naturally overbearing."

From that moment he loved her no longer. She had ruffled his self-esteem; she had disappointed his hope of triumph, defeated his anticipations of pleasure. In his eyes she was no more than Noun had been. Poor Indiana! who longed to be so much more! Her passionate love was misunderstood, her blind confidence was spurned. Raymon had never understood her; how could he have continued to love her?

Thereupon he swore, in his irritation, that he would triumph over her; he swore it not from a feeling of pride but in a revengeful spirit. It was no longer a matter of snatching a new pleasure, but of punishing an insult; of possessing a woman, but of subduing her. He swore that he would be her master, were it for but a single day, and that then he would abandon her, to have the satisfaction of seeing her at his feet.

On the spur of the moment he wrote this letter:

"You want me to promise. Foolish girl, can you think of such a thing? I will promise whatever you choose, because I can do nothing but obey you; but, if I break my promises I shall be guilty neither to God nor to you. If you loved me, Indiana, you would not inflict these cruel torments on me, you would not expose me to the risk of perjuring myself, you would not blush at the thought of being my mistress. But you think that in my arms you would be degraded–"

He felt that his bitterness was making itself manifest, despite his efforts; he tore up this sheet, and, after taking time to reflect, began anew:

"You admit that you nearly lost your reason last night; for my part, I lost mine altogether. I was culpable–but no, I was mad! Forget those hours of suffering and excitement. I am calm now; I have reflected; I am still worthy of you. Bless you, my angel from heaven, for saving me from myself, for reminding me how I ought to love you. Now, Indiana, command me! I am your slave, as you well know. I would give my life for an hour in your arms; but I can suffer a whole lifetime to obtain a smile from you. I will be your friend, your brother, nothing more. If I suffer, you shall not know it. If my blood boils when I am near you, if my breast takes fire, if a cloud passes before my eyes when I touch your hand, if a sweet kiss from your lips, a sisterly kiss, scorches my forehead, I will order my blood to be calm, my brain to grow cool, my mouth to respect you. I will be gentle, I will be submissive, I will be unhappy,–if you will be the happier therefor and enjoy my agony,–if only I may hear you tell me again that you love me! Oh! tell me so! give me back your confidence and my joy! tell me when we shall meet again. I know not what result the events of last night may have had; how does it happen that you do not refer to the subject, that you leave me in an agony of suspense? Carle saw you all three walking together in the park. The colonel seemed ill or depressed, but not angry. In that case that Ralph did not betray us! What a strange man! But to what extent can we rely on his discretion, and how shall I dare show myself at Lagny now that our fate is in his hands? But I will dare. If it is necessary to stoop so low as to implore him, I will silence my pride, I will overcome my aversion, I will do anything rather than lose you. A word from you and I will burden my life with as much remorse as I am able to carry; for you I would abandon my mother herself; for you I would commit any crime. Ah! if you realized the depth of my love, Indiana!"

The pen fell from Raymon's hands; he was terribly fatigued, he was falling asleep. But he read over his letter to make sure that his ideas had not suffered from the influence of drowsiness; but it was impossible for him to understand his own meaning, his brain was so affected by his physical exhaustion. He rang for his servant, bade him go to Lagny before daybreak; then slept that deep, refreshing sleep whose tranquil delights only those who are thoroughly satisfied with themselves really know. Madame Delmare had not retired; she was unconscious of fatigue and passed the night writing. When she received Raymon's letter she answered it in haste:

"Thanks, Raymon, thanks! you restore my strength and my life. Now I can dare anything, endure anything; for you love me, and the most severe tests do not alarm you. Yes, we will meet again–we will defy everybody. Ralph may do what he will with our secret. I am no longer disturbed about anything since you love me; I am not even afraid of my husband.

"You want to know about our affairs? I forgot to mention them yesterday, and yet they have taken a turn which has an important bearing on my fortunes. We are ruined. There is some talk of selling Lagny, and even of going to live in the colonies. But of what consequence is all that? I cannot make up my mind to think about it. I know that we shall never be parted. You have sworn it, Raymon; I rely on your promise, do you rely on my courage. Nothing will frighten me, nothing will turn me back. My place is established at your side, and death alone can tear me from it."

"Mere woman's effervescence!" said Raymon, crumpling the letter. "Romantic projects, perilous undertakings, appeal to their feeble imaginations as bitter substances arouse a sick man's appetite. I have succeeded; I have recovered my influence; and, as for all this imprudent folly with which she threatens me, we will see! It is all characteristic of the light-headed, false creatures, always ready to undertake the impossible and making of generosity a show virtue which must be attended with scandal! Who would think, to read this letter, that she counts her kisses and doles out her caresses like a miser!"

XVIII

That same day he went to Lagny. Ralph was not there, and the colonel received him amicably and talked to him confidentially. He took him into the park, where they were less likely to be disturbed, and told him that he was utterly ruined and that the factory would be offered for sale on the following day. Raymon made generous offers of assistance, but Delmare declined them.

"No, my friend," he said, "I have suffered too much from the thought that I owed my fate to Ralph's kindness; I was in too much of a hurry to repay him. The sale of this property will enable me to pay all my debts at once. To be sure, I shall have nothing left, but I have courage, energy and business experience; the future is before us. I have built up my little fortune once, and I can begin it again. I must do it for my wife's sake, for she is young, and I don't wish to leave her in poverty. She still owns an estate of some little value at Ile Bourbon, and I propose to go into retirement there and start in business afresh. In a few years–in ten years at most–I hope that we shall meet again."

Raymon pressed the colonel's hand, smiling inwardly at his confidence, at his speaking of ten years as of a single day, when his bald head and enfeebled body indicated a feeble hold upon existence, a life near its close. Nevertheless he pretended to share his hopes.

"I am delighted to see," he said, "that you do not allow yourself to be cast down by these reverses. I recognize your manly heart, your undaunted courage. But does Madame Delmare display the same courage? Do you not anticipate some resistance on her part to your project of expatriation?"

"I shall be very sorry," the colonel replied, "but wives are made to obey, not to advise. I have not yet definitely made my purpose known to Indiana. With the exception of yourself, my friend, I do not know what there is here that she should feel any regret at leaving; and yet I anticipate tears and nervous attacks, from a spirit of contradiction, if nothing else. The devil take the women! However, my dear Raymon, I rely upon you all the same to make my wife listen to reason. She has confidence in you; use your influence to prevent her from crying. I detest tears."

Raymon promised to come again the next day and inform Madame Delmare of her husband's decision.

"You will do me a very great favor," said the colonel. "I will take Ralph to the farm, so that you may have a good chance to talk with her."

"Well, luck is on my side!" thought Ralph, as he took his leave.

XIX

Monsieur Delmare's plans fell in perfectly with Raymon's wishes. He foresaw that this love affair which, so far as he was concerned, was drawing near its close, would soon bring him nothing but annoyance and importunity, so that he was very glad to see events arranging themselves in such a way as to save him from the wearisome but inevitable results of a played-out intrigue. It only remained for him to take advantage of Madame Delmare's last moments of excitement, and then to leave to his complaisant destiny the task of ridding him of her tears and reproaches.

So he returned to Lagny the next day, intending to exalt the unhappy woman's enthusiasm to its apogee.

"Do you know, Indiana," he said, when they met, "the part that your husband has requested me to play with respect to you? A strange commission, upon my word! I am to entreat you to go with him to Ile Bourbon; to urge you to leave me; to tear out my heart and my life. Do you think that he made a good choice of an advocate?"

Madame Delmare's sombre gravity imposed a sort of respect on Raymon's cunning.

"Why do you come and tell me all this?" she said. "Are you afraid that I shall allow myself to be moved? Are you afraid that I shall obey? Never fear, Raymon, my mind is made up; I have passed two nights looking at it on every side; I know to what I expose myself; I know what I must defy, what I must sacrifice, what I must disdain to notice; I am ready to pass through this stormy period of my destiny. Will not you be my support and my guide?"

Raymon was tempted to take fright at this cool determination and to take these insane threats seriously; but in a moment he recurred to his former opinion that Indiana did not really love him, and that she was applying now to her situation the exaggerated sentiments she had learned from books. He strove to be eloquent with passion, he devoted his energies to dramatic improvisation, in order to maintain himself on his romantic mistress's level, and he succeeded in prolonging her error. But, to a calm and impartial auditor, this love scene would have seemed a contest between stage illusion and reality. The grandiloquence of Raymon's sentiments, the poesy of his ideas would have seemed a cold and cruel parody of the real sentiments which Indiana expressed so simply: in the one case mind, in the other heart.

XIX

Raymon, who however had some little fear that she might carry out her promises if he did not shrewdly undermine the plan of resistance she had formed, persuaded her to counterfeit submission or indifference until such time as she could come forth in open rebellion. It was essential, he said, that they should have left Lagny before she declared herself, in order to avoid a scandal in presence of the servants, and Ralph's dangerous intervention in the affair.

But Ralph did not leave his unfortunate friends. In vain did he offer his whole fortune, his Bellerive estate, his English consols, and whatever his plantations in the colonies would bring; the colonel was inflexible. His affection for Ralph had diminished; he was no longer willing to owe anything to him. Ralph might perhaps have been able to move him had he possessed Raymon's wit and address; but when he had plainly set forth his ideas and declared his sentiments, the poor baronet believed that he had said everything, and he never attempted to secure the retraction of a refusal. So he let Bellerive and followed Monsieur and Madame Delmare to Paris, pending their departure for Ile Bourbon

Lagny was offered for sale with the factory and the appurtenances. The winter was a melancholy and depressing one to Madame Delmare. To be sure, Raymon was in Paris, he saw her every day, he was attentive and affectionate; but he remained barely an hour with her. He arrived just after dinner, and when the colonel went out on business, he also took his leave to attend some social function or other. Society, you know, was Raymon's element, his life; he must have the noise, the bustle, the crowd, to breathe freely, to display all his intellectual power, all his ease of manner, all his superiority. In the privacy of the boudoir he could make himself attractive, in society he became brilliant; and then he was no longer the man of a small coterie, the friend of this one or that one; he was the man of intellect who belongs to all alike, and to whom society is a sort of fatherland.

And then, as we have said, Raymon had some principle. When the colonel manifested such confidence in him and esteem for him, when he saw that he regarded him as the very type of honor and sincerity and desired him to act as mediator between his wife and himself, he determined to justify that confidence, to deserve that esteem, to reconcile that husband and wife, to repel any attachment on the part of the latter which might endanger the repose of the other. He became once more a moral, virtuous, philosophical person. You will see for how long.

Indiana, who did not understand this conversion, suffered horribly to be so neglected; and yet she still had the satisfaction of feeling that her hopes were not entirely destroyed. She was easily deceived; she asked nothing better than to be deceived, her real life was so bitter and desolate! Her husband had become almost impossible to live with. In public he affected the heroic courage and indifference of a brave man; but when he returned to the privacy of his own home he was simply an irritable, severe, absurd child. Indiana was the victim of his disgust with life, and, we must confess, she was largely to blame. If she had raised her voice, if she had complained, affectionately but forcibly, Delmare, who was only rough, would have blushed at the idea of being considered unkind. Nothing was easier than to touch his heart and govern him absolutely, if one chose to descend to his level and enter into the circle of ideas that were within the scope of his mind. But Indiana was stiff and haughty in her submissiveness; she always obeyed in silence; but it was the silence and submissiveness of the slave who has made of hatred a virtue and of unhappiness a merit. Her resignation was the dignity of a king who accepts fetters and a dungeon rather than voluntarily abdicate his throne and lay aside a vain title. A woman of a commoner mould would have mastered that commonplace man; she would have said what he said and reserved the right to think differently; she would have pretended to respect his prejudices and secretly have trampled them under foot; she would have caressed him and deceived him. Indiana saw many women who acted thus; but she felt so far above them that she would have blushed to imitate them. Being virtuous and chaste, she thought that she was not called upon to flatter her master by her words so long as she respected him in his actions. She did not care for his affection because she could not respond to it. She would have considered it far more blameworthy to make a show of love for the husband whom she did not love, than to give her heart to the lover who inspired love in her. To deceive was the crime in her eyes, and twenty times a day she felt that she must declare her love for Raymon; naught detained her but the fear of ruining him. Her impassive obedience irritated the colonel much more than a cleverly managed rebellion would have done. Although his self-esteem would have suffered if he had ceased to be master in his own house, it suffered much more from the consciousness that he was master in a hateful and absurd fashion. He would have liked to convince and he simply commanded; to reign, and he governed. Sometimes he gave an order that was awkwardly expressed, or, without reflection, issued orders that were injurious to his own interests. Madame Delmare saw that they were carried out without scrutiny, without question, with the indifference of the horse that draws the plough in one direction or another. Delmare, when he saw the result of the failure to understand his ideas, of the misconstruction of his wishes, would fly into a rage; but when she had proved to him with a few tranquil, icy words that she had simply caused his orders to be obeyed, he was reduced to the necessity of turning his wrath against himself. It was a cruel pang, a bitter affront to that man of petty self-esteem and of violent passions.

Several times he would have killed his wife, if he had been at Smyrna or at Cairo. And yet he loved with all his heart that weak woman who lived in subjection to him and kept the secret of his ill-treatment with religious prudence. He loved her or pitied her–I do not know which. He would have liked to win her love, for he was proud of her education and of her superiority. He would have risen in his own eyes if she would have stooped so far as to parley with his ideas and his principles. When he went to her apartments in the morning with the purpose of picking a quarrel with her, he sometimes found her asleep and dared not wake her. He would gaze at her in silence; he would take fright at the delicacy of her constitution, the pallor of her cheeks, at the air of calm melancholy, of resignation to misfortune expressed by that motionless and silent face. He would find in her features innumerable subjects of self-reproach, remorse, anger and dread.

He would blush at the thought of the influence which so frail a creature had exerted over his destiny–he, a man of iron, accustomed to command others, to see whole battalions, spirited horses and frightened men march at a word from his lips.

And a wife who was still but a child had made him unhappy! She forced him to look within himself–to scrutinize his own decisions, to modify many of them, to retract some of them–and all this without saying: "You are wrong; I beg that you will do thus or thus." She had never implored, she had never deigned to show herself his equal and to avow herself his companion. That woman, whom he could have crushed in his hand if he had chosen, lay there, an insignificant creature, dreaming of another before his eyes, perhaps, and defying him even in her sleep. He was tempted to strangle her–to drag her out of bed by the hair, to trample on her and force her to shriek for mercy and to implore his forgiveness; but she was so pretty, so dainty and so fair, that he would suddenly take pity on her, as a child is moved to pity as he gazes at the bird he intended to kill. And he would weep like a woman, man of bronze as he was, and would steal away so that she might not enjoy the triumph of seeing him weep. In truth I know not which was the unhappier, he or she. She was cruel from virtue, as he was kind from weakness; she had too much patience, of which he had not enough; she had the failings of her good qualities and he the good qualities of his failings.

Around these two ill-assorted beings swarmed a multitude of friends who strove to bring them nearer together, some in order to have something to occupy their minds, others to give themselves importance, others as the result of ill-advised affection. Some took the wife's part, others the husband's. They quarrelled among themselves on the subject of Monsieur and Madame Delmare, who, on the other hand, did not quarrel at all; for, with Indiana's systematic submission, the colonel could never succeed in picking a quarrel, whatever he might do. And then there were those who knew nothing, but wanted to make themselves necessary. They counselled submission to Madame Delmare and did not see that she was only too submissive; others advised the husband to be inflexible and not to allow his authority to pass into his wife's hands. These last, stupid mortals who have so little feeling that they are always afraid that some one is treading on them and who mistake cause and effect for each other, belong to a species which you will find everywhere, which is constantly getting entangled in other people's legs and makes a deal of noise in order to attract attention.

Monsieur and Madame Delmare had made a particularly large number of acquaintances at Melun and at Fontainebleau. They met these people again at Paris, and they were the keenest in the game of evil-speaking that was being played about them. The wit of small towns is, as you doubtless know, the most ill-natured in the world. Good people are always misunderstood there, superior minds are sworn foes of the public. If a battle is to be fought for a fool or a boor you will see them running from all directions. If you have a dispute with any one, they come to look on as at the theatre; they make bets; they crowd upon your heels, so eager are they to see and hear. The one who falls they will cover with mud and maledictions; the weakest is always in the wrong. If you make war on prejudices, petty foibles, vices, you insult them personally, you attack them in what they hold most dear, you are a treacherous and dangerous man. You will be summoned before the courts to make reparations by people whose names you do not know, but whom you will be convicted of having referred to in your slurring allusions. What advice shall I give you? If you meet one of those people, avoid stepping in his shadow, even at sunset, when a man's shadow is thirty feet long; all that ground belong to the inhabitant of the small town, and you have no right to set a foot upon it. If you breathe the air that he breathes, you injure him, you destroy his health; if you drink at his fountain, you cause it to run dry; if you lend a hand to business in his province, you increase the price of the articles he purchases; if you offer him snuff, you poison it; if you think his daughter pretty, you intend to seduce her; if you extol his wife's domestic virtues, it is insulting irony, and in your heart you despise her for her ignorance; if you are so ill-advised as to pay him a compliment in his own house, he will not understand it, and he will go about everywhere saying that you have insulted him. Take your penates and carry them into the woods or to the desolate moors. There only will the man of the small town leave you in peace.

Even behind the manifold girdle of the walls of Paris the small town pursued this ill-starred couple. Well-to-do families from Melun and Fontainebleau took up their abode in the capital for the winter and brought thither the blessing of their provincial manners. Cliques were formed around Delmare and his wife, and all that was humanly possible was attempted in order to make their position with respect to each other more uncomfortable. Their unhappiness was increased thereby and their mutual obstinacy did not diminish.

Ralph had the good sense not to meddle in their dissensions. Madame Delmare had suspected him of embittering her husband against her, or at least of seeking to put an end to Raymon's intimacy with her; but she soon realized the injustice of her suspicions. The colonel's perfect tranquility with respect to Monsieur de Ramière was irrefutable evidence of his cousin's silence. Thereupon she felt that she must thank him; but he sedulously avoided any conversation on that subject; whenever she was alone with him, he eluded her hints and pretended not to understand them. It was such a delicate subject that Madame Delmare had not the courage to force Ralph to discuss it; she simply endeavored, by her loving attentions, by her delicate and affectionate deference to him, to make him understand her gratitude; but Ralph seemed to pay no heed, and Indiana's pride was wounded by this display of supercilious generosity. She was afraid that she should seem to play the rôle of the guilty wife imploring the indulgence of a stern witness; she became cold and constrained once more with poor Ralph. It seemed to her that his conduct in this matter was the natural consequence of his selfishness; that he loved her still, although he no longer esteemed her; that he simply desired her society for his own diversion, that he disliked to abandon habits which she had formed for him in her home and to deprive himself of the attentions that she was never weary of bestowing upon him. She fancied that he was by no means anxious to invent grievances against her husband or herself.

"That is just like his contempt for women," she thought; "in his eyes they are simply domestic animals, useful to keep a house in order, prepare meals and serve tea. He doesn't do them the honor of entering into a discussion with them; their faults have no effect on him provided that they do not interfere with his comfort or his mode of life. Ralph has no need of my heart; as long as my hands retain the knack of preparing his pudding and of touching the strings of the harp for him, what does he care for my love for another man, my secret suffering, my deathly impatience under the yoke that is crushing me? I am his servant, he asks nothing more of me than that."

XX

Indiana had ceased to reproach Raymon; he defended himself so badly that she was afraid of finding him too worthy of blame. There was one thing which she dreaded much more than being deceived, and that was being abandoned. She could not live without her belief in him, without her hope of the future he had promised her; for her life with Monsieur Delmare and Ralph had become hateful to her, and if she had not expected soon to escape from the power of those two men, she would have drowned herself at once. She often thought of it; she said to herself that if Raymon treated her as he had treated Noun there would be no other way for her to avoid an unendurable future than to join Noun. That sombre thought followed her everywhere and she took pleasure in it.

Meanwhile the time fixed for their departure from France drew near. The colonel seemed to have no suspicion of the resistance which his wife was meditating; every day he made some progress in the settlement of his affairs, every day he paid off one more creditor; and Madame Delmare looked on with a tranquil eye at all these preparations, sure as she was of her own courage. She was preparing, too, for her struggle with the difficulties she anticipated. She sought to procure an ally in her aunt, Madame de Carvajal, and dilated to her upon her repugnance to the journey; and the old marchioness who–to give her no more than her due–built great hopes of attracting *custom* to her salon upon her niece's beauty, declared that it was the colonel's duty to leave his wife in France; that it would be downright barbarity to expose her to the fatigues and dangers of an ocean voyage when her health had just begun to show some slight improvement; in a word, that it was his place to go to work at rebuilding his fortune, Indiana's to remain with her old aunt and take care of her. At first Monsieur Delmare looked upon these insinuations as the doting talk of an old woman; but he was forced to pay more attention to them when Madame de Carvajal gave him clearly to understand that her inheritance was to be had only at that price. Although Delmare loved money like a man who had worked hard all his life to amass it, he had some pride in his composition; he pronounced his ultimatum with decision, and declared that his wife should go with him at any risk. The marchioness, who could not believe that money was not the absolute sovereign of every man of good sense, did not look upon this as Monsieur Delmare's last word; she continued to encourage her niece in her resistance, proposing to assume the responsibility for her action in the eyes of the world. It needed all the indelicacy of a mind corrupted by intrigue and ambition, all the shuffling of a heart distorted by constant devotion to mere external show, to close her eyes thus to the real causes of Indiana's rebellion. Her passion for Monsieur de Ramière was a secret to no one but her husband; but as Indiana had as yet given scandal nothing to seize upon, the secret was mentioned only in undertones, and Madame de Carvajal had been confidentially informed of it by more than a score of persons. The foolish old woman was flattered by it; all that she desired was to have her niece *à la mode* in society, and an intrigue with Raymon was a fine beginning. And yet Madame de Carvajal's moral character was not of the Regency type; the Restoration had given a virtuous impulse to minds of that stamp; and as *conduct* was demanded at court, the marchioness detested nothing so much as the scandal that ruins and destroys. Under Madame du Barry she would been less rigid in her principles; under the Dauphiness she became one of the *high-necked.* But all this was for show, for the sake of appearances; she kept her disapprobation and her scorn for notorious misconduct, and she always awaited the result of an intrigue before condemning it. Those infidelities which did not cross the threshold were venial in her eyes. She became a Spaniard once more to pass judgment on passions inside the blinds; in her eyes there was no guilt save that which was placarded on the streets for passers-by to see. So that Indiana, passionate but chaste, enamored but reserved, was a precious subject to exhibit and exploit; such a woman as she was might fascinate the strongest brains in that hypocritical society and withstand the perils of the most delicate missions. This was an excellent chance to speculate on the responsibility of so pure a mind and so passionate a heart. Poor Indiana! luckily her fatal destiny surpassed all her hopes and led her into an abyss of misery where her aunt's pernicious protection did not seek her out.

Raymon was not disturbed as to what was to become of her. This intrigue had already reached the last stage of distaste, deathly ennui, so far as he was concerned. To cause ennui is to descend as low as possible in the regard of the person whom one loves. Luckily for the last days of her illusion, Indiana had no suspicion of it.

One morning, on returning from a ball, he found Madame Delmare in his room. She had come at midnight; for five mortal hours she had been waiting! It was in the coldest part of the year; she had no fire, but sat with her head resting on her hand, enduring cold and anxiety with the gloomy patience which the whole course of her life has taught her. She raised her head when he entered, and Raymon, speechless with amazement, could detect on her pale face no indication of anger or reproach.

"I was waiting for you," she said gently; "as you had not come to see me for three days, and as things have happened which it is important that you should know without delay, I came here last night in order to tell you of them."

"It is imprudent beyond belief!" said Raymon, cautiously locking the door behind him; "and my people know that you are here! They just told me so."

"I made no attempt at concealment," she replied coldly; "and as for the word you use, I consider it ill-chosen."

"I said imprudent, I should have said insane."

"And I should say *courageous.* But no matter; listen to me. Monsieur Delmare starts for Bordeaux in three days, and sails thence for the colony. You and I agreed that you should protect me from violence if he employed it; there is no question that he will, for I made known my determination last evening and he locked me into my room. I escaped through a window; see, my hands are bleeding. They may be looking for me at this moment, but Ralph is at Bellerive so that he will not be able to tell where I am. I have decided to remain in hiding until Monsieur Delmare has made up his mind to leave me behind. Have you thought about making ready for my flight, of preparing a hiding-place for me? It is so long since I have been able to see you alone, that I do not know what your present inclinations are; but one day, when I expressed some doubt concerning your resolution, you told me that you could not imagine love without confidence; you reminded me that you had never doubted me, you proved to me that I was unjust, and thereupon I was afraid of remaining below your level if I did not cast aside such puerile suspicions and the innumerable little exactions by which women degrade ordinary love-affairs. I have endured with resignation the brevity of your calls, the embarrassment of our interviews, the eagerness with which you seemed to avoid any free exchange of sentiment with me; I have retained my confidence in you. Heaven is my witness that when anxiety and fear were gnawing at my heart I spurned them as criminal thoughts. I have come now to seek the reward of my faith; the time has come; tell me, do you accept my sacrifices? "

The crisis was so urgent that Raymon did not feel bold enough to pretend any longer. Desperate, frantic to find himself caught in his own trap, he lost his head and vented his temper in coarse and brutal maledictions.

"You are a mad woman!" he cried, throwing himself into a chair. "Where have you dreamed of love? in what romance written for the entertainment of lady's-maids, have you studied society, I pray to know?"

He paused, realizing that he had been far too rough, and cudgelling his brains to find a way of saying the same things in other terms and of sending her away without insulting her.

But she was calm, like one prepared to listen to anything.

"Go on," she said, folding her arms over her heart, whose throbbing gradually grew less violent; "I am listening; I presume that you have something more than that to say to me?"

"Still another effort of the imagination, another love scene," thought Raymon.– "Never," he cried, springing excitedly to his feet, "never will I accept such sacrifices! When I told you that I should have the strength to do it, Indiana, I boasted too much, or rather I slandered myself; for the man is no better than a dastard who will consent to dishonor the woman he loves. In your ignorance of life, you failed to realize the importance of such a plan, and I, in my despair at the thought of losing you, did not choose to reflect–"

"Your power of reflection has returned very suddenly!" she said, withdrawing her hand, which he tried to take.

"Indiana," he rejoined, "do you not see that you impose the dishonorable part on me, while you reserve the heroic part for yourself, and that you condemn me because I desire to remain worthy of your love? Could you continue to love me, ignorant and simple-hearted woman as you are, if I sacrificed your life to my pleasure, your reputation to my selfish interests?"

"You say things that are very contradictory," said Indiana; "if I made you happy by remaining with you, what do you care for the public opinion? Do you care more for it than for me?"

"Oh! I do not care for it on my account, Indiana!"

"Is it on my account then? I anticipated your scruples and to spare you anything like remorse I have taken the initiative; I did not wait for you to come and carry me away from my home, I did not even consult you with regard to crossing my husband's threshold forever. The decisive step is taken, and your conscience cannot reproach you for it. At the moment, Raymon, I am dishonored. In your absence I counted on yonder clock the hours that consummated my disgrace; and now, although the dawn finds my brow as pure as it was yesterday, I am a lost creature in public opinion. Yesterday there was still some compassion for me in the hearts of other women; to-day there will be no feeling left but contempt. I considered all these things before acting."

"Infernal female foresight!" thought Raymon.

And then, struggling against her as he would have done against a bailiff who has come to levy on his furniture, he said in a caressing fatherly tone:

"You exaggerate the importance of what you have done. No, my love, all is not lost because of one rash step. I will enjoin silence on my servants."

"Will you enjoin silence on mine who, I doubt not, are anxiously looking for me at this moment. And my husband, do you think he will quietly keep the secret? do you think he will consent to receive me to-morrow, when I have passed a whole night under your roof? Will you advise me to go back and throw myself at his feet, and ask him, as a proof of his forgiveness, to be kind enough to replace on my neck the chain which has crushed my life and withered my youth? You would consent, without regret, to see the woman which you loved so dearly go back and resume another man's yoke, when you have her fate in your hands, when you can keep her in your arms all your life, when she is in your power, offering to remain here forever! You would not feel the least repugnance, the least alarm in surrendering her at once to the implacable master, who perhaps awaits her coming only to kill her!"

A thought flashed through Raymon's brain. The moment had come to subdue that womanly pride, or it would never come. She had offered him all the sacrifices that he did not want, and she stood before him in overweening confidence that she ran no other risks than those she had foreseen. Raymon conceived a scheme for ridding himself of her embarrassing devotion or of deriving some profit of it. He was too good a friend of Delmare, he owed too much consideration to the man's unbounded confidence to steal his wife from him; he must content himself with seducing her.

"You are right, my Indiana," he cried with animation, "you bring me back to myself, you rekindle my transports with the thought of your danger and the dread of injuring you has cooled. Forgive my childish solicitude and let me prove to you how much of tenderness and genuine love it denotes. Your sweet voice makes my blood quiver, your burning words pour fire into my veins; forgive, oh! forgive me for having thought of anything else than this ineffable moment when I at last possess you. Let me forget all the dangers that threaten us and thank you on my knees for the happiness you bring me; let me live entirely in this hour of bliss which I pass at your feet and for which all my blood would not pay. Let him come, that dolt of a husband who locks you up and goes to sleep upon his vulgar brutality, let him come and snatch you from my transports! let him come and snatch you from my arms, my treasure, my life ! Henceforth you do not belong to him; you are my sweetheart, my companion, my mistress–"

As he pleaded thus, Raymon gradually worked himself up, as he was accustomed to do when *arguing* his passions. It was a powerful, a romantic situation; it offered some risks. Raymon loved danger, like a genuine descendant of a race of valiant knights. Every sound that he heard in the street seemed to denote the coming of the husband to claim his wife and his rival's blood. To seek the joys of love in the stirring emotions of such a situation was a diversion worthy of Raymon. For a quarter of an hour he loved Madame Delmare passionately, he lavished upon her the seductions of burning eloquence. He was truly powerful in his language and sincere in his behavior–this man whose ardent brain considered love-making a polite accomplishment. He played at passion so well that he deceived himself. Shame upon this foolish woman! She abandoned herself in ecstasy to those treacherous demonstrations; she was happy, she was radiant with hope and joy; she forgave everything, she almost accorded everything.

But Raymon ruined himself by over-precipitation. If he had carried his art so far as to prolong for twenty-four hours the situation in which Indiana had risked herself, she would perhaps have been his. But the day was breaking, bright and rosy; the sun poured floods of light into the room, and the noise in the street increased with every moment. Raymon cast a glance at the clock; it was nearly seven.

"It is time to have done with it," he thought; "Delmare may appear at any moment, and before that happens I must induce her to return home voluntarily."

He became more urgent and less tender; the pallor of his lips betrayed the working of an impatience more imperious than delicate. There was in his kisses a sort of abruptness, almost anger. Indiana was afraid. A good angel spread his wings over that wavering and bewildered soul; she came to herself and repelled the attacks of cold and selfish vice.

"Leave me," she said; "I do not propose to yield through weakness what I am willing to accord for love or gratitude. You cannot need proofs of my affection: my presence here is a sufficiently decisive one, and I bring the future with me. But allow me to keep all the strength of my conscience to contend against powerful obstacles that still separate us; I need stoicism and tranquility."

"What are you talking about?" angrily demanded Raymon, who was furious at her resistance and had not listened to her.

And, losing his heart altogether in that moment of torture and wrath, he pushed her roughly away and strode up and down the room, with heaving bosom and head on fire; then he took a carafe and drank a large glass of water which suddenly calmed his excitement and cooled his love. Whereupon he looked at her ironically and said:

"Come, madame, it is time for you to retire."

A ray of light at last enlightened Indiana and laid Raymon's heart bare before her.

"You are right," she said.

And she walked toward the door.

"Pray take your cloak and boa," he said, detaining her.

"To be sure," she retorted, "those traces of my presence might compromise you."

"You are a child," he said, in a coaxing tone, as he adjusted her cloak with ostentatious care; "you know very well that I love you; but really you take pleasure in torturing me, and you drive me mad. Wait until I go and call a cab. If I could, I would escort you home; but that would ruin you."

"Pray, do you not think that I am ruined already?" she asked bitterly.

"No, my darling," replied Raymon, who asked nothing better than to persuade her to leave him in peace. "Nobody has noticed your absence, as they have not yet come here in search of you. Although I should be the last one to be suspected, it would be natural to inquire at the houses of all of your acquaintances. And then you can go and place yourself under your aunt's protection; indeed, that is the course I advise you to take; she will arrange everything. You will be supposed to have passed the night at her house."

Madame Delmare was not listening; she was gazing stupidly at the sun, as it rose, huge and red, over an expanse of gleaming roofs. Raymon tried to rouse her from her preoccupation. She turned her eyes on him, but seemed not to recognize him. Her cheeks had a greenish tinge and her parched lips seemed paralyzed.

Raymon was terrified. He remembered the other's suicide, and, in his alarm, not knowing which way to turn, dreading lest he should become twice a criminal in his own eyes, but feeling too exhausted mentally to be able to deceive her again, he pushed her gently into an easy-chair, locked the door, and went up to his mother's room.

XXI

He found her awake; she was accustomed to rise early, the result of habits of hard-working activity which she has formed during the emigration, and which she had not abandoned when she recovered her wealth.

Seeing Raymon enter her room so late, pale and excited, and in full dress, she realized that he was struggling in one of the frequent crises of his stormy life. She had always been his refuge and salvation in these periods of agitation, of which no trace remained save a deep and sorrowful one in her mother-heart. Her life had been withered and used up by all that Raymon had acquired and reacquired. Her son's character, impetuous yet cold, reflective yet passionate, was a consequence of her inexhaustible love and generous indulgence. He would have been a better man with a mother less kind; but she had accustomed him to make the most of all the sacrifices that she consented to make for him; she had taught him to seek and to advance his own well-being as zealously and as powerfully as she sought it. Because she deemed herself created to preserve him from all sorrows and to sacrifice all her own interests to him, he had accustomed himself to believe that the whole world was created for him and would place itself in his hand at a word from his mother. By an abundance of generosity she had succeeded only in forming a selfish heart.

She turned pale, did the poor mother, and, sitting up in bed, gazed anxiously at him. Her glance said at once: "What can I do for you? Where must I go?"

"Mother," he said grasping the dry, transparent hand that she held out to him, "I am horribly unhappy, I need your help. Save me from the troubles by which I am surrounded. I love Madame Delmare, as you know–"

"I did not know it," said Madame de Ramière, in a tone of affectionate reproof.

"Don't try to deny it, dear mother," said Raymon, who had no time to waste; "you did know it, and your admirable delicacy prevented you speaking it first. Well, that woman is driving me to despair, and my brain is going."

"Tell me what you mean !" said Madame de Ramière, with the youthful vivacity born of ardent maternal love.

"I do not mean to conceal anything from you, especially as I am not guilty this time. For several months I have been trying to calm her romantic brain and bring her back to a sense of her duties; but all my efforts serve only to intensify this thirst for danger, this craving for adventure that ferments in the brains of all the women of her country. At this moment she is here, in my room, against my will, and I cannot induce her to go away."

XXI

"Unhappy child!" said Madame de Ramière, dressing herself in haste. "Such a timid, gentle creature! I will go and see her, talk to her! that is what you came to ask me to do, isn't it?"

"Yes, yes," said Raymon, moved involuntarily by his mother's goodness of heart; "go and make her understand the language of reason and kindness. She will love virtue from your lips, I doubt not; perhaps she will give way to your caresses; she will recover her self-control, poor creature! she suffers so keenly!"

Raymon threw himself into a chair and began to weep, the divers emotions of the morning had so shaken his nerves. His mother wept for him and could not make up her mind to go down until she had forced him to take a few drops of ether.

Indiana was not weeping and rose with a calm and dignified air when she recognized her. Madame de Ramière was so little prepared for such a dignified and noble bearing, that she felt embarrassed before the younger woman, as if she had shown lack of consideration for her by taking her by surprise in her son's bedroom. She yielded to the deep and true emotion of her heart and opened her arms impulsively. Madame Delmare threw herself into them; her despair found vent in bitter sobs and the two women wept a long while on each other's bosom.

But when Madame de Ramière would have spoken, Indiana checked her.

"Do not say anything to me, madame," she said, wiping away her tears; "you could find no words to say that would not cause me pain. Your interest and your kisses are enough to prove your generous affection; my heart is as much relieved as it can be. I will go now; I do not need your urging to realize what I have to do."

"But I did not come to send you away, but to comfort you," said Madame de Ramière.

"I cannot be comforted," she replied, kissing her once more; "love me, that will help me a little; but do not speak to me. Adieu, madame; you believe in God–pray for me."

"You shall not go alone!" cried Madame de Ramière; "I will myself go with you to your husband, to justify you, defend you and protect you."

"Generous woman!" said Indiana, embracing her warmly, "you cannot do it. You alone are ignorant of Raymon's secret; all Paris will be talking about it to-night, and you would play an incongruous part in such a story. Let me bear the scandal of it alone; I shall not suffer long."

"What do you mean? would you commit the crime of taking your own life? Dear child! you too believe in God, do you not?"

"And so, madame, I start for Ile Bourbon in three days."

"Come to my arms, my darling child! come and let me bless you! God will reward your courage."

"I trust so," said Indiana, looking up at the sky.

Madame de Ramière insisted on sending for a carriage; but Indiana resisted. She was resolved to return alone and without causing a sensation. In vain did

Raymon's mother express her alarm at the idea of her undertaking so long a journey on foot in her exhausted, agitated condition.

"I have strength enough," she said; "a word from Raymon sufficed to give me all I need."

She wrapped herself in her cloak, lowered her black lace veil and left the house by a secret door to which Madame de Ramière showed her the way. As soon as she stepped into the street she felt as if her trembling legs would refuse to carry her; it seemed to her every moment that she could feel her furious husband's brutal hand seize her, throw her down and drag her in the gutter. Soon the noise in the street, the indifference of the faces that passed her on every side and the penetrating chill of the morning air restored her strength and tranquillity, but it was a pitiable sort of strength and a tranquillity as depressing as that which sometimes prevails on the ocean and alarms the far-sighted sailor more than the howling of the tempest. She walked along the quays from the Institute to the Corps Législatif; but she forgot to cross the bridge and continued to wander by the river, absorbed in a bewildered reverie, in meditation without ideas, and walking aimlessly on and on.

She gradually drew nearer to the river, which washed pieces of ice ashore at her feet and shattered them on the stones along the shore with a dry sound that suggested cold. The greenish water exerted an attractive force on Indiana's senses. One becomes accustomed to horrible ideas; by dint of dwelling on them one takes pleasure in them. The thought of Noun's suicide had soothed her hours of despair for so many months, that suicide had assumed in her mind the form of a tempting pleasure. A single thought, a religious thought, had prevented her from deciding definitely upon it; but at this moment no well-defined thought controlled her exhausted brain. She hardly remembered that God existed, that Raymon ever existed, and she walked on, still drawing nearer the bank, obeying the instinct of unhappiness and the magnetic force of suffering.

When she felt the stinging cold of the water on her feet, she woke as if from a fit of somnambulism, and on looking about to discover where she was, saw Paris behind her and the Seine rushing by at her feet, bearing in its oily depths the white reflection of the houses and the grayish blue of the sky. This constant movement of the water and the immobility of the ground became confused in her bewildered mind, and it seemed to her that the water was sleeping and the ground moving. In that moment of vertigo she leaned against a wall and bent forward, fascinated, over what seemed to her a solid mass. But the bark of a dog that was capering about her distracted her thoughts and delayed for some seconds the accomplishment of her design. Meanwhile a man ran to the spot, guided by the dog's voice, seized her around the waist, dragged her back and laid her on the ruins of an abandoned boat on the shore. She looked in his face and did not recognize him. He knelt at her foot, unfastened his cloak and wrapped it about her, took her hands in his to warm them and called her by name. But her brain was too weak to make an effort; for forty-eight hours she had forgotten to eat.

XXI

SIR RALPH SAVES INDIANA

In that moment of vertigo she leaned against a wall and bent forward, fascinated, over what seemed to her a solid mass. But the bark of a dog that was capering about her distracted her thoughts and delayed for some seconds the accomplishment of her design. Meanwhile, a man ran to the spot, guided by the dog's voice, seized her around the waist, dragged her back, and laid her on the ruins of an abandoned boat on the shore.

However, when the blood began to circulate in her benumbed limbs, she saw Ralph kneeling beside her, holding her hands and watching for the return of consciousness.

"Did you meet Noun?" she asked him. "I saw her pass along there," she added, pointing to the river, distracted by her fixed idea. "I tried to follow her, but she walked too fast, and I am not strong enough to walk. It was like a nightmare."

Ralph looked at her in sore distress. He too felt as if his head were bursting and his brain running wild.

"Let us go," she continued; "but first see if you can find my feet; I lost them on the stones."

Ralph saw that her feet were wet and paralyzed by cold. He carried her in his arms to a house near by, where the kindly care of a hospitable woman restored her to consciousness. Meanwhile Ralph sent word to Monsieur Delmare that his wife was found; but the colonel had not returned home when the news arrived. He was continuing his search in a frenzy of anxiety and wrath. Ralph, being more perspicacious, had gone to Monsieur de Ramière's, but he had found Raymon, who had just gone to bed and who was very cool and ironical in his reception of him. Then he had thought of Noun and had followed the river in one direction, while his servant did the same in the other direction. Ophelia had speedily found her mistress's scent and had led Ralph to the place where he found her.

When Indiana was able to recall what had taken place during that wretched night, she tried in vain to remember the occurrences of her moments of delirium. She was unable therefore to explain to her cousin what thoughts had guided her action during the last hour; but he divined them and understood the state of her heart without questioning her. He simply took her hand and said to her in a gentle but grave tone:

"Cousin, I require one promise from you; it is the last proof of friendship which I shall ever ask at your hands."

"Tell me what it is," she replied; "to oblige you is the only pleasure that is left to me."

"Well then," rejoiced Ralph, "swear to me that you will not resort to suicide without notifying me. I swear to you on my honor that I will not oppose your design in any way. I simply insist on being notified: as for life, I care about it as little as you do, and you know that I have often had the same idea."

"Why do you talk of suicide?" said Madame Delmare. "I have never intended to take my own life. I am afraid of God; if it weren't for that!–"

"Just now, Indiana, when I seized you in my arms, when this poor beast"–and he patted Ophelia–"caught your dress, you had forgotten God and the whole universe, poor Ralph with the rest."

A tear stood in Indiana's eye. She pressed Sir Ralph's hand.

"Why did you stop me?" she said sadly; "I should be on God's bosom now, for I was not guilty, I did not know what I was doing."

"I saw that, and I thought that it was better to commit suicide after due reflection. We will talk about it again if you choose."

XXI

Indiana shuddered. The cab stopped in front of the house where she was to confront her husband. She had not the strength to mount the steps and Ralph carried her to her room. Their whole retinue was reduced to a single maid servant, who had gone to discuss Madame Delmare's flight with the neighbors, and Lelièvre, who, in despair, had gone to the morgue to inspect the bodies brought in that morning. So Ralph remained with Madame Delmare to nurse her. She was suffering intensely when a loud peal of the bell announced the colonel's return. A shudder of terror and hatred ran through her every vein. She seized her cousin's arm.

"Listen, Ralph," she said; "if you have the slightest affection for me, you will spare me the sight of that man in my present condition. I do not want to arouse his pity, I prefer his anger to that. Do not open the door, or else send him away; tell him that I haven't been found."

Her lips quivered, her arms clung to Ralph with convulsive strength, to detain him. Torn by two conflicting feelings, the poor baronet could not make up his mind what to do. Delmare was jangling the bell as if he would break it, and his wife was almost dying in his chair.

"You think only of his anger," said Ralph at last; "you do not think of his misery, his anxiety; you still believe that he hates you. If you had seen his grief this morning!"

Indiana dropped her arms, thoroughly exhausted, and Ralph went and opened the door.

"Is she here?" cried the colonel, rushing in. "Ten thousand devils! I have run about enough after her; I am deeply obliged to her for putting such a pleasant duty on me! Deuce take her! I don't want to see her, for I should kill her!"

"You forget that she can hear you," replied Ralph in an undertone. "She is in no condition to bear any painful excitement. Be calm."

"Twenty-five thousand maledictions!" roared the colonel. "I have endured enough myself since this morning. It's a good thing for me that my nerves are like cables. Which of us is the more injured, the more exhausted, which of us has the better right to be sick, I pray to know,–she or I? And where did you find her? what was she doing? She is responsible for my having outrageously insulted that foolish old woman, Carvajal, who gave me ambiguous answers and blamed me for this charming freak! Damnation! I am dead beat!"

As he spoke thus in his harsh, hoarse voice, Delmare had thrown himself on a chair in the ante-room; he wiped his brow from which the perspiration was streaming despite the intense cold; he described with many oaths his fatigues, his anxieties, his sufferings; he asked a thousand questions, and, luckily, did not listen to the answers, for poor Ralph could not lie, and he could think of nothing in what he had to tell that was likely to appease the colonel. So he sat on a table, as silent and unmoved as if he were absolutely without interest in the sufferings of those two, and yet he was really more unhappy in their unhappiness than they themselves were.

Madame Delmare, when she heard her husband's imprecations, felt stronger than she expected. She preferred this fierce wrath, which reconciled her with herself, to a generous forbearance which would have aroused her remorse. She wiped away the last trace of her tears and summoned what remained of her strength, which she was well content to expend in a day, so heavy a burden had life become to her. Her husband accosted her in a harsh and imperious tone, but suddenly changed his expression and his manner and seemed sorely embarrassed, overmatched by the superiority of her character. He tried to be as cool and dignified as she was; but he could not succeed.

"Will you condescend to inform me, madame," he said, "where you passed the morning and perhaps the night?"

That *perhaps* indicated to Madame Delmare that her absence had not been discovered until late. Her courage increased with that knowledge.

"No, monsieur," she replied, "I do not propose to tell you."

Delmare turned green with anger and amazement.

"Do you really hope to conceal the truth from me?" he said, in a trembling voice.

"I care very little about it," she replied in an icy tone. "I refuse to tell you solely for form's sake. I propose to convince you that you have no right to ask me that question?"

"I have no right, ten thousand devils. Who is master here, pray tell, you or I? Which of us wears a petticoat and ought to be running a distaff? Do you propose to take the beard off my chin? It would look well on you, hussy!"

"I know that I am the slave and you the master. The laws of this country make you my master. You can bind my body, tie my hands, govern my acts. You have the right of the stronger, and society confirms you in it; but you cannot command my will, monsieur; God alone can bend it and subdue it. Try to find a law, a dungeon, an instrument of torture that gives you any hold on it! you might as well try to handle the air and grasp space."

"Hold your tongue, you foolish, impertinent creature; your high-flown novelist's phrases weary me."

"You can impose silence on me, but not prevent me from thinking."

"Silly pride! pride of a poor worm! you abuse the compassion I have had for you! But you will soon see that this mighty will can be subdued without too much difficulty."

"I don't advise you to try it; your repose would suffer, and you would gain nothing in dignity."

"Do you think so?" he said, crushing her hand between his thumb and forefinger.

"I do think so," she said, without wincing.

Ralph stepped forward, grasped the colonel's arm in his iron hand and bent it like a reed, saying in a pacific tone:

"I beg that you will not touch a hair of that woman's head."

Delmare longed to fly at him; but he felt that he was in the wrong and he dreaded nothing in the world so much as having to blush for himself. So he simply pushed him away, saying:

"Attend to your own business."

Then he returned to his wife.

"So, madame," he said, holding his arms tightly against his sides to resist the temptation to strike her, "you rebel against me, you refuse to go to Ile Bourbon with me, you desire a separation? Very well! *Mordieu!* I too–"

"I desire it no longer," she replied. "I did desire it yesterday, it was my will; it is not so this morning. You resorted to violence and locked me in my room; I went out through the window to show you that there is a difference between exerting an absurd control over a woman's actions and reigning over her will. I passed several hours away from your domination; I breathed the air of liberty in order to show you that you are not morally my master, and that I look to no one on earth but myself for orders. As I walked along I reflected that I owed it to my duty and my conscience to return and place myself under your control once more. I did it of my own free will. My cousin *accompanied* me here, he did not *bring me back.* If I had not chosen to come with him, he could not have forced me to do it, as you can imagine. So, monsieur, do not waste your time fighting against my determination; you will never control it, you lost all right to change it as soon as you undertook to assert your right by force. Make your preparations for departure; I am ready to assist you and to accompany you, not because it is your will, but because it is my pleasure. You may condemn me, but I will never obey anyone but myself."

"I am sorry for the derangement of your mind," said the colonel, shrugging his shoulders.

And he went to his room to put his papers in order, well satisfied in his heart with Madame Delmare's resolution and anticipating no further obstacles; for he respected her word as much as he despised her ideas.

XXII

Raymon, yielding to fatigue, slept soundly after his curt reception of Sir Ralph, who came to his house to make inquiries. When he awoke, his heart was full of a feeling of intense relief; he believed that the worst crisis of his intrigue had finally come and gone. For a long time he had foreseen that there would come a time when he would be brought face to face with that woman's love and would have to defend his liberty against the exacting demands of a romantic passion; and he encouraged himself in advance by arguing against such pretensions. He had at last reached and crossed that dangerous spot: he had said no, he would have no occasion to go there again, for everything had happened for the best. Indiana had not wept overmuch, had not been too insistent. She had been quite reasonable; she had understood at the first word and had made up her mind quickly and proudly.

Raymon was very well pleased with his providence; for he had one of his own, in whom he believed like a good son, and upon whom he relied to arrange everything to other people's detriment rather than his own. That providence had treated him so well thus far that he did not choose to doubt it. To anticipate the result of his wrong-doing and to be anxious concerning it would have been in his eyes a crime against the good Lord who watched over him.

He rose, still very much fatigued by the efforts of the imagination which the circumstances of that painful scene had compelled him to make. His mother returned; she had been to Madame de Carvajal to inquire as to Madame Delmare's health and frame of mind. The marchioness was not disturbed about her; she was, however, very much disgusted when Madame de Ramière shrewdly questioned her. But the only thing that impressed her in Madame Delmare's disappearance was the scandal that would result from it. She complained very bitterly of her niece, whom, only the day before, she had extolled to the skies; and Madame de Ramière understood that the unfortunate Indiana had, by this performance, alienated her kinswoman and lost the only natural prop that she still possessed.

To one who could read in the depths of the marchioness's soul, this would have seemed no great loss; but Madame de Carvajal was esteemed virtuous beyond reproach, even by Madame de Ramière. Her youth had been enveloped in the mysteries of prudence, or lost in the whirlwind of revolutions.

"But what will become of the unhappy creature?" said Madame de Ramière. "If her husband maltreats her, who will protect her?"

"That will be as God wills," replied the marchioness; "for my part, I'll have nothing more to do with her and I never wish to see her again."

XXII

Madame de Ramière, kind-hearted and anxious, determined to obtain news of Madame Delmare at any price. She bade her coachman drive to the end of the street on which she lived and sent a footman to question the concierge, instructing him to try to see Sir Ralph if he were in the house. She awaited in her carriage the result of this manoeuvre, and Ralph himself soon joined her there.

The only person, perhaps, who judged Ralph accurately was Madame de Ramière; a few words sufficed to make each of them understand the other's sincere and unselfish interest in the matter. Ralph narrated what had passed during the morning; and, as he had nothing more than suspicions concerning the events of the night, he did not seek confirmation of them. But Madame de Ramière deemed it her duty to inform him of what she knew, imparting to him her desire to break off this ill-omened and impossible liaison. Ralph, who felt more at ease with her than with anybody else, allowed the profound emotion which her information caused him to appear on his face.

"You say, madame," he murmured, repressing a sort of nervous shudder that ran through his veins, "that she passed the night in your house?"

"A solitary and sorrowful night, no doubt. Raymon, who certainly was not guilty of complicity, did not come home until six o'clock, and at seven he came up to me to ask me to go down and soothe the poor child's mind."

"She meant to leave her husband! she meant to destroy her good name!" rejoined Ralph, his eyes fixed on vacancy and a strange oppression at his heart. "Then she must love this man, who is so unworthy of her, very dearly!"

Ralph forgot that he was talking to Raymon's mother.

"I have suspected this a long while," he continued; "why could I not have foretold the day on which she would consummate her ruin! I would have killed her first!"

Such language in Ralph's mouth surprised Madame de Ramière beyond measure; she supposed that she was speaking to a calm, indulgent man, and she regretted that she had trusted to appearances.

"*Mon Dieu!* " she said in dismay, "do you judge her without mercy? will you abandon her as her aunt has? Are you incapable of pity or forgiveness? Will she not have a single friend left after a fault which has already caused her such bitter suffering?"

"Have no fear of anything of the sort on my part, madame," Ralph replied; "I have known all for six months and I have said nothing. I surprised their first kiss and I did not hurl Monsieur de Ramière from his horse; I often intercepted their love messages in the woods and did not tear them in pieces with my whip. I met Monsieur de Ramière on the bridge he must cross to go to join her; it was night, we were alone and I am four times as strong as he; and yet I did not throw the man into the river; and when, after allowing him to escape, I discovered that he had eluded my vigilance and had stolen into her house, instead of bursting in the doors and throwing him out of the window, I quietly warned them of the husband's approach and saved the life of one in order to save the other's honor. You see, madame, that I am indulgent and merciful. This morning I had that man under my hand; I was well aware that he was the cause of all our misery, and, if I had not the right to accuse him without proofs, I certainly should have been justified in quarreling with him for his arrogant and mocking manner. But I bore with his insulting contempt because I knew that his death would kill Indiana; I allowed him to turn over and fall asleep again on the other side, while Indiana, insane and almost dead, was on the shore of the Seine, preparing to join his other victim. You see, madame, that I practise patience with those whom I hate and indulgence with those I love."

Madame de Ramière, sitting in her carriage opposite Ralph, gazed at him in surprise mingled with alarm. He was so different from what she had always seen him that she almost believed that he had suddenly become deranged. The allusion he had just made to Noun's death confirmed her in that idea; for she knew absolutely nothing of that story and took the words that Ralph had let fall in his indignation for a fragment of thought unconnected with his subject. He was, in very truth, passing through one of those periods of intense excitement which occur at least once in the lives of the most placid men, and which border so closely on madness that one step farther would carry them across the line. His wrath was restrained and concentrated like that of all cold temperaments; but it was deep, like the wrath of all noble souls; and the novelty of this frame of mind, which was truly portentous in him, made him terrible to look upon.

Madame de Ramière took his hand and said gently:

"You must suffer terribly, my dear Monsieur Ralph, for you wound me without mercy: you forget that the man of whom you speak is my son and that his wrong-doing, if he has been guilty of any, must be infinitely more painful to me than to you."

Ralph at once came to himself, and said, kissing Madame de Ramière's hand with an effusive warmth of regard, which was almost as unusual a manifestation on his part as that of his wrath:

"Forgive me, madame; you are right, I do suffer terribly, and I forget those things which I should respect. Pray, forget yourself the bitterness I have allowed to appear! my heart will not fail to lock itself up again."

Madame de Ramière, although somewhat reassured by this reply, could not rid herself of all anxiety when she saw with what profound hatred Ralph regarded her son. She tried to excuse him in his enemy's eyes, but he checked her.

"I divine your thoughts, madame," he said; "but have no fear, Monsieur de Ramière and I are not likely to meet again at present. As for my cousin, do not regret having enlightened me. If the whole world abandons her, I swear that she will always have at least one friend."

When Madame de Ramière returned home, toward evening, she found Raymon luxuriously ensconced in front of the fire, warming his slippered feet and drinking tea to banish the last vestiges of the nervous excitement of the morning. He was still cast down by that artificial emotion; but pleasant thoughts of the future revivified his faculties; he felt that he had become free once more, and he abandoned himself unreservedly to blissful mediations upon that priceless condition, which he had hitherto been so unsuccessful in maintaining.

"Why am I destined," he said to himself, "to weary so quickly of this priceless freedom of the heart which I always have to buy so dearly? When I feel that I am caught in a woman's net, I cannot break it quickly enough, in order to recover my repose and mental tranquillity. May I be cursed if I sacrifice them in such a hurry again! The trouble these two creoles have caused me will serve as a warning, and hereafter I do not propose to meddle with any but easy-going, laughing Parisian women–genuine women of the world. Perhaps I should do well to marry and have done with it, as they say–"

He was absorbed by such comforting, commonplace thoughts as these, when his mother entered, tired and deeply moved.

"She is better," she said; "everything has gone off as well as possible; I hope that she will grow calmer and–"

"Who?" inquired Raymon, waking with a start among his castles in Spain.

However, he concluded on the following day that he still had a duty to perform, namely, to regain that woman's esteem, if not her love. He did not choose that she should boast of having left him; he proposed that she should be persuaded that she had yielded to the influence of his good sense and his generosity. He desired to govern her even after he had spurned her; and he wrote to her as follows:

"I do not write to ask your pardon, my dear, for a few cruel or audacious words that escaped me in the delirium of my passion. In the derangement of fever no man can form perfectly coherent ideas or express himself in a proper manner. It is not my fault that I am not a god, that I cannot control in your presence the turbulent ardor of my blood, that my brain whirls, that I go mad. Perhaps I may have a right to complain of the merciless *sang-froid* with which you condemned me to frightful torture and never took pity on me; but that was not your fault. You are too perfect to play the same rôle in this world that we common mortals play, subject as we are to human passions, slaves of our less-refined organization. As I have often told you, Indiana, you are not a woman, and, when I think of you tranquilly and without excitement, you are an angel. I adore you in my heart as a divinity. But alas! in your presence the *old Adam* has often reasserted his rights. Often, under the perfumed breath from your lips, a scorching flame has consumed mine; often when, as I leaned toward you, my hair has brushed against yours, a thrill of indescribable bliss has run through my veins, and thereupon I have forgotten that you were an emanation from Heaven, a dream of everlasting felicity, an angel sent from God's bosom to guide my steps in this life and to describe to me the joys of another existence. Why, O chaste spirit, did you assume the alluring form of a woman? Why, O angel of light, did you clothe yourself in the seductions of hell? Often have I thought that I held happiness in my arms, and it was only virtue.

"Forgive me these reprehensible regrets, my love; I was not worthy of you, but perhaps we should both have been happier if you would have consented to stoop to my level. But my inferiority has constantly caused you pain and you have imputed your own virtues to me as crimes.

"Now that you absolve me–as I am sure that you do, for perfection implies mercy–let me still raise my voice to thank you and bless you. Thank you, do I say? Ah! no, my life, that is not the word; for my heart is more torn than yours by the courage that snatches you from my arms. But I admire you; and, through my tears, I congratulate you. Yes, my Indiana, you have mustered strength to accomplish this heroic sacrifice. It tears out my heart and my life; it renders my future desolate, it ruins my existence. But I love you well enough to endure it without a complaint; for my honor is nothing, yours is all in all. I would sacrifice my honor to you a thousand times; but yours is dearer to me than all the joys you have given me. No, no! I could not have enjoyed such a sacrifice. In vain should I have tried to blunt my conscience by delirious transports; in vain would you have opened your arms to intoxicate me with celestial joys–remorse would have found me out; it would have poisoned every hour of my life, and I should have been more humiliated than you by the contempt of men. O God! to see you degraded and brought to shame by me! to see you deprived of the veneration which encompassed you! to see you insulted in my arms and to be unable to wipe out the insult! for, though I should have shed all my blood for you, it would not have availed you. I might have avenged you, perhaps, but could never have justified you. My zeal in your defence would have been an additional accusation against you; my death an unquestionable proof of your crime. Poor Indiana! I should have ruined you! Ah! how miserably unhappy I should be!

"Go, therefore, my beloved; go and reap under another sky the fruits of virtue and religion. God will reward us for such an effort, for God is good. He will reunite us in a happier life, and perhaps–but the mere thought is a crime; and yet I cannot refrain from hoping! Adieu, Indiana, adieu! You see that our love is a sin! Alas! my heart is broken. Where could I find strength to say adieu to you!"

Raymon himself carried this letter to Madame Delmare's; but she shut herself up in her room and refused to see him. So he left the house after handing the letter secretly to the servant and cordially embracing the husband. As he left the last step behind him, he felt much better-hearted than usual; the weather was finer, the women fairer, the shops more brilliant. It was a red-letter day in Raymon's life.

Madame Delmare placed the letter, with the seal unbroken, in a box which she did not propose to open until she reached her destination. She wished to go to take leave of her aunt, but Sir Ralph with downright obstinacy opposed her doing so. He had seen Madame de Carvajal; he knew that she would overwhelm Indiana with reproaches and scorn; he was indignant at this hypocritical severity, and could not endure the thought of Madame Delmare exposing herself to it.

On the following day, as Delmare and his wife were about entering the diligence, Sir Ralph said to them with his accustomed *sang-froid:*

"I have often given you to understand, my friends, that it was my wish to accompany you; but you have refused to understand, or, at all events, to give me an answer. Will you allow me to go with you?"

"To Bordeaux?" queried Monsieur Delmare.

"To Bourbon," replied Sir Ralph.

"You cannot think of it," rejoined Monsieur Delmare; "you cannot shift your establishment about from place to place at the caprice of a couple whose situation is precarious and whose future is uncertain. It would be abusing your friendship shamefully to accept the sacrifice of your whole life and of your position in society. You are rich and young and free; you ought to marry again, found a family–"

"That is not the question," said Sir Ralph, coldly. "As I have not the art of enveloping my ideas in words which change their meaning, I will tell you frankly what I think. It has seemed to me that in the last six months our friendship has fallen off perceptibly. Perhaps I have made mistakes which my dulness of perception has prevented me from detecting. If I am wrong, a word from you will suffice to set my mind at rest; allow me to go with you. If I have deserved severe treatment at your hands, it is time to tell me so; you ought not, by abandoning me thus, to leave me to suffer remorse for having failed to make reparation for my faults."

The colonel was so touched by this artless and generous appeal that he forgot all the wounds to his self-esteem which had alienated him from his friend. He offered him his hand, swore that his friendship was more sincere than ever, and that he refused his offers only from delicacy.

Madame Delmare held her peace. Ralph made an effort to obtain a word from her.

"And you, Indiana," he said in a stifled voice, "have you still a friendly feeling for me?"

That question reawoke all the filial affection, all the memories of childhood, of years of intimacy, which bound their hearts together. They threw themselves weeping into each other's arms, and Ralph nearly swooned; for strong emotions were constantly fermenting in that robust body, beneath that calm and reserved exterior. He sat down to avoid falling and remained for a few moments without speaking, pale as death; then he seized the colonel's hand in one of his and his wife's in the other.

"At this moment, when we are about to part, perhaps forever, be frank with me. You refuse my proposal to accompany you on my account and not on your own?"

"I give you my word of honor," said Delmare, "that in refusing you I sacrifice my happiness to yours."

"For my part," said Indiana, "you know that I would like never to leave you."

"God forbid that I should doubt your sincerity at such a moment!" rejoined Ralph; "your word is enough for me; I am content with you both."

And he disappeared.

Six weeks later the brig *Coraly* sailed from the port of Bordeaux. Ralph had written to his friends that he would be in that city just prior to their sailing; but, as his custom was, in such a laconic style that it was impossible to determine whether he intended to bid them adieu for the last time or to accompany them. They waited in vain for him until the last moment, and when the captain gave the signal to weigh anchor he had not appeared. Gloomy presentiments added their bitterness to the dull pain that gnawed at Indiana's heart, when the last houses of the town vanished amid the trees on the shore. She shuddered at the thought that she was thenceforth alone in the world with the husband whom she hated! that she must live and die with him, without a friend to comfort her, without a kinsman to protect her against his brutal domination.

But, as she turned, she saw on the deck behind her Ralph's placid and kindly face smiling into hers.

"So you have not abandoned me after all?" she said, as she threw her arms about his neck, her face bathed in tears.

"Never!" replied Ralph, straining her to his heart.

XXIII

LETTER FROM MADAME DELMARE TO MONSIEUR DE RAMIÈRE

"Ile Bourbon, June 3d, 18—

"I had determined to weary you no more with reminders of me; but, after reading on my arrival here the letter you sent me just before I left Paris, I feel that I owe you a reply because, in the agitation caused by horrible suffering, I went too far. I was mistaken with regard to you, and I owe you an apology, not as a lover but as a *man.*

"Forgive me, Raymon, for in the most ghastly moment of my life I took you for a monster. A single word, a single glance from you banished all confidence and all hope from my heart forever. I know that I can never be happy again; but I still hope that I may not be driven to despise you; that would be the last blow.

"Yes, I took you for a dastard, for the worst of all human creatures, an *egotist.* I conceived a horror of you. I regretted that Bourbon was not so far away as I longed to fly from you, and indignation gave me strength to drain the cup to the dregs.

"But since I have read your letter I feel better. I do not regret you, but I no longer hate you, and I do not wish to leave your life a prey to remorse for having ruined mine. Be happy, be free from care; forget me. I am still alive and I may live a long while.

"It is a fact that you are not to blame; I was the one who was mad. Your heart was not dry, but it was closed to me. You did not lie to me, but I deceived myself. You were neither perjured nor cold; you simply did not love me.

"Oh! *mon Dieu!* you did not love me! In heaven's name how must you be loved? But I will not stoop to complaints; I am not writing to you for the purpose of poisoning with hateful memories the repose of your present life; nor do I propose to implore your compassion for sorrows which I am strong enough to bear alone. On the contrary, knowing better the rôle for which you are suited, I absolve you and forgive you.

"I will not amuse myself by refuting the charges in your letter; it would be too easy a matter; I will not reply to your observations with regard to my duties. Never fear, Raymon; I am familiar with them and I did not love you little enough to disregard them without due reflection. It is not necessary to tell me that the scorn of mankind would have been the reward of my downfall; I was well aware of it. I knew too that the stain would be deep, indelible and painful beyond words; that I should be spurned on all sides, cursed, covered with shame, and that I should not find a single friend to pity me and comfort me. The only mistake I had made was the feeling confident that you would open your arms to me, and that you would assist me to forget the scorn, the misery and the desertion of my friends. The only thing I had not anticipated was that you might refuse to accept my sacrifice after I had consummated it. I had imagined that that was impossible. I went to your house with the expectation that you would repel me at first from principle and a sense of duty, but firmly convinced that when you learned the inevitable consequences of what I had done, you would feel bound to assist me to endure them. No, upon my word I would never have believed that you would abandon me undefended to the consequences of such a dangerous resolution, and that you would leave me to gather its bitter fruits instead of taking me to your bosom and making a rampart of your love.

"In that case how gladly I would have defied the distant mutterings of a world that was powerless to injure me! how I would have defied hatred, being strong in your love! how feeble my remorse would have been, and how easily the passion you would have inspired would have stifled its voice! Engrossed by you alone, I would have forgotten myself; proud in the possession of your heart, I should have had no time to blush for my own. A word from you, a glance, a kiss would have sufficed to absolve me, and the memory of men and laws could have found no place in such a life. You see I was mad; according to your cynical expression I had acquired my knowledge of life from novels written for lady's-maids, from those gay, childish works of fiction in which the heart is interested in the success of wild enterprises and in impossible felicities. What you said, Raymon, was horribly true! The thing that terrifies and crushes me is that you are right.

"One thing that I cannot understand so well is that the impossibility was not the same for both of us; that I, a weak woman, derived from the exaltation of my feelings sufficient strength to place myself alone in a romantic, improbable situation, and that you, a brave man, could not find in your will-power, sufficient courage to follow me. And yet you had shared my dreams of the future, you had assented to my illusions, you had nourished in me that hope impossible of realization. For a long while you had listened to my childish plans, my pygmy-like aspirations, with a smile on your lips and joy in your eyes, and your words were all love and gratitude. You too were blind, short-sighted, boastful. How did it happen that your reason did not return until the danger was in sight? Why, I thought that danger charmed the eyes, strengthened the resolution, put fear to flight; and yet you trembled like a leaf when the crisis came! Have you men no courage except the physical courage that defies death? are you not capable of the moral courage that welcomes misfortune? Do you, who explain everything so admirably, explain that to me, I beg.

"It may be that your dream was not like mine; in my case, you see, courage was love. You had fancied that you loved me, and you had awakened, surprised to find that you had made such a mistake, on the day that I went forward trusting in the shelter of my mistake. Great God! what an extraordinary delusion it was of yours, since you did not then foresee all the obstacles that struck you when the time for action came! since you did not mention them to me until it was too late!

"But why should I reproach you now? Are we responsible for the impulses of our hearts? was it in your power to say that you would always love me? No, of course not. My misfortune consists in my inability to make myself agreeable to you longer and more really. I look about for the cause of it and find none in my heart; but it apparently exists, none the less. Perhaps I loved you too well, perhaps my affection was annoying and tiresome. You were a man, you loved liberty and pleasure. I was a burden to you. Sometimes I tried to put fetters on your life. Alas! those were very paltry offences to plead in justification of such a cruel desertion!

"Enjoy, therefore, the liberty you have purchased at the expense of my whole life; I will interfere with it no more. Why did you not give me this lesson sooner? My wound would have been less deep, and yours also, perhaps.

"Be happy! that is the last wish my broken heart will ever form! Do not exhort me to think of God, leave that for the priests, who have to soften the hard hearts of the guilty. For my part, I have more faith than you; I do not serve the same God, but I serve Him more loyally and with a purer heart. Yours is the God of men, the king, the founder and the upholder of your race; mine is the God of the universe, the creator, the preserver and the hope of all creatures. Yours made everything for you alone; mine made all created things for one another. You deem yourselves the masters of the world; I deem you only its tyrants. You think that God protects you and authorizes you to possess the empire of the earth; I think that He permits that for a little time, and that the day will come when His breath will scatter you like grains of sand. No, Raymon, you do not know God; or rather let me repeat what Ralph said to you one day at Lagny: you believe in nothing. Your education and your craving for an irresistible power to oppose to the brute force of the people, have led you to adopt without scrutiny the beliefs of your fathers; but the conviction of God's existence has never reached your heart–I doubt if you have ever prayed to Him. For my part, I have but one belief, the only one probably that you have not: I believe in Him; but the religion you have devised I will have nothing to do with; all your morality, all your principles, are simply the interests of your social order which you have raised to the dignity of laws and which you claim to trace back to God himself, just as your priests instituted the rites and ceremonies of the church to establish their power over the nations and amass wealth. But it is all falsehood and impiety. I, who invoke God and understand Him, know that there is nothing in common between Him and you, and that by clinging to Him with all my strength I separate myself from you, whose constant aim it is to overthrow His works and sully His gifts. I tell you, it ill becomes you to invoke His name to crush the resistance of a poor, weak woman, to stifle the lamentations of a broken heart. God does not choose that the creations of His hands shall be oppressed and trodden under foot. If He vouchsafed to descend so far as to intervene in our paltry quarrels, He would crush the strong and raise the weak; He would pass His mighty hand over our uneven heads and level them like the surface of the sea; He would say to the slave: 'Cast off thy chains and fly to the mountains where I have placed water and flowers and sunshine for thee.' He would say to the kings: 'Throw your purple robes to the beggars to sit upon, and go to sleep in the valleys where I have spread for you carpets of moss and heather.' To the powerful He would say: 'Bend your knees and bear the burdens of your weaker brethren; for henceforth you will need them and I will give them strength and courage.' Yes, those are my dreams; they are all of another life, of another world, where the laws of the brutal will not have passed over the heads of the peaceably inclined; where resistance and flight will not be crimes; where man can escape man as the gazelle escapes the panther; where the chain of the law will not be stretched about him to force him to throw himself under his enemy's feet; and where the voice of prejudice will not be raised in his distress to insult his sufferings and to say to him: 'You shall be deemed cowardly and base because you did not bend the knee and crawl.'

"No, do not talk to me about God, you of all men, Raymon; do not invoke His name to send me into exile and reduce me to silence. In submitting as I do I yield to the power of men. If I listened to the voice which God has placed in the depths of my heart, and to the noble instinct of a bold and strong nature, which perhaps is the genuine conscience, I should fly to the desert, I should learn to do without help, protection and love: I should go and live for myself in the heart of our beautiful mountains: I should forget the tyrants, the unjust and the ungrateful. But alas! man cannot do without his fellowman, and even Ralph cannot live alone.

"Adieu, Raymon! may you be happy without me! I forgive you for the harm you have done me. Talk of me sometimes to your mother, the best woman I have ever known. Understand that there is neither anger nor vengeance in my heart against you; my grief is worthy of the love I had for you.

"INDIANA."

The unfortunate creature was over-boastful. This profound and calm sorrow was due simply to a sense of what her own dignity demanded when she addressed Raymon; but, when she was alone, she gave way freely to its consuming violence. Sometimes, however, a vague gleam of hope shone in her troubled eyes. Perhaps she never lost the last vestige of confidence in Raymon's love, despite the cruel lessons of experience, despite the distressing thoughts which placed before her mind every day his indifference and indolence when his interests or his pleasures were not concerned. It is my belief that, if Indiana could have persuaded herself to face the bald truth, she would not have dragged out her hopeless, ruined life so long.

Woman is naturally foolish; it is as if Heaven, to counterbalance the eminent superiority over us men which she owes to her delicacy of perception, had implanted a blind vanity, an idiotic credulity in her heart. It may be that one need only be an adept in the art of bestowing praise and flattering the self-esteem, to obtain dominion over that subtle, supple and perspicacious being. Sometimes the men who are most incapable of obtaining any sort of ascendancy over other men, obtain an unbounded ascendancy over the minds of women. Flattery is the yoke that bends those ardent but frivolous heads so low. Woe to him who undertakes to be frank and outspoken in love! he will have Ralph's fate.

This is what I should reply if you should tell me that Indiana is an exceptional character, and that the ordinary woman displays neither her stoical coolness nor her exasperating patience in resistance to conjugal despotism. I should tell you to look at the reverse of the medal, and see the miserable weakness, the stupid blindness she displays in her relations with Raymon. I should ask you where you ever found a woman who was not as ready to deceive as to be deceived; who had not the art to confine for ten years in the depths of her heart the secret of a hope sacrificed so thoughtlessly in a day of frenzied excitement, and who would not become, in one man's arms, as pitiably weak as she could be strong and invincible in another man's.

XXIV

Madame Delmare's home had become more peaceable, however. With their false friends had disappeared many of the difficulties which, under the fostering hand of those officious meddlers, had been envenomed with all the warmth of their zeal. Sir Ralph, with his silence and his apparent noninterference, was more skilful than all of them in letting drop those airy trifles of intimate companionship which float about in the favoring breeze of pleasant gossip. But Indiana lived almost alone. Her house was in the mountains above the town, and Monsieur Delmare, who had a warehouse in the port, went down every morning for the whole day, to superintend his business with the Indies and with France. Sir Ralph, who had no other home than theirs, but who found ways to add to their comfort without their suspecting his gifts, devoted himself to the study of natural history or to superintending the plantation; Indiana, resuming the easy-going habits of creole life, passed the scorching hours of the day in her straw chair, and the long evenings in the solitude of the mountains.

Bourbon is in truth, simply a huge cone, the base of which is about forty leagues in circumference, while its gigantic mountain peaks rise to the height of ten thousand feet. From almost every part of that imposing mass, the eye can see in the distance, beyond the beetling rocks, beyond the narrow valleys and stately forests, the unbroken horizon surrounding the azure-hued sea like a girdle. From her window, Indiana could see between the twin peaks of a wooded mountain opposite that on which their house was built, the white sails on the Indian Ocean. During the silent hours of the day, that spectacle attracted her eyes and gave to her melancholy a fixed and uniform tinge of despair. That splendid sight made her musings bitter and gloomy, instead of casting its poetical influence upon them; and she would lower the curtain that hung at her window and shun the very daylight, in order to shed bitter, scalding tears in the secrecy of her heart.

But when the land breeze began to blow, toward evening, and to bring to her nostrils the fragrance of the flowering rice-fields, she would go forth into the wilderness, leaving Delmare and Ralph on the veranda, to enjoy the aromatic infusion of the *faham* and to loiter over their cigars. She would climb to the top of some accessible peak, the extinct crater of a former volcano, and gaze at the setting sun as it kindled the red vapors of the atmosphere into flame and spread a sort of dust of gold and rubies over the murmuring stalks of the sugar cane and the glistening walls of the cliff. She rarely went down into the gorges of the St. Gilles River, because the sight of the sea, although it distressed her, fascinated her with its magnetic mirage. It seemed to her that beyond those waves and that distant haze the magic apparition of another land would burst upon her gaze. Sometimes the clouds on the shore assumed strange forms in her eyes: at one time she would see a white wave rise upon the ocean and describe a gigantic line which she took for the facade of the Louvre; again two square sails would emerge suddenly from the mist and recall to her mind the towers of Notre-Dame at Paris, when the Seine sends up a dense mist which surrounds their foundations and leaves them as if suspended in the sky; at other times there were patches of pink clouds which, in their changing shapes, imitated all the caprices of architecture in a great city. That woman's mind slumbered in the illusions of the past, and she would quiver with joy at sight of that magnificent Paris, whose realities were connected with the most unhappy period of her life. A curious sort of vertigo would take possession of her brain. Standing at a great height above the shore, and watching the gorges that separated her from the ocean recede before her eyes, it seemed as if she were flying swiftly through space toward the fascinating city of her imagination. Dreaming thus, she would cling to the rock against which she was leaning, and to one who had at such times seen her eager eyes, her bosom heaving with impatient longing and the horrifying expression of joy on her face, she would have seemed to manifest all the symptoms of madness. And yet those were her hours of pleasure, the only moments of well-being to which she looked forward hopefully during the day. If her husband had taken it into his head to forbid these solitary walks, I do not know what thought she would have lived upon; for in her everything centred in a certain faculty of inventing allusions, in an eager striving toward a point which was neither memory, nor anticipation, nor hope, nor regret, but longing in all its devouring intensity. Thus she lived for weeks and months beneath the tropical sky, recognizing, loving, caressing but one shade, cherishing but one chimera.

Ralph, for his part, was attracted to gloomy, secluded spots in his walks, where the wind from the sea could not reach him; for the sight of the ocean had become as antipathetic to him as the thought of crossing it again. France held only an accursed place in his heart's memory. There it was that he had been unhappy to the point of losing courage, accustomed as he was to unhappiness and patient with his misery. He strove with all his might to forget it; for, although he was intensely disgusted with life, he wished to live as long as he should feel that he was necessary. He was very careful therefore never to utter a word relating to the time he had passed in that country. What would he not have given to tear that ghastly memory from Madame Delmare's mind! But he had so little confidence of his ability, he felt that he was so awkward, so lacking in eloquence, that he avoided her instead of trying to divert her thoughts. In the excess of his delicate reserve, he continued to maintain the outward appearance of indifference and selfishness. He went off and suffered alone, and, to see him scouring woods and mountains in pursuit of birds and insects, one would have taken him for a naturalist sportsman engrossed by his innocent passion and utterly indifferent to the passions of the heart that were stirring in his neighborhood. And yet hunting and study were merely the pretext behind which he concealed his long and bitter reveries.

This conical island is split at the base on all sides and conceals in its embrasures deep gorges through which flow pure and turbulent streams. One of these gorges is called Bernica. It is a picturesque spot, a sort of deep and narrow valley, hidden between two perpendicular walls of rock, the surface of which is studded with clumps of saxatile shrubs and tufts of ferns.

A stream flows in the narrow trough formed by the meeting of the two sides. At the point where they meet it plunges down into frightful depths, and, where it falls, forms a basin surrounded by reeds and covered with a damp mist. Around its banks and along the edges of the tiny stream fed by the overflow of the basin grow bananas and oranges, whose dark and healthy green clothe the inner walls of the gorge. Thither Ralph fled to avoid the heat and companionship. All his walks led to that favorite goal; the cool, monotonous plash of the waterfall lulled his melancholy to sleep, When his heart was torn by the secret agony so long concealed, so cruelly misunderstood, it was there that he expended in unknown tears, in silent lamentations, the useless energy of his heart and the concentrated activity of his youth.

In order that you may understand Ralph's character, it will be well to tell you that at least half of his life had been passed in the depths of that ravine. Thither he had gone, in his early childhood, to steel his courage against the injustice with which he had been treated in his family. It was there that he had put forth all the energies of his soul to endure the destiny arbitrarily imposed upon him, and that he had acquired the habit of stoicism which he had carried to such a point that it had become a second nature to him. There too, in his youth, he had carried little Indiana on his shoulders; he had laid her on the grass by the stream while he fished in the clear water or tried to scale the cliff in search of birds' nests.

The only dwellers in that solitude were the gulls, petrels, coots and sea-swallows. Those birds were incessantly flying up and down, hovering overhead or circling about, having chosen the holes and clefts in those inaccessible walls to rear their wild broods. Toward night they would assemble in restless groups and fill the echoing gorge with their hoarse, savage cries. Ralph liked to follow their majestic flight, to listen to their melancholy voices. He taught his little pupil their names and their habits; he showed her the lovely Madagascar teal, with its orange breast and emerald back; he bade her admire the flight of the red-winged tropic-bird, which sometimes strays to those regions and flies in a few hours from Mauritius to Rodrigues, whither, after a journey of two hundred leagues, it returns to sleep under the *veloutier* in which its nest is hidden. The petrel, harbinger of the tempest, also spread its tapering wings over those cliffs; and the queen of the sea, the frigate-bird, with its forked tail, its slate-colored coat and its jagged beak, which lights so rarely that it would seem that the air is its country, and constant movement its nature, raised its cry of distress above all the rest. These wild inhabitants were apparently accustomed to seeing the two children playing about the dwellings, for they hardly condescended to take fright at their approach; and when

Ralph reached the shelf on which they had installed their families, they would rise in black clouds and light, as if in derision, a few feet above him. Indiana would laugh at their evolutions, and would carry home, carefully, in her hat of rice-straw, the eggs Ralph had succeeded in stealing for her, and for which he had often to fight stoutly against powerful blows from the wings of the great amphibious creatures.

These memories rushed tumultuously to Ralph's mind, but they were extremely bitter to him; for times had changed greatly, and the little girl who had always been his companion had ceased to be his friend, or at all events was no longer his friend, as formerly, in absolute simpleness of heart. Although she returned his affection, his devotion, his regard, there was one thing which prevented any confidence between them, one memory upon which all the emotions of their lives turned as upon a pivot. Ralph felt that he could not refer to it; he had ventured to do it once, on a day of danger, and his bold act had availed nothing. To recur to it now would be nothing more than cold-blooded barbarity, and Ralph had made up his mind to forgive Raymon, the man for whom he had less esteem than for any man on earth, rather than add to Indiana's sorrow by condemning him according to his own ideas of what justice demanded.

So he held his peace and even avoided her. Although living under the same roof, he had managed so that he hardly saw her except at meals; and yet he watched over her like a mysterious providence. He left the house only when the heat confined her to her hammock; but at night, when she had gone out, he would invent an excuse for leaving Delmare on the veranda and would go and wait for her at the foot of the cliffs where he knew she was in the habit of sitting. He would remain there whole hours, sometimes gazing at her through the branches upon which the moon cast its white light, but respecting the narrow space which separated them, and never venturing to shorten her sad reverie by an instant. When she came down into the valley she always found him on the edge of a little stream along which ran the path to the house. Several broad flat stones, around which the water rippled in silver threads, served him as a seat. When Indiana's white dress appeared on the bank, Ralph would rise silently, offer her his arm and take her back to the house without speaking to her, unless Indiana, being more discouraged and depressed than usual, herself opened the conversation. Then, when he had left her, he would go to his own room and wait until the whole house was asleep before going to bed. If he heard Delmare scolding, Ralph would grasp the first pretext that came to his mind to go to him, and would succeed in pacifying him or diverting his thoughts without ever allowing him to suspect that such was his purpose.

The construction of the house, which was transparent, so to speak, compared with the houses in our climate, and the consequent necessity of being always under the eyes of everybody else, compelled the colonel to put more restraint upon his temper. Ralph's inevitable appearance, at the slightest sound, to stand between him and his wife, forced him to keep a check upon himself; for Delmare had sufficient self-esteem to retain control of himself before that acute but stern censor.

And so he waited until the hour for retiring had delivered him from his judge before venting the ill-humor which business vexations had heaped up during the day. But it was of no avail; the secret influence kept vigil with him, and, at the first harsh word, at the first loud tone that was audible through the thin partitions, the sound of moving furniture or of somebody walking about, as if by accident, in Ralph's room, seemed to impose silence on him and to warn him that the silent and patient solicitude of Indiana's protector was not asleep.

PART FOURTH

XXV

Now it happened that the ministry of the 8th of August, which overturned so many things in France, dealt a serious blow at Raymon's security. Monsieur de Ramière was not one of those blindly vain mortals who triumph on a day of victory. He had made politics the mainspring of all his ideas, the basis of all his dreams of the future. He had flattered himself that the king, by adopting a policy of shrewd concessions, would maintain for a long time to come the equilibrium which assured the existence of the noble families. But the rise to power of the Prince de Polignac destroyed that hope. Raymon saw too far ahead, he was too well acquainted with the new society not to stand on his guard against momentary triumphs. He understood that his whole future trembled in the balance with that of the monarchy, and that his fortune, perhaps his life, hung by a thread.

Thereupon he found himself in a delicate and embarrassing position. Honor made it his duty to devote himself, despite all the risks of such devotion, to the family whose interests had been thus far closely connected with his own. In that respect he could hardly disregard his conscience and the memory of his forefathers. But this new order of things, this tendency toward an absolute despotism, offended his prudence, his common-sense, and, so he said, his convictions. It compromised his whole existence, it did worse than that, it made him ridiculous, him, a renowned publicist who had ventured so many times to promise, in the name of the crown, justice for all and fidelity to the sworn compact. But now all the acts of the government gave a formal contradiction to the young eclectic politician's imprudent assertions; all the calm and slothful minds who, two days earlier, asked nothing better than to cling to the constitutional throne, began to throw themselves into the opposition and to denounce as rascality the efforts of Raymon and his fellows. The most courteous accused him of lack of foresight and incapacity. Raymon felt that it was humiliating to be considered a dupe after playing such a brilliant rôle in the game. He began secretly to curse and despise this royalty which thus degraded itself and involved him in its downfall; he would have liked to be able to cut loose from it without disgrace before the hour of battle. For some time he made incredible efforts to gain the confidence of both camps. The opposition ranks of that period were not squeamish concerning the admission of new recruits. They needed them, and the credentials they required were so trivial, that they enlisted considerable numbers. Nor did they disdain the support of great names, and day after day adroitly flattering allusions in their newspapers tended to detach the brightest gems from that worn-out crown. Raymon was not deceived by these demonstrations of esteem; but he did not reject them, for he was certain of their utility. On the other hand, the champions of the throne became more intolerant as their situation became more desperate. They drove from their ranks, without prudence and without regard for propriety, their strongest defenders. They soon began to manifest their dissatisfaction and distrust to Raymon. He, in his embarrassment, attached to his reputation as the principal ornament of his existence, was very opportunely taken down with an acute attack of rheumatism, which compelled him to abandon work of every sort for the moment and to go into the country with his mother.

In his isolation Raymon really suffered to feel that he was like a corpse amid the devouring activity of a society on the brink of dissolution, to feel that he was prevented, by his embarrassment as to the color he should assume no less than by illness, from enlisting under the warlike banners that waved on all sides, summoning the most obscure and the least experienced to the great conflict. The intense pains of his malady, solitude, ennui and fever insensibly turned his ideas into another channel. He asked himself, for the first time, perhaps, if society had deserved all the pains he had taken to make himself agreeable to it, and he judged society justly when he saw that it was so indifferent with regard to him, so forgetful of his talents and his glory. Then he took comfort for having been its dupe by assuring himself that he had never sought anything but his personal gratification; and that he had found it there, thanks to himself. Nothing so confirms us in egotism as reflection. Raymon drew this conclusion from it: that man, in the social state, requires two sorts of happiness, happiness in public life and in private life, social triumphs and domestic joys.

His mother, who nursed him assiduously, fell dangerously ill; it was his turn to forget his own sufferings and to take care of her; but his strength was not sufficient. Ardent, passionate souls display miraculous stores of health in times of danger; but lukewarm, indolent souls do not arouse such supernatural outbursts of bodily strength. Although Raymon was a good son, as the phrase is understood in society, he succumbed physically under the weight of fatigue. Lying on his bed of pain, with no one at his pillow save hirelings and now and then a friend who was in haste to return to the excitements of social life, he began to think of Indiana, and he sincerely regretted her, for at that time she would have been most useful to him. He remembered the dutiful attentions she had lavished on her crabbed old husband and he imagined the gentle and beneficent care with which she would have encompassed her lover.

"If I had accepted her sacrifice," he thought, "she would be dishonored; but what would it matter to me now? Abandoned as I am by a frivolous, selfish world, I should not be alone; she whom everybody spurned with contumely would be at my feet, impelled by love; she would weep over my sufferings and would find a way to allay them. Why did I discard that woman? She loved me so dearly that she would have found consolation for the insults of her fellows by bringing a little happiness into my domestic life."

XXV

He determined to marry when he recovered, and he mentally reviewed the names and faces that had impressed him in the salons of the two divisions of society. Fascinating apparitions flitted through his dreams; head-dresses laden with flowers, snowy shoulders enveloped in swansdown capes, supple forms imprisoned in muslin or satin: such alluring phantoms fluttered their gauze wings before Raymon's heavy, burning eyes; but he had seen these peris only in the perfumed whirl of the ballroom. On waking, he asked himself whether their rosy lips knew any other smiles than those of coquetry; whether their white hands could dress the wounds of sorrow; whether their refined and brilliant wit could stoop to the painful task of consoling and diverting a horribly bored invalid. Raymon was a man of keen intelligence and he was more distrustful than other men of the coquetry of women; he had a more intense hatred of selfishness because he knew that from a selfish person he could obtain nothing to advance his own happiness. And then Raymon was no less embarrassed concerning the choice of a wife than concerning the choice of his political colors. The same reasons imposed moderation and prudence on him. He belonged to a family of high rank and unbending pride which would brook no mésalliance, and yet wealth could no longer be considered secure except in plebeian hands. According to all appearance that class was destined to rise over the ruins of the other, and in order to maintain oneself on the surface of the movement one must be the son-in-law of a manufacturer or a stock-broker. Raymon concluded therefore that it would be wise to wait and see which way the wind blew before entering upon a course of action which would decide his whole future.

These positive reflections made plain to him the utter lack of affection which characterizes marriages of convenience, so-called, and the hope of having some day a companion worthy of his love entered only incidentally into his prospects of happiness. Meanwhile his illness might be prolonged, and the hope of better days to come does not efface the keen consciousness of present pains. He recurred to the unpleasant thought of his blindness on the day he had declined to kidnap Madame Delmare, and he cursed himself for having comprehended so imperfectly his real interests.

At this juncture he received the letter Indiana wrote him from Ile Bourbon. The sombre and inflexible energy which she retained, amid shocks which might well have crushed her spirit, made a profound impression on Raymon.

"I judged her ill," he thought; "she really loved me, she still loves me; for my sake she would have been capable of those heroic efforts which I considered to be beyond a woman's strength; and now I probably need say but a word to draw her, like an irresistible magnet, from one end of the world to the other. If six months, eight months, perhaps, were not necessary to obtain that result, I would like to make the trial!"

He fell asleep meditating that idea: but he was soon awakened by a great commotion in the next room. He rose with difficulty, put on a dressing-gown, and dragged himself to his mother's apartment. She was very ill.

Toward morning she found strength to talk with him; she was under no illusion as to the brief time she had yet to live and her mind was busy with her son's future.

"You are about to lose your best friend," she said; "may Heaven replace her by a companion worthy of you! But be prudent, Raymon, and do not risk the repose of your whole life for a mere chimera of your ambition. I have known but one woman, alas! whom I should have cared to call my daughter; but Heaven has disposed of her. But listen, my son. Monsieur Delmare is old and broken; who knows if that long voyage did not exhaust the rest of his vitality? Respect his wife as long as he lives; but if, as I believe will be the case, he is summoned soon to follow me to the grave, remember there is still one woman in the world who loves you almost as dearly as your mother loved you."

That evening Madame de Ramière died in her son's arms. Raymon's grief was deep and bitter; in the face of such a loss there could be neither false emotion nor selfish scheming. His mother was really necessary to him; with her he lost all the moral comfort of his life. He shed despairing tears upon her pallid forehead, her lifeless eyes. He maligned Heaven, he cursed his destiny, he wept for Indiana. He called God to account for the happiness He owed him. He reproached Him for treating him like other men and tearing everything from him at once. Then he doubted the existence of this God who chastised him; he chose to deny Him rather than submit to His decrees. He lost all the illusions with all the realities of life; and he returned to his bed of fever and suffering, as crushed and hopeless as a deposed king, as a fallen angel.

When he was nearly restored to health, he cast a glance at the condition of France. Matters were going from bad to worse; on all sides there were threats of refusal to pay taxes. Raymon was amazed at the foolish confidence of his party, and deeming it wise not to plunge into the mêlée as yet, he shut himself up at Cercy with the melancholy memory of his mother and Madame Delmare.

By dint of pondering the idea to which he had attached little importance at its first conception, he accustomed himself to the thought that Indiana was not lost to him, if he chose to take the trouble to beckon her back. He detected many inconveniences in the scheme but many more advantages. It was not in accord with his interest to wait until she was a widow before marrying her, as Madame de Ramière had suggested. Delmare might live twenty years longer, and Raymon did not choose to renounce forever the chance of a brilliant marriage. He conceived a better plan than that in his cheerful and fertile imagination. He could, by taking a little trouble, exert an unbounded influence over his Indiana; he felt that he possessed sufficient mental cunning and knavery to make of that enthusiastic and sublime creature a devoted and submissive mistress. He could shield her from the ferocity of public opinion, conceal her behind the impenetrable wall of his private life, keep her as a precious treasure in the depths of his retreat, and employ her to sweeten his moments of solitude and meditation with the joys of a pure and generous affection. He would not have to exert himself overmuch to escape the husband's wrath; he would not come three thousand leagues in pursuit of his wife when his business interests made his presence absolutely necessary in the other hemisphere. Indiana would demand little in the way of pleasure and liberty after the bitter trials which had bent her neck to the yoke. She was ambitious only for love, and Raymon felt that he would love her from gratitude as soon as she made herself useful to him. He remembered also the constancy and gentleness she had shown during the long days of his coldness and neglect. He promised himself that he would cleverly retain his liberty, so that she would not dare to complain. He flattered himself that he could acquire sufficient control over her convictions to make her consent to anything, even to his marriage; and he based that hope upon numerous examples of secret liaisons which he had known to continue despite the laws of society, by virtue of the prudence and skill with which the parties had succeeded in avoiding the judgment of public opinion.

"Besides," he said to himself, "that woman will have made an irrevocable, boundless sacrifice for me. She will have travelled the world over for me and have left behind her all means of existence–all possibility of pardon. Society is stern and unforgiving only to paltry, commonplace faults. Uncommon audacity takes it by surprise, notorious misfortune disarms it; it will pity, perhaps admire this woman who will have done for me what no other woman would have dared to try. It will blame her, but it will not laugh at her, and I shall not be blamed for taking her in and protecting her after such a signal proof of her love. Perhaps, on the contrary, my courage will be extolled, at all events I shall have defenders, and my reputation will undergo a glorious and indecisive trial. Society likes to be defied sometimes; it does not accord its admiration to those who crawl along the beaten paths. In these days public opinion must be driven with a whip."

Under the influence of these thoughts he wrote to Madame Delmare. His letter was what it was sure to be from the pen of so adroit and experienced a man. It breathed love, grief, and, above all, truth. Alas! what a slender reed the truth is, to bend thus with every breath!

However, Raymon was wise enough not to express the object of his letter in so many words. He pretended to look upon Indiana's return as a joy of which he had no hope; but he had but little to say of her duty. He repeated his mother's last words; he described with much warmth the state of despair to which his loss had reduced him, the ennui of solitude and the danger of his position politically. He drew a dismal and terrifying picture of the revolution that was rising above the horizon, and, while feigning to rejoice that he was to meet its coming alone, he gave Indiana to understand that the moment had come for her to manifest that enthusiastic loyalty, that perilous devotion of which she had boasted so confidently. He cursed his destiny and said that virtue had cost him very dear, that his yoke was very heavy: that he had held happiness in his hand and had had the strength of will to doom himself to eternal solitude.

"Do not tell me again that you once loved me," he added; "I am so weak and discouraged that I curse my courage and hate my duties. Tell me that you are happy, that you have forgotten me, so that I may have strength not to come and tear you away from the bonds that keep you from me."

In a word, he said that he was unhappy; that was equivalent to telling Indiana that he expected her.

XXVI

During the three months that elapsed between the despatch of this letter and its arrival at Ile Bourbon, Madame Delmare's situation had become almost intolerable, as the result of a domestic incident of the greatest importance to her. She had adopted the depressing habit of writing down every evening a narrative of the sorrowful thoughts of the day. This journal of her sufferings was addressed to Raymon, and, although she had no intention of sending it to him, she talked with him, sometimes passionately, sometimes bitterly, of the misery of her life and of the sentiments which she could not overcome. These papers fell into Delmare's hands, that is to say, he broke open the box which contained them as well as Raymon's letters, and devoured them with a jealous, frenzied eye. In the first outbreak of his wrath he lost the power to restrain himself and went outside, with fast-beating heart and clenched fists, to await her return from her walk. Perhaps, if she had been a few minutes later, the unhappy man would have had time to recover himself; but their evil star decreed that she should appear before him almost immediately. Thereupon, unable to utter a word, he seized her by the hair, threw her down and stamped on her forehead with his heel.

He had no sooner made that bloody mark of his brutal nature upon a poor, weak creature, than he was horrified at what he had done. He fled in dire dismay, and locked himself in his room, where he cocked his pistol preparatory to blowing out his brains; but as he was about to pull the trigger he looked out on the veranda and saw that Indiana had risen and, with a calm, self-possessed air, was wiping away the blood that covered her face. As he thought that he had killed her, his first feeling was of joy when he saw her on her feet; then his wrath blazed up anew.

"It is only a scratch," he cried, "and you deserve a thousand deaths! No, I will not kill myself; for then you would go and rejoice over it in your lover's arms. I do not propose to assure the happiness of both of you; I propose to live to make you suffer, to see you die by inches of deathly ennui, to dishonor the infamous creature who has made a fool of me!"

He was battling with the tortures of jealous rage, when Ralph entered the veranda by another door and found Indiana in the disheveled condition in which that horrible scene had left her. But she had not manifested the slightest alarm, she had not uttered a cry, she had not raised her hand to ask for mercy. Weary of life as she was, it seemed that she had been desirous to give Delmare time to commit murder by refraining from calling for help. It is certain that when the assault took place Ralph was within twenty yards, and that he had not heard the slightest sound.

"Indiana!" he cried, recoiling in horror and surprise; "who has wounded you thus?"

"Do you ask?" she replied with a bitter smile; "what other *than your friend* has the *right* and the inclination?"

Ralph dropped the cane he held; he needed no other weapons than his great hands to strangle Delmare. He reached his door in two leaps and burst it open with his fist. But he found Delmare lying on the floor, with purple cheeks and swollen throat, struggling in the noiseless convulsions of apoplexy.

He seized the papers that were scattered over the floor. When he recognized Raymon's handwriting and saw the ruins of the letter-box, he understood what had happened; and, carefully collecting the accusing documents, he hastened to hand them to Madame Delmare and urged her to burn them at once. Delmare had probably not taken time to read them all.

Then he begged her to go to her room while he summoned the slaves to look after the colonel; but she would neither burn the papers nor hide the wound.

"No," she said haughtily, "I will not do it! That man did not scruple to tell Madame de Carvajal of my flight long ago; he made haste to publish what he called my dishonor. I propose to show to everybody this token of his own dishonor which he has taken pains to stamp on my face. It is a strange sort of justice that requires one to keep secret another's crimes, when that other assumes the right to brand one without mercy!"

When Ralph found the colonel was in a condition to listen to him, he heaped reproaches upon him with more energy and severity than one would have thought him capable of exhibiting. Thereupon Delmare, who certainly was not an evil-minded man, wept like a child over what he had done; but he wept without dignity, as a man can do when he abandons himself to the sensation of the moment, without reasoning as to its causes and effects. Prompt to jump to the opposite extreme, he would have called his wife and solicited her pardon; but Ralph objected and tried to make him understand that such a puerile reconciliation would impair the authority of one without wiping out the injury done to the other. He was well aware that there are injuries which are never forgiven and miseries which one can never forget.

From that moment, the husband's personality became hateful in the wife's eyes. All that he did to atone for his treatment of her deprived him of the slight consideration he had retained thus far. He had in very truth made a tremendous mistake; the man who does not feel strong enough to be cold and implacable in his vengeance should abjure all thought of impatience or resentment. There is no possible rôle between that of the Christian who forgives and that of the man of the world who spurns. But Delmare had his share of selfishness too; he felt that he was growing old, that his wife's care was becoming more necessary to him every day. He was terribly afraid of solitude, and if, in the paroxysm of his wounded pride, he recurred to his habits as a soldier and maltreated her, reflection soon led him back to the characteristic weakness of old men, whom the thought of desertion terrifies. Too enfeebled by age and hardships to aspire to become a father, he had remained an old bachelor in his home, and had taken a wife as he would have taken a housekeeper. It was not from affection for her, therefore, that he forgave her for not loving him, but from regard for his own comfort: and if he grieved at his failure to command her affections, it was because he was afraid that he should be less carefully tended in his old age.

When Madame Delmare, for her part, being deeply aggrieved by the operation of the laws of society, summoned all her strength of mind to hate and despise them, there was a wholly personal feeling at the bottom of her thoughts. But it may be that this craving for happiness which consumes us, this hatred of injustice, this thirst for liberty which ends only with life, are the constituent elements of *egotism*, a name by which the English designate love of self, considered as one of the privileges of mankind and not as a vice. It seems to me that the individual who is selected out of all the rest to suffer from the working of institutions that are advantageous to his fellowmen ought, if he has the least energy in his soul, to struggle against this arbitrary yoke. I also think that the greater and more noble his soul is, the more it should rankle and fester under the blows of injustice. If he has ever dreamed that happiness was to be the reward of virtue, into what ghastly doubts, what desperate perplexity must he be cast by the disappointments which experience brings!

Thus all Indiana's reflections, all her acts, all her sorrows were a part of this great and terrible struggle between nature and civilization. If the desert mountains of the island could have concealed her long, she would assuredly have taken refuge among them on the day of the assault upon her; but Bourbon was not of sufficient extent to afford her a secure hiding-place, and she determined to place the sea and uncertainty as to her place of refuge between her tyrant and herself. When she had formed this resolution, she felt more at ease and was almost gay and unconcerned at home. Delmare was so surprised and delighted that he indulged apart in this brutal reasoning: that it was a good thing to make women feel the law of the strongest now and then.

Thereafter she thought of nothing but flight, solitude and independence; she considered in her tortured, grief-stricken brain innumerable plans of a romantic establishment in the deserts of India or Africa. At night she followed the flight of the birds to their resting-place at Ile Rodrigue. That deserted island promised her all the pleasures of solitude, the first craving of a broken heart. But the same reasons that prevented her from flying to the interior of Bourbon caused her to abandon the idea of seeking refuge in the small islands near by. She often met at the house tradesmen from Madagascar, who had business relations with her husband; dull, vulgar, copper-colored fellows who had no tact or shrewdness except in forwarding their business interests. Their stories attracted Madame Delmare's attention, none the less; she enjoyed questioning them concerning the marvelous products of that island, and what they told her of the prodigies performed by nature there intensified more and more the desire that she felt to go and hide herself away there. The size of the island and the fact that Europeans occupied so small a portion of it led her to hope that she would never be discovered. She decided upon that place, therefore, and fed her idle mind upon dreams of a future which she proposed to create for herself, unassisted. She was already building her solitary cabin under the shade of a primeval forest, on the bank of a nameless river; she fancied herself taking refuge under the protection of those savage tribes whom the yoke of our laws and our prejudices has not debased. Ignorant creature that she was, she hoped to find there the virtues that are banished from our hemisphere, and to live in peace, unvexed by any social constitution; she imagined that she could avoid the dangers of isolation, escape the malignant diseases of the climate. A weak woman, who could not endure the anger of one man, but flattered herself that she could defy the hardships of uncivilized life!

Amid these romantic thoughts and extravagant plans she forgot her present ills; she made for herself a world apart, which consoled her for that in which she was compelled to live; she accustomed herself to think less of Raymon, who was soon to cease to be a part of her solitary and philosophical existence. She was so busily occupied in constructing for herself a future according to her fancy that she let the past rest a little; and already, as she felt that her heart was freer and braver, she imagined that she was reaping in advance the fruits of her solitary life. But Raymon's letter arrived, and that edifice of chimeras vanished like a breath. She felt, or fancied that she felt, that she loved him more than before. For my part, I like to think that she never loved him with all the strength of her soul. It seems to me that misplaced affection is as different from requited affection as an error from the truth. It seems to me that, although the excitement and ardor of our sentiments abuse us to the point of believing that that is love in all its power, we learn later, when we taste the delights of a true love, how entirely we deceived ourselves.

But Raymon's situation, as he described it, rekindled in Indiana's heart that generous flame which was a necessity of her nature. Fancying him alone and unhappy, she considered it her duty to forget the past and not to anticipate the future. A few hours earlier, she intended to leave her husband under the spur of hatred and resentment; now, she regretted that she did not esteem him so that she might make a real sacrifice for Raymon's sake. So great was her enthusiasm that she feared that she was doing too little for him in fleeing from an irascible master at the peril of her life, and subjecting herself to the miseries of a four months' voyage. She would have given her life, with the idea that it was too small a price to pay for a smile from Raymon. Women are made that way.

Thus it was simply a question of leaving the island. It was very difficult to elude Delmare's distrust and Ralph's clear-sightedness. But those were not the principal obstacles; it was necessary to avoid giving the notice of her proposed departure, which, according to law, every passenger is compelled to give through the newspapers.

Among the few vessels lying in the dangerous roadstead of Bourbon was the ship *Eugène*, soon to sail for Europe. For a long while Indiana sought an opportunity to speak with the captain without her husband's knowledge, but whenever she expressed a wish to walk down to the port, he ostentatiously placed her in Ralph's charge, and followed them with his own eyes with maddening persistence. However, by dint of picking up with the greatest care every scrap of information favorable to her plan, Indiana learned that the captain of the vessel bound for France had a kinswoman at the village of Saline in the interior of the island, and that he often returned from her house on foot, to sleep on board. From that moment she hardly left the cliff that served as her post of observation. To avert suspicion, she went thither by roundabout paths, and returned in the same way at night when she had failed to discover the person in whom she was interested on the road to the mountains.

She had but two days of hope remaining, for the landwind had already begun to blow. The anchorage threatened to become untenable, and Captain Random was impatient to be at sea.

However, she prayed earnestly to the God of the weak and oppressed, and went and stationed herself on the very road to Saline, disregarding the danger of being seen, and risking her last hope. She had not been waiting an hour when Captain Random came down the path. He was a genuine sailor, always rough-spoken and cynical, whether he was in good or bad humor; his expression froze Indiana's blood with terror. Nevertheless, she mustered all her courage and walked to meet him with a dignified and resolute air.

"Monsieur," she said, "I place my honor and my life in your hands. I wish to leave the colony and return to France. If, instead of granting me your protection, you betray the secret I confide to you, there is nothing left for me to do but throw myself into the sea."

The captain replied with an oath that the sea would refuse to sink such a pretty lugger, and that, as she had come of her own accord and hove to under his lee, he would promise to tow her to the end of the world.

"You consent then, monsieur?" said Madame Delmare anxiously. "In that case here is the pay for my passage in advance."

And she handed him a casket containing the jewels Madame de Carvajal had given her long before; they were the only fortune that she still possessed. But the sailor had different ideas, and he returned the casket with words that brought the blood to her cheeks.

"I am very unfortunate, monsieur," she replied, restraining the tears of wrath that glistened behind her long lashes; "the proposition I am making to you justifies you in insulting me; and yet, if you knew how odious my life in this country is to me, you would have more pity than contempt for me."

Indiana's noble and touching countenance imposed respect on Captain Random. Those who do not wear out their natural delicacy by over-use sometimes find it healthy and unimpaired in an emergency. He recalled Colonel Delmare's unattractive features and the sensation that his attack on his wife had caused in the colonies. While ogling with a lustful eye that fragile, pretty creature, he was struck by her air of innocence and sincerity. He was especially moved when he noticed on her forehead a white mark which the deep flush on her face brought out in bold relief. He had had some business relations with Delmare which had left him ill-disposed toward him; he was so close-fisted and unyielding in business matters.

"Damnation!" he cried, "I have nothing but contempt for a man who is capable of kicking such a pretty woman in the face! Delmare's a pirate, and I am not sorry to play this trick on him; but be prudent, madame, and remember that I am compromising my good name. You must make your escape quietly when the moon has set, and fly like a poor petrel from the foot of some sombre reef."

"I know, monsieur," she replied, "that you cannot do me this very great favor without transgressing the law; you may perhaps have to pay a fine; that is why I offer you this casket, the contents of which are worth at least twice the price of a passage."

The captain took the casket with a smile.

"This is not the time to settle our account," he said; "I am willing to take charge of your little fortune. Under the circumstances I suppose you won't have very much luggage; on the night we are to sail, hide among the rocks at the *Anse aux Lataniers*; between one and two o'clock in the morning a boat will come ashore pulled by two stout rowers, and bring you aboard."

XXVII

The day preceding her departure passed away like a dream. Indiana was afraid that it would be long and painful; it seemed to last but a moment. The silence of the neighborhood, the peaceful tranquillity within the house were in striking contrast to the internal agitation by which Madame Delmare was consumed. She locked herself into her room to prepare the few clothes she intended to carry; then she concealed them under her dress and carried them one by one to the rocks at the *Anse aux Lataniers*, where she placed them in a bark basket and buried them in the sand. The sea was rough and the wind increased from hour to hour. As a precautionary measure the *Eugène* had left the roadstead, and Madame Delmare could see in the distance her white sails bellied out by the breeze, as she stood on and off, making short tacks, in order to hold the land. Her heart went out eagerly toward the vessel, which seemed to be pawing the air impatiently, like a race-horse, full of fire and ardor, as the word is about to be given. But when she returned to the interior of the island she found in the mountain gorges a calm, soft atmosphere, bright sunlight, the song of birds and humming of insects, and everything going on as on the day before, heedless of the intense emotions by which she was tortured. Then she could not believe in the reality of her situation, and wondered if her approaching departure were not the illusion of a dream.

Toward night the wind fell. The *Eugène* approached the shore, and at sunset Madame Delmare on her rocky perch heard the report of a cannon echoing among the cliffs. It was the signal of departure on the following day, on the return of the orb then sinking below the horizon.

After dinner Monsieur Delmare complained of not feeling well. His wife thought that her opportunity had gone, that he would keep the whole house awake all night, and that her plan would be defeated; and then he was suffering, he needed her; that was not the moment to leave him. Thereupon remorse entered her soul and she wondered who would have pity on that old man when she had abandoned him. She shuddered at the thought that she was about to commit what was a crime in her own eyes, and that the voice of conscience would rise even louder than the voice of society, to condemn her. If Delmare, as usual, had harshly demanded her services, if he had displayed an imperious and capricious spirit in his sufferings, resistance would have seemed natural and lawful to the down-trodden slave; but, for the first time in his life, he submitted to the pain with gentleness, and seemed grateful and affectionate to his wife. At ten o'clock he declared that he felt entirely well, insisted that she should go to her own room, and that no one should pay any further attention to him. Ralph, too, assured her that every symptom of illness had disappeared and that a quiet night's sleep was the only remedy that he needed.

When the clock struck eleven all was silent and peaceful in the house. Madame Delmare fell on her knees and prayed, weeping bitterly; for she was about to burden her heart with a grievous sin, and from God alone could come such forgiveness as she could hope to receive. She stole softly into her husband's room. He was sleeping soundly; his features were composed, his breathing regular. As she was about to withdraw, she noticed in the shadows another person asleep in a chair. It was Ralph, who had risen noiselessly and come to watch over her husband in his sleep, to guard against accident.

"Poor Ralph!" thought Indiana; "what an eloquent and cruel reproach to me!"

She longed to wake him, to confess everything to him, to implore him to save her from herself; and then she thought of Raymon.

"One more sacrifice," she said to herself, "and the most cruel of all–the sacrifice of my duty."

Love is woman's virtue; it is for love that she glories in her sins, it is from love that she acquires the heroism to defy her remorse. The more dearly it costs her to commit, the crime, the more she will have deserved at the hands of the man she loves. It is like the fanaticism that places the dagger in the hand of the religious enthusiast.

She took from her neck a gold chain which came to her from her mother and which she had always worn; she gently placed it around Ralph's neck, as the last pledge of an everlasting friendship, then lowered the lamp so that she could see her old husband's face once more, and make sure that he was no longer ill. He was dreaming at that moment and said in a faint, sad voice:

"Beware of that man, he will ruin you."

Indiana shuddered from head to foot and fled to her room. She wrung her hands in pitiable uncertainty; then suddenly seized upon the thought that she was no longer acting in her own interest but in Raymon's; that she was going to him, not in search of happiness, but to make him happy, and that, even though she were to be accursed for all eternity, she would be sufficiently recompensed if she embellished her lover's life. She rushed from the house and walked swiftly to the *Anse aux Lataniers*, not daring to turn and look at what she left behind her.

She at once set about disinterring her bark basket and sat upon it, trembling and silent, listening to the whistling of the wind, to the plashing of the waves as they died at her feet, and to the shrill groaning of the *satanite* among the great bunches of seaweed that clung to the steep sides of the cliffs; but all these noises were drowned by the throbbing of her heart, which rang in her ears like a funeral knell.

She waited a long while; she looked at her watch and found that the appointed time had passed. The sea was so high, and navigation about the shores of the island is so difficult in the best of weather, that she was beginning to despair of the courage of the men who were to take her aboard, when she spied on the gleaming waves the black shadow of a *pirogue*, trying to make the land. But the swell was so strong and the sea so rough that the frail craft constantly disappeared, burying itself as it were in the dark folds of a shroud studded with silver stars. She rose and answered their signal several times with cries which the wind whisked away before carrying them to the ears of the oarsmen. At last, when they were near enough to hear her, they pulled toward her with much difficulty; then paused to wait for a wave. As soon as they felt it raise the skiff they redoubled their efforts, and the wave broke and threw them up on the beach.

The ground on which Saint-Paul is built is composed of sea sand and gravel from the mountains, which the Des Galets river brings from a long distance from its mouth by the strength of its current. These heaps of rounded pebbles form submarine mountains near the shore which the waves overthrow and rebuild at their pleasure. Their constant shifting makes it impossible to avoid them, and the skill of the pilot is useless among these constantly appearing and disappearing obstacles. Large vessels lying in the harbor of Saint-Denis often drag their anchors and are cast on shore by the force of the currents; they have no other resource when this off-shore wind begins to blow, and to make the turbulent receding waves perilous, than to put to sea as quickly as possible, and that is what the *Eugène* had done.

The skiff bore Indiana and her fortunes amid the wild waves, the howling of the storm and the oaths of the two rowers, who had no hesitation in cursing loudly the danger to which they exposed themselves for her sake. Two hours ago, they said, the ship should have been under way, and on her account the captain had obstinately refused to give the order. They added divers insulting and cruel reflections, but the unhappy fugitive consumed her shame in silence; and when one of them suggested to the other that they might be punished if they were lacking in the respect they had been ordered to pay the *captain's mistress:*

"Never you fear!" was the reply; "the sharks are the lads we've got to settle accounts with this night. If we ever see the captain again, I don't believe he'll be any uglier than them."

"Talking of sharks," said the first, "I don't know whether one of 'em has got scent of us already, but I can see a face in our wake that don't belong to a Christian."

"You fool! to take a dog's face for a sea-wolf's! Hold! my four-legged passenger, we forgot you and left you on shore; but, blast my eyes, if you shall eat up the ship's biscuit! Our orders only mentioned a young woman, nothing was said about a cur–"

MADAME DELMARE'S FLIGHT

She waited a long while; she looked at her watch and found that the appointed time had passed. The sea was so high, and navigation about the shores of the island is so difficult in the best of weather, that she was beginning to despair of the courage of the men who were to take her aboard, when she spied on the gleaming waves the black shadow of a pirogue, *trying to make the land.*

As he spoke he raised his oar to hit the beast on the head; but Madame Delmare, casting her tearful, distraught eyes upon the sea, recognized her beautiful Ophelia, who had found her scent on the rocks and was swimming after her. As the sailor was about to strike her, the waves, against which she was struggling painfully, carried her away from the skiff, and her mistress heard her moaning with impatience and exhaustion. She begged the oarsmen to take her into the boat and they pretended to comply; but, as the faithful beast approached, they dashed out her brains with loud shouts of laughter, and Indiana saw before her the dead body of the creature who had loved her better than Raymon. At the same time a huge wave drew the skiff down as it were into the depths of an abyss, and the laughter of the sailors changed to imprecations and yells of terror. However, thanks to its buoyancy and lightness the *pirogue* righted itself like a duck and climbed to the summit of the wave, to plunge into another ravine and mount again to another foaming crest. As they left the shore behind, the sea became less rough, and soon the skiff flew along swiftly and without danger toward the ship. Thereupon, the oarsmen recovered their good humor and with it the power of reflection. They strove to atone for their brutal treatment of Indiana; but their cajolery was more insulting than their anger.

"Come, come, my young lady," said one of them, "take courage, you're safe now; of course the captain will give us a glass of the best wine in the locker for the pretty parcel we've fished up for him."

The other affected to sympathize with the young lady because her clothes were wet; but, he said, the captain was waiting for her and would take good care of her. Indiana listened to their remarks in deadly terror, without speaking or moving; she realized the horror of her situation, and could see no other way of escaping the outrages which awaited her than to throw herself into the sea. Two or three times she was on the point of jumping out of the boat; but she recovered courage, a sublime courage, with the thought:

" It is for him, Raymon, that I suffer all these indignities. I must live though I were crushed with shame!"

She put her hand to her oppressed heart and touched the hilt of a dagger which she had concealed there in the morning, with a sort of instinctive prevision of danger. The possession of that weapon restored all her confidence; it was a short, pointed stiletto, which her father used to carry; an old Spanish weapon which had belonged to a Medina-Sidonia, whose name was cut on the blade, with the date 1300. Doubtless it had rusted in noble blood, had washed out more than one affront, punished more than one insolent knave. With it in her possession, Indiana felt that she became a Spaniard once more, and she went aboard the ship with a resolute heart, saying to herself that a woman incurred no risk so long as she had a sure means of taking her own life before submitting to dishonor. She avenged herself for the harsh treatment of her guides only by rewarding them handsomely for their fatigue; then she went to her cabin and anxiously awaited the hour of departure.

At last the day broke, and the sea was covered with small boats bringing the passengers aboard. Indiana looked with terror through the port-hole at the faces of those who came aboard the *Eugène*; she dreaded lest she should see her husband, coming to claim her. At last the echoes of the last gun died away on the island which had been her prison. The ship began to cut her way through the waves, and the sun, rising from the ocean, cast its cheerful, rosy light on the white peaks of the Salazes as they sank lower and lower on the horizon.

When they were a few leagues from port, a sort of comedy was played on board to avoid a confession of trickery. Captain Random pretended to discover Madame Delmare on his vessel; he feigned surprise, questioned the sailors, went through the form of losing his temper and of quieting down again, and ended by drawing up a report of the finding of a *stowaway* on board; that is the technical term used on such occasions.

Allow me to go no farther with the story of this voyage. It will be enough for me to tell you, for Captain Random's justification, that, despite his rough training, he had enough natural good sense to understand Madame Delmare's character very quickly; he ventured upon very few attempts to abuse her unprotected condition and eventually was touched by it and acted as her friend and protector. But that worthy man's loyal behavior and Indiana's dignity did not restrain the comments of the crew, the mocking glances, the insulting suspicions and the broad and stinging jests. These were the real torments of the unhappy woman during that journey, for I say nothing of the fatigue, the discomforts, the dangers, the tedium and the sea-sickness; she paid no heed to them.

XXVIII

Three days after the despatch of his letter to Ile Bourbon, Raymon had entirely forgotten both the letter and its purpose. He had felt decidedly better and had ventured to make a visit in the neighborhood. The estate of Lagny, which Monsieur Delmare had left to be sold for the benefit of his creditors, had been purchased by a wealthy manufacturer, Monsieur Hubert, a shrewd and estimable man, not like all wealthy manufacturers, but like a small number of the newly-rich. Raymon found the new owner comfortably settled in that house which recalled so many memories. He took pleasure in giving a free rein to his emotion as he wandered through the garden where Noun's light footprints seemed to be still visible on the gravel, and through those great rooms which seemed still to retain the echoes of Indiana's soft words; but soon the presence of a new hostess changed the current of his thoughts.

In the main salon, on the spot where Madame Delmare was accustomed to sit and work, a tall, slender young woman, with a glance that was at once pleasant and mischievous, caressing and mocking, sat before an easel, amusing herself by copying in water-colors the odd hangings on the walls. The copy was a fascinating thing, a delicate satire instinct with the bantering yet refined nature of the artist. She had amused herself by exaggerating the pretentious finicalness of the old frescoes; she had grasped the false and shifting character of the age of Louis XIV. on those stilted figures. While refreshing the colors that time had faded, she had restored their affected graces, their perfume of courtiership, their costumes of the boudoir and the shepherd's hut, so curiously identical. Beside that work of historical raillery she had written the word *copy*.

She raised her long eyes, instinct with merriment of a caustic, treacherous, yet attractive sort, slowly to Raymon's face. For some reason she reminded him of Shakespeare's Anne Page. There was in her manner neither timidity nor boldness, nor affectation, nor self-distrust. Their conversation turned upon the influence of fashion in the arts.

"Is it not true, monsieur, that the moral coloring of the period was in that brush?" she said, pointing to the wainscoting, covered with rustic cupids after the style of Boucher. "Isn't it true that those sheep do not walk or sleep or browse like sheep of to-day? And that pretty landscape, so false and so orderly, those clumps of many-petalled roses in the middle of the forest where naught but a bit of eglantine grows in our days, those tame birds of a species that has apparently disappeared, and those pink satin gowns which the sun never faded–is there not in all these a deal of poesy, ideas of luxury and pleasure, of a whole useless, harmless, joyous life? Doubtless these absurd fictions were quite as valuable as our gloomy political deliverances! If only I had been born in those days!" she added with a smile; "frivolous and narrow-minded creature that I am, I should have been much better fitted to paint fans and produce masterpieces of thread-work than to read the newspapers and understand the debates in the Chambers!"

Monsieur Hubert left the young people together; and their conversation drifted from one subject to another, until it fell at last upon Madame Delmare.

"You were very intimate with our predecessors in this house," said the young woman, "and it is generous on your part to come and see new faces here. Madame Delmare," she added, with a penetrating glance at him, "was a remarkable woman, so they say; she must have left memories here which place us at a disadvantage, so far as you are concerned."

"She was an excellent woman," Raymon replied, unconcernedly, "and her husband was a worthy man."

"But," rejoined the reckless girl, "she was something more than an excellent woman, I should judge. If I remember rightly there was a charm about her personality which calls for a more enthusiastic and more poetic description. I saw her two years ago, at a ball at the Spanish ambassador's. She was fascinating that night; do you remember?"

Raymon started at this reminder of the evening that he spoke to Indiana for the first time. He remembered at the same moment that he had noticed at that ball the distingué features and clever eyes of the young woman with whom he was now talking; but he did not then ask who she was.

Not until he had taken his leave of her and was congratulating Monsieur Hubert on his daughter's charms, did he learn her name.

"I have not the good fortune to be her father," said the manufacturer; "but I did the best I could by adopting her. Do you not know my story?"

"I have been ill for several months," Raymon replied, "and have heard nothing of you beyond the good you have already done in the province."

"There are people," said Monsieur Hubert with a smile, "who consider that I did a most meritorious thing in adopting Mademoiselle de Nangy; but you, monsieur, who have elevated ideas, will judge whether I did anything more than true delicacy required. Ten years ago, a widower and childless, I found myself possessed of funds to a considerable amount, the results of my labors, which I was anxious to invest. I found that the estate and château of Nangy in Bourgogne, national property, were for sale and suited me perfectly. I had been in possession some time when I learned that the former lord of the manor and his seven-year-old granddaughter were living in a hovel, in extreme destitution. The old man had received some indemnity, but he had religiously devoted it to the payment of debts incurred during the emigration. I tried to better his condition and to give him a home in my house; but he had retained in his poverty all the pride of his rank. He refused to return to the house of his ancestors as an object of charity, and died shortly after my arrival, having steadfastly refused to accept any favors at my hands. Then I took his child there. The little patrician was proud already and accepted my assistance most unwillingly; but at that age prejudices are not deeply rooted and resolutions do not last long. She soon accustomed herself to look upon me as her father and I brought her up as my own daughter. She has rewarded me handsomely by the happiness she has showered on my old age. And so, to make sure of my happiness, I have adopted Mademoiselle de Nangy, and my only hope now is to find her a husband worthy of her and able to manage prudently the property I shall leave her."

Encouraged by the interest with which Raymon listened to his confidences, the excellent man, in true bourgeois fashion, gradually confided all his business affairs to him. His attentive auditor found that he had a fine, large fortune administered with the most minute care, and which simply awaited a younger proprietor, of more fashionable tastes than the worthy Hubert, to shine forth in all its splendor. He felt that he might be the man destined to perform that agreeable task, and he gave thanks to the ingenious fate which reconciled all his interests by offering him, by favor of divers romantic incidents, a woman of his own rank possessed of a fine plebian fortune. It was a chance not to be let slip, and he put forth all his skill in the effort to grasp it. Moreover, the heiress was charming; Raymon became more kindly disposed toward his providence.

As for Madame Delmare, he would not think of her. He drove away the fears which the thought of his letter aroused from time to time; he tried to persuade himself that poor Indiana would not grasp his meaning or would not have the courage to respond to it; and he finally succeeded in deceiving himself and believing that he was not blameworthy, for Raymon would have been horrified to find that he was selfish. He was not one of those artless villains who come on the stage to make a naïve confession of their vices to their own hearts. Vice is not reflected in its own ugliness, or it would frighten itself; and Shakespeare's Iago, who is so true to life in his acts, is false in his words, being forced by our stage conventions to lay bare himself the secret recesses of his deep and tortuous heart. Man rarely tramples his conscience under foot thus coolly. He turns it over, squeezes it, pinches it, disfigures it; and when he has distorted it and exhausted it and worn it out, he carries it about with him as an indulgent and obliging mentor which accommodates itself to his passions and his interests, but which he pretends always to consult and to fear.

He went often to Lagny, therefore, and his visits were agreeable to Monsieur Hubert; for, as you know, Raymon had the art of winning affection, and soon the rich bourgeois's one desire was to call him his son-in-law. But he wished that his adopted daughter should choose him freely and that they should be allowed every opportunity to know and judge each other.

Laure de Nangy was in no haste to assure Raymon's happiness; she kept him perfectly balanced between fear and hope. Being less generous than Madame Delmare, but more adroit, distant yet flattering, haughty yet cajoling, she was the very woman to subjugate Raymon; for she was as superior to him in cunning as he was to Indiana. She soon realized that her admirer craved her fortune much more than herself. Her placid imagination anticipated nothing better in the way of homage; she had too much sense, too much knowledge of the world to dream of love when two millions were at stake. She had chosen her course calmly and philosophically, and she was not inclined to blame Raymon; she did not hate him because he was of a calculating, unsentimental temper like the age in which he lived; but she knew him too well to love him. She made it a matter of pride not to fall below the standard of that cold and scheming epoch; her self-esteem would have suffered had she been swayed by the foolish illusions of an ignorant boarding-school miss; she would have blushed at being deceived as at being detected in a foolish act; in a word, she made her heroism consist in steering clear of love, as Madame Delmare's consisted in sacrificing everything to it.

Mademoiselle de Nangy was fully resolved, therefore, to submit to marriage as a social necessity; but she took a malicious pleasure in making use of the liberty which still belonged to her, and in imposing her authority for some time on the man who aspired to deprive her of it. No youth, no sweet dreams, no brilliant and deceptive future for that girl, who was doomed to undergo all the miseries of wealth. For her, life was a matter of stoical calculation, happiness a childish delusion against which she must defend herself as a weakness and an absurdity.

While Raymon was at work building up his fortune, Indiana was drawing near the shores of France. But imagine her surprise and alarm, when she landed, to see the tri-colored flag floating on the walls of Bordeaux! The city was in a state of violent agitation; the prefect had been almost murdered the night before; the populace were rising on all sides; the garrison seemed to be preparing for a bloody conflict, and the result of the revolution was still unknown.

"I have come too late!" was the thought that fell upon Madame Delmare like a stroke of lightning.

In her alarm she left on board the little money and the few clothes that she possessed, and ran about through the city in a state of frenzy. She tried to find a diligence for Paris, but the public conveyances were crowded with people who were either escaping or going to claim a share in the spoils of the vanquished. Not until evening did she succeed in finding a place. As she was stepping into the coach an improvised patrol of National Guards objected to the departure of the passengers and demanded to see their papers. Indiana had none. While she argued against the absurd suspicions of the triumphant party, she heard it stated all about her that the monarchy had fallen, that the king was a fugitive, and that the ministers had been massacred with all their adherents. This news, proclaimed with laughter and stamping and shouts of joy, dealt Madame Delmare a deadly blow. In the whole revolution she was personally interested in but one fact; in all France she knew but one man. She fell on the ground in a swoon, and came to herself in a hospital–several days later.

After two months she was discharged, without money or linen or effects, weak and trembling, exhausted by an inflammatory brain fever which had caused her life to be despaired of several times. When she found herself in the street, alone, hardly able to walk, without friends, resources or strength, when she made an effort to recall the particulars of her situation and realized that she was hopelessly lost in that great city, she had an indescribable thrill of terror and despair as she thought that Raymon's fate had long since been decided and that there was not a solitary person about her who could put an end to her horrible uncertainty. The horror of desertion bore down with all its might upon her crushed spirit, and the apathetic despair born of hopeless misery gradually deadened all her faculties. In the mental numbness which she felt stealing over her, she dragged herself to the harbor, and, shivering with fever, sat down on a stone to warm herself in the sunshine, gazing listlessly at the water plashing at her feet. She sat there several hours, devoid of energy, of hope, of purpose; but suddenly she remembered her clothes and her money, which she had left on the *Eugène*, and which she might possibly recover; but it was nightfall, and she dared not go among the sailors who were just leaving their work with much rough merriment and question them concerning the ship. Desiring, on the other hand, to avoid the attention she was beginning to attract, she left the quay and concealed herself in the ruins of a house recently demolished behind the great esplanade of Les Quinconces. There, cowering in a corner, she passed that cold October night, a night laden with bitter thoughts and alarms. At last the day broke; hunger made itself felt insistent and implacable. She decided to ask alms. Her clothes, although in wretched condition, still indicated more comfortable circumstances than a beggar is supposed to enjoy. People looked at her curiously, suspiciously, ironically, and gave her nothing. Again she dragged herself to the quays, inquired about the *Eugène* and learned from the first waterman she addressed that she was still in the roadstead. She hired him to put her aboard and found Random at breakfast.

"Well, well, my fair passenger," he cried, "so you have returned from Paris already! You have come in good time, for I sail to-morrow. Shall I take you back to Bourbon?"

He informed Madame Delmare that he had caused search to be made for her everywhere, that he might return what belonged to her. But Indiana had not a scrap of paper upon her from which her name could be learned when she was taken to the hospital. She had been entered on the books there and also on the police books under the designation *unknown*; so the captain had been unable to learn anything about her.

The next day, despite her weakness and exhaustion, Indiana started for Paris. Her anxiety should have diminished when she saw the turn political affairs had taken; but anxiety does not reason, and love is fertile in childish fears.

On the very evening of her arrival at Paris she hurried to Raymon's house and questioned the concierge in an agony of apprehension.

"Monsieur is quite well," was the reply; "he is at Lagny."

"At Lagny! you mean at Cercy, do you not?"

"No, madame, at Lagny, which he owns now."

"Dear Raymon!" thought Indiana, "he has bought that estate to afford me a refuge where public malice cannot reach me. He knew that I would come!"

Drunk with joy, she hastened, light of heart and instinct with new life, to take apartments in a furnished house, and devoted the night and part of the next day to rest. It was so long since the unfortunate creature had enjoyed a peaceful sleep! Her dreams were sweet and deceptive, and when she woke she did not regret them, for she found hope at her pillow. She dressed with care; she knew that Raymon was particular about all the minutiæ of the toilet, and she had ordered the night before a pretty new dress which was brought to her just as she rose. But, when she was ready to arrange her hair, she sought in vain the long and magnificent tresses she had once had; during her illness they had fallen under the nurse's shears. She noticed it then for the first time, her all-engrossing thoughts had diverted her mind so completely from small things.

Nevertheless, when she had curled her short black locks about her pale and melancholy brow, when she had placed upon her shapely head a little English hat, called then, by way of allusion to the recent blow to great fortunes, a *three per cent.;* when she had fastened at her girdle a bunch of the flowers whose perfume Raymond loved, she hoped that she would still find favor in his sight; for she was as pale and fragile as in the first days of their acquaintance, and the effect of her illness had effaced the traces of the tropical sunshine.

She hired a cab in the afternoon and arrived about nine at night at a village on the outskirts of Fontainebleau. There she ordered the driver to put up his horse and wait for her until the next day, and started off alone, on foot, by a path which led to Lagny park by a walk of less than quarter of an hour through the woods. She tried to open the small gate but found it locked on the inside. It was her wish to enter by stealth, to avoid the eyes of the servants and take Raymon by surprise. She skirted the park wall. It was quite old; she remembered that there were frequent breaches, and, by good luck, she found one and passed over without much difficulty.

When she stood upon ground which belonged to Raymon and was to be thenceforth her refuge, her sanctuary, her fortress and her home, her heart leaped for joy. With light, triumphant foot she hastened along the winding paths she knew so well. She reached the English garden, which was dark and deserted on that side. Nothing was changed in the flower-beds; but the bridge, the painful sight of which she dreaded, had disappeared, and the course of the stream had been altered; the spots which might have recalled Noun's death had been changed, and no others.

"He wished to banish that cruel memory," thought Indiana. "He was wrong, I could have endured it. Was it not for my sake that he planted the seeds of remorse in his life? Henceforth we are quits, for I too have committed a crime. I may have caused my husband's death. Raymon can open his arms to me, we will take the place of innocence and virtue to each other."

She crossed the stream on boards laid across where a bridge was to be built and passed through the flower-garden. She was forced to stop, for her heart was beating as if it would burst; she looked up at the windows of her old bedroom. O bliss! a light was shining through the blue curtains, Raymon was there. As if he could occupy any other room! The door to the secret stairway was open.

"He expects me at any time," she thought; "he will be happy but not surprised."

At the top of the staircase she paused again to take breath; she felt less strong to endure joy than sorrow. She stooped and looked through the keyhole. Raymon was alone, reading. It was really he, it was Raymon overflowing with life and vigor; his trials had not aged him, the tempests of politics had not taken a single hair from his head; there he sat, placid and handsome, his head resting on his white hand which was buried in his black hair.

Indiana impulsively tried the door, which opened without resistance.

"You expected me!" she cried, falling on her knees and resting her feeble head upon Raymon's bosom; "you counted the months and days, you knew that the time had passed, but you knew too that I could not fail to come at your call. You called me and I am here, I am here! I am dying!"

Her ideas became tangled in her brain; for some time she knelt there, silent, gasping for breath, incapable of speech or thought. Then she opened her eyes, recognized Raymon as if just waking from a dream, uttered a cry of frantic joy, and pressed her lips to his, wild, ardent and happy. He was pale, dumb, motionless, as if struck by lightning.

"Speak to me, in Heaven's name," she cried; "it is I, your Indiana, your slave whom you recalled from exile and who has travelled three thousand leagues to love you and serve you; it is your chosen companion, who has left everything, risked everything, defied everything, to bring you this moment of joy! You are happy, you are content with her, are you not? I am waiting for my reward; with a word, a kiss I shall be paid a hundredfold."

But Raymon did not reply; his admirable presence of mind had abandoned him. He was crushed with surprise, remorse and terror when he saw that woman at his feet; he hid his face in his hands and longed for death.

"My God! my God! you don't speak to me, you don't kiss me, you have nothing to say to me!" cried Madame Delmare, pressing Raymon's knees to her breast; "is it because you cannot? Joy makes people ill, it kills sometimes, I know! Ah! you are not well, you are suffocating, I surprised you too suddenly! Try to look at me; see how pale I am, how old I have grown, how I have suffered! But it was for you, and you will love me all the better for it! Say one word to me, Raymon, just one."

"I would like to weep," said Raymon in a stifled tone.

"And so would I," said she, covering his hands with kisses. "Ah! yes, that would do you good. Weep, weep on my bosom, and I will wipe your tears away with my kisses. I have come to bring you happiness, to be whatever you choose–your companion, your servant or your mistress. Formerly I was very cruel, very foolish, very selfish. I made you suffer terribly, and I refused to understand that I demanded what was beyond your strength. But since then I have reflected, and as you are not afraid to defy public opinion with me, I have no right to refuse to make any sacrifice. Dispose of me, of my blood, of my life, as you will; I am yours body and soul. I have travelled three thousand leagues to tell you this, to give myself to you. Take me, I am your property, you are my master."

I cannot say what infernal project passed rapidly through Raymon's brain. He removed his clenched hands from his face and looked at Indiana with diabolical *sang-froid;* then a wicked smile played about his lips and made his eyes gleam, for Indiana was still lovely.

"First of all, we must conceal you," he said, rising.

"Why conceal me here?" she said; "aren't you at liberty to take me in and protect me, who have no one but you on earth, and who, without you, shall be compelled to beg on the public highway? Why, even society can no longer call it a crime for you to love me; I have taken everything on my own shoulders! But where are you going?" she cried, as she saw him walking toward the door.

She clung to him with the terror of a child who does not wish to be left alone a single instant, and dragged herself along on her knees behind him.

His purpose was to lock the door; but he was too late. The door opened before he could reach it, and Laure de Nangy entered. She seemed less surprised than exasperated, and did not utter an exclamation, but stooped a little to look with snapping eyes at the half-fainting woman on the floor; then, with a cold, bitter, scornful smile, she said:

"Madame Delmare, you seem to enjoy placing three persons in a very strange situation; but I thank you for assigning me the least ridiculous rôle of the three, and this is how I discharge it. Be good enough to retire."

Indignation renewed Indiana's strength; she rose and drew herself up to her full height.

"Who is this woman, pray?" she said to Raymon, "and by what right does she give me orders in your house?"

"You are in my house, madame," retorted Laure.

"Speak, in heaven's name, monsieur," cried Indiana fiercely, shaking the wretched man's arm; "tell me whether she is your mistress or your wife!"

"She is my wife," Raymon replied with a dazed air.

"I forgive your uncertainty," said Madame de Ramière with a cruel smile. "If you had remained where your duty required you to remain, you would have received cards to monsieur's marriage. Come, Raymon," she added in a tone of sarcastic amiability, "I am moved to pity by your embarrassment. You are rather young; you will realize now, I trust, that more prudence is advisable. I leave it for you to put an end to this absurd scene. I would laugh at it if you didn't look so utterly wretched."

With that she withdrew, well satisfied with the dignity she had displayed, and secretly triumphant because the incident had placed her husband in a position of inferiority and dependence with regard to her.

When Indiana recovered the use of her faculties she was alone in a close carriage, being driven rapidly toward Paris.

XXIX

The carriage stopped at the barrier. A servant whom Madame Delmare recognized as a man who had formerly been in Raymon's service came to the door and asked where he should leave *madame*. Indiana instinctively gave the name and street number of the lodging-house at which she had slept the night before. On arriving there, she fell into a chair and remained there until morning, without a thought of going to bed, without moving, longing for death but too crushed, too inert to summon strength to kill herself. She believed that it was impossible to live after such terrible blows, and that death would of its own motion come in search of her. She remained there all the following day, taking no sustenance, making no reply to the offers of service that were made her.

I do not know that there is anything more horrible on earth than life in a furnished lodging-house in Paris, especially when it is situated, as this one was, in a dark, narrow street, and only a dull, hazy light crawls regretfully, as it were, over the smoky ceilings and soiled windows. And then there is something chilly and repellent in the sight of the furniture to which you are unaccustomed and to which your idle glance turns in vain for a memory, a touch of sympathy. All those objects which belong, so to speak, to no one, because they belong to all comers; that room where no one has left any trace of his passage save now and then a strange name, found on a card in the mirror-frame; that mercenary roof, which has sheltered so many poor travellers, so many lonely strangers, with hospitality for none; which looks with indifference upon so many human agitations and can describe none of them: the discordant, never-ending noise from the street, which does not even allow you to sleep and thus escape grief or ennui: all these are causes of disgust and irritation even to one who does not bring to the horrible place such a frame of mind as Madame Delmare's. You ill-starred provincial, who have left your fields, your blue sky, your verdure, your house and your family, to come and shut yourself up in this dungeon of the mind and the heart–see Paris, lovely Paris, which in your dreams has seemed to you such a marvel of beauty! see it stretch away yonder, black with mud and rainy, as noisy and pestilent and rapid as a torrent of slime! There is the perpetual revel, always brilliant and perfumed, which was promised you; there are the intoxicating pleasures, the wonderful surprises, the treasures of sight and taste and hearing which were to contend for the possession of your passions and faculties, which are of limited capacity and powerless to enjoy them all at once! See, yonder, the affable, winning, hospitable Parisian, as he was described to you, always in a hurry, always careworn! Tired out before you have seen the whole of this ever-moving population, this inextricable labyrinth, you take refuge, over-whelmed with dismay, in the cheerful precincts of a furnished lodging-house, where, after hastily installing you, the only servant of a house that is often of immense size leaves you to die in peace, if fatigue or sorrow deprive you of the strength to attend to the thousand necessities of life.

But to be a woman and to find oneself in such a place, spurned by everybody, three thousand leagues from all human affection; to be without money, which is much worse than being abandoned in a vast desert without water; to have in all one's past not a single happy memory that is not poisoned or withered, in the whole future not a single hope to divert one's thoughts from the emptiness of the present, is the last degree of misery and hopelessness. And so Madame Delmare, making no attempt to contend against a destiny that was fulfilled, against a broken, ruined life, submitted to the gnawings of hunger, fever and sorrow without uttering a complaint, without shedding a tear, without making an effort to die an hour earlier, to suffer an hour less.

They found her on the morning of the second day, lying on the floor, stiff with cold, with clenched teeth, blue lips and lustreless eyes; but she was not dead. The landlady examined her secretary and, seeing how poorly supplied it was, considered whether the hospital was not the proper place for this stranger, who certainly had not the means to pay the expenses of a long and costly illness. However, as she was a woman *overflowing with humanity*, she caused her to be put to bed and sent for a doctor to ascertain if the illness would last more than a day or two.

A doctor appeared who had not been sent for. Indiana, on opening her eyes, found him beside her bed. I need not tell you his name.

"Oh! you here! you here!", she cried, throwing herself, almost fainting, on his breast. "You are my good angel! But you come too late, and I can do nothing for you except to die blessing you."

"You will not die, my dear," replied Ralph with deep emotion; "life may still smile upon you. The laws which interfered with your happiness no longer fetter your affection. I would have preferred to destroy the invincible spell which a man whom I neither like nor esteem has cast upon you; but that is not in my power, and I am tired of seeing you suffer. Hitherto your life has been perfectly frightful; it cannot be more so. Besides, even if my gloomy forebodings are realized and the happiness of which you have dreamed is destined to be of short duration, you will at least have enjoyed it for some little time, you will not die without a taste of it. So I sacrifice all my repugnance and dislike. The destiny which casts you, all alone as you are, into my arms, imposes upon me the duties of a father and a guardian toward you. I come to tell you that you are free and that you may unite your lot to Monsieur de Ramière's. Delmare is no more."

Tears rolled slowly down Ralph's cheeks while he was speaking. Indiana suddenly sat up in bed and cried, wringing her hands in despair:

"My husband is dead! and it was I who killed him! And you talk to me of the future and happiness, as if such a thing were possible for the heart that detests and despises itself! But be sure that God is just and that I am cursed. Monsieur de Ramière is married."

She fell back, utterly exhausted, into her cousin's arms. They were unable to resume conversation until several hours later.

"Your justly disturbed conscience may be set at rest," said Ralph, in a solemn, but sad and gentle tone. "Delmare was at death's door when you deserted him: he did not wake from the sleep in which you left him, he never knew of your flight, he died without cursing you or weeping for you. Toward morning, when I woke from the heavy sleep into which I had fallen beside his bed, I found his face purple and he was burning hot and breathing stertorously in his sleep; he was already stricken with apoplexy. I ran to your room and was surprised not to find you there; but I had no time to try to discover the explanation of your absence; I was not seriously alarmed about it until after Delmare's death. Everything that skill could do was of no avail, the disease progressed with startling rapidity, and he died an hour later, in my arms, without recovering the use of his senses. At the last moment, however, his benumbed, clouded mind seemed to make an effort to come to life; he felt for my hand which he took for yours–his were already stiff and numb–he tried to press it, and died, stammering your name."

"I heard his last words," said Indiana gloomily; "at the moment that I left him forever, he spoke to me in his sleep. 'That man will ruin you,' he said. Those words are here," she added, putting one hand to her heart and the other to her head.

"When I succeeded in taking my eyes and my thoughts from that dead body," continued Ralph, "I thought of you; of you, Indiana, who were free thenceforth, and who could not weep for your master unless from kindness of heart or religious feeling. I was the only one whom his death deprived of something, for I was his friend, and, even if he was not always very sociable, at all events I had no rival in his heart. I feared the effect of breaking the news to you too suddenly, and I went to the door to wait for you, thinking that you would soon return from your morning walk. I waited a long while. I will not attempt to describe my anxiety, my search, and my alarm when I found Ophelia's body, all bleeding and bruised by the rocks; the waves had washed it upon the beach. I looked a long while, alas! expecting to discover yours; for I thought that you had taken your own life, and for three days I believed that there was nothing left on earth for me to love. It is useless to speak of my grief; you must have foreseen it when you abandoned me.

"Meanwhile, a rumor that you had fled spread swiftly through the colony. A vessel came into port that had passed the *Eugéne* in Mozambique Channel; some of the ship's company had been aboard your ship. A passenger had recognized you, and in less than three days the whole island knew of your departure.

"I spare you the absurd and insulting reports that resulted from the coincidence of those two events on the same night, your flight and your husband's death. I was not spared in the charitable conclusions that people amused themselves by drawing; but I paid no attention to them. I had still one duty to perform on earth, to make sure of your welfare and to lend you a helping hand if necessary. I sailed soon after you; but I had a horrible voyage and have been in France only a week. My first thought was to go to Monsieur de Ramière to inquire about you; but by good luck I met his servant Carle, who had just brought you here. I asked him no questions except where you were living, and I came here with the conviction that I should not find you alone."

"Alone, alone! shamefully abandoned!" cried Madame Delmare. "But let us not speak of that man, let us never speak of him. I can never love him again, for I despise him; but you must not tell me that I once loved him, for that reminds me of my shame and my crime; it casts a terrible reproach upon my last moments. Ah! be my angel of consolation; you who never fail to come and offer me a friendly hand in all the crises of my miserable life. Fulfil with pity your last mission; say to me words of affection and forgiveness, so that I may die at peace, and hope for pardon from the Judge who awaits me on high."

She hoped to die; but grief rivets the chain of life instead of breaking it. She was not even dangerously ill; she simply had no strength, and lapsed into a state of languor and apathy which resembled imbecility.

Ralph tried to distract her; he took her away from everything that could remind her of Raymon. He took her to Touraine, he surrounded her with all the comforts of life; he devoted all his time to making a portion of hers endurable; and when he failed, when he had exhausted all the resources of his art and his affection without bringing a feeble gleam of pleasure to that gloomy, careworn face, he deplored the powerlessness of his words and blamed himself bitterly for the ineptitude of his affection.

One day he found her more crushed and hopeless than ever. He dared not speak to her, but sat down beside her with a melancholy air. Thereupon, Indiana turned to him and said, pressing his hand tenderly:

"I cause you a vast deal of pain, poor Ralph! and you must be patient beyond words to endure the spectacle of such egotistical, cowardly misery as mine! Your unpleasant task was finished long ago. The most insanely exacting woman could not ask of friendship more than you have done for me. Now leave me to the misery that is gnawing at my heart; do not spoil your pure and holy life by contact with an accursed life; try to find elsewhere the happiness which cannot exist near me."

"I do in fact give up all hope of curing you, Indiana," he replied; "but I will never abandon you even if you should tell me that I annoy you; for you still require bodily care, and if you are not willing that I should be your friend, I will at all events be your servant. But listen to me; I have an expedient to propose to you which I have kept in reserve for the last stage of the disease, but which certainly is infallible."

"I know but one remedy for sorrow," she replied, "and that is forgetting; for I have had time to convince myself that argument is unavailing. Let us hope everything from time, therefore. If my will could obey the gratitude which you inspire in me, I should be now as cheerful and calm as in the days of our childhood; believe me, my friend, I take no pleasure in nourishing my trouble and inflaming my wound; do I not know that all my sufferings rebound on your heart? Alas! I would like to forget, to be cured! but I am only a weak woman. Ralph, be patient and do not think me ungrateful."

She burst into tears. Sir Ralph took her hand.

"Listen, dear Indiana," he said; "to forget is not in our power; I do not accuse you! I can suffer patiently; but to see you suffer is beyond my strength. Indeed why should we struggle thus, weak creatures that we are, against a destiny of iron? It is quite enough to drag this cannon-ball; the God whom you and I adore did not condemn man to undergo so much misery without giving him the instinct to escape from it; and what constitutes, in my opinion, man's most marked superiority over the brute is his ability to understand what the remedy is for all his ills. The remedy is suicide; that is what I propose, what I advise."

"I have often thought of it," Indiana replied after a short silence. "Long ago I was violently tempted to resort to it, but religious scruples arrested me. Since then my ideas have reached a higher level, in solitude. Misfortune clung to me and gradually taught me a different religion from that taught by men. When you came to my assistance I had determined to allow myself to die of hunger; but you begged me to live, and I had not the right to refuse you that sacrifice. Now, what holds me back is your existence, your future. What will you do all alone, poor Ralph, without family, without passions, without affections? Since I have received these horrible wounds in my heart I am no longer good for anything to you; but perhaps I shall recover. Yes, Ralph, I will do my utmost, I swear. Have patience a little longer; soon, perhaps, I shall be able to smile. I long to become tranquil and light-hearted once more in order to devote to you this life for which you have fought so stoutly with misfortune."

"No, my dear, no; I do not desire such a sacrifice; I will never accept it," said Ralph. "Wherein is my life more precious than yours, pray? Why must you inflict a hateful future upon yourself in order that mine may be pleasant? Do you think that it will be possible for me to enjoy it while feeling that your heart has no share in it? No, I am not so selfish as that. Let us not attempt, I beg you, an impossible heroism; it is overweening pride and presumption to hope to renounce all self-love thus. Let us view our situation calmly and dispose of our remaining days as common property which neither of us has the right to appropriate at the other's expense. For a long time, ever since my birth, I may say, life has been a bore and a burden to me; now I no longer feel the courage to endure it without bitterness of heart and impiety. Let us go together; let us return to God, who exiled us in this world of trials, in this vale of tears, but who will surely not refuse to open His arms to us when, bruised and weary, we go to Him and implore His indulgence and His mercy. I believe in God, Indiana, and it was I who first taught you to believe in Him. So have confidence in me; an upright heart cannot deceive one who questions it with sincerity. I feel that we have both suffered enough here on earth to be cleansed of our sins. The baptism of unhappiness has surely purified our souls sufficiently; let us give them back to Him who gave them."

This idea engrossed Ralph and Indiana for several days, at the end of which it was decided that they should commit suicide together. It only remained to choose what sort of death they would die.

"It is a matter of some importance," said Ralph; "but I have already considered it, and this is what I have to suggest. The act that we are about to undertake not being the result of a momentary mental aberration, but of a deliberate determination formed after calm and pious reflection, it is important that we should bring to it the meditative seriousness of a Catholic receiving the sacraments of his Church. For us the universe is the temple in which we adore God. In the bosom of majestic, virgin nature we are impressed by the consciousness of His power, pure of all human profanation. Let us go back to the desert, therefore, so that we may be able to pray. Here, in this country swarming with men and vices, in the bosom of this civilization which denies God or disfigures Him, I feel that I should be ill at ease, distraught and depressed. I would like to die cheerfully, with a serene brow and with my eyes gazing heavenward. But where can we find heaven here? I will tell you, therefore, the spot where suicide appeared to me in its noblest and most solemn aspect. It is in Ile Bourbon, on the verge of a precipice, on the summit of the cliff from which the transparent cascade, surmounted by a gorgeous rainbow, plunges into the lonely ravine of Bernica. That is where we passed the sweetest hours of our childhood; that is where I bewailed the bitterest sorrows of my life; that is where I learned to pray, to hope; that is where I would like, during one of the lovely nights of that latitude, to bury myself in those pure waters and go down into the cool, flower-decked grave formed by the depths of the verdure-lined abyss. If you have no predilection for any other spot, give me the satisfaction of offering up our twofold sacrifice on the spot which witnessed the games of our childhood and the sorrows of our youth."

"I agree," said Madame Delmare, placing her hand in Ralph's to seal the compact. "I have always been drawn to the banks of the stream by an invincible attraction, by the memory of my poor Noun. To die as she died will be sweet to me; it will be an atonement for her death, which I caused."

"Moreover," said Ralph, "another sea voyage, made under the influence of other feelings than those which have agitated us hitherto, is the best preparation we could imagine for communing with ourselves, for detaching ourselves from earthly affections, for raising ourselves in unalloyed purity to the feet of the Supreme Being. Isolated from the whole world, always ready to leave this life with glad hearts, we shall watch with enchanted eyes the tempest arouse the elements and unfold its magnificent spectacles before us. Come, Indiana, let us go; let us shake the dust of this ungrateful land from our feet. To die here, under Raymon's eyes, would be to all appearance a mere commonplace, cowardly revenge. Let us leave that man's punishment to God; and let us go and beseech Him to open the treasures of His mercy to that barren and ungrateful heart."

They left France. The schooner *Nahandove*, as fleet and nimble as a bird, bore them to their twice-abandoned country. Never was there so pleasant and fast a passage. It seemed as if a favorable wind had undertaken to guide safely into port those two ill-fated beings who had been tossed about so long among the reefs and shoals of life. During those three months Indiana reaped the fruit of her docile compliance with Ralph's advice. The sea air, so bracing and so penetrating, restored her impaired health; a wave of peace overflowed her wearied heart. The certainty that she would soon have done with her sufferings produced upon her the effect of a doctor's assurances upon a credulous patient. Forgetting her past life, she opened her heart to the profound emotions of religious hope. Her thoughts were all impregnated with a mysterious charm, a celestial perfume. Never had the sea and sky seemed to her so beautiful. It seemed to her that she saw them for the first time, she discovered so many new splendors and glories in them. Her brow became serene once more, and one would have said that a ray of the Divine essence had passed into her sweetly melancholy eyes.

A change no less extraordinary took place in Ralph's soul and in his outward aspect; the same causes produced almost the same results. His heart, so long hardened against sorrow, softened in the revivifying warmth of hope. Heaven descended also into that bitter, wounded heart. His words took on the stamp of his feelings and for the first time Indiana became acquainted with his real character. The reverent, filial intimacy that bound them together took from the one his painful shyness, from the other her unjust prejudices. Every day cured Ralph of some *gaucherie* of his nature, Indiana of some error of her judgment. At the same time the painful memory of Raymon faded away and gradually vanished in face of Ralph's unsuspected virtues, his sublime sincerity. As the one grew greater in her estimation, the other fell away. At last, by dint of comparing the two men, every vestige of her blind and fatal love was effaced from her heart.

XXX

It was last year, one evening during the never-ending summer that reigns in those latitudes, that two passengers from the schooner *Nahandove* journeyed into the mountains of Ile Bourbon three days after landing. These two persons had devoted the interval to repose, a precaution quite inconsistent with the plan which had brought them to the colony. But such was evidently not their opinion; for, after taking *faham* together on the veranda, they dressed with especial care as if they intended to pass the evening in society, and, taking the road to the mountain, they reached the ravine of Bernica after about an hour's walk.

Chance willed that it should be one of the loveliest evenings for which the moon ever furnished light in the tropics. That luminary had just risen from the dark waves and was beginning to cast a long band of quick-silver on the sea; but its rays did not shine into the gorge, and the edges of the basin reflected only the trembling gleam of a few stars. Even the lemon-trees on the higher slopes of the mountain were not covered with the pale diamonds with which the moon sprinkles their polished, brittle leaves. The ebony trees and the tamarinds murmured softly in the darkness; only the bushy tufts at the summit of the huge palm-trees, whose slender trunks rose a hundred feet from the ground, shone with a greenish tinge in the silvery beams.

The sea-birds were resting quietly in the crevices of the cliffs, and only a few blue pigeons, concealed behind the projections of the mountain, raised their melancholy, passionate note in the distance. Lovely beetles, living jewels, rustled gently in the branches of the coffee-trees, or skimmed the surface of the lake with a buzzing noise, and the regular plashing of the cascade seemed to exchange mysterious words with the echoes on its shores.

The two solitary promenaders ascended by a steep and winding path to the top of the gorge, to the spot where the torrent plunges down in a white column of vapor to the foot of the precipice. They found themselves on a small platform admirably adapted to their purpose. A number of convolvuli hanging from the trunks of trees formed a natural cradle suspended over the waterfall. Sir Ralph, with wonderful self-possession, cut away several branches which might impede their spring, then took his companion's hand and drew her to a seat beside him on a moss-covered rock from which in the daytime the beautiful view from that spot could be seen in all its wild and charming grandeur. But at that moment the darkness and the dense vapor from the cascade enveloped everything and made the height of the precipice seem immeasurable and awe-inspiring.

XXX

"Let me remind you, my dear Indiana," said Ralph, "that the success of our undertaking requires the greatest self-possession on our part. If you jump hastily in a direction where, because of the darkness, you see no obstacles, you will inevitably bruise yourself on the rocks and your death will be slow and painful; but, if you take care to throw yourself in the direction of the white line which marks the course of the waterfall you will fall into the lake with it, and the water itself will see to it that you do not miss your aim. But, if you prefer to wait an hour, the moon will rise high enough to give us light."

"I am willing," Indiana replied, "especially as we ought to devote these last moments to religious thoughts."

"You are right, my dear," said Ralph. "This last hour should be one of meditation and prayer. I do not say that we ought to make our peace with the Eternal, that would be to forget the distance that separates us from His sublime power; but we ought, I think, to make our peace with the men who have caused our suffering, and to confide to the wind which blows toward the north-east words of pity for those from whom three thousand leagues of ocean separate us."

Indiana received this suggestion without surprise or emotion. For several months past her thoughts had become more and more elevated in direct proportion to the change that had taken place in Ralph. She no longer listened to him simply as a phlegmatic adviser; she followed him in silence as a good spirit whose mission it was to take her from the earth and deliver her from her torments.

"I agree," she said; "I am overjoyed to feel that I can forgive without an effort, that I have neither hatred nor regret nor love nor resentment in my heart; indeed, at this moment, I hardly remember the sorrows of my sad life and the ingratitude of those who surrounded me. Almighty God! Thou seest the deepest recesses of my heart; Thou knowest that it is pure and calm, and that all my thoughts of love and hope have turned to Thee."

Thereupon, Ralph seated himself at Indiana's feet and began to pray in a loud voice that rose above the roar of the cascade. It was the first time perhaps since he was born that his whole thought came to his lips. The hour of his death had struck; his heart was no longer held in check by fetters or mysteries; it belonged to God alone; the chains of society no longer weighed it down. Its ardor was no longer a crime, it was free to soar upward to God who awaited it; the veil that concealed so much virtue, grandeur and power fell away, and the man's mind rose at its first leap to the level of his heart.

As a bright flame burns amid dense clouds of smoke and scatters them, so did the sacred fire that glowed in the depths of his being send forth its brilliant light. The first time that that inflexible conscience found itself delivered from its trammels and its fears, words came of themselves to the assistance of his thoughts, and the man of mediocre talents, who had never said any but commonplace things in his life, became, in his last hour, eloquent and convincing as Raymon had never been. Do not expect me to repeat to you the strange harangue that he confided to the echoes of the vast solitude; not even he himself, if he were here, could repeat it. There are moments of mental exaltation and ecstasy when our thoughts are purified, subtilised, etherealised as it were. These infrequent moments raise us so high, carry us so far out of ourselves, that when we fall back upon the earth we lose all consciousness and memory of that intellectual debauch. Who can understand the anchorite's mysterious visions? Who can tell the dreams of the poet before his exaltation cooled so that he could write them down for us? Who can say what marvellous things are revealed to the soul of the just man when Heaven opens to receive him? Ralph, a man so utterly commonplace to all outward appearance–and yet an exceptional man, for he firmly believed in God and consulted the book of his conscience day by day–Ralph at that moment was adjusting his accounts with eternity. It was the time to be himself, to lay bare his whole moral being, to lay aside, before the Judge, the disguise that men had forced upon him. Casting away the haircloth in which sorrow had enveloped his bones, he stood forth sublime and radiant as if he had already entered into the abode of divine rewards.

As she listened to him, it did not occur to Indiana to be surprised; she did not ask herself if it were really Ralph who talked like that. The Ralph she had known had ceased to exist, and he to whom she was listening now seemed to be a friend whom she had formerly seen in her dreams and who finally became incarnate for her on the brink of the grave. She felt her own pure soul soar upward in the same flight. A profound religious sympathy aroused in her the same emotions, and tears of enthusiasm fell from her eyes upon Ralph's hair.

Thereupon, the moon rose over the tops of the great palms, and its beams, shining between the branches of the convolvuli, enveloped Indiana in a pale, misty light which made her resemble, in her white dress and with her long hair falling over her shoulders, the wraith of some maiden lost in the desert.

Sir Ralph knelt before her and said:

"Now, Indiana, you must forgive me for all the injury I have done you, so that I may forgive myself for it."

"Alas!" she replied, "what can I possibly have to forgive you, my poor Ralph? Ought I not, on the contrary, to bless you to the last moment of my life, as you have forced me to do in all the days of misery that have fallen to my lot?"

"I do not know how far I have been blameworthy," rejoined Ralph; "but it is impossible that, in the course of such a long and terrible battle with my destiny, I should not have been many times without my own volition."

"Of what battle are you speaking?" queried Indiana.

"That is what I must explain to you before we die; that is the secret of my life. You asked me to tell it to you on the ship that brought us here, and I promised to do so on the shore of Bernica Lake, when the moon should rise upon us for the last time."

"That moment has come," she said, "and I am listening."

"Summon all your patience then, for I have a long story to tell you, Indiana, and that story is my own."

"I thought that I knew it, inasmuch as I have hardly ever been separated from you."

"You do not know it; you do not know it for a single day, a single hour," said Ralph sadly. "When could I have told it to you, pray? It is Heaven's will that the only suitable moment for me to do so, should be the last moment of your life and my own. But it is as innocent and proper to-day as it would formerly have been insane and criminal. It is a personal gratification for which no one has the right to blame me at this hour, which you accord to me in order to complete the task of patience and gentleness which you have taken upon yourself with regard to me. Endure to the end, therefore, the burden of my unhappiness; and if my words tire you and annoy you, listen to the waterfall as it sings the hymn of the dead over me.

"I was born to love; none of you chose to believe it, and your error in that regard had a decisive influence on my character. It is true that nature, while giving me an ardent heart, was guilty of a strange inconsistency; she placed on my face a stone mask and on my tongue a weight that it could not raise; she refused me what she grants to the most ordinary mortals, the power to express my feelings by the glance or by speech. That made me selfish. People judged the mental being by the outer envelope and, like an imperfect fruit I was compelled to dry up under the rough husk which I could not cast off. I was hardly born when I was cast out of the heart which I most needed. My mother put me away from her breast with disgust, because my baby face could not return her smile. At an age when one can hardly distinguish a thought from a desire, I was already branded with the hateful designation of egotist.

"Thereupon it was decided that no one would love me, because I was unable to put in words my affection for anyone. They made me unhappy, they declared that I did not feel my unhappiness; I was almost banished from my father's house; they sent me to live among the rocks like a lonely shore-bird. You know what my childhood was, Indiana. I passed the long days in the desert, with no anxious mother to come there in search of me, with no friendly voice amid the silence of the ravines to remind me that the approach of night called me back to the cradle. I grew up alone, I lived alone; but God would not permit me to be unhappy to the end, for I shall not die alone.

"Heaven however sent me a gift, a consolation, a hope. You came into my life as if Heaven had created you for me. Poor child! abandoned like me, like me set adrift in life without love and without protectors, you seemed to be destined for me–at least I flattered myself that it was so. Was I too presumptuous? For ten years you were mine, absolutely mine; I had no rivals, no misgivings. At that time I had had no experience of what jealousy is.

"That time, Indiana, was the least dismal period of my life. I made of you my sister, my daughter, my companion, my pupil, my whole society. Your need of me made my life something more than that of a wild beast; for your sake I threw off the gloom into which the contempt of my own family had cast me. I began to esteem myself by becoming useful to you. I must tell you everything, Indiana; after accepting the burden of life for you, my imagination suggested the hope of a reward. I accustomed myself–forgive the words I am about to use; even to-day I cannot utter them without fear and trembling–I accustomed myself to think that you would be my wife; child that you were, I looked upon you as my betrothed; my imagination arrayed you in the charms of young womanhood; I was impatient to see you in your maturity. My brother, who had usurped my share of the family affection and who took pleasure in peaceful avocations, had a garden on the hillside which we can see from here by daylight, and which subsequent owners have transformed into a rice-field. The care of his flowers occupied his pleasantest moments, and every morning he went out to watch their progress with an impatient eye, and to wonder, child that he was, because they had not grown so much as he expected in a single night. You, Indiana, were my whole vocation, my only joy, my only treasure; you were the young plant that I cultivated, the bud that I was impatient to see bloom. I, too, looked eagerly every morning for the effect of another day that had passed over your head; for I was already a young man and you were but a child. Already passions of which you did not know the name were stirring my bosom; my fifteen years played havoc with my imagination, and you were surprised to see me so often in a melancholy mood, sharing your games, but taking no pleasure in them. You could not imagine that a fruit or a bird was no longer a priceless treasure to me as it was to you, and I already seemed cold and odd to you. And yet you loved me such as I was; for, despite my melancholy, there was not a moment of my life that was not devoted to you; my sufferings made you dearer to my heart; I cherished the insane hope that it would be your mission to change them to joys some day.

"Alas! forgive me for the sacrilegious thought which kept me alive for ten years; if it were a crime in the accursed child to hope for you, lovely, simple-hearted child of the mountains, God alone is guilty of giving him, for his only sustenance, that audacious thought. Upon what could that wounded, misunderstood heart subsist, who encountered new necessities at every turn and found a refuge nowhere? from whom could he expect a glance, a smile of love, if not from you, whose lover and father he was at the same time?

"Do not be shocked to find that you grew up under the wing of a poor bird consumed by love; never did any impure homage, any blameworthy thought endanger the virginity of your soul; never did my mouth brush from your cheeks that bloom of innocence which covered them as the fruit is covered with a moist vapor in the morning. My kisses were the kisses of a father, and when your innocent and playful lips met mine they did not find there the stinging flame of virile desire. No, it was not with you, a tiny blue-eyed child, that I was in love. As I held you in my arms, with your innocent smile and your dainty caresses, you were simply my child, or at most my little sister; but I was in love with your fifteen years, when, yielding to the ardor of my own youth, I devoured the future with a greedy eye.

"When I read you the story of Paul and Virginie, you only half understood it. You wept, however; you saw only the story of a brother and sister where I had quivered with sympathy, realizing the torments of two lovers. That book made me miserable, whereas it was your joy. You enjoyed hearing me read of the attachment of a faithful dog, of the beauty of the cocoa-palms and the songs of Dominique the negro. But I, when I was alone, read over and over the conversations between Paul and his sweetheart, the impulsive suspicions of the one, the secret sufferings of the other. Oh! how well I understood those first anxieties of youth, seeking in his own heart an explanation of the mysteries of life, and seizing enthusiastically on the first object of love that presents itself to him! But do me justice, Indiana–I did not commit the crime of hastening by a single day the placid development of your childhood; I did not let a word escape me which could suggest to you that there were such things as tears and misery in life. I left you, at the age of ten, in all the ignorance, all the security that were yours when your nurse placed you in my arms, one day when I had determined to die.

"Often as I sat alone on this cliff I wrung my hands frantically as I listened to all the sounds of spring time and of love which the mountain gives forth, as I saw the creepers chase each other to and fro, the insects sleeping in a voluptuous embrace in the calyx of a flower, as I inhaled the burning dust which the palm-trees sent to one another–etheral transports, subtle joys to which the gentle summer breeze serves as a couch. At such times I was frantic, I was mad. I appealed for love to the flowers, to the birds, to the voice of the torrent. I called wildly upon that unknown bliss, the mere thought of which made my brain whirl. But I would see you running toward me, along yonder path, merry and laughing, so tiny in the distance and so awkward about climbing the rocks that one might have taken you for a penguin, with your white dress and your brown hair. Then my blood would grow calm, my lips cease to burn. In presence of the little Indiana of seven I would forget the Indiana of fifteen of whom I had just been dreaming. I would open my arms to you with pure delight; your kisses would cool my forehead. At those times I was happy; I was a father.

"How many free, peaceful days we have passed in this ravine! How many times I have bathed your feet in the pure water of yonder basin! How many times I have watched you sleeping among the reeds, shaded by the leaf of a palm for an umbrella! It was at those times that my tortures would occasionally begin anew. It was a sore affliction to me that you were so small. I would ask myself whether, suffering as I did, I could live until the day when you could understand me and respond to my love. I would gently lift your silken locks and kiss them with passion. I would compare them with curls I had cut from your head in preceding years and which I kept in my wallet. I would joyously make sure of the darker shade that each recurring spring gave to them. Then I would examine the marks on the trunk of a date-tree nearby, that I had made to show the progressive increase in your height for four or five years. The tree still bears those scars, Indiana; I found them on it the last time I came here to suffer. Alas! in vain did you grow taller and taller; in vain did your beauty keep all its promises; in vain did your hair become black as ebony. You did not grow for me; not for me did your charms develop. The first time that your heart beat faster it was for another than me.

"Do you remember how we ran, as light of foot as two turtle-doves, among the thickets of wild rose bushes? Do you remember, too, that we sometimes went astray in the forests over our heads? Once we tried to reach the mist-enveloped peaks of the Salazes; but we had not foreseen that the higher we went the scarcer the fruit became, the less accessible the streams, the more terrible and more penetrating the cold.

"When we saw the vegetation receding behind us you would have returned; but when we had crossed the fern belt we found a quantity of wild strawberries, and you were so busy filling your basket with them that you thought no more about leaving the place. But we had to abandon the idea of going on. We were walking on volcanic rocks covered with little brown spots, and with woolly plants growing among them. Those wretched wind-beaten weeds made us think of the goodness of God, who has given them a warm garment to withstand the violence of the storm. Then the mist became so dense that we could not tell where we were going, and we had to go down again. I carried you in my arms. I crept carefully down the deep slopes of the mountain. Darkness surprised us as we entered the first woods, in the third belt of vegetation. I picked some pomegranates for you and made shift to quench my own thirst with the convolvuli, the stalks of which contain an abundant supply of cool, pure water. Thereupon we recalled the adventure of our favorite heroes, when they lost themselves in the forests of the Rivière-Rouge. But we had no loving mothers, nor zealous servants, nor faithful dog to search for us. But I was content; I was proud. I shared with no one the duty of watching over you, and I considered myself more fortunate than Paul.

"Yes, it was a profound and pure and true passion that you inspired in me even then. Noun, at ten years, was a head taller than you; a creole in the fullest acceptation of the word, she was already developed. Her melting eyes already shone with a curious expression; her bearing and character were those of a young woman. But I did not love Noun, or I loved her only because of you, with whom she always played. It never occurred to me to wonder whether she was beautiful already; whether she would be more beautiful some day. I never looked at her. In my eyes she was more of a child than you; for, you see, I loved you. I staked all my hopes upon you; you were the companion of my life, the dream of my youth.

"Those days of exile in England, that period of pain and grief, I will not describe. If I treated any one badly, it was not you; and if any one treated me badly, I do not propose to complain. There I became more *egotistical,* that is to say more depressed and more distrustful than ever. By being suspicious of me, people had compelled me to become self-sufficient and to rely upon myself. Thus I had only the testimony of my own heart to support me in those trials. It was attributed to me as a crime that I did not love a woman who married me only because she was forced to and who never treated me with anything but contempt. It was afterwards remarked that one of the principal characteristics of my egotism was the aversion I seemed to feel for children. Raymon more than once bantered me cruelly concerning that supposed peculiarity, observing that the care necessary for the education of children was quite inconsistent with the rigidly methodical ways of an old bachelor. I fancy that he did not know that I had been a father, and that it was I who educated you. But none of you would ever understand that the memory of my son was as intensely painful to me after many years as on the first day, and that my sore heart swelled at the sight of flaxen heads that reminded me of him. When a man is unhappy, people are terribly afraid of not finding him blameworthy enough, because they dread being compelled to pity him.

"But what no one will ever be able to understand is the profound indignation, the black despair which took possession of me when I, a poor child of the desert, upon whom no one had ever deigned to cast a pitying glance, was forced to leave this spot and take upon myself the burdens of society; when I was told that I must fill an empty place that had spurned me; when they tried to make me understand that I had duties to fulfil toward those men and women who had disregarded their duties toward me. Think of it! no one of all my kindred had chosen to be my protector and now they all called upon me to undertake the defence of their interests! They would not even leave me to enjoy in peace what pariahs enjoy, the air of solitude! I had but one thing in life that I cherished, one thought, one hope–that you would belong to me forever; they deprived me of that, they told me that you were not rich enough for me. Bitter mockery! for me whom the mountains had nourished and whom my father's roof had cast out! me, who had never been allowed to learn the use of riches, and upon whom was now laid the duty of managing to advantage the riches of other people!

"However I submitted. I had no right to pray that my paltry happiness might be spared; I was despised enough, Heaven knows! to resist would have been to make myself odious. My mother, inconsolable for her other son's death, threatened to die herself if I did not follow out my destiny. My father, who accused me of not knowing how to comfort him, as if I were to blame because he loved me so little, was ready to curse me if I tried to escape from his yoke. I bent my head; but what I suffered even you yourself, although you too have been very unhappy, could never understand. If, after being hunted and maltreated and oppressed as I have been, I have not returned mankind evil for evil, perhaps it is a fair conclusion that my heart is not so cold and sterile as it has been accused of being.

"When I came back here, when I saw the man to whom you had been married–forgive me, Indiana, that was the time when I was genuinely selfish; there must always be selfishness in love, since there was a touch of it even in mine–I felt an indescribably cruel joy in the thought that that legal sham would give you a master and not a husband. You were surprised at the species of affection for him I displayed; it was because I did not look upon him as a rival. I knew well enough that that old man could neither feel nor inspire love, and that your heart would come forth untouched from that marriage. I was grateful to him for your coldness and your melancholy. If he had remained here, I should perhaps have become a very guilty man; but you left me alone and it was not in my power to live without you. I tried to conquer the indomitable love which had sprung to life again in all its force when I found you as fair and sad as I had dreamed of you in your childhood. But solitude only intensified my suffering and I yielded to the craving I felt to see you, to live under the same roof, to breathe the same air, to drink my fill every hour of the melodious tones of your voice. You know what obstacles I had to meet, what distrust I had to overcome; I realized then what duties I had voluntarily undertaken; I could not connect my life with yours without quieting your husband's suspicions by a sacred promise, and I have never known what it was to trifle with my word. I pledged myself therefore with my mind and my heart never to forget my rôle of brother, and I ask you, Indiana, if I ever was false to my oath.

"I realized also that it would be difficult, perhaps impossible, for me to perform that painful task, if I laid aside the disguise that precluded any intimate relations, any profound sentiment; I realized that I must not play with the danger, for my passion was too intense to come forth victorious from a battle. I felt that I must erect about myself a triple wall of ice, in order to repel your interest in me, in order to deprive myself of your compassion, which would have ruined me. I said to myself that on the day that you pitied me, I should be already guilty, and I made up my mind to live under the weight of that horrible accusation of indifference and selfishness, which, thank Heaven! you did not fail to bring against me. The success of my ruse surpassed my hopes; you lavished upon me a sort of insulting pity like that which is accorded to eunuchs; you denied me the possession of a heart and passions; you trampled me under foot, and I had not the right to display energy enough to be angry and vow vengeance, for that would have betrayed me and shown you that I was a man.

"I complain of mankind at large and not of you, Indiana. You were always kind and merciful; you tolerated me under this despicable disguise I had adopted in order to be near you; you never made me blush for my rôle, you were all in all to me, and sometimes I thought with pride that if you looked kindly upon me in the guise I had assumed in order that you might misunderstand me, you might perhaps love me if you should know me some day as I really was. Alas! what other than you would not have spurned me? what other would have held out her hand to that speechless, witless clown? Everybody but you held aloof with disgust from the *egotist!* Ah! there was one being in the world generous enough not to tire of that profitless exchange; there was one heart large enough to shed something of the blessed flame that animated it upon the narrow, benumbed heart of the poor abandoned wretch. It required a heart that had too much of that of which I had not enough. There was under Heaven but one Indiana capable of caring for a Ralph.

"Next to you the person who showed me the most indulgence was Delmare. You accused me of preferring him to you, of sacrificing your comfort to my own by refusing to interfere in your domestic quarrels. Unjust, blind woman! you did not see that I served you as well as it was possible to do; and, above all, you did not understand that I could not raise my voice in your behalf without betraying myself. What would have become of you if Delmare had turned me out of his house? who would have protected you, patiently, silently, but with the persevering steadfastness of an undying love? Not Raymon surely. And then I was fond of him from a feeling of gratitude, I confess;–yes, fond of that rough, vulgar creature who had it in his power to deprive me of my only remaining joy, and who did not do it; that man whose misfortune it was not to be loved by you, so that there was a secret bond of sympathy between us! I was fond of him too for the very reason that he had never caused me the tortures of jealousy.

"But I have come now to the most ghastly sorrow of my life, to the fatal time when your love, of which I had dreamed so long, belonged to another. Then and not till then did I fully realize the nature of the sentiment that I had held in check so many years. Then did hatred pour poison into my breast and jealousy consume what was left of my strength. Hitherto my imagination had kept you pure; my respect encompassed you with a veil which the innocent audacity of dreams dared not even raise; but when I was assailed by the horrible thought that another had involved you in his destiny, had snatched you from my power and was intoxicating himself with deep draughts of the bliss of which I dared not even dream, I became frantic; I would have rejoiced to see that detested man at the foot of this precipice and to roll stones down upon his head.

"However your sufferings were so great that I forgot my own. I did not choose to kill him, because you would have wept for him. Indeed I was tempted twenty times, Heaven forgive me! to be a vile and despicable wretch, to betray Delmare and serve my enemy. Yes, Indiana, I was so insane, so miserable at the sight of your suffering, that I repented having tried to enlighten you and that I would have given my life to bequeath my heart to that man! Oh! the villain! may God forgive him for the injury he has done me! but may He punish him for the misery he has heaped upon your head! It is for that that I hate him; for, so far as I am concerned, I forget what my life has been, when I see what he has made of yours. He is a man whom society should have branded on the forehead on the day of his birth! whom it should have spat upon and cast out as the hardest-hearted and vilest of men! But on the contrary, she bore it aloft in triumph. Ah! I recognize mankind in that, and I ought not to be indignant; for man simply obeys his nature in adoring the deformed creature who destroys the happiness and consideration of another.

"Forgive me, Indiana, forgive me! it is cruel perhaps to complain before you, but this is the first time and the last; let me curse the ungrateful wretch who has driven you to the grave. This terrible lesson was necessary to open your eyes. In vain did a voice from Noun's deathbed and Delmare's cry out to you: 'Beware of him, he will ruin you!'–you were deaf: your evil genius led you on and, dishonored as you are, public opinion condemns you and absolves him. He did all sorts of evil and no heed was paid to it. He killed Noun and you forgot it; he ruined you and you forgave him. You see, he had the art to dazzle the eyes and deceive the mind; his adroit, deceitful words found their way to the heart; his viper's glance fascinated; and if nature had given him my metallic features and my dull intelligence she would have made a perfect man of him.

"Yes, I say, may God punish him, for he was barbarous to you! or, rather, may He forgive him, for perhaps he was more stupid than wicked! He did not understand you; he did not appreciate the happiness he might have enjoyed! Oh! you loved him so dearly! He might have made your life so beautiful! In his place I would not have been virtuous; I would have fled with you into the heart of the mountains; I would have torn you from society to have you all to myself, and I should have had but one fear, that you would not be accursed and abandoned sufficiently so that I might be all in all to you. I would have been jealous of your consideration, but not in the same way that he was; my aim would have been to destroy it in order to replace it by my love. I should have suffered intensely to see another man give you the slightest morsel of pleasure, a moment's gratification; it would have been a theft from me; for your happiness would have been my care, my property, my life, my honor! Oh! how vain and how wealthy I would have been with this wild ravine for my only home, these mountain trees for my only fortune, if heaven had given them to me with your love! Let us weep, Indiana; it is the first time in my life that I have wept; it is God's will that I should not die without knowing that melancholy pleasure."

Ralph was weeping like a child. It was in very truth the first time that stoical soul had ever given way to self-compassion; and yet there was in those tears more sorrow for Indiana's fate than for his own.

"Do not weep for me," he said, seeing that her face too was bathed in tears. "Do not pity me; your pity wipes out the whole past, and the present is no longer bitter. Why should I suffer now? You no longer love him."

"If I had known you as you are, Ralph, I should never have loved him," cried Madame Delmare; "it was your virtue that was my ruin."

"And then," continued Ralph, looking at her with a sorrowful smile, "I have many other causes of joy. You unwittingly confided something to me during the hours that we poured out our hearts to each other on board ship. You told me that this Raymon was never so fortunate as he had the presumption to claim to be, and you relieved me of a part of my torments. You took away my remorse for having watched over you so ineffectually; for I had the insolence to try to protect you from his fascinations; and therein I insulted you, Indiana. I did not have faith in your strength; that is another crime for you to forgive."

"Alas!" said Indiana, "you ask me to forgive! me who have made your whole life miserable, who have rewarded so pure and generous a love with incredible blindness, barbarous ingratitude! Why, I am the one who should crawl at your feet and implore forgiveness."

"Then this love of mine arouses neither disgust nor anger in your breast, Indiana? O my God! I thank Thee! I shall die happy! Listen, Indiana; cease to blame yourself for my sufferings. At this moment I regret none of Raymon's joys, and I think that my fate would arouse his envy if he had the heart of a man. Now I am your brother, your husband, your lover for all eternity. Since the day that you promised to leave this life with me, I have cherished the sweet thought that you belonged to me, that you had returned to me never to leave me again. I began once more to call you my betrothed under my breath. It would have been too much happiness–or, it may be, not enough–to possess you on earth. In God's bosom the bliss awaits me of which my childhood dreamed. There, Indiana, you will love me; there, your divine intellect, stripped of all the lying fictions of this life, will make up to me for a whole life of sacrifices, suffering and self-denial; there, you will be mine, O my Indiana! for you are heaven! and if I deserve to be saved, I deserve to possess you. This is what I had in mind when I asked you to put on this white dress; it is the wedding dress; and yonder rock jutting out into the basin is the altar that awaits us."

He rose and plucked a branch from a flowering orange tree in a neighboring thicket and placed it on Indiana's black hair; then he knelt at her feet.

"Make me happy," he said; "tell me that your heart consents to this marriage in another world. Give me eternity; do not compel me to pray for absolute annihilation."

If the story of Ralph's inward life has produced no effect upon you, if you have not come to love that virtuous man, it is because I have proved to be an unfaithful interpreter of his memories, because I have not been able to exert the power possessed by a man who is profoundly in earnest in his passion. Moreover, the moon does not lend me its melancholy influence, nor do the song of the grosbeak, the perfume of the cinnamon-tree, and all the luxurious and intoxicating seductions of a night in the tropics appeal to your head and heart. It may be, too, that you do not know by experience what powerful and novel sensations awake in the heart at the thought of suicide, and how all the things of this life appear in their true light at the moment of severing our connection with them. This sudden light filled all the inmost recesses of Indiana's heart; the bandage, which had long been loosened, fell from her eyes altogether. Newly awake to the truth and to nature, she saw Ralph's heart as it really was. She also saw his features as she had never seen them; for the mental exaltation of his position had produced the same effect on him that the Voltaic battery produces on paralyzed limbs; it had set him free from the paralysis that had fettered his eyes and his voice. Arrayed in all the glory of his frankness and his virtue he was much handsomer than Raymon, and Indiana felt that he was the man she should have loved.

"Be my husband in heaven and on earth," she said, "and let this kiss bind me to you for all eternity!"

Their lips met; and doubtless there is in a love that comes from the heart a greater power than in the ardor of a fugitive desire; for that kiss, on the threshold of another life, summed up for them all the joys of this.

Thereupon Ralph took his fiancée in his arms and bore her away to plunge with her in the torrent.

RALPH AND INDIANA SEEK DEATH TOGETHER

Their lips met; and doubtless there is in a love that comes from the heart a greater power than in the ardor of a fugitive desire; for that kiss, on the threshold of another life, summed up for them all the joys of this.

Thereupon Ralph took his fiancée in his arms and bore her away to plunge with her in the torrent.

CONCLUSION

TO J. NERAUD

On a hot, sunshiny day in January last I started from Saint-Paul and wandered into the wild forests of Ile Bourbon to muse and dream. I dreamed of you, my friend; those virgin forests had retained for me the memory of your wanderings and your studies, the ground had kept the imprint of your feet. I found everywhere the marvellous things with which your magical tales charmed the tedium of my vigils in the old days, and, in order that we might enjoy them together, I called upon old Europe, where obscurity encompasses you with its modest advantages, to send you to me. Happy man, whose intellect and merits no treacherous friend has made known to the world!

I walked in the direction of a lonely spot in the highest part of the island, called *Brulé de Saint-Paul.*

A huge fragment of mountain, which was dislodged and fell during some volcanic disturbance, has formed on the slope of the principle mountain a sort of long arena studded with rocks arranged in the most magical disorder, in the most extraordinary confusion. Here, a huge boulder balances itself on a number of small fragments; there, rises a wall of slender, light, porous rocks with dentilated edges and openwork decoration like a Moorish building; farther on, an obelisk of basalt, whose sides an artist seems to have carved and polished, stands upon a crenelated bastion; in another place, a gothic fortress is crumbling to decay beside a curious, shapeless pagoda. That spot is the rendezvous of all the rough drafts of art, all the sketches of architecture; it would seem that all the geniuses of all nations and of all ages went for their inspiration to that vast work of hazard and demolition. There, doubtless some magically elaborate design of chance gave birth to the Moorish style of sculpture. In the heart of the forests, art found in the palm-tree one of its most beautiful models. The *vacoa* which anchors itself in the ground and clings to it with a hundred arms branched from its main stalk, evidently furnished the first suggestion of the plan of a cathedral supported by its lightly flying buttresses. In the *Brulé de Saint-Paul* all shapes, all types of beauty, all humorous and bold conceits were assembled, piled upon one another, arranged and constructed in one tempestuous night. The spirits of air and fire undoubtedly presided over this diabolical operation; they alone could give to their productions that awe-inspiring, fanciful, incomplete character which distinguishes their works from those of man; they alone could have piled up those monstrous boulders, moved those gigantic masses, toyed with mountains as with grains of sand, and strewn, amid creations which man has tried to copy, those grand conceptions of art, those sublime contrasts impossible of realization, which seem to defy the audacity of the artist and to say to him derisively: "Try it again."

I halted at the foot of a crystallized basaltic monument, about sixty feet high and cut with facets as if by a lapidary. At the top of this strange object an inscription seemed to have been traced in bold characters by an immortal hand. Those vulcanized rocks often present that phenomenon; long ago, when their substance, softened by the action of fire, was still warm and malleable, they received and retained the imprint of the shells and climbing plants that clung to them. These chance contacts have resulted in some strange freaks, curious hieroglyphics, mysterious characters which seem to have been stamped there like the seal of some supernatural being, written in cabalistic letters.

I stood there a long time, detained by a foolish idea that I might find a meaning for those ciphers. This profitless search caused me to fall into a profound meditation, during which I forgot that time was flying.

Already the mists were gathering about the peaks of the mountains, creeping down the sides and rapidly shutting out their outlines. Before I had descended half way to the plateau, they reached the belt that I was crossing and enveloped it in an impenetrable curtain. A moment later a high wind came up and swept the mist away in a twinkling. Then it fell; the mist settled down once more, to be once more driven away by a terrific squall.

I sought shelter from the storm in a grotto which afforded me some protection; but another scourge came to the assistance of the wind. Torrents of rain swelled the streams, all of which flow from the summit of the mountain. In an hour, everything was inundated and the sides of the mountain, with water pouring down on every side, formed one vast cascade which rushed madly down toward the lowlands.

After two days of most painful and dangerous travelling, I found myself, guided by Providence, I doubt not, at the door of a house built in an exceedingly wild locality. The simple but attractive cottage had withstood the tempest, being sheltered by a rampart of cliffs which leaned over it as if to act as an umbrella. A little lower, a waterfall plunged madly down into a ravine and formed at the bottom a brimming lake, above which, clumps of lovely trees still reared their storm-tossed, tired heads.

I knocked vigorously; but the face that appeared in the doorway made me recoil. Before I had opened my mouth to ask for shelter the master of the house had welcomed me gravely and silently with a wave of his hand. I entered and found myself alone with him, face to face with Sir Ralph Brown.

In the year that had passed since the *Nahandove* brought Sir Ralph and his companion back to the colony, he had not been seen in the town three times; and, as for Madame Delmare, her seclusion had been so absolute that her existence was still a problematical matter to many of the people. It was about the same time that I first landed at Bourbon, and my present interview with Monsieur Brown was the second one I had had in my life.

The first had left an ineradicable impression on me; it was at Saint-Paul, on the seashore. His features and bearing had impressed me only slightly at first; but when, through mere idle curiosity, I questioned the colonists concerning him, their replies were so strange, so contradictory, that I scrutinized the recluse of Bernica more closely.

"He's a clown–a man of no education," said one; "an absolute nullity, who has only one good quality–that of keeping his mouth shut."

"He's an extremely well educated and profound man," said another, "but too strongly persuaded of his own superiority, contemptuous and conceited–so much so that he considers any words wasted that he happens to exchange with the common herd."

"He's a man who cares for nobody but himself," said a third; "a man of inferior capacity, but not stupid; profoundly selfish and, they say, hopelessly unsociable."

"Why, don't you know?" said a young man brought up in the colony and thoroughly imbued with the characteristic narrow-mindedness of provincials, "he's a knave, a villain who poisoned his friend in the most dastardly way in order to marry his wife."

This assertion bewildered me so that I turned to another, older colonist, whom I knew to be possessed of considerable common sense.

As my glance eagerly requested a solution of these enigmas, he answered:

"Sir Ralph was formerly an excellent man, who was not a favorite because he was not communicative, but whom everybody esteemed. That is all I can say about him; for, since his unfortunate experience, I have had no relations with him."

"What experience?" I inquired.

He told me about Colonel Delmare's sudden death, his wife's flight during the same night, and Monsieur Brown's departure and return. The obscurity which surrounded all these circumstances had been in nowise lessened by the investigations of the authorities; there was no evidence that the fugitive had committed the crime. The king's attorney had refused to prosecute; but the partiality of the magistrates for Monsieur Brown was well known, and they had been severely criticised for not having at least enlightened public opinion concerning an affair which left the reputations of two persons marred by a hateful suspicion.

A fact that seemed to justify these suspicions was the furtive return of the two accused persons and their mysterious establishment in the depths of the ravine of Bernica. They had run away at first, so it was said, to give the affair time to die out; but public opinion had been so cold in France that they had been driven to return and take refuge in the desert, to gratify their criminal attachment in peace.

But all these theories were set at naught by another fact which was vouched for by persons who seemed better informed: Madame Delmare, I was told, had always manifested a decided coolness, almost downright aversion for her cousin Monsieur Brown.

I had thereupon scrutinized the hero of so many strange tales carefully–conscientiously, if I may say so. He was sitting on a bale of merchandise, awaiting the return of a sailor whom he had sent to make some purchase or other for him. His eyes, blue as the sea, were gazing pensively at the horizon, with such a placid and honest expression; all the lines of his face were so perfectly in harmony with one another; nerves, muscles, blood, all seemed so tranquil, so perfect, so well-ordered in that robust and healthy individual, that I would have sworn that all the tales were deadly insults, that he had no crime on his conscience, that he had never had one in his mind, that his heart and his hands were as pure as his brow.

But suddenly the baronet's distraught glance had fallen upon me, as I was staring at him with eager and impertinent curiosity. Confused and embarrassed as a thief caught in the act, I lowered my eyes, for Sir Ralph's expression conveyed a stern rebuke. Since then I had often thought of him, involuntarily; he had appeared in my dreams. I was conscious, as I thought of him, of that vague feeling of uneasiness, that indescribable emotion, which are like the magnetic fluid with which an unusual destiny is encompassed.

My desire to know Sir Ralph was very real, therefore, and very keen; but I should have preferred to watch him furtively, without being seen myself. It seemed to me that I had wronged him. The crystalline appearance of his eyes froze me with terror. It was so evident that he was a man of towering superiority, either in virtue or in villainy, that I felt very small and mean in his presence.

His hospitality was neither showy nor vulgar. He took me to his room, lent me some clothes and clean linen; then led me to his companion, who was awaiting us to take supper.

As I saw how young and lovely she still was–she seemed barely eighteen–and admired her bloom, her grace, and her sweet voice, I felt a thrill of painful emotion. I reflected that that woman was either very guilty or very unfortunate: guilty of a detestable crime or dishonored by a detestable accusation.

I was detained at Bernica for a week by the overflowing of the rivers, the inundation of the plains, the rain and the wind; and then came the sun, and it never occurred to me to leave my hosts.

Neither of them could be called brilliant. They had little wit, I should say–perhaps indeed they had none at all; but they had that quality which makes one's words impressive and pleasant to hear; they had intellect of the heart. Indiana is ignorant, but not with that narrow, vulgar ignorance which proceeds from indolence, from carelessness or nullity of character. She is eager to learn what the engrossing preoccupations of her life had prevented her from finding out; and then, too, there may have been a little coquetry in the way she questioned Sir Ralph, in order to bring into the light her friend's vast stores of knowledge.

I found her playful, but without petulance; her manners have retained a trace of the languor and melancholy natural to creoles, but in her they seemed to me to have a more abiding charm; her eyes especially have an incomparably soft expression and seem to tell the story of a life of suffering; and when her mouth smiles, there is still a touch of melancholy in those eyes, but the melancholy that seems to be the contemplation of happiness or the emotion of gratitude.

One morning I said to them that at last I was going away.

"Already!" was their answer.

The accent of regret was so genuine, so touching, that I felt encouraged. I had determined that I would not leave Sir Ralph without asking him to tell me his story; but I felt an insurmountable timidity because of the horrible suspicion that had been planted in my mind.

I tried to overcome it.

"Men are great villains," I said to him; "they have spoken ill of you to me. I am not surprised, now that I know you. Your life must have been a very beautiful one, to be so slandered–"

I stopped abruptly when I detected an expression of innocent surprise on Madame Delmare's features. I understood that she knew nothing of the atrocious calumnies current in the colony, and I encountered upon Sir Ralph's face an unequivocal look of haughty displeasure. I rose at once to take my leave of them, shamefaced and sad, crushed by Monsieur Brown's glance, which reminded me of our first meeting and the silent interview of the same sort we had had on the seashore.

Bitterly chagrined to leave that excellent man in such a frame of mind, regretting that I had annoyed and wounded him in return for the happy days I owed to him, I felt my heart swell within me and I burst into tears.

"Young man," he said, taking my hand, "remain with us another day; I have not the courage to let the only friend we have on the island leave us in this way–I understand you," he added, after Madame Delmare had left the room; "I will tell you my story, but not before Indiana. There are wounds which one must not reopen."

That evening we went for a walk in the woods. The trees, which had been so fresh and lovely a fortnight earlier, were entirely stripped of their leaves, but they were already covered with great resinous buds. The birds and insects had resumed possession of their empire. The withered flowers already had young buds to replace them. The streams perseveringly carried seaward the gravel with which their beds were filled. Everything was returning to life and health and happiness.

"Just see," said Ralph to me, "with what astounding rapidity this kindly, fecund nature repairs its losses! Does it not seem as if it were ashamed of the time wasted, and were determined, by dint of a lavish expenditure of sap and vigor, to do over in a few days the work of a year?"

"And it will succeed," rejoined Madame Delmare. "I remember last year's storms; at the end of a month there was no trace of them."

"It is the image of a heart broken by sorrow," I said to her; "when happiness comes back, it renews its youth and blooms again very quickly."

Indiana gave me her hand and looked at Monsieur Brown with an indescribable expression of affection and joy.

When night fell she went to her room, and Sir Ralph, bidding me sit beside him on a bench in the garden, told me his history to the point at which we dropped it in the last chapter.

There he made a long pause and seemed to have forgotten my presence completely.

Impelled by my interest in his narrative, I decided to interrupt his meditation by one last question.

He started like a man suddenly awakened; then, smiling pleasantly, he said:

"My young friend, there are memories which we rob of their bloom by putting them in words. Let it suffice you to know that I was fully determined to kill Indiana with myself. But doubtless the consummation of our sacrifice was still unrecorded in the archives of Heaven. A doctor would tell you perhaps that a very natural attack of vertigo took possession of my wits and led me astray as to the location of the path. For my own part, who am not a doctor at all in such matters, I prefer to believe that the angel of Abraham and Tobias, that beautiful white angel with the blue eyes and the girdle of gold, whom you often saw in your childish dreams, came down from Heaven on a moonbeam, and, as he hovered in the trembling vapor of the cataract, stretched his silvery wings over my gentle companion's head. The only thing that I am able to tell you is that the moon sank behind the great peaks of the mountain and no ominous sound disturbed the peaceful murmur of the waterfall; the birds on the cliff did not take their flight until a white streak appeared on the horizon; and the first ruddy beam that fell upon the clump of orange-trees found me on my knees blessing God.

"Do not think, however, that I accepted instantly the unhoped-for happiness which gave a new turn to my destiny. I was afraid to sound the radiant future that was dawning for me; and when Indiana raised her eyes and smiled upon me, I pointed to the waterfall and talked of dying.

"'If you do not regret having lived until this morning,' I said to her, 'we can both declare that we have tasted happiness in all its plentitude; and it is an additional reason for ceasing to live, for perhaps my star would pale to-morrow. Who can say that, on leaving this spot, on coming forth from this intoxicating situation to which thoughts of death and love have brought me, I shall not become once more the detestable brute whom you despised yesterday? Will you not blush for yourself when you find me again as you have always known me? Oh! Indiana, spare me that horrible agony; it would be the complement of my destiny.'

"'Do you doubt your heart, Ralph?' said Indiana with an adorable expression of love and confidence, 'or does not mine offer you sufficient guarantee?'

"Shall I tell you? I was not happy at first. I did not doubt Madame Delmare's sincerity, but I was terrified by thought of the future. Having distrusted myself beyond measure for thirty years, I could not feel assured in a single day of my ability to please and to retain her love. I had moments of uncertainty, alarm and bitterness; I sometimes regretted that I had not jumped into the lake when a word from Indiana had made me so happy.

"She too must have had attacks of melancholy. She found it difficult to break herself of the habit of suffering, for the heart becomes used to unhappiness, it takes root in it and cuts loose from it only with an effort. However, I must do her heart the justice to say that she never had a regret for Raymon; she did not even remember him enough to hate him.

"At last, as always happens in deep and true attachments, time, instead of weakening our love, established it firmly and sealed it; each day gave it added intensity, because each day brought fresh obligations on both sides to esteem and to bless. All our fears vanished one by one; and when we saw how easy it was to destroy those causes of distrust, we smilingly confessed to each other that we took our happiness like cowards and that neither of us deserved it. From that moment we have loved each other in perfect security."

Ralph paused; then, after a few moments of profound meditation in which we were equally absorbed, he continued, pressing my hand:

"I say nothing of my happiness; if there are griefs that never betray their existence and envelop the heart like a shroud, so there are joys that remain buried in the heart of a man because no earthly voice can describe them. Moreover, if some angel from heaven should light upon one of these flowering branches and describe those joys in the language of his native land, you would not understand them, young man, for the tempest has not bruised and shattered you. Alas! what can the heart that has not suffered understand of happiness? As to our crimes–" he added with a smile.

"Oh!" I cried, my eyes wet with tears.

"Listen, monsieur," he continued, interrupting me; "you have lived but a few hours with the two outlaws of Bernica, but a single hour would suffice for you to learn their whole life. All our days resemble one another; they are all calm and lovely; they pass by as swiftly and as pure as those of our childhood. Every night we bless God; we pray to him every morning, we implore at his hands the sunshine and shade of the day before. The greater part of our income is devoted to the redemption of poor and infirm blacks. That is the principle cause of the evil that the colonists say of us. Would that we were rich enough to set free all those who live in slavery! Our servants are our friends; they share our joys, we nurse them in sickness. This is the way our life is spent, without vexations, without remorse. We rarely speak of the past, rarely of the future; but always of the former without bitterness, of the latter without alarm. If we sometimes surprise ourselves with tears in our eyes, it is because great joys always cause tears to flow; the eyes are dry in great misery."

"My friend," I said after a long silence, "if the accusations of the world should reach your ears, your happiness would answer loudly enough."

"You are young," he replied, "in your eyes, for your conscience is ingenuous and pure and unsoiled by the world, our happiness is the proof of our virtue; in the eyes of the world it is our crime. Solitude is sweet, I tell you, and men are not worth a regret."

"All do not accuse you," I said; "but even those who appreciate your true character blame you for despising public opinion, and those who acknowledge your virtue say that you are arrogant and proud."

"Believe me," replied Ralph, "there is more pride in that reproach than in any alleged scorn. As for public opinion, monsieur, judging from those whom it exalts, ought we not always to hold out our hand to those whom it tramples upon? It is said that its approval is necessary to happiness; they who think so should respect it. For my part, I sincerely pity any happiness that rises or falls with its capricious breath."

"Some moralists criticise your solitary life; they claim that every man belongs to society, which demands his presence. They add that you set an example which it is dangerous to follow."

"Society should demand nothing of the man who expects nothing from it," Sir Ralph replied. "As for the contagion of example, I do not believe in it, monsieur; too much energy is required to break with the world, and too much suffering to acquire that energy. So let this unknown happiness flow on in peace, for it costs nobody anything, and conceals itself for fear of making others envious. Go, young man, follow the course of your destiny; have friends, a profession, a reputation, a fatherland. As for me, I have Indiana. Do not break the chains that bind you to society, respect its judgments if they are fair to you: but if some day it calumniates you and spurns you, have pride enough to find a way to do without it."

"Yes," said I, "a pure heart will enable us to endure exile; but, to make us love it, one must have such a companion as yours."

"Ah!" he said, "if you knew how I pity this world of yours, which looks down on me!"

The next day I left Ralph and Indiana; one embraced me, the other shed a few tears.

"Adieu," they said to me; "return to the world; if some day it banishes you, remember our Indian cottage."

The Brontë Sisters: Famous Novels - unabridged - Wuthering Heights, Agnes Grey, The Tenant of Wildfell Hall, Jane Eyre
Charlotte Brontë
Benediction Classics, 2012
1130 pages
ISBN: 978-1-78139-250-8

Available from www.amazon.com, www.amazon.co.uk

The Brontë sisters, Charlotte (1816-55), Emily (1818-48), and Anne (1820-49), achieved literary renown for their novels which were passionate and original. Contained in this volume are the famous (or complete) novels - Wuthering Heights, Agnes Grey, The Tenant of Wildfell Hall, Jane Eyre.

Five Novels by Thomas Hardy - Far From The Madding Crowd, The Return of the Native, The Mayor of Casterbridge, Tess of the d'Urbervilles, Jude the Obscure (complete and unabridged)
Thomas Hardy
Benediction Classics, 2013
1114 pages
ISBN: 978-1-78139-356-7

Available from www.amazon.com, www.amazon.co.uk

Thomas Hardy, (1840 - 1928) was an English novelist and poet. He was highly critical of Victorian society and focussed mainly on the declining rural communities.

E M Forster - Collected Works, including A Room with a View, Howards End, The Longest Journey, Where Angels Fear to Tread and The Celestial Omnibus and other Stories
E M Forster
Oxford City Press, 2013
808 pages
ISBN: 978-1-78139-373-4

Available from www.amazon.com, www.amazon.co.uk

Edward Morgan Forster (1879 - 1970) is best known for his beautiful novels - ironic with delicious plots, highlighting the hypocrisy and discrimination in early 20th-century British society.

The Complete Novels of Jane Austen (unabridged): Sense and Sensibility, Pride and Prejudice, Mansfield Park, Emma, Northanger Abbey, Persuasion, Love and Freindship, and Lady Susan
Jane Austen
Benediction Classics, 2012
1118 pages
ISBN: 978-1-78139-211-9

Available from www.amazon.com, www.amazon.co.uk

This edition contains Jane Austen's six novels unabridged: Sense and Sensibility (1811), Pride and Prejudice (1813), Mansfield Park (1814), Emma (1815), Northanger Abbey (1818, posthumous), Persuasion (1818, posthumous). It also contains the short fiction story, Lady Susan (1794, 1805). In addition one of the Juvenilia stories is included, Love and Freindship.

Gomez Arias;
Or The Moors Of The Alpujarras.
A Spanish Historical Romance
Joaquín Telesforo De Trueba Y Cosío
Benediction Classics, 2011
354 pages
ISBN: 978-1-84902-462-4

Available from www.amazon.com, www.amazon.co.uk

This paperback includes all three Volumes of the novel 'Gomez Arias The Moors of the Alpujarras, A Spanish Historical Romance'. It was written in 1826 by the Spaniard Joaquín Telesforo de Trueba y Cosío who wrote in English and belonged to the Romantic movement. It is set in the province of Granada. A censored version was produced in 1831

Also from Benediction Books ...

Wandering Between Two Worlds: Essays on Faith and Art
Anita Mathias
Benediction Books, 2007
152 pages
ISBN: 0955373700

Available from www.amazon.com, www.amazon.co.uk

In these wide-ranging lyrical essays, Anita Mathias writes, in lush, lovely prose, of her naughty Catholic childhood in Jamshedpur, India; her large, eccentric family in Mangalore, a sea-coast town converted by the Portuguese in the sixteenth century; her rebellion and atheism as a teenager in her Himalayan boarding school, run by German missionary nuns, St. Mary's Convent, Nainital; and her abrupt religious conversion after which she entered Mother Teresa's convent in Calcutta as a novice. Later rich, elegant essays explore the dualities of her life as a writer, mother, and Christian in the United States-- Domesticity and Art, Writing and Prayer, and the experience of being "an alien and stranger" as an immigrant in America, sensing the need for roots.

About the Author

Anita Mathias is the author of *Wandering Between Two Worlds: Essays on Faith and Art*. She has a B.A. and M.A. in English from Somerville College, Oxford University, and an M.A. in Creative Writing from the Ohio State University, USA. Anita won a National Endowment of the Arts fellowship in Creative Non-fiction in 1997. She lives in Oxford, England with her husband, Roy, and her daughters, Zoe and Irene.

Anita's website:
http://www.anitamathias.com, and
Anita's blog Dreaming Beneath the Spires:
http://dreamingbeneaththespires.blogspot.com

The Church That Had Too Much
Anita Mathias
Benediction Books, 2010
52 pages
ISBN: 9781849026567

Available from www.amazon.com, www.amazon.co.uk

The Church That Had Too Much was very well-intentioned. She wanted to love God, she wanted to love people, but she was both hampered by her muchness and the abundance of her possessions, and beset by ambition, power struggles and snobbery. Read about the surprising way The Church That Had Too Much began to resolve her problems in this deceptively simple and enchanting fable.

About the Author

Anita Mathias is the author of *Wandering Between Two Worlds: Essays on Faith and Art*. She has a B.A. and M.A. in English from Somerville College, Oxford University, and an M.A. in Creative Writing from the Ohio State University, USA. Anita won a National Endowment of the Arts fellowship in Creative Non-fiction in 1997. She lives in Oxford, England with her husband, Roy, and her daughters, Zoe and Irene.

Anita's website:
http://www.anitamathias.com, and
Anita's blog Dreaming Beneath the Spires:
http://dreamingbeneaththespires.blogspot.com

www.ingramcontent.com/pod-product-compliance
Lightning Source LLC
Chambersburg PA
CBHW080811020826
48982CB00017B/887

* 9 7 8 1 7 8 1 3 9 4 2 2 9 *